THE
CENTENARY EDITION
OF THE WORKS OF
NATHANIEL HAWTHORNE

Volume X

MOSSES FROM AN OLD MANSE

EDITORS

General Editors

WILLIAM CHARVAT, 1905–1966

ROY HARVEY PEARCE

CLAUDE M. SIMPSON

FREDSON BOWERS, *Textual Editor*

L. NEAL SMITH, *Associate Textual Editor*

JOHN MANNING, *Assistant Textual Editor*

J. DONALD CROWLEY, *Editor for the Tales*

A PUBLICATION OF
THE OHIO STATE UNIVERSITY CENTER
FOR TEXTUAL STUDIES

NATHANIEL HAWTHORNE

MOSSES FROM
AN OLD MANSE

Ohio State University Press

CENTER FOR EDITIONS OF
AMERICAN AUTHORS

AN APPROVED TEXT

MODERN LANGUAGE
ASSOCIATION OF AMERICA

®

*Editorial expenses for this volume have been supported by
grants from the National Endowment for the Humanities
administered through the
Center for Editions of American Authors of the
Modern Language Association*

*International Standard Book Number 0-8142-0203-9
Library of Congress Catalogue Card Number 73-5364
Copyright© 1974 by the Ohio State University Press
All Rights Reserved*

ACKNOWLEDGEMENTS

T HE EDITORS express their appreciation to all scholars, librarians, and bibliophiles for generous aid, and in particular to W. H. Bond and Carolyn E. Jakeman, Houghton Library, Harvard University; Douglas Ewing, the Pierpont Morgan Library; Harriet C. Jameson, University of Michigan, Ann Arbor; Katherine Ommen, University of Texas, Austin; Norman Holmes Pearson, Yale University; David Randall, the Lilly Library, Indiana University; Lola L. Szladits, the Berg Collection, New York Public Library, and to Parkman D. Howe, Boston. For permission to edit manuscript material we are indebted to the Manuscript Division, New York Public Library, Astor, Lenox, and Tilden Foundation; the Pierpont Morgan Library; the Lilly Library, Indiana University; and to C. E. Frazer Clark, Jr., Bloomfield Hills, Mich.

Our thanks go to Marianne Bailey, Frances Lappe, Nancy Long, and Don Nigro for their assistance, and special recognition to Ann Jackowski for her work in preparation of this volume.

We are grateful for support from the National Endowment for the Humanities of the National Foundation on the Arts and Humanities, the University of Missouri Research Council, and the following divisions of the Ohio State University: the Department of English, the Graduate School, the University Libraries, and the Research Foundation.

THE EDITORS

CONTENTS

· ix ·

*An alphabetical list and a chronological list of the
complete tales will be found at the end of Volume XI.*

MOSSES FROM AN OLD MANSE

THE OLD MANSE

THE AUTHOR MAKES THE READER ACQUAINTED
WITH HIS ABODE

BETWEEN two tall gate-posts of rough-hewn stone, (the gate itself having fallen from its hinges, at some unknown epoch,) we beheld the gray front of the old parsonage, terminating the vista of an avenue of black-ash trees. It was now a twelvemonth since the funeral procession of the venerable clergyman, its last inhabitant, had turned from that gate-way towards the village burying-ground. The wheel-track, leading to the door, as well as the whole breadth of the avenue, was almost overgrown with grass, affording dainty mouthfuls to two or three vagrant cows, and an old white horse, who had his own living to pick up along the roadside. The glimmering shadows, that lay half-asleep between the door of the house and the public highway, were a kind of spiritual medium, seen through which, the edifice had not quite the aspect of belonging to the material world. Certainly it had little in common with those ordinary abodes, which stand so imminent upon the road that every passer-by can thrust his head, as it were, into the domestic circle. From these quiet windows, the figures of passing travellers looked too remote and dim to disturb the sense of privacy. In its near retirement, and accessible seclusion, it was the very spot for the residence of a clergyman; a man not estranged from human life, yet enveloped, in the midst of it, with a veil woven of intermingled gloom and brightness. It was worthy to have been one of the time-honored parsonages of England, in which, through many generations, a succession of holy occupants pass from youth to age, and bequeath each an inheritance of sanctity to pervade the house and hover over it, as with an atmosphere.

Nor, in truth, had the old Manse ever been prophaned by a lay occupant, until that memorable summer-afternoon when I entered it as my home. A priest had built it; a priest had succeeded to it; other priestly men, from time to time, had dwelt in it; and children, born in its chambers, had grown up to assume the priestly character. It was awful to reflect how many sermons must have been written there. The latest inhabitant alone—he, by whose translation to Paradise the dwelling was left vacant—had penned nearly three thousand discourses, besides the better, if not the greater number, that gushed living from his lips. How often, no doubt, had he paced to-and-fro along the avenue, attuning his meditations, to the sighs and gentle murmurs, and deep and solemn peals of the wind, among the lofty tops of the trees! In that variety of natural utterances, he could find something accordant with every passage of his sermon, were it of tenderness or reverential fear. The boughs over my head seemed shadowy with solemn thoughts, as well as with rustling leaves. I took shame to myself for having been so long a writer of idle stories, and ventured to hope that wisdom would descend upon me with the falling leaves of the avenue; and that I should light upon an intellectual treasure in the old Manse, well worth those hoards of long-hidden gold, which people seek for in moss-grown houses. Profound treatises of morality;—a layman's unprofessional, and therefore unprejudiced views of religion;—histories, (such as Bancroft might have written, had he taken up his abode here, as he once purposed,) bright with picture, gleaming over a depth of philosophic thought;—these were the works that might fitly have flowed from such a retirement. In the humblest event, I resolved at least to achieve a novel, that should evolve some deep lesson, and should possess physical substance enough to stand alone.

In furtherance of my design, and as if to leave me no pretext for not fulfilling it, there was, in the rear of the house, the most delightful little nook of a study that ever afforded its snug seclusion to a scholar. It was here that Emerson wrote 'Nature'; for he was then an inhabitant of the Manse, and used to watch the Assyrian dawn and the Paphian sunset and moonrise, from the summit of our eastern hill. When I first saw the room, its walls were blackened with the smoke of unnumbered years, and made still blacker by the grim prints of Puritan ministers that hung around. These worthies looked strangely like bad angels, or, at least, like men who had wrestled so continually and so sternly with the devil, that somewhat of his sooty fierceness had been imparted to their own visages. They had all vanished now. A cheerful coat of paint, and golden-tinted paper-hangings, lighted up the small apartment; while the shadow of a willow-tree, that swept against the overhanging eaves, attempered the cheery western sunshine. In place of the grim prints, there was the sweet and lovely head of one of Raphael's Madonnas, and two pleasant little pictures of the Lake of Como. The only other decorations were a purple vase of flowers, always fresh, and a bronze one containing graceful ferns. My books (few, and by no means choice; for they were chiefly such waifs as chance had thrown in my way) stood in order about the room, seldom to be disturbed.

The study had three windows, set with little, old-fashioned panes of glass, each with a crack across it. The two on the western side looked, or rather peeped, between the willow-branches, down into the orchard, with glimpses of the river through the trees. The third, facing northward, commanded a broader view of the river, at a spot where its hitherto obscure waters gleam forth into the light of history. It was at this window that the clergyman, who then dwelt in the Manse, stood watching the outbreak of a long and deadly struggle between two nations; he saw the irregular array of his parishioners on the farther side of the river, and the glittering line of the British, on the hither bank. He awaited, in an agony of suspense, the rattle of the musketry. It came— and there needed but a gentle wind to sweep the battle-smoke around this quiet house.

Perhaps the reader—whom I cannot help considering as my guest in the old Manse, and entitled to all courtesy in the way of sight-showing—perhaps he will choose to take a nearer view of the memorable spot. We stand now on the river's brink. It may well be called the Concord—the river of peace and quietness—for it is certainly the most unexcitable and sluggish stream that ever loitered, imperceptibly, towards its eternity, the sea. Positively, I had lived three weeks beside it, before it grew quite clear to my perception which way the current flowed. It never has a vivacious aspect, except when a north-western breeze is vexing its surface, on a sun-shiny day. From the incurable indolence of its nature, the stream is happily incapable of becoming the slave of human ingenuity, as is the fate of so many a wild, free mountain-torrent. While all things else are compelled to subserve some useful purpose, it idles its sluggish life away, in lazy liberty, without turning a solitary spindle, or affording even water-power enough to grind the corn that grows upon its banks. The torpor of its movement allows it nowhere a bright pebbly shore, nor so much as a narrow strip of glistening sand, in any part of its course. It slumbers between broad prairies, kissing the long meadow-grass, and bathes the overhanging boughs of elder-bushes and willows, or the roots of elms and ash-trees, and clumps of maples. Flags and rushes grow along its plashy shore; the yellow water-lily spreads its broad, flat leaves on the margin; and the fragrant white pond-lily abounds, generally selecting a position just so far from the river's brink, that it cannot be grasped, save at the hazard of plunging in.

It is a marvel whence this perfect flower derives its loveliness and perfume, springing, as it does, from the black mud over which the river sleeps, and where lurk the slimy eel, and speckled frog, and the mud turtle, whom continual washing cannot cleanse. It is the very same black mud out of which the yellow lily sucks its obscene life and noisome odor. Thus we see, too, in the world, that some persons assimilate only what is ugly and evil from the same moral circumstances which supply good and beautiful results—the fragrance of celestial flowers—to the daily life of others.

The reader must not, from any testimony of mine, contract a dislike towards our slumberous stream. In the light of a calm and golden sunset, it becomes lovely beyond expression; the more lovely for the quietude that so well accords with the hour, when even the wind, after blustering all day long, usually hushes itself to rest. Each tree and rock, and every blade of grass, is distinctly imaged, and, however unsightly in reality, assumes ideal beauty in the reflection. The minutest things of earth, and the broad aspect of the firmament, are pictured equally without effort, and with the same felicity of success. All the sky glows downward at our feet; the rich clouds float through the unruffled bosom of the stream, like heavenly thoughts through a peaceful heart. We will not, then, malign our river as gross and impure, while it can glorify itself with so adequate a picture of the heaven that broods above it; or, if we remember its tawny hue and the muddiness of its bed, let it be a symbol that the earthliest human soul has an infinite spiritual capacity, and may contain the better world within its depths. But, indeed, the same lesson might be drawn out of any mud-puddle in the streets of a city—and, being taught us everywhere, it must be true.

Come; we have pursued a somewhat devious track, in our walk to the battle-ground. Here we are, at the point where the river was crossed by the old bridge, the possession of which was the immediate object of the contest. On the hither side, grow two or three elms, throwing a wide circumference of shade, but which must have been planted at some period within the threescore years and ten, that have passed since the battle-day. On the farther shore, overhung by a clump of elder-bushes, we discern the stone abutment of the bridge. Looking down into the river, I once discovered some heavy fragments of the timbers, all green with half-a-century's growth of water-moss; for, during that length of time, the tramp of horses and human footsteps have ceased, along this ancient highway. The stream has here about the breadth of twenty strokes of a swimmer's arm; a space not too wide, when the bullets were whistling across. Old people, who dwell hereabouts, will point out the very spots, on the western bank, where our countrymen fell down and died; and, on this side of the river, an obelisk of granite has grown up from the soil that was fertilized with British blood. The monument, not more than twenty feet in height, is such as it befitted the inhabitants of a village to erect, in illustration of a matter of local interest, rather than what was suitable to commemorate an epoch of national history. Still, by the fathers of the village this famous deed was done; and their descendants might rightfully claim the privilege of building a memorial.

A humbler token of the fight, yet a more interesting one than the granite obelisk, may be seen close under the stone-wall, which separates the battle-ground from the precincts of the parsonage. It is the grave—marked by a small, moss-grown fragment of stone at the head, and another at the foot—the grave of two British soldiers, who were slain in the skirmish, and have ever since slept peacefully where Zechariah Brown and Thomas Davis buried them. Soon was their warfare ended;—a weary night-march from Boston—a rattling volley of musketry across the river;—and then these many years of rest! In the long procession of slain invaders, who passed into eternity from the battle-fields of the Revolution, these two nameless soldiers led the way.

Lowell, the poet, as we were once standing over this grave, told me a tradition in reference to one of the inhabitants below. The story has something deeply impressive, though its circumstances cannot altogether be reconciled with probability. A youth, in the service of the clergyman, happened to be chopping wood, that April morning, at the back door of the Manse; and when the noise of battle rang from side to side of the bridge, he hastened across the intervening field, to see what might be going forward. It is rather strange, by the way, that this lad should have been so diligently at work, when the whole population of town and county were startled out of their customary business, by the advance of the British troops. Be that as it might, the tradition says that the lad now left his task, and hurried to the battle-field, with the axe still in his hand. The British had by this time retreated—the Americans were in pursuit—and the late scene of strife was thus deserted by both parties. Two soldiers lay on the ground; one was a corpse; but, as the young New-Englander drew nigh, the other Briton raised himself painfully upon his hands and knees, and gave a ghastly stare into his face. The boy—it must have been a nervous impulse, without purpose, without thought, and betokening a sensitive and impressible nature, rather than a hardened one—the boy uplifted his axe, and dealt the wounded soldier a fierce and fatal blow upon the head.

I could wish that the grave might be opened; for I would fain know whether either of the skeleton soldiers have the mark of an axe in his skull. The story comes home to me like truth. Oftentimes, as an intellectual and moral exercise, I have sought to follow that poor youth through his subsequent career, and observe how his soul was tortured by the blood-stain, contracted, as it had been, before the long custom of war had robbed human life of its sanctity, and while it still seemed murderous to slay a brother man. This one circumstance has borne more fruit for me, than all that history tells us of the fight.

Many strangers come, in the summer-time, to view the battle-ground. For my own part, I have never found my imagination much excited by this, or any other scene of historic celebrity; nor would the placid margin of the river have lost any of its charm for me, had men never fought and died there. There is a wilder interest in the tract of land—perhaps a hundred yards in breadth—which extends between the battle-field and the northern face of our old Manse, with its contiguous avenue and orchard. Here, in some unknown age, before the white man came, stood an Indian village, convenient to the river, whence its inhabitants must have drawn so large a part of their subsistence. The site is identified by the spear and arrow-heads, the chisels, and other implements of war, labor, and the chase, which the plough turns up from the soil. You see a splinter of stone, half hidden beneath a sod; it looks like nothing worthy of note; but, if you have faith enough to pick it up—behold a relic! Thoreau, who has a strange faculty of finding what the Indians have left behind them, first set me on the search; and I afterwards enriched myself with some very perfect specimens, so rudely wrought that it seemed almost as if chance had fashioned them. Their great charm consists in this rudeness, and in the individuality of each article, so different from the productions of civilized machinery, which shapes everything on one pattern. There is an exquisite delight, too, in picking up, for one's self, an arrow-head that was dropt centuries ago, and has never been handled since, and which we thus receive directly from the hand of the red hunter, who purposed to shoot it at his game, or at an enemy. Such an incident builds up again the Indian village, amid its encircling forest, and recalls to life the painted chiefs and warriors, the squaws at their household toil, and the children sporting among the wigwams; while the little wind-rocked papoose swings from the branch of a tree. It can hardly be told whether it is a joy or a pain, after such a momentary vision, to gaze around in the broad daylight of reality, and see stone-fences, white houses, potatoe-fields, and men doggedly hoeing, in their shirt-sleeves and homespun pantaloons. But this is nonsense. The old Manse is better than a thousand wigwams.

The old Manse! We had almost forgotten it, but will return thither through the orchard. This was set out by the last clergyman, in the decline of his life, when the neighbors laughed at the hoary-headed man for planting trees, from which he could have no prospect of gathering fruit. Even had that been the case, there was only so much the better motive for planting them, in the pure and unselfish hope of benefitting his successors—an end so seldom achieved by more ambitious efforts. But the old minister, before reaching his patriarchal age of ninety, ate the apples from this orchard during many years, and added silver and gold to his annual stipend, by disposing of the superfluity. It is pleasant to think of him, walking among the trees in the quiet afternoons of early autumn, and picking up here and there a windfall; while he observes how heavily the branches are weighed down, and computes the number of empty flour-barrels that will be filled by their burthen. He loved each tree, doubtless, as if it had been his own child. An orchard has a relation to mankind, and readily connects itself with matters of the heart. The trees possess a domestic character; they have lost the wild nature of their forest-kindred, and have grown humanized by receiving the care of man, as well as by contributing to his wants. There is so much individuality of character, too, among apple-trees, that it gives them an additional claim to be the objects of human interest. One is harsh and crabbed in its manifestations; another gives us fruit as mild as charity. One is churlish and illiberal, evidently grudging the few apples that it bears; another exhausts itself in free-hearted benevolence. The variety of grotesque shapes, into which apple-trees contort themselves, has its effect on those who get acquainted with them; they stretch out their crooked branches, and take such hold of the imagination that we remember them as humorists and odd fellows. And what is more melancholy than the old apple-trees, that linger about the spot where once stood a homestead, but where there is now only a ruined chimney, rising out of a grassy and weed-grown cellar? They offer their fruit to every wayfarer—apples that are bitter-sweet with the moral of time's vicissitude.

I have met with no other such pleasant trouble in the world, as that of finding myself, with only the two or three mouths which it was my privilege to feed, the sole inheritor of the old clergyman's wealth of fruits. Throughout the summer, there were cherries and currants; and then came Autumn, with this immense burthen of apples, dropping them continually from his over-laden shoulders, as he trudged along. In the stillest afternoon, if I listened, the thump of a great apple was audible, falling without a breath of wind, from the mere necessity of perfect ripeness. And, besides, there were pear-trees, that flung down bushels upon bushels of heavy pears, and peach-trees, which, in a good year, tormented me with peaches, neither to be eaten nor kept, nor, without labor and perplexity, to be given away. The idea of an infinite generosity and exhaustless bounty, on the part of our Mother Nature, was well worth obtaining through such cares as these. That feeling can be enjoyed in perfection only by the natives of the summer islands, where the bread-fruit, the cocoa, the palm, and the orange, grow spontaneously, and hold forth the ever-ready meal; but, likewise, almost as well, by a man long habituated to city-life, who plunges into such a solitude as that of the old Manse, where he plucks the fruit of trees that he did not plant, and which therefore, to my heterodox taste, bear the closest resemblance to those that grew in Eden. It has been an apophthegm, these five thousand years, that toil sweetens the bread it earns. For my part, (speaking from hard experience, acquired while belaboring the rugged furrows of Brook Farm,) I relish best the free gifts of Providence.

Not that it can be disputed, that the light toil, requisite to cultivate a moderately sized garden, imparts such zest to kitchen-vegetables as is never found in those of the market-gardener. Childless men, if they would know something of the bliss of paternity, should plant a seed—be it squash, bean, Indian corn, or perhaps a mere flower, or worthless weed—should plant it with their own hands, and nurse it from infancy to maturity, altogether by their own care. If there be not too many of them, each individual plant becomes an object of separate interest. My garden, that skirted the avenue of the Manse, was of precisely the right extent. An hour or two of morning labor was all that it required. But I used to visit and re-visit it, a dozen times a day, and stand in deep contemplation over my vegetable progeny, with a love that nobody could share nor conceive of, who had never taken part in the process of creation. It was one of the most bewitching sights in the world, to observe a hill of beans thrusting aside the soil, or a row of early peas, just peeping forth sufficiently to trace a line of delicate green. Later in the season, the humming-birds were attracted by the blossoms of a peculiar variety of bean; and they were a joy to me, those little spiritual visitants, for deigning to sip airy food out of my nectar-cups. Multitudes of bees used to bury themselves in the yellow blossoms of the summer-squashes. This, too, was a deep satisfaction; although, when they had laden themselves with sweets, they flew away to some unknown hive, which would give back nothing in requital of what my garden had contributed. But I was glad thus to fling a benefaction upon the passing breeze, with the certainty that somebody must profit by it, and that there would be a little more honey in the world, to allay the sourness and bitterness which mankind is always complaining of. Yes, indeed; my life was the sweeter for that honey.

Speaking of summer-squashes, I must say a word of their beautiful and varied forms. They presented an endless diversity of urns and vases, shallow or deep, scalloped or plain, moulded in patterns which a sculptor would do well to copy, since Art has never invented anything more graceful. A hundred squashes in the garden were worthy—in my eyes, at least—of being rendered indestructible in marble. If ever Providence (but I know it never will) should assign me a superfluity of gold, part of it shall be expended for a service of plate, or most delicate porcelain, to be wrought into the shapes of summer-squashes, gathered from vines which I will plant with my own hands. As dishes for containing vegetables, they would be peculiarly appropriate.

But, not merely the squeamish love of the Beautiful was gratified by my toil in the kitchen-garden. There was a hearty enjoyment, likewise, in observing the growth of the crook-necked winter squashes, from the first little bulb, with the withered blossom adhering to it, until they lay strewn upon the soil, big, round fellows, hiding their heads beneath the leaves, but turning up their great yellow rotundities to the noontide sun. Gazing at them, I felt that, by my agency, something worth living for had been done. A new substance was borne into the world. They were real and tangible existences, which the mind could seize hold of and rejoice in. A cabbage, too,—especially the early Dutch cabbage, which swells to a monstrous circumference, until its ambitious heart often bursts asunder,—is a matter to be proud of, when we can claim a share with the earth and sky in producing it. But, after all, the hugest pleasure is reserved, until these vegetable children of ours are smoking on the table, and we, like Saturn, make a meal of them.

What with the river, the battle-field, the orchard, and the garden, the reader begins to despair of finding his way back into the old Manse. But, in agreeable weather, it is the truest hospitality to keep him out of doors. I never grew quite acquainted with my habitation, till a long spell of sulky rain had confined me beneath its roof. There could not be a more sombre aspect of external Nature, than as then seen from the windows of my study. The great willow-tree had caught, and retained among its leaves, a whole cataract of water, to be shaken down, at intervals, by the frequent gusts of wind. All day long, and for a week together, the rain was drip-drip-dripping and splash-splash-splashing from the eaves, and bubbling and foaming into the tubs beneath the spouts. The old, unpainted shingles of the house and outbuildings were black with moisture; and the mosses, of ancient growth upon the walls, looked green and fresh, as if they were the newest things and after-thought of Time. The usually mirrored surface of the river was blurred by an infinity of rain-drops; the whole landscape had a completely water-soaked appearance, conveying the impression that the earth was wet through, like a sponge; while the summit of a wooded hill, about a mile distant, was enveloped in a dense mist, where the demon of the tempest seemed to have his abiding-place, and to be plotting still direr inclemencies.

Nature has no kindness—no hospitality—during a rain. In the fiercest heat of sunny days, she retains a secret mercy, and welcomes the wayfarer to shady nooks of the woods, whither the sun cannot penetrate; but she provides no shelter against her storms. It makes us shiver to think of those deep, umbrageous recesses—those overshadowing banks—where we found such enjoyment during the sultry afternoons. Not a twig of foliage there, but would dash a little shower into our faces. Looking reproachfully towards the impenetrable sky—if sky there be, above that dismal uniformity of cloud— we are apt to murmur against the whole system of the universe, since it involves the extinction of so many summer days, in so short a life, by the hissing and spluttering rain. In such spells of weather—and, it is to be supposed, such weather came—Eve's bower in Paradise must have been but a cheerless and aguish kind of shelter, nowise comparable to the old parsonage, which had resources of its own, to beguile the week's imprisonment. The idea of sleeping on a couch of wet roses!

Happy the man who, in a rainy day, can betake himself to a huge garret, stored, like that of the Manse, with lumber that each generation has left behind it, from a period before the Revolution. Our garret was an arched hall, dimly illuminated through small and dusty windows; it was but a twilight at the best; and there were nooks, or rather caverns of deep obscurity, the secrets of which I never learned, being too reverent of their dust and cobwebs. The beams and rafters, roughly hewn, and with strips of bark still on them, and the rude masonry of the chimneys, made the garret look wild and uncivilized; an aspect unlike what was seen elsewhere, in the quiet and decorous old house. But, on one side, there was a little white-washed apartment, which bore the traditionary title of the Saints' Chamber, because holy men, in their youth, had slept, and studied, and prayed there. With its elevated retirement, its one window, its small fireplace, and its closet, convenient for an oratory, it was the very spot where a young man might inspire himself with solemn enthusiasm, and cherish saintly dreams. The occupants, at various epochs, had left brief records and ejaculations, inscribed upon the walls. There, too, hung a tattered and shrivelled roll of canvass, which, on inspection, proved to be the forcibly wrought picture of a clergyman, in wig, band, and gown, holding a Bible in his hand. As I turned his face towards the light, he eyed me with an air of authority such as men of his profession seldom assume, in our days. The original had been pastor of the parish, more than a century ago, a friend of Whitefield, and almost his equal in fervid eloquence. I bowed before the effigy of the dignified divine, and felt as if I had now met face to face with the ghost, by whom, as there was reason to apprehend, the Manse was haunted.

Houses of any antiquity, in New England, are so invariably possessed with spirits, that the matter seems hardly worth alluding to. Our ghost used to heave deep sighs in a particular corner of the parlor; and sometimes rustled paper, as if he were turning over a sermon, in the long upper entry;—where, nevertheless, he was invisible, in spite of the bright moonshine that fell through the eastern window. Not improbably, he wished me to edit and publish a selection from a chest full of manuscript discourses, that stood in the garret. Once, while Hillard and other friends sat talking with us in the twilight, there came a rustling noise, as of a minister's silk gown, sweeping through the very midst of the company, so closely as almost to brush against the chairs. Still, there was nothing visible. A yet stranger business was that of a ghostly servant-maid, who used to be heard in the kitchen, at deepest midnight, grinding coffee, cooking, ironing—performing, in short, all kinds of domestic labor—although no traces of anything accomplished could be detected, the next morning. Some neglected duty of her servitude—some ill-starched ministerial band—disturbed the poor damsel in her grave, and kept her at work without any wages.

But, to return from this digression. A part of my predecessor's library was stored in the garret; no unfit receptacle, indeed, for such dreary trash as comprised the greater number of volumes. The old books would have been worth nothing at an auction. In this venerable garret, however, they possessed an interest quite apart from their literary value, as heirlooms, many of which had been transmitted down through a series of consecrated hands, from the days of the mighty Puritan divines. Autographs of famous names were to be seen, in faded ink, on some of their fly-leaves; and there were marginal observations, or interpolated pages closely covered with manuscript, in illegible short-hand, perhaps concealing matter of profound truth and wisdom. The world will never be the better for it. A few of the books were Latin folios, written by Catholic authors; others demolished Papistry as with a sledge-hammer, in plain English. A dissertation on the book of Job—which only Job himself could have had patience to read—filled at least a score of small, thickset quartos, at the rate of two or three volumes to a chapter. Then there was a vast folio Body of Divinity; too corpulent a body, it might be feared, to comprehend the spiritual element of religion. Volumes of this form dated back two hundred years, or more, and were generally bound in black leather, exhibiting precisely such an appearance as we should attribute to books of enchantment. Others, equally antique, were of a size proper to be carried in the large waistcoat-pockets of old times; diminutive, but as black as their bulkier brethren, and abundantly interfused with Greek and Latin quotations. These little old volumes impressed me as if they had been intended for very large ones, but had been unfortunately blighted, at an early stage of their growth.

The rain pattered upon the roof, and the sky gloomed through the dusty garret-windows; while I burrowed among these venerable books, in search of any living thought, which should burn like a coal of fire, or glow like an inextinguishable gem, beneath the dead trumpery that had long hidden it. But I found no such treasure; all was dead alike; and I could not but muse deeply and wonderingly upon the humiliating fact, that the works of man's intellect decay like those of his hands. Thought grows mouldy. What was good and nourishing food for the spirits of one generation, affords no sustenance for the next. Books of religion, however, cannot be considered a fair test of the enduring and vivacious properties of human thought; because such books so seldom really touch upon their ostensible subject, and have therefore so little business to be written at all. So long as an unlettered soul can attain to saving grace, there would seem to be no deadly error in holding theological libraries to be accumulations of, for the most part, stupendous impertinence.

Many of the books had accrued in the latter years of the last clergyman's lifetime. These threatened to be of even less interest than the elder works, a century hence, to any curious inquirer who should then rummage among them, as I was doing now. Volumes of the Liberal Preacher and Christian Examiner, occasional sermons, controversial pamphlets, tracts, and other productions of a like fugitive nature, took the place of the thick and heavy volumes of past time. In a physical point of view, there was much the same difference as between a feather and a lump of lead; but, intellectually regarded, the specific gravity of old and new was about upon a par. Both, also, were alike frigid. The elder books, nevertheless, seemed to have been earnestly written, and might be conceived to have possessed warmth, at some former period; although, with the lapse of time, the heated masses had cooled down even to the freezing point. The frigidity of the modern productions, on the other hand, was characteristic and inherent, and evidently had little to do with the writer's qualities of mind and heart. In fine, of this whole dusty heap of literature, I tossed aside all the sacred part, and felt myself none the less a Christian for eschewing it. There appeared no hope of either mounting to the better world on a Gothic staircase of ancient folios, or of flying thither on the wings of a modern tract.

Nothing, strange to say, retained any sap, except what had been written for the passing day and year, without the remotest pretension or idea of permanence. There were a few old newspapers, and still older almanacs, which reproduced, to my mental eye, the epochs when they had issued from the press, with a distinctness that was altogether unaccountable. It was as if I had found bits of magic looking-glass among the books, with the images of a vanished century in them. I turned my eyes towards the tattered picture, above-mentioned, and asked of the austere divine, wherefore it was that he and his brethren, after the most painful rummaging and groping into their minds, had been able to produce nothing half so real, as these newspaper scribblers and almanac-makers had thrown off, in the effervescence of a moment. The portrait responded not; so I sought an answer for myself. It is the Age itself that writes newspapers and almanacs, which therefore have a distinct purpose and meaning, at the time, and a kind of intelligible truth for all times; whereas, most other works—being written by men who, in the very act, set themselves apart from their age—are likely to possess little significance when new, and none at all, when old. Genius, indeed, melts many ages into one, and thus effects something permanent, yet still with a similarity of office to that of the more ephemeral writer. A work of genius is but the newspaper of a century, or perchance of a hundred centuries.

Lightly as I have spoken of these old books, there yet lingers with me a superstitious reverence for literature of all kinds. A bound volume has a charm in my eyes, similar to what scraps of manuscript possess, for the good Mussulman. He imagines, that those wind-wafted records are perhaps hallowed by some sacred verse; and I, that every new book, or antique one, may contain the 'Open Sesame'—the spell to disclose treasures, hidden in some unsuspected cave of Truth. Thus, it was not without sadness, that I turned away from the library of the old Manse.

Blessed was the sunshine when it came again, at the close of another stormy day, beaming from the edge of the western horizon; while the massive firmament of clouds threw down all the gloom it could, but served only to kindle the golden light into a more brilliant glow, by the strongly contrasted shadows. Heaven smiled at the earth, so long unseen, from beneath its heavy eyelid. Tomorrow for the hill-tops and the wood-paths!

Or it might be that Ellery Channing came up the avenue, to join me in a fishing-excursion on the river. Strange and happy times were those, when we cast aside all irksome forms and straight-laced habitudes, and delivered ourselves up to the free air, to live like the Indians or any less conventional race, during one bright semi-circle of the sun. Rowing our boat against the current, between wide meadows, we turned aside into the Assabeth. A more lovely stream than this, for a mile above its junction with the Concord, has never flowed on earth—nowhere, indeed, except to lave the interior regions of a poet's imagination. It is sheltered from the breeze by woods and a hill-side; so that elsewhere there might be a hurricane, and here scarcely a ripple across the shaded water. The current lingers along so gently, that the mere force of the boatman's will seems sufficient to propel his craft against it. It comes flowing softly through the midmost privacy and deepest heart of a wood, which whispers it to be quiet, while the stream whispers back again from its sedgy borders, as if river and wood were hushing one another to sleep. Yes; the river sleeps along its course, and dreams of the sky, and of the clustering foliage, amid which fall showers of broken sunlight, imparting specks of vivid cheerfulness, in contrast with the quiet depth of the prevailing tint. Of all this scene, the slumbering river has a dream-picture in its bosom. Which, after all, was the most real—the picture, or the original?— the objects palpable to our grosser senses, or their apotheosis in the stream beneath? Surely, the disembodied images stand in closer relation to the soul. But, both the original and the reflection had here an ideal charm; and, had it been a thought more wild, I could have fancied that this river had strayed forth out of the rich scenery of my companion's inner world;—only the vegetation along its banks should then have had an Oriental character.

Gentle and unobtrusive as the river is, yet the tranquil woods seem hardly satisfied to allow it passage. The trees are rooted on the very verge of the water, and dip their pendent branches into it. At one spot, there is a lofty bank, on the slope of which grow some hemlocks, declining across the stream, with outstretched arms, as if resolute to take the plunge. In other places, the banks are almost on a level with the water; so that the quiet congregation of trees set their feet in the flood, and are fringed with foliage down to the surface. Cardinal-flowers kindle their spiral flames, and illuminate the dark nooks among the shrubbery. The pond-lily grows abundantly along the margin; that delicious flower which, as Thoreau tells me, opens its virgin bosom to the first sunlight, and perfects its being through the magic of that genial kiss. He has beheld beds of them unfolding in due succession, as the sunrise stole gradually from flower to flower; a sight not to be hoped for, unless when a poet adjusts his inward eye to a proper focus with the outward organ. Grape-vines, here and there, twine themselves around shrub and tree, and hang their clusters over the water, within reach of the boatman's hand. Oftentimes, they unite two trees of alien race in an inextricable twine, marrying the hemlock and the maple against their will, and enriching them with a purple offspring, of which neither is the parent. One of these ambitious parasites has climbed into the upper branches of a tall white-pine, and is still ascending from bough to bough, unsatisfied, till it shall crown the tree's airy summit with a wreath of its broad foliage and a cluster of its grapes.

The winding course of the stream continually shut out the scene behind us, and revealed as calm and lovely a one before. We glided from depth to depth, and breathed new seclusion at every turn. The shy kingfisher flew from the withered branch, close at hand, to another at a distance, uttering a shrill cry of anger or alarm. Ducks—that had been floating there, since the preceding eve—were startled at our approach, and skimmed along the glassy river, breaking its dark surface with a bright streak. The pickerel leaped from among the lily-pads. The turtle, sunning itself upon a rock, or at the root of a tree, slid suddenly into the water with a plunge. The painted Indian, who paddled his canoe along the Assabeth, three hundred years ago, could hardly have seen a wilder gentleness, displayed upon its banks and reflected in its bosom, than we did. Nor could the same Indian have prepared his noontide meal with more simplicity. We drew up our skiff at some point where the overarching shade formed a natural bower, and there kindled a fire with the pine-cones and decayed branches that lay strewn plentifully around. Soon, the smoke ascended among the trees, impregnated with a savory incense, not heavy, dull, and surfeiting, like the steam of cookery within doors, but sprightly and piquant. The smell of our feast was akin to the woodland odors with which it mingled; there was no sacrilege committed by our intrusion there; the sacred solitude was hospitable, and granted us free leave to cook and eat, in the recess that was at once our kitchen and banquetting-hall. It is strange what humble offices may be performed, in a beautiful scene, without destroying its poetry. Our fire, red-gleaming among the trees, and we beside it, busied with culinary rites and spreading out our meal on a moss-grown log, all seemed in unison with the river gliding by, and the foliage rustling over us. And, what was strangest, neither did our mirth seem to disturb the propriety of the solemn woods; although the hobgoblins of the old wilderness, and the will-of-the-whisps that glimmered in the marshy places, might have come trooping to share our table-talk, and have added their shrill laughter to our merriment. It was the very spot in which to utter the extremest nonsense, or the profoundest wisdom—or that ethereal product of the mind which partakes of both, and may become one or the other, in correspondence with the faith and insight of the auditor.

So, amid sunshine and shadow, rustling leaves, and sighing waters, up-gushed our talk, like the babble of a fountain. The evanescent spray was Ellery's; and his, too, the lumps of golden thought, that lay glimmering in the fountain's bed, and brightened both our faces by the reflection. Could he have drawn out that virgin gold, and stamped it with the

mint-mark that alone gives currency, the world might have
had the profit, and he the fame. My mind was the richer,
merely by the knowledge that it was there. But the chief
profit of those wild days, to him and me, lay—not in any
definite idea—not in any angular or rounded truth, which
we dug out of the shapeless mass of problematical stuff—
but in the freedom which we thereby won from all custom
and conventionalism, and fettering influences of man on
man. We were so free to-day, that it was impossible to be
slaves again tomorrow. When we crossed the threshold of
a house, or trod the thronged pavements of a city, still the
leaves of the trees, that overhung the Assabeth, were whispering to us—'Be free! Be free!' Therefore, along that shady
river-bank, there are spots, marked with a heap of ashes and
half-consumed brands, only less sacred in my remembrance
than the hearth of a household-fire.

And yet how sweet—as we floated homeward adown the
golden river, at sunset—how sweet was it to return within
the system of human society, not as to a dungeon and a
chain, but as to a stately edifice, whence we could go forth
at will into statelier simplicity! How gently, too, did the
sight of the old Manse—best seen from the river, overshadowed with its willow, and all environed about with the
foliage of its orchard and avenue—how gently did its gray,
homely aspect rebuke the speculative extravagances of the
day! It had grown sacred, in connection with the artificial
life against which we inveighed; it had been a home, for
many years, in spite of all; it was my home, too;—and, with
these thoughts, it seemed to me that all the artifice and
conventionalism of life was but an impalpable thinness upon
its surface, and that the depth below was none the worse for
it. Once, as we turned our boat to the bank, there was a
cloud in the shape of an immensely gigantic figure of a
hound, couched above the house, as if keeping guard over

it. Gazing at this symbol, I prayed that the upper influences might long protect the institutions that had grown out of the heart of mankind.

If ever my readers should decide to give up civilized life, cities, houses, and whatever moral or material enormities, in addition to these, the perverted ingenuity of our race has contrived,—let it be in the early autumn. Then, Nature will love him better than at any other season, and will take him to her bosom with a more motherly tenderness. I could scarcely endure the roof of the old house above me, in those first autumnal days. How early in the summer, too, the prophecy of autumn comes!—earlier in some years than in others,—sometimes, even in the first weeks of July. There is no other feeling like what is caused by this faint, doubtful, yet real perception, if it be not rather a foreboding, of the year's decay—so blessedly sweet and sad, in the same breath.

Did I say that there was no feeling like it? Ah, but there is a half-acknowledged melancholy, like to this, when we stand in the perfected vigor of our life, and feel that Time has now given us all his flowers, and that the next work of his never idle fingers must be—to steal them, one by one, away!

I have forgotten whether the song of the cricket be not as early a token of autumn's approach, as any other;—that song, which may be called an audible stillness; for, though very loud and heard afar, yet the mind does not take note of it as a sound; so completely is its individual existence merged among the accompanying characteristics of the season. Alas, for the pleasant summer-time! In August, the grass is still verdant on the hills and in the vallies; the foliage of the trees is as dense as ever, and as green; the flowers gleam forth in richer abundance along the margin of the river, and by the stone-walls, and deep among the woods; the days, too, are as fervid now as they were a month ago;—and yet, in every breath of wind, and in every beam of sunshine, we hear the whispered farewell, and behold the parting smile, of a dear friend. There is a coolness amid all the heat; a mildness in the blazing noon. Not a breeze can stir, but it thrills us with the breath of autumn. A pensive glory is seen in the far, golden gleams, among the shadows of the trees. The flowers—even the brightest of them, and they are the most gorgeous of the year—have this gentle sadness wedded to their pomp, and typify the character of the delicious time, each within itself. The brilliant cardinal-flower has never seemed gay to me.

Still later in the season, Nature's tenderness waxes stronger. It is impossible not to be fond of our Mother now; for she is so fond of us! At other periods, she does not make this impression on me, or only at rare intervals; but, in these genial days of autumn, when she has perfected her harvests, and accomplished every needful thing that was given her to do, then she overflows with a blessed super-fluity of love. She has leisure to caress her children now.

It is good to be alive, at such times. Thank heaven for breath!—yes, for mere breath!—when it is made up of a heavenly breeze like this! It comes with a real kiss upon our cheeks; it would linger fondly around us, if it might; but, since it must be gone, it embraces us with its whole kindly heart, and passes onward, to embrace likewise the next thing that it meets. A blessing is flung abroad, and scattered far and wide over the earth, to be gathered up by all who choose. I recline upon the still unwithered grass, and whisper to myself:—'Oh, perfect day!—Oh, beautiful world!—Oh, beneficent God!' And it is the promise of a blissful Eternity; for our Creator would never have made such lovely days, and have given us the deep hearts to enjoy them, above and beyond all thought, unless we were meant to be immortal.

This sunshine is the golden pledge thereof. It beams through the gates of Paradise, and shows us glimpses far inward.

By-and-by—in a little time—the outward world puts on a drear austerity. On some October morning, there is a heavy hoar-frost on the grass, and along the tops of the fences; and, at sunrise, the leaves fall from the trees of our avenue without a breath of wind, quietly descending by their own weight. All summer long, they have murmured like the noise of waters; they have roared loudly, while the branches were wrestling with the thunder-gust; they have made music, both glad and solemn; they have attuned my thoughts by their quiet sound, as I paced to-and-fro beneath the arch of intermingling boughs. Now, they can only rustle under my feet. Henceforth, the gray parsonage begins to assume a larger importance, and draws to its fireside—for the abomination of the air-tight stove is reserved till wintry weather—draws closer and closer to its fireside the vagrant impulses, that had gone wandering about, through the summer.

When summer was dead and buried, the old Manse became as lonely as a hermitage. Not that ever—in my time, at least—it had been thronged with company; but, at no rare intervals, we welcomed some friend out of the dusty glare and tumult of the world, and rejoiced to share with him the transparent obscurity that was flung over us. In one respect, our precincts were like the Enchanted Ground, through which the pilgrim travelled on his way to the Celestial City. The guests, each and all, felt a slumberous influence upon them; they fell asleep in chairs, or took a more deliberate siesta on the sofa, or were seen stretched among the shadows of the orchard, looking up dreamily through the boughs. They could not have paid a more acceptable compliment to my abode, nor to my own qualities as a host. I held it as a proof, that they left their cares behind them, as they passed between the stone gate-posts, at the entrance of our avenue; and that the so powerful opiate was the abundance of peace and quiet, within and all around us. Others could give them pleasure and amusement, or instruction—these could be picked up anywhere—but it was for me to give them rest— rest, in a life of trouble. What better could be done for those weary and world-worn spirits?—for him, whose career of per- petual action was impeded and harassed by the rarest of his powers, and the richest of his acquirements?—for another, who had thrown his ardent heart, from earliest youth, into the strife of politics, and now, perchance, began to suspect that one lifetime is too brief for the accomplishment of any lofty aim?—for her, on whose feminine nature had been imposed the heavy gift of intellectual power, such as a strong man might have staggered under, and with it the necessity to act upon the world?—in a word, not to multiply instances, what better could be done for anybody, who came within our magic circle, than to throw the spell of a tranquil spirit over him? And when it had wrought its full effect, then we dismissed him, with but misty reminiscences, as if he had been dreaming of us.

Were I to adopt a pet idea, as so many people do, and fondle it in my embraces to the exclusion of all others, it would be, that the great want which mankind labors under, at this present period, is—sleep! The world should recline its vast head on the first convenient pillow, and take an age- long nap. It has gone distracted, through a morbid activity, and, while preternaturally wide-awake, is nevertheless tor- mented by visions, that seem real to it now, but would assume their true aspect and character, were all things once set right by an interval of sound repose. This is the only method of getting rid of old delusions, and avoiding new ones—of regenerating our race, so that it might in due time awake, as an infant out of dewy slumber—of restoring to us the simple perception of what is right, and the single-hearted desire to achieve it; both of which have long been lost, in consequence of this weary activity of brain, and torpor or passion of the heart, that now afflicts the universe. Stimulants, the only mode of treatment hitherto attempted, cannot quell the disease; they do but heighten the delirium.

Let not the above paragraph ever be quoted against the author; for, though tinctured with its modicum of truth, it is the result and expression of what he knew, while he was writing, to be but a distorted survey of the state and prospects of mankind. There were circumstances around me, which made it difficult to view the world precisely as it exists; for, serene and sober as was the old Manse, it was necessary to go but a little way beyond its threshold, before meeting with stranger moral shapes of men than might have been encountered elsewhere, in a circuit of a thousand miles.

These hobgoblins of flesh and blood were attracted thither by the wide-spreading influence of a great original Thinker, who had his earthly abode at the opposite extremity of our village. His mind acted upon other minds, of a certain constitution, with wonderful magnetism, and drew many men upon long pilgrimages, to speak with him face to face. Young visionaries—to whom just so much of insight had been imparted, as to make life all a labyrinth around them—came to seek the clue that should guide them out of their self-involved bewilderment. Gray-headed theorists—whose systems, at first air, had finally imprisoned them in an iron frame-work—travelled painfully to his door, not to ask deliverance, but to invite this free spirit into their own thraldom. People that had lighted on a new thought, or a thought that they fancied new, came to Emerson, as the finder of a glittering gem hastens to a lapidary, to ascertain its quality and value. Uncertain, troubled, earnest wanderers, through the midnight of the moral world, beheld his intellectual fire, as a beacon burning on a hill-top, and, climbing the difficult ascent, looked forth into the surrounding obscurity, more hopefully than hitherto. The light revealed objects unseen before—mountains, gleaming lakes, glimpses of a creation among the chaos—but also, as was unavoidable, it attracted bats and owls, and the whole host of night-birds, which flapped their dusky wings against the gazer's eyes, and sometimes were mistaken for fowls of angelic feather. Such delusions always hover nigh, whenever a beacon-fire of truth is kindled.

For myself, there had been epochs of my life, when I, too, might have asked of this prophet the master-word, that should solve me the riddle of the universe; but now, being happy, I felt as if there were no question to be put, and therefore admired Emerson as a poet of deep beauty and austere tenderness, but sought nothing from him as a philosopher. It was good, nevertheless, to meet him in the wood-paths, or sometimes in our avenue, with that pure, intellectual gleam diffused about his presence, like the garment of a shining-one; and he so quiet, so simple, so without pretension, encountering each man alive as if expecting to receive more than he could impart. And, in truth, the heart of many an ordinary man had, perchance, inscriptions which he could not read. But it was impossible to dwell in his vicinity, without inhaling, more or less, the mountain-atmosphere of his lofty thought, which, in the brains of some people, wrought a singular giddiness—new truth being as heady as new wine. Never was a poor little country village infested with such a variety of queer, strangely dressed, oddly behaved mortals, most of whom took upon themselves to be important agents of the world's destiny, yet were simply bores of a very intense water. Such, I imagine, is the invariable character of persons who crowd so closely about an original thinker, as to draw in his unuttered breath, and thus become imbued with a false originality. This triteness of novelty is enough to make any man, of common sense, blaspheme at all ideas of less than a century's standing; and pray that the world may be petrified and rendered immovable, in precisely the worst moral and physical state that it ever yet arrived at, rather than be benefitted by such schemes of such philosophers.

And now, I begin to feel—and perhaps should have sooner felt—that we have talked enough of the old Manse. Mine honored reader, it may be, will vilify the poor author as an egotist, for babbling through so many pages about a moss-grown country parsonage, and his life within its walls, and on the river, and in the woods,—and the influences that wrought upon him, from all these sources. My conscience, however, does not reproach me with betraying anything too sacredly individual to be revealed by a human spirit, to its brother or sister spirit. How narrow—how shallow and scanty too—is the stream of thought that has been flowing from my pen, compared with the broad tide of dim emotions, ideas, and associations, which swell around me from that portion of my existence! How little have I told!—and, of that little, how almost nothing is even tinctured with any quality that makes it exclusively my own! Has the reader gone wandering, hand in hand with me, through the inner passages of my being, and have we groped together into all its chambers, and examined their treasures or their rubbish? Not so. We have been standing on the green sward, but just within the cavern's mouth, where the common sunshine is free to penetrate, and where every footstep is therefore free to come. I have appealed to no sentiment or sensibilities, save such as are diffused among us all. So far as I am a man of really individual attributes, I veil my face; nor am I, nor have ever been, one of those supremely hospitable people, who serve up their own hearts delicately fried, with brain-sauce, as a tidbit for their beloved public.

Glancing back over what I have written, it seems but the scattered reminiscences of a single summer. In fairy-land, there is no measurement of time; and, in a spot so sheltered from the turmoil of life's ocean, three years hastened away with a noiseless flight, as the breezy sunshine chases the cloud-shadows across the depths of a still valley. Now came hints, growing more and more distinct, that the owner of the old house was pining for his native air. Carpenters next appeared, making a tremendous racket among the out-buildings, strewing the green grass with pine-shavings and chips of chestnut joists, and vexing the whole antiquity of the place with their discordant renovations. Soon, moreover, they divested our abode of the veil of woodbine, which had crept over a large portion of its southern face. All the aged mosses were cleaned unsparingly away; and there were horrible whispers about brushing up the external walls with a coat of paint—a purpose as little to my taste, as might be that of rouging the venerable cheeks of one's grandmother. But the hand that renovates is always more sacrilegious than that which destroys. In fine, we gathered up our household goods, drank a farewell cup of tea in our pleasant little breakfast-room—delicately fragrant tea, an unpurchaseable luxury, one of the many angel-gifts that had fallen like dew upon us—and passed forth between the tall stone gate-posts, as uncertain as the wandering Arabs where our tent might next be pitched. Providence took me by the hand, and—an oddity of dispensation which, I trust, there is no irreverence in smiling at—has led me, as the newspapers announce while

I am writing, from the Old Manse into a Custom-House! As a storyteller, I have often contrived strange vicissitudes for my imaginary personages, but none like this.

The treasure of intellectual gold, which I hoped to find in our secluded dwelling, had never come to light. No profound treatise of ethics—no philosophic history—no novel, even, that could stand, unsupported, on its edges. All that I had to show, as a man of letters, were these few tales and essays, which had blossomed out like flowers in the calm summer of my heart and mind. Save editing (an easy task) the journal of my friend of many years, the African Cruiser, I had done nothing else. With these idle weeds and withering blossoms, I have intermixed some that were produced long ago—old, faded things, reminding me of flowers pressed between the leaves of a book—and now offer the bouquet, such as it is, to any whom it may please. These fitful sketches, with so little of external life about them, yet claiming no profundity of purpose,—so reserved, even while they sometimes seem so frank,—often but half in earnest, and never, even when most so, expressing satisfactorily the thoughts which they profess to image—such trifles, I truly feel, afford no solid basis for a literary reputation. Nevertheless, the public—if my limited number of readers, whom I venture to regard rather as a circle of friends, may be termed a public—will receive them the more kindly, as the last offering, the last collection of this nature, which it is my purpose ever to put forth. Unless I could do better, I have done enough in this kind. For myself, the book will always retain one charm, as reminding me of the river, with its delightful solitudes, and of the avenue, the garden, and the orchard, and especially the dear old Manse, with the little study on its western side, and the sunshine glimmering through the willow-branches while I wrote.

Let the reader, if he will do me so much honor, imagine himself my guest, and that, having seen whatever may be worthy of notice, within and about the old Manse, he has finally been ushered into my study. There, after seating him in an antique elbow-chair, an heirloom of the house, I take forth a roll of manuscript, and intreat his attention to the following tales:—an act of personal inhospitality, however, which I never was guilty of, nor ever will be, even to my worst enemy.

THE BIRTH-MARK

I N THE latter part of the last century, there lived a man of science—an eminent proficient in every branch of natural philosophy—who, not long before our story opens, had made experience of a spiritual affinity, more attractive than any chemical one. He had left his laboratory to the care of an assistant, cleared his fine countenance from the furnace-smoke, washed the stain of acids from his fingers, and persuaded a beautiful woman to become his wife. In those days, when the comparatively recent discovery of electricity, and other kindred mysteries of nature, seemed to open paths into the region of miracle, it was not unusual for the love of science to rival the love of woman, in its depth and absorbing energy. The higher intellect, the imagination, the spirit, and even the heart, might all find their congenial aliment in pursuits which, as some of their ardent votaries believed, would ascend from one step of powerful intelligence to another, until the philosopher should lay his hand on the secret of creative force, and perhaps make new worlds for himself. We know not whether Aylmer possessed this degree of faith in man's ultimate control over nature. He had devoted himself, however, too unreservedly to scientific studies, ever to be weaned from them by any second passion.

His love for his young wife might prove the stronger of the two; but it could only be by intertwining itself with his love of science, and uniting the strength of the latter to its own.

Such a union accordingly took place, and was attended with truly remarkable consequences, and a deeply impressive moral. One day, very soon after their marriage, Aylmer sat gazing at his wife, with a trouble in his countenance that grew stronger, until he spoke.

"Georgiana," said he, "has it never occurred to you that the mark upon your cheek might be removed?"

"No, indeed," said she, smiling; but perceiving the seriousness of his manner, she blushed deeply. "To tell you the truth, it has been so often called a charm, that I was simple enough to imagine it might be so."

"Ah, upon another face, perhaps it might," replied her husband. "But never on yours! No, dearest Georgiana, you came so nearly perfect from the hand of Nature, that this slightest possible defect—which we hesitate whether to term a defect or a beauty—shocks me, as being the visible mark of earthly imperfection."

"Shocks you, my husband!" cried Georgiana, deeply hurt; at first reddening with momentary anger, but then bursting into tears. "Then why did you take me from my mother's side? You cannot love what shocks you!"

To explain this conversation, it must be mentioned, that, in the centre of Georgiana's left cheek, there was a singular mark, deeply interwoven, as it were, with the texture and substance of her face. In the usual state of her complexion,— a healthy, though delicate bloom,—the mark wore a tint of deeper crimson, which imperfectly defined its shape amid the surrounding rosiness. When she blushed, it gradually became more indistinct, and finally vanished amid the triumphant rush of blood, that bathed the whole cheek with its brilliant glow. But, if any shifting emotion caused her to turn pale, there was the mark again, a crimson stain upon the snow, in what Aylmer sometimes deemed an almost fearful distinctness. Its shape bore not a little similarity to the human hand, though of the smallest pigmy size. Georgiana's lovers were wont to say, that some fairy, at her birth-hour, had laid her tiny hand upon the infant's cheek, and left this impress there, in token of the magic endowments that were to give her such sway over all hearts. Many a desperate swain would have risked life for the privilege of pressing his lips to the mysterious hand. It must not be concealed, however, that the impression wrought by this fairy sign-manual varied exceedingly, according to the difference of temperament in the beholders. Some fastidious persons— but they were exclusively of her own sex—affirmed that the Bloody Hand, as they chose to call it, quite destroyed the effect of Georgiana's beauty, and rendered her countenance even hideous. But it would be as reasonable to say, that one of those small blue stains, which sometimes occur in the purest statuary marble, would convert the Eve of Powers to a monster. Masculine observers, if the birth-mark did not heighten their admiration, contented themselves with wishing it away, that the world might possess one living specimen of ideal loveliness, without the semblance of a flaw. After his marriage—for he thought little or nothing of the matter before—Aylmer discovered that this was the case with himself.

Had she been less beautiful—if Envy's self could have found aught else to sneer at—he might have felt his affection heightened by the prettiness of this mimic hand, now vaguely portrayed, now lost, now stealing forth again, and glimmering to-and-fro with every pulse of emotion that throbbed within her heart. But, seeing her otherwise so perfect, he found this one defect grow more and more intolerable, with every moment of their united lives. It was the fatal flaw of humanity, which Nature, in one shape or another, stamps ineffaceably on all her productions, either to imply that they are temporary and finite, or that their perfection must be wrought by toil and pain. The Crimson Hand expressed the ineludible gripe, in which mortality clutches the highest and purest of earthly mould, degrading them into kindred with the lowest, and even with the very brutes, like whom their visible frames return to dust. In this manner, selecting it as the symbol of his wife's liability to sin, sorrow, decay, and death, Alymer's sombre imagination was not long in rendering the birth-mark a frightful object, causing him more trouble and horror than ever Georgiana's beauty, whether of soul or sense, had given him delight.

At all the seasons which should have been their happiest, he invariably, and without intending it—nay, in spite of a purpose to the contrary—reverted to this one disastrous topic. Trifling as it at first appeared, it so connected itself with innumerable trains of thought, and modes of feeling, that it became the central point of all. With the morning twilight, Aylmer opened his eyes upon his wife's face, and recognized the symbol of imperfection; and when they sat together at the evening hearth, his eyes wandered stealthily to her cheek, and beheld, flickering with the blaze of the wood fire, the spectral Hand that wrote mortality, where he would fain have worshipped. Georgiana soon learned to shudder at his gaze. It needed but a glance, with the peculiar expression that his face often wore, to change the roses of her cheek into a deathlike paleness, amid which the Crimson Hand was brought strongly out, like a bas-relief of ruby on the whitest marble.

Late, one night, when the lights were growing dim, so as hardly to betray the stain on the poor wife's cheek, she herself, for the first time, voluntarily took up the subject.

"Do you remember, my dear Aylmer," said she, with a feeble attempt at a smile—"have you any recollection of a dream, last night, about this odious Hand?"

"None!—none whatever!" replied Aylmer, starting; but then he added in a dry, cold tone, affected for the sake of concealing the real depth of his emotion:—"I might well dream of it; for before I fell asleep, it had taken a pretty firm hold of my fancy."

"And you did dream of it," continued Georgiana, hastily; for she dreaded lest a gush of tears should interrupt what she had to say—"A terrible dream! I wonder that you can forget it. Is it possible to forget this one expression?—'It is in her heart now—we must have it out!'—Reflect, my husband; for by all means I would have you recall that dream."

The mind is in a sad note, when Sleep, the all-involving, cannot confine her spectres within the dim region of her sway, but suffers them to break forth, affrighting this actual life with secrets that perchance belong to a deeper one. Aylmer now remembered his dream. He had fancied himself, with his servant Aminadab, attempting an operation for the removal of the birth-mark. But the deeper went the knife, the deeper sank the Hand, until at length its tiny grasp appeared to have caught hold of Georgiana's heart; whence, however, her husband was inexorably resolved to cut or wrench it away.

When the dream had shaped itself perfectly in his memory, Aylmer sat in his wife's presence with a guilty feeling. Truth often finds its way to the mind close-muffled in robes of sleep, and then speaks with uncompromising directness of matters in regard to which we practise an unconscious self-deception, during our waking moments. Until now, he had not been aware of the tyrannizing influence acquired by one idea over his mind, and of the lengths which he might find in his heart to go, for the sake of giving himself peace.

"Aylmer," resumed Georgiana, solemnly, "I know not what may be the cost to both of us, to rid me of this fatal birth-mark. Perhaps its removal may cause cureless deformity. Or, it may be, the stain goes as deep as life itself. Again, do we know that there is a possibility, on any terms, of unclasping the firm gripe of this little Hand, which was laid upon me before I came into the world?"

"Dearest Georgiana, I have spent much thought upon the subject," hastily interrupted Aylmer—"I am convinced of the perfect practicability of its removal."

"If there be the remotest possibility of it," continued Georgiana, "let the attempt be made, at whatever risk. Danger is nothing to me; for life—while this hateful mark makes me the object of your horror and disgust—life is a burthen which I would fling down with joy. Either remove this dreadful Hand, or take my wretched life! You have deep science! All the world bears witness of it. You have achieved great wonders! Cannot you remove this little, little mark, which I cover with the tips of two small fingers? Is this beyond your power, for the sake of your own peace, and to save your poor wife from madness?"

"Noblest—dearest—tenderest wife!" cried Aylmer, rapturously. "Doubt not my power. I have already given this matter the deepest thought—thought which might almost have enlightened me to create a being less perfect than yourself. Georgiana, you have led me deeper than ever into the heart of science. I feel myself fully competent to render this dear cheek as faultless as its fellow; and then, most beloved, what will be my triumph, when I shall have corrected what Nature left imperfect, in her fairest work! Even Pygmalion, when his sculptured woman assumed life, felt not greater ecstasy than mine will be."

"It is resolved, then," said Georgiana, faintly smiling,—
"And, Aylmer, spare me not, though you should find the
birth-mark take refuge in my heart at last."

Her husband tenderly kissed her cheek—her right cheek—
not that which bore the impress of the Crimson Hand.

The next day, Aylmer apprized his wife of a plan that he
had formed, whereby he might have opportunity for the
intense thought and constant watchfulness, which the proposed operation would require; while Georgiana, likewise,
would enjoy the perfect repose essential to its success. They
were to seclude themselves in the extensive apartments occupied by Aylmer as a laboratory, and where, during his toilsome youth, he had made discoveries in the elemental powers
of nature, that had roused the admiration of all the learned
societies in Europe. Seated calmly in this laboratory, the pale
philosopher had investigated the secrets of the highest cloud-
region, and of the profoundest mines; he had satisfied himself
of the causes that kindled and kept alive the fires of the
volcano; and had explained the mystery of fountains, and
how it is that they gush forth, some so bright and pure, and
others with such rich medicinal virtues, from the dark bosom
of the earth. Here, too, at an earlier period, he had studied
the wonders of the human frame, and attempted to fathom
the very process by which Nature assimilates all her precious
influences from earth and air, and from the spiritual world,
to create and foster Man, her masterpiece. The latter pursuit,
however, Aylmer had long laid aside, in unwilling recognition of the truth, against which all seekers sooner or later
stumble, that our great creative Mother, while she amuses us
with apparently working in the broadest sunshine, is yet
severely careful to keep her own secrets, and, in spite of her
pretended openness, shows us nothing but results. She permits us indeed, to mar, but seldom to mend, and, like a
jealous patentee, on no account to make. Now, however,

Aylmer resumed these half-forgotten investigations; not, of course, with such hopes or wishes as first suggested them; but because they involved much physiological truth, and lay in the path of his proposed scheme for the treatment of Georgiana.

As he led her over the threshold of the laboratory, Georgiana was cold and tremulous. Aylmer looked cheerfully into her face, with intent to reassure her, but was so startled with the intense glow of the birth-mark upon the whiteness of her cheek, that he could not restrain a strong convulsive shudder. His wife fainted.

"Aminadab! Aminadab!" shouted Aylmer, stamping violently on the floor.

Forthwith, there issued from an inner apartment a man of low stature, but bulky frame, with shaggy hair hanging about his visage, which was grimed with the vapors of the furnace. This personage had been Aylmer's under-worker during his whole scientific career, and was admirably fitted for that office by his great mechanical readiness, and the skill with which, while incapable of comprehending a single principle, he executed all the practical details of his master's experiments. With his vast strength, his shaggy hair, his smoky aspect, and the indescribable earthiness that incrusted him, he seemed to represent man's physical nature; while Aylmer's slender figure, and pale, intellectual face, were no less apt a type of the spiritual element.

"Throw open the door of the boudoir, Aminadab," said Aylmer, "and burn a pastille."

"Yes, master," answered Aminadab, looking intently at the lifeless form of Georgiana; and then he muttered to himself: —"If she were my wife, I'd never part with that birth-mark."

When Georgiana recovered consciousness, she found herself breathing an atmosphere of penetrating fragrance, the gentle potency of which had recalled her from her deathlike faintness. The scene around her looked like enchantment. Aylmer had converted those smoky, dingy, sombre rooms, where he had spent his brightest years in recondite pursuits, into a series of beautiful apartments, not unfit to be the secluded abode of a lovely woman. The walls were hung with gorgeous curtains, which imparted the combination of grandeur and grace, that no other species of adornment can achieve; and as they fell from the ceiling to the floor, their rich and ponderous folds, concealing all angles and straight lines, appeared to shut in the scene from infinite space. For aught Georgiana knew, it might be a pavilion among the clouds. And Aylmer, excluding the sunshine, which would have interfered with his chemical processes, had supplied its place with perfumed lamps, emitting flames of various hue, but all uniting in a soft, empurpled radiance. He now knelt by his wife's side, watching her earnestly, but without alarm; for he was confident in his science, and felt that he could draw a magic circle round her, within which no evil might intrude.

"Where am I?—Ah, I remember!" said Georgiana, faintly; and she placed her hand over her cheek, to hide the terrible mark from her husband's eyes.

"Fear not, dearest!" exclaimed he. "Do not shrink from me! Believe me, Georgiana, I even rejoice in this single imperfection, since it will be such rapture to remove it."

"Oh, spare me!" sadly replied his wife—"Pray do not look at it again. I never can forget that convulsive shudder."

In order to soothe Georgiana, and, as it were, to release her mind from the burthen of actual things, Aylmer now put in practice some of the light and playful secrets, which science had taught him among its profounder lore. Airy figures, absolutely bodiless ideas, and forms of unsubstantial beauty, came and danced before her, imprinting their momentary footsteps on beams of light. Though she had some indistinct idea of the method of these optical phenomena, still the illusion was almost perfect enough to warrant the belief, that her husband possessed sway over the spiritual world. Then again, when she felt a wish to look forth from her seclusion, immediately, as if her thoughts were answered, the procession of external existence flitted across a screen. The scenery and the figures of actual life were perfectly represented, but with that bewitching, yet indescribable difference, which always makes a picture, an image, or a shadow, so much more attractive than the original. When wearied of this, Aylmer bade her cast her eyes upon a vessel, containing a quantity of earth. She did so, with little interest at first, but was soon startled, to perceive the germ of a plant, shooting upward from the soil. Then came the slender stalk—the leaves gradually unfolded themselves—and amid them was a perfect and lovely flower.

"It is magical!" cried Georgiana, "I dare not touch it."

"Nay, pluck it," answered Aylmer, "pluck it, and inhale its brief perfume while you may. The flower will wither in a few moments, and leave nothing save its brown seed-vessels— but thence may be perpetuated a race as ephemeral as itself."

But Georgiana had no sooner touched the flower than the whole plant suffered a blight, its leaves turning coal-black, as if by the agency of fire.

"There was too powerful a stimulus," said Aylmer thoughtfully.

To make up for this abortive experiment, he proposed to take her portrait by a scientific process of his own invention. It was to be effected by rays of light striking upon a polished plate of metal. Georgiana assented—but, on looking at the result, was affrighted to find the features of the portrait blurred and indefinable; while the minute figure of a hand appeared where the cheek should have been. Aylmer snatched the metallic plate, and threw it into a jar of corrosive acid.

Soon, however, he forgot these mortifying failures. In the intervals of study and chemical experiment, he came to her, flushed and exhausted, but seemed invigorated by her presence, and spoke in glowing language of the resources of his art. He gave a history of the long dynasty of the Alchemists, who spent so many ages in quest of the universal solvent, by which the Golden Principle might be elicted from all things vile and base. Aylmer appeared to believe, that, by the plainest scientific logic, it was altogether within the limits of possibility to discover this long-sought medium; but, he added, a philosopher who should go deep enough to acquire the power, would attain too lofty a wisdom to stoop to the exercise of it. Not less singular were his opinions in regard to the Elixir Vitæ. He more than intimated, that it was his option to concoct a liquid that should prolong life for years—perhaps interminably—but that it would produce a discord in nature, which all the world, and chiefly the quaffer of the immortal nostrum, would find cause to curse.

"Aylmer, are you in earnest?" asked Georgiana, looking at him with amazement and fear; "it is terrible to possess such power, or even to dream of possessing it!"

"Oh, do not tremble, my love!" said her husband, "I would not wrong either you or myself by working such inharmonious effects upon our lives. But I would have you consider how trifling, in comparison, is the skill requisite to remove this little Hand."

At the mention of the birth-mark, Georgiana, as usual, shrank, as if a red-hot iron had touched her cheek.

Again Aylmer applied himself to his labors. She could hear his voice in the distant furnace-room, giving directions to Aminadab, whose harsh, uncouth, misshapen tones were audible in response, more like the grunt or growl of a brute than human speech. After hours of absence, Aylmer reappeared, and proposed that she should now examine his cabinet of chemical products, and natural treasures of the earth. Among the former he showed her a small vial, in which, he remarked, was contained a gentle yet most powerful fragrance, capable of impregnating all the breezes that blow across a kingdom. They were of inestimable value, the contents of that little vial; and, as he said so, he threw some of the perfume into the air, and filled the room with piercing and invigorating delight.

"And what is this?" asked Georgiana, pointing to a small crystal globe, containing a gold-colored liquid. "It is so beautiful to the eye, that I could imagine it the Elixir of Life."

"In one sense it is," replied Aylmer, "or rather the Elixir of Immortality. It is the most precious poison that ever was concocted in this world. By its aid, I could apportion the lifetime of any mortal at whom you might point your finger. The strength of the dose would determine whether he were to linger out years, or drop dead in the midst of a breath. No king, on his guarded throne, could keep his life, if I, in my private station, should deem that the welfare of millions justified me in depriving him of it."

"Why do you keep such a terrific drug?" inquired Georgiana in horror.

"Do not mistrust me, dearest!" said her husband, smiling; "its virtuous potency is yet greater than its harmful one. But, see! here is a powerful cosmetic. With a few drops of this, in a vase of water, freckles may be washed away as easily as the hands are cleansed. A stronger infusion would take the blood out of the cheek, and leave the rosiest beauty a pale ghost."

"Is it with this lotion that you intend to bathe my cheek?" asked Georgiana anxiously.

"Oh, no!" hastily replied her husband—"this is merely superficial. Your case demands a remedy that shall go deeper."

In his interviews with Georgiana, Aylmer generally made minute inquiries as to her sensations, and whether the con-

finement of the rooms, and the temperature of the atmosphere, agreed with her. These questions had such a particular
drift, that Georgiana began to conjecture that she was already
subjected to certain physical influences, either breathed in
with the fragrant air, or taken with her food. She fancied,
likewise—but it might be altogether fancy—that there was
a stirring up of her system,—a strange indefinite sensation
creeping through her veins, and tingling, half painfully, half
pleasurably, at her heart. Still, whenever she dared to look
into the mirror, there she beheld herself, pale as a white
rose, and with the crimson birth-mark stamped upon her
cheek. Not even Aylmer now hated it so much as she.

To dispel the tedium of the hours which her husband
found it necessary to devote to the processes of combination
and analysis, Georgiana turned over the volumes of his
scientific library. In many dark old tomes, she met with
chapters full of romance and poetry. They were the works of
the philosophers of the middle ages, such as Albertus Magnus,
Cornelius Agrippa, Paracelsus, and the famous friar who
created the prophetic Brazen Head. All these antique natural-
ists stood in advance of their centuries, yet were imbued with
some of their credulity, and therefore were believed, and
perhaps imagined themselves, to have acquired from the investigation of nature a power above nature, and from physics
a sway over the spiritual world. Hardly less curious and imaginative were the early volumes of the Transactions of the
Royal Society, in which the members, knowing little of the
limits of natural possibility, were continually recording wonders, or proposing methods whereby wonders might be
wrought.

But, to Georgiana, the most engrossing volume was a large
folio from her husband's own hand, in which he had recorded
every experiment of his scientific career, with its original aim,
the methods adopted for its development, and its final success

or failure, with the circumstances to which either event was attributable. The book, in truth, was both the history and emblem of his ardent, ambitious, imaginative, yet practical and laborious, life. He handled physical details, as if there were nothing beyond them; yet spiritualized them all, and redeemed himself from materialism, by his strong and eager aspiration towards the infinite. In his grasp, the veriest clod of earth assumed a soul. Georgiana, as she read, reverenced Aylmer, and loved him more profoundly than ever, but with a less entire dependence on his judgment than heretofore. Much as he had accomplished, she could not but observe that his most splendid successes were almost invariably failures, if compared with the ideal at which he aimed. His brightest diamonds were the merest pebbles, and felt to be so by himself, in comparison with the inestimable gems which lay hidden beyond his reach. The volume, rich with achievements that had won renown for its author, was yet as melancholy a record as ever mortal hand had penned. It was the sad confession, and continual exemplification, of the short-comings of the composite man—the spirit burthened with clay and working in matter—and of the despair that assails the higher nature, at finding itself so miserably thwarted by the earthly part. Perhaps every man of genius, in whatever sphere, might recognize the image of his own experience in Aylmer's journal.

So deeply did these reflections affect Georgiana, that she laid her face upon the open volume, and burst into tears. In this situation she was found by her husband.

"It is dangerous to read in a sorcerer's books," said he, with a smile, though his countenance was uneasy and displeased. "Georgiana, there are pages in that volume, which I can scarcely glance over and keep my senses. Take heed lest it prove as detrimental to you!"

"It has made me worship you more than ever," said she.

"Ah! wait for this one success," rejoined he, "then worship me if you will. I shall deem myself hardly unworthy of it. But, come! I have sought you for the luxury of your voice. Sing to me, dearest!"

So she poured out the liquid music of her voice to quench the thirst of his spirit. He then took his leave, with a boyish exuberance of gaiety, assuring her that her seclusion would endure but a little longer, and that the result was already certain. Scarcely had he departed, when Georgiana felt irresistibly impelled to follow him. She had forgotten to inform Aylmer of a symptom, which, for two or three hours past, had begun to excite her attention. It was a sensation in the fatal birth-mark, not painful, but which induced a restlessness throughout her system. Hastening after her husband, she intruded, for the first time, into the laboratory.

The first thing that struck her eye was the furnace, that hot and feverish worker, with the intense glow of its fire, which, by the quantities of soot clustered above it, seemed to have been burning for ages. There was a distilling apparatus in full operation. Around the room were retorts, tubes, cylinders, crucibles, and other apparatus of chemical research. An electrical machine stood ready for immediate use. The atmosphere felt oppressively close, and was tainted with gaseous odors, which had been tormented forth by the processes of science. The severe and homely simplicity of the apartment, with its naked walls and brick pavement, looked strange, accustomed as Georgiana had become to the fantastic elegance of her boudoir. But what chiefly, indeed almost solely, drew her attention, was the aspect of Aylmer himself.

He was pale as death, anxious, and absorbed, and hung over the furnace as if it depended upon his utmost watchfulness whether the liquid, which it was distilling, should be the draught of immortal happiness or misery. How different from the sanguine and joyous mien that he had assumed for Georgiana's encouragement!

"Carefully now, Aminadab! Carefully, thou human machine! Carefully, thou man of clay!" muttered Aylmer, more to himself than his assistant. "Now, if there be a thought too much or too little, it is all over!"

"Hoh! hoh!" mumbled Aminadab—"look, master, look!"

Aylmer raised his eyes hastily, and at first reddened, then grew paler than ever, on beholding Georgiana. He rushed towards her, and seized her arm with a gripe that left the print of his fingers upon it.

"Why do you come hither? Have you no trust in your husband?" cried he impetuously. "Would you throw the blight of that fatal birth-mark over my labors? It is not well done. Go, prying woman, go!"

"Nay, Aylmer," said Georgiana, with the firmness of which she possessed no stinted endowment, "it is not you that have a right to complain. You mistrust your wife! You have concealed the anxiety with which you watch the development of this experiment. Think not so unworthily of me, my husband! Tell me all the risk we run; and fear not that I shall shrink, for my share in it is far less than your own!"

"No, no, Georgiana!" said Aylmer impatiently, "it must not be."

"I submit," replied she calmly. "And, Aylmer, I shall quaff whatever draught you bring me; but it will be on the same principle that would induce me to take a dose of poison, if offered by your hand."

"My noble wife," said Aylmer, deeply moved, "I knew not the height and depth of your nature, until now. Nothing shall be concealed. Know, then, that this Crimson Hand, superficial as it seems, has clutched its grasp into your being, with a strength of which I had no previous conception. I have already administered agents powerful enough to do aught except to change your entire physical system. Only one thing remains to be tried. If that fail us, we are ruined!"

"Why did you hesitate to tell me this?" asked she.

"Because, Georgiana," said Aylmer, in a low voice, "there is danger!"

"Danger? There is but one danger—that this horrible stigma shall be left upon my cheek!" cried Georgiana. "Remove it! remove it!—whatever be the cost—or we shall both go mad!"

"Heaven knows, your words are too true," said Aylmer, sadly. "And now, dearest, return to your boudoir. In a little while, all will be tested."

He conducted her back, and took leave of her with a solemn tenderness, which spoke far more than his words how much was now at stake. After his departure, Georgiana became wrapt in musings. She considered the character of Aylmer, and did it completer justice than at any previous moment. Her heart exulted, while it trembled, at his honorable love, so pure and lofty that it would accept nothing less than perfection, nor miserably make itself contented with an earthlier nature than he had dreamed of. She felt how much more precious was such a sentiment, than that meaner kind which would have borne with the imperfection for her sake, and have been guilty of treason to holy love, by degrading its perfect idea to the level of the actual. And, with her whole spirit, she prayed, that, for a single moment, she might satisfy his highest and deepest conception. Longer than one moment, she well knew, it could not be; for his spirit was ever on the march—ever ascending—and each instant required something that was beyond the scope of the instant before.

The sound of her husband's footsteps aroused her. He bore a crystal goblet, containing a liquor colorless as water, but bright enough to be the draught of immortality. Aylmer was pale; but it seemed rather the consequence of a highly wrought state of mind, and tension of spirit, than of fear or doubt.

"The concoction of the draught has been perfect," said he, in answer to Georgiana's look. "Unless all my science have deceived me, it cannot fail."

"Save on your account, my dearest Aylmer," observed his wife, "I might wish to put off this birth-mark of mortality by relinquishing mortality itself, in preference to any other mode. Life is but a sad possession to those who have attained precisely the degree of moral advancement at which I stand. Were I weaker and blinder, it might be happiness. Were I stronger, it might be endured hopefully. But, being what I find myself, methinks I am of all mortals the most fit to die."

"You are fit for heaven without tasting death!" replied her husband. "But why do we speak of dying? The draught cannot fail. Behold its effect upon this plant!"

On the window-seat there stood a geranium, diseased with yellow blotches, which had overspread all its leaves. Aylmer poured a small quantity of the liquid upon the soil in which it grew. In a little time, when the roots of the plant had taken up the moisture, the unsightly blotches began to be extinguished in a living verdure.

"There needed no proof," said Georgiana, quietly. "Give me the goblet. I joyfully stake all upon your word."

"Drink, then, thou lofty creature!" exclaimed Aylmer, with fervid admiration. "There is no taint of imperfection on thy spirit. Thy sensible frame, too, shall soon be all perfect!"

She quaffed the liquid, and returned the goblet to his hand.

"It is grateful," said she, with a placid smile. "Methinks it is like water from a heavenly fountain; for it contains I know not what of unobtrusive fragrance and deliciousness. It allays a feverish thirst, that had parched me for many days. Now, dearest, let me sleep. My earthly senses are closing over my spirit, like the leaves round the heart of a rose, at sunset."

She spoke the last words with a gentle reluctance, as if it required almost more energy than she could command to pronounce the faint and lingering syllables. Scarcely had they loitered through her lips, ere she was lost in slumber. Aylmer sat by her side, watching her aspect with the emotions proper to a man, the whole value of whose existence was involved in the process now to be tested. Mingled with this mood, however, was the philosophic investigation, characteristic of the man of science. Not the minutest symptom escaped him. A heightened flush of the cheek—a slight irregularity of breath —a quiver of the eyelid—a hardly perceptible tremor through the frame—such were the details which, as the moments passed, he wrote down in his folio volume. Intense thought had set its stamp upon every previous page of that volume; but the thoughts of years were all concentrated upon the last.

While thus employed, he failed not to gaze often at the fatal Hand, and not without a shudder. Yet once, by a strange and unaccountable impulse, he pressed it with his lips. His spirit recoiled, however, in the very act, and Georgiana, out of the midst of her deep sleep, moved uneasily and murmured, as if in remonstrance. Again, Aylmer resumed his watch. Nor was it without avail. The Crimson Hand, which at first had been strongly visible upon the marble paleness of Georgiana's cheek now grew more faintly outlined. She remained not less pale than ever; but the birth-mark, with every breath that came and went, lost somewhat of its former distinctness. Its presence had been awful; its departure was more awful still. Watch the stain of the rainbow fading out of the sky; and you will know how that mysterious symbol passed away.

"By Heaven, it is well nigh gone!" said Aylmer to himself, in almost irrepressible ecstasy. "I can scarcely trace it now. Success! Success! And now it is like the faintest rose-color. The slightest flush of blood across her cheek would overcome it. But she is so pale!"

He drew aside the window-curtain, and suffered the light of natural day to fall into the room, and rest upon her cheek. At the same time, he heard a gross, hoarse chuckle, which he had long known as his servant Aminadab's expression of delight.

"Ah, clod! Ah, earthly mass!" cried Aylmer, laughing in a sort of frenzy. "You have served me well! Matter and Spirit —Earth and Heaven—have both done their part in this! Laugh, thing of senses! You have earned the right to laugh."

These exclamations broke Georgiana's sleep. She slowly unclosed her eyes, and gazed into the mirror, which her husband had arranged for that purpose. A faint smile flitted over her lips, when she recognized how barely perceptible was now that Crimson Hand, which had once blazed forth with such disastrous brilliancy as to scare away all their happiness. But then her eyes sought Aylmer's face, with a trouble and anxiety that he could by no means account for.

"My poor Aylmer!" murmured she.

"Poor? Nay, richest! Happiest! Most favored!" exclaimed he. "My peerless bride, it is successful! You are perfect!"

"My poor Aylmer!" she repeated, with a more than human tenderness. "You have aimed loftily!—you have done nobly! Do not repent, that, with so high and pure a feeling, you have rejected the best that earth could offer. Aylmer—dearest Aylmer—I am dying!"

Alas, it was too true! The fatal Hand had grappled with the mystery of life, and was the bond by which an angelic spirit kept itself in union with a mortal frame. As the last crimson tint of the birth-mark—that sole token of human imperfection—faded from her cheek, the parting breath of the now perfect woman passed into the atmosphere, and her soul, lingering a moment near her husband, took its heavenward flight. Then a hoarse, chuckling laugh was heard again! Thus ever does the gross Fatality of Earth exult in its invariable triumph over the immortal essence, which, in this dim sphere of half-development, demands the completeness of a higher state. Yet, had Aylmer reached a profounder wisdom, he need not thus have flung away the happiness, which would have woven his mortal life of the self-same texture with the celestial. The momentary circumstance was too strong for him; he failed to look beyond the shadowy scope of Time, and living once for all in Eternity, to find the perfect Future in the present.

A SELECT PARTY

A MAN of Fancy made an entertainment at one of of his castles in the air, and invited a select number of distinguished personages to favor him with their presence. The mansion, though less splendid than many that have been situated in the same region, was, nevertheless, of a magnificence such as is seldom witnessed by those acquainted only with terrestrial architecture. Its strong foundations and massive walls were quarried out of a ledge of heavy and sombre clouds, which had hung brooding over the earth, apparently as dense and ponderous as its own granite, throughout a whole autumnal day. Perceiving that the general effect was gloomy—so that the airy castle looked like a feudal fortress, or a monastery of the middle ages, or a state-prison of our own times, rather than the home of pleasure and repose which he intended it to be—the owner, regardless of expense, resolved to gild the exterior from top to bottom. Fortunately, there was just then a flood of evening sunshine in the air. This being gathered up and poured abundantly upon the roof and walls, imbued them with a kind of solemn cheerfulness; while the cupolas and pinnacles were made to glitter with the purest gold, and all the hundred windows gleamed with a glad light, as if the edifice itself were rejoicing in its heart. And now, if the people of the lower world chanced to be looking upward, out of the turmoil of their petty perplexities, they probably mistook the castle in the air for a heap of sunset clouds, to which the magic of light and shade had imparted the aspect of a fantastically constructed mansion. To such beholders it was unreal, because they lacked the imaginative faith. Had they been worthy to pass within its portal, they would have recognized the truth, that the dominions which the spirit conquers for itself among unrealities, become a thousand times more real than the earth whereon they stamp their feet, saying, "This is solid and substantial!—this may be called a fact!"

At the appointed hour, the host stood in his great saloon to receive the company. It was a vast and noble room, the vaulted ceiling of which was supported by double rows of gigantic pillars, that had been hewn entire out of masses of variegated clouds. So brilliantly were they polished, and so exquisitely wrought by the sculptor's skill, as to resemble the finest specimens of emerald, porphyry, opal, and chrysolite, thus producing a delicate richness of effect, which their immense size rendered not incompatible with grandeur. To each of these pillars a meteor was suspended. Thousands of these ethereal lustres are continually wandering about the firmament, burning out to waste, yet capable of imparting a useful radiance to any person who has the art of converting them to domestic purposes. As managed in the saloon, they are far more economical than ordinary lamp-light. Such, however, was the intensity of their blaze, that it had been found expedient to cover each meteor with a globe of evening mist, thereby muffling the too potent glow, and soothing it into a mild and comfortable splendor. It was like the brilliancy of a powerful, yet chastened, imagination; a light which seemed to hide whatever was unworthy to be noticed, and give effect to every beautiful and noble attribute. The guests, therefore, as they advanced up the centre of the saloon, appeared to better advantage than ever before in their lives.

The first that entered, with old-fashioned punctuality, was a venerable figure in the costume of by-gone days, with his white hair flowing down over his shoulders, and a reverend beard upon his breast. He leaned upon a staff, the tremulous stroke of which, as he set it carefully upon the floor, re-echoed through the saloon at every footstep. Recognizing at once this celebrated personage, whom it had cost him a vast deal of trouble and research to discover, the host advanced nearly three-fourths of the distance, down between the pillars, to meet and welcome him.

"Venerable sir," said the Man of Fancy, bending to the floor, "the honor of this visit would never be forgotten, were my term of existence to be as happily prolonged as your own."

The old gentleman received the compliment with gracious condescension; he then thrust up his spectacles over his forehead, and appeared to take a critical survey of the saloon.

"Never, within my recollection," observed he, "have I entered a more spacious and noble hall. But are you sure that it is built of solid materials, and that the structure will be permanent?"

"Oh, never fear, my venerable friend," replied the host. "In reference to a lifetime like your own, it is true, my castle may well be called a temporary edifice. But it will endure long enough to answer all the purposes for which it was erected."

But we forget that the reader has not yet been made acquainted with the guest. It was no other than that universally accredited character, so constantly referred to in all seasons of intense cold or heat—he that remembers the hot Sunday and the cold Friday—the witness of a past age, whose negative reminiscences find their way into every newspaper, yet whose antiquated and dusky abode is so overshadowed by accumulated years, and crowded back by modern edifices, that none but the Man of Fancy could have discovered it—it was, in short, that twin-brother of Time, and great-grandsire of mankind, and hand-and-glove associate of all forgotten men and things, the Oldest Inhabitant! The host would willingly have drawn him into conversation, but succeeded only in eliciting a few remarks as to the oppressive atmosphere of this present summer evening, compared with one which the guest had experienced, about four-score years ago. The old gentleman, in fact, was a good deal overcome by his journey among the clouds, which, to a frame so earth-incrusted by long continuance in a lower region, was unavoidably more fatiguing than to younger spirits. He was therefore conducted to an easy-chair, well cushioned, and stuffed with vaporous softness, and left to take a little repose.

The Man of Fancy now discerned another guest, who stood so quietly in the shadow of one of the pillars, that he might easily have been overlooked.

"My dear sir," exclaimed the host, grasping him warmly by the hand, "allow me to greet you as the hero of the evening. Pray do not take it as an empty compliment; for if there were not another guest in my castle, it would be entirely pervaded with your presence!"

"I thank you," answered the unpretending stranger, "but, though you happened to overlook me, I have not just arrived. I came very early, and, with your permission, shall remain after the rest of the company have retired."

And who does the reader imagine was this unobtrusive guest? It was the famous performer of acknowledged impossibilities; a character of superhuman capacity and virtue, and, if his enemies are to be credited, of no less remarkable weaknesses and defects. With a generosity of which he alone sets us the example, we will glance merely at his nobler attributes. He it is, then, who prefers the interests of others to his own, and a humble station to an exalted one. Careless of fashion, custom, the opinions of men, and the influence of the press, he assimilates his life to the standard of ideal rectitude, and thus proves himself the one independent citizen of our free country. In point of ability, many people declare him to be the only mathematician capable of squaring the circle; the only mechanic acquainted with the principle of perpetual motion; the only scientific philosopher who can compel water to run up hill; the only writer of the age whose genius is equal to the production of an epic poem; and, finally—so various are his accomplishments—the only professor of gymnastics who has succeeded in jumping down his own throat. With all these talents, however, he is so far from being considered a member of good society, that it is the severest censure of any fashionable assemblage, to affirm that this remarkable individual was present. Public orators, lecturers, and theatrical performers, particularly eschew his company. For especial reasons, we are not at liberty to disclose his name, and shall mention only one other trait—a most singular phenomenon in natural philosophy—that when he happens to cast his eyes upon a looking-glass, he beholds Nobody reflected there!

Several other guests now made their appearance, and among them, chattering with immense volubility, a brisk little gentleman of universal vogue in private society, and not unknown in the public journals, under the title of Monsieur On-Dit. The name would seem to indicate a Frenchman; but, whatever be his country, he is thoroughly versed in all the languages of the day, and can express himself quite as much to the purpose in English as in any other tongue. No sooner were the ceremonies of salutation over, than this talkative little person put his mouth to the host's ear, and whispered three secrets of state, an important piece of commercial intelligence, and a rich item of fashionable scandal. He then assured the Man of Fancy that he would not fail to circulate in the society of the lower world a minute description of this magnificent castle in the air, and of the festivities at which he had the honor to be a guest. So saying, Monsieur On-Dit made his bow and hurried from one to another of the company, with all of whom he seemed to be acquainted, and to possess some topic of interest or amusement for every individual. Coming at last to the Oldest Inhabitant, who was slumbering comfortably in the easy-chair, he applied his mouth to that venerable ear.

"What do you say?" cried the old gentleman, starting from his nap, and putting up his hand to serve the purpose of an ear-trumpet.

Monsieur On-Dit bent forward again, and repeated his communication.

"Never, within my memory," exclaimed the Oldest Inhabitant, lifting his hands in astonishment, "has so remarkable an incident been heard of!"

Now came in the Clerk of the Weather, who had been invited out of deference to his official station, although the host was well aware that his conversation was likely to contribute but little to the general enjoyment. He soon, indeed, got into a corner with his acquaintance of long ago, the Oldest Inhabitant, and began to compare notes with him in reference to the great storms, gales of wind, and other atmospherical facts that had occurred during a century past. It rejoiced the Man of Fancy, that his venerable and much respected guest had met with so congenial an associate. Entreating them both to make themselves perfectly at home, he now turned to receive the Wandering Jew. This personage, however, had latterly grown so common, by mingling in all sorts of society, and appearing at the beck of every entertainer, that he could hardly be deemed a proper guest in a very exclusive circle. Besides, being covered with dust from his continual wanderings along the highways of the world, he really looked out of place in a dress party, so that the host felt relieved of an incommodity, when the restless individual in question, after a brief stay, took his departure on a ramble towards Oregon.

The portal was now thronged by a crowd of shadowy people, with whom the Man of Fancy had been acquainted in his visionary youth. He had invited them hither for the sake of observing how they would compare, whether advantageously or otherwise, with the real characters to whom his maturer life had introduced him. They were beings of crude imagination, such as glide before a young man's eye, and pretend to be actual inhabitants of the earth; the wise and witty, with whom he would hereafter hold intercourse; the generous and heroic friends, whose devotion would be requited with his own; the beautiful dream-woman, who would become the help-mate of his human toils and sorrows, and at once the source and partaker of his happiness. Alas! it is not good for the full grown man to look too closely at these old acquaintances, but rather to reverence them at a distance, through the medium of years that have gathered duskily between. There was something laughably untrue in their pompous stride and exaggerated sentiment; they were neither human, nor tolerable likenesses of humanity, but fantastic masquers, rendering heroism and nature alike ridiculous by the grave absurdity of their pretensions to such attributes. And as for the peerless dream-lady, behold! there advanced up the saloon, with a movement like a jointed-doll, a sort of wax figure of an angel—a creature as cold as moonshine—an artifice in petticoats, with an intellect of pretty phrases, and only the semblance of a heart—yet, in all these particulars, the true type of a young man's imaginary mistress. Hardly could the host's punctilious courtesy restrain a smile, as he paid his respects to this unreality, and met the sentimental glance with which the Dream sought to remind him of their former love-passages.

"No, no, fair lady," murmured he, betwixt sighing and smiling; "my taste is changed! I have learned to love what Nature makes, better than my own creations in the guise of womanhood."

"Ah, false one!" shrieked the dream-lady, pretending to faint, but dissolving into thin air, out of which came the deplorable murmur of her voice—"your inconstancy has annihilated me!"

"So be it," said the cruel Man of Fancy to himself—"and a good riddance, too!"

Together with these shadows, and from the same region, there came an uninvited multitude of shapes, which, at any time during his life, had tormented the Man of Fancy in his moods of morbid melancholy, or had haunted him in the delirium of fever. The walls of his castle in the air were not dense enough to keep them out; nor would the strongest of earthly architecture have availed to their exclusion. Here were those forms of dim terror, which had beset him at the entrance of life, waging warfare with his hopes. Here were strange uglinesses of earlier date, such as haunt children in the night time. He was particularly startled by the vision of a deformed old black woman, whom he imagined as lurking in the garret of his native home, and who, when he was an infant, had once come to his bedside and grinned at him, in the crisis of a scarlet fever. This same black shadow, with others almost as hideous, now glided among the pillars of the magnificent saloon, grinning recognition, until the man shuddered anew at the forgotten terrors of his childhood. It amused him, however, to observe the black woman, with the mischievous caprice peculiar to such beings, steal up to the chair of the Oldest Inhabitant, and peep into his half-dreamy mind.

"Never within my memory," muttered that venerable personage, aghast, "did I see such a face!"

Almost immediately after the unrealities just described, arrived a number of guests, whom incredulous readers may be inclined to rank equally among creatures of imagination. The most noteworthy were an incorruptible Patriot; a Scholar without pedantry; a Priest without worldly ambition, and a Beautiful Woman without pride or coquetry; a Married Pair, whose life had never been disturbed by incongruity of feeling; a Reformer, untrammelled by his theory; and a Poet, who felt no jealousy towards other votaries of the lyre. In truth, however, the host was not one of the cynics who consider these patterns of excellence, without the fatal flaw, such rarities in the world; and he had invited them to his select party chiefly out of humble deference to the judgment of society, which pronounces them almost impossible to be met with.

"In my younger days," observed the Oldest Inhabitant, "such characters might be seen at the corner of every street."

Be that as it might, these specimens of perfection proved to be not half so entertaining companions as people with the ordinary allowance of faults.

But now appeared a stranger, whom the host had no sooner recognized, than, with an abundance of courtesy unlavished on any other, he hastened down the whole length of the saloon, in order to pay him emphatic honor. Yet he was a young man in poor attire, with no insignia of rank or acknowledged eminence, nor anything to distinguish him among the crowd except a high, white forehead, beneath which a pair of deep-set eyes were glowing with warm light. It was such a light as never illuminates the earth, save when a great heart burns as the household fire of a grand intellect. And who was he? Who, but the Master Genius, for whom our country is looking anxiously into the mist of time, as destined to fulfil the great mission of creating an American literature, hewing it, as it were, out of the unwrought granite of our intellectual quarries. From him, whether moulded in the form of an epic poem, or assuming a guise altogether new, as the spirit itself may determine, we are to receive our first great original work, which shall do all that remains to be achieved for our glory among the nations. How this child of a mighty destiny had been discovered by the Man of Fancy, it is of little consequence to mention. Suffice it, that he dwells as yet unhonored among men, unrecognized by those who have known him from his cradle;—the noble countenance, which should be distinguished by a halo diffused around it, passes daily amid the throng of people, toiling and troubling themselves about the trifles of a moment—and none pay reverence to the worker of immortality. Nor does it matter much to him, in his triumph over all the ages, though a generation or two of his own times shall do themselves the wrong to disregard him.

By this time, Monsieur On-Dit had caught up the stranger's name and destiny, and was busily whispering the intelligence among the other guests.

"Pshaw!" said one, "there can never be an American Genius."

"Pish!" cried another, "we have already as good poets as any in the world. For my part, I desire to see no better."

And the Oldest Inhabitant, when it was proposed to introduce him to the Master Genius, begged to be excused, observing, that a man who had been honored with the acquaintance of Dwight, and Freneau, and Joel Barlow, might be allowed a little austerity of taste.

The saloon was now fast filling up, by the arrival of other remarkable characters; among whom were noticed Davy Jones, the distinguished nautical personage, and a rude, carelessly dressed, harum-scarum sort of elderly fellow, known by the nickname of Old Harry. The latter, however, after being shown to a dressing room, re-appeared with his grey hair nicely combed, his clothes brushed, a clean dicky on his neck, and altogether so changed in aspect as to merit the more respectful appellation of Venerable Henry. John Doe and Richard Roe came arm-in-arm, accompanied by a Man of Straw, a fictitious endorser, and several persons who had no existence except as voters in closely contested elections. The celebrated Seatsfield, who now entered, was at first supposed to belong to the same brotherhood, until he made it apparent that he was a real man of flesh and blood, and had his earthly domicile in Germany. Among the latest comers, as might reasonably be expected, arrived a guest from the far future.

"Do you know him?—do you know him?" whispered Monsieur On-Dit, who seemed to be acquainted with everybody. "He is the representative of Posterity—the man of an age to come!"

"And how came he here?" asked a figure who was evidently the prototype of the fashion-plate in a magazine, and might be taken to represent the vanities of the passing moment. "The fellow infringes upon our rights by coming before his time."

"But you forget where we are," answered the Man of Fancy, who overheard the remark; "the lower earth, it is true, will be forbidden ground to him for many long years hence; but a castle in the air is a sort of no-man's land, where Posterity may make acquaintance with us on equal terms."

No sooner was his identity known, than a throng of guests gathered about Posterity, all expressing the most generous interest in his welfare, and many boasting of the sacrifices which they had made, or were willing to make, in his behalf. Some, with as much secrecy as possible, desired his judgment upon certain copies of verses, or great manuscript rolls of prose; others accosted him with the familiarity of old friends, taking it for granted that he was perfectly cognizant of their names and characters. At length, finding himself thus beset, Posterity was put quite beside his patience.

"Gentlemen, my good friends," cried he, breaking loose from a misty poet, who strove to hold him by the button, "I pray you to attend to your own business, and leave me to take care of mine! I expect to owe you nothing, unless it be certain national debts, and other incumbrances and impediments, physical and moral, which I shall find it troublesome enough to remove from my path. As to your verses, pray read them to your contemporaries. Your names are as strange to me as your faces; and even were it otherwise—let me whisper you a secret—the cold, icy memory which one generation may retain of another, is but a poor recompense to barter life for. Yet, if your heart is set on being known to me, the surest, the only method, is, to live truly and wisely for your own age, whereby, if the native force be in you, you may likewise live for posterity!"

"It is nonsense," murmured the Oldest Inhabitant, who, as a man of the past, felt jealous that all notice should be withdrawn from himself, to be lavished on the future,—"sheer nonsense, to waste so much thought on what only is to be!"

To divert the minds of his guests, who were considerably abashed by this little incident, the Man of Fancy led them through several apartments of the castle, receiving their compliments upon the taste and varied magnificence that were displayed in each. One of these rooms was filled with moonlight, which did not enter through the window, but was the aggregate of all the moon-shine that is scattered around the earth on a summer night, while no eyes are awake to enjoy its beauty. Airy spirits had gathered it up, wherever they found it gleaming on the broad bosom of a lake, or silvering the meanders of a stream, or glimmering among the wind-stirred boughs of a wood, and had garnered it in this one spacious hall. Along the walls, illuminated by the mild intensity of the moon-shine, stood a multitude of ideal statues, the original conceptions of the great works of ancient or modern art, which the sculptors did but imperfectly succeed in putting into marble. For it is not to be supposed that the pure idea of an immortal creation ceases to exist; it is only necessary to know where they are deposited, in order to obtain possession of them. In the alcoves of another vast apartment was arranged a splendid library, the volumes of which were inestimable, because they consisted not of actual performances, but of the works which the authors only planned, without ever finding the happy season to achieve them. To take familiar instances, here were the untold tales of Chaucer's Canterbury Pilgrims; the unwritten Cantos of the Fairy Queen; the conclusion of Coleridge's Christabel; and the whole of Dryden's projected Epic on the subject of King Arthur. The shelves were crowded; for it would not be too much to affirm that every author has imagined, and shaped out in his thought, more and far better works than those which actually proceeded from his pen. And here, likewise, were the unrealized conceptions of youthful poets, who died of the very strength of their own genius, before the world had caught one inspired murmur from their lips.

When the peculiarities of the library and statue-gallery were explained to the Oldest Inhabitant, he appeared infinitely perplexed, and exclaimed, with more energy than usual, that he had never heard of such a thing within his memory, and, moreover, did not at all understand how it could be.

"But my brain, I think," said the good old gentleman, is getting not so clear as it used to be. You young folks, I suppose, can see your way through these strange matters. For my part, I give it up."

"And so do I," muttered the Old Harry. "It is enough to puzzle the——ahem!"

Making as little reply as possible to these observations, the Man of Fancy preceded the company to another noble saloon, the pillars of which were solid golden sunbeams, taken out of the sky in the first hour in the morning. Thus, as they retained all their living lustre, the room was filled with the most cheerful radiance imaginable, yet not too dazzling to be borne with comfort and delight. The windows were beautifully adorned with curtains, made of the many-colored clouds of sunrise, all imbued with virgin light, and hanging in magnificent festoons from the ceiling to the floor. Moreover, there were fragments of rainbows scattered through the room; so that the guests, astonished at one another, reciprocally saw their heads made glorious by the seven primary hues; or, if they chose—as who would not?—they could grasp a rainbow in the air, and convert it to their own apparel and adornment. But the morning light and scattered rainbows were only a type and symbol of the real wonders of the apartment. By an influence akin to magic, yet perfectly natural, whatever means and opportunities of joy are neglected in the lower world, had been carefully gathered up, and deposited in the saloon of morning sunshine. As may well be conceived, therefore, there was material enough to supply not merely a joyous evening, but also a happy lifetime, to more than as many people as that spacious apartment could contain. The company seemed to renew their youth; while that pattern and proverbial standard of innocence, the Child Unborn, frolicked to and fro among them, communicating his own unwrinkled gaiety to all who had the good fortune to witness his gambols.

"My honored friends," said the Man of Fancy, after they had enjoyed themselves awhile, "I am now to request your presence in the banqueting-hall, where a slight collation is awaiting you."

"Ah, well said!" ejaculated a cadaverous figure, who had been invited for no other reason than that he was pretty constantly in the habit of dining with Duke Humphrey. "I was beginning to wonder whether a castle in the air were provided with a kitchen."

It was curious, in truth, to see how instantaneously the guests were diverted from the high moral enjoyments which they had been tasting with so much apparent zest, by a suggestion of the more solid as well as liquid delights of the festive board. They thronged eagerly in the rear of the host, who now ushered them into a lofty and extensive hall, from end to end of which was arranged a table, glittering all over with innumerable dishes and drinking-vessels of gold. It is an uncertain point, whether these rich articles of plate were made for the occasion, out of molten sunbeams, or recovered from the wrecks of Spanish galleons, that had lain for ages at the bottom of the sea. The upper end of the table was overshadowed by a canopy, beneath which was placed a chair of elaborate magnificence, which the host himself declined to occupy, and besought his guests to assign it to the worthiest among them. As a suitable homage to his incalculable antiquity and eminent distinction, the post of honor was at first tendered to the Oldest Inhabitant. He, however, eschewed it, and requested the favor of a bowl of gruel at a side-table, where he could refresh himself with a quiet nap. There was some little hesitation as to the next candidate, until Posterity took the Master Genius of our country by the hand, and led him to the chair of state, beneath the princely canopy. When once they beheld him in his true place, the company acknowledged the justice of the selection by a long thunder-roll of vehement applause.

Then was served up a banquet, combining, if not all the delicacies of the season, yet all the rarities which careful purveyors had met with in the flesh, fish, and vegetable markets of the land of Nowhere. The bill of fare being unfortunately lost, we can only mention a Phœnix, roasted in its own flames, cold potted birds of Paradise, ice-creams from the Milky Way, and whip-syllabubs and flummery from the Paradise of Fools, whereof there was a very great consumption. As for drinkables, the temperance-people contented themselves with water, as usual, but it was the water of the Fountain of Youth; the ladies sipped Nepenthe; the love-lorn, the care-worn, and the sorrow-stricken, were supplied with brimming goblets of Lethe; and it was shrewdly conjectured that a certain golden vase, from which only the more distinguished guests were invited to partake, contained nectar that had been mellowing ever since the days of classical mythology. The cloth being removed, the company, as usual, grew eloquent over their liquor, and delivered themselves of a succession of brilliant speeches; the task of reporting which we resign to the more adequate ability of Counsellor Gill, whose indispensable co-operation the Man of Fancy had taken the precaution to secure.

When the festivity of the banquet was at its most ethereal point, the Clerk of the Weather was observed to steal from the table, and thrust his head between the purple and golden curtains of one of the windows.

"My fellow-guests," he remarked aloud, after carefully noting the signs of the night, "I advise such of you as live at a distance, to be going as soon as possible; for a thunderstorm is certainly at hand."

"Mercy on me!" cried Mother Carey, who had left her brood of chickens, and come hither in gossamer drapery, with pink silk stockings, "How shall I ever get home?"

All now was confusion and hasty departure, with but little superfluous leave-taking. The Oldest Inhabitant, however, true to the rule of those long-past days in which his courtesy had been studied, paused on the threshold of the meteor-lighted hall, to express his vast satisfaction at the entertainment.

"Never, within my memory," observed the gracious old gentleman, "has it been my good fortune to spend a pleasanter evening, or in more select society."

The wind here took his breath away, whirled his three-cornered hat into infinite space, and drowned what further compliments it had been his purpose to bestow. Many of the company had bespoken Will o' the Whisps to convoy them home; and the host, in his general beneficence, had engaged the Man in the Moon, with an immense horn lantern, to be the guide of such desolate spinsters as could do no better for themselves. But a blast of the rising tempest blew out all their lights in the twinkling of an eye. How, in the darkness that ensued, the guests contrived to get back to earth, or whether the greater part of them contrived to get back at all, or are still wandering among clouds, mists, and puffs of tempestuous wind, bruised by the beams and rafters of the overthrown castle in the air, and deluded by all sorts of unrealities, are points that concern themselves, much more than the writer or the public. People should think of these matters, before they trust themselves on a pleasure-party into the realm of Nowhere.

YOUNG GOODMAN BROWN

YOUNG Goodman Brown came forth, at sunset, into the street of Salem village, but put his head back, after crossing the threshold, to exchange a parting kiss with his young wife. And Faith, as the wife was aptly named, thrust her own pretty head into the street, letting the wind play with the pink ribbons of her cap, while she called to Goodman Brown.

'Dearest heart,' whispered she, softly and rather sadly, when her lips were close to his ear, 'pr'y thee, put off your journey until sunrise, and sleep in your own bed to-night. A lone woman is troubled with such dreams and such thoughts, that she's afeard of herself, sometimes. Pray, tarry with me this night, dear husband, of all nights in the year!'

'My love and my Faith,' replied young Goodman Brown, 'of all nights in the year, this one night must I tarry away from thee. My journey, as thou callest it, forth and back again, must needs be done 'twixt now and sunrise. What, my sweet, pretty wife, dost thou doubt me already, and we but three months married!'

'Then, God bless you!' said Faith, with the pink ribbons, 'and may you find all well, when you come back.'

'Amen!' cried Goodman Brown. 'Say thy prayers, dear Faith, and go to bed at dusk, and no harm will come to thee.'

So they parted; and the young man pursued his way, until, being about to turn the corner by the meeting-house, he looked back, and saw the head of Faith still peeping after him, with a melancholy air, in spite of her pink ribbons.

'Poor little Faith!' thought he, for his heart smote him. 'What a wretch am I, to leave her on such an errand! She talks of dreams, too. Methought, as she spoke, there was trouble in her face, as if a dream had warned her what work is to be done to-night. But, no, no! 'twould kill her to think it. Well; she's a blessed angel on earth; and after this one night, I'll cling to her skirts and follow her to Heaven.'

With this excellent resolve for the future, Goodman Brown felt himself justified in making more haste on his present evil purpose. He had taken a dreary road, darkened by all the gloomiest trees of the forest, which barely stood aside to let the narrow path creep through, and closed immediately behind. It was all as lonely as could be; and there is this peculiarity in such a solitude, that the traveller knows not who may be concealed by the innumerable trunks and the thick boughs overhead; so that, with lonely footsteps, he may yet be passing through an unseen multitude.

'There may be a devilish Indian behind every tree,' said Goodman Brown, to himself; and he glanced fearfully behind him, as he added, 'What if the devil himself should be at my very elbow!'

His head being turned back, he passed a crook of the road, and looking forward again, beheld the figure of a man, in grave and decent attire, seated at the foot of an old tree. He arose, at Goodman Brown's approach, and walked onward, side by side with him.

'You are late, Goodman Brown,' said he. 'The clock of the Old South was striking as I came through Boston; and that is full fifteen minutes agone.'

'Faith kept me back awhile,' replied the young man, with a tremor in his voice, caused by the sudden appearance of his companion, though not wholly unexpected.

It was now deep dusk in the forest, and deepest in that part of it where these two were journeying. As nearly as could be discerned, the second traveller was about fifty years old, apparently in the same rank of life as Goodman Brown, and bearing a considerable resemblance to him, though perhaps more in expression than features. Still, they might have been taken for father and son. And yet, though the elder person was as simply clad as the younger, and as simple in manner too, he had an indescribable air of one who knew the world, and would not have felt abashed at the governor's dinner-table, or in King William's court, were it possible that his affairs should call him thither. But the only thing about him, that could be fixed upon as remarkable, was his staff, which bore the likeness of a great black snake, so curiously wrought, that it might almost be seen to twist and wriggle itself, like a living serpent. This, of course, must have been an ocular deception, assisted by the uncertain light.

'Come, Goodman Brown!' cried his fellow-traveller, 'this is a dull pace for the beginning of a journey. Take my staff, if you are so soon weary.'

'Friend,' said the other, exchanging his slow pace for a full stop, 'having kept covenant by meeting thee here, it is my purpose now to return whence I came. I have scruples, touching the matter thou wot'st of.'

'Sayest thou so?' replied he of the serpent, smiling apart. 'Let us walk on, nevertheless, reasoning as we go, and if I convince thee not, thou shalt turn back. We are but a little way in the forest, yet.'

'Too far, too far!' exclaimed the goodman, unconsciously resuming his walk. 'My father never went into the woods on such an errand, nor his father before him. We have been a race of honest men and good Christians, since the days of the martyrs. And shall I be the first of the name of Brown, that ever took this path, and kept—'

'Such company, thou wouldst say,' observed the elder person, interpreting his pause. 'Well said, Goodman Brown! I have been as well acquainted with your family as with ever a one among the Puritans; and that's no trifle to say. I helped your grandfather, the constable, when he lashed the Quaker woman so smartly through the streets of Salem. And it was I that brought your father a pitch-pine knot, kindled at my own hearth, to set fire to an Indian village, in King Philip's war. They were my good friends, both; and many a pleasant walk have we had along this path, and returned merrily after midnight. I would fain be friends with you, for their sake.'

'If it be as thou sayest,' replied Goodman Brown, 'I marvel they never spoke of these matters. Or, verily, I marvel not, seeing that the least rumor of the sort would have driven them from New-England. We are a people of prayer, and good works, to boot, and abide no such wickedness.'

'Wickedness or not,' said the traveller with the twisted staff, 'I have a very general acquaintance here in New-England. The deacons of many a church have drunk the communion wine with me; the selectmen, of divers towns, make me their chairman; and a majority of the Great and General Court are firm supporters of my interest. The governor and I, too—but these are state-secrets.'

'Can this be so!' cried Goodman Brown, with a stare of amazement at his undisturbed companion. 'Howbeit, I have nothing to do with the governor and council; they have their own ways, and are no rule for a simple husbandman, like me. But, were I to go on with thee, how should I meet the eye of that good old man, our minister, at Salem village? Oh, his voice would make me tremble, both Sabbath-day and lecture-day!'

Thus far, the elder traveller had listened with due gravity, but now burst into a fit of irrepressible mirth, shaking himself so violently, that his snake-like staff actually seemed to wriggle in sympathy.

'Ha! ha! ha!' shouted he, again and again; then composing himself, 'Well, go on, Goodman Brown, go on; but pr'y thee, don't kill me with laughing!'

'Well, then, to end the matter at once,' said Goodman Brown, considerably nettled, 'there is my wife, Faith. It would break her dear little heart; and I'd rather break my own!'

'Nay, if that be the case,' answered the other, 'e'en go thy ways, Goodman Brown. I would not, for twenty old women like the one hobbling before us, that Faith should come to any harm.'

As he spoke, he pointed his staff at a female figure on the path, in whom Goodman Brown recognized a very pious and exemplary dame, who had taught him his catechism, in youth, and was still his moral and spiritual adviser, jointly with the minister and Deacon Gookin.

'A marvel, truly, that Goody Cloyse should be so far in the wilderness, at night-fall!' said he. 'But, with your leave, friend, I shall take a cut through the woods, until we have left this Christian woman behind. Being a stranger to you, she might ask whom I was consorting with, and whither I was going.'

'Be it so,' said his fellow-traveller. 'Betake you to the woods, and let me keep the path.'

Accordingly, the young man turned aside, but took care to watch his companion, who advanced softly along the road, until he had come within a staff's length of the old dame. She, meanwhile, was making the best of her way, with singular speed for so aged a woman, and mumbling some indistinct words, a prayer, doubtless, as she went. The traveller put forth his staff, and touched her withered neck with what seemed the serpent's tail.

'The devil!' screamed the pious old lady.

'Then Goody Cloyse knows her old friend?' observed the traveller, confronting her, and leaning on his writhing stick.

'Ah, forsooth, and is it your worship, indeed?' cried the good dame. 'Yea, truly is it, and in the very image of my old gossip, Goodman Brown, the grandfather of the silly fellow that now is. But—would your worship believe it?— my broomstick hath strangely disappeared, stolen, as I suspect, by that unhanged witch, Goody Cory, and that, too, when I was all anointed with the juice of smallage and cinque-foil and wolf's-bane—'

'Mingled with fine wheat and the fat of a new-born babe,' said the shape of old Goodman Brown.

'Ah, your worship knows the receipt,' cried the old lady, cackling aloud. 'So, as I was saying, being all ready for the meeting, and no horse to ride on, I made up my mind to foot it; for they tell me, there is a nice young man to be taken into communion to-night. But now your good worship will lend me your arm, and we shall be there in a twinkling.'

'That can hardly be,' answered her friend. 'I may not spare you my arm, Goody Cloyse, but here is my staff, if you will.'

So saying, he threw it down at her feet, where, perhaps, it assumed life, being one of the rods which its owner had formerly lent to the Egyptian Magi. Of this fact, however, Goodman Brown could not take cognizance. He had cast up his eyes in astonishment, and looking down again, beheld neither Goody Cloyse nor the serpentine staff, but his fellow-traveller alone, who waited for him as calmly as if nothing had happened.

'That old woman taught me my catechism!' said the young man; and there was a world of meaning in this simple comment.

They continued to walk onward, while the elder traveller exhorted his companion to make good speed and persevere in the path, discoursing so aptly, that his arguments seemed rather to spring up in the bosom of his auditor, than to be suggested by himself. As they went, he plucked a branch of maple, to serve for a walking-stick, and began to strip it of the twigs and little boughs, which were wet with evening dew. The moment his fingers touched them, they became strangely withered and dried up, as with a week's sunshine. Thus the pair proceeded, at a good free pace, until suddenly, in a gloomy hollow of the road, Goodman Brown sat himself down on the stump of a tree, and refused to go any farther.

'Friend,' said he, stubbornly, 'my mind is made up. Not another step will I budge on this errand. What if a wretched old woman do choose to go to the devil, when I thought she was going to Heaven! Is that any reason why I should quit my dear Faith, and go after her?'

'You will think better of this, by-and-by,' said his acquaintance, composedly. 'Sit here and rest yourself awhile; and when you feel like moving again, there is my staff to help you along.'

Without more words, he threw his companion the maple stick, and was as speedily out of sight, as if he had vanished into the deepening gloom. The young man sat a few moments, by the road-side, applauding himself greatly, and thinking with how clear a conscience he should meet the minister, in his morning-walk, nor shrink from the eye of good old Deacon Gookin. And what calm sleep would be his, that very night, which was to have been spent so wickedly, but purely and sweetly now, in the arms of Faith! Amidst these pleasant and praiseworthy meditations, Goodman Brown heard the tramp of horses along the road, and deemed it advisable to conceal himself within the verge of the forest, conscious of the guilty purpose that had brought him thither, though now so happily turned from it.

On came the hoof-tramps and the voices of the riders, two grave old voices, conversing soberly as they drew near. These mingled sounds appeared to pass along the road, within a few yards of the young man's hiding-place; but owing, doubtless, to the depth of the gloom, at that particular spot, neither the travellers nor their steeds were visible. Though their figures brushed the small boughs by the way-side, it could not be seen that they intercepted, even for a moment, the faint gleam from the strip of bright sky, athwart which they must have passed. Goodman Brown alternately crouched and stood on tip-toe, pulling aside the branches, and thrusting forth his head as far as he durst, without discerning so much as a shadow. It vexed him the more, because he could have sworn, were such a thing possible, that he recognized the voices of the minister and Deacon Gookin, jogging along quietly, as they were wont to do, when bound to some ordination or ecclesiastical council. While yet within hearing, one of the riders stopped to pluck a switch.

'Of the two, reverend Sir,' said the voice like the deacon's, 'I had rather miss an ordination-dinner than to-night's meeting. They tell me that some of our community are to be here from Falmouth and beyond, and others from Connecticut and Rhode-Island; besides several of the Indian powows, who, after their fashion, know almost as much deviltry as the best of us. Moreover, there is a goodly young woman to be taken into communion.'

'Mighty well, Deacon Gookin!' replied the solemn old tones of the minister. 'Spur up, or we shall be late. Nothing can be done, you know, until I get on the ground.'

The hoofs clattered again, and the voices, talking so strangely in the empty air, passed on through the forest, where no church had ever been gathered, nor solitary Christian prayed. Whither, then, could these holy men be journeying, so deep into the heathen wilderness? Young Goodman Brown caught hold of a tree, for support, being ready to sink down on the ground, faint and overburthened with the heavy sickness of his heart. He looked up to the sky, doubting whether there really was a Heaven above him. Yet, there was the blue arch, and the stars brightening in it.

'With Heaven above, and Faith below, I will yet stand firm against the devil!' cried Goodman Brown.

While he still gazed upward, into the deep arch of the firmament, and had lifted his hands to pray, a cloud, though no wind was stirring, hurried across the zenith, and hid the brightening stars. The blue sky was still visible, except directly overhead, where this black mass of cloud was sweeping swiftly northward. Aloft in the air, as if from the depths of the cloud, came a confused and doubtful sound of voices. Once, the listener fancied that he could distinguish the accents of town's-people of his own, men and women, both pious and ungodly, many of whom he had met at the communion-table, and had seen others rioting at the tavern. The next moment, so indistinct were the sounds, he doubted whether he had heard aught but the murmur of the old forest, whispering without a wind. Then came a stronger swell of those familiar tones, heard daily in the sunshine, at Salem village, but never, until now, from a cloud of night. There was one voice, of a young woman, uttering lamentations, yet with an uncertain sorrow, and entreating for some favor, which, perhaps, it would grieve her to obtain. And all the unseen multitude, both saints and sinners, seemed to encourage her onward.

'Faith!' shouted Goodman Brown, in a voice of agony and desperation; and the echoes of the forest mocked him, crying

—'Faith! Faith!' as if bewildered wretches were seeking her, all through the wilderness.

The cry of grief, rage, and terror, was yet piercing the night, when the unhappy husband held his breath for a response. There was a scream, drowned immediately in a louder murmur of voices, fading into far-off laughter, as the dark cloud swept away, leaving the clear and silent sky above Goodman Brown. But something fluttered lightly down through the air, and caught on the branch of a tree. The young man seized it, and beheld a pink ribbon.

'My Faith is gone!' cried he, after one stupefied moment. 'There is no good on earth; and sin is but a name. Come, devil! for to thee is this world given.'

And maddened with despair, so that he laughed loud and long, did Goodman Brown grasp his staff and set forth again, at such a rate, that he seemed to fly along the forest-path, rather than to walk or run. The road grew wilder and drearier, and more faintly traced, and vanished at length, leaving him in the heart of the dark wilderness, still rushing onward, with the instinct that guides mortal man to evil. The whole forest was peopled with frightful sounds; the creaking of the trees, the howling of wild beasts, and the yell of Indians; while, sometimes, the wind tolled like a distant church-bell, and sometimes gave a broad roar around the traveller, as if all Nature were laughing him to scorn. But he was himself the chief horror of the scene, and shrank not from its other horrors.

'Ha! ha! ha!' roared Goodman Brown, when the wind laughed at him. 'Let us hear which will laugh loudest! Think not to frighten me with your deviltry! Come witch, come wizard, come Indian powow, come devil himself! and here comes Goodman Brown. You may as well fear him as he fear you!'

In truth, all through the haunted forest, there could be nothing more frightful than the figure of Goodman Brown.

On he flew, among the black pines, brandishing his staff with frenzied gestures, now giving vent to an inspiration of horrid blasphemy, and now shouting forth such laughter, as set all the echoes of the forest laughing like demons around him. The fiend in his own shape is less hideous, than when he rages in the breast of man. Thus sped the demoniac on his course, until, quivering among the trees, he saw a red light before him, as when the felled trunks and branches of a clearing have been set on fire, and throw up their lurid blaze against the sky, at the hour of midnight. He paused, in a lull of the tempest that had driven him onward, and heard the swell of what seemed a hymn, rolling solemnly from a distance, with the weight of many voices. He knew the tune; it was a familiar one in the choir of the village meeting-house. The verse died heavily away, and was lengthened by a chorus, not of human voices, but of all the sounds of the benighted wilderness, pealing in awful harmony together. Goodman Brown cried out; and his cry was lost to his own ear, by its unison with the cry of the desert.

In the interval of silence, he stole forward, until the light glared full upon his eyes. At one extremity of an open space, hemmed in by the dark wall of the forest, arose a rock, bearing some rude, natural resemblance either to an altar or a pulpit, and surrounded by four blazing pines, their tops aflame, their stems untouched, like candles at an evening meeting. The mass of foliage, that had overgrown the summit of the rock, was all on fire, blazing high into the night, and fitfully illuminating the whole field. Each pendent twig and leafy festoon was in a blaze. As the red light arose and fell, a numerous congregation alternately shone forth, then disappeared in shadow, and again grew, as it were, out of the darkness, peopling the heart of the solitary woods at once.

'A grave and dark-clad company!' quoth Goodman Brown.

In truth, they were such. Among them, quivering to-and-

fro, between gloom and splendor, appeared faces that would
be seen, next day, at the council-board of the province, and
others which, Sabbath after Sabbath, looked devoutly heavenward, and benignantly over the crowded pews, from the
holiest pulpits in the land. Some affirm, that the lady of the
governor was there. At least, there were high dames well
known to her, and wives of honored husbands, and widows,
a great multitude, and ancient maidens, all of excellent
repute, and fair young girls, who trembled, lest their mothers
should espy them. Either the sudden gleams of light, flashing
over the obscure field, bedazzled Goodman Brown, or he
recognized a score of the church-members of Salem village,
famous for their especial sanctity. Good old Deacon Gookin
had arrived, and waited at the skirts of that venerable saint,
his revered pastor. But, irreverently consorting with these
grave, reputable, and pious people, these elders of the church,
these chaste dames and dewy virgins, there were men of
dissolute lives and women of spotted fame, wretches given
over to all mean and filthy vice, and suspected even of
horrid crimes. It was strange to see, that the good shrank
not from the wicked, nor were the sinners abashed by the
saints. Scattered, also, among their pale-faced enemies, were
the Indian priests, or powows, who had often scared their
native forest with more hideous incantations than any known
to English witchcraft.

'But, where is Faith?' thought Goodman Brown; and, as
hope came into his heart, he trembled.

Another verse of the hymn arose, a slow and mournful
strain, such as the pious love, but joined to words which
expressed all that our nature can conceive of sin, and darkly
hinted at far more. Unfathomable to mere mortals is the
lore of fiends. Verse after verse was sung, and still the chorus
of the desert swelled between, like the deepest tone of a
mighty organ. And, with the final peal of that dreadful

anthem, there came a sound, as if the roaring wind, the rushing streams, the howling beasts, and every other voice of the unconverted wilderness, were mingling and according with the voice of guilty man, in homage to the prince of all. The four blazing pines threw up a loftier flame, and obscurely discovered shapes and visages of horror on the smoke-wreaths, above the impious assembly. At the same moment, the fire on the rock shot redly forth, and formed a glowing arch above its base, where now appeared a figure. With reverence be it spoken, the figure bore no slight similitude, both in garb and manner, to some grave divine of the New-England churches.

'Bring forth the converts!' cried a voice, that echoed through the field and rolled into the forest.

At the word, Goodman Brown stept forth from the shadow of the trees, and approached the congregation, with whom he felt a loathful brotherhood, by the sympathy of all that was wicked in his heart. He could have well nigh sworn, that the shape of his own dead father beckoned him to advance, looking downward from a smoke-wreath, while a woman, with dim features of despair, threw out her hand to warn him back. Was it his mother? But he had no power to retreat one step, nor to resist, even in thought, when the minister and good old Deacon Gookin seized his arms, and led him to the blazing rock. Thither came also the slender form of a veiled female, led between Goody Cloyse, that pious teacher of the catechism, and Martha Carrier, who had received the devil's promise to be queen of hell. A rampant hag was she! And there stood the proselytes, beneath the canopy of fire.

'Welcome, my children,' said the dark figure, 'to the communion of your race! Ye have found, thus young, your nature and your destiny. My children, look behind you!'

They turned; and flashing forth, as it were, in a sheet of flame, the fiend-worshippers were seen; the smile of welcome gleamed darkly on every visage.

'There,' resumed the sable form, 'are all whom ye have reverenced from youth. Ye deemed them holier than your-selves, and shrank from your own sin, contrasting it with their lives of righteousness, and prayerful aspirations heaven-ward. Yet, here are they all, in my worshipping assembly! This night it shall be granted you to know their secret deeds; how hoary-bearded elders of the church have whispered wanton words to the young maids of their households; how many a woman, eager for widow's weeds, has given her husband a drink at bed-time, and let him sleep his last sleep in her bosom; how beardless youths have made haste to inherit their fathers' wealth; and how fair damsels—blush not, sweet ones!—have dug little graves in the garden, and bidden me, the sole guest, to an infant's funeral. By the sympathy of your human hearts for sin, ye shall scent out all the places—whether in church, bed-chamber, street, field, or forest—where crime has been committed, and shall exult to behold the whole earth one stain of guilt, one mighty blood-spot. Far more than this! It shall be yours to penetrate, in every bosom, the deep mystery of sin, the fountain of all wicked arts, and which inexhaustibly supplies more evil impulses than human power—than my power, at its utmost! —can make manifest in deeds. And now, my children, look upon each other.'

They did so; and, by the blaze of the hell-kindled torches, the wretched man beheld his Faith, and the wife her husband, trembling before that unhallowed altar.

'Lo! there ye stand, my children,' said the figure, in a deep and solemn tone, almost sad, with its despairing awful-ness, as if his once angelic nature could yet mourn for our miserable race. 'Depending upon one another's hearts, ye had still hoped, that virtue were not all a dream. Now are ye undeceived! Evil is the nature of mankind. Evil must be your only happiness. Welcome, again, my children, to the communion of your race!'

'Welcome!' repeated the fiend-worshippers, in one cry of despair and triumph.

And there they stood, the only pair, as it seemed, who were yet hesitating on the verge of wickedness, in this dark world. A basin was hollowed, naturally, in the rock. Did it contain water, reddened by the lurid light? or was it blood? or, perchance, a liquid flame? Herein did the Shape of Evil dip his hand, and prepare to lay the mark of baptism upon their foreheads, that they might be partakers of the mystery of sin, more conscious of the secret guilt of others, both in deed and thought, than they could now be of their own. The husband cast one look at his pale wife, and Faith at him. What polluted wretches would the next glance shew them to each other, shuddering alike at what they disclosed and what they saw!

'Faith! Faith!' cried the husband. 'Look up to Heaven, and resist the Wicked One!'

Whether Faith obeyed, he knew not. Hardly had he spoken, when he found himself amid calm night and solitude, listening to a roar of the wind, which died heavily away through the forest. He staggered against the rock and felt it chill and damp, while a hanging twig, that had been all on fire, besprinkled his cheek with the coldest dew.

The next morning, young Goodman Brown came slowly into the street of Salem village, staring around him like a bewildered man. The good old minister was taking a walk along the grave-yard, to get an appetite for breakfast and meditate his sermon, and bestowed a blessing, as he passed, on Goodman Brown. He shrank from the venerable saint, as if to avoid an anathema. Old Deacon Gookin was at domestic worship, and the holy words of his prayer were heard through the open window. 'What God doth the wizard pray to?' quoth Goodman Brown. Goody Cloyse, that excellent old Christian, stood in the early sunshine, at her own lattice, catechising a little girl, who had brought her a pint of morning's milk. Goodman Brown snatched away the child, as from the grasp of the fiend himself. Turning the corner by the meeting-house, he spied the head of Faith, with the pink ribbons, gazing anxiously forth, and bursting into such joy at sight of him, that she skipt along the street, and almost kissed her husband before the whole village. But, Goodman Brown looked sternly and sadly into her face, and passed on without a greeting.

Had Goodman Brown fallen asleep in the forest, and only dreamed a wild dream of a witch-meeting?

Be it so, if you will. But, alas! it was a dream of evil omen for young Goodman Brown. A stern, a sad, a darkly meditative, a distrustful, if not a desperate man, did he become, from the night of that fearful dream. On the Sabbath-day, when the congregation were singing a holy psalm, he could not listen, because an anthem of sin rushed loudly upon his ear, and drowned all the blessed strain. When the minister spoke from the pulpit, with power and fervid eloquence, and, with his hand on the open Bible, of the sacred truths of our religion, and of saint-like lives and triumphant deaths, and of future bliss or misery unutterable, then did Goodman Brown turn pale, dreading, lest the roof should thunder down upon the gray blasphemer and his hearers. Often, awakening suddenly at midnight, he shrank from the bosom of Faith, and at morning or eventide, when the family knelt down at prayer, he scowled, and muttered to himself, and gazed sternly at his wife, and turned away. And when he had lived long, and was borne to his grave, a hoary corpse, followed by Faith, an aged woman, and children and grand-children, a goodly procession, besides neighbors, not a few, they carved no hopeful verse upon his tomb-stone; for his dying hour was gloom.

RAPPACCINI'S DAUGHTER

FROM THE WRITINGS OF AUBÉPINE

W E DO NOT remember to have seen any translated specimens of the productions of M. de
l'Aubépine; a fact the less to be wondered at,
as his very name is unknown to many of his own countrymen, as well as to the student of foreign literature. As a
writer, he seems to occupy an unfortunate position between
the Transcendentalists (who, under one name or another,
have their share in all the current literature of the world),
and the great body of pen-and-ink men who address the
intellect and sympathies of the multitude. If not too refined,
at all events too remote, too shadowy and unsubstantial in
his modes of development, to suit the taste of the latter class,
and yet too popular to satisfy the spiritual or metaphysical
requisitions of the former, he must necessarily find himself
without an audience; except here and there an individual,
or possibly an isolated clique. His writings, to do them
justice, are not altogether destitute of fancy and originality;
they might have won him greater reputation but for an
inveterate love of allegory, which is apt to invest his plots
and characters with the aspect of scenery and people in the

clouds, and to steal away the human warmth out of his conceptions. His fictions are sometimes historical, sometimes of the present day, and sometimes, so far as can be discovered, have little or no reference either to time or space. In any case, he generally contents himself with a very slight embroidery of outward manners,—the faintest possible counterfeit of real life,—and endeavors to create an interest by some less obvious peculiarity of the subject. Occasionally, a breath of nature, a rain-drop of pathos and tenderness, or a gleam of humor, will find its way into the midst of his fantastic imagery, and make us feel as if, after all, we were yet within the limits of our native earth. We will only add to this very cursory notice, that M. de l'Aubépine's productions, if the reader chance to take them in precisely the proper point of view, may amuse a leisure hour as well as those of a brighter man; if otherwise, they can hardly fail to look excessively like nonsense.

Our author is voluminous; he continues to write and publish with as much praiseworthy and indefatigable prolixity, as if his efforts were crowned with the brilliant success that so justly attends those of Eugene Sue. His first appearance was by a collection of stories, in a long series of volumes, entitled "Contes deux fois racontées." The titles of some of his more recent works (we quote from memory) are as follows:— "Le Voyage Céleste à Chemin de Fer," 3 tom. 1838. "Le nouveau Père Adam et la nouvelle Mère Eve," 2 tom. 1839. "Roderic; ou le Serpent à l'estomac," 2 tom. 1840. "Le Culte du Feu," a folio volume of ponderous research into the religion and ritual of the old Persian Ghebers, published in 1841. "La Soirée du Chateau en Espagne," 1 tom. 8vo. 1842; and "L'Artiste du Beau; ou le Papillon Mécanique," 5 tom. 4to. 1843. Our somewhat wearisome perusal of this startling catalogue of volumes has left behind it a certain personal affection and sympathy, though by no means admiration, for M. de l'Aubépine; and we would fain do the little in our power towards introducing him favorably to the American public. The ensuing tale is a translation of his *"Beatrice; ou la Belle Empoisonneuse,"* recently published in *"La Revue Anti-Aristo-cratique."* This journal, edited by the Comte de Bearhaven, has, for some years past, led the defence of liberal principles and popular rights, with a faithfulness and ability worthy of all praise.

A YOUNG man, named Giovanni Guasconti, came, very long ago, from the more southern region of Italy, to pursue his studies at the University of Padua. Giovanni, who had but a scanty supply of gold ducats in his pocket, took lodgings in a high and gloomy chamber of an old edifice, which looked not unworthy to have been the palace of a Paduan noble, and which, in fact, exhibited over its entrance the armorial bearings of a family long since extinct. The young stranger, who was not unstudied in the great poem of his country, recollected that one of the ancestors of this family, and perhaps an occupant of this very mansion, had been pictured by Dante as a partaker of the immortal agonies of his Inferno. These reminiscences and associations, together with the tendency to heart-break natural to a young man for the first time out of his native sphere, caused Giovanni to sigh heavily, as he looked around the desolate and ill-furnished apartment.

"Holy Virgin, Signor," cried old dame Lisabetta, who, won by the youth's remarkable beauty of person, was kindly endeavoring to give the chamber a habitable air, "what a sigh was that to come out of a young man's heart! Do you find this old mansion gloomy? For the love of heaven, then, put your head out of the window, and you will see as bright sunshine as you have left in Naples."

Guasconti mechanically did as the old woman advised, but could not quite agree with her that the Paduan sunshine was as cheerful as that of southern Italy. Such as it was, however, it fell upon a garden beneath the window, and expended its fostering influences on a variety of plants, which seemed to have been cultivated with exceeding care.

"Does this garden belong to the house?" asked Giovanni.

"Heaven forbid, Signor!—unless it were fruitful of better pot-herbs than any that grow there now," answered old Lisabetta. "No; that garden is cultivated by the own hands of Signor Giacomo Rappaccini, the famous Doctor, who, I warrant him, has been heard of as far as Naples. It is said that he distils these plants into medicines that are as potent as a charm. Oftentimes you may see the Signor Doctor at work, and perchance the Signora his daughter, too, gathering the strange flowers that grow in the garden."

The old woman had now done what she could for the aspect of the chamber, and, commending the young man to the protection of the saints, took her departure.

Giovanni still found no better occupation than to look down into the garden beneath his window. From its appearance, he judged it to be one of those botanic gardens, which were of earlier date in Padua than elsewhere in Italy, or in the world. Or, not improbably, it might once have been the pleasure-place of an opulent family; for there was the ruin of a marble fountain in the centre, sculptured with rare art, but so wofully shattered that it was impossible to trace the original design from the chaos of remaining fragments. The water, however, continued to gush and sparkle into the sunbeams as cheerfully as ever. A little gurgling sound ascended to the young man's window, and made him feel as if the fountain were an immortal spirit, that sung its song unceasingly, and without heeding the vicissitudes around it; while one century embodied it in marble, and another scattered the perishable garniture on the soil. All about the pool into which the water subsided, grew various plants, that seemed to require a plentiful supply of moisture for the nourishment of gigantic leaves, and, in some instances, flowers gorgeously magnificent. There was one shrub in particular, set in a marble vase in the midst of the pool, that bore a profusion of purple blossoms, each of which had the lustre and richness of a gem; and the whole together made a show so resplendent that it seemed enough to illuminate the garden, even had there been no sunshine. Every portion of the soil was peopled with plants and herbs, which, if less beautiful, still bore tokens of assiduous care; as if all had their individual virtues, known to the scientific mind that fostered them. Some were placed in urns, rich with old carving, and others in common garden-pots; some crept serpent-like along the ground, or climbed on high, using whatever means of ascent was offered them. One plant had wreathed itself round a statue of Vertumnus, which was thus quite veiled and shrouded in a drapery of hanging foliage, so happily arranged that it might have served a sculptor for a study.

While Giovanni stood at the window, he heard a rustling behind a screen of leaves, and became aware that a person was at work in the garden. His figure soon emerged into view, and showed itself to be that of no common laborer, but a tall, emaciated, sallow, and sickly-looking man, dressed in a scholar's garb of black. He was beyond the middle term of life, with grey hair, a thin grey beard, and a face singularly marked with intellect and cultivation, but which could never, even in his more youthful days, have expressed much warmth of heart.

Nothing could exceed the intentness with which this scientific gardener examined every shrub which grew in his path; it seemed as if he was looking into their inmost nature, making observations in regard to their creative essence, and discovering why one leaf grew in this shape, and another in that, and wherefore such and such flowers differed among themselves in hue and perfume. Nevertheless, in spite of this deep intelligence on his part, there was no approach to intimacy between himself and these vegetable existences. On the contrary, he avoided their actual touch, or the direct inhaling of their odors, with a caution that impressed Giovanni most disagreeably; for the man's demeanor was that of one walking among malignant influences, such as savage beasts, or deadly snakes, or evil spirits, which, should he allow them one moment of license, would wreak upon him some terrible fatality. It was strangely frightful to the young man's imagination, to see this air of insecurity in a person cultivating a garden, that most simple and innocent of human toils, and which had been alike the joy and labor of the unfallen parents of the race. Was this garden, then, the Eden of the present world?—and this man, with such a perception of harm in what his own hands caused to grow, was he the Adam?

The distrustful gardener, while plucking away the dead leaves or pruning the too luxuriant growth of the shrubs, defended his hands with a pair of thick gloves. Nor were these his only armor. When, in his walk through the garden, he came to the magnificent plant that hung its purple gems beside the marble fountain, he placed a kind of mask over his mouth and nostrils, as if all this beauty did but conceal a deadlier malice. But finding his task still too dangerous, he drew back, removed the mask, and called loudly, but in the infirm voice of a person affected with inward disease:

"Beatrice!—Beatrice!"

"Here am I, my father! What would you?" cried a rich and youthful voice from the window of the opposite house; a voice as rich as a tropical sunset, and which made Giovanni, though he knew not why, think of deep hues of purple or crimson, and of perfumes heavily delectable.—"Are you in the garden?"

"Yes, Beatrice," answered the gardener, "and I need your help."

Soon there emerged from under a sculptured portal the figure of a young girl, arrayed with as much richness of taste as the most splendid of the flowers, beautiful as the day, and with a bloom so deep and vivid that one shade more would have been too much. She looked redundant with life, health, and energy; all of which attributes were bound down and compressed, as it were, and girdled tensely, in their luxuriance, by her virgin zone. Yet Giovanni's fancy must have grown morbid, while he looked down into the garden; for the impression which the fair stranger made upon him was as if here were another flower, the human sister of those vegetable ones, as beautiful as they—more beautiful than the richest of them—but still to be touched only with a glove, nor to be approached without a mask. As Beatrice came down the garden path, it was observable that she handled and inhaled the odor of several of the plants, which her father had most sedulously avoided.

"Here, Beatrice," said the latter,—"see how many needful offices require to be done to our chief treasure. Yet, shattered as I am, my life might pay the penalty of approaching it so closely as circumstances demand. Henceforth, I fear, this plant must be consigned to your sole charge."

"And gladly will I undertake it," cried again the rich tones of the young lady, as she bent towards the magnificent plant, and opened her arms as if to embrace it. "Yes, my sister, my splendor, it shall be Beatrice's task to nurse and serve thee; and thou shalt reward her with thy kisses and perfumed breath, which to her is as the breath of life!"

Then, with all the tenderness in her manner that was so strikingly expressed in her words, she busied herself with such attentions as the plant seemed to require; and Giovanni, at his lofty window, rubbed his eyes, and almost doubted whether it were a girl tending her favorite flower, or one sister performing the duties of affection to another. The scene soon terminated. Whether Doctor Rappaccini had finished his labors in the garden, or that his watchful eye had caught the stranger's face, he now took his daughter's arm and retired. Night was already closing in; oppressive exhalations seemed to proceed from the plants, and steal upward past the open window; and Giovanni, closing the lattice, went to his couch, and dreamed of a rich flower and beautiful girl. Flower and maiden were different and yet the same, and fraught with some strange peril in either shape.

But there is an influence in the light of morning that tends to rectify whatever errors of fancy, or even of judgment, we may have incurred during the sun's decline, or among the shadows of the night, or in the less wholesome glow of moonshine. Giovanni's first movement on starting from sleep, was to throw open the window, and gaze down into the garden which his dreams had made so fertile of mysteries. He was surprised, and a little ashamed, to find how real and matter-of-fact an affair it proved to be, in the first rays of the sun, which gilded the dew-drops that hung upon leaf and blossom, and, while giving a brighter beauty to each rare flower, brought everything within the limits of ordinary experience. The young man rejoiced, that, in the heart of the barren city, he had the privilege of overlooking this spot of lovely and luxuriant vegetation. It would serve, he said to himself, as a symbolic language, to keep him in communion with Nature. Neither the sickly and thought-worn Doctor Giacomo Rappaccini, it is true, nor his brilliant daughter, were now visible; so that Giovanni could not determine how much of the singularity which he attributed to both, was due to their own qualities, and how much to his wonder-working fancy. But he was inclined to take a most rational view of the whole matter.

In the course of the day, he paid his respects to Signor Pietro Baglioni, professor of medicine in the University, a physician of eminent repute, to whom Giovanni had brought a letter of introduction. The Professor was an elderly personage, apparently of genial nature, and habits that might almost be called jovial; he kept the young man to dinner, and made himself very agreeable by the freedom and liveliness of his conversation, especially when warmed by a flask or two of Tuscan wine. Giovanni, conceiving that men of science, inhabitants of the same city, must needs be on familiar terms with one another, took an opportunity to mention the name of Doctor Rappaccini. But the Professor did not respond with so much cordiality as he had anticipated.

"Ill would it become a teacher of the divine art of medicine," said Professor Pietro Baglioni, in answer to a question of Giovanni, "to withhold due and well-considered praise of a physician so eminently skilled as Rappaccini. But, on the other hand, I should answer it but scantily to my conscience, were I to permit a worthy youth like yourself, Signor Giovanni, the son of an ancient friend, to imbibe erroneous ideas respecting a man who might hereafter chance to hold your life and death in his hands. The truth is, our worshipful Doctor Rappaccini has as much science as any member of the faculty—with perhaps one single exception—in Padua, or all Italy. But there are certain grave objections to his professional character."

"And what are they?" asked the young man.

"Has my friend Giovanni any disease of body or heart, that he is so inquisitive about physicians?" said the Professor, with a smile. "But as for Rappaccini, it is said of him—and I, who know the man well, can answer for its truth—that he cares infinitely more for science than for mankind. His patients are interesting to him only as subjects for some new experiment. He would sacrifice human life, his own among the rest, or whatever else was dearest to him, for the sake of adding so much as a grain of mustard-seed to the great heap of his accumulated knowledge."

"Methinks he is an awful man, indeed," remarked Guasconti, mentally recalling the cold and purely intellectual aspect of Rappaccini. "And yet, worshipful Professor, is it not a noble spirit? Are there many men capable of so spiritual a love of science?"

"God forbid," answered the Professor, somewhat testily— "at least, unless they take sounder views of the healing art than those adopted by Rappaccini. It is his theory, that all medicinal virtues are comprised within those substances which we term vegetable poisons. These he cultivates with his own hands, and is said even to have produced new varieties of poison, more horribly deleterious than Nature, without the assistance of this learned person, would ever have plagued the world withal. That the Signor Doctor does less mischief than might be expected, with such dangerous substances, is undeniable. Now and then, it must be owned, he has effected—or seemed to effect—a marvellous cure. But, to tell you my private mind, Signor Giovanni, he should receive little credit for such instances of success—they being probably the work of chance—but should be held strictly accountable for his failures, which may justly be considered his own work."

The youth might have taken Baglioni's opinions with many grains of allowance, had he known that there was a professional warfare of long continuance between him and Doctor Rappaccini, in which the latter was generally thought to have gained the advantage. If the reader be inclined to judge for himself, we refer him to certain black-letter tracts on both sides, preserved in the medical department of the University of Padua.

"I know not, most learned Professor," returned Giovanni, after musing on what had been said of Rappaccini's exclusive zeal for science—"I know not how dearly this physician may love his art; but surely there is one object more dear to him. He has a daughter."

"Aha!" cried the Professor with a laugh. "So now our friend Giovanni's secret is out. You have heard of this daughter, whom all the young men in Padua are wild about, though not half a dozen have ever had the good hap to see her face. I know little of the Signora Beatrice, save that Rappaccini is said to have instructed her deeply in his science, and that, young and beautiful as fame reports her, she is already qualified to fill a professor's chair. Perchance her father destines her for mine! Other absurd rumors there be, not worth talking about, or listening to. So now, Signor Giovanni, drink off your glass of Lacryma."

Guasconti returned to his lodgings somewhat heated with the wine he had quaffed, and which caused his brain to swim with strange fantasies in reference to Doctor Rappaccini and the beautiful Beatrice. On his way, happening to pass by a florist's, he bought a fresh bouquet of flowers.

Ascending to his chamber, he seated himself near the window, but within the shadow thrown by the depth of the wall, so that he could look down into the garden with little risk of being discovered. All beneath his eye was a solitude. The strange plants were basking in the sunshine, and now and then nodding gently to one another, as if in acknowledgment of sympathy and kindred. In the midst, by the shattered fountain, grew the magnificent shrub, with its purple gems clustering all over it; they glowed in the air, and gleamed back again out of the depths of the pool, which thus seemed to overflow with colored radiance from the rich reflection that was steeped in it. At first, as we have said, the garden was a solitude. Soon, however,—as Giovanni had half-hoped, half-feared, would be the case,—a figure appeared beneath the antique sculptured portal, and came down between the rows of plants, inhaling their various perfumes, as if she were one of those beings of old classic fable, that lived upon sweet odors. On again beholding Beatrice, the young man was even startled to perceive how much her beauty exceeded his recollection of it; so brilliant, so vivid was its character, that she glowed amid the sunlight, and, as Giovanni whispered to himself, positively illuminated the more shadowy intervals of the garden path. Her face being now more revealed than on the former occasion, he was struck by its expression of simplicity and sweetness; qualities that had not entered into his idea of her character, and which made him ask anew, what manner of mortal she might be. Nor did he fail again to observe, or imagine, an analogy between the beautiful girl and the gorgeous shrub that hung its gem-like flowers over the fountain; a resemblance which Beatrice seemed to have indulged a fantastic humor in heightening, both by the arrangement of her dress and the selection of its hues.

Approaching the shrub, she threw open her arms, as with a passionate ardor, and drew its branches into an intimate embrace; so intimate, that her features were hidden in its leafy bosom, and her glistening ringlets all intermingled with the flowers.

"Give me thy breath, my sister," exclaimed Beatrice; "for I am faint with common air! And give me this flower of thine, which I separate with gentlest fingers from the stem, and place it close beside my heart."

With these words, the beautiful daughter of Rappaccini plucked one of the richest blossoms of the shrub, and was about to fasten it in her bosom. But now, unless Giovanni's draughts of wine had bewildered his senses, a singular incident occurred. A small orange-colored reptile, of the lizard or chameleon species, chanced to be creeping along the path, just at the feet of Beatrice. It appeared to Giovanni—but,

at the distance from which he gazed, he could scarcely have
seen anything so minute—it appeared to him, however, that
a drop or two of moisture from the broken stem of the flower
descended upon the lizard's head. For an instant, the reptile
contorted itself violently, and then lay motionless in the
sunshine. Beatrice observed this remarkable phenomenon,
and crossed herself, sadly, but without surprise; nor did she
therefore hesitate to arrange the fatal flower in her bosom.
There it blushed, and almost glimmered with the dazzling
effect of a precious stone, adding to her dress and aspect
the one appropriate charm, which nothing else in the world
could have supplied. But Giovanni, out of the shadow of
his window, bent forward and shrank back, and murmured
and trembled.

"Am I awake? Have I my senses?" said he to himself.
"What is this being?—beautiful, shall I call her?—or inexpressibly terrible?"

Beatrice now strayed carelessly through the garden, approaching closer beneath Giovanni's window, so that he was
compelled to thrust his head quite out of its concealment in
order to gratify the intense and painful curiosity which she
excited. At this moment, there came a beautiful insect over
the garden wall; it had perhaps wandered through the city
and found no flowers nor verdure among those antique
haunts of men, until the heavy perfumes of Doctor Rappaccini's shrubs had lured it from afar. Without alighting on
the flowers, this winged brightness seemed to be attracted
by Beatrice, and lingered in the air and fluttered about her
head. Now, here it could not be but that Giovanni Guasconti's eyes deceived him. Be that as it might, he fancied
that while Beatrice was gazing at the insect with childish
delight, it grew faint and fell at her feet;—its bright wings
shivered; it was dead—from no cause that he could discern,
unless it were the atmosphere of her breath. Again Beatrice

crossed herself and sighed heavily, as she bent over the dead insect.

An impulsive movement of Giovanni drew her eyes to the window. There she beheld the beautiful head of the young man—rather a Grecian than an Italian head, with fair, regular features, and a glistening of gold among his ringlets —gazing down upon her like a being that hovered in mid-air. Scarcely knowing what he did, Giovanni threw down the bouquet which he had hitherto held in his hand.

"Signora," said he, "there are pure and healthful flowers. Wear them for the sake of Giovanni Guasconti!"

"Thanks, Signor," replied Beatrice, with her rich voice, that came forth as it were like a gush of music; and with a mirthful expression half childish and half woman-like. "I accept your gift, and would fain recompense it with this precious purple flower; but if I toss it into the air, it will not reach you. So Signor Guasconti must even content himself with my thanks."

She lifted the bouquet from the ground, and then as if inwardly ashamed at having stepped aside from her maidenly reserve to respond to a stranger's greeting, passed swiftly homeward through the garden. But, few as the moments were, it seemed to Giovanni when she was on the point of vanishing beneath the sculptured portal, that his beautiful bouquet was already beginning to wither in her grasp. It was an idle thought; there could be no possibility of distinguishing a faded flower from a fresh one at so great a distance.

For many days after this incident, the young man avoided the window that looked into Doctor Rappaccini's garden, as if something ugly and monstrous would have blasted his eye-sight, had he been betrayed into a glance. He felt conscious of having put himself, to a certain extent, within the influence of an unintelligible power, by the communication

which he had opened with Beatrice. The wisest course would
have been, if his heart were in any real danger, to quit his
lodgings and Padua itself, at once; the next wiser, to have
accustomed himself, as far as possible, to the familiar and
day-light view of Beatrice; thus bringing her rigidly and
systematically within the limits of ordinary experience. Least
of all, while avoiding her sight, ought Giovanni to have
remained so near this extraordinary being, that the proximity
and possibility even of intercourse, should give a kind of
substance and reality to the wild vagaries which his imagination ran riot continually in producing. Guasconti had not a
deep heart—or at all events, its depths were not sounded
now—but he had a quick fancy, and an ardent southern
temperament, which rose every instant to a higher fever-pitch.
Whether or no Beatrice possessed those terrible attributes—
that fatal breath—the affinity with those so beautiful and
deadly flowers—which were indicated by what Giovanni had
witnessed, she had at least instilled a fierce and subtle poison
into his system. It was not love, although her rich beauty was
a madness to him; nor horror, even while he fancied her
spirit to be imbued with the same baneful essence that
seemed to pervade her physical frame; but a wild offspring
of both love and horror that had each parent in it, and
burned like one and shivered like the other. Giovanni knew
not what to dread; still less did he know what to hope; yet
hope and dread kept a continual warfare in his breast, alternately vanquishing one another and starting up afresh to
renew the contest. Blessed are all simple emotions, be they
dark or bright! It is the lurid intermixture of the two that
produces the illuminating blaze of the infernal regions.

Sometimes he endeavored to assuage the fever of his spirit
by a rapid walk through the streets of Padua, or beyond its
gates; his footsteps kept time with the throbbings of his brain,

so that the walk was apt to accelerate itself to a race. One day, he found himself arrested; his arm was seized by a portly personage who had turned back on recognizing the young man, and expended much breath in overtaking him.

"Signor Giovanni!—stay, my young friend!" cried he. "Have you forgotten me? That might well be the case, if I were as much altered as yourself."

It was Baglioni, whom Giovanni had avoided, ever since their first meeting, from a doubt that the Professor's sagacity would look too deeply into his secrets. Endeavoring to recover himself, he stared forth wildly from his inner world into the outer one, and spoke like a man in a dream:

"Yes; I am Giovanni Guasconti. You are Professor Pietro Baglioni. Now let me pass!"

"Not yet—not yet, Signor Giovanni Guasconti," said the Professor, smiling, but at the same time scrutinizing the youth with an earnest glance.—"What; did I grow up side by side with your father, and shall his son pass me like a stranger, in these old streets of Padua? Stand still, Signor Giovanni; for we must have a word or two, before we part."

"Speedily, then, most worshipful Professor, speedily!" said Giovanni, with feverish impatience. "Does not your worship see that I am in haste?"

Now, while he was speaking, there came a man in black along the street, stooping and moving feebly, like a person in inferior health. His face was all overspread with a most sickly and sallow hue, but yet so pervaded with an expression of piercing and active intellect, that an observer might easily have overlooked the merely physical attributes, and have seen only this wonderful energy. As he passed, this person exchanged a cold and distant salutation with Baglioni, but fixed his eyes upon Giovanni with an intentness that seemed to bring out whatever was within him worthy of notice. Nevertheless, there was a peculiar quietness in the look, as if taking merely a speculative, not a human, interest in the young man.

"It is Doctor Rappaccini!" whispered the Professor, when the stranger had passed.—"Has he ever seen your face before?"

"Not that I know," answered Giovanni, starting at the name.

"He *has* seen you!—he must have seen you!" said Baglioni, hastily. "For some purpose or other, this man of science is making a study of you. I know that look of his! It is the same that coldly illuminates his face, as he bends over a bird, a mouse, or a butterfly, which, in pursuance of some experiment, he has killed by the perfume of a flower;—a look as deep as Nature itself, but without Nature's warmth of love. Signor Giovanni, I will stake my life upon it, you are the subject of one of Rappaccini's experiments!"

"Will you make a fool of me?" cried Giovanni, passionately. "*That*, Signor Professor, were an untoward experiment."

"Patience, patience!" replied the imperturbable Professor.— "I tell thee, my poor Giovanni, that Rappaccini has a scientific interest in thee. Thou hast fallen into fearful hands! And the Signora Beatrice? What part does she act in this mystery?"

But Guasconti, finding Baglioni's pertinacity intolerable, here broke away, and was gone before the Professor could again seize his arm. He looked after the young man intently, and shook his head.

"This must not be," said Baglioni to himself. "The youth is the son of my old friend, and shall not come to any harm from which the arcana of medical science can preserve him.

Besides, it is too insufferable an impertinence in Rappaccini, thus to snatch the lad out of my own hands, as I may say, and make use of him for his infernal experiments. This daughter of his! It shall be looked to. Perchance, most learned Rappaccini, I may foil you where you little dream of it!"

Meanwhile, Giovanni had pursued a circuitous route, and at length found himself at the door of his lodgings. As he crossed the threshold, he was met by old Lisabetta, who smirked and smiled, and was evidently desirous to attract his attention; vainly, however, as the ebullition of his feelings had momentarily subsided into a cold and dull vacuity. He turned his eyes full upon the withered face that was puckering itself into a smile, but seemed to behold it not. The old dame, therefore, laid her grasp upon his cloak.

"Signor!—Signor!" whispered she, still with a smile over the whole breadth of her visage, so that it looked not unlike a grotesque carving in wood, darkened by centuries—"Listen, Signor! There is a private entrance into the garden!"

"What do you say?" exclaimed Giovanni, turning quickly about, as if an inanimate thing should start into feverish life.—"A private entrance into Doctor Rappaccini's garden!"

"Hush! hush!—not so loud!" whispered Lisabetta, putting her hand over his mouth. "Yes; into the worshipful Doctor's garden, where you may see all his fine shrubbery. Many a young man in Padua would give gold to be admitted among those flowers."

Giovanni put a piece of gold into her hand.

"Show me the way," said he.

A surmise, probably excited by his conversation with Baglioni, crossed his mind, that this interposition of old Lisabetta might perchance be connected with the intrigue, whatever were its nature, in which the Professor seemed to suppose that Doctor Rappaccini was involving him. But such a suspicion, though it disturbed Giovanni, was inadequate to restrain him. The instant that he was aware of the possibility of approaching Beatrice, it seemed an absolute necessity of his existence to do so. It mattered not whether she were angel or demon; he was irrevocably within her sphere, and must obey the law that whirled him onward, in ever lessening circles, towards a result which he did not attempt to foreshadow. And yet, strange to say, there came across him a sudden doubt, whether this intense interest on his part were not delusory—whether it were really of so deep and positive a nature as to justify him in now thrusting himself into an incalculable position—whether it were not merely the fantasy of a young man's brain, only slightly, or not at all, connected with his heart!

He paused—hesitated—turned half about—but again went on. His withered guide led him along several obscure passages, and finally undid a door, through which, as it was opened, there came the sight and sound of rustling leaves, with the broken sunshine glimmering among them. Giovanni stepped forth, and forcing himself through the entanglement of a shrub that wreathed its tendrils over the hidden entrance, he stood beneath his own window, in the open area of Doctor Rappaccini's garden.

How often is it the case, that, when impossibilities have come to pass, and dreams have condensed their misty substance into tangible realities, we find ourselves calm, and even coldly self-possessed, amid circumstances which it would have been a delirium of joy or agony to anticipate! Fate delights to thwart us thus. Passion will choose his own time to rush upon the scene, and lingers sluggishly behind, when an appropriate adjustment of events would seem to summon his appearance. So was it now with Giovanni. Day after day, his pulses had throbbed with feverish blood, at the improbable idea of an interview with Beatrice, and of standing with her, face to face, in this very garden, basking in the Oriental sunshine of her beauty, and snatching from her full gaze the mystery which he deemed the riddle of his own existence. But now there was a singular and untimely equanimity within his breast. He threw a glance around the garden to discover if Beatrice or her father were present, and perceiving that he was alone, began a critical observation of the plants.

The aspect of one and all of them dissatisfied him; their gorgeousness seemed fierce, passionate, and even unnatural. There was hardly an individual shrub which a wanderer, straying by himself through a forest, would not have been startled to find growing wild, as if an unearthly face had glared at him out of the thicket. Several, also, would have shocked a delicate instinct by an appearance of artificialness, indicating that there had been such commixture, and, as it were, adultery of various vegetable species, that the production was no longer of God's making, but the monstrous off-spring of man's depraved fancy, glowing with only an evil mockery of beauty. They were probably the result of experiment, which, in one or two cases, had succeeded in mingling plants individually lovely into a compound possessing the questionable and ominous character that distinguished the whole growth of the garden. In fine, Giovanni recognized but two or three plants in the collection, and those of a kind that he well knew to be poisonous. While busy with these contemplations, he heard the rustling of a silken garment, and turning, beheld Beatrice emerging from beneath the sculptured portal.

Giovanni had not considered with himself what should be his deportment; whether he should apologize for his intrusion into the garden, or assume that he was there with the privity, at least, if not by the desire, of Doctor Rappaccini or his daughter. But Beatrice's manner placed him at his ease, though leaving him still in doubt by what agency he had gained admittance. She came lightly along the path, and met him near the broken fountain. There was surprise in her face, but brightened by a simple and kind expression of pleasure.

"You are a connoisseur in flowers, Signor," said Beatrice with a smile, alluding to the bouquet which he had flung her from the window. "It is no marvel, therefore, if the sight of my father's rare collection has tempted you to take a nearer view. If he were here, he could tell you many strange and interesting facts as to the nature and habits of these shrubs, for he has spent a life-time in such studies, and this garden is his world."

"And yourself, lady"—observed Giovanni—"if fame says true—you, likewise, are deeply skilled in the virtues indicated by these rich blossoms, and these spicy perfumes. Would you deign to be my instructress, I should prove an apter scholar than if taught by Signor Rappaccini himself."

"Are there such idle rumors?" asked Beatrice, with the music of a pleasant laugh. "Do people say that I am skilled in my father's science of plants? What a jest is there! No; though I have grown up among these flowers, I know no more of them than their hues and perfume; and sometimes, methinks I would fain rid myself of even that small knowledge. There are many flowers here, and those not the least brilliant, that shock and offend me, when they meet my eye. But, pray, Signor, do not believe these stories about my science. Believe nothing of me save what you see with your own eyes."

"And must I believe all that I have seen with my own eyes?" asked Giovanni pointedly, while the recollection of former scenes made him shrink. "No, Signora, you demand too little of me. Bid me believe nothing, save what comes from your own lips."

It would appear that Beatrice understood him. There came a deep flush to her cheek; but she looked full into Giovanni's eyes, and responded to his gaze of uneasy suspicion with a queen-like haughtiness.

"I do so bid you, Signor!" she replied. "Forget whatever you may have fancied in regard to me. If true to the outward senses, still it may be false in its essence. But the words of Beatrice Rappaccini's lips are true from the depths of the heart outward. Those you may believe!"

A fervor glowed in her whole aspect, and beamed upon Giovanni's consciousness like the light of truth itself. But while she spoke, there was a fragrance in the atmosphere around her, rich and delightful, though evanescent, yet which the young man, from an indefinable reluctance, scarcely dared to draw into his lungs. It might be the odor of the flowers. Could it be Beatrice's breath, which thus embalmed her words with a strange richness, as if by steeping them in her heart? A faintness passed like a shadow over Giovanni, and flitted away; he seemed to gaze through the beautiful girl's eyes into her transparent soul, and felt no more doubt or fear.

The tinge of passion that had colored Beatrice's manner vanished; she became gay, and appeared to derive a pure delight from her communion with the youth, not unlike what the maiden of a lonely island might have felt, conversing with a voyager from the civilized world. Evidently her experience of life had been confined within the limits of that garden. She talked now about matters as simple as the daylight or summer-clouds, and now asked questions in reference to the city, or Giovanni's distant home, his friends, his mother, and his sisters; questions indicating such seclusion, and such lack of familiarity with modes and forms, that Giovanni responded as if to an infant. Her spirit gushed out before him like a fresh rill, that was just catching its first glimpse of the sunlight, and wondering at the reflections of earth and sky which were flung into its bosom. There came thoughts, too, from a deep source, and fantasies of a gem-like brilliancy, as if diamonds and rubies sparkled upward among the bubbles of the fountain. Ever and anon, there gleamed across the young man's mind a sense of wonder, that he should be walking side by side with the being who had so wrought upon his imagination—whom he had idealized in such hues of terror—in whom he had positively witnessed such manifestations of dreadful attributes—that he should be conversing with Beatrice like a brother, and should find her so human and so maiden-like. But such reflections were only momentary; the effect of her character was too real, not to make itself familiar at once.

In this free intercourse, they had strayed through the garden, and now, after many turns among its avenues, were come to the shattered fountain, beside which grew the magnificent shrub with its treasury of glowing blossoms. A fragrance was diffused from it, which Giovanni recognized as identical with that which he had attributed to Beatrice's breath, but incomparably more powerful. As her eyes fell upon it, Giovanni beheld her press her hand to her bosom, as if her heart were throbbing suddenly and painfully.

"For the first time in my life," murmured she, addressing the shrub, "I had forgotten thee!"

"I remember, Signora," said Giovanni, "that you once promised to reward me with one of these living gems for the bouquet, which I had the happy boldness to fling to your feet. Permit me now to pluck it as a memorial of this interview."

He made a step towards the shrub, with extended hand. But Beatrice darted forward, uttering a shriek that went through his heart like a dagger. She caught his hand, and drew it back with the whole force of her slender figure. Giovanni felt her touch thrilling through his fibres.

"Touch it not!" exclaimed she, in a voice of agony. "Not for thy life! It is fatal!"

Then, hiding her face, she fled from him, and vanished beneath the sculptured portal. As Giovanni followed her with his eyes, he beheld the emaciated figure and pale intelligence of Doctor Rappaccini, who had been watching the scene, he knew not how long, within the shadow of the entrance.

No sooner was Guasconti alone in his chamber, than the image of Beatrice came back to his passionate musings, invested with all the witchery that had been gathering around it ever since his first glimpse of her, and now likewise imbued with a tender warmth of girlish womanhood. She was human: her nature was endowed with all gentle and feminine qualities; she was worthiest to be worshipped; she was capable, surely, on her part, of the height and heroism of love. Those tokens, which he had hitherto considered as proofs of a frightful peculiarity in her physical and moral system, were now either forgotten, or, by the subtle sophistry of passion, transmuted into a golden crown of enchantment, rendering Beatrice the more admirable, by so much as she was the more unique. Whatever had looked ugly, was now beautiful; or, if incapable of such a change, it stole away and hid itself among those shapeless half-ideas, which throng the dim region beyond the daylight of our perfect consciousness. Thus did he spend the night, nor fell asleep, until the dawn had begun to awake the slumbering flowers in Doctor Rappaccini's garden, whither Giovanni's dreams doubtless led him. Up rose the sun in his due season, and flinging his beams upon the young man's eyelids, awoke him to a sense of pain. When thoroughly aroused, he became sensible of a burning and tingling agony in his hand—in his right hand—the very hand which Beatrice had grasped in her own, when he was on the point of plucking one of the gem-like flowers. On the back of that hand there was now a purple print, like that of four small fingers, and the likeness of a slender thumb upon his wrist.

Oh, how stubbornly does love—or even that cunning semblance of love which flourishes in the imagination, but strikes no depth of root into the heart—how stubbornly does it hold its faith, until the moment come, when it is doomed to vanish into thin mist! Giovanni wrapt a handkerchief about his hand, and wondered what evil thing had stung him, and soon forgot his pain in a reverie of Beatrice.

After the first interview, a second was in the inevitable course of what we call fate. A third; a fourth; and a meeting with Beatrice in the garden was no longer an incident in Giovanni's daily life, but the whole space in which he might be said to live; for the anticipation and memory of that ecstatic hour made up the remainder. Nor was it otherwise with the daughter of Rappaccini. She watched for the youth's appearance, and flew to his side with confidence as unreserved as if they had been playmates from early infancy— as if they were such playmates still. If, by any unwonted chance, he failed to come at the appointed moment, she stood beneath the window, and sent up the rich sweetness of her tones to float around him in his chamber, and echo and reverberate throughout his heart—"Giovanni! Giovanni! Why tarriest thou? Come down!"—And down he hastened into that Eden of poisonous flowers.

But, with all this intimate familiarity, there was still a reserve in Beatrice's demeanor, so rigidly and invariably sustained, that the idea of infringing it scarcely occurred to his imagination. By all appreciable signs, they loved; they had looked love, with eyes that conveyed the holy secret from the depths of one soul into the depths of the other, as if it were too sacred to be whispered by the way; they had even spoken love, in those gushes of passion when their spirits darted forth in articulated breath, like tongues of long-hidden flame; and yet there had been no seal of lips, no clasp of hands, nor any slightest caress, such as love claims and hallows. He had never touched one of the gleaming ringlets of her hair; her garment—so marked was the physical barrier between them—had never been waved against him by a breeze. On the few occasions when Giovanni had seemed tempted to overstep the limit, Beatrice grew so sad, so stern, and withal wore such a look of desolate separation, shuddering at itself, that not a spoken word was requisite to repel him. At such times, he was startled at the horrible suspicions that rose, monster-like, out of the caverns of his heart, and stared him in the face; his love grew thin and faint as the morning-mist; his doubts alone had substance. But when Beatrice's face brightened again, after the momentary shadow, she was transformed at once from the mysterious, questionable being, whom he had watched with so much awe and horror; she was now the beautiful and unsophisticated girl, whom he felt that his spirit knew with a certainty beyond all other knowledge.

A considerable time had now passed since Giovanni's last meeting with Baglioni. One morning, however, he was disagreeably surprised by a visit from the Professor, whom he had scarcely thought of for whole weeks, and would willingly have forgotten still longer. Given up, as he had long been, to a pervading excitement, he could tolerate no companions, except upon condition of their perfect sympathy with his present state of feeling. Such sympathy was not to be expected from Professor Baglioni.

The visitor chatted carelessly, for a few moments, about the gossip of the city and the University, and then took up another topic.

"I have been reading an old classic author lately," said he, "and met with a story that strangely interested me. Possibly you may remember it. It is of an Indian prince, who sent a beautiful woman as a present to Alexander the Great. She was as lovely as the dawn, and gorgeous as the sunset; but what especially distinguished her was a certain rich perfume in her breath—richer than a garden of Persian roses. Alexander, as was natural to a youthful conqueror, fell in love at first sight with this magnificent stranger. But a certain sage physician, happening to be present, discovered a terrible secret in regard to her."

"And what was that?" asked Giovanni, turning his eyes downward to avoid those of the Professor.

"That this lovely woman," continued Baglioni, with emphasis, "had been nourished with poisons from her birth upward, until her whole nature was so imbued with them, that she herself had become the deadliest poison in existence. Poison was her element of life. With that rich perfume of her breath, she blasted the very air. Her love would have been poison!—her embrace death! Is not this a marvellous tale?"

"A childish fable," answered Giovanni, nervously starting from his chair. "I marvel how your worship finds time to read such nonsense, among your graver studies."

"By the bye," said the Professor, looking uneasily about him, "what singular fragrance is this in your apartment? Is it the perfume of your gloves? It is faint, but delicious, and yet, after all, by no means agreeable. Were I to breathe it long, methinks it would make me ill. It is like the breath of a flower—but I see no flowers in the chamber."

"Nor are there any," replied Giovanni, who had turned pale as the Professor spoke; "nor, I think, is there any fragrance, except in your worship's imagination. Odors, being a sort of element combined of the sensual and the spiritual, are apt to deceive us in this manner. The recollection of a perfume—the bare idea of it—may easily be mistaken for a present reality."

"Aye; but my sober imagination does not often play such tricks," said Baglioni; "and were I to fancy any kind of odor, it would be that of some vile apothecary drug, wherewith my fingers are likely enough to be imbued. Our worshipful friend Rappaccini, as I have heard, tinctures his medicaments with odors richer than those of Araby. Doubtless, likewise, the fair and learned Signora Beatrice would minister to her patients with draughts as sweet as a maiden's breath. But wo to him that sips them!"

Giovanni's face evinced many contending emotions. The tone in which the Professor alluded to the pure and lovely daughter of Rappaccini was a torture to his soul; and yet, the intimation of a view of her character, opposite to his own, gave instantaneous distinctness to a thousand dim suspicions, which now grinned at him like so many demons. But he strove hard to quell them, and to respond to Baglioni with a true lover's perfect faith.

"Signor Professor," said he, "you were my father's friend—perchance, too, it is your purpose to act a friendly part towards his son. I would fain feel nothing towards you, save respect and deference. But I pray you to observe, Signor, that there is one subject on which we must not speak. You know not the Signora Beatrice. You cannot, therefore, estimate the wrong—the blasphemy, I may even say—that is offered to her character by a light or injurious word."

"Giovanni!—my poor Giovanni!" answered the Professor, with a calm expression of pity, "I know this wretched girl far better than yourself. You shall hear the truth in respect to the poisoner Rappaccini, and his poisonous daughter. Yes; poisonous as she is beautiful! Listen; for even should you do violence to my grey hairs, it shall not silence me. That old fable of the Indian woman has become a truth, by the deep and deadly science of Rappaccini, and in the person of the lovely Beatrice!"

Giovanni groaned and hid his face.

"Her father," continued Baglioni, "was not restrained by natural affection from offering up his child, in this horrible manner, as the victim of his insane zeal for science. For— let us do him justice—he is as true a man of science as ever distilled his own heart in an alembic. What, then, will be your fate? Beyond a doubt, you are selected as the material of some new experiment. Perhaps the result is to be death— perhaps a fate more awful still! Rappaccini, with what he calls the interest of science before his eyes, will hesitate at nothing."

"It is a dream!" muttered Giovanni to himself, "surely it is a dream!"

"But," resumed the Professor, "be of good cheer, son of my friend! It is not yet too late for the rescue. Possibly, we may even succeed in bringing back this miserable child within the limits of ordinary nature, from which her father's madness has estranged her. Behold this little silver vase! It was wrought by the hands of the renowned Benvenuto Cellini, and is well worthy to be a love-gift to the fairest dame in Italy. But its contents are invaluable. One little sip of this antidote would have rendered the most virulent poisons of the Borgias innocuous. Doubt not that it will be as efficacious against those of Rappaccini. Bestow the vase, and the precious liquid within it, on your Beatrice, and hope-fully await the result."

Baglioni laid a small, exquisitely wrought silver phial on the table, and withdrew, leaving what he had said to produce its effect upon the young man's mind.

"We will thwart Rappaccini yet!" thought he, chuckling to himself, as he descended the stairs. "But, let us confess the truth of him, he is a wonderful man!—a wonderful man

indeed! A vile empiric, however, in his practice, and therefore not to be tolerated by those who respect the good old
rules of the medical profession!"

Throughout Giovanni's whole acquaintance with Beatrice,
he had occasionally, as we have said, been haunted by dark
surmises as to her character. Yet, so thoroughly had she made
herself felt by him as a simple, natural, most affectionate and
guileless creature, that the image now held up by Professor
Baglioni, looked as strange and incredible, as if it were not
in accordance with his own original conception. True, there
were ugly recollections connected with his first glimpses of
the beautiful girl; he could not quite forget the bouquet that
withered in her grasp, and the insect that perished amid the
sunny air, by no ostensible agency, save the fragrance of her
breath. These incidents, however, dissolving in the pure light
of her character, had no longer the efficacy of facts, but were
acknowledged as mistaken fantasies, by whatever testimony
of the senses they might appear to be substantiated. There is
something truer and more real, than what we can see with
the eyes, and touch with the finger. On such better evidence,
had Giovanni founded his confidence in Beatrice, though
rather by the necessary force of her high attributes, than by
any deep and generous faith, on his part. But, now, his spirit
was incapable of sustaining itself at the height to which the
early enthusiasm of passion had exalted it; he fell down,
grovelling among earthly doubts, and defiled therewith the
pure whiteness of Beatrice's image. Not that he gave her up;
he did but distrust. He resolved to institute some decisive
test that should satisfy him, once for all, whether there were
those dreadful peculiarities in her physical nature, which
could not be supposed to exist without some corresponding
monstrosity of soul. His eyes, gazing down afar, might have
deceived him as to the lizard, the insect, and the flowers. But

if he could witness, at the distance of a few paces, the sudden blight of one fresh and healthful flower in Beatrice's hand, there would be room for no further question. With this idea, he hastened to the florist's, and purchased a bouquet that was still gemmed with the morning dew-drops.

It was now the customary hour of his daily interview with Beatrice. Before descending into the garden, Giovanni failed not to look at his figure in the mirror; a vanity to be expected in a beautiful young man, yet, as displaying itself at that troubled and feverish moment, the token of a certain shallowness of feeling and insincerity of character. He did gaze, however, and said to himself, that his features had never before possessed so rich a grace, nor his eyes such vivacity, nor his cheeks so warm a hue of superabundant life.

"At least," thought he, "her poison has not yet insinuated itself into my system. I am no flower to perish in her grasp!"

With that thought, he turned his eyes on the bouquet, which he had never once laid aside from his hand. A thrill of indefinable horror shot through his frame, on perceiving that those dewy flowers were already beginning to droop; they wore the aspect of things that had been fresh and lovely, yesterday. Giovanni grew white as marble, and stood motionless before the mirror, staring at his own reflection there, as at the likeness of something frightful. He remembered Baglioni's remark about the fragrance that seemed to pervade the chamber. It must have been the poison in his breath! Then he shuddered—shuddered at himself! Recovering from his stupor, he began to watch, with curious eye, a spider that was busily at work, hanging its web from the antique cornice of the apartment, crossing and re-crossing the artful system of interwoven lines, as vigorous and active a spider as ever dangled from an old ceiling. Giovanni bent towards the insect, and emitted a deep, long breath. The spider suddenly ceased its toil; the web vibrated with a tremor originating in the body of the small artizan. Again Giovanni sent forth a breath, deeper, longer, and imbued with a venomous feeling out of his heart; he knew not whether he were wicked or only desperate. The spider made a convulsive gripe with his limbs, and hung dead across the window.

"Accursed! Accursed!" muttered Giovanni, addressing himself. "Hast thou grown so poisonous, that this deadly insect perishes by thy breath?"

At that moment, a rich, sweet voice came floating up from the garden:—

"Giovanni! Giovanni! It is past the hour! Why tarriest thou! Come down!"

"Yes," muttered Giovanni again. "She is the only being whom my breath may not slay! Would that it might!"

He rushed down, and in an instant, was standing before the bright and loving eyes of Beatrice. A moment ago, his wrath and despair had been so fierce that he could have desired nothing so much as to wither her by a glance. But, with her actual presence, there came influences which had too real an existence to be at once shaken off; recollections of the delicate and benign power of her feminine nature, which had so often enveloped him in a religious calm; recollections of many a holy and passionate outgush of her heart, when the pure fountain had been unsealed from its depths, and made visible in its transparency to his mental eye; recollections which, had Giovanni known how to estimate them, would have assured him that all this ugly mystery was but an earthly illusion, and that, whatever mist of evil might seem to have gathered over her, the real Beatrice was a heavenly angel. Incapable as he was of such high faith, still her presence had not utterly lost its magic. Giovanni's rage was quelled into an aspect of sullen insensibility. Beatrice, with a quick spiritual sense, immediately felt that there was a gulf of blackness between them, which neither he nor she could pass. They walked on together, sad and silent, and came thus to the marble fountain, and to its pool of water on the ground, in the midst of which grew the shrub that bore gem-like blossoms. Giovanni was affrighted at the eager enjoyment—the appetite, as it were—with which he found himself inhaling the fragrance of the flowers.

"Beatrice," asked he abruptly, "whence came this shrub?"

"My father created it," answered she, with simplicity.

"Created it! created it!" repeated Giovanni. "What mean you, Beatrice?"

"He is a man fearfully acquainted with the secrets of nature," replied Beatrice; "and, at the hour when I first drew breath, this plant sprang from the soil, the offspring of his science, of his intellect, while I was but his earthly child. Approach it not!" continued she, observing with terror that Giovanni was drawing nearer to the shrub. "It has qualities that you little dream of. But I, dearest Giovanni,—I grew up and blossomed with the plant, and was nourished with its breath. It was my sister, and I loved it with a human affection: for—alas! hast thou not suspected it? there was an awful doom."

Here Giovanni frowned so darkly upon her that Beatrice paused and trembled. But her faith in his tenderness reassured her, and made her blush that she had doubted for an instant.

"There was an awful doom," she continued,—"the effect of my father's fatal love of science—which estranged me from all society of my kind. Until Heaven sent thee, dearest Giovanni, Oh! how lonely was thy poor Beatrice!"

"Was it a hard doom?" asked Giovanni, fixing his eyes upon her.

"Only of late have I known how hard it was," answered she tenderly. "Oh, yes; but my heart was torpid, and therefore quiet."

Giovanni's rage broke forth from his sullen gloom like a lightning-flash out of a dark cloud.

"Accursed one!" cried he, with venomous scorn and anger. "And finding thy solitude wearisome, thou hast severed me, likewise, from all the warmth of life, and enticed me into thy region of unspeakable horror!"

"Giovanni!" exclaimed Beatrice, turning her large bright eyes upon his face. The force of his words had not found its way into her mind; she was merely thunder-struck.

"Yes, poisonous thing!" repeated Giovanni, beside himself with passion. "Thou hast done it! Thou hast blasted me! Thou hast filled my veins with poison! Thou hast made me as hateful, as ugly, as loathsome and deadly a creature as thyself,—a world's wonder of hideous monstrosity! Now—if our breath be happily as fatal to ourselves as to all others— let us join our lips in one kiss of unutterable hatred, and so die!"

"What has befallen me?" murmured Beatrice, with a low moan out of her heart. "Holy Virgin pity me, a poor heart-broken child!"

"Thou! Dost thou pray?" cried Giovanni, still with the same fiendish scorn. "Thy very prayers, as they come from thy lips, taint the atmosphere with death. Yes, yes; let us pray! Let us to church, and dip our fingers in the holy water at the portal! They that come after us will perish as by a pestilence. Let us sign crosses in the air! It will be scattering curses abroad in the likeness of holy symbols!"

"Giovanni," said Beatrice calmly, for her grief was beyond passion, "why dost thou join thyself with me thus in those terrible words? I, it is true, am the horrible thing thou namest me. But thou!—what hast thou to do, save with one other shudder at my hideous misery, to go forth out of the garden and mingle with thy race, and forget that there ever crawled on earth such a monster as poor Beatrice?"

"Dost thou pretend ignorance?" asked Giovanni, scowling upon her. "Behold! This power have I gained from the pure daughter of Rappaccini!"

There was a swarm of summer-insects flitting through the air, in search of the food promised by the flower-odors of the fatal garden. They circled round Giovanni's head, and were evidently attracted towards him by the same influence which had drawn them, for an instant, within the sphere of several of the shrubs. He sent forth a breath among them, and smiled bitterly at Beatrice, as at least a score of the insects fell dead upon the ground.

"I see it! I see it!" shrieked Beatrice. "It is my father's fatal science! No, no, Giovanni; it was not I! Never, never! I dreamed only to love thee, and be with thee a little time, and so to let thee pass away, leaving but thine image in mine heart. For, Giovanni—believe it—though my body be nourished with poison, my spirit is God's creature, and craves love as its daily food. But my father!—he has united us in this fearful sympathy. Yes; spurn me!—tread upon me!—kill me! Oh, what is death, after such words as thine? But it was not I! Not for a world of bliss would I have done it!"

Giovanni's passion had exhausted itself in its outburst from his lips. There now came across him a sense, mournful, and not without tenderness, of the intimate and peculiar relationship between Beatrice and himself. They stood, as it were, in an utter solitude, which would be made none the less solitary by the densest throng of human life. Ought not, then, the desert of humanity around them to press this insulated pair closer together? If they should be cruel to one another, who was there to be kind to them? Besides, thought Giovanni, might there not still be a hope of his returning within the limits of ordinary nature, and leading Beatrice—the redeemed Beatrice—by the hand? Oh, weak, and selfish, and unworthy spirit, that could dream of an earthly union and earthly happiness as possible, after such deep love had been so bitterly wronged as was Beatrice's love by Giovanni's blighting words! No, no; there could be no such hope. She must pass heavily, with that broken heart, across the borders of Time—she must bathe her hurts in some fount of Paradise, and forget her grief in the light of immortality—and *there* be well!

But Giovanni did not know it.

"Dear Beatrice," said he, approaching her, while she shrank away, as always at his approach, but now with a different impulse—"dearest Beatrice, our fate is not yet so desperate. Behold! There is a medicine, potent, as a wise physician has assured me, and almost divine in its efficacy. It is composed of ingredients the most opposite to those by which thy awful father has brought this calamity upon thee and me. It is distilled of blessed herbs. Shall we not quaff it together, and thus be purified from evil?"

"Give it me!" said Beatrice, extending her hand to receive the little silver phial which Giovanni took from his bosom. She added, with a peculiar emphasis: "I will drink—but do thou await the result."

She put Baglioni's antidote to her lips; and, at the same moment, the figure of Rappaccini emerged from the portal, and came slowly towards the marble fountain. As he drew near, the pale man of science seemed to gaze with a triumphant expression at the beautiful youth and maiden, as might an artist who should spend his life in achieving a picture or a group of statuary, and finally be satisfied with his success. He paused—his bent form grew erect with conscious power, he spread out his hands over them, in the attitude of a father imploring a blessing upon his children.

But those were the same hands that had thrown poison into the stream of their lives! Giovanni trembled. Beatrice shuddered nervously, and pressed her hand upon her heart.

"My daughter," said Rappaccini, "thou art no longer lonely in the world! Pluck one of those precious gems from thy sister shrub, and bid thy bridegroom wear it in his bosom. It will not harm him now! My science, and the sympathy between thee and him, have so wrought within his system, that he now stands apart from common men, as thou dost, daughter of my pride and triumph, from ordinary women. Pass on, then, through the world, most dear to one another, and dreadful to all besides!"

"My father," said Beatrice, feebly—and still, as she spoke, she kept her hand upon her heart—"wherefore didst thou inflict this miserable doom upon thy child?"

"Miserable!" exclaimed Rappaccini. "What mean you, foolish girl? Dost thou deem it misery to be endowed with marvellous gifts, against which no power nor strength could avail an enemy? Misery, to be able to quell the mightiest with a breath? Misery, to be as terrible as thou art beautiful? Wouldst thou, then, have preferred the condition of a weak woman, exposed to all evil, and capable of none?"

"I would fain have been loved, not feared," murmured Beatrice, sinking down upon the ground.—"But now it matters not; I am going, father, where the evil, which thou hast striven to mingle with my being, will pass away like a dream—like the fragrance of these poisonous flowers, which will no longer taint my breath among the flowers of Eden. Farewell, Giovanni! Thy words of hatred are like lead within my heart—but they, too, will fall away as I ascend. Oh, was there not, from the first, more poison in thy nature than in mine?"

To Beatrice—so radically had her earthly part been wrought upon by Rappaccini's skill—as poison had been life, so the powerful antidote was death. And thus the poor victim of man's ingenuity and of thwarted nature, and of the fatality that attends all such efforts of perverted wisdom, perished there, at the feet of her father and Giovanni. Just at that moment, Professor Pietro Baglioni looked forth from the window, and called loudly, in a tone of triumph mixed with horror, to the thunder-stricken man of science:

"Rappaccini! Rappaccini! And is *this* the upshot of your experiment?"

MRS. BULLFROG

I T MAKES me melancholy to see how like fools some very sensible people act, in the matter of choosing wives. They perplex their judgments by a most undue attention to little niceties of personal appearance, habits, disposition, and other trifles, which concern nobody but the lady herself. An unhappy gentleman, resolving to wed nothing short of perfection, keeps his heart and hand till both get so old and withered, that no tolerable woman will accept them.—Now, this is the very height of absurdity. A kind Providence has so skilfully adapted sex to sex, and the mass of individuals to each other, that, with certain obvious exceptions, any male and female may be moderately happy in the married state. The true rule is, to ascertain that the match is fundamentally a good one, and then to take it for granted that all minor objections, should there be such, will vanish, if you let them alone. Only put yourself beyond hazard, as to the real basis of matrimonial bliss, and it is scarcely to be imagined what miracles, in the way of reconciling smaller incongruities, connubial love will effect.

For my own part, I freely confess, that, in my bachelorship, I was precisely such an over-curious simpleton, as I now advise the reader not to be. My early habits had gifted me with a feminine sensibility, and too exquisite refinement.—I was the accomplished graduate of a dry-goods store, where, by dint of ministering to the whims of fine ladies, and suiting silken hose to delicate limbs, and handling satins, ribbons, chintzes, calicoes, tapes, gauze, and cambric needles, I grew up a very lady-like sort of a gentleman. It is not assuming too much, to affirm, that the ladies themselves were hardly so lady-like as Thomas Bullfrog. So painfully acute was my sense of female imperfection, and such varied excellence did I require in the woman whom I could love, that there was an awful risk of my getting no wife at all, or of being driven to perpetrate matrimony with my own image in the looking-glass. Besides the fundamental principle, already hinted at, I demanded the fresh bloom of youth, pearly teeth, glossy ringlets, and the whole list of lovely items, with the utmost delicacy of habits and sentiments, a silken texture of mind, and, above all, a virgin heart. In a word, if a young angel,○ just from Paradise, yet dressed in earthly fashion, had come and offered me her hand, it is by no means certain that I should have taken it. There was every chance of my becoming a most miserable old bachelor, when, by the best luck in the world, I made a journey into another state, and was smitten by, and smote again, and wooed, won, and married the present Mrs. Bullfrog, all in the space of a fortnight. Owing to these extempore measures, I not only gave my bride credit for certain perfections, which have not as yet come to light, but also overlooked a few trifling defects, which, however, glimmered on my perception, long before the close of the honey-moon. Yet, as there was no mistake about the fundamental principle aforesaid, I soon learned, as will be seen, to estimate Mrs. Bullfrog's deficiencies and superfluities at exactly their proper value.

The same morning that Mrs. Bullfrog and I came together as a unit, we took two seats in the stage-coach, and began our

journey towards my place of business. There being no other
passengers, we were as much alone, and as free to give vent
to our raptures, as if I had hired a hack for the matrimonial
jaunt. My bride looked charmingly, in a green silk calash,
and riding-habit of pelisse cloth, and whenever her red lips
parted with a smile, each tooth appeared like an inestimable
pearl. Such was my passionate warmth, that—we had rattled
out of the village, gentle reader, and were lonely as Adam
and Eve in Paradise—I plead guilty to no less freedom than
a kiss!—The gentle eye of Mrs. Bullfrog scarcely rebuked me
for the profanation. Emboldened by her indulgence, I threw
back the calash from her polished brow, and suffered my
fingers, white and delicate as her own, to stray among those
dark and glossy curls, which realized my day-dreams of
rich hair.

'My love,' said Mrs. Bullfrog, tenderly, 'you will disarrange
my curls.'

'Oh, no, my sweet Laura!' replied I, still playing with the
glossy ringlet. 'Even your fair hand could not manage a curl
more delicately than mine.—I propose myself the pleasure of
doing up your hair in papers, every evening, at the same time
with my own.'

'Mr. Bullfrog,' repeated she, 'you must not disarrange my
curls.'

This was spoken in a more decided tone than I had
happened to hear, until then, from my gentlest of all gentle
brides. At the same time, she put up her hand and took mine
prisoner, but merely drew it away from the forbidden ringlet,
and then immediately released it. Now, I am a fidgetty little
man, and always love to have something in my fingers; so
that, being debarred from my wife's curls, I looked about me
for any other plaything. On the front seat of the coach, there
was one of those small baskets in which travelling ladies, who
are too delicate to appear at a public table, generally carry a

supply of gingerbread, biscuits and cheese, cold ham, and other light refreshments, merely to sustain nature to the journey's end. Such airy diet will sometimes keep them in pretty good flesh, for a week together. Laying hold of this same little basket, I thrust my hand under the newspaper, with which it was carefully covered.

'What's this, my dear?' cried I; for the black neck of a bottle had popped out of the basket.

'A bottle of Kalydor, Mr. Bullfrog,' said my wife, coolly taking the basket from my hands, and replacing it on the front seat.

There was no possibility of doubting my wife's word; but I never knew genuine Kalydor, such as I use for my own complexion, to smell so much like cherry-brandy. I was about to express my fears that the lotion would injure her skin, when an accident occurred, which threatened more than a skin-deep injury. Our Jehu had carelessly driven over a heap of gravel, and fairly capsized the coach, with the wheels in the air, and our heels where our heads should have been. What became of my wits, I cannot imagine; they have always had a perverse trick of deserting me, just when they were most needed; but so it chanced, that, in the confusion of our overthrow, I quite forgot that there was a Mrs. Bullfrog in the world. Like many men's wives, the good lady served her husband as a stepping-stone. I had scrambled out of the coach, and was instinctively settling my cravat, when somebody brushed roughly by me, and I heard a smart thwack upon the coachman's ear.

'Take that, you villain!' cried a strange, hoarse voice. 'You have ruined me, you blackguard! I shall never be the woman I have been!'

And then came a second thwack, aimed at the driver's other ear, but which missed it, and hit him on the nose, causing a terrible effusion of blood. Now, who, or what fearful apparition, was inflicting this punishment on the poor fellow, remained an impenetrable mystery to me. The blows were given by a person of grisly aspect, with a head almost bald, and sunken cheeks, apparently of the feminine gender, though hardly to be classed in the gentler sex. There being no teeth to modulate the voice, it had a mumbled fierceness, not passionate, but stern, which absolutely made me quiver like a calves foot jelly. Who could the phantom be? The most awful circumstance of the affair is yet to be told; for this ogre, or whatever it was, had a riding-habit like Mrs. Bullfrog's, and also a green silk calash, dangling down her back by the strings. In my terror and turmoil of mind, I could imagine nothing less, than that the Old Nick, at the moment of our overturn, had annihilated my wife and jumped into her petticoats. This idea seemed the more probable, since I could nowhere perceive Mrs. Bullfrog alive, nor, though I looked very sharp about the coach, could I detect any traces of that beloved woman's dead body. There would have been a comfort in giving her Christian burial!

'Come, sir, bestir yourself! Help this rascal to set up the coach,' said the hobgoblin to me; then, with a terrific screech to three countrymen, at a distance—'Here, you fellows, an't you ashamed to stand off, when a poor woman is in distress?'

The countrymen, instead of fleeing for their lives, came running at full speed, and laid hold of the topsy-turvy coach. I, also, though a small-sized man, went to work like a son of Anak. The coachman, too, with the blood still streaming from his nose, tugged and toiled most manfully, dreading, doubtless, that the next blow might break his head. And yet, bemauled as the poor fellow had been, he seemed to glance at me with an eye of pity, as if my case were more deplorable than his. But I cherished a hope that all would turn out a dream, and seized the opportunity, as we raised the coach, to jam two of my fingers under the wheel, trusting that the pain would awaken me.

'Why, here we are all to rights again!' exclaimed a sweet voice, behind. 'Thank you for your assistance, gentlemen. My dear Mr. Bullfrog, how you perspire! Do let me wipe your face. Don't take this little accident too much to heart, good driver. We ought to be thankful that none of our necks are broke!'

'We might have spared one neck out of the three,' muttered the driver, rubbing his ear and pulling his nose, to ascertain whether he had been cuffed or not.—'Why, the woman's a witch!'

I fear that the reader will not believe, yet it is positively a fact, that there stood Mrs. Bullfrog, with her glossy ringlets curling on her brow, and two rows of orient pearls gleaming between her parted lips, which wore a most angelic smile. She had regained her riding-habit and calash from the grisly phantom, and was, in all respects, the lovely woman who had been sitting by my side, at the instant of our overturn. How she had happened to disappear, and who had supplied her place, and whence did she now return, were problems too knotty for me to solve. There stood my wife. That was the one thing certain among a heap of mysteries. Nothing remained, but to help her into the coach, and plod on, through the journey of the day and the journey of life, as comfortably as we could. As the driver closed the door upon us, I heard him whisper to the three countrymen—

'How do you suppose a fellow feels, shut up in a cage with a she-tiger?'

Of course, this query could have no reference to my situation. Yet, unreasonable as it may appear, I confess that my feelings were not altogether so ecstatic as when I first called Mrs. Bullfrog mine. True, she was a sweet woman, and an angel of a wife; but what if a gorgon should return, amid the transports of our connubial bliss, and take the angel's place! I recollected the tale of a fairy, who half the time was a beautiful woman, and half the time a hideous monster. Had I taken that very fairy to be the wife of my bosom? While such whims and chimeras were flitting across my fancy, I began to look askance at Mrs. Bullfrog, almost expecting that the transformation would be wrought before my eyes.

To divert my mind, I took up the newspaper which had covered the little basket of refreshments, and which now lay at the bottom of the coach, blushing with a deep-red stain, and emitting a potent spirituous fume, from the contents of the broken bottle of Kalydor. The paper was two or three years old, but contained an article of several columns, in which I soon grew wonderfully interested. It was the report of a trial for breach of promise of marriage, giving the testimony in full, with fervid extracts from both the gentleman's and lady's amatory correspondence. The deserted damsel had personally appeared in court, and had borne energetic evidence to her lover's perfidy, and the strength of her blighted affections.—On the defendant's part, there had been an attempt, though insufficiently sustained, to blast the plaintiff's character, and a plea in mitigation of damages, on account of her unamiable temper. A horrible idea was suggested by the lady's name.

'Madam,' said I, holding the newspaper before Mrs. Bullfrog's eyes—and, though a small, delicate, and thin-visaged man, I feel assured that I looked very terrific—'Madam,' repeated I, through my shut teeth, 'were you the plaintiff in this cause?'

'Oh, my dear Mr. Bullfrog,' replied my wife, sweetly, 'I thought all the world knew that.'

'Horror! horror!' exclaimed I, sinking back on the seat.

Covering my face with both hands, I emitted a deep and deathlike groan, as if my tormented soul were rending me asunder. I, the most exquisitely fastidious of men, and whose wife was to have been the most delicate and refined of women, with all the fresh dew-drops glittering on her virgin rosebud of a heart! I thought of the glossy ringlets and pearly teeth—I thought of the Kalydor—I thought of the coach-man's bruised ear and bloody nose—I thought of the tender love-secrets, which she had whispered to the judge and jury, and a thousand tittering auditors—and gave another groan!

'Mr. Bullfrog,' said my wife.

As I made no reply, she gently took my hands within her own, removed them from my face, and fixed her eyes stead-fastly on mine.

'Mr. Bullfrog,' said she, not unkindly, yet with all the decision of her strong character, 'let me advise you to over-come this foolish weakness, and prove yourself, to the best of your ability, as good a husband as I will be a wife. You have discovered, perhaps, some little imperfections in your bride. Well—what did you expect? Women are not angels. If they were, they would go to Heaven for husbands—or, at least, be more difficult in their choice on earth.'

'But why conceal those imperfections?' interposed I, tremu-lously.

'Now, my love, are not you a most unreasonable little man?' said Mrs. Bullfrog, patting me on the cheek. 'Ought a woman to disclose her frailties earlier than the wedding-day? Few husbands, I assure you, make the discovery in such good season, and still fewer complain that these trifles are con-cealed too long. Well, what a strange man you are! Poh! you are joking.'

'But the suit for breach of promise!' groaned I.

'Ah! and is that the rub?' exclaimed my wife. 'Is it possible that you view that affair in an objectionable light? Mr. Bullfrog, I never could have dreamt it! Is it an objection, that I have triumphantly defended myself against slander, and vindicated my purity in a court of justice? Or, do you complain, because your wife has shown the proper spirit of a woman, and punished the villain who trifled with her affections?'

'But,' persisted I—shrinking into a corner of the coach, however; for I did not know precisely how much contradiction the proper spirit of a woman would endure—'but, my love, would it not have been more dignified to treat the villain with the silent contempt he merited?'

'That is all very well, Mr. Bullfrog,' said my wife, slily; 'but, in that case, where would have been the five thousand dollars, which are to stock your dry-goods store?'

'Mrs. Bullfrog, upon your honor,' demanded I, as if my life hung upon her words, 'is there no mistake about those five thousand dollars?'

'Upon my word and honor, there is none,' replied she. 'The jury gave me every cent the rascal had—and I have kept it all for my dear Bullfrog!'

'Then, thou dear woman,' cried I, with an overwhelming gush of tenderness, 'let me fold thee to my heart! The basis of matrimonial bliss is secure, and all thy little defects and frailties are forgiven. Nay, since the result has been so fortunate, I rejoice at the wrongs which drove thee to this blessed law-suit. Happy Bullfrog that I am!'

FIRE-WORSHIP

I T IS a great revolution in social and domestic life—
and no less so in the life of the secluded student—this
almost universal exchange of the open fire-place for the
cheerless and ungenial stove. On such a morning as now
lowers around our old grey parsonage, I miss the bright face
of my ancient friend, who was wont to dance upon the
hearth, and play the part of a more familiar sunshine. It is
sad to turn from the clouded sky and sombre landscape—
from yonder hill, with its crown of rusty, black pines, the
foliage of which is so dismal in the absence of the sun; that
bleak pasture-land, and the broken surface of the potato field,
with the brown clods partly concealed by the snow-fall of last
night; the swollen and sluggish river, with ice-encrusted borders, dragging its blueish grey stream along the verge of our
orchard, like a snake half torpid with the cold—it is sad to
turn from an outward scene of so little comfort, and find the
same sullen influences brooding within the precincts of my
study. Where is that brilliant guest—that quick and subtle
spirit whom Prometheus lured from Heaven to civilize mankind, and cheer them in their wintry desolation—that comfortable inmate, whose smile, during eight months of the

year, was our sufficient consolation for summer's lingering advance and early flight? Alas! blindly inhospitable, grudging the food that kept him cheery and mercurial, we have thrust him into an iron prison, and compel him to smoulder away his life on a daily pittance which once would have been too scanty for his breakfast! Without a metaphor, we now make our fire in an air-tight stove, and supply it with some half-a-dozen sticks of wood between dawn and nightfall.

I never shall be reconciled to this enormity. Truly may it be said, that the world looks darker for it. In one way or another, here and there, and all around us, the inventions of mankind are fast blotting the picturesque, the poetic, and the beautiful out of human life. The domestic fire was a type of all these attributes, and seemed to bring might and majesty, and wild Nature, and a spiritual essence, into our inmost home, and yet to dwell with us in such friendliness, that its mysteries and marvels excited no dismay. The same mild companion, that smiled so placidly in our faces, was he that comes roaring out of Ætna, and rushes madly up the sky, like a fiend breaking loose from torment, and fighting for a place among the upper angels. He it is, too, that leaps from cloud to cloud amid the crashing thunder-storm. It was he whom the Gheber worshipped, with no unnatural idolatry; and it was he who devoured London and Moscow, and many another famous city, and who loves to riot through our own dark forests, and sweep across our prairies, and to whose ravenous maw, it is said, the universe shall one day be given as a final feast. Meanwhile he is the great artizan and laborer by whose aid men are enabled to build a world within a world, or, at least, to smoothe down the rough creation which Nature flung to us. He forges the mighty anchor, and every lesser instrument. He drives the steamboat and drags the rail-car. And it was he—this creature of terrible might, and so

many-sided utility, and all-comprehensive destructiveness—
that used to be the cheerful, homely friend of our wintry
days, and whom we have made the prisoner of this iron cage!

How kindly he was, and, though the tremendous agent of
change, yet bearing himself with such gentleness, so rendering
himself a part of all life-long and age-coeval associations, that
it seemed as if he were the great conservative of Nature!
While a man was true to the fireside, so long would he be
true to country and law—to the God whom his fathers
worshipped—to the wife of his youth—and to all things else
which instinct or religion have taught us to consider sacred.
With how sweet humility did this elemental spirit perform
all needful offices for the household in which he was domesti-
cated! He was equal to the concoction of a grand dinner, yet
scorned not to roast a potato, or toast a bit of cheese. How
humanely did he cherish the schoolboy's icy fingers, and
thaw the old man's joints with a genial warmth, which almost
equalled the glow of youth! And how carefully did he dry
the cow-hide boots that had trudged through mud and snow,
and the shaggy outside garment, stiff with frozen sleet; taking
heed, likewise, to the comfort of the faithful dog who had
followed his master through the storm! When did he refuse
a coal to light a pipe, or even a part of his own substance to
kindle a neighbor's fire? And then, at twilight, when laborer
or scholar, or mortal of whatever age, sex, or degree, drew a
chair beside him, and looked into his glowing face, how
acute, how profound, how comprehensive was his sympathy
with the mood of each and all! He pictured forth their very
thoughts. To the youthful, he showed the scenes of the
adventurous life before them; to the aged, the shadows of
departed love and hope; and, if all earthly things had grown
distasteful, he could gladden the fireside muser with golden
glimpses of a better world. And, amid this varied communion
with the human soul, how busily would the sympathizer,

the deep moralist, the painter of magic pictures, be causing the tea-kettle to boil!

Nor did it lessen the charm of his soft, familiar courtesy and helpfulness, that the mighty spirit, were opportunity offered him, would run riot through the peaceful house, wrap its inmates in his terrible embrace, and leave nothing of them save their whitened bones. This possibility of mad destruction only made his domestic kindness the more beautiful and touching. It was so sweet of him, being endowed with such power, to dwell, day after day, and one long, lonesome night after another, on the dusky hearth, only now and then betraying his wild nature, by thrusting his red tongue out of the chimney-top! True, he had done much mischief in the world, and was pretty certain to do more; but his warm heart atoned for all. He was kindly to the race of man; and they pardoned his characteristic imperfections.

The good old clergyman, my predecessor in this mansion, was well acquainted with the comforts of the fireside. His yearly allowance of wood, according to the terms of his settlement, was no less than sixty cords. Almost an annual forest was converted from oak logs into ashes, in the kitchen, the parlor, and this little study, where now an unworthy successor —not in the pastoral office, but merely in his earthly abode— sits scribbling beside an air-tight stove. I love to fancy one of those fireside days, while the good man, a contemporary of the Revolution, was in his early prime, some five-and-sixty years ago. Before sunrise, doubtless, the blaze hovered upon the grey skirts of night, and dissolved the frost-work that had gathered like a curtain over the small window-panes. There is something peculiar in the aspect of the morning fireside; a fresher, brisker glare; the absence of that mellowness, which can be produced only by half-consumed logs, and shapeless brands with the white ashes on them, and mighty coals, the remnant of tree-trunks that the hungry element has gnawed for hours. The morning hearth, too, is newly swept, and the brazen andirons well brightened, so that the cheerful fire may see its face in them. Surely it was happiness, when the pastor, fortified with a substantial breakfast, sat down in his arm-chair and slippers, and opened the Whole Body of Divinity, or the Commentary on Job, or whichever of his old folios or quartos might fall within the range of his weekly sermons. It must have been his own fault, if the warmth and glow of this abundant hearth did not permeate the discourse, and keep his audience comfortable, in spite of the bitterest northern blast that ever wrestled with the church-steeple. He reads, while the heat warps the stiff covers of the volume; he writes, without numbness either in his heart or fingers; and, with unstinted hand, he throws fresh sticks of wood upon the fire.

A parishioner comes in. With what warmth of benevolence —how should he be otherwise than warm, in any of his attributes?—does the minister bid him welcome, and set a chair for him in so close proximity to the hearth, that soon the guest finds it needful to rub his scorched shins with his great red hands. The melted snow drips from his steaming boots, and bubbles upon the hearth. His puckered forehead unravels its entanglement of crisscross wrinkles. We lose much of the enjoyment of fireside heat, without such an opportunity of marking its genial effect upon those who have been looking the inclement weather in the face. In the course of the day our clergyman himself strides forth, per-chance to pay a round of pastoral visits, or, it may be, to visit his mountain of a wood-pile, and cleave the monstrous logs into billets suitable for the fire. He returns with fresher life to his beloved hearth. During the short afternoon, the western sunshine comes into the study, and strives to stare the ruddy blaze out of countenance, but with only a brief triumph, soon to be succeeded by brighter glories of its rival.

Beautiful it is to see the strengthening gleam—the deepening light—that gradually casts distinct shadows of the human figure, the table, and the high-backed chairs, upon the opposite wall, and at length, as twilight comes on, replenishes the room with living radiance, and makes life all rose-color. Afar, the wayfarer discerns the flickering flame, as it dances upon the windows, and hails it as a beacon-light of humanity, reminding him, in his cold and lonely path, that the world is not all snow, and solitude, and desolation. At eventide, probably, the study was peopled with the clergyman's wife and family; and children tumbled themselves upon the hearth-rug, and grave Puss sat with her back to the fire, or gazed, with a semblance of human meditation, into its fervid depths. Seasonably, the plenteous ashes of the day were raked over the mouldering brands, and from the heap came jets of flame, and an incense of night-long smoke, creeping quietly up the chimney.

Heaven forgive the old clergyman! In his latter life, when, for almost ninety winters, he had been gladdened by the fire-light—when it had gleamed upon him from infancy to extreme age, and never without brightening his spirits as well as his visage, and perhaps keeping him alive so long—he had the heart to brick up his chimney-place, and bid farewell to the face of his old friend for ever! Why did not he take an eternal leave of the sunshine too? His sixty cords of wood had probably dwindled to a far less ample supply, in modern times; and it is certain that the parsonage had grown crazy with time and tempest, and pervious to the cold; but still, it was one of the saddest tokens of the decline and fall of open fire-places, that the grey patriarch should have deigned to warm himself at an air-tight stove.

And I, likewise—who have found a home in this ancient owl's nest, since its former occupant took his heavenward flight—I, to my shame, have put up stoves in kitchen, and

parlor, and chamber. Wander where you will about the
house, not a glimpse of the earth-born, heaven-aspiring fiend
of Ætna—him that sports in the thunder-storm—the idol of
the Ghebers—the devourer of cities, the forest rioter, and
prairie sweeper—the future destroyer of our earth—the old
chimney-corner companion, who mingled himself so sociably
with household joys and sorrows—not a glimpse of this
mighty and kindly one will greet your eyes. He is now an
invisible presence. There is his iron cage. Touch it, and he
scorches your fingers. He delights to singe a garment, or perpetrate any other little unworthy mischief; for his temper is
ruined by the ingratitude of mankind, for whom he cherished
such warmth of feeling, and to whom he taught all their
arts, even that of making his own prison-house. In his fits of
rage, he puffs volumes of smoke and noisome gas through the
crevices of the door, and shakes the iron walls of his dungeon,
so as to overthrow the ornamental urn upon its summit. We
tremble, lest he should break forth amongst us. Much of his
time is spent in sighs, burthened with unutterable grief, and
long-drawn through the funnel. He amuses himself, too, with
repeating all the whispers, the moans, and the louder utterances or tempestuous howls of the wind; so that the stove
becomes a microcosm of the aërial world. Occasionally, there
are strange combinations of sounds—voices, talking almost
articulately within the hollow chest of iron—insomuch that
fancy beguiles me with the idea, that my fire wood must
have grown in that infernal forest of lamentable trees, which
breathed their complaints to Dante. When the listener is half-
asleep, he may readily take these voices for the conversation
of spirits, and assign them an intelligible meaning. Anon,
there is a pattering noise—drip, drip, drip—as if a summer
shower were falling within the narrow circumference of
the stove.

These barren and tedious eccentricities are all that the air-tight stove can bestow, in exchange for the invaluable moral influences which we have lost by our desertion of the open fire-place. Alas! is this world so very bright, that we can afford to choke up such a domestic fountain of gladsomeness, and sit down by its darkened source, without being conscious of a gloom?

It is my belief, that social intercourse cannot long continue what it has been, now that we have subtracted from it so important and vivifying an element as fire-light. The effects will be more perceptible on our children, and the generations that shall succeed them, than on ourselves, the mechanism of whose life may remain unchanged, though its spirit be far other than it was. The sacred trust of the household-fire has been transmitted in unbroken succession from the earliest ages, and faithfully cherished, in spite of every discouragement, such as the Curfew law of the Norman conquerors; until, in these evil days, physical science has nearly succeeded in extinguishing it. But we at least have our youthful recollections tinged with the glow of the hearth, and our life-long habits and associations arranged on the principle of a mutual bond in the domestic fire. Therefore, though the sociable friend be for ever departed, yet in a degree he will be spiritually present to us; and still more will the empty forms, which were once full of his rejoicing presence, continue to rule our manners. We shall draw our chairs together, as we and our forefathers have been wont, for thousands of years back, and sit around some blank and empty corner of the room, babbling, with unreal cheerfulness, of topics suitable to the homely fireside. A warmth from the past—from the ashes of by-gone years, and the raked-up embers of long ago—will sometimes thaw the ice about our hearts. But it must be otherwise with our successors. On the most favorable supposition, they will be acquainted with the fireside in no better shape than that of the sullen stove; and more probably, they will have grown up amid furnace-heat, in houses which might be fancied to have their foundation over the infernal pit, whence sulphurous steams and unbreathable exhalations ascend through the apertures of the floor. There will be nothing to attract these poor children to one centre. They will never behold one another through that peculiar medium of vision—the ruddy gleam of blazing wood or bituminous coal—which gives the human spirit so deep an insight into its fellows, and melts all humanity into one cordial heart of hearts. Domestic life—if it may still be termed domestic—will seek its separate corners, and never gather itself into groups. The easy gossip—the merry, yet unambitious jest—the life-long, practical discussion of real matters in a casual way—the soul of truth, which is so often incarnated in a simple fireside word—will disappear from earth. Conversation will contract the air of a debate, and all moral intercourse be chilled with a fatal frost.

In classic times, the exhortation to fight "pro aris et focis"—for the altars and the hearths—was considered the strongest appeal that could be made to patriotism. And it seemed an immortal utterance; for all subsequent ages and people have acknowledged its force, and responded to it with the full portion of manhood that Nature had assigned to each. Wisely were the Altar and the Hearth conjoined in one mighty sentence! For the hearth, too, had its kindred sanctity. Religion sat down beside it, not in the priestly robes which decorated, and perhaps disguised, her at the altar, but arrayed in a simple matron's garb, and uttering her lessons with the tenderness of a mother's voice and heart. The holy Hearth! If any earthly and material thing—or rather, a divine idea, embodied in brick and mortar—might be supposed to possess the permanence of mortal truth, it was this. All revered it.

The man, who did not put off his shoes upon this holy ground, would have deemed it pastime to trample upon the altar. It has been our task to uproot the hearth. What further reform is left for our children to achieve, unless they overthrow the altar too? And by what appeal, hereafter, when the breath of hostile armies may mingle with the pure, cold breezes of our country, shall we attempt to rouse up native valor? Fight for your hearths? There will be none throughout the land. FIGHT FOR YOUR STOVES! Not I, in faith. If, in such a cause, I strike a blow, it shall be on the invader's part; and Heaven grant that it may shatter the abomination all to pieces!

BUDS AND BIRD-VOICES

BALMY SPRING—weeks later than we expected, and months later than we longed for her—comes at last, to revive the moss on the roof and walls of our old mansion. She peeps brightly into my study-window, inviting me to throw it open, and create a summer atmosphere by the intermixture of her genial breath with the black and cheerless comfort of the stove. As the casement ascends, forth into infinite space fly the innumerable forms of thought or fancy, that have kept me company in the retirement of this little chamber, during the sluggish lapse of wintry weather;—visions, gay, grotesque, and sad; pictures of real life, tinted with nature's homely gray and russet; scenes in dream-land, bedizened with rainbow-hues, which faded before they were well laid on;—all these may vanish now, and leave me to mould a fresh existence out of sunshine. Brooding meditation may flap her dusky wings, and take her owl-like flight, blinking amid the cheerfulness of noontide. Such companions befit the season of frosted window-panes and crackling fires, when the blast howls through the black ash-trees of our avenue, and the drifting snow-storm chokes up the wood-paths, and fills the highway from stone-wall to stone-wall. In the spring and summer time, all sombre thoughts should follow the winter northward, with the sombre and thoughtful crows. The old, paradisiacal economy of life is again in force; we live, not to think, nor to labor, but for the simple end of being happy; nothing, for the present hour, is worthy of man's infinite capacity, save to imbibe the warm smile of heaven, and sympathize with the reviving earth.

The present Spring comes onward with fleeter footsteps, because winter lingered so unconscionably long, that, with her best diligence, she can hardly retrieve half the allotted period of her reign. It is but a fortnight, since I stood on the brink of our swollen river, and beheld the accumulated ice of four frozen months go down the stream. Except in streaks here and there upon the hill-sides, the whole visible universe was then covered with deep snow, the nethermost layer of which had been deposited by an early December storm. It was a sight to make the beholder torpid, in the impossibility of imagining how this vast white napkin was to be removed from the face of the corpselike world, in less time than had been required to spread it there. But who can estimate the power of gentle influences, whether amid material desolation, or the moral winter of man's heart! There have been no tempestuous rains, —even, no sultry days,—but a constant breath of southern winds, with now a day of kindly sunshine, and now a no less kindly mist, or a soft descent of showers, in which a smile and a blessing seemed to have been steeped. The snow has vanished as if by magic; whatever heaps may be hidden in the woods and deep gorges of the hills, only two solitary specks remain in the landscape; and those I shall almost regret to miss, when, to-morrow, I look for them in vain. Never before, methinks, has spring pressed so closely on the footsteps of retreating winter. Along the road-side, the green blades of grass have sprouted on the very edge of the snow-drifts. The pastures and mowing fields have not yet assumed a general aspect of verdure; but neither have they the cheerless brown tint which they wear in latter autumn, when vegetation has entirely ceased; there is now a faint shadow of life, gradually brightening into the warm reality. Some tracts, in a happy exposure—as, for instance, yonder south-western slope of an orchard, in front of that old red farm-house, beyond the river—such patches of land already wear a beautiful and tender green, to which no future luxuriance can add a charm. It looks unreal—a prophecy—a hope—a transitory effect of some peculiar light, which will vanish with the slightest motion of the eye. But beauty is never a delusion; not these verdant tracts, but the dark and barren landscape, all around them, is a shadow and a dream. Each moment wins some portion of the earth from death to life; a sudden gleam of verdure brightens along the sunny slope of a bank, which, an instant ago, was brown and bare. You look again, and behold an apparition of green grass!

The trees, in our orchard and elsewhere, are as yet naked, but already appear full of life and vegetable blood. It seems as if, by one magic touch, they might instantaneously burst into full foliage, and that the wind, which now sighs through their naked branches, might make sudden music amid innumerable leaves. The moss-grown willow-tree, which, for forty years past, has overshadowed these western windows, will be among the first to put on its green attire. There are some objections to the willow; it is not a dry and cleanly tree, and impresses the beholder with an association of sliminess. No trees, I think, are perfectly agreeable as companions, unless they have glossy leaves, dry bark, and a firm and hard texture of trunk and branches. But the willow is almost the earliest to gladden us with the promise and reality of beauty, in its graceful and delicate foliage, and the last to scatter its yellow, yet scarcely withered leaves, upon the ground. All through the winter, too, its yellow twigs give it a sunny aspect, which is not without a cheering influence, even in the grayest and gloomiest day. Beneath a clouded sky, it faithfully remembers the sunshine. Our old house would lose a charm, were the willow to be cut down, with its golden crown over the snow-covered roof, and its heap of summer verdure.

The lilac-shrubs, under my study-window, are likewise almost in leaf; in two or three days more, I may put forth my hand, and pluck the topmost bough in its freshest green. These lilacs are very aged, and have lost the luxuriant foliage of their prime. The heart, or the judgment, or the moral sense, or the taste, is dissatisfied with their present aspect. Old age is not venerable, when it embodies itself in lilacs, rose-bushes, or any other ornamental shrubs; it seems as if such plants, as they grow only for beauty, ought to flourish in immortal youth, or, at least, to die before their sad decrepitude. Trees of beauty are trees of Paradise, and therefore not subject to decay, by their original nature, though they have lost that precious birth-right by being transplanted to an earthly soil. There is a kind of ludicrous unfitness in the idea of a time-stricken and grandfatherly lilac-bush. The analogy holds good in human life. Persons who can only be graceful and ornamental—who can give the world nothing but flowers —should die young, and never be seen with gray hair and wrinkles, any more than the flower-shrubs with mossy bark and blighted foliage, like the lilacs under my window. Not that beauty is worthy of less than immortality—no; the beautiful should live forever—and thence, perhaps, the sense of impropriety, when we see it triumphed over by time. Apple-trees, on the other hand, grow old without reproach. Let them live as long as they may, and contort themselves into whatever perversity of shape they please, and deck their withered limbs with a springtime gaudiness of pink-blossoms, still they are respectable, even if they afford us only an apple or two in a season. Those few apples—or, at all events, the

remembrance of apples in by-gone years—are the atonement
which utilitarianism inexorably demands, for the privilege of
lengthened life. Human flower-shrubs, if they will grow old
on earth, should, beside their lovely blossoms, bear some kind
of fruit that will satisfy earthly appetites; else neither man,
nor the decorum of nature, will deem it fit that the moss
should gather on them.

One of the first things that strike the attention, when the
white sheet of winter is withdrawn, is the neglect and disarray
that lay hidden beneath it. Nature is not cleanly, according
to our prejudices. The beauty of preceding years, now transformed to brown and blighted deformity, obstructs the brightening loveliness of the present hour. Our avenue is strewn
with the whole crop of Autumn's withered leaves. There are
quantities of decayed branches, which one tempest after another has flung down, black and rotten; and one or two with
the ruin of a bird's nest clinging to them. In the garden are
the dried bean-vines, the brown stalks of the asparagus-bed,
and melancholy old cabbages, which were frozen into the soil
before their unthrifty cultivator could find time to gather
them. How invariably, throughout all the forms of life, do we
find these intermingled memorials of death! On the soil of
thought, and in the garden of the heart, as well as in the
sensual world, lie withered leaves; the ideas and feelings that
we have done with. There is no wind strong enough to sweep
them away; infinite space will not garner them from our sight.
What mean they? Why may we not be permitted to live and
enjoy, as if this were the first life, and our own the primal
enjoyment, instead of treading always on these dry bones
and mouldering relics, from the aged accumulation of which
springs all that now appears so young and new? Sweet must
have been the springtime of Eden, when no earlier year had
strewn its decay upon the virgin turf, and no former experience had ripened into summer, and faded into autumn,

in the hearts of its inhabitants! That was a world worth living in! Oh, thou murmurer, it is out of the very wantonness of such a life, that thou feignest these idle lamentations! There is no decay. Each human soul is the first created inhabitant of its own Eden. We dwell in an old moss-covered mansion, and tread in the worn footprints of the past, and have a gray clergyman's ghost for our daily and nightly inmate; yet all these outward circumstances are made less than visionary, by the renewing power of the spirit. Should the spirit ever lose this power—should the withered leaves, and the rotten branches, and the moss-covered house, and the ghost of the gray past, ever become its realities, and the verdure and the freshness merely its faint dream—then let it pray to be released from earth. It will need the air of heaven, to revive its pristine energies!

What an unlooked-for flight was this, from our shadowy avenue of black ash and Balm of Gilead trees, into the infinite! Now we have our feet again upon the turf. Nowhere does the grass spring up so industriously as in this homely yard, along the base of the stone-wall, and in the sheltered nooks of the buildings, and especially around the southern door-step; a locality which seems particularly favorable to its growth; for it is already tall enough to bend over, and wave in the wind. I observe that several weeds—and, most frequently, a plant that stains the fingers with its yellow juice—have survived, and retained their freshness and sap throughout the winter. One knows not how they have deserved such an exception from the common lot of their race. They are now the patriarchs of the departed year, and may preach mortality to the present generation of flowers and weeds.

Among the delights of spring, how is it possible to forget the birds! Even the crows were welcome, as the sable harbingers of a brighter and livelier race. They visited us before the snow was off, but seem mostly to have departed now, or else to have betaken themselves to remote depths of the woods, which they haunt all summer long. Many a time shall I disturb them there, and feel as if I had intruded among a company of silent worshippers, as they sit in sabbath-stillness among the tree-tops. Their voices, when they speak, are in admirable accordance with the tranquil solitude of a summer afternoon; and, resounding so far above the head, their loud clamor increases the religious quiet of the scene, instead of breaking it. A crow, however, has no real pretensions to religion, in spite of his gravity of mien and black attire; he is certainly a thief, and probably an infidel. The gulls are far more respectable, in a moral point of view. These denizens of sea-beaten rocks, and haunters of the lonely beach, come up our inland river, at this season, and soar high overhead, flapping their broad wings in the upper sunshine. They are among the most picturesque of birds, because they so float and rest upon the air as to become almost stationary parts of the landscape. The imagination has time to grow acquainted with them; they have not flitted away in a moment. You go up among the clouds, and greet these lofty-flighted gulls, and repose confidently with them upon the sustaining atmosphere. Ducks have their haunts along the solitary places of the river, and alight in flocks upon the broad bosom of the overflowed meadows. Their flight is too rapid and determined for the eye to catch enjoyment from it, although it never fails to stir up the heart with the sportsman's ineradicable instinct. They have now gone farther northward, but will visit us again in autumn.

The smaller birds—the little songsters of the woods, and those that haunt man's dwellings, and claim human friendship by building their nests under the sheltering eaves, or among the orchard-trees—these require a touch more delicate and a gentler heart than mine, to do them justice. Their outburst of melody is like a brook let loose from wintry chains. We need not deem it a too high and solemn word, to call it a hymn of praise to the Creator; since Nature, who pictures the reviving year in so many sights of beauty, has expressed the sentiment of renewed life in no other sound, save the notes of these blessed birds. Their musick, however, just now, seems to be incidental, and not the result of a set purpose. They are discussing the economy of life and love, and the site and architecture of their summer residences, and have no time to sit on a twig, and pour forth solemn hymns, or overtures, operas, symphonies, and waltzes. Anxious questions are asked; grave subjects are settled in quick and animated debate; and only by occasional accident, as from pure ecstasy, does a rich warble roll its tiny waves of golden sound through the atmosphere. Their little bodies are as busy as their voices; they are in a constant flutter and restlessness. Even when two or three retreat to a tree-top, to hold council, they wag their tails and heads all the time, with the irrepressible activity of their nature, which perhaps renders their brief span of life in reality as long as the patriarchal age of sluggish man. The black-birds, three species of which consort together, are the noisiest of all our feathered citizens. Great companies of them—more than the famous 'four-and-twenty,' whom Mother Goose has immortalized—congregate in contiguous tree-tops, and vociferate with all the clamor and confusion of a turbulent political meeting. Politics, certainly, must be the occasion of such tumultuous debates; but still— unlike all other politicians—they instil melody into their individual utterances, and produce harmony as a general effect. Of all bird-voices, none are more sweet and cheerful to my ear than those of swallows, in the dim, sun-streaked interior of a lofty barn; they address the heart with even a closer sympathy than Robin Redbreast. But, indeed, all these winged people, that dwell in the vicinity of homesteads, seem to partake of human nature, and possess the germ, if not the developement, of immortal souls. We hear them saying their melodious prayers, at morning's blush and eventide. A little while ago, in the deep of night, there came the lively thrill of a bird's note from a neighboring tree; a real song, such as greets the purple dawn, or mingles with the yellow sunshine. What could the little bird mean, by pouring it forth at midnight? Probably the music gushed out of the midst of a dream, in which he fancied himself in Paradise with his mate, but suddenly awoke on a cold, leafless bough, with a New-England mist penetrating through his feathers. That was a sad exchange of imagination for reality!

Insects are among the earliest births of spring. Multitudes, of I know not what species, appeared long ago, on the surface of the snow. Clouds of them, almost too minute for sight, hover in a beam of sunshine, and vanish, as if annihilated, when they pass into the shade. A musquitoe has already been heard to sound the small horror of his bugle-horn. Wasps infest the sunny windows of the house. A bee entered one of the chambers, with a prophecy of flowers. Rare butterflies came before the snow was off, flaunting in the chill breeze, and looking forlorn and all astray, in spite of the magnificence of their dark velvet cloaks, with golden borders.

The fields and wood-paths have as yet few charms to entice the wanderer. In a walk, the other day, I found no violets nor anemones, nor anything in the likeness of a flower. It was worth while, however, to ascend our opposite hill, for the sake of gaining a general idea of the advance of spring, which I had hitherto been studying in its minute developements. The river lay around me in a semi-circle, overflowing all the meadows which give it its Indian name, and offering a noble breadth to sparkle in the sunbeams. Along the hither shore, a row of trees stood up to their knees in water; and afar off, on the surface of the stream, tufts of bushes thrust up their heads, as it were, to breathe. The most striking objects were great solitary trees, here and there, with a mile-wide waste of water all around them. The curtailment of the trunk, by its immersion in the river, quite destroys the fair proportions of the tree, and thus makes us sensible of a regularity and propriety in the usual forms of nature. The flood of the present season—though it never amounts to a freshet, on our quiet stream—has encroached farther upon the land than any previous one, for at least a score of years. It has overflowed stone-fences, and even rendered a portion of the highway navigable for boats. The waters, however, are now gradually subsiding; islands become annexed to the mainland; and other islands emerge, like new creations, from the watery waste. The scene supplies an admirable image of the receding of the Nile—except that there is no deposit of black slime;—or of Noah's flood—only that there is a freshness and novelty in these recovered portions of the continent, which give the impression of a world just made, rather than of one so polluted that a deluge had been requisite to purify it. These upspringing islands are the greenest spots in the landscape; the first gleam of sunlight suffices to cover them with verdure.

Thank Providence for Spring! The earth—and man himself, by sympathy with his birth-place—would be far other than we find them, if life toiled wearily onward, without this periodical infusion of the primal spirit. Will the world ever be so decayed, that spring may not renew its greenness? Can man be so dismally age-stricken, that no faintest sunshine of his youth may revisit him once a year? It is impossible. The moss on our time-worn mansion brightens into beauty; the good old pastor, who once dwelt here, renewed his prime, regained his boyhood, in the genial breezes of his ninetieth spring. Alas for the worn and heavy soul, if, whether in youth or age, it have outlived its privilege of springtime sprightliness! From such a soul, the world must hope no reformation of its evil—no sympathy with the lofty faith and gallant struggles of those who contend in its behalf. Summer works in the present, and thinks not of the future; Autumn is a rich conservative; Winter has utterly lost its faith, and clings tremulously to the remembrance of what has been; but Spring, with its outgushing life, is the true type of the Movement!

MONSIEUR DU MIROIR

T HAN the gentleman above-named, there is nobody, in the whole circle of my acquaintance, whom I have more attentively studied, yet of whom I have less real knowledge, beneath the surface which it pleases him to present. Being anxious to discover who and what he really is, and how connected with me, and what are to be the results, to him and to myself, of the joint interest, which, without any choice on my part, seems to be permanently established between us—and incited, furthermore, by the propensities of a student of human nature, though doubtful whether M. du Miroir have aught of humanity but the figure—I have determined to place a few of his remarkable points before the public, hoping to be favored with some clew to the explanation of his character.—Nor let the reader condemn any part of the narrative as frivolous, since a subject of such grave reflection diffuses its importance through the minutest particulars, and there is no judging, beforehand, what odd little circumstance may do the office of a blind man's dog, among the perplexities of this dark investigation. And however extraordinary, marvellous, preternatural, and utterly incredible, some of the meditated disclosures may appear, I pledge my honor to maintain as sacred a regard to fact, as if my testimony were given on oath, and involved the dearest interests of the personage in question. Not that there is matter for a criminal accusation against M. du Miroir; nor am I the man to bring it forward, if there were. The chief that I complain of is his impenetrable mystery, which is no better than nonsense, if it conceal anything good, and much worse, in the contrary case.

But, if undue partialities could be supposed to influence me, M. du Miroir might hope to profit, rather than to suffer by them; for, in the whole of our long intercourse, we have seldom had the slightest disagreement; and, moreover, there are reasons for supposing him a near relative of mine, and consequently entitled to the best word that I can give him. He bears, indisputably, a strong personal resemblance to myself, and generally puts on mourning at the funerals of the family. On the other hand, his name would indicate a French descent; in which case, infinitely preferring that my blood should flow from a bold British and pure Puritan source, I beg leave to disclaim all kindred with M. du Miroir. Some genealogists trace his origin to Spain, and dub him a knight of the order of the CABALLEROS DE LOS ESPEJOS, one of whom was overthrown by Don Quixote. But what says M. du Miroir, himself, of his paternity and his father-land? Not a word did he ever say about the matter; and herein, perhaps, lies one of his most especial reasons for maintaining such a vexatious mystery—that he lacks the faculty of speech to expound it. His lips are sometimes seen to move; his eyes and countenance are alive with shifting expression, as if corresponding by visible hieroglyphics to his modulated breath; and anon, he will seem to pause, with as satisfied an air, as if he had been talking excellent sense. Good sense or bad, M. du Miroir is the sole judge of his own conversational powers, never having whispered so much as a syllable, that reached the ears of any other auditor. Is he really dumb?—

or is all the world deaf?—or is it merely a piece of my
friend's waggery, meant for nothing but to make fools of us?
If so, he has the joke all to himself.

This dumb devil, which possesses M. du Miroir, is, I am
persuaded, the sole reason that he does not make me the
most flattering protestations of friendship. In many particulars—indeed, as to all his cognizable and not preternatural
points, except that, once in a great while, I speak a word or
two—there exists the greatest apparent sympathy between us.
Such is his confidence in my taste, that he goes astray from
the general fashion, and copies all his dresses after mine.
I never try on a new garment, without expecting to meet
M. du Miroir in one of the same pattern. He has duplicates of
all my waistcoats and cravats, shirt-bosoms of precisely a
similar plait, and an old coat for private wear, manufactured,
I suspect, by a Chinese tailor, in exact imitation of a beloved
old coat of mine, with a facsimile, stitch by stitch, of a patch
upon the elbow. In truth, the singular and minute coinci-
dences that occur, both in the accidents of the passing day
and the serious events of our lives, remind me of those
doubtful legends of lovers, or twin-children, twins of fate,
who have lived, enjoyed, suffered, and died, in unison, each
faithfully repeating the least tremor of the other's breath,
though separated by vast tracts of sea and land. Strange to
say, my incommodities belong equally to my companion,
though the burthen is nowise alleviated by his participation.
The other morning, after a night of torment from the tooth-
ache, I met M. du Miroir with such a swollen anguish in his
cheek, that my own pangs were redoubled, as were also his,
if I might judge by a fresh contortion of his visage. All the
inequalities of my spirits are communicated to him, causing
the unfortunate M. du Miroir to mope and scowl through a
whole summer's day, or to laugh as long, for no better reason
than the gay or gloomy crotchets of my brain. Once we were

joint sufferers of a three months' sickness, and met like mutual
ghosts in the first days of convalescence. Whenever I have
been in love, M. du Miroir has looked passionate and tender,
and never did my mistress discard me, but this too susceptible
gentleman grew lack-a-daisical. His temper, also, rises to
blood-heat, fever-heat, or boiling-water heat, according to the
measure of any wrong which might seem to have fallen
entirely on myself. I have sometimes been calmed down, by
the sight of my own inordinate wrath, depicted on his frown-
ing brow. Yet, however prompt in taking up my quarrels, I
cannot call to mind that he ever struck a downright blow in
my behalf; nor, in fact, do I perceive that any real and
tangible good has resulted from his constant interference in
my affairs; so that, in my distrustful moods, I am apt to
suspect M. du Miroir's sympathy to be mere outward show,
not a whit better nor worse than other people's sympathy.
Nevertheless, as mortal man must have something in the
guise of sympathy, and whether the true metal, or merely
copper-washed, is of less moment, I choose rather to content
myself with M. du Miroir's, such as it is, than to seek the
sterling coin, and perhaps miss even the counterfeit.

In my age of vanities, I have often seen him in the ball-
room, and might again, were I to seek him there. We have
encountered each other at the Tremont theatre, where, however, he took his seat neither in the dress-circle, pit, nor
upper regions, nor threw a single glance at the stage, though
the brightest star, even Fanny Kemble herself, might be
culminating there. No; this whimsical friend of mine chose
to linger in the saloon, near one of the large looking-glasses
which throw back their pictures of the illuminated room. He
is so full of these unaccountable eccentricities, that I never
like to notice M. du Miroir, nor to acknowledge the slightest
connection with him, in places of public resort. He, however,
has no scruple about claiming my acquaintance, even when

his common sense, if he had any, might teach him that I would as willingly exchange a nod with the Old Nick. It was but the other day, that he got into a large brass kettle, at the entrance of a hardware store, and thrust his head, the moment afterwards, into a bright new warming-pan, whence he gave me a most merciless look of recognition. He smiled, and so did I; but these childish tricks make decent people rather shy of M. du Miroir, and subject him to more dead cuts than any other gentleman in town.

One of this singular person's most remarkable peculiarities is his fondness for water, wherein he excels any temperance-man whatever. His pleasure, it must be owned, is not so much to drink it, (in which respect, a very moderate quantity will answer his occasions,) as to souse himself over head and ears, wherever he may meet with it. Perhaps he is a merman, or born of a mermaid's marriage with a mortal, and thus amphibious by hereditary right, like the children which the old river deities, or nymphs of fountains, gave to earthly love. When no cleaner bathing-place happened to be at hand, I have seen the foolish fellow in a horse-pond. Sometimes he refreshes himself in the trough of a town-pump, without caring what the people think about him. Often, while carefully picking my way along the street, after a heavy shower, I have been scandalized to see M. du Miroir, in full dress, paddling from one mud-puddle to another, and plunging into the filthy depths of each. Seldom have I peeped into a well, without discerning this ridiculous gentleman at the bottom, whence he gazes up, as through a long telescopic tube, and probably makes discoveries among the stars by daylight. Wandering along lonesome paths, or in pathless forests, when I have come to virgin-fountains, of which it would have been pleasant to deem myself the first discoverer, I have started to find M. du Miroir there before me. The solitude seemed lonelier for his presence. I have leaned from a precipice that frowns over Lake George—which the French called Nature's font of sacramental water, and used it in their log-churches here, and their cathedrals beyond the sea—and seen him far below, in that pure element. At Niagara, too, where I would gladly have forgotten both myself and him, I could not help observing my companion, in the smooth water, on the very verge of the cataract, just above the Table Rock. Were I to reach the sources of the Nile, I should expect to meet him there. Unless he be another Ladurlad, whose garments the depths of ocean could not moisten, it is difficult to conceive how he keeps himself in any decent pickle; though I am bound to confess, that his clothes seem always as dry and comfortable as my own. But, as a friend, I could wish that he would not so often expose himself in liquor.

All that I have hitherto related may be classed among those little personal oddities which agreeably diversify the surface of society; and, though they may sometimes annoy us, yet keep our daily intercourse fresher and livelier than if they were done away. By an occasional hint, however, I have endeavored to pave the way for stranger things to come, which, had they been disclosed at once, M. du Miroir might have been deemed a shadow, and myself a person of no veracity, and this truthful history a fabulous legend. But, now that the reader knows me worthy of his confidence, I will begin to make him stare.

To speak frankly, then, I could bring the most astounding proofs that M. du Miroir is at least a conjuror, if not one of that unearthly tribe with whom conjurors deal. He has inscrutable methods of conveying himself from place to place, with the rapidity of the swiftest steam-boat, or rail-car. Brick walls, and oaken doors, and iron bolts, are no impediment to his passage. Here in my chamber, for instance, as the evening deepens into night, I sit alone—the key turned and withdrawn from the lock—the key-hole stuffed with paper, to keep out a peevish little blast of wind. Yet, lonely as I seem, were I to lift one of the lamps and step five paces eastward, M. du Miroir would be sure to meet me, with a lamp also in his hand. And, were I to take the stage coach to-morrow, without giving him the least hint of my design, and post onward till the week's end, at whatever hotel I might find myself, I should expect to share my private apartment with this inevitable M. du Miroir. Or, out of a mere wayward fantasy, were I to go, by moonlight, and stand beside the stone font of the Shaker Spring at Canterbury, M. du Miroir would set forth on the same fool's errand, and would not fail to meet me there. Shall I heighten the reader's wonder? While writing these latter sentences, I happened to glance towards the large round globe of one of the brass andirons; and lo!— a miniature apparition of M. du Miroir, with his face widened and grotesquely contorted, as if he were making fun of my amazement. But he has played so many of these jokes, that they begin to lose their effect. Once, presumptuous that he was, he stole into the heaven of a young lady's eyes, so that while I gazed, and was dreaming only of herself, I found him also in my dream. Years have so changed him since, that he need never hope to enter those heavenly orbs again.

From these veritable statements, it will be readily concluded, that, had M. du Miroir played such pranks in old witch times, matters might have gone hard with him; at least, if the constable and posse comitatus could have executed a warrant, or the jailor had been cunning enough to keep him. But it has often occurred to me as a very singular circumstance, and as betokening either a temperament morbidly suspicious, or some weighty cause of apprehension, that he never trusts himself within the grasp even of his most intimate friend. If you step forward to meet him, he readily advances; if you offer him your hand, he extends his own, with an air of the utmost frankness; but though you calculate upon a hearty shake, you do not get hold of his little finger. Ah, this M. du Miroir is a slippery fellow!

These, truly, are matters of special admiration. After vainly endeavoring, by the strenuous exertion of my own wits, to gain a satisfactory insight into the character of M. du Miroir, I had recourse to certain wise men, and also to books of abstruse philosophy, seeking who it was that haunted me, and why. I heard long lectures, and read huge volumes, with little profit beyond the knowledge that many former instances are recorded, in successive ages, of similar connections between ordinary mortals and beings possessing the attributes of M. du Miroir. Some now alive, perhaps, besides myself, have such attendants. Would that M. du Miroir could be persuaded to transfer his attachment to one of those, and allow some other of his race to assume the situation that he now holds in regard to me! If I must needs have so instrusive an intimate, who stares me in the face in my closest privacy, and follows me even to my bed-chamber, I should prefer—scandal apart—the laughing bloom of a young girl, to the dark and bearded gravity of my present companion. But such desires are never to be gratified. Though the members of M. du Miroir's family have been accused, perhaps justly, of visiting their friends often in splendid halls and seldom in darksome dungeons, yet they exhibit a rare constancy to the objects of their first attachment, however unlovely in person or unamiable in disposition, however unfortunate, or even infamous, and deserted by all the world besides. So will it be with my associate. Our fates appear inseparably blended. It is my belief, as I find him mingling with my earliest recollections, that we came into existence together, as my shadow follows me into the sunshine, and that, hereafter, as heretofore, the brightness or gloom of my fortunes will shine upon, or darken, the face of M. du Miroir. As we have been young together, and as it is now near the summer noon with both of us, so, if long life be granted, shall each count his own wrinkles on the other's brow, and his white hairs on the other's head. And when the coffin lid shall have closed over me, and that face and form, which, more truly than the lover swears it to his beloved, are the sole light of his existence, when they shall be laid in that dark chamber, whither his swift and secret footsteps cannot bring him,—then what is to become of poor M. du Miroir! Will he have the fortitude, with my other friends, to take a last look at my pale countenance? Will he walk foremost in the funeral train? Will he come often and haunt around my grave, and weed away the nettles, and plant flowers amid the verdure, and scrape the moss out of the letters of my burial-stone? Will he linger where I have lived, to remind the neglectful world of one who staked much to win a name, but will not then care whether he lost or won?

Not thus will he prove his deep fidelity. Oh, what terror, if this friend of mine, after our last farewell, should step into the crowded street, or roam along our old frequented path, by the still waters, or sit down in the domestic circle, where our faces are most familiar and beloved! No; but when the ray of Heaven shall bless me no more, nor the thoughtful lamplight gleam upon my studies, nor the cheerful fireside gladden the meditative man, then, his task fulfilled, shall this mysterious being vanish from the earth forever. He will pass to the dark realm of Nothingness, but will not find me there.

There is something fearful in bearing such a relation to a creature so imperfectly known, and in the idea that, to a certain extent, all which concerns myself will be reflected in its consequences upon him. When we feel that another is to share the self-same fortune with ourselves, we judge more severely of our prospects, and withhold our confidence from that delusive magic which appears to shed an infallibility of happiness over our own pathway. Of late years, indeed, there has been much to sadden my intercourse with M. du Miroir. Had not our union been a necessary condition of our life, we must have been estranged ere now. In early youth, when my affections were warm and free, I loved him well, and could always spend a pleasant hour in his society, chiefly because it gave me an excellent opinion of myself. Speechless as he was, M. du Miroir had then a most agreeable way of calling me a handsome fellow; and I, of course, returned the compliment; so that, the more we kept each other's company, the greater coxcombs we mutually grew. But neither of us need apprehend any such misfortune now. When we chance to meet—for it is chance oftener than design—each glances sadly at the other's forehead, dreading wrinkles there, and at our temples, whence the hair is thinning away too early, and at the sunken eyes, which no longer shed a gladsome light over the whole face. I involuntarily peruse him as a record of my heavy youth, which has been wasted in sluggishness, for lack of hope and impulse, or equally thrown away in toil, that had no wise motive, and has accomplished no good end. I perceive that the tranquil gloom of a disappointed soul has darkened through his countenance, where the blackness of the future seems to mingle with the shadows of the past, giving him the aspect of a fated man. Is it too wild a thought, that my fate may have assumed this image of myself, and therefore haunts me with such inevitable pertinacity, originating every act which it appears to imitate, while it deludes me by pretending to share the events, of which it is merely the emblem and the prophecy? I must banish this idea, or it will throw too deep an awe round my companion. At our next meeting, especially if it be at midnight or in solitude, I fear that I shall glance aside and shudder; in which case, as M. du Miroir is extremely sensitive to ill-treatment, he also will avert his eyes, and express horror or disgust.

But no! This is unworthy of me. As, of old, I sought his society for the bewitching dreams of woman's love which he inspired, and because I fancied a bright fortune in his aspect, so now will I hold daily and long communion with him, for the sake of the stern lessons that he will teach my manhood. With folded arms, we will sit face to face, and lengthen out our silent converse, till a wiser cheerfulness shall have been wrought from the very texture of despondency. He will say, perhaps indignantly, that it befits only him to mourn for the decay of outward grace, which, while he possessed it, was his all. But have not you, he will ask, a treasure in reserve, to which every year may add far more value than age, or death itself, can snatch from that miserable clay? He will tell me, that, though the bloom of life has been nipt with a frost, yet the soul must not sit shivering in its cell, but bestir itself manfully, and kindle a genial warmth from its own exercise, against the autumnal and the wintry atmosphere. And I, in return, will bid him be of good cheer, nor take it amiss that I must blanch his locks and wrinkle him up like a wilted apple, since it shall be my endeavor so to beautify his face with intellect and mild benevolence, that he shall profit immensely by the change. But here a smile will glimmer somewhat sadly over M. du Miroir's visage.

When this subject shall have been sufficiently discussed, we may take up others as important. Reflecting upon his power of following me to the remotest regions and into the deepest privacy, I will compare the attempt to escape him to the hopeless race that men sometimes run with memory, or their own hearts, or their moral selves, which, though burthened with cares enough to crush an elephant, will never be one step behind. I will be self-contemplative, as nature bids me, and make him the picture or visible type of what I muse upon, that my mind may not wander so vaguely as heretofore, chasing its own shadow through a chaos, and catching only the monsters that abide there. Then will we turn our thoughts to the spiritual world, of the reality of which, my companion shall furnish me an illustration, if not an argument. For, as we have only the testimony of the eye to M. du Miroir's existence, while all the other senses would fail to inform us that such a figure stands within arm's length, wherefore should there not be beings innumerable, close beside us, and filling heaven and earth with their multitude, yet of whom no corporeal perception can take cognizance? A blind man might as reasonably deny that M. du Miroir exists, as we, because the Creator has hitherto withheld the spiritual perception, can therefore contend that there are no spirits. Oh, there are! And, at this moment, when the subject of which I write has grown strong within me, and surrounded itself with those solemn and awful associations which might have seemed most alien to it, I could fancy that M. du Miroir is himself a wanderer from the spiritual world, with nothing human, except his illusive garment of visibility. Methinks I should tremble now, were his wizard power, of gliding through all impediments in search of me, to place him suddenly before my eyes.

Ha! What is yonder? Shape of mystery, did the tremor of my heart-strings vibrate to thine own, and call thee from thy home, among the dancers of the Northern Lights, and shadows flung from departed sunshine, and giant spectres that appear on clouds at daybreak, and affright the climber of the Alps? In truth, it startled me, as I threw a wary glance eastward across the chamber, to discern an unbidden guest, with his eyes bent on mine. The identical MONSIEUR DU MIROIR! Still, there he sits, and returns my gaze with as much of awe and curiosity, as if he, too, had spent a solitary evening in fantastic musings, and made me his theme. So inimitably does he counterfeit, that I could almost doubt which of us is the visionary form, or whether each be not the other's mystery, and both twin brethren of one fate, in mutually reflected spheres. Oh, friend, canst thou not hear and answer me? Break down the barrier between us! Grasp my hand! Speak! Listen! A few words, perhaps, might satisfy the feverish yearning of my soul for some master-thought, that should guide me through this labyrinth of life, teaching wherefore I was born, and how to do my task on earth, and what is death. Alas! Even that unreal image should forget to ape me, and smile at these vain questions.—Thus do mortals deify, as it were, a mere shadow of themselves, a spectre of human reason, and ask of that to unveil the mysteries, which Divine Intelligence has revealed so far as needful to our guidance, and hid the rest.

Farewell, Monsieur du Miroir! Of you, perhaps, as of many men, it may be doubted whether you are the wiser, though your whole business is REFLECTION.

THE HALL OF FANTASY

I
T HAS happened to me, on various occasions, to find myself in a certain edifice, which would appear to have some of the characteristics of a public Exchange. Its interior is a spacious hall, with a pavement of white marble. Overhead is a lofty dome, supported by long rows of pillars, of fantastic architecture, the idea of which was probably taken from the Moorish ruins of the Alhambra, or perhaps from some enchanted edifice in the Arabian Tales. The windows of this hall have a breadth and grandeur of design, and an elaborateness of workmanship, that have nowhere been equalled, except in the Gothic cathedrals of the old world. Like their prototypes, too, they admit the light of heaven only through stained and pictured glass, thus filling the hall with many-colored radiance, and painting its marble floor with beautiful or grotesque designs; so that its inmates breathe, as it were, a visionary atmosphere, and tread upon the fantasies of poetic minds. These peculiarities, combining a wilder mixture of styles than even an American architect usually recognizes as allowable—Grecian, Gothic, Oriental, and nondescript—cause the whole edifice to give the impression of a dream, which might be dissipated and shattered to fragments, by merely stamping the foot upon the pave-

ment. Yet, with such modifications and repairs as successive ages demand, the Hall of Fantasy is likely to endure longer than the most substantial structure that ever cumbered the earth.

It is not at all times that one can gain admittance into this edifice; although most persons enter it at some period or other of their lives—if not in their waking moments, then by the universal passport of a dream. At my last visit, I wandered thither unawares, while my mind was busy with an idle tale, and was startled by the throng of people who seemed suddenly to rise up around me.

"Bless me! Where am I?" cried I, with but a dim recognition of the place.

"You are in a spot," said a friend, who chanced to be near at hand, "which occupies, in the world of fancy, the same position which the Bourse, the Rialto, and the Exchange, do in the commercial world. All who have affairs in that mystic region, which lies above, below, or beyond the Actual, may here meet, and talk over the business of their dreams."

"It is a noble hall," observed I.

"Yes," he replied. "Yet we see but a small portion of the edifice. In its upper stories are said to be apartments, where the inhabitants of earth may hold converse with those of the moon. And beneath our feet are gloomy cells, which communicate with the infernal regions, and where monsters and chimeras are kept in confinement, and fed with all unwholesomeness."

In niches and on pedestals, around about the hall, stood the statues or busts of men, who, in every age, have been rulers and demi-gods in the realms of imagination, and its kindred regions. The grand old countenance of Homer; the shrunken and decrepit form, but vivid face of Æsop; the dark presence of Dante; the wild Ariosto; Rabelais's smile of deep-wrought mirth; the profound, pathetic humor of

Cervantes; the all-glorious Shakespeare; Spenser, meet guest for an allegoric structure; the severe divinity of Milton; and Bunyan, moulded of homeliest clay, but instinct with celestial fire—were those that chiefly attracted my eye. Fielding, Richardson, and Scott, occupied conspicuous pedestals. In an obscure and shadowy niche was reposited the bust of our countryman, the author of Arthur Mervyn.

"Besides these indestructible memorials of real genius," remarked my companion, "each century has erected statues of its own ephemeral favorites, in wood."

"I observe a few crumbling relics of such," said I. "But ever and anon, I suppose, Oblivion comes with her huge broom, and sweeps them all from the marble floor. But such will never be the fate of this fine statue of Goethe."

"Nor of that next to it—Emanuel Swedenborg," said he. "Were ever two men of transcendent imagination more unlike?"

In the centre of the hall springs an ornamental fountain, the water of which continually throws itself into new shapes, and snatches the most diversified hues from the stained atmosphere around. It is impossible to conceive what a strange vivacity is imparted to the scene by the magic dance of this fountain, with its endless transformations, in which the imaginative beholder may discern what form he will. The water is supposed by some to flow from the same source as the Castalian spring, and is extolled by others as uniting the virtues of the Fountain of Youth with those of many other enchanted wells, long celebrated in tale and song. Having never tasted it, I can bear no testimony to its quality.

"Did you ever drink this water?" I inquired of my friend.

"A few sips, now and then," answered he. "But there are men here who make it their constant beverage—or, at least, have the credit of doing so. In some instances, it is known to have intoxicating qualities."

"Pray let us look at these water-drinkers," said I.

So we passed among the fantastic pillars, till we came to a spot where a number of persons were clustered together, in the light of one of the great stained windows, which seemed to glorify the whole group, as well as the marble that they trod on. Most of them were men of broad foreheads, meditative countenances, and thoughtful, inward eyes; yet it required but a trifle to summon up mirth, peeping out from the very midst of grave and lofty musings. Some strode about, or leaned against the pillars of the hall, alone and in silence; their faces wore a rapt expression, as if sweet music were in the air around them, or as if their inmost souls were about to float away in song. One or two, perhaps, stole a glance at the bystanders, to watch if their poetic absorption were observed. Others stood talking in groups, with a liveliness of expression, a ready smile, and a light, intellectual laughter, which showed how rapidly the shafts of wit were glancing to-and-fro among them.

A few held higher converse, which caused their calm and melancholy souls to beam moonlight from their eyes. As I lingered near them—for I felt an inward attraction towards these men, as if the sympathy of feeling, if not of genius, had united me to their order—my friend mentioned several of their names. The world has likewise heard those names; with some it has been familiar for years; and others are daily making their way deeper into the universal heart.

"Thank heaven," observed I to my companion, as we passed to another part of the hall, "we have done with this techy, wayward, shy, proud, unreasonable set of laurel-gatherers. I love them in their works, but have little desire to meet them elsewhere."

"You have adopted an old prejudice, I see," replied my friend, who was familiar with most of these worthies, being himself a student of poetry, and not without the poetic flame.

"But so far as my experience goes, men of genius are fairly gifted with the social qualities; and in this age, there appears to be a fellow-feeling among them, which had not heretofore been developed. As men, they ask nothing better than to be on equal terms with their fellow-men; and as authors, they have thrown aside their proverbial jealousy, and acknowledge a generous brotherhood."

"The world does not think so," answered I. "An author is received in general society pretty much as we honest citizens are in the Hall of Fantasy. We gaze at him as if he had no business among us, and question whether he is fit for any of our pursuits."

"Then it is a very foolish question," said he. "Now, here are a class of men, whom we may daily meet on 'Change. Yet what poet in the hall is more a fool of fancy than the sagest of them?"

He pointed to a number of persons, who, manifest as the fact was, would have deemed it an insult to be told that they stood in the Hall of Fantasy. Their visages were traced into wrinkles and furrows, each of which seemed the record of some actual experience in life. Their eyes had the shrewd, calculating glance, which detects so quickly and so surely all that it concerns a man of business to know, about the characters and purposes of his fellow-men. Judging them as they stood, they might be honored and trusted members of the Chamber of Commerce, who had found the genuine secret of wealth, and whose sagacity gave them the command of fortune. There was a character of detail and matter-of-fact in their talk, which concealed the extravagance of its purport, insomuch that the wildest schemes had the aspect of every-day realities. Thus the listener was not startled at the idea of cities to be built, as if by magic, in the heart of pathless forests; and of streets to be laid out, where now the sea was tossing; and of mighty rivers to be staid in their courses, in order to turn the machinery of a cotton-mill. It was only by an effort—and scarcely then—that the mind convinced itself that such speculations were as much matter of fantasy as the old dream of Eldorado, or as Mammon's Cave, or any other vision of gold, ever conjured up by the imagination of needy poet or romantic adventurer.

"Upon my word," said I, "it is dangerous to listen to such dreamers as these! Their madness is contagious."

"Yes," said my friend, "because they mistake the Hall of Fantasy for actual brick and mortar, and its purple atmosphere for unsophisticated sunshine. But the poet knows his where-about, and therefore is less likely to make a fool of himself in real life."

"Here again," observed I, as we advanced a little further, "we see another order of dreamers—peculiarly characteristic, too, of the genius of our country."

These were the inventors of fantastic machines. Models of their contrivances were placed against some of the pillars of the hall, and afforded good emblems of the result generally to be anticipated from an attempt to reduce day-dreams to practice. The analogy may hold in morals, as well as physics. For instance, here was the model of a railroad through the air, and a tunnel under the sea. Here was a machine—stolen, I believe—for the distillation of heat from moonshine; and another for the condensation of morning-mist into square blocks of granite, wherewith it was proposed to rebuild the entire Hall of Fantasy. One man exhibited a sort of lens, whereby he had succeeded in making sunshine out of a lady's smile; and it was his purpose wholly to irradiate the earth, by means of this wonderful invention.

"It is nothing new," said I, "for most of our sunshine comes from woman's smile already."

"True," answered the inventor; "but my machine will secure a constant supply for domestic use—whereas, hitherto, it has been very precarious."

Another person had a scheme for fixing the reflections of objects in a pool of water, and thus taking the most life-like portraits imaginable; and the same gentleman demonstrated the practicability of giving a permanent dye to ladies' dresses, in the gorgeous clouds of sunset. There were at least fifty kinds of perpetual motion, one of which was applicable to the wits of newspaper editors and writers of every description. Professor Espy was here, with a tremendous storm in a gum-elastic bag. I could enumerate many more of these Utopian inventions; but, after all, a more imaginative collection is to be found in the Patent Office at Washington.

Turning from the inventors, we took a more general survey of the inmates of the hall. Many persons were present, whose right of entrance appeared to consist in some crochet of the brain, which, so long as it might operate, produced a change in their relation to the actual world. It is singular how very few there are, who do not occasionally gain admittance on such a score, either in abstracted musings, or momentary thoughts, or bright anticipations, or vivid remembrances; for even the actual becomes ideal, whether in hope or memory, and beguiles the dreamer into the Hall of Fantasy. Some unfortunates make their whole abode and business here, and contract habits which unfit them for all the real employments of life. Others—but these are few—possess the faculty, in their occasional visits, of discovering a purer truth than the world can impart, among the lights and shadows of these pictured windows.

And with all its dangerous influences, we have reason to thank God, that there is such a place of refuge from the gloom and chillness of actual life. Hither may come the prisoner, escaping from his dark and narrow cell, and cankerous chain, to breathe free air in this enchanted atmosphere. The sick man leaves his weary pillow, and finds strength to wander hither, though his wasted limbs might not support him even to the threshold of his chamber. The exile passes through the Hall of Fantasy, to revisit his native soil. The burthen of years rolls down from the old man's shoulders, the moment that the door uncloses. Mourners leave their heavy sorrows at the entrance, and here rejoin the lost ones, whose faces would else be seen no more, until thought shall have become the only fact. It may be said, in truth, that there is but half a life—the meaner and earthlier half—for those who never find their way into the hall. Nor must I fail to mention, that, in the observatory of the edifice, is kept that wonderful perspective glass, through which the shepherds of the Delectable Mountains showed Christian the far-off gleam of the Celestial City. The eye of Faith still loves to gaze through it.

"I observe some men here," said I to my friend, "who might set up a strong claim to be reckoned among the most real personages of the day."

"Certainly," he replied. "If a man be in advance of his age, he must be content to make his abode in this hall, until the lingering generations of his fellow-men come up with him. He can find no other shelter in the universe. But the fantasies of one day are the deepest realities of a future one."

"It is difficult to distinguish them apart, amid the gorgeous and bewildering light of this hall," rejoined I. "The white sunshine of actual life is necessary in order to test them. I am rather apt to doubt both men and their reasonings, till I meet them in that truthful medium."

"Perhaps your faith in the ideal is deeper than you are aware," said my friend. "You are at least a Democrat; and methinks no scanty share of such faith is essential to the adoption of that creed."

Among the characters who had elicited these remarks, were most of the noted reformers of the day, whether in physics, politics, morals, or religion. There is no surer method of arriving at the Hall of Fantasy, than to throw oneself into the current of a theory; for, whatever landmarks of fact may be set up along the stream, there is a law of nature that impels it thither. And let it be so; for here the wise head and capacious heart may do their work; and what is good and true becomes gradually hardened into fact, while error melts away and vanishes among the shadows of the hall. Therefore may none, who believe and rejoice in the progress of mankind, be angry with me because I recognized their apostles and leaders, amid the fantastic radiance of those pictured windows. I love and honor such men, as well as they.

It would be endless to describe the herd of real or self-styled reformers, that peopled this place of refuge. They were the representatives of an unquiet period, when mankind is seeking to cast off the whole tissue of ancient custom, like a tattered garment. Many of them had got possession of some crystal fragment of truth, the brightness of which so dazzled them, that they could see nothing else in the wide universe. Here were men, whose faith had embodied itself in the form of a potatoe; and others whose long beards had a deep spiritual significance. Here was the abolitionist, brandishing his one idea like an iron flail. In a word, there were a thousand shapes of good and evil, faith and infidelity, wisdom and nonsense,—a most incongruous throng.

Yet, withal, the heart of the stanchest conservative, unless he abjured his fellowship with man, could hardly have helped throbbing in sympathy with the spirit that pervaded these innumerable theorists. It was good for the man of un-quickened heart to listen even to their folly. Far down, beyond the fathom of the intellect, the soul acknowledged that all these varying and conflicting developments of humanity were united in one sentiment. Be the individual theory as wild as fancy could make it, still the wiser spirit would recognize the struggle of the race after a better and purer life, than had yet been realized on earth. My faith revived, even while I rejected all their schemes. It could not be, that the world should continue forever what it has been; a soil where Happiness is so rare a flower, and Virtue so often a blighted fruit; a battle-field where the good principle, with its shield flung above its head, can hardly save itself amid the rush of adverse influences. In the enthusiasm of such thoughts, I gazed through one of the pictured windows; and, behold! the whole external world was tinged with the dimly glorious aspect that is peculiar to the Hall of Fantasy; insomuch that it seemed practicable, at that very instant, to realize some plan for the perfection of mankind. But, alas! if reformers would understand the sphere in which their lot is cast, they must cease to look through pictured windows. Yet they not only use this medium, but mistake it for the whitest sunshine.

"Come," said I to my friend, starting from a deep reverie,— "let us hasten hence, or I shall be tempted to make a theory— after which, there is little hope of any man."

"Come hither, then," answered he. "Here is one theory, that swallows up and annihilates all others."

He led me to a distant part of the hall, where a crowd of deeply attentive auditors were assembled round an elderly man, of plain, honest, trustworthy aspect. With an earnestness that betokened the sincerest faith in his own doctrine, he announced that the destruction of the world was close at hand.

"It is Father Miller himself!" exclaimed I.

"No less a man," said my friend, "and observe how picturesque a contrast between his dogma, and those of the reformers whom we have just glanced at. They look for the earthly perfection of mankind, and are forming schemes, which imply that the immortal spirit will be connected with a physical nature, for innumerable ages of futurity. On the other hand, here comes good Father Miller, and, with one puff of his relentless theory, scatters all their dreams like so many withered leaves upon the blast."

"It is, perhaps, the only method of getting mankind out of the various perplexities, into which they have fallen," I replied. "Yet I could wish that the world might be permitted to endure, until some great moral shall have been evolved. A riddle is propounded. Where is the solution? The sphinx did not slay herself, until her riddle had been guessed. Will it not be so with the world? Now, if it should be burnt to-morrow morning, I am at a loss to know what purpose will have been accomplished, or how the universe will be wiser or better for our existence and destruction."

"We cannot tell what mighty truths may have been embodied in act, through the existence of the globe and its inhabitants," rejoined my companion. "Perhaps it may be revealed to us, after the fall of the curtain over our catastrophe; or not impossibly, the whole drama, in which we are involuntary actors, may have been performed for the instruction of another set of spectators. I cannot perceive that our own comprehension of it is at all essential to the matter. At any rate, while our view is so ridiculously narrow and superficial, it would be absurd to argue the continuance of the world from the fact, that it seems to have existed hitherto in vain."

"The poor old Earth," murmured I. "She has faults enough, in all conscience; but I cannot bear to have her perish."

"It is no great matter," said my friend. "The happiest of us has been weary of her, many a time and oft."

"I doubt it," answered I, pertinaciously; "the root of human nature strikes down deep into this earthly soil; and it is but reluctantly that we submit to be transplanted, even for a higher cultivation in Heaven. I query whether the destruction of the earth would gratify any one individual; except, perhaps, some embarrassed man of business, whose notes fall due a day after the day of doom."

Then, methought, I heard the expostulating cry of a multitude against the consummation, prophesied by Father Miller. The lover wrestled with Providence for his fore-shadowed bliss. Parents entreated that the earth's span of endurance might be prolonged by some seventy years, so that their new-born infant should not be defrauded of his life-time. A youthful poet murmured, because there would be no posterity to recognize the inspiration of his song. The reformers, one and all, demanded a few thousand years, to test their theories, after which the universe might go to wreck. A mechanician, who was busied with an improvement of the steam-engine, asked merely time to perfect his model. A miser insisted that the world's destruction would be a personal wrong to himself, unless he should first be permitted to add a specified sum to his enormous heap of gold. A little boy made dolorous inquiry whether the last day would come before Christmas, and thus deprive him of his anticipated dainties. In short, nobody seemed satisfied that this mortal scene of things should have its close just now. Yet, it must be confessed, the motives of the crowd for desiring its continuance were mostly so absurd, that, unless Infinite Wisdom had been aware of much better reasons, the solid Earth must have melted away at once.

For my own part, not to speak of a few private and personal ends, I really desired our old Mother's prolonged existence, for her own dear sake.

"The poor old Earth!" I repeated. "What I should chiefly regret in her destruction would be that very earthliness, which no other sphere or state of existence can renew or compensate. The fragrance of flowers, and of new-mown hay;

the genial warmth of sunshine, and the beauty of a sunset among clouds; the comfort and cheerful glow of the fireside; the deliciousness of fruits, and of all good cheer; the magnificence of mountains, and seas, and cataracts, and the softer charm of rural scenery; even the fast-falling snow, and the gray atmosphere through which it descends—all these, and innumerable other enjoyable things of earth, must perish with her. Then the country frolics; the homely humor; the broad, open-mouthed roar of laughter, in which body and soul conjoin so heartily! I fear that no other world can show us anything just like this. As for purely moral enjoyments, the good will find them in every state of being. But where the material and the moral exist together, what is to happen then? And then our mute four-footed friends, and the winged songsters of our woods! Might it not be lawful to regret them, even in the hallowed groves of Paradise?"

"You speak like the very spirit of earth, imbued with a scent of freshly-turned soil!" exclaimed my friend.

"It is not that I so much object to giving up these enjoyments, on my own account," continued I; "but I hate to think that they will have been eternally annihilated from the list of joys."

"Nor need they be," he replied. "I see no real force in what you say. Standing in this Hall of Fantasy, we perceive what even the earth-clogged intellect of man can do, in creating circumstances, which, though we call them shadowy and visionary, are scarcely more so than those that surround us in actual life. Doubt not, then, that man's disembodied spirit may recreate Time and the World for itself, with all their peculiar enjoyments, should there still be human yearnings amid life eternal and infinite. But I doubt whether we shall be inclined to play such a poor scene over again."

"Oh, you are ungrateful to our Mother Earth!" rejoined I. "Come what may, I never will forget her! Neither will it satisfy me to have her exist merely in idea. I want her great, round, solid self to endure interminably, and still to be peopled with the kindly race of man, whom I uphold to be much better than he thinks himself. Nevertheless, I confide the whole matter to Providence, and shall endeavor so to live, that the world may come to an end at any moment, without leaving me at a loss to find foothold somewhere else."

"It is an excellent resolve," said my companion, looking at his watch. "But come; it is the dinner hour. Will you partake of my vegetable diet?"

A thing so matter-of-fact as an invitation to dinner, even when the fare was to be nothing more substantial than vegetables and fruit, compelled us forthwith to remove from the Hall of Fantasy. As we passed out of the portal, we met the spirits of several persons, who had been sent thither in magnetic sleep. I looked back among the sculptured pillars, and at the transformations of the gleaming fountain, and almost desired that the whole of life might be spent in that visionary scene, where the actual world, with its hard angles, should never rub against me, and only be viewed through the medium of pictured windows. But, for those who waste all their days in the Hall of Fantasy, good Father Miller's prophecy is already accomplished, and the solid earth has come to an untimely end. Let us be content, therefore, with merely an occasional visit, for the sake of spiritualizing the grossness of this actual life, and prefiguring to ourselves a state, in which the Idea shall be all in all.

THE CELESTIAL RAIL-ROAD

NOT A great while ago, passing through the gate of dreams, I visited that region of the earth in which lies the famous city of Destruction. It interested me much to learn, that, by the public spirit of some of the inhabitants, a rail-road has recently been established between this populous and flourishing town, and the Celestial City. Having a little time upon my hands, I resolved to gratify a liberal curiosity by making a trip thither. Accordingly, one fine morning, after paying my bill at the hotel, and directing the porter to stow my luggage behind a coach, I took my seat in the vehicle, and set out for the Station House. It was my good fortune to enjoy the company of a gentleman—one Mr. Smooth-it-away—who, though he had never actually visited the Celestial City, yet seemed as well acquainted with its laws, customs, policy, and statistics, as with those of the city of Destruction, of which he was a native townsman. Being, moreover, a director of the rail-road corporation, and one of its largest stockholders, he had it in his power to give me all desirable information respecting that praiseworthy enterprise.

Our coach rattled out of the city, and, at a short distance from its outskirts, passed over a bridge, of elegant construction, but somewhat too slight, as I imagined, to sustain any considerable weight. On both sides lay an extensive quagmire, which could not have been more disagreeable either to sight or smell, had all the kennels of the earth emptied their pollution there.

"This," remarked Mr. Smooth-it-away, "is the famous Slough of Despond—a disgrace to all the neighborhood; and the greater, that it might so easily be converted into firm ground."

"I have understood," said I, "that efforts have been made for that purpose, from time immemorial. Bunyan mentions that above twenty thousand cart-loads of wholesome instructions had been thrown in here, without effect."

"Very probably!—and what effect could be anticipated from such unsubstantial stuff?" cried Mr. Smooth-it-away. "You observe this convenient bridge. We obtained a sufficient foundation for it by throwing into the slough some editions of books of morality, volumes of French philosophy and German rationalism, tracts, sermons, and essays of modern clergymen, extracts from Plato, Confucius, and various Hindoo sages, together with a few ingenious commentaries upon texts of Scripture—all of which, by some scientific process, have been converted into a mass like granite. The whole bog might be filled up with similar matter."

It really seemed to me, however, that the bridge vibrated and heaved up and down, in a very formidable manner; and, spite of Mr. Smooth-it-away's testimony to the solidity of its foundation, I should be loth to cross it in a crowded omnibus; especially if each passenger were encumbered with as heavy luggage as that gentleman and myself. Nevertheless, we got over without accident, and soon found ourselves at the Station House. This very neat and spacious edifice is erected on the site of the little Wicket-Gate, which formerly, as all old pilgrims will recollect, stood directly across the highway, and, by its inconvenient narrowness, was a great obstruction to the traveller of liberal mind and expansive stomach. The reader of John Bunyan will be glad to know, that Christian's old friend Evangelist, who was accustomed to supply each pilgrim with a mystic roll, now presides at the ticket-office. Some malicious persons, it is true, deny the identity of this reputable character with the Evangelist of old times, and even pretend to bring competent evidence of an imposture. Without involving myself in the dispute, I shall merely observe, that, so far as my experience goes, the square pieces of pasteboard, now delivered to passengers, are much more convenient and useful along the road, than the antique roll of parchment. Whether they will be as readily received at the gate of the Celestial City, I decline giving an opinion.

A large number of passengers were already at the Station House, awaiting the departure of the cars. By the aspect and demeanor of these persons, it was easy to judge that the feelings of the community had undergone a very favorable change, in reference to the Celestial pilgrimage. It would have done Bunyan's heart good to see it. Instead of a lonely and ragged man, with a huge burthen on his back, plodding along sorrowfully on foot, while the whole city hooted after him, here were parties of the first gentry and most respectable people in the neighborhood, setting forth towards the Celestial City, as cheerfully as if the pilgrimage were merely a summer tour. Among the gentlemen were characters of deserved eminence, magistrates, politicians, and men of wealth, by whose example religion could not but be greatly recommended to their meaner brethren. In the ladies' apartment, too, I rejoiced to distinguish some of those flowers of fashionable society, who are so well fitted to adorn the most elevated circles of the Celestial City. There was much pleasant conversation about the news of the day, topics of business, politics, or the lighter matters of amusement; while religion, though indubitably the main thing at heart, was thrown tastefully into the back-ground. Even an infidel would have heard little or nothing to shock his sensibility.

One great convenience of the new method of going on pilgrimage, I must not forget to mention. Our enormous burthens, instead of being carried on our shoulders, as had been the custom of old, were all snugly deposited in the baggage-car, and, as I was assured, would be delivered to their respective owners, at the journey's end. Another thing, likewise, the benevolent reader will be delighted to understand. It may be remembered that there was an ancient feud between Prince Beelzebub and the keeper of the Wicket-Gate, and that the adherents of the former distinguished personage were accustomed to shoot deadly arrows at honest pilgrims, while knocking at the door. This dispute, much to the credit as well of the illustrious potentate above-mentioned as of the worthy and enlightened Directors of the rail-road, has been pacifically arranged, on the principle of mutual compromise. The prince's subjects are now pretty numerously employed about the Station House, some in taking care of the baggage, others in collecting fuel, feeding the engines, and such congenial occupations; and I can conscientiously affirm, that persons more attentive to their business, more willing to accommodate, or more generally agreeable to the passengers, are not to be found on any rail-road. Every good heart must surely exult at so satisfactory an arrangement of an immemorial difficulty.

"Where is Mr. Greatheart?" inquired I. "Beyond a doubt, the Directors have engaged that famous old champion to be chief engineer on the rail-road?"

"Why, no," said Mr. Smooth-it-away, with a dry cough. "He was offered the situation of brake-man; but, to tell you the truth, our friend Greatheart has grown preposterously stiff and narrow, in his old age. He has so often guided pilgrims over the road, on foot, that he considers it a sin to travel in any other fashion. Besides, the old fellow had entered so heartily into the ancient feud with Prince Beelzebub, that he would have been perpetually at blows or ill language with some of the prince's subjects, and thus have embroiled us anew. So, on the whole, we were not sorry when honest Greatheart went off to the Celestial City in a huff, and left us at liberty to choose a more suitable and accommodating man. Yonder comes the engineer of the train. You will probably recognize him at once."

The engine at this moment took its station in advance of the cars, looking, I must confess, much more like a sort of mechanical demon, that would hurry us to the infernal regions, than a laudable contrivance for smoothing our way to the Celestial City. On its top sat a personage almost enveloped in smoke and flame, which—not to startle the reader—appeared to gush from his own mouth and stomach, as well as from the engine's brazen abdomen.

"Do my eyes deceive me?" cried I. "What on earth is this! A living creature?—if so, he is own brother to the engine that he rides upon!"

"Poh, poh; you are obtuse!" said Mr. Smooth-it-away, with a hearty laugh. "Don't you know Apollyon, Christian's old enemy, with whom he fought so fierce a battle in the Valley of Humiliation? He was the very fellow to manage the engine; and so we have reconciled him to the custom of going on pilgrimage, and engaged him as chief engineer."

"Bravo, bravo!" exclaimed I, with irrepressible enthusiasm. "This shows the liberality of the age; this proves, if anything can, that all musty prejudices are in a fair way to be obliterated. And how will Christian rejoice to hear of this happy transformation of his old antagonist! I promise myself great pleasure in informing him of it, when we reach the Celestial City."

The passengers being all comfortably seated, we now rattled away merrily, accomplishing a greater distance in ten minutes, than Christian probably trudged over, in a day. It was laughable, while we glanced along, as it were, at the tail of a thunder-bolt, to observe two dusty foot-travellers, in the old pilgrim-guise, with cockle-shell and staff, their mystic rolls of parchment in their hands, and their intolerable burthens on their backs. The preposterous obstinacy of these honest people, in persisting to groan and stumble along the difficult pathway, rather than take advantage of modern improvements, excited great mirth among our wiser brotherhood. We greeted the two pilgrims with many pleasant gibes and a roar of laughter; whereupon, they gazed at us with such woeful and absurdly compassionate visages, that our merriment grew tenfold more obstreperous. Apollyon, also, entered heartily into the fun, and contrived to flirt the smoke and flame of the engine, or of his own breath, into their faces, and enveloped them in an atmosphere of scalding steam. These little practical jokes amused us mightily, and doubtless afforded the pilgrims the gratification of considering themselves martyrs.

At some distance from the rail-road, Mr. Smooth-it-away pointed to a large, antique edifice, which, he observed, was a tavern of long standing, and had formerly been a noted stopping-place for pilgrims. In Bunyan's road-book, it is mentioned as the Interpreter's House.

"I have long had a curiosity to visit that old mansion," remarked I.

"It is not one of our stations, as you perceive," said my companion. "The keeper was violently opposed to the rail-road; and well he might be, as the track left his house of entertainment on one side, and thus was pretty certain to deprive him of all his reputable customers. But the foot-path still passes his door; and the old gentleman now and then receives a call from some simple traveller, and entertains him with fare as old-fashioned as himself."

Before our talk on this subject came to a conclusion, we were rushing by the place where Christian's burthen fell from his shoulders, at the sight of the cross. This served as a theme for Mr. Smooth-it-away, Mr. Live-for-the-world, Mr. Hide-sin-in-the-heart, Mr. Scaly Conscience, and a knot of gentlemen from the town of Shun Repentance, to descant upon the inestimable advantages resulting from the safety of our baggage. Myself, and all the passengers indeed, joined with great unanimity in this view of the matter; for our burthens were rich in many things, esteemed precious throughout the world; and, especially, we each of us possessed a great variety of favorite Habits, which we trusted would not be out of fashion, even in the polite circles of the Celestial City. It would have been a sad spectacle, to see such an assortment of valuable articles tumbling into the sepulchre. Thus pleasantly conversing on the favorable circumstances of our position, as compared with those of past pilgrims, and of narrow-minded ones at the present day, we soon found ourselves at the foot of the Hill Difficulty. Through the very heart of this rocky mountain a tunnel has been constructed, of most admirable architecture, with a lofty arch and a spacious double-track; so that, unless the earth and rocks should chance to crumble down, it will remain an eternal monument of the builder's skill and enterprise. It is a great, though incidental advantage, that the materials from the heart of the Hill Difficulty have been employed in filling up the Valley of Humiliation; thus obviating the necessity of descending into that disagreeable and unwholesome hollow.

"This is a wonderful improvement, indeed," said I. "Yet I should have been glad of an opportunity to visit the Palace Beautiful, and be introduced to the charming young ladies— Miss Prudence, Miss Piety, Miss Charity, and the rest—who have the kindness to entertain pilgrims there."

"Young ladies!" cried Mr. Smooth-it-away, as soon as he could speak for laughing. "And charming young ladies! Why, my dear fellow, they are old maids, every soul of them—prim, starched, dry, and angular—and not one of them, I will venture to say, has altered so much as the fashion of her gown, since the days of Christian's pilgrimage."

"Ah, well," said I, much comforted. "Then I can very readily dispense with their acquaintance."

The respectable Apollyon was now putting on the steam at a prodigious rate, anxious, perhaps, to get rid of the unpleasant reminiscences, connected with the spot where he had so disastrously encountered Christian. Consulting Mr. Bunyan's road-book, I perceived that we must now be within a few miles of the Valley of the Shadow of Death; into which doleful region, at our present speed, we should plunge much sooner than seemed at all desirable. In truth, I expected nothing better than to find myself in the ditch on one side, or the quag on the other. But, on communicating my apprehensions to Mr. Smooth-it-away, he assured me that the difficulties of this passage, even in its worst condition, had been vastly exaggerated, and that, in its present state of improvement, I might consider myself as safe as on any rail-road in Christendom.

Even while we were speaking, the train shot into the entrance of this dreaded Valley. Though I plead guilty to some foolish palpitations of the heart, during our headlong rush over the causeway here constructed, yet it were unjust to withhold the highest encomiums on the boldness of its original conception, and the ingenuity of those who executed it. It was gratifying, likewise, to observe how much care had been taken to dispel the everlasting gloom, and supply the defect of cheerful sunshine; not a ray of which has ever penetrated among these awful shadows. For this purpose, the inflammable gas, which exudes plentifully from the soil, is collected by means of pipes, and thence communicated to a quadruple row of lamps, along the whole extent of the passage. Thus a radiance has been created, even out of the fiery and sulphurous curse that rests forever upon the Valley; a radiance hurtful, however, to the eyes, and somewhat bewildering, as I discovered by the changes which it wrought in the visages of my companions. In this respect, as compared with natural daylight, there is the same difference as between truth and falsehood; but, if the reader have ever travelled through the Dark Valley, he will have learned to be thankful for any light that he could get; if not from the sky above, then from the blasted soil beneath. Such was the red brilliancy of these lamps, that they appeared to build walls of fire on both sides of the track, between which we held our course at lightning-speed, while a reverberating thunder filled the Valley with its echoes. Had the engine run off the track—a catastrophe, it is whispered, by no means unprecedented— the bottomless pit, if there be any such place, would undoubtedly have received us. Just as some dismal fooleries of this nature had made my heart quake, there came a tremendous shriek, careering along the Valley as if a thousand devils had burst their lungs to utter it, but which proved to be merely the whistle of the engine, on arriving at a stopping-place.

The spot, where we had now paused, is the same that our friend Bunyan—a truthful man, but infected with many fantastic notions—has designated, in terms plainer than I like to repeat, as the mouth of the infernal region. This, however, must be a mistake; inasmuch as Mr. Smooth-it-away, while we remained in the smoky and lurid cavern, took occasion to prove that Tophet has not even a metaphorical existence. The place, he assured us, is no other than the crater of a half-extinct volcano, in which the Directors had caused forges to be set up, for the manufacture of rail-road iron. Hence, also, is obtained a plentiful supply of fuel for

the use of the engines. Whoever had gazed into the dismal
obscurity of the broad cavern-mouth, whence, ever and anon,
darted huge tongues of dusky flame,—and had seen the
strange, half-shaped monsters, and visions of faces horribly
grotesque, into which the smoke seemed to wreathe itself,—
and had heard the awful murmurs, and shrieks, and deep
shuddering whispers of the blast, sometimes forming itself
into words almost articulate,—he would have seized upon
Mr. Smooth-it-away's comfortable explanation, as greedily as
we did. The inhabitants of the cavern, moreover, were unlovely personages, dark, smoke-begrimed, generally deformed,
with misshapen feet, and a glow of dusky redness in their
eyes; as if their hearts had caught fire, and were blazing
out of the upper windows. It struck me as a peculiarity, that
the laborers at the forge, and those who brought fuel to the
engine, when they began to draw short breath, positively
emitted smoke from their mouth and nostrils.

Among the idlers about the train, most of whom were
puffing cigars which they had lighted at the flame of the
crater, I was perplexed to notice several, who, to my certain
knowledge, had heretofore set forth by rail-road for the
Celestial City. They looked dark, wild, and smoky, with a
singular resemblance, indeed, to the native inhabitants; like
whom, also, they had a disagreeable propensity to ill-natured
gibes and sneers; the habit of which had wrought a settled
contortion of their visages. Having been on speaking terms
with one of these persons—an indolent, good-for-nothing
fellow, who went by the name of Take-it-easy—I called to
him, and inquired what was his business there.

"Did you not start," said I, "for the Celestial City?"

"That's a fact," said Mr. Take-it-easy, carelessly puffing
some smoke into my eyes. "But I heard such bad accounts,
that I never took pains to climb the hill, on which the city
stands. No business doing—no fun going on—nothing to

drink, and no smoking allowed—and a thrumming of church-music from morning till night! I would not stay in such a place, if they offered me house-room and living free."

"But, my good Mr. Take-it-easy," cried I, "why take up your residence here, of all places in the world?"

"Oh," said the loafer, with a grin, "it is very warm here-abouts, and I meet with plenty of old acquaintances, and altogether the place suits me. I hope to see you back again, some day soon. A pleasant journey to you!"

While he was speaking, the bell of the engine rang, and we dashed away, after dropping a few passengers, but re-ceiving no new ones. Rattling onward through the Valley, we were dazzled with the fiercely gleaming gas-lamps, as before. But sometimes, in the dark of intense brightness, grim faces, that bore the aspect and expression of individual sins, or evil passions, seemed to thrust themselves through the veil of light, glaring upon us, and stretching forth a great dusky hand, as if to impede our progress. I almost thought, that they were my own sins that appalled me there. These were freaks of imagination—nothing more, certainly,—mere delusions, which I ought to be heartily ashamed of—but, all through the Dark Valley, I was tormented, and pestered, and dolefully bewildered, with the same kind of waking dreams. The mephitic gasses of that region intoxicate the brain. As the light of natural day, however, began to struggle with the glow of the lanterns, these vain imaginations lost their vividness, and finally vanished with the first ray of sunshine that greeted our escape from the Valley of the Shadow of Death. Ere we had gone a mile beyond it, I could well nigh have taken my oath that this whole gloomy passage was a dream.

At the end of the Valley, as John Bunyan mentions, is a cavern, where, in his days, dwelt two cruel giants, Pope and Pagan, who had strewn the ground about their residence with the bones of slaughtered pilgrims. These vile old troglodytes are no longer there; but into their deserted cave another terrible giant has thrust himself, and makes it his business to seize upon honest travellers, and fat them for his table with plentiful meals of smoke, mist, moonshine, raw potatoes, and saw-dust. He is a German by birth, and is called Giant Transcendentalist; but as to his form, his features, his substance, and his nature generally, it is the chief peculiarity of this huge miscreant, that neither he for himself, nor anybody for him, has ever been able to describe them. As we rushed by the cavern's mouth, we caught a hasty glimpse of him, looking somewhat like an ill-proportioned figure, but considerably more like a heap of fog and duskiness. He shouted after us, but in so strange a phraseology that we knew not what he meant, nor whether to be encouraged or affrighted.

It was late in the day, when the train thundered into the ancient city of Vanity, where Vanity Fair is still at the height of prosperity, and exhibits an epitome of whatever is brilliant, gay, and fascinating, beneath the sun. As I purposed to make a considerable stay here, it gratified me to learn that there is no longer the want of harmony between the townspeople and pilgrims, which impelled the former to such lamentably mistaken measures as the persecution of Christian, and the fiery martyrdom of Faithful. On the contrary, as the new rail-road brings with it great trade and a constant influx of strangers, the lord of Vanity Fair is its chief patron, and the capitalists of the city are among the largest stockholders. Many passengers stop to take their pleasure or make their profit in the Fair, instead of going onward to the Celestial City. Indeed, such are the charms of the place, that people often affirm it to be the true and only heaven; stoutly contending that there is no other, that those who seek further are mere dreamers, and that, if the fabled brightness of the Celestial City lay but a bare mile beyond the gates of Vanity, they

would not be fools enough to go thither. Without subscrib-
ing to these, perhaps, exaggerated encomiums, I can truly
say, that my abode in the city was mainly agreeable, and my
intercourse with the inhabitants productive of much amusement and instruction.

Being naturally of a serious turn, my attention was directed
to the solid advantages derivable from a residence here,
rather than to the effervescent pleasures, which are the grand
object with too many visitants. The Christian reader, if he
have had no accounts of the city later than Bunyan's time,
will be surprised to hear that almost every street has its
church, and that the reverend clergy are nowhere held in
higher respect than at Vanity Fair. And well do they deserve
such honorable estimation; for the maxims of wisdom and
virtue, which fall from their lips, come from as deep a spiritual source, and tend to us as lofty a religious aim, as those
of the sagest philosophers of old. In justification of this high
praise, I need only mention the names of the Rev. Mr.
Shallow-deep; the Rev. Mr. Stumble-at-truth; that fine old
clerical character, the Rev. Mr. This-to-day, who expects
shortly to resign his pulpit to the Rev. Mr. That-to-morrow;
together with the Rev. Mr. Bewilderment; the Rev. Mr. Clog-
the-spirit; and, last and greatest, the Rev. Dr. Wind-of-
doctrine. The labors of these eminent divines are aided by
those of innumerable lecturers, who diffuse such a various
profundity, in all subjects of human or celestial science, that
any man may acquire an omnigenous erudition, without the
trouble of even learning to read. Thus literature is etherealized by assuming for its medium the human voice; and
knowledge, depositing all its heavier particles—except, doubtless, its gold—becomes exhaled into a sound, which forthwith steals into the ever-open ear of the community. These
ingenious methods constitute a sort of machinery, by which
thought and study are done to every person's hand, without

his putting himself to the slightest inconvenience in the matter. There is another species of machine for the whole-sale manufacture of individual morality. This excellent result is effected by societies for all manner of virtuous purposes; with which a man has merely to connect himself, throwing, as it were, his quota of virtue into the common stock; and the president and directors will take care that the aggregate amount be well applied. All these, and other wonderful improvements in ethics, religion, and literature, being made plain to my comprehension by the ingenious Mr. Smooth-it-away, inspired me with a vast admiration of Vanity Fair.

It would fill a volume, in an age of pamphlets, were I to record all my observations in this great capital of human business and pleasure. There was an unlimited range of society—the powerful, the wise, the witty, and the famous in every walk of life—princes, presidents, poets, generals, artists, actors, and philanthropists, all making their own market at the Fair, and deeming no price too exorbitant for such commodities as hit their fancy. It was well worth one's while, even if he had no idea of buying or selling, to loiter through the bazaars, and observe the various sorts of traffic that were going forward.

Some of the purchasers, I thought, made very foolish bargains. For instance, a young man, having inherited a splendid fortune, laid out a considerable portion of it in the purchase of diseases, and finally spent all the rest for a heavy lot of repentance and a suit of rags. A very pretty girl bartered a heart as clear as crystal, and which seemed her most valuable possession, for another jewel of the same kind, but so worn and defaced as to be utterly worthless. In one shop, there were a great many crowns of laurel and myrtle, which soldiers, authors, statesmen, and various other people, pressed eagerly to buy; some purchased these paltry wreaths with their lives; others by a toilsome servitude of years; and many sacrificed whatever was most valuable, yet finally slunk away without the crown. There was a sort of stock or scrip, called Conscience, which seemed to be in great demand, and would purchase almost anything. Indeed, few rich commodities were to be obtained without paying a heavy sum in this particular stock; and a man's business was seldom very lucrative, unless he knew precisely when and how to throw his hoard of Conscience into the market. Yet, as this stock was the only thing of permanent value, whoever parted with it was sure to find himself a loser, in the long run. Several of the speculations were of a questionable character. Occasionally, a member of congress recruited his pocket by the sale of his constituents; and I was assured that public officers have often sold their country, at very moderate prices. Thousands sold their happiness for a whim. Gilded chains were in great demand, and purchased with almost any sacrifice. In truth, those who desired, according to the old adage, to sell anything valuable for a song, might find customers all over the Fair; and there were innumerable messes of pottage, piping hot, for such as chose to buy them with their birth-rights. A few articles, however, could not be found genuine, at Vanity Fair. If a customer wished to renew his stock of youth, the dealers offered him a set of false teeth and an auburn wig; if he demanded peace of mind, they recommended opium or a brandy-bottle.

Tracts of land and golden mansions, situate in the Celestial City, were often exchanged, at very disadvantageous rates, for a few years lease of small, dismal, inconvenient tenements in Vanity Fair. Prince Beelzebub himself took great interest in this sort of traffic, and sometimes condescended to meddle with smaller matters. I once had the pleasure to see him bargaining with a miser for his soul, which, after much ingenious skirmishing on both sides, his Highness succeeded in obtaining at about the value of sixpence. The prince remarked, with a smile, that he was a loser by the transaction.

Day after day, as I walked the streets of Vanity, my manners and deportment became more and more like those of the inhabitants. The place began to seem like home; the idea of pursuing my travels to the Celestial City was almost obliterated from my mind. I was reminded of it, however, by the sight of the same pair of simple pilgrims at whom we had laughed so heartily, when Apollyon puffed smoke and steam into their faces, at the commencement of our journey. There they stood amid the densest bustle of Vanity—the dealers offering them their purple, and fine linen, and jewels; the men of wit and humor gibing at them; a pair of buxom ladies ogling them askance; while the benevolent Mr. Smooth-it-away whispered some of his wisdom at their elbows, and pointed to a newly erected temple—but there were these worthy simpletons, making the scene look wild and monstrous, merely by their sturdy repudiation of all part in its business or pleasures.

One of them—his name was Stick-to-the-right—perceived in my face, I suppose, a species of sympathy and almost admiration, which, to my own great surprise, I could not help feeling for this pragmatic couple. It prompted him to address me.

"Sir," inquired he, with a sad, yet mild and kindly voice, "do you call yourself a pilgrim?"

"Yes," I replied. "My right to that appellation is indubitable. I am merely a sojourner here in Vanity Fair, being bound for the Celestial City, by the new rail-road."

"Alas, friend," rejoined Mr. Stick-to-the-right, "I do assure you, and beseech you to receive the truth of my words, that

that whole concern is a bubble. You may travel on it all your life-time, were you to live thousands of years, and yet never get beyond the limits of Vanity Fair! Yea; though you should deem yourself entering the gates of the Blessed City, it will be nothing but a miserable delusion."

"The Lord of the Celestial City," began the other pilgrim, whose name was Mr. Foot-it-to-Heaven, "has refused, and will ever refuse, to grant an act of incorporation for this rail-road; and unless that be obtained, no passenger can ever hope to enter his dominions. Wherefore, every man, who buys a ticket, must lay his account with losing the purchase-money —which is the value of his own soul."

"Poh, nonsense!" said Mr. Smooth-it-away, taking my arm and leading me off. "These fellows ought to be indicted for a libel. If the law stood as it once did in Vanity Fair, we should see them grinning through the iron-bars of the prison-window."

This incident made a considerable impression on my mind, and contributed with other circumstances to indispose me to a permanent residence in the city of Vanity; although, of course, I was not simple enough to give up my original plan of gliding along easily and commodiously by rail-road. Still, I grew anxious to be gone. There was one strange thing that troubled me; amid the occupations or amusements of the Fair, nothing was more common than for a person—whether at a feast, theatre, or church, or trafficking for wealth and honors, or whatever he might be doing, and however unseasonable the interruption—suddenly to vanish like a soap-bubble, and be never more seen of his fellows; and so accustomed were the latter to such little accidents, that they went on with their business, as quietly as if nothing had happened. But it was otherwise with me.

Finally, after a pretty long residence at the Fair, I resumed my journey towards the Celestial City, still with Mr. Smooth-it-away at my side. At a short distance beyond the suburbs of Vanity, we passed the ancient silver-mine, of which Demas was the first discoverer, and which is now wrought to great advantage, supplying nearly all the coined currency of the world. A little further onward was the spot where Lot's wife had stood for ages, under the semblance of a pillar of salt. Curious travellers have long since carried it away piece-meal. Had all regrets been punished as rigorously as this poor dame's were, my yearning for the relinquished delights of Vanity Fair might have produced a similar change in my own corporeal substance, and left me a warning to future pilgrims.

The next remarkable object was a large edifice, constructed of moss-grown stone, but in a modern and airy style of architecture. The engine came to a pause in its vicinity, with the usual tremendous shriek.

"This was formerly the castle of the redoubted giant Despair," observed Mr. Smooth-it-away; "but, since his death, Mr. Flimsy-faith has repaired it, and now keeps an excellent house of entertainment here. It is one of our stopping-places."

"It seems but slightly put together," remarked I, looking at the frail, yet ponderous walls. "I do not envy Mr. Flimsy-faith his habitation. Some day, it will thunder down upon the heads of the occupants."

"We shall escape, at all events," said Mr. Smooth-it-away; "for Apollyon is putting on the steam again."

The road now plunged into a gorge of the Delectable Mountains, and traversed the field where, in former ages, the blind men wandered and stumbled among the tombs. One of these ancient tomb-stones had been thrust across the track, by some malicious person, and gave the train of cars a terrible jolt. Far up the rugged side of a mountain, I perceived a rusty iron-door, half-overgrown with bushes and creeping-plants, but with smoke issuing from its crevices.

"Is that," inquired I, "the very door in the hill-side, which the shepherds assured Christian was a by-way to hell?"

"That was a joke on the part of the shepherds," said Mr. Smooth-it-away, with a smile. "It is neither more nor less than the door of a cavern, which they use as a smoke-house for the preparation of mutton-hams."

My recollections of the journey are now, for a little space, dim and confused; inasmuch as a singular drowsiness here overcame me, owing to the fact that we were passing over the Enchanted Ground, the air of which encourages a disposition to sleep. I awoke, however, as soon as we crossed the borders of the pleasant land of Beulah. All the passengers were rubbing their eyes, comparing watches, and congratulating one another on the prospect of arriving so seasonably at the journey's end. The sweet breezes of this happy clime came refreshingly to our nostrils; we beheld the glimmering gush of silver fountains, overhung by trees of beautiful foliage and delicious fruit, which were propagated by grafts from the Celestial gardens. Once, as we dashed onward like a hurricane, there was a flutter of wings, and the bright appearance of an angel in the air, speeding forth on some heavenly mission. The engine now announced the close vicinity of the final Station House, by one last and horrible scream, in which there seemed to be distinguishable every kind of wailing and woe, and bitter fierceness of wrath, all mixed up with the wild laughter of a devil or a madman. Throughout our journey, at every stopping-place, Apollyon had exercised his ingenuity in screwing the most abominable sounds out of the whistle of the steam-engine; but, in this closing effort, he outdid himself, and created an infernal uproar, which, besides disturbing the peaceful inhabitants of Beulah, must have sent its discord even through the Celestial gates.

While the horrid clamor was still ringing in our ears, we heard an exulting strain, as if a thousand instruments of music, with height, and depth, and sweetness in their tones, at once tender and triumphant, were struck in unison, to greet the approach of some illustrious hero, who had fought the good fight, and won a glorious victory, and was come to lay aside his battered arms forever. Looking to ascertain what might be the occasion of this glad harmony, I perceived, on alighting from the cars, that a multitude of Shining Ones had assembled on the other side of the river, to welcome two poor pilgrims, who were just emerging from its depths. They were the same whom Apollyon and ourselves had persecuted with taunts and gibes, and scalding steam, at the commencement of our journey; the same whose unworldly aspect and impressive words had stirred my conscience, amid the wild revellers of Vanity Fair.

"How amazingly well those men have got on!" cried I to Mr. Smooth-it-away. "I wish we were secure of as good a reception."

"Never fear—never fear!" answered my friend. "Come!—make haste!—the ferry-boat will be off directly; and in three minutes you will be on the other side of the river. No doubt you will find coaches to carry you up to the city-gates."

A steam ferry-boat, the last improvement on this important route, lay at the river-side, puffing, snorting, and emitting all those other disagreeable utterances, which betoken the departure to be immediate. I hurried on board, with the rest of the passengers, most of whom were in great perturbation; some bawling out for their baggage; some tearing their hair, and exclaiming that the boat would explode or sink; some already pale with the heaving of the stream; some gazing affrighted at the ugly aspect of the steersman; and some still dizzy with the slumberous influences of the Enchanted Ground. Looking back to the shore, I was amazed to discern Mr. Smooth-it-away, waving his hand in token of farewell!

"Don't you go over to the Celestial City?" exclaimed I.

"Oh, no!" answered he with a queer smile, and that same disagreeable contortion of visage, which I had remarked in the inhabitants of the Dark Valley. "Oh, no! I have come thus far only for the sake of your pleasant company. Good bye! We shall meet again."

And then did my excellent friend, Mr. Smooth-it-away, laugh outright; in the midst of which cachinnation, a smoke-wreath issued from his mouth and nostrils; while a twinkle of lurid flame darted out of either eye, proving indubitably that his heart was all of a red blaze. The impudent Fiend! To deny the existence of Tophet, when he felt its fiery tortures raging within his breast! I rushed to the side of the boat, intending to fling myself on shore. But the wheels, as they began their revolutions, threw a dash of spray over me, so cold—so deadly cold, with the chill that will never leave those waters, until Death be drowned in his own river—that, with a shiver and a heart-quake, I awoke. Thank Heaven, it was a Dream!

THE PROCESSION OF LIFE

L IFE figures itself to me as a festal or funereal procession. All of us have our places, and are to move onward under the direction of a Chief-Marshal. The grand difficulty results from the invariably mistaken principles on which the deputy-marshals seek to arrange this immense concourse of people, so much more numerous than those that train their interminable length through streets and highways in times of political excitement. Their scheme is ancient, far beyond the memory of man, or even the record of history, and has hitherto been very little modified by the innate sense of something wrong, and the dim perception of better methods, that have disquieted all the ages through which the procession has taken its march. Its members are classified by the merest external circumstances, and thus are more certain to be thrown out of their true positions, than if no principle of arrangement were attempted. In one part of the procession we see men of landed estate or moneyed capital, gravely keeping each other company, for the preposterous reason that they chance to have a similar standing in the tax-gatherer's book. Trades and professions march together with scarcely a more real bond of union. In this manner, it cannot be denied, people are disentangled from the mass, and separated into various classes according to certain apparent relations; all have some artificial badge, which the world, and themselves among the first, learn to consider as a genuine characteristic. Fixing our attention on such outside shows of similarity or difference, we lose sight of those realities by which nature, fortune, fate, or Providence, has constituted for every man a brotherhood, wherein it is one great office of human wisdom to classify him. When the mind has once accustomed itself to a proper arrangement of the Procession of Life, or a true classification of society, even though merely speculative, there is thenceforth a satisfaction which pretty well suffices for itself, without the aid of any actual reformation in the order of march.

For instance, assuming to myself the power of marshalling the aforesaid procession, I direct a trumpeter to send forth a blast loud enough to be heard from hence to China; and a herald, with world-pervading voice, to make proclamation for a certain class of mortals to take their places. What shall be their principle of union? After all, an external one, in comparison with many that might be found, yet far more real than those which the world has selected for a similar purpose. Let all who are afflicted with like physical diseases form themselves into ranks!

Our first attempt at classification is not very successful. It may gratify the pride of aristocracy to reflect, that Disease, more than any other circumstance of human life, pays due observance to the distinctions which rank and wealth, and poverty and lowliness, have established among mankind. Some maladies are rich and precious, and only to be acquired by the right of inheritance, or purchased with gold. Of this kind is the gout, which serves as a bond of brotherhood to the purple-visaged gentry, who obey the herald's voice, and painfully hobble from all civilized regions of the globe to take their post in the grand procession. In mercy to their toes, let us hope that the march may not be long! The Dyspeptics, too, are people of good standing in the world. For them the earliest salmon is caught in our eastern rivers, and the shy woodcock stains the dry leaves with his blood, in his remotest haunts; and the turtle comes from the far Pacific islands to be gobbled up in soup. They can afford to flavor all their dishes with indolence, which, in spite of the general opinion, is a sauce more exquisitely piquant than appetite won by exercise. Apoplexy is another highly respectable disease. We will rank together all who have the symptom of dizziness in the brain, and, as fast as any drop by the way, supply their places with new members of the board of aldermen.

On the other hand, here come whole tribes of people, whose physical lives are but a deteriorated variety of life, and themselves a meaner species of mankind; so sad an effect has been wrought by the tainted breath of cities, scanty and unwholesome food, destructive modes of labor, and the lack of those moral supports that might partially have counteracted such bad influences. Behold here a train of house-painters, all afflicted with a peculiar sort of colic. Next in place we will marshal those workmen in cutlery, who have breathed a fatal disorder into their lungs, with the impalpable dust of steel. Tailors and shoemakers, being sedentary men, will chiefly congregate into one part of the procession, and march under similar banners of disease; but among them we may observe here and there a sickly student, who has left his health between the leaves of classic volumes; and clerks, likewise, who have caught their deaths on high official stools; and men of genius, too, who have written sheet after sheet, with pens dipped in their heart's blood. These are a wretched, quaking, short-breathed set. But what is this crowd of pale-cheeked, slender girls, who disturb the ear with the multiplicity of their short, dry coughs? They are seamstresses, who have plied the daily and nightly needle in the service of master-tailors and close-fisted contractors, until now it is almost time for each to hem the borders of her own shroud. Consumption points their place in the procession. With their sad sisterhood are intermingled many youthful maidens, who have sickened in aristocratic mansions, and for whose aid science has unavailingly searched its volumes, and whom breathless love has watched. In our ranks the rich maiden and the poor seamstress may walk arm in arm. We might find innumerable other instances, where the bond of mutual disease—not to speak of nation-sweeping pestilences—embraces high and low, and makes the king a brother of the clown. But it is not hard to own that Disease is the natural aristocrat. Let him keep his state, and have his established orders of rank, and wear his royal mantle of the color of a fever-flush; and let the noble and wealthy boast their own physical infirmities, and display their symptoms as the badges of high station! All things considered, these are as proper subjects of human pride as any relations of human rank that men can fix upon.

Sound again, thou deep-breathed trumpeter! and herald, with thy voice of might, shout forth another summons, that shall reach the old baronial castles of Europe, and the rudest cabin of our western wilderness! What class is next to take its place in the procession of mortal life? Let it be those whom the gifts of intellect have united in a noble brotherhood!

Aye, this is a reality, before which the conventional distinctions of society melt away, like a vapor when we would grasp it with the hand. Were Byron now alive, and Burns, the first would come from his ancestral Abbey, flinging aside, although unwillingly, the inherited honors of a thousand years, to take the arm of the mighty peasant, who grew immortal while he stooped behind his plough. These are gone; but the hall, the farmer's fireside, the hut, perhaps the palace, the counting-room, the workshop, the village, the city, life's high places and low ones, may all produce their poets, whom a common temperament pervades like an electric sympathy. Peer or ploughman, we will muster them, pair by pair, and shoulder to shoulder. Even society, in its most artificial state, consents to this arrangement. These factory girls from Lowell shall mate themselves with the pride of drawing-rooms and literary circles—the bluebells in fashion's nose-gay, the Sapphos, and Montagues, and Nortons, of the age. Other modes of intellect bring together as strange companies. Silk-gowned professor of languages, give your arm to this sturdy blacksmith, and deem yourself honored by the conjunction, though you behold him grimy from the anvil. All varieties of human speech are like his mother tongue to this rare man. Indiscriminately, let those take their places, of whatever rank they come, who possess the kingly gifts to lead armies, or to sway a people,—Nature's generals, her lawgivers, her kings, —and with them, also, the deep philosophers, who think the thought in one generation that is to revolutionize society in the next. With the hereditary legislator, in whom eloquence is a far-descended attainment—a rich echo repeated by powerful voices, from Cicero downward—we will match some wondrous backwoodsman, who has caught a wild power of language from the breeze among his native forest boughs. But we may safely leave brethren and sisterhood to settle their own congenialities. Our ordinary distinctions become so trifling, so impalpable, so ridiculously visionary, in comparison with a classification founded on truth, that all talk about the matter is immediately a common-place.

Yet, the longer I reflect, the less am I satisfied with the idea of forming a separate class of mankind on the basis of high intellectual power. At best, it is but a higher development of innate gifts common to all. Perhaps, moreover, he, whose genius appears deepest and truest, excels his fellows in nothing save the knack of expression; he throws out, occasionally, a lucky hint at truths of which every human soul is profoundly, though unutterably, conscious. Therefore, though we suffer the brotherhood of intellect to march onward together, it may be doubted whether their peculiar relation will not begin to vanish, as soon as the procession shall have passed beyond the circle of this present world. But we do not classify for eternity.

And next, let the trumpet pour forth a funereal wail, and the herald's voice give breath, in one vast cry, to all the groans and grievous utterances that are audible throughout the earth. We appeal now to the sacred bond of sorrow, and summon the great multitude who labor under similar afflictions, to take their places in the march.

How many a heart, that would have been insensible to any other call, has responded to the doleful accents of that voice! It has gone far and wide, and high and low, and left scarcely a mortal roof unvisited. Indeed, the principle is only too universal for our purpose, and, unless we limit it, will quite break up our classification of mankind, and convert the whole procession into a funeral train. We will therefore be at some pains to discriminate. Here comes a lonely rich man; he has built a noble fabric for his dwelling-house, with a front of stately architecture, and marble floors, and doors of precious woods; the whole structure is as beautiful as a dream, and as substantial as the native rock. But the visionary shapes of a long posterity, for whose home this mansion was intended, have faded into nothingness, since the death of the founder's only son. The rich man gives a glance at his sable garb in one of the splendid mirrors of his drawing-room, and, descending a flight of lofty steps, instinctively offers his arm to yonder poverty-stricken widow, in the rusty black bonnet, and with a check-apron over her patched gown. The sailor-boy, who was her sole earthly stay, was washed overboard in a late tempest. This couple, from the palace and the alms-house, are but the types of thousands more, who represent the dark tragedy of life, and seldom quarrel for the upper parts. Grief is such a leveller, with its own dignity and its own humility, that the noble and the peasant, the beggar and the monarch, will waive their pretensions to external rank, without the officiousness of interference on our part. If pride—the influence of the world's false distinctions—remain in the heart, then sorrow lacks the earnestness which makes it holy and reverend. It loses its reality, and becomes a miser-able shadow. On this ground, we have an opportunity to assign over multitudes who would willingly claim places here, to other parts of the procession. If the mourner have any-thing dearer than his grief, he must seek his true position elsewhere. There are so many unsubstantial sorrows, which the necessity of our mortal state begets on idleness, that an observer, casting aside sentiment, is sometimes led to question whether there be any real woe, except absolute physical suf-fering, and the loss of closest friends. A crowd, who exhibit what they deem to be broken hearts—and among them many love-lorn maids and bachelors, and men of disappointed ambition in arts, or politics, and the poor who were once rich, or who have sought to be rich in vain—the great majority of these may ask admittance into some other fra-ternity. There is no room here. Perhaps we may institute a separate class, where such unfortunates will naturally fall into the procession. Meanwhile let them stand aside, and patiently await their time.

If our trumpeter can borrow a note from the doomsday trumpet-blast, let him sound it now! The dread alarum should make the earth quake to its centre, for the herald is about to address mankind with a summons, to which even the purest mortal may be sensible of some faint responding echo in his breast. In many bosoms it will awaken a still, small voice, more terrible than its own reverberating uproar.

The hideous appeal has swept around the globe. Come, all ye guilty ones, and rank yourselves in accordance with the brotherhood of crime! This, indeed, is an awful summons. I almost tremble to look at the strange partnerships that begin to be formed, reluctantly, but by the invincible necessity of like to like, in this part of the procession. A forger from the state prison seizes the arm of a distinguished financier. How indignantly does the latter plead his fair reputation upon 'Change, and insist that his operations, by their magnificence of scope, were removed into quite another sphere of morality than those of his pitiful companion! But, let him cut the connection if he can. Here comes a murderer, with his clanking chains, and pairs himself—horrible to tell!—with as pure and upright a man, in all observable respects, as ever partook of the consecrated bread and wine. He is one of those, perchance the most hopeless of all sinners, who practise such an exemplary system of outward duties, that even a deadly crime may be hidden from their own sight and remembrance, under this unreal frost-work. Yet he now finds his place. Why do that pair of flaunting girls, with the pert, affected laugh, and the sly leer at the bystanders, intrude themselves into the same rank with yonder decorous matron, and that somewhat prudish maiden? Surely, these poor creatures, born to vice, as their sole and natural inheritance, can be no fit associates for women who have been guarded round about by all the proprieties of domestic life, and who could not err, unless they first created the opportunity! Oh, no; it must be merely the impertinence of those unblushing hussies; and we can only wonder how such respectable ladies should have responded to a summons that was not meant for them.

We shall make short work of this miserable class, each member of which is entitled to grasp any other member's hand, by that vile degradation wherein guilty error has buried all alike. The foul fiend, to whom it properly belongs, must relieve us of our loathsome task. Let the bond-servants of sin pass on. But neither man nor woman, in whom good predominates, will smile or sneer, nor bid the Rogues' March be played, in derision of their array. Feeling within their breasts a shuddering sympathy, which at least gives token of the sin that might have been, they will thank God for any place in the grand procession of human existence, save among those most wretched ones. Many, however, will be astonished at the fatal impulse that drags them thitherward. Nothing is more remarkable than the various deceptions by which guilt conceals itself from the perpetrator's conscience, and oftenest, perhaps, by the splendor of its garments. Statesmen, rulers, generals, and all men who act over an extensive sphere, are most liable to be deluded in this way; they commit wrong, devastation, and murder, on so grand a scale, that it impresses them as speculative rather than actual; but, in our procession, we find them linked in detestable conjunction with the meanest criminals, whose deeds have the vulgarity of petty details. Here, the effect of circumstance and accident is done away, and a man finds his rank according to the spirit of his crime, in whatever shape it may have been developed.

We have called the Evil; now let us call the Good. The trumpet's brazen throat should pour heavenly music over the earth, and the herald's voice go forth with the sweetness of an angel's accents, as if to summon each upright man to his reward. But, how is this? Do none answer to the call? Not one: for the just, the pure, the true, and all who might most worthily obey it, shrink sadly back, as most conscious of error and imperfection. Then let the summons be to those whose pervading principle is Love. This classification will embrace all the truly good, and none in whose souls there exists not something that may expand itself into a heaven, both of well-doing and felicity.

The first that presents himself is a man of wealth, who has bequeathed the bulk of his property to a hospital; his ghost, methinks, would have a better right here than his living body. But here they come, the genuine benefactors of their race. Some have wandered about the earth, with pictures of bliss in their imagination, and with hearts that shrank sensitively from the idea of pain and woe, yet have studied all varieties of misery that human nature can endure. The prison, the insane asylum, the squalid chambers of the alms-house, the manufactory where the demon of machinery annihilates the human soul, and the cotton-field where God's image becomes a beast of burthen; to these, and every other scene where man wrongs or neglects his brother, the apostles of humanity have penetrated. This missionary, black with India's burning sunshine, shall give his arm to a pale-faced brother who has made himself familiar with the infected alleys and loathsome haunts of vice, in one of our own cities. The generous founder of a college shall be the partner of a maiden lady, of narrow substance, one of whose good deeds it has been, to gather a little school of orphan children. If the mighty merchant whose benefactions are reckoned by thousands of dollars, deem himself worthy, let him join the procession with her whose love has proved itself by watchings at the sick-bed, and all those lowly offices which bring her into actual contact with disease and wretchedness. And with those whose impulses have guided them to benevolent actions, we will rank others, to whom Providence has assigned a different tendency and different powers. Men who have spent their lives in generous and holy contemplation for the human race; those who, by a certain heavenliness of spirit, have purified the atmosphere around them, and thus supplied a medium in which good and high things may be projected

and performed,—give to these a lofty place among the benefactors of mankind, although no deed, such as the world
calls deeds, may be recorded of them. There are some individuals, of whom we cannot conceive it proper that they
should apply their hands to any earthly instrument, or work
out any definite act; and others, perhaps not less high, to
whom it is an essential attribute to labor, in body as well as
spirit, for the welfare of their brethren. Thus, if we find
a spiritual sage, whose unseen, inestimable influence has
exalted the moral standard of mankind, we will choose for
his companion some poor laborer, who has wrought for love
in the potatoe-field of a neighbor poorer than himself.

We have summoned this various mulitude—and, to the
credit of our nature, it is a large one—on the principle of
Love. It is singular, nevertheless, to remark the shyness that
exists among many members of the present class, all of whom
we might expect to recognize one another by the free-masonry
of mutual goodness, and to embrace like brethren, giving
God thanks for such various specimens of human excellence.
But it is far otherwise. Each sect surrounds its own righteousness with a hedge of thorns. It is difficult for the good Christian to acknowledge the good Pagan; almost impossible for
the good Orthodox to grasp the hand of the good Unitarian,
leaving to their Creator to settle the matters in dispute, and
giving their mutual efforts strongly and trustingly to whatever right thing is too evident to be mistaken. Then again,
though the heart be large, yet the mind is often of such
moderate dimensions as to be exclusively filled up with one
idea. When a good man has long devoted himself to a
particular kind of beneficence—to one species of reform—he
is apt to become narrowed into the limits of the path wherein
he treads, and to fancy that there is no other good to be done
on earth but that self-same good to which he has put his
hand, and in the very mode that best suits his own concep-

tions. All else is worthless; his scheme must be wrought out by the united strength of the whole world's stock of love, or the world is no longer worthy of a position in the universe. Moreover, powerful Truth, being the rich grape-juice expressed from the vineyard of the ages, has an intoxicating quality, when imbibed by any save a powerful intellect, and often, as it were, impels the quaffer to quarrel in his cups. For such reasons, strange to say, it is harder to contrive a friendly arrangement of these brethren of love and righteousness, in the procession of life, than to unite even the wicked, who, indeed, are chained together by their crimes. The fact is too preposterous for tears, too lugubrious for laughter.

But, let good men push and elbow one another as they may, during their earthly march, all will be peace among them when the honorable array of their procession shall tread on heavenly ground. There they will doubtless find, that they have been working each for the other's cause, and that every well-delivered stroke, which, with an honest purpose, any mortal struck, even for a narrow object, was indeed stricken for the universal cause of good. Their own view may be bounded by country, creed, profession, the diversities of individual character—but above them all is the breadth of Providence. How many, who have deemed themselves antagonists, will smile hereafter, when they look back upon the world's wide harvest field, and perceive that, in unconscious brotherhood, they were helping to bind the self-same sheaf!

But, come! The sun is hastening westward, while the march of human life, that never paused before, is delayed by our attempt to re-arrange its order. It is desirable to find some comprehensive principle, that shall render our task easier by bringing thousands into the ranks, where hitherto we have brought one. Therefore let the trumpet, if possible, split its brazen throat with a louder note than ever, and the herald summon all mortals who, from whatever cause, have lost, or never found, their proper places in the world.

Obedient to this call, a great multitude come together, most of them with a listless gait, betokening weariness of soul, yet with a gleam of satisfaction in their faces, at the prospect of at length reaching those positions which, hitherto, they have vainly sought. But here will be another disappointment; for we can attempt no more than merely to associate, in one fraternity, all who are afflicted with the same vague trouble. Some great mistake in life is the chief condition of admittance into this class. Here are members of the learned professions, whom Providence endowed with special gifts for the plough, the forge, and the wheel-barrow, or for the routine of unintellectual business. We will assign to them, as partners in the march, those lowly laborers and handicraftsmen, who have pined, as with a dying thirst, after the unattainable fountains of knowledge. The latter have lost less than their companions; yet more, because they deem it infinite. Perchance the two species of unfortunates may comfort one another. Here are Quakers with the instinct of battle in them; and men of war who should have worn the broadbrim. Authors shall be ranked here, whom some freak of Nature, making game of her poor children, has imbued with the confidence of genius, and strong desire of fame, but has favored with no corresponding power; and others, whose lofty gifts were unaccompanied with the faculty of expression, or any of that earthly machinery, by which ethereal endowments must be manifested to mankind. All these, therefore, are melancholy laughing-stocks. Next, here are honest and well-intentioned persons, who, by a want of tact—by inaccurate perceptions—by a distorting imagination—have been kept continually at cross-purposes with the world, and bewildered upon the path of life. Let us see, if they can confine themselves within the line of our procession. In this class, likewise, we must assign places to those who have encountered that worst of ill-success, a higher fortune than their abilities could vindicate; writers, actors, painters, the pets of a day, but whose laurels wither unrenewed amid their hoary hair; politicians, whom some malicious contingency of affairs has thrust into conspicuous station, where, while the world stands gazing at them, the dreary consciousness of imbecility makes them curse their birth-hour. To such men, we give for a companion him whose rare talents, which perhaps require a revolution for their exercise, are buried in the tomb of sluggish circumstances.

Not far from these, we must find room for one whose success has been of the wrong kind; the man who should have lingered in the cloisters of a university, digging new treasures out of the Herculaneum of antique lore, diffusing depth and accuracy of literature throughout his country, and thus making for himself a great and quiet fame. But the outward tendencies around him have proved too powerful for his inward nature, and have drawn him into the arena of political tumult, there to contend at disadvantage, whether front to front, or side by side, with the brawny giants of actual life. He becomes, it may be, a name for brawling parties to bandy to and fro, a legislator of the Union; a governor of his native State; an ambassador to the courts of kings or queens; and the world may deem him a man of happy stars. But not so the wise; and not so himself, when he looks through his experience, and sighs to miss that fitness, the one invaluable touch, which makes all things true and real. So much achieved, yet how abortive is his life! Whom shall we choose for his companion? Some weak-framed blacksmith, perhaps, whose delicacy of muscle might have suited a tailor's shop-board better than the anvil.

Shall we bid the trumpet sound again? It is hardly worth the while. There remain a few idle men of fortune, tavern and grog-shop loungers, lazzaroni, old bachelors, decaying maidens, and people of crooked intellect or temper, all of whom may find their like, or some tolerable approach to it, in the plentiful diversity of our latter class. There, too, as his ultimate destiny, must we rank the dreamer, who, all his life long, has cherished the idea that he was peculiarly apt for something, but never could determine what it was; and there the most unfortunate of men, whose purpose it has been to enjoy life's pleasures, but to avoid a manful struggle with its toil and sorrow. The remainder, if any, may connect themselves with whatever rank of the procession they shall find best adapted to their tastes and consciences. The worst possible fate would be, to remain behind, shivering in the solitude of time, while all the world is on the move towards eternity. Our attempt to classify society is now complete. The result may be anything but perfect; yet better—to give it the very lowest praise—than the antique rule of the herald's office, or the modern one of the tax-gatherer, whereby the accidents and superficial attributes, with which the real nature of individuals has least to do, are acted upon as the deepest characteristics of mankind. Our task is done. Now let the grand procession move!

Yet pause awhile! We had forgotten the Chief-Marshal.

Hark! That world-wide swell of solemn music, with the clang of a mighty bell breaking forth through its regulated uproar, announces his approach. He comes; a severe, sedate, immovable, dark rider, waving his truncheon of universal sway, as he passes along the lengthened line, on the pale horse of the Revelations. It is Death! Who else could assume the guidance of a procession that comprehends all humanity? And if some, among these many millions, should deem themselves classed amiss, yet let them take to their hearts the comfortable truth, that Death levels us all into one great brotherhood, and that another state of being will surely rectify the wrong of this. Then breathe thy wail upon the earth's wailing wind, thou band of melancholy music, made up of every sigh that the human heart, unsatisfied, has uttered! There is yet triumph in thy tones. And now we move! Beggars in their rags, and Kings trailing the regal purple in the dust; the Warrior's gleaming helmet; the Priest in his sable robe; the hoary Grandsire, who has run life's circle and come back to childhood; the ruddy School-boy with his golden curls, frisking along the march; the Artisan's stuff-jacket; the Noble's star-decorated coat;—the whole presenting a motley spectacle, yet with a dusky grandeur brooding over it. Onward, onward, into that dimness where the lights of Time, which have blazed along the procession, are flickering in their sockets! And whither? We know not; and Death, hitherto our leader, deserts us by the wayside, as the tramp of our innumerable footsteps echoes beyond his sphere. He knows not, more than we, our destined goal. But God, who made us, knows, and will not leave us on our toilsome and doubtful march, either to wander in infinite uncertainty, or perish by the way!

FEATHERTOP

A MORALIZED LEGEND

D ICKON," cried Mother Rigby, "a coal for my pipe!"

The pipe was in the old dame's mouth, when she said these words. She had thrust it there after filling it with tobacco, but without stooping to light it at the hearth; where, indeed, there was no appearance of a fire having been kindled, that morning. Forthwith, however, as soon as the order was given, there was an intense red glow out of the bowl of the pipe, and a whiff of smoke from Mother Rigby's lips. Whence the coal came, and how brought thither by an invisible hand, I have never been able to discover.

"Good!" quoth Mother Rigby, with a nod of her head. "Thank ye, Dickon! And now for making this scarecrow. Be within call, Dickon, in case I need you again."

The good woman had risen thus early, (for, as yet, it was scarcely sunrise,) in order to set about making a scarecrow, which she intended to put in the middle of her corn-patch. It was now the latter week of May, and the crows and blackbirds had already discovered the little, green, rolled-up leaf of the Indian corn, just peeping out of the soil. She was determined, therefore, to contrive as lifelike a scarecrow as ever was seen, and to finish it immediately, from top to toe, so that it should begin its sentinel's duty that very morning. Now, Mother Rigby (as everybody must have heard) was one of the most cunning and potent witches in New England, and might, with very little trouble, have made a scarecrow ugly enough to frighten the minister himself. But, on this occasion, as she had awakened in an uncommonly pleasant humor, and was further dulcified by her pipe of tobacco, she resolved to produce something fine, beautiful, and splendid, rather than hideous and horrible.

"I don't want to set up a hobgoblin in my own corn-patch and almost at my own door-step," said Mother Rigby to herself, puffing out a whiff of smoke. "I could do it if I pleased; but I'm tired of doing marvellous things, and so I'll keep within the bounds of every-day business, just for variety's sake. Besides, there's no use in scaring the little children, for a mile roundabout, though 'tis true I'm a witch!"

It was settled, therefore, in her own mind, that the scarecrow should represent a fine gentleman of the period, so far as the materials at hand would allow. Perhaps it may be as well to enumerate the chief of the articles that went to the composition of this figure.

The most important item of all, probably, although it made so little show, was a certain broomstick, on which Mother Rigby had taken many an airy gallop at midnight, and which now served the scarecrow by way of a spinal column, or, as the unlearned phrase it, a backbone. One of its arms was a disabled flail, which used to be wielded by Goodman Rigby, before his spouse worried him out of this troublesome world; the other, if I mistake not, was composed of the pudding-stick and a broken rung of a chair, tied loosely together at the elbow. As for its legs, the right was a hoe-handle, and the left, an undistinguished and miscellaneous stick from the wood-pile. Its lungs, stomach, and other affairs of that kind, were nothing better than a meal-bag stuffed with straw.

Thus, we have made out the skeleton and entire corporosity of the scarecrow, with the exception of its head; and this was admirably supplied by a somewhat withered and shrivelled pumpkin in which Mother Rigby cut two holes for the eyes and a slit for the mouth, leaving a bluish-colored knob, in the middle, to pass for a nose. It was really quite a respectable face.

"I've seen worse ones on human shoulders, at any rate," said Mother Rigby. "And many a fine gentleman has a pumpkin-head, as well as my scarecrow!"

But the clothes, in this case, were to be the making of the man. So the good old woman took down from a peg an ancient plum-colored coat, of London make, and with relics of embroidery on its seams, cuffs, pocket-flaps, and button-holes, but lamentably worn and faded, patched at the elbows, tattered at the skirts, and threadbare all over. On the left breast was a round hole, whence either a star of nobility had been rent away, or else the hot heart of some former wearer had scorched it through and through. The neighbors said, that this rich garment belonged to the Black Man's wardrobe, and that he kept it at Mother Rigby's cottage for the convenience of slipping it on, whenever he wished to make a grand appearance at the governor's table. To match the coat, there was a velvet waistcoat of very ample size, and formerly embroidered with foliage, that had been as brightly golden as the maple-leaves in October, but which had now quite vanished out of the substance of the velvet. Next came a pair of scarlet breeches, once worn by the French governor of Louisbourg, and the knees of which had touched the lower step of the throne of Louis le Grand. The Frenchman had given these small-clothes to an Indian powwow, who parted with them to the old witch for a gill of strong-waters, at one of their dances in the forest. Furthermore, Mother Rigby produced a pair of silk stockings and put them on the figure's legs, where they showed as unsubstantial as a dream, with the wooden reality of the two sticks making itself miserably apparent through the holes. Lastly, she put her dead husband's wig on the bare scalp of the pumpkin, and surmounted the whole with a rusty three-cornered hat, in which was stuck the longest tail-feather of a rooster.

Then the old dame stood the figure up in a corner of her cottage, and chuckled to behold its yellow semblance of a visage, with its knobby little nose thrust into the air. It had a strangely self-satisfied aspect, and seemed to say—"Come look at me!"

"And you are well worth looking at—that's a fact!" quoth Mother Rigby, in admiration at her own handiwork. "I've made many a puppet, since I've been a witch; but methinks this is the finest of them all. 'Tis almost too good for a scarecrow. And, by the by, I'll just fill a fresh pipe of tobacco, and then take him out to the corn-patch."

While filling her pipe, the old woman continued to gaze with almost motherly affection at the figure in the corner. To say the truth—whether it were chance, or skill, or downright witchcraft—there was something wonderfully human in this ridiculous shape, bedizened with its tattered finery; and as for the countenance, it appeared to shrivel its yellow surface into a grin—a funny kind of expression, betwixt scorn and merriment, as if it understood itself to be a jest at mankind. The more Mother Rigby looked, the better she was pleased.

"Dickon," cried she, sharply, "another coal for my pipe!"

Hardly had she spoken, than, just as before, there was a red glowing coal on the top of the tobacco. She drew in a long whiff, and puffed it forth again into the bar of morning sunshine, which struggled through the one dusty pane of her cottage window. Mother Rigby always liked to flavor her pipe with a coal of fire from the particular chimney-corner, whence this had been brought. But where that chimney-corner might be, or who brought the coal from it—further than that the invisible messenger seemed to respond to the name of Dickon—I cannot tell.

"That puppet yonder," thought Mother Rigby, still with her eyes fixed on the scarecrow, "is too good a piece of work to stand all summer in a corn-patch, frightening away the crows and blackbirds. He's capable of better things. Why, I've danced with a worse one, when partners happened to be scarce, at our witch meetings in the forest! What if I should let him take his chance among the other men of straw and empty fellows, who go bustling about the world?"

The old witch took three or four more whiffs of her pipe, and smiled.

"He'll meet plenty of his brethren, at every street-corner!" continued she. "Well; I didn't mean to dabble in witchcraft to-day, further than the lighting of my pipe; but a witch I am, and a witch I'm likely to be, and there's no use trying to shirk it. I'll make a man of my scarecrow, were it only for the joke's sake!"

While muttering these words, Mother Rigby took the pipe from her own mouth, and thrust it into the crevice which represented the same feature in the pumpkin-visage of the scarecrow.

"Puff, darling, puff!" said she. "Puff away, my fine fellow! Your life depends on it!"

This was a strange exhortation, undoubtedly, to be addressed to a mere thing of sticks, straw, and old clothes, with nothing better than a shrivelled pumpkin for a head; as we know to have been the scarecrow's case. Nevertheless, as we must carefully hold in remembrance, Mother Rigby was a witch of singular power and dexterity; and, keeping this fact duly before our minds, we shall see nothing beyond credibility in the remarkable incidents of our story. Indeed, the great difficulty will be at once got over, if we can only bring ourselves to believe, that, as soon as the old dame bade him puff, there came a whiff of smoke from the scarecrow's mouth. It was the very feeblest of whiffs, to be sure; but it was followed by another and another, each more decided than the preceding one.

"Puff away, my pet! Puff away, pretty one!" Mother Rigby kept repeating, with her pleasantest smile. "It is the breath of life to ye; and that you may take my word for!"

Beyond all question, the pipe was bewitched. There must have been a spell, either in the tobacco, or in the fiercely glowing coal that so mysteriously burned on top of it, or in the pungently aromatic smoke, which exhaled from the kindled weed. The figure, after a few doubtful attempts, at length blew forth a volley of smoke, extending all the way from the obscure corner into the bar of sunshine. There it eddied and melted away among the motes of dust. It seemed a convulsive effort; for the two or three next whiffs were fainter, although the coal still glowed, and threw a gleam over the scarecrow's visage. The old witch clapt her skinny palms together, and smiled encouragingly upon her handiwork. She saw that the charm worked well. The shrivelled, yellow face, which heretofore had been no face at all, had already a thin, fantastic haze, as it were, of human likeness, shifting to-and-fro across it; sometimes vanishing entirely, but growing more perceptible than ever, with the next whiff from the pipe. The whole figure, in like manner, assumed a show of life, such as we impart to ill-defined shapes among the clouds, and half-deceive ourselves with the pastime of our own fancy.

If we must needs pry closely into the matter, it may be doubted whether there was any real change, after all, in the sordid, worn-out, worthless, and ill-joined substance of the scarecrow; but merely a spectral illusion, and a cunning effect of light and shade, so colored and contrived as to delude the eyes of most men. The miracles of witchcraft seem always to have had a very shallow subtlety; and, at least, if the above explanation do not hit the truth of the process, I can suggest no better.

"Well puffed, my pretty lad!" still cried old Mother Rigby. "Come; another good, stout whiff; and let it be with might and main! Puff for thy life, I tell thee! Puff out of the very bottom of thy heart; if any heart thou hast, or any bottom to it! Well done, again! Thou didst suck in that mouthfull, as if for the pure love of it."

And then the witch beckoned to the scarecrow, throwing so much magnetic potency into her gesture, that it seemed as if it must inevitably be obeyed, like the mystic call of the loadstone, when it summons the iron.

"Why lurkest thou in the corner, lazy one?" said she. "Step forth! Thou hast the world before thee!"

Upon my word, if the legend were not one which I heard on my grandmother's knee, and which had established its place among things credible before my childish judgment could analyze its probability, I question whether I should have the face to tell it now!

In obedience to Mother Rigby's word, and extending its arm as if to reach her outstretched hand, the figure made a step forward—a kind of hitch and jerk, however, rather than a step—then tottered, and almost lost its balance. What could the witch expect? It was nothing, after all, but a scarecrow, stuck upon two sticks. But the strong-willed old beldam scowled, and beckoned, and flung the energy of her purpose so forcibly at this poor combination of rotten wood, and musty straw, and ragged garments, that it was compelled to show itself a man, in spite of the reality of things. So it stept into the bar of sunshine. There it stood—poor devil of a contrivance that it was!—with only the thinnest vesture of human similitude about it, through which was evident the stiff, rickety, incongruous, faded, tattered, good-for-nothing patchwork of its substance, ready to sink in a heap upon the floor, as conscious of its own unworthiness to be erect. Shall I confess the truth? At its present point of vivification, the scarecrow reminds me of some of the lukewarm and abortive characters, composed of heterogeneous materials, used for the thousandth time, and never worth using, with which romance-writers (and myself, no doubt, among the rest) have so over-peopled the world of fiction.

But the fierce old hag began to get angry and show a glimpse of her diabolic nature, (like a snake's head peeping with a hiss out of her bosom,) at this pusillanimous behavior of the thing, which she had taken the trouble to put together.

"Puff away, wretch!" cried she wrathfully. "Puff, puff, puff, thou thing of straw and emptiness!—thou rag or two!—thou meal bag!—thou pumpkin-head!—thou nothing!—where shall I find a name vile enough to call thee by! Puff, I say, and suck in thy fantastic life along with the smoke; else I snatch the pipe from thy mouth, and hurl thee where that red coal came from!"

Thus threatened, the unhappy scarecrow had nothing for it, but to puff away for dear life. As need was, therefore, it applied itself lustily to the pipe, and sent forth such abundant vollies of tobacco-smoke that the small cottage-kitchen became all vaporous. The one sunbeam struggled mistily through, and could but imperfectly define the image of the cracked and dusty window-pane on the opposite wall. Mother Rigby, meanwhile, with one brown arm akimbo and the other stretched towards the figure, loomed grimly amid the obscurity, with such port and expression as when she was wont to heave a ponderous nightmare on her victims, and stand at the bedside to enjoy their agony. In fear and trembling did this poor scarecrow puff. But its efforts, it must be acknowledged, served an excellent purpose; for, with each successive whiff, the figure lost more and more of its dizzy and perplexing tenuity, and seemed to take denser substance. Its very garments, moreover, partook of the magical change, and shone with the gloss of novelty, and glistened with the skilfully embroidered gold that had long ago been rent away. And, half-revealed among the smoke, a yellow visage bent its lustreless eyes on Mother Rigby.

At last, the old witch clenched her fist, and shook it at the figure. Not that she was positively angry, but merely acting on the principle—perhaps untrue, or not the only truth, though as high a one as Mother Rigby could be expected to attain—that feeble and torpid natures, being incapable of better inspiration, must be stirred up by fear. But, here was the crisis. Should she fail in what she now sought to effect, it was her ruthless purpose to scatter the miserable simulacre into its original elements.

"Thou hast a man's aspect," said she sternly. "Have also the echo and mockery of a voice! I bid thee speak!"

The scarecrow gasped, struggled, and at length emitted a murmur, which was so incorporated with its smoky breath that you could scarcely tell whether it were indeed a voice, or only a whiff of tobacco. Some narrators of this legend hold the opinion, that Mother Rigby's conjurations, and the fierceness of her will, had compelled a familiar spirit into the figure, and that the voice was his.

"Mother," mumbled the poor, stifled voice, "be not so awful with me! I would fain speak; but being without wits, what can I say?"

"Thou canst speak, darling, canst thou?" cried Mother Rigby, relaxing her grim countenance into a smile. "And what shalt thou say, quoth-a! Say, indeed! Art thou of the brotherhood of the empty skull, and demandest of me what thou shalt say? Thou shalt say a thousand things, and saying

them a thousand times over, thou shalt still have said nothing!
Be not afraid, I tell thee! When thou comest into the world,
(whither I purpose sending thee, forthwith,) thou shalt not
lack the wherewithal to talk. Talk! Why, thou shalt babble
like a mill-stream, if thou wilt. Thou hast brains enough for
that, I trow!"

"At your service, mother," responded the figure.

"And that was well said, my pretty one!" answered Mother
Rigby. "Then thou spakest like thyself, and meant nothing.
Thou shalt have a hundred such set phrases, and five hundred
to the boot of them. And now, darling, I have taken so much
pains with thee, and thou art so beautiful, that, by my troth,
I love thee better than any witch's puppet in the world; and
I've made them of all sorts—clay, wax, straw, sticks, night-
fog, morning-mist, sea-foam, and chimney-smoke! But thou
art the very best. So give heed to what I say!"

"Yes, kind mother," said the figure, "with all my heart!"

"With all thy heart!" cried the old witch, setting her hands
to her sides, and laughing loudly. "Thou hast such a pretty
way of speaking! With all thy heart! And thou didst put thy
hand to the left side of thy waistcoat, as if thou really
hadst one!"

So now, in high good-humor with this fantastic contrivance
of hers, Mother Rigby told the scarecrow that it must go and
play its part in the great world, where not one man in a
hundred, she affirmed, was gifted with more real substance
than itself. And, that he might hold up his head with the
best of them, she endowed him, on the spot, with an unreckonable amount of wealth. It consisted partly of a gold
mine in Eldorado, and of ten thousand shares in a broken
bubble, and of half a million acres of vineyard at the North
pole, and of a castle in the air and a chateau in Spain, together with all the rents and income therefrom accruing. She
further made over to him the cargo of a certain ship, laden

with salt of Cadiz, which she herself, by her necromantic arts, had caused to founder, ten years before, in the deepest of mid-ocean. If the salt were not dissolved, and could be brought to market, it would fetch a pretty penny among the fishermen. That he might not lack ready money, she gave him a copper farthing, of Birmingham manufacture, being all the coin she had about her, and likewise a great deal of brass, which she applied to his forehead, thus making it yellower than ever.

"With that brass alone," quoth Mother Rigby, "thou canst pay thy way all over the earth. Kiss me, pretty darling! I have done my best for thee."

Furthermore, that the adventurer might lack no possible advantage towards a fair start in life, this excellent old dame gave him a token, by which he was to introduce himself to a certain magistrate, member of the council, merchant, and elder of the church, (the four capacities constituting but one man,) who stood at the head of society in the neighboring metropolis. The token was neither more nor less than a single word, which Mother Rigby whispered to the scarecrow, and which the scarecrow was to whisper to the merchant.

"Gouty as the old fellow is, he'll run thy errands for thee, when once thou hast given him that word in his ear," said the old witch. "Mother Rigby knows the worshipful Justice Gookin, and the worshipful justice knows Mother Rigby!"

Here the witch thrust her wrinkled face close to the puppet's, chuckling irrepressibly, and fidgetting all through her system, with delight at the idea which she meant to communicate.

"The worshipful Master Gookin," whispered she, "hath a comely maiden to his daughter! And hark ye, my pet! Thou hast a fair outside, and a pretty wit enough of thine own. Yea; a pretty wit enough! Thou wilt think better of it, when thou hast seen more of other people's wits. Now, with thy outside and thy inside, thou art the very man to win a young girl's heart. Never doubt it! I tell thee it shall be so. Put but a bold face on the matter, sigh, smile, flourish thy hat, thrust forth thy leg like a dancing-master, put thy right hand to the left side of thy waistcoat—and pretty Polly Gookin is thine own!"

All this while, the new creature had been sucking in and exhaling the vapory fragrance of his pipe, and seemed now to continue this occupation as much for the enjoyment which it afforded, as because it was an essential condition of his existence. It was wonderful to see how exceedingly like a human being it behaved. Its eyes (for it appeared to possess a pair) were bent on Mother Rigby, and at suitable junctures, it nodded or shook its head. Neither did it lack words proper for the occasion—'Really! Indeed! Pray tell me! Is it possible! Upon my word! By no means! Oh! Ah! Hem!'—and other such weighty utterances as imply attention, inquiry, acquiescence, or dissent, on the part of the auditor. Even had you stood by, and seen the scarecrow made, you could scarcely have resisted the conviction that it perfectly understood the cunning counsels, which the old witch poured into its counterfeit of an ear. The more earnestly it applied its lips to the pipe, the more distinctly was its human likeness stamped among visible realities; the more sagacious grew its expression; the more lifelike its gestures and movements, and the more intelligibly audible its voice. Its garments, too, glistened so much the brighter with an illusory magnificence. The very pipe, in which burned the spell of all this wonderwork, ceased to appear as a smoke-blackened earthen stump, and became a meerschaum, with painted bowl and amber mouth-piece.

It might be apprehended, however, that, as the life of the illusion seemed identical with the vapor of the pipe, it would terminate simultaneously with the reduction of the tobacco to ashes. But the beldam foresaw the difficulty.

"Hold thou the pipe, my precious one," said she, "while I fill it for thee again."

It was sorrowful to behold how the fine gentleman began to fade back into a scarecrow, while Mother Rigby shook the ashes out of the pipe, and proceeded to replenish it from her tobacco-box.

"Dickon," cried she, in her high, sharp tone, "another coal for this pipe!"

No sooner said than the intensely red speck of fire was glowing within the pipe-bowl; and the scarecrow, without waiting for the witch's bidding, applied the tube to its lips, and drew in a few short, convulsive whiffs, which soon, however, became regular and equable.

"Now, mine own heart's darling," quoth Mother Rigby, "whatever may happen to thee, thou must stick to thy pipe. Thy life is in it; and that, at least, thou knowest well, if thou knowest naught besides. Stick to thy pipe, I say! Smoke, puff, blow thy cloud; and tell the people, if any question be made, that it is for thy health, and that so the physician orders thee to do. And, sweet one, when thou shalt find thy pipe getting low, go apart into some corner, and (first filling thyself with smoke) cry sharply—'Dickon, a fresh pipe of tobacco!' and—'Dickon, another coal for my pipe!'—and have it into thy pretty mouth, as speedily as may be. Else, instead of a gallant gentleman in a gold-laced coat, thou wilt be but a jumble of sticks, and tattered clothes, and a bag of straw, and a withered pumpkin! Now depart, my treasure, and good luck go with thee!"

"Never fear, mother!" said the figure, in a stout voice, and sending forth a courageous whiff of smoke. "I will thrive, if an honest man and a gentleman may!"

"Oh, thou wilt be the death of me!" cried the old witch, convulsed with laughter. "That was well said! If an honest man and a gentleman may! Thou playest thy part to perfection. Get along with thee for a smart fellow; and I will wager on thy head, as a man of pith and substance, with a brain, and what they call a heart, and all else that a man should have, against any other thing on two legs. I hold myself a better witch than yesterday, for thy sake. Did not I make thee? And I defy any witch in New England to make such another! Here; take my staff along with thee!"

The staff, though it was but a plain oaken stick, immediately took the aspect of a gold-headed cane.

"That gold-head has as much sense in it as thine own," said Mother Rigby, "and it will guide thee straight to worshipful Master Gookin's door. Get thee gone, my pretty pet, my darling, my precious one, my treasure; and if any ask thy name, it is Feathertop. For thou hast a feather in thy hat, and I have thrust a handfull of feathers into the hollow of thy head, and thy wig, too, is of the fashion they call Feathertop—so be Feathertop thy name!"

And, issuing from the cottage, Feathertop strode manfully towards town. Mother Rigby stood at the threshold, well pleased to see how the sunbeams glistened on him, as if all his magnificence were real, and how diligently and lovingly he smoked his pipe, and how handsomely he walked, in spite of a little stiffness of his legs. She watched him, until out of sight, and threw a witch-benediction after her darling, when a turn of the road snatched him from her view.

Betimes in the forenoon, when the principal street of the neighboring town was just at its acme of life and bustle, a stranger of very distinguished figure was seen on the sidewalk. His port, as well as his garments, betokened nothing short of nobility. He wore a richly embroidered plum-colored coat, a waistcoat of costly velvet, magnificently adorned with golden foliage, a pair of splendid scarlet breeches, and the finest and glossiest of white silk stockings. His head was covered with a peruque, so daintily powdered and adjusted that it would

have been sacrilege to disorder it with a hat; which, therefore, (and it was a gold-laced hat, set off with a snowy
feather,) he carried beneath his arm. On the breast of his
coat glistened a star. He managed his gold-headed cane with
an airy grace, peculiar to the fine gentleman of the period;
and, to give the highest possible finish to his equipment, he
had lace ruffles at his wrists, of a most ethereal delicacy,
sufficiently avouching how idle and aristocratic must be the
hands which they half concealed.

It was a remarkable point in the accoutrement of this
brilliant personage, that he held in his left hand a fantastic
kind of a pipe, with an exquisitely painted bowl, and an
amber mouth-piece. This he applied to his lips, as often as
every five or six paces, and inhaled a deep whiff of smoke,
which, after being retained a moment in his lungs, might be
seen to eddy gracefully from his mouth and nostrils.

As may well be supposed, the street was all a-stir to find
out the stranger's name.

"It is some great nobleman, beyond question," said one of
the townspeople. "Do you see the star at his breast?"

"Nay; it is too bright to be seen," said another. "Yes; he
must needs be a nobleman, as you say. But, by what conveyance, think you, can his lordship have voyaged or travelled
hither? There has been no vessel from the old country for
a month past; and if he have arrived overland from the
southward, pray where are his attendants and equipage?"

"He needs no equipage to set off his rank," remarked a
third. "If he came among us in rags, nobility would shine
through a hole in his elbow. I never saw such dignity of
aspect. He has the old Norman blood in his veins, I warrant
him!"

"I rather take him to be a Dutchman, or one of your High
Germans," said another citizen. "The men of those countries
have always the pipe at their mouths."

"And so has a Turk," answered his companion. "But, in my judgment, this stranger hath been bred at the French court, and hath there learned politeness and grace of manner, which none understand so well as the nobility of France. That gait, now! A vulgar spectator might deem it stiff—he might call it a hitch and jerk—but, to my eye, it hath an unspeakable majesty, and must have been acquired by constant observation of the deportment of the Grand Monarque. The stranger's character and office are evident enough. He is a French ambassador, come to treat with our rulers about the cession of Canada."

"More probably a Spaniard," said another, "and hence his yellow complexion. Or, most likely, he is from the Havana, or from some port on the Spanish Main, and comes to make investigation about the piracies which our Governor is thought to connive at. Those settlers in Peru and Mexico have skins as yellow as the gold which they dig out of their mines."

"Yellow or not," cried a lady, "he is a beautiful man!—so tall—so slender!—such a fine, noble face, with so well-shaped a nose, and all that delicacy of expression about the mouth! And, bless me, how bright his star is! It positively shoots out flames!"

"So do your eyes, fair lady!" said the stranger, with a bow, and a flourish of his pipe; for he was just passing at the instant. "Upon my honor, they have quite dazzled me!"

"Was ever so original and exquisite a compliment?" murmured the lady, in an ecstasy of delight.

Amid the general admiration, excited by the stranger's appearance, there were only two dissenting voices. One was that of an impertinent cur, which, after snuffing at the heels of the glistening figure, put its tail between its legs and skulked into its master's back-yard, vociferating an execrable howl. The other dissentient was a young child, who squalled at the fullest stretch of his lungs, and babbled some unintelligible nonsense about a pumpkin.

Feathertop, meanwhile, pursued his way along the street. Except for the few complimentary words to the lady, and, now and then, a slight inclination of the head, in requital of the profound reverences of the by-standers, he seemed wholly absorbed in his pipe. There needed no other proof of his rank and consequence, than the perfect equanimity with which he comported himself, while the curiosity and admiration of the town swelled almost into clamor around him. With a crowd still gathering behind his footsteps, he finally reached the mansion-house of the worshipful Justice Gookin, entered the gate, ascended the steps of the front-door, and knocked. In the interim, before his summons was answered, the stranger was observed to shake the ashes out of his pipe.

"What did he say, in that sharp voice?" inquired one of the spectators.

"Nay, I know not," answered his friend. "But the sun dazzles my eyes strangely! How dim and faded his lordship looks, all of a sudden! Bless my wits, what is the matter with me!"

"The wonder is," said the other, "that his pipe, (which was out only an instant ago,) should be all a-light again, and with the reddest coal I ever saw! There is something mysterious about this stranger. What a whiff of smoke was that! Dim and faded, do you call him? Why, as he turns about, the star on his breast is all a-blaze."

"It is, indeed," said his companion; "and it will go near to dazzle pretty Polly Gookin, whom I see peeping at it out of the chamber-window."

The door being now opened, Feathertop turned to the crowd, made a stately bend of his body, like a great man acknowledging the reverence of the meaner sort, and vanished into the house. There was a mysterious kind of a smile, if it might not better be called a grin or grimace, upon his visage; but of all the throng that beheld him, not an individual appears to have possessed insight enough to detect the illusive character of the stranger, except a little child and a cur-dog.

Our legend here loses somewhat of its continuity, and, passing over the preliminary explanation between Feathertop and the merchant, goes in quest of the pretty Polly Gookin. She was a damsel of a soft, round figure, with light hair and blue eyes, and a fair rosy face, which seemed neither very shrewd nor very simple. This young lady had caught a glimpse of the glistening stranger, while standing at the threshold, and had forthwith put on a laced cap, a string of beads, her finest kerchief, and her stiffest damask petticoat, in preparation for the interview. Hurrying from her chamber to the parlor, she had ever since been viewing herself in the large looking-glass, and practising pretty airs—now a smile, now a ceremonious dignity of aspect, and now a softer smile than the former—kissing her hand, likewise, tossing her head, and managing her fan; while, within the mirror, an unsubstantial little maid repeated every gesture, and did all the foolish things that Polly did, but without making her ashamed of them. In short, it was the fault of pretty Polly's ability, rather than her will, if she failed to be as complete an artifice as the illustrious Feathertop himself; and when she thus tampered with her own simplicity, the witch's phantom might well hope to win her.

No sooner did Polly hear her father's gouty footsteps approaching the parlor-door, accompanied with the stiff clatter of Feathertop's high-heeled shoes, than she seated herself bolt upright, and innocently began warbling a song.

"Polly! Daughter Polly!" cried the old merchant. "Come hither, child!"

Master Gookin's aspect, as he opened the door, was doubtful and troubled.

"This gentleman," continued he, presenting the stranger, "is the Chevalier Feathertop—nay, I beg his pardon, my Lord Feathertop!—who hath brought me a token of remembrance from an ancient friend of mine. Pay your duty to his lordship, child, and honor him as his quality deserves."

After these few words of introduction, the worshipful magistrate immediately quitted the room. But, even in that brief moment, (had the fair Polly glanced aside at her father, instead of devoting herself wholly to the brilliant guest,) she might have taken warning of some mischief nigh at hand. The old man was nervous, fidgetty, and very pale. Purposing a smile of courtesy, he had deformed his face with a sort of galvanic grin, which, when Feathertop's back was turned, he exchanged for a scowl; at the same time shaking his fist, and stamping his gouty foot—an incivility which brought its retribution along with it. The truth appears to have been, that Mother Rigby's word of introduction, whatever it might be, had operated far more on the rich merchant's fears, than on his good-will. Moreover, being a man of wonderfully acute observation, he had noticed that the painted figures, on the bowl of Feathertop's pipe, were in motion. Looking more closely, he became convinced, that these figures were a party of little demons, each duly provided with horns and a tail, and dancing hand in hand, with gestures of diabolical merriment, round the circumference of the pipe-bowl. As if to confirm his suspicions, while Master Gookin ushered his guest along a dusky passage, from his private room to the parlor, the star on Feathertop's breast had scintillated actual flames, and threw a flickering gleam upon the wall, the ceiling, and the floor.

With such sinister prognostics manifesting themselves on all hands, it is not to be marvelled at that the merchant should have felt that he was committing his daughter to a very questionable acquaintance. He cursed, in his secret soul, the insinuating elegance of Feathertop's manners, as this brilliant personage bowed, smiled, put his hand on his heart, inhaled a long whiff from his pipe, and enriched the atmosphere with the smoky vapor of a fragrant and visible sigh. Gladly would poor Master Gookin have thrust his dangerous guest into the street. But there was a constraint and terror within him. This respectable old gentleman, we fear, at an earlier period of life, had given some pledge or other to the Evil Principle, and perhaps was now to redeem it by the sacrifice of his daughter.

It so happened that the parlor-door was partly of glass, shaded by a silken curtain, the folds of which hung a little awry. So strong was the merchant's interest in witnessing what was to ensue between the fair Polly and the gallant Feathertop, that, after quitting the room, he could by no means refrain from peeping through the crevice of the curtain.

But there was nothing very miraculous to be seen; nothing —except the trifles previously noticed—to confirm the idea of a supernatural peril, environing the pretty Polly. The stranger, it is true, was evidently a thorough and practised man of the world, systematic and self-possessed, and therefore the sort of person to whom a parent ought not to confide a simple young girl, without due watchfulness for the result. The worthy magistrate, who had been conversant with all degrees and qualities of mankind, could not but perceive that every motion and gesture of the distinguished Feathertop came in its proper place; nothing had been left rude or native in him; a well-digested conventionalism had incorporated itself thoroughly with his substance, and transformed him into a work of art. Perhaps it was this peculiarity that invested him with a species of ghastliness and awe. It is the effect of anything completely and consummately artificial, in human shape, that the person impresses us as an unreality, and as having hardly pith enough to cast a shadow upon the floor. As regarded Feathertop, all this resulted in a wild, extravagant, and fantastical impression, as if his life and being were akin to the smoke that curled upward from his pipe.

But pretty Polly Gookin felt not thus. The pair were now promenading the room; Feathertop with his dainty stride, and no less dainty grimace; the girl with a native maidenly grace, just touched, not spoiled, by a slightly affected manner, which seemed caught from the perfect artifice of her companion. The longer the interview continued, the more charmed was pretty Polly, until, within the first quarter of an hour, (as the old magistrate noted by his watch,) she was evidently beginning to be in love. Nor need it have been witchcraft that subdued her in such a hurry; the poor child's heart, it may be, was so very fervent, that it melted her with its own warmth, as reflected from the hollow semblance of a lover. No matter what Feathertop said, his words found depth and reverberation in her ear; no matter what he did, his action was heroic to her eye. And, by this time, it is to be supposed, there was a blush on Polly's cheek, a tender smile about her mouth, and a liquid softness in her glance; while the star kept coruscating on Feathertop's breast, and the little demons careered, with more frantic merriment than ever, about the circumference of his pipe-bowl. Oh, pretty Polly Gookin, why should these imps rejoice so madly that a silly maiden's heart was about to be given to a shadow! Is it so unusual a misfortune?—so rare a triumph?

By and by, Feathertop paused, and throwing himself into an imposing attitude, seemed to summon the fair girl to survey his figure, and resist him longer, if she could. His star, his embroidery, his buckles, glowed, at that instant, with unutterable splendor; the picturesque hues of his attire took a richer depth of coloring; there was a gleam and polish over his whole presence, betokening the perfect witchery of well-ordered manners. The maiden raised her eyes, and suffered them to linger upon her companion with a bashful and admiring gaze. Then, as if desirous of judging what value her own simple comeliness might have, side by side with so much brilliancy, she cast a glance towards the full-length looking-glass, in front of which they happened to be standing. It was one of the truest plates in the world, and incapable of flattery. No sooner did the images, therein reflected, meet Polly's eye, than she shrieked, shrank from the stranger's side, gazed at him, for a moment, in the wildest dismay, and sank insensible upon the floor. Feathertop, likewise, had looked towards the mirror, and there beheld, not the glittering mockery of his outside show, but a picture of the sordid patchwork of his real composition, stript of all witchcraft.

The wretched simulacrum! We almost pity him. He threw up his arms, with an expression of despair, that went farther than any of his previous manifestations, towards vindicating his claims to be reckoned human. For perchance the only time, since this so often empty and deceptive life of mortals began its course, an Illusion had seen and fully recognized itself.

Mother Rigby was seated by her kitchen-hearth, in the twilight of this eventful day, and had just shaken the ashes out of a new pipe, when she heard a hurried tramp along the road. Yet it did not seem so much the tramp of human footsteps, as the clatter of sticks or the rattling of dry bones.

"Ha!" thought the old witch. "What step is that? Whose skeleton is out of its grave now, I wonder!"

A figure burst headlong into the cottage-door. It was Feathertop! His pipe was still a-light; the star still flamed upon his breast; the embroidery still glowed upon his garments; nor had he lost, in any degree or manner that could be estimated, the aspect that assimilated him with our mortal-brotherhood. But yet, in some indescribable way, (as is the case with all that has deluded us, when once found out,) the poor reality was felt beneath the cunning artifice.

"What has gone wrong?" demanded the witch. "Did yonder snuffling hypocrite thrust my darling from his door? The villain! I'll set twenty fiends to torment him, till he offer thee his daughter on his bended knees!"

"No, mother," said Feathertop despondingly, "it was not that!"

"Did the girl scorn my precious one?" asked Mother Rigby, her fierce eyes glowing like two coals of Tophet. "I'll cover her face with pimples! Her nose shall be as red as the coal in thy pipe! Her front teeth shall drop out! In a week hence, she shall not be worth thy having!"

"Let her alone, mother!" answered poor Feathertop. "The girl was half-won; and methinks a kiss from her sweet lips might have made me altogether human! But," he added, after a brief pause, and then a howl of self-contempt, "I've seen myself, mother!—I've seen myself for the wretched, ragged, empty thing I am! I'll exist no longer!"

Snatching the pipe from his mouth, he flung it with all his might against the chimney, and, at the same instant, sank upon the floor, a medley of straw and tattered garments, with some sticks protruding from the heap; and a shrivelled pumpkin in the midst. The eye-holes were now lustreless; but the rudely-carved gap, that just before had been a mouth, still seemed to twist itself into a despairing grin, and was so far human.

"Poor fellow!" quoth Mother Rigby, with a rueful glance at the relics of her ill-fated contrivance. "My poor, dear, pretty Feathertop! There are thousands upon thousands of coxcombs and charlatans in the world, made up of just such a jumble of worn-out, forgotten, and good-for-nothing trash, as he was! Yet they live in fair repute, and never see themselves for what they are! And why should my poor puppet be the only one to know himself, and perish for it?"

While thus muttering, the witch had filled a fresh pipe of tobacco, and held the stem between her fingers, as doubtful whether to thrust it into her own mouth or Feathertop's.

"Poor Feathertop!" she continued. "I could easily give him another chance, and send him forth again to-morrow. But, no! his feelings are too tender; his sensibilities too deep. He seems to have too much heart to bustle for his own advantage, in such an empty and heartless world. Well, well! I'll make a scarecrow of him, after all. 'Tis an innocent and a useful vocation, and will suit my darling well; and if each of his human brethren had as fit a one, 'twould be the better for mankind; and as for this pipe of tobacco, I need it more than he!"

So saying, Mother Rigby put the stem between her lips. "Dickon!" cried she, in her high, sharp tone, "another coal for my pipe!"

THE NEW ADAM AND EVE

W E, WHO ARE BORN into the world's artificial system, can never adequately know how little in our present state and circumstances is natural, and how much is merely the interpolation of the perverted mind and heart of man. Art has become a second and stronger Nature; she is a step-mother, whose crafty tenderness has taught us to despise the bountiful and wholesome ministrations of our true parent. It is only through the medium of the imagination that we can loosen those iron fetters, which we call truth and reality, and make ourselves even partially sensible what prisoners we are. For instance, let us conceive good Father Miller's interpretation of the prophecies to have proved true. The Day of Doom has burst upon the globe, and swept away the whole race of men. From cities and fields, sea-shore and mid-land mountain region, vast continents, and even the remotest islands of the ocean—each living thing is gone. No breath of a created being disturbs this earthly atmosphere. But the abodes of man, and all that he has accomplished, the foot-prints of his wanderings, and the results of his toil, the visible symbols of his intellectual cultivation and moral progress—in short, everything physical that can give evidence of his present position—shall remain untouched by the hand of destiny. Then, to inherit and repeople this waste and deserted earth, we will suppose a new Adam and a new Eve to have been created, in the full development of mind and heart, but with no knowledge of their predecessors, nor of the diseased circumstances that had become encrusted around them. Such a pair would at once distinguish between art and nature. Their instincts and intuitions would immediately recognize the wisdom and simplicity of the latter; while the former, with its elaborate perversities, would offer them a continual succession of puzzles.

Let us attempt, in a mood half-sportive and half-thoughtful, to track these imaginary heirs of our mortality through their first day's experience. No longer ago than yesterday, the flame of human life was extinguished; there has been a breathless night; and now another morn approaches, expecting to find the earth no less desolate than at eventide.

It is dawn. The east puts on its immemorial blush, although no human eye is gazing at it; for all the phenomena of the natural world renew themselves, in spite of the solitude that now broods around the globe. There is still beauty of earth, sea, and sky, for beauty's sake. But soon there are to be spectators. Just when the earliest sunshine gilds earth's mountain tops, two beings have come into life, not in such an Eden as bloomed to welcome our first parents, but in the heart of a modern city. They find themselves in existence, and gazing into one another's eyes. Their emotion is not astonishment; nor do they perplex themselves with efforts to discover what, and whence, and why they are. Each is satisfied to be, because the other exists likewise; and their first consciousness is of calm and mutual enjoyment, which seems not to have been the birth of that very moment, but prolonged from a past eternity. Thus content with an inner sphere which they inhabit together, it is not immediately that the outward world can obtrude itself upon their notice.

Soon, however, they feel the invincible necessity of this earthly life, and begin to make acquaintance with the objects and circumstances that surround them. Perhaps no other stride so vast remains to be taken, as when they first turn from the reality of their mutual glance, to the dreams and shadows that perplex them everywhere else.

"Sweetest Eve, where are we?" exclaims the new Adam,— for speech, or some equivalent mode of expression, is born with them, and comes just as natural as breath;—"Methinks I do not recognize this place."

"Nor I, dear Adam," replies the new Eve. "And what a strange place too! Let me come closer to thy side, and behold thee only; for all other sights trouble and perplex my spirit."

"Nay, Eve," replies Adam, who appears to have the stronger tendency towards the material world; "it were well that we gain some insight into these matters. We are in an odd situation here! Let us look about us."

Assuredly, there are sights enough to throw the new inheritors of earth into a state of hopeless perplexity. The long lines of edifices, their windows glittering in the yellow sunrise, and the narrow street between, with its barren pavement, tracked and battered by wheels that have now rattled into an irrevocable past! The signs, with their unintelligible hieroglyphics! The squareness and ugliness, and regular or irregular deformity, of everything that meets the eye! The marks of wear and tear, and unrenewed decay, which distinguish the works of man from the growth of nature! What is there in all this, capable of the slightest significance to minds that know nothing of the artificial system which is implied in every lamp-post and each brick of the houses? Moreover, the utter loneliness and silence, in a scene that originally grew out of noise and bustle, must needs impress a feeling of desolation even upon Adam and Eve, unsuspicious as they are of the recent extinction of human existence. In a forest, solitude would be life; in the city, it is death.

The new Eve looks round with a sensation of doubt and distrust, such as a city dame, the daughter of numberless generations of citizens, might experience, if suddenly transported to the garden of Eden. At length, her downcast eye discovers a small tuft of grass, just beginning to sprout among the stones of the pavement; she eagerly grasps it, and is sensible that this little herb awakens some response within her heart. Nature finds nothing else to offer her. Adam, after staring up and down the street, without detecting a single object that his comprehension can lay hold of, finally turns his forehead to the sky. There, indeed, is something which the soul within him recognizes.

"Look up yonder, mine own Eve!" he cries; "surely we ought to dwell among those gold-tinged clouds, or in the blue depths beyond them. I know not how nor when, but evidently we have strayed away from our home; for I see nothing hereabouts that seems to belong to us."

"Can we not ascend thither?" inquires Eve.

"Why not?" answers Adam, hopefully. "But no! Something drags us down in spite of our best efforts. Perchance we may find a path hereafter."

In the energy of new life, it appears no such impracticable feat to climb into the sky! But they have already received a woful lesson, which may finally go far towards reducing them to the level of the departed race, when they acknowledge the necessity of keeping the beaten track of earth. They now set forth on a ramble through the city, in the hope of making their escape from this uncongenial sphere. Already, in the fresh elasticity of their spirits they have found the idea of weariness. We will watch them as they enter some of the shops, and public or private edifices; for every door, whether of alderman or beggar, church or hall of state, has been flung wide open by the same agency that swept away the inmates.

It so happens—and not unluckily for an Adam and Eve who are still in the costume that might better have befitted Eden—it so happens, that their first visit is to a fashionable dry-good store. No courteous and importunate attendants hasten to receive their orders; no throng of ladies are tossing over the rich Parisian fabrics. All is deserted; trade is at a stand-still; and not even an echo of the national watch-word—"Go ahead!"—disturbs the quiet of the new customers. But specimens of the latest earthly fashions, silks of every shade, and whatever is most delicate or splendid for the decoration of the human form, lie scattered around, profusely as bright autumnal leaves in a forest. Adam looks at a few of the articles, but throws them carelessly aside, with whatever exclamation may correspond to "Pish!" or "Pshaw!" in the new vocabulary of nature. Eve, however,—be it said without offence to her native modesty,—examines these treasures of her sex with somewhat livelier interest. A pair of corsets chance to lie upon the counter; she inspects them curiously, but knows not what to make of them. Then she handles a fashionable silk with dim yearnings—thoughts that wander hither and thither—instincts groping in the dark.

"On the whole, I do not like it," she observes, laying the glossy fabric upon the counter. "But, Adam, it is very strange! What can these things mean? Surely I ought to know—yet they put me in a perfect maze!"

"Poh! my dear Eve, why trouble thy little head about such nonsense?" cries Adam, in a fit of impatience. "Let us go somewhere else. But stay! How very beautiful! My loveliest Eve, what a charm you have imparted to that robe, by merely throwing it over your shoulders!"

For Eve, with the taste that nature moulded into her composition, has taken a remnant of exquisite silver gauze and drawn it around her form, with an effect that gives Adam his first idea of the witchery of dress. He beholds his spouse in a new light and with renewed admiration, yet is hardly reconciled to any other attire than her own golden locks. However, emulating Eve's example, he makes free with a mantle of blue velvet, and puts it on so picturesquely, that it might seem to have fallen from Heaven upon his stately figure. Thus garbed, they go in search of new discoveries.

They next wander into a Church, not to make a display of their fine clothes, but attracted by its spire, pointing upward to the sky, whither they have already yearned to climb. As they enter the portal, a clock, which it was the last earthly act of the sexton to wind up, repeats the hour in deep reverberating tones; for Time has survived his former progeny, and, with the iron tongue that man gave him, is now speaking to his two grandchildren. They listen, but understand him not. Nature would measure time by the succession of thoughts and acts which constitute real life, and not by hours of emptiness. They pass up the church aisle, and raise their eyes to the ceiling. Had our Adam and Eve become mortal in some European city, and strayed into the vastness and sublimity of an old cathedral, they might have recognized the purpose for which the deep-souled founders reared it. Like the dim awfulness of an ancient forest, its very atmosphere would have incited them to prayer. Within the snug walls of a metropolitan church there can be no such influence.

Yet some odor of religion is still lingering here, the bequest of pious souls, who had grace to enjoy a foretaste of immortal life. Perchance, they breathe a prophecy of a better world to their successors, who have become obnoxious to all their own cares and calamities in the present one.

"Eve, something impels me to look upward," says Adam. "But it troubles me to see this roof between us and the sky. Let us go forth, and perhaps we shall discern a Great Face looking down upon us."

"Yes; a Great Face, with a beam of love brightening over it, like sunshine," responds Eve. "Surely, we have seen such a countenance somewhere!"

They go out of the church, and kneeling at its threshold give way to the spirit's natural instinct of adoration towards a beneficent Father. But, in truth, their life thus far has been a continual prayer. Purity and simplicity hold converse, at every moment, with their Creator.

We now observe them entering a Court of Justice. But what remotest conception can they attain of the purposes of such an edifice? How should the idea occur to them, that human brethren, of like nature with themselves, and originally included in the same law of love which is their only rule of life, should ever need an outward enforcement of the true voice within their souls? And what, save a woful experience, the dark result of many centuries, could teach them the sad mysteries of crime? Oh, Judgment Seat, not by the pure in heart wast thou established, nor in the simplicity of nature; but by hard and wrinkled men, and upon the accumulated heap of earthly wrong! Thou art the very symbol of man's perverted state.

On as fruitless an errand our wanderers next visit a Hall of Legislature, where Adam places Eve in the Speaker's chair, unconscious of the moral which he thus exemplifies. Man's intellect, moderated by Woman's tenderness and moral sense! Were such the legislation of the world, there would be no need of State Houses, Capitols, Halls of Parliament, nor even of those little assemblages of patriarchs beneath the shadowy trees, by whom freedom was first interpreted to mankind on our native shores.

Whither go they next? A perverse destiny seems to perplex them with one after another of the riddles which mankind put forth to the wandering universe, and left unsolved in their own destruction. They enter an edifice of stern grey stone, standing insulated in the midst of others, and gloomy even in the sunshine, which it barely suffers to penetrate through its iron-grated windows. It is a Prison. The jailer has left his post at the summons of a stronger authority than the sheriff's. But the prisoners? Did the messenger of fate, when he shook open all the doors, respect the magistrate's warrant and the judge's sentence, and leave the inmates of the dungeons to be delivered by due course of earthly law? No; a new trial has been granted, in a higher court, which may set judge, jury, and prisoner at its bar all in a row, and perhaps find one no less guilty than another. The jail, like the whole earth, is now a solitude, and has thereby lost something of its dismal gloom. But here are the narrow cells, like tombs, only drearier and deadlier because in these the immortal spirit was buried with the body. Inscriptions appear on the walls, scribbled with a pencil, or scratched with a rusty nail; brief words of agony, perhaps, or guilt's desperate defiance to the world, or merely a record of a date, by which the writer strove to keep up with the march of life. There is not a living eye that could now decipher these memorials.

Nor is it while so fresh from their Creator's hand, that the new denizens of earth—no, nor their descendants for a thousand years—could discover that this edifice was a hospital for the direst disease which could afflict their predecessors. Its patients bore the outward marks of that leprosy with which all were more or less infected. They were sick—and so were the purest of their brethren—with the plague of sin. A deadly sickness, indeed! Feeling its symptoms within the breast, men concealed it with fear and shame, and were only the more cruel to those unfortunates whose pestiferous sores were flagrant to the common eye. Nothing, save a rich garment, could ever hide the plague-spot. In the course of the world's lifetime, every remedy was tried for its cure and extirpation, except the single one, the flower that grew in Heaven, and was sovereign for all the miseries of earth. Man never had attempted to cure sin by LOVE! Had he but once made the effort, it might well have happened, that there would have been no more need of the dark lazar-house into which Adam and Eve have wandered. Hasten forth, with your native innocence, lest the damps of these still conscious walls infect you likewise, and thus another fallen race be propagated!

Passing from the interior of the prison into the space within its outward wall, Adam pauses beneath a structure of the simplest contrivance, yet altogether unaccountable to him. It consists merely of two upright posts, supporting a transverse beam, from which dangles a cord.

"Eve, Eve!" cries Adam, shuddering with a nameless horror. "What can this thing be?"

"I know not," answers Eve; "but, Adam, my heart is sick! There seems to be no more sky!—no more sunshine!"

Well might Adam shudder, and poor Eve be sick at heart; for this mysterious object was the type of mankind's whole system, in regard to the great difficulties which God had given to be solved—a system of fear and vengeance, never successful, yet followed to the last. Here, on the morning when the final summons came, a criminal—one criminal, where none were guiltless—had died upon the gallows. Had the world heard the foot-fall of its own approaching doom, it would have been no inappropriate act, thus to close the record of its deeds by one so characteristic.

The two pilgrims now hurry from the prison. Had they known how the former inhabitants of earth were shut up in artificial error, and cramped and chained by their perversions, they might have compared the whole moral world to a prison-house, and have deemed the removal of the race a general jail-delivery.

They next enter, unannounced—but they might have rung at the door in vain—a private mansion, one of the stateliest in Beacon street. A wild and plaintive strain of music is quivering through the house, now rising like a solemn organ peal, and now dying into the faintest murmur; as if some spirit, that had felt an interest in the departed family, were bemoaning itself in the solitude of hall and chamber. Perhaps, a virgin, the purest of mortal race, has been left behind, to perform a requiem for the whole kindred of humanity? Not so! These are the tones of an Æolian harp, through which Nature pours the harmony that lies concealed in her every breath, whether of summer breeze or tempest. Adam and Eve are lost in rapture, unmingled with surprise. The passing wind, that stirred the harp-strings, has been hushed, before they can think of examining the splendid furniture, the gorgeous carpets, and the architecture of the rooms. These things amuse their unpractised eyes, but appeal to nothing within their hearts. Even the pictures upon the walls scarcely excite a deeper interest; for there is something radically artificial and deceptive in painting, with which minds in the primal simplicity cannot sympathize. The unbidden guests examine a row of family portraits, but are too dull to recognize them as men and women, beneath the disguise of a pre- posterous garb, and with features and expression debased, because inherited through ages of moral and physical decay.

Chance, however, presents them with pictures of human beauty, fresh from the hand of Nature. As they enter a magnificent apartment, they are astonished, but not affrighted, to perceive two figures advancing to meet them. Is it not awful to imagine that any life, save their own, should remain in the wide world?

"How is this?" exclaims Adam. "My beautiful Eve, are you in two places at once?"

"And you, Adam!" answers Eve, doubtful, yet delighted. "Surely that noble and lovely form is yours. Yet here you are by my side! I am content with one—methinks there should not be two!"

This miracle is wrought by a tall looking-glass, the mystery of which they soon fathom, because Nature creates a mirror for the human face in every pool of water, and for her own great features in waveless lakes. Pleased and satisfied with gazing at themselves, they now discover the marble statue of a child in a corner of the room, so exquisitely idealized, that it is almost worthy to be the prophetic likeness of their first-born. Sculpture, in its highest excellence, is more genuine than painting, and might seem to be evolved from a natural germ, by the same law as a leaf or flower. The statue of the child impresses the solitary pair as if it were a companion; it likewise hints at secrets both of the past and future.

"My husband!" whispers Eve.

"What would you say, dearest Eve?" inquires Adam.

"I wonder if we are alone in the world," she continues, with a sense of something like fear at the thought of other inhabitants. "This lovely little form! Did it ever breathe? Or is it only the shadow of something real, like our pictures in the mirror?"

"It is strange!" replies Adam, pressing his hand to his brow. "There are mysteries all around us. An idea flits continually before me—would that I could seize it! Eve, Eve, are we treading in the footsteps of beings that bore a likeness to ourselves? If so, whither are they gone?—and why is their world so unfit for our dwelling-place?"

"Our great Father only knows," answers Eve. "But something tells me that we shall not always be alone. And how sweet if other beings were to visit us in the shape of this fair image!"

Then they wander through the house, and everywhere find tokens of human life, which now, with the idea recently suggested, excite a deeper curiosity in their bosoms. Woman has here left traces of her delicacy and refinement, and of her gentle labors. Eve ransacks a work-basket, and instinctively thrusts the rosy tip of her finger into a thimble. She takes up a piece of embroidery, glowing with mimic flowers, in one of which a fair damsel of the departed race has left

her needle. Pity that the Day of Doom should have anticipated the completion of such a useful task! Eve feels almost
conscious of the skill to finish it. A piano-forte has been left
open. She flings her hand carelessly over the keys, and strikes
out a sudden melody, no less natural than the strains of the
Æolian harp, but joyous with the dance of her yet un-
burthened life. Passing through a dark entry, they find a
broom behind the door; and Eve, who comprises the whole
nature of womanhood, has a dim idea that it is an instrument
proper for her hand. In another apartment they behold a
canopied bed, and all the appliances of luxurious repose. A
heap of forest-leaves would be more to the purpose. They
enter the nursery, and are perplexed with the sight of little
gowns and caps, tiny shoes, and a cradle; amid the drapery
of which is still to be seen the impress of a baby's form.
Adam slightly notices these trifles; but Eve becomes involved
in a fit of mute reflection, from which it is hardly possible
to rouse her.

By a most unlucky arrangement, there was to have been
a grand dinner-party in this mansion on the very day when
the whole human family, including the invited guests, were
summoned to the unknown regions of illimitable space. At
the moment of fate, the table was actually spread, and the
company on the point of sitting down. Adam and Eve come
unbidden to the banquet; it has now been some time cold,
but otherwise furnishes them with highly favorable specimens
of the gastronomy of their predecessors. But it is difficult to
imagine the perplexity of the unperverted couple, in endeavoring to find proper food for their first meal, at a table
where the cultivated appetites of a fashionable party were
to have been gratified. Will Nature teach them the mystery
of a plate of turtle soup? Will she embolden them to attack
a haunch of venison? Will she initiate them into the merits
of a Parisian pasty, imported by the last steamer that ever

crossed the Atlantic? Will she not, rather, bid them turn with disgust from fish, fowl, and flesh, which, to their pure nostrils, steam with a loathsome odor of death and corruption?—Food? The bill of fare contains nothing which they recognize as such.

Fortunately, however, the dessert is ready upon a neighboring table. Adam, whose appetite and animal instincts are quicker than those of Eve, discovers this fitting banquet.

"Here, dearest Eve," he exclaims, "here is food."

"Well," answers she, with the germ of a housewife stirring within her, "we have been so busy to-day, that a picked-up dinner must serve."

So Eve comes to the table, and receives a red-cheeked apple from her husband's hand, in requital of her predecessor's fatal gift to our common grandfather. She eats it without sin, and, let us hope, with no disastrous consequences to her future progeny. They make a plentiful, yet temperate meal of fruit, which, though not gathered in Paradise, is legitimately derived from the seeds that were planted there. Their primal appetite is satisfied.

"What shall we drink, Eve?" inquires Adam.

Eve peeps among some bottles and decanters, which, as they contain fluids, she naturally conceives must be proper to quench thirst. But never before did claret, hock, and madeira, of rich and rare perfume, excite such disgust as now.

"Pah!" she exclaims, after smelling at various wines. "What stuff is here? The beings who have gone before us could not have possessed the same nature that we do; for neither their hunger nor thirst were like our own!"

"Pray hand me yonder bottle," says Adam. "If it be drinkable by any manner of mortal, I must moisten my throat with it."

After some remonstrances, she takes up a champagne bottle, but is frightened by the sudden explosion of the cork, and drops it upon the floor. There the untasted liquor effervesces. Had they quaffed it, they would have experienced that brief delirium, whereby, whether excited by moral or physical causes, man sought to recompense himself for the calm, life-long joys which he had lost by his revolt from Nature. At length, in a refrigerator, Eve finds a glass pitcher of water, pure, cold, and bright, as ever gushed from a fountain among the hills. Both drink; and such refreshment does it bestow, that they question one another if this precious liquid be not identical with the stream of life within them.

"And now," observes Adam, "we must again try to discover what sort of a world this is, and why we have been sent hither."

"Why?—To love one another!" cries Eve. "Is not that employment enough?"

"Truly is it," answers Adam, kissing her; "but still—I know not—something tells us there is labor to be done. Perhaps our allotted task is no other than to climb into the sky, which is so much more beautiful than earth."

"Then would we were there now," murmurs Eve, "that no task or duty might come between us!"

They leave the hospitable mansion; and we next see them passing down State street. The clock on the old State House points to high noon, when the Exchange should be in its glory, and present the liveliest emblem of what was the sole business of life, as regarded a multitude of the fore-gone worldlings. It is over now. The Sabbath of eternity has shed its stillness along the street. Not even a news-boy assails the two solitary passers-by, with an extra penny-paper from the office of the Times or Mail, containing a full account of yesterday's terrible catastrophe. Of all the dull times that merchants and speculators have known, this is the very worst; for, so far as they were concerned, creation itself has taken the benefit of the bankrupt-act. After all, it is a pity.

Those mighty capitalists, who had just attained the wished-for wealth! Those shrewd men of traffic, who had devoted so many years to the most intricate and artificial of sciences, and had barely mastered it, when the universal bankruptcy was announced by peal of trumpet! Can they have been so incautious as to provide no currency of the country whither they have gone, nor any bills of exchange, or letters of credit, from the needy on earth to the cash-keepers of Heaven?

Adam and Eve enter a Bank. Start not, ye whose funds are treasured there! You will never need them now. Call not for the police! The stones of the street and the coin of the vaults are of equal value to this simple pair. Strange sight! They take up the bright gold in handfuls, and throw it sportively into the air, for the sake of seeing the glittering worthlessness descend again in a shower. They know not that each of those small yellow circles was once a magic spell, potent to sway men's hearts, and mystify their moral sense. Here let them pause in the investigation of the past. They have discovered the main-spring, the life, the very essence, of the system that had wrought itself into the vitals of mankind, and choked their original nature in its deadly gripe. Yet how powerless over these young inheritors of earth's hoarded wealth! And here, too, are huge packages of bank-notes, those talismanic slips of paper, which once had the efficacy to build up enchanted palaces, like exhalations, and work all kinds of perilous wonders, yet were themselves but the ghosts of money, the shadows of a shade. How like is this vault to a magician's cave, when the all-powerful wand is broken, and the visionary splendor vanished, and the floor strewn with fragments of shattered spells, and lifeless shapes once animated by demons!

"Everywhere, my dear Eve," observes Adam, "we find heaps of rubbish of one kind or another. Somebody, I am convinced, has taken pains to collect them—but for what purpose? Perhaps, hereafter, we shall be moved to do the like. Can that be our business in the world?"

"Oh, no, no, Adam!" answers Eve. "It would be better to sit down quietly and look upward to the sky."

They leave the Bank, and in good time; for had they tarried later, they would probably have encountered some gouty old goblin of a capitalist, whose soul could not long be anywhere, save in the vault with his treasure.

Next, they drop into a jeweller's shop. They are pleased with the glow of gems; and Adam twines a string of beautiful pearls around the head of Eve, and fastens his own mantle with a magnificent diamond brooch. Eve thanks him, and views herself with delight in the nearest looking-glass. Shortly afterward, observing a boquet of roses and other brilliant flowers in a vase of water, she flings away the inestimable pearls, and adorns herself with these lovelier gems of nature. They charm her with sentiment as well as beauty.

"Surely they are living beings," she remarks to Adam.

"I think so," replies Adam, "and they seem to be as little at home in the world as ourselves."

We must not attempt to follow every footstep of these investigators whom their Creator has commissioned to pass unconscious judgment upon the works and ways of the vanished race. By this time, being endowed with quick and accurate perceptions, they begin to understand the purpose of the many things around them. They conjecture, for instance, that the edifices of the city were erected, not by the immediate hand that made the world, but by beings somewhat similar to themselves, for shelter and convenience. But how will they explain the magnificence of one habitation, as compared with the squalid misery of another? Through what medium can the idea of servitude enter their minds? When will they comprehend the great and miserable fact,— the evidences of which appeal to their senses everywhere,—

that one portion of earth's lost inhabitants was rolling in luxury, while the multitude was toiling for scanty food? A wretched change, indeed, must be wrought in their own hearts, ere they can conceive the primal decree of Love to have been so completely abrogated, that a brother should ever want what his brother had. When their intelligence shall have reached so far, Earth's new progeny will have little reason to exult over her old rejected one!

Their wanderings have now brought them into the suburbs of the city. They stand on a grassy brow of a hill, at the foot of a granite obelisk, which points its great finger upward, as if the human family had agreed, by a visible symbol of age-long endurance, to offer some high sacrifice of thanksgiving or supplication. The solemn height of the monument, its deep simplicity, and the absence of any vulgar and practical use, all strengthen its effect upon Adam and Eve, and lead them to interpret it by a purer sentiment than the builders thought of expressing.

"Eve, it is a visible prayer," observes Adam.

"And we will pray too," she replies.

Let us pardon these poor children of neither father nor mother, for so absurdly mistaking the purport of the memorial, which man founded and woman finished, on far-famed Bunker Hill. The idea of war is not native to their souls. Nor have they sympathies for the brave defenders of liberty, since oppression is one of their unconjectured mysteries. Could they guess that the green sward on which they stand so peacefully, was once strewn with human corpses and purple with their blood, it would equally amaze them, that one generation of men should perpetrate such carnage, and that a subsequent generation should triumphantly commemorate it.

With a sense of delight, they now stroll across green fields and along the margin of a quiet river. Not to track them too closely, we next find the wanderers entering a Gothic edifice of grey stone, where the by-gone world has left whatever it deemed worthy of record, in the rich library of Harvard University.

No student ever yet enjoyed such solitude and silence as now broods within its deep alcoves. Little do the present visitors understand what opportunities are thrown away upon them. Yet Adam looks anxiously at the long rows of volumes, those storied heights of human lore, ascending one above another from floor to ceiling. He takes up a bulky folio. It opens in his hands, as if spontaneously to impart the spirit of its author to the yet unworn and untainted intellect of the fresh-created mortal. He stands poring over the regular columns of mystic characters, seemingly in studious mood; for the unintelligible thought upon the page has a mysterious relation to his mind, and makes itself felt, as if it were a burthen flung upon him. He is even painfully perplexed, and grasps vainly at he knows not what. Oh, Adam, it is too soon, too soon by at least five thousand years, to put on spectacles, and busy yourself in the alcoves of a library!

"What can this be?" he murmurs at last. "Eve, methinks nothing is so desirable as to find out the mystery of this big and heavy object with its thousand thin divisions. See! it stares me in the face, as if it were about to speak!"

Eve, by a feminine instinct, is dipping into a volume of fashionable poetry, the production of certainly the most fortunate of earthly bards, since his lay continues in vogue when all the great masters of the lyre have passed into oblivion. But let not his ghost be too exultant! The world's one lady tosses the book upon the floor, and laughs merrily at her husband's abstracted mien.

"My dear Adam," cries she, "you look pensive and dismal! Do fling down that stupid thing; for even if it should speak, it would not be worth attending to. Let us talk with one another, and with the sky, and the green earth, and its trees and flowers. They will teach us better knowledge than we can find here."

"Well, Eve, perhaps you are right," replies Adam, with a sort of sigh. "Still, I cannot help thinking that the interpretation of the riddles amid which we have been wandering all day long might here be discovered."

"It may be better not to seek the interpretation," persists Eve. "For my part, the air of this place does not suit me. If you love me, come away!"

She prevails, and rescues him from the mysterious perils of the library. Happy influence of woman! Had he lingered there long enough to obtain a clue to its treasures,—as was not impossible, his intellect being of human structure, indeed, but with an untransmitted vigor and acuteness,—had he then and there become a student, the annalist of our poor world would soon have recorded the downfall of a second Adam. The fatal apple of another Tree of Knowledge would have been eaten. All the perversions and sophistries, and false wisdom so aptly mimicking the true; all the narrow truth, so partial that it becomes more deceptive than falsehood; all the wrong principles and worse practice, the pernicious examples and mistaken rules of life; all the specious theories, which turn earth into cloud-land, and men into shadows; all the sad experience, which it took mankind so many ages to accumulate, and from which they never drew a moral for their future guidance—the whole heap of this disastrous lore would have tumbled at once upon Adam's head. There would have been nothing left for him, but to take up the already abortive experiment of life, where we had dropped it, and toil onward with it a little further.

But, blessed in his ignorance, he may still enjoy a new world in our worn-out one. Should he fall short of good, even as far as we did, he has at least the freedom—no worthless one—to make errors for himself. And his literature, when the progress of centuries shall create it, will be no interminably repeated echo of our own poetry, and reproduction of the images that were moulded by our great fathers of song and fiction, but a melody never yet heard on earth, and intellectual forms unbreathed upon by our conceptions. Therefore let the dust of ages gather upon the volumes of the library, and, in due season, the roof of the edifice crumble down upon the whole. When the second Adam's descendants shall have collected as much rubbish of their own, it will be time enough to dig into our ruins, and compare the literary advancement of two independent races.

But we are looking forward too far. It seems to be the vice of those who have a long past behind them. We will return to the new Adam and Eve, who, having no reminiscences, save dim and fleeting visions of a pre-existence, are content to live and be happy in the present.

The day is near its close, when these pilgrims, who derive their being from no dead progenitors, reach the cemetery of Mount Auburn. With light hearts—for earth and sky now gladden each other with beauty—they tread along the winding paths, among marble pillars, mimic temples, urns, obelisks, and sarcophagi, sometimes pausing to contemplate these fantasies of human growth, and sometimes to admire the flowers wherewith Nature converts decay to loveliness. Can Death, in the midst of his old triumphs, make them sensible that they have taken up the heavy burthen of mortality, which a whole species had thrown down? Dust kindred to their own has never lain in the grave. Will they then recognize, and so soon, that Time and the elements have an indefeasible claim upon their bodies? Not improbably, they may. There must have been shadows enough, even amid the primal sunshine of their existence, to suggest the thought of the soul's incongruity with its circumstances.

They have already learned that something is to be thrown aside. The idea of Death is in them, or not far off. But were they to choose a symbol for him, it would be the Butterfly soaring upward, or the bright Angel beckoning them aloft, or the Child asleep, with soft dreams visible through her transparent purity.

Such a Child, in whitest marble, they have found among the monuments of Mount Auburn.

"Sweetest Eve," observes Adam, while hand in hand they contemplate this beautiful object, "yonder sun has left us, and the whole world is fading from our sight. Let us sleep, as this lovely little figure is sleeping. Our Father only knows, whether what outward things we have possessed to-day are to be snatched from us for ever. But should our earthly life be leaving us with the departing light, we need not doubt that another morn will find us somewhere beneath the smile of God. I feel that He has imparted the boon of existence, never to be resumed."

"And no matter where we exist," replies Eve, "for we shall always be together."

EGOTISM;* OR, THE BOSOM-SERPENT

FROM THE UNPUBLISHED
"ALLEGORIES OF THE HEART"

HERE HE COMES!" shouted the boys along the street.—"Here comes the man with a snake in his bosom!"

This outcry, saluting Herkimer's ears, as he was about to enter the iron gate of the Elliston mansion, made him pause. It was not without a shudder that he found himself on the point of meeting his former acquaintance, whom he had known in the glory of youth, and whom now, after an interval of five years, he was to find the victim either of a diseased fancy, or a horrible physical misfortune.

"A snake in his bosom!" repeated the young sculptor to himself. "It must be he. No second man on earth has such a bosom-friend! And now, my poor Rosina, Heaven grant me wisdom to discharge my errand aright! Woman's faith must be strong indeed, since thine has not yet failed."

Thus musing, he took his stand at the entrance of the gate, and waited until the personage, so singularly announced, should make his appearance. After an instant or two, he beheld the figure of a lean man, of unwholesome look, with glittering eyes and long black hair, who seemed to imitate

---

*The physical fact, to which it is here attempted to give a moral signification, has been known to occur in more than one instance.

the motion of a snake; for, instead of walking straight forward with open front, he undulated along the pavement in a curved line. It may be too fanciful to say, that something, either in his moral or material aspect, suggested the idea that a miracle had been wrought, by transforming a serpent into a man; but so imperfectly, that the snaky nature was yet hidden, and scarcely hidden, under the mere outward guise of humanity. Herkimer remarked that his complexion had a greenish tinge over its sickly white, reminding him of a species of marble out of which he had once wrought a head of Envy, with her snaky locks.

The wretched being approached the gate, but, instead of entering, stopt short, and fixed the glitter of his eye full upon the compassionate, yet steady countenance of the sculptor.

"It gnaws me! It gnaws me!" he exclaimed.

And then there was an audible hiss, but whether it came from the apparent lunatic's own lips, or was the real hiss of a serpent, might admit of discussion. At all events, it made Herkimer shudder to his heart's core.

"Do you know me, George Herkimer?" asked the snake-possessed.

Herkimer did know him. But it demanded all the intimate and practical acquaintance with the human face, acquired by modelling actual likenesses in clay, to recognize the features of Roderick Elliston in the visage that now met the sculptor's gaze. Yet it was he. It added nothing to the wonder, to reflect that the once brilliant young man had undergone this odious and fearful change, during the no more than five brief years of Herkimer's abode at Florence. The possibility of such a transformation being granted, it was as easy to conceive it effected in a moment as in an age. Inexpressibly shocked and startled, it was still the keenest pang, when Herkimer remembered that the fate of his cousin

Rosina, the ideal of gentle womanhood, was indissolubly interwoven with that of a being whom Providence seemed to have unhumanized.

"Elliston! Roderick!" cried he, "I had heard of this; but my conception came far short of the truth. What has befallen you? Why do I find you thus?"

"Oh, 'tis a mere nothing! A snake! A snake! The commonest thing in the world. A snake in the bosom—that's all," answered Roderick Elliston. "But how is your own breast?" continued he, looking the sculptor in the eye, with the most acute and penetrating glance that it had ever been his fortune to encounter. "All pure and wholesome? No reptile there? By my faith and conscience, and by the devil within me, here is a wonder! A man without a serpent in his bosom!"

"Be calm, Elliston," whispered George Herkimer, laying his hand upon the shoulder of the snake-possessed. "I have crossed the ocean to meet you. Listen!—let us be private— I bring a message from Rosina!—from your wife!"

"It gnaws me! It gnaws me!" muttered Roderick.

With this exclamation, the most frequent in his mouth, the unfortunate man clutched both hands upon his breast, as if an intolerable sting or torture impelled him to rend it open, and let out the living mischief, even were it intertwined with his own life. He then freed himself from Herkimer's grasp, by a subtle motion, and gliding through the gate, took refuge in his antiquated family residence. The sculptor did not pursue him. He saw that no available intercourse could be expected at such a moment, and was desirous, before another meeting, to inquire closely into the nature of Roderick's disease, and the circumstances that had reduced him to so lamentable a condition. He succeeded in obtaining the necessary information from an eminent medical gentleman.

Shortly after Elliston's separation from his wife—now nearly four years ago—his associates had observed a singular gloom spreading over his daily life, like those chill, grey mists that sometimes steal away the sunshine from a summer's morning. The symptoms caused them endless perplexity. They knew not whether ill health were robbing his spirits of elasticity; or whether a canker of the mind was gradually eating, as such cankers do, from his moral system into the physical frame, which is but the shadow of the former. They looked for the root of this trouble in his shattered schemes of domestic bliss—wilfully shattered by himself—but could not be satisfied of its existence there. Some thought that their once brilliant friend was in an incipient stage of insanity, of which his passionate impulses had perhaps been the forerunners; others prognosticated a general blight and gradual decline. From Roderick's own lips, they could learn nothing. More than once, it is true, he had been heard to say, clutching his hands convulsively upon his breast—"It gnaws me! It gnaws me!"—but, by different auditors, a great diversity of explanation was assigned to this ominous expression. What could it be, that gnawed the breast of Roderick Elliston? Was it sorrow? Was it merely the tooth of physical disease? Or, in his reckless course, often verging upon profligacy, if not plunging into its depths, had he been guilty of some deed, which made his bosom a prey to the deadlier fangs of remorse? There was plausible ground for each of these conjectures; but it must not be concealed that more than one elderly gentleman, the victim of good cheer and slothful habits, magisterially pronounced the secret of the whole matter to be Dyspepsia!

Meanwhile, Roderick seemed aware how generally he had become the subject of curiosity and conjecture, and, with a morbid repugnance to such notice, or to any notice whatsoever, estranged himself from all companionship. Not merely the eye of man was a horror to him; not merely the light of a friend's countenance; but even the blessed sunshine, likewise, which, in its universal beneficence, typifies the radiance of the Creator's face, expressing his love for all the creatures of his hand. The dusky twilight was now too transparent for Roderick Elliston; the blackest midnight was his chosen hour to steal abroad; and if ever he were seen, it was when the watchman's lantern gleamed upon his figure, gliding along the street, with his hands clutched upon his bosom, still muttering:—"It gnaws me! It gnaws me!" What could it be that gnawed him?

After a time, it became known that Elliston was in the habit of resorting to all the noted quacks that infested the city, or whom money would tempt to journey thither from a distance. By one of these persons, in the exultation of a supposed cure, it was proclaimed far and wide, by dint of hand-bills and little pamphlets on dingy paper, that a distinguished gentleman, Roderick Elliston, Esq., had been relieved of a SNAKE in his stomach! So here was the monstrous secret, ejected from its lurking-place into public view, in all its horrible deformity. The mystery was out; but not so the bosom-serpent. He, if it were anything but a delusion, still lay coiled in his living den. The empiric's cure had been a sham, the effect, it was supposed, of some stupefying drug, which more nearly caused the death of the patient than of the odious reptile that possessed him. When Roderick Elliston regained entire sensibility, it was to find his misfortune the town talk—the more than nine days' wonder and horror—while, at his bosom, he felt the sickening motion of a thing alive, and the gnawing of that restless fang, which seemed to gratify at once a physical appetite and a fiendish spite.

He summoned the old black servant, who had been bred up in his father's house, and was a middle-aged man while Roderick lay in his cradle.

"Scipio!" he began; and then paused, with his arms folded over his heart—"What do people say of me, Scipio?"

"Sir! my poor master! that you had a serpent in your bosom," answered the servant, with hesitation.

"And what else?" asked Roderick, with a ghastly look at the man.

"Nothing else, dear master," replied Scipio;—"only that the Doctor gave you a powder, and that the snake leapt out upon the floor."

"No, no!" muttered Roderick to himself, as he shook his head, and pressed his hands with a more convulsive force upon his breast,—"I feel him still. It gnaws me! It gnaws me!"

From this time, the miserable sufferer ceased to shun the world, but rather solicited and forced himself upon the notice of acquaintances and strangers. It was partly the result of desperation, on finding that the cavern of his own bosom had not proved deep and dark enough to hide the secret, even while it was so secure a fortress for the loathsome fiend that had crept into it. But still more, this craving for notoriety was a symptom of the intense morbidness which now pervaded his nature. All persons, chronically diseased, are egotists, whether the disease be of the mind or body; whether it be sin, sorrow, or merely the more tolerable calamity of some endless pain, or mischief among the cords of mortal life. Such individuals are made acutely conscious of a self, by the torture in which it dwells. Self, therefore, grows to be so prominent an object with them, that they cannot but present it to the face of every casual passer-by. There is a pleasure—perhaps the greatest of which the sufferer is susceptible—in displaying the wasted or ulcerated limb, or the cancer in the breast; and the fouler the crime, with so much the more difficulty does the perpetrator prevent it from thrusting up its snake-like head, to frighten the world; for it is that cancer, or that crime, which constitutes their respective individuality. Roderick Elliston, who, a little while before, had held himself so scornfully above the common lot of men, now paid full allegiance to this humiliating law. The snake in his bosom seemed the symbol of a monstrous egotism, to which everything was referred, and which he pampered, night and day, with a continual and exclusive sacrifice of devil-worship.

He soon exhibited what most people considered indubitable tokens of insanity. In some of his moods, strange to say, he prided and gloried himself on being marked out from the ordinary experience of mankind, by the possession of a double nature, and a life within a life. He appeared to imagine that the snake was a divinity—not celestial, it is true, but darkly infernal—and that he thence derived an eminence and a sanctity, horrid, indeed, yet more desirable than whatever ambition aims at. Thus he drew his misery around him like a regal mantle, and looked down triumphantly upon those whose vitals nourished no deadly monster. Oftener, however, his human nature asserted its empire over him, in the shape of a yearning for fellowship. It grew to be his custom to spend the whole day in wandering about the streets, aimlessly, unless it might be called an aim, to establish a species of brotherhood between himself and the world. With cankered ingenuity, he sought out his own disease in every breast. Whether insane or not, he showed so keen a perception of frailty, error, and vice, that many persons gave him credit for being possessed not merely with a serpent, but with an actual fiend, who imparted this evil faculty of recognizing whatever was ugliest in man's heart.

For instance, he met an individual, who, for thirty years, had cherished a hatred against his own brother. Roderick, amidst the throng of the street, laid his hand on this man's chest, and looking full into his forbidding face,

"How is the snake to-day?"—he inquired, with a mock expression of sympathy.

"The snake!" exclaimed the brother-hater—"What do you mean?"

"The snake! The snake! Does he gnaw you?" persisted Roderick. "Did you take counsel with him, this morning, when you should have been saying your prayers? Did he sting, when you thought of your brother's health, wealth, and good repute? Did he caper for joy, when you remembered the profligacy of his only son? And whether he stung, or whether he frolicked, did you feel his poison throughout your body and soul, converting everything to sourness and bitterness? That is the way of such serpents. I have learned the whole nature of them from my own!"

"Where is the police?" roared the object of Roderick's persecution, at the same time giving an instinctive clutch to his breast. "Why is this lunatic allowed to go at large?"

"Ha, ha!" chuckled Roderick, releasing his grasp of the man.—"His bosom-serpent has stung him then!"

Often, it pleased the unfortunate young man to vex people with a lighter satire, yet still characterized by somewhat of snake-like virulence. One day, he encountered an ambitious statesman, and gravely inquired after the welfare of his boa constrictor; for of that species, Roderick affirmed, this gentleman's serpent must needs be, since its appetite was enormous enough to devour the whole country and constitution. At another time, he stopped a close-fisted old fellow, of great wealth, but who skulked about the city, in the guise of a scare-crow, with a patched blue surtout, brown hat, and mouldy boots, scraping pence together, and picking up rusty nails. Pretending to look earnestly at this respectable person's stomach, Roderick assured him that his snake was a copper-head, and had been generated by the immense quantities of that base metal, with which he daily defiled his fingers. Again, he assaulted a man of rubicund visage, and told him that few bosom-serpents had more of the devil in them, than those that breed in the vats of a distillery. The next whom Roderick honored with his attention was a distinguished clergyman, who happened just then to be engaged in a theological controversy, where human wrath was more perceptible than divine inspiration.

"You have swallowed a snake, in a cup of sacramental wine," quoth he.

"Profane wretch!" exclaimed the divine; but nevertheless, his hand stole to his breast.

He met a person of sickly sensibility, who, on some early disappointment, had retired from the world, and thereafter held no intercourse with his fellow-men, but brooded sullenly or passionately over the irrevocable past. This man's very heart, if Roderick might be believed, had been changed into a serpent, which would finally torment both him and itself to death. Observing a married couple, whose domestic troubles were matter of notoriety, he condoled with both on having mutually taken a house-adder to their bosoms. To an envious author, who depreciated works which he could never equal, he said, that his snake was the slimiest and filthiest of all the reptile tribe, but was fortunately without a sting. A man of impure life, and a brazen face, asking Roderick if there were any serpent in his breast, he told him that there was, and of the same species that once tortured Don Rodrigo, the Goth. He took a fair young girl by the hand, and gazing sadly into her eyes, warned her that she cherished a serpent of the deadliest kind within her gentle breast; and the world found the truth of those ominous words, when, a few months afterwards, the poor girl died of love and shame. Two ladies, rivals in fashionable life, who tormented one another with a thousand little stings of womanish spite, were given to understand, that each of their hearts was a nest of diminutive snakes, which did quite as much mischief as one great one.

But nothing seemed to please Roderick better, than to lay hold of a person infected with jealousy, which he represented as an enormous green reptile, with an ice-cold length of body, and the sharpest sting of any snake save one.

"And what one is that?" asked a bystander, overhearing him.

It was a dark-browed man, who put the question; he had an evasive eye, which, in the course of a dozen years, had looked no mortal directly in the face. There was an ambiguity about this person's character—a stain upon his reputation—yet none could tell precisely of what nature; although the city-gossips, male and female, whispered the most atrocious surmises. Until a recent period, he had followed the sea, and was, in fact, the very ship-master whom George Herkimer had encountered, under such singular circumstances, in the Grecian Archipelago.

"What bosom-serpent has the sharpest sting?" repeated this man; but he put the question as if by a reluctant necessity, and grew pale while he was uttering it.

"Why need you ask?" replied Roderick, with a look of dark intelligence. "Look into your own breast! Hark, my serpent bestirs himself! He acknowledges the presence of a master-fiend!"

And then, as the bystanders afterwards affirmed, a hissing sound was heard, apparently in Roderick Elliston's breast. It was said, too, that an answering hiss came from the vitals of the shipmaster, as if a snake were actually lurking there, and had been aroused by the call of its brother-reptile. If there were in fact any such sound, it might have been caused by a malicious exercise of ventriloquism, on the part of Roderick.

Thus, making his own actual serpent—if a serpent there actually was in his bosom—the type of each man's fatal error, or hoarded sin, or unquiet conscience, and striking his sting so unremorsefully into the sorest spot, we may well imagine that Roderick became the pest of the city. Nobody could elude him; none could withstand him. He grappled with the ugliest truth that he could lay his hand on, and compelled his adversary to do the same. Strange spectacle in human life, where it is the instinctive effort of one and all to hide those sad realities, and leave them undisturbed beneath a heap of superficial topics, which constitute the materials of intercourse between man and man! It was not to be tolerated that Roderick Elliston should break through the tacit compact, by which the world has done its best to secure repose, without relinquishing evil. The victims of his malicious remarks, it is true, had brothers enough to keep them in countenance; for, by Roderick's theory, every mortal bosom harbored either a brood of small serpents, or one overgrown monster, that had devoured all the rest. Still, the city could not bear this new apostle. It was demanded by nearly all, and particularly by the most respectable inhabitants, that Roderick should no longer be permitted to violate the received rules of decorum, by obtruding his own bosom-serpent to the public gaze, and dragging those of decent people from their lurking-places.

Accordingly, his relatives interfered, and placed him in a private asylum for the insane. When the news was noised abroad, it was observed that many persons walked the streets with freer countenances, and covered their breasts less carefully with their hands.

His confinement, however, although it contributed not a little to the peace of the town, operated unfavorably upon Roderick himself. In solitude, his melancholy grew more black and sullen. He spent whole days—indeed, it was his sole occupation—in communing with the serpent. A conversation was sustained, in which as it seemed, the hidden monster bore a part, though unintelligibly to the listeners, and inaudible, except in a hiss. Singular as it may appear, the sufferer had now contracted a sort of affection for his tormentor; mingled, however, with the intensest loathing and horror. Nor were such discordant emotions incompatible;

each, on the contrary, imparted strength and poignancy to its opposite. Horrible love—horrible antipathy—embracing one another in his bosom, and both concentrating themselves upon a being that had crept into his vitals, or been engendered there, and which was nourished with his food, and lived upon his life, and was as intimate with him as his own heart, and yet was the foulest of all created things! But not the less was it the true type of a morbid nature.

Sometimes, in his moments of rage and bitter hatred against the snake and himself, Roderick determined to be the death of him, even at the expense of his own life. Once he attempted it by starvation. But, while the wretched man was on the point of famishing, the monster seemed to feed upon his heart, and to thrive and wax gamesome, as if it were his sweetest and most congenial diet. Then he privily took a dose of active poison, imagining that it would not fail to kill either himself, or the devil that possessed him, or both together. Another mistake; for if Roderick had not yet been destroyed by his own poisoned heart, nor the snake by gnawing it, they had little to fear from arsenic or corrosive sublimate. Indeed, the venomous pest appeared to operate as an antidote against all other poisons. The physicians tried to suffocate the fiend with tobacco-smoke. He breathed it as freely as if it were his native atmosphere. Again, they drugged their patient with opium, and drenched him with intoxicating liquors, hoping that the snake might thus be reduced to stupor, and perhaps be ejected from the stomach. They succeeded in rendering Roderick insensible; but, placing their hands upon his breast, they were inexpressibly horror-stricken to feel the monster wriggling, twining, and darting to and fro, within his narrow limits, evidently enlivened by the opium or alcohol, and incited to unusual feats of activity. Thenceforth, they gave up all attempts at cure or palliation. The doomed sufferer submitted to his fate, resumed his former loathsome affection for the bosom-fiend, and spent whole miserable days before a looking glass, with his mouth wide open, watching, in hope and horror, to catch a glimpse of the snake's head, far down within his throat. It is supposed that he succeeded; for the attendants once heard a frenzied shout, and rushing into the room, found Roderick lifeless upon the floor.

He was kept but little longer under restraint. After minute investigation, the medical directors of the asylum decided that his mental disease did not amount to insanity, nor would warrant his confinement; especially as its influence upon his spirits was unfavorable, and might produce the evil which it was meant to remedy. His eccentricities were doubtless great —he had habitually violated many of the customs and prejudices of society; but the world was not, without surer ground, entitled to treat him as a madman. On this decision of such competent authority, Roderick was released, and had returned to his native city, the very day before his encounter with George Herkimer.

As soon as possible after learning these particulars, the sculptor, together with a sad and tremulous companion, sought Elliston at his own house. It was a large, sombre edifice of wood with pilasters and a balcony, and was divided from one of the principal streets by a terrace of three elevations, which was ascended by successive flights of stone steps. Some immense old elms almost concealed the front of the mansion. This spacious and once magnificent family-residence was built by a grandee of the race, early in the past century; at which epoch, land being of small comparative value, the garden and other grounds had formed quite an extensive domain. Although a portion of the ancestral heritage had been alienated, there was still a shadowy enclosure in the rear of the mansion, where a student, or a dreamer, or a man of stricken heart, might lie all day upon the grass, amid the solitude of murmuring boughs, and forget that a city had grown up around him.

Into this retirement, the sculptor and his companion were ushered by Scipio, the old black servant, whose wrinkled visage grew almost sunny with intelligence and joy, as he paid his humble greetings to one of the two visitors.

"Remain in the arbor," whispered the sculptor to the figure that leaned upon his arm, "you will know whether, and when, to make your appearance."

"God will teach me," was the reply. "May he support me too!"

Roderick was reclining on the margin of a fountain, which gushed into the fleckered sunshine with the same clear sparkle, and the same voice of airy quietude, as when trees of primeval growth flung their shadows across its bosom. How strange is the life of a fountain, born at every moment, yet of an age coeval with the rocks, and far surpassing the venerable antiquity of a forest!

"You are come! I have expected you," said Elliston, when he became aware of the sculptor's presence.

His manner was very different from that of the preceding day—quiet, courteous, and, as Herkimer thought, watchful both over his guest and himself. This unnatural restraint was almost the only trait that betokened anything amiss. He had just thrown a book upon the grass, where it lay half-opened, thus disclosing itself to be a natural history of the serpent-tribe, illustrated by life-like plates. Near it lay that bulky volume, the Ductor Dubitantium of Jeremy Taylor, full of cases of conscience, and in which most men, possessed of a conscience, may find something applicable to their purpose.

"You see," observed Elliston, pointing to the book of serpents, while a smile gleamed upon his lips, "I am making an effort to become better acquainted with my bosom-friend. But I find nothing satisfactory in this volume. If I mistake not, he will prove to be *sui generis*, and akin to no other reptile in creation."

"Whence came this strange calamity?" inquired the sculptor.

"My sable friend, Scipio, has a story," replied Roderick, "of a snake that had lurked in this fountain—pure and innocent as it looks—ever since it was known to the first settlers. This insinuating personage once crept into the vitals of my great-grandfather, and dwelt there many years, tormenting the old gentleman beyond mortal endurance. In short, it is a family peculiarity. But, to tell you the truth, I have no faith in this idea of the snake's being an heir-loom. He is my own snake, and no man's else."

"But what was his origin?" demanded Herkimer.

"Oh! there is poisonous stuff in any man's heart, sufficient to generate a brood of serpents," said Elliston, with a hollow laugh. "You should have heard my homilies to the good townspeople. Positively, I deem myself fortunate in having bred but a single serpent. You, however, have none in your bosom, and therefore, cannot sympathize with the rest of the world. It gnaws me! It gnaws me!"

With this exclamation, Roderick lost his self-control and threw himself upon the grass, testifying his agony by intricate writhings, in which Herkimer could not but fancy a resemblance to the motions of a snake. Then, likewise, was heard that frightful hiss, which often ran through the sufferer's speech, and crept between the words and syllables, without interrupting their succession.

"This is awful indeed!" exclaimed the sculptor—"an awful infliction, whether it be actual or imaginary! Tell me, Roderick Elliston, is there any remedy for this loathsome evil?"

"Yes, but an impossible one," muttered Roderick, as he lay wallowing with his face in the grass. "Could I, for one instant, forget myself, the serpent might not abide within me.

It is my diseased self-contemplation that has engendered and nourished him!"

"Then forget yourself, my husband," said a gentle voice above him—"forget yourself in the idea of another!"

Rosina had emerged from the arbor, and was bending over him, with the shadow of his anguish reflected in her countenance, yet so mingled with hope and unselfish love, that all anguish seemed but an earthly shadow and a dream. She touched Roderick with her hand. A tremor shivered through his frame. At that moment, if report be trustworthy, the sculptor beheld a waving motion through the grass, and heard a tinkling sound, as if something had plunged into the fountain. Be the truth as it might, it is certain that Roderick Elliston sat up, like a man renewed, restored to his right mind, and rescued from the fiend, which had so miserably overcome him in the battle-field of his own breast.

"Rosina!" cried he, in broken and passionate tones, but with nothing of the wild wail that had haunted his voice so long. "Forgive! Forgive!"

Her happy tears bedewed his face.

"The punishment has been severe," observed the sculptor. "Even Justice might now forgive—how much more a woman's tenderness! Roderick Elliston, whether the serpent was a physical reptile, or whether the morbidness of your nature suggested that symbol to your fancy, the moral of the story is not the less true and strong. A tremendous Egotism—manifesting itself, in your case, in the form of jealousy—is as fearful a fiend as ever stole into the human heart. Can a breast, where it has dwelt so long, be purified?"

"Oh, yes!" said Rosina, with a heavenly smile. "The serpent was but a dark fantasy, and what it typified was as shadowy as itself. The past, dismal as it seems, shall fling no gloom upon the future. To give it its due importance, we must think of it but as an anecdote in our Eternity!"

THE CHRISTMAS BANQUET

FROM THE UNPUBLISHED
"ALLEGORIES OF THE HEART"

I HAVE here attempted," said Roderick, unfolding a few sheets of manuscript, as he sat with Rosina and the sculptor in the summer-house—"I have attempted to seize hold of a personage who glides past me, occasionally, in my walk through life. My former sad experience, as you know, has gifted me with some degree of insight into the gloomy mysteries of the human heart, through which I have wandered like one astray in a dark cavern, with his torch fast flickering to extinction. But this man—this class of men —is a hopeless puzzle."

"Well, but propound him," said the sculptor. "Let us have an idea of him, to begin with."

"Why, indeed," replied Roderick, "he is such a being as I could conceive you to carve out of marble, and some yet unrealized perfection of human science to endow with an exquisite mockery of intellect; but still there lacks the last inestimable touch of a divine Creator. He looks like a man, and, perchance, like a better specimen of man than you ordinarily meet. You might esteem him wise—he is capable of cultivation and refinement, and has at least an external conscience—but the demands that spirit makes upon spirit, are precisely those to which he cannot respond. When, at last, you come close to him, you find him chill and unsubstantial—a mere vapor."

"I believe," said Rosina, "I have a glimmering idea of what you mean."

"Then be thankful," answered her husband, smiling; "but do not anticipate any further illumination from what I am about to read. I have here imagined such a man to be—what, probably, he never is—conscious of the deficiency in his spiritual organization. Methinks the result would be a sense of cold unreality, wherewith he would go shivering through the world, longing to exchange his load of ice for any burthen of real grief that fate could fling upon a human being."

Contenting himself with this preface, Roderick began to read.

In a certain old gentleman's last will and testament, there appeared a bequest, which, as his final thought and deed, was singularly in keeping with a long life of melancholy eccentricity. He devised a considerable sum for establishing a fund, the interest of which was to be expended, annually forever, in preparing a Christmas Banquet for ten of the most miserable persons that could be found. It seemed not to be the testator's purpose to make these half-a-score of sad hearts merry, but to provide that the stern or fierce expression of human discontent should not be drowned, even for that one holy and joyful day, amid the acclamations of festal gratitude which all Christendom sends up. And he desired, likewise, to perpetuate his own remonstrance against the earthly course of Providence, and his sad and sour dissent from those systems of religion or philosophy which either find sunshine in the world, or draw it down from heaven.

The task of inviting the guests, or of selecting among such as might advance their claims to partake of this dismal hospitality, was confided to the two trustees or stewards of the fund. These gentlemen, like their deceased friend, were sombre humorists, who made it their principal occupation to number the sable threads in the web of human life, and drop all the golden ones out of the reckoning. They performed their present office with integrity and judgment. The aspect of the assembled company, on the day of the first festival, might not, it is true, have satisfied every beholder that these were especially the individuals, chosen forth from all the world, whose griefs were worthy to stand as indicators of the mass of human suffering. Yet, after due consideration, it could not be disputed that here was a variety of hopeless discomfort, which, if it sometimes arose from causes apparently inadequate, was thereby only the shrewder imputation against the nature and mechanism of life.

The arrangements and decorations of the banquet were probably intended to signify that death-in-life which had been the testator's definition of existence. The hall, illuminated by torches, was hung round with curtains of deep and dusky purple, and adorned with branches of cypress and wreaths of artificial flowers, imitative of such as used to be strewn over the dead. A sprig of parsley was laid by every plate. The main reservoir of wine was a sepulchral urn of silver, whence the liquor was distributed around the table in small vases, accurately copied from those that held the tears of ancient mourners. Neither had the stewards—if it were their taste that arranged these details—forgotten the fantasy of the old Egyptians, who seated a skeleton at every festive board, and mocked their own merriment with the imperturbable grin of a death's-head. Such a fearful guest, shrouded in a black mantle, sat now at the head of the table. It was whispered, I know not with what truth, that the testator himself had once walked the visible world with the machinery of that same skeleton, and that it was one of the stipulations of his will, that he should thus be permitted to sit, from year to year, at the banquet which he had instituted. If so, it was perhaps covertly implied that he had cherished no hopes of bliss beyond the grave to compensate for the evils which he felt or imagined here. And if, in their bewildered conjectures as to the purpose of earthly existence, the banqueters should throw aside the veil, and cast an inquiring glance at this figure of death, as seeking thence the solution otherwise unattainable, the only reply would be a stare of the vacant eye-caverns, and a grin of the skeleton-jaws. Such was the response that the dead man had fancied himself to receive, when he asked of Death to solve the riddle of his life; and it was his desire to repeat it when the guests of his dismal hospitality should find themselves perplexed with the same question.

"What means that wreath?" asked several of the company, while viewing the decorations of the table.

They alluded to a wreath of cypress, which was held on high by a skeleton-arm, protruding from within the black mantle.

"It is a crown," said one of the stewards, "not for the worthiest, but for the wofullest, when he shall prove his claim to it."

The guest earliest bidden to the festival, was a man of soft and gentle character, who had not energy to struggle against the heavy despondency to which his temperament rendered him liable; and therefore, with nothing outwardly to excuse him from happiness, he had spent a life of quiet misery, that made his blood torpid, and weighed upon his breath, and sat like a ponderous night-fiend upon every throb of his unresisting heart. His wretchedness seemed as deep as his original nature, if not identical with it. It was the misfortune of a second guest to cherish within his bosom a diseased heart, which had become so wretchedly sore, that the continual and unavoidable rubs of the world, the blow of an enemy, the careless jostle of a stranger, and even the faithful and loving touch of a friend, alike made ulcers in it. As is the habit of people thus afflicted, he found his chief employment in exhibiting these miserable sores to any who would give themselves the pain of viewing them. A third guest was a hypochondriac, whose imagination wrought necromancy in his outward and inward world, and caused him to see monstrous faces in the household fire, and dragons in the clouds of sunset, and fiends in the guise of beautiful women, and something ugly or wicked beneath all the pleasant surfaces of nature. His neighbor at table was one who, in his early youth, had trusted mankind too much, and hoped too highly in their behalf, and, in meeting with many disappointments, had become desperately soured. For several years back, this misanthrope had employed himself in accumulating motives for hating and despising his race—such as murder, lust, treachery, ingratitude, faithlessness of trusted friends, instinctive vices of children, impurity of women, hidden guilt in men of saint-like aspect—and, in short, all manner of black realities that sought to decorate themselves with outward grace or glory. But, at every atrocious fact that was added to his catalogue—at every increase of the sad knowledge which he spent his life to collect—the native impulses of the poor man's loving and confiding heart made him groan with anguish. Next, with his heavy brow bent downward, there stole into the hall a man naturally earnest and impassioned, who, from his immemorial infancy, had felt the consciousness of a high message to the world, but, essaying to deliver it, had found either no voice or form of speech, or else no ears to listen. Therefore his whole life was a bitter questioning of himself—"Why have not men acknowledged my mission? Am I not a self-deluding fool? What business have I on earth? Where is my grave?" Throughout the festival, he quaffed frequent draughts from the sepulchral urn of wine, hoping thus to quench the celestial fire that tortured his own breast, and could not benefit his race.

Then there entered—having flung away a ticket for a ball —a gay gallant of yesterday, who had found four or five wrinkles in his brow, and more grey hairs than he could well number, on his head. Endowed with sense and feeling, he had nevertheless spent his youth in folly, but had reached at last that dreary point in life, where Folly quits us of her own accord, leaving us to make friends with Wisdom if we can. Thus, cold and desolate, he had come to seek Wisdom at the banquet, and wondered if the skeleton were she. To eke out the company, the stewards had invited a distressed poet from his home in the alms-house, and a melancholy idiot from the street corner. The latter had just the glimmering of sense that was sufficient to make him conscious of a vacancy, which the poor fellow, all his life long, had mistily sought to fill up with intelligence, wandering up and down the streets, and groaning miserably, because his attempts were ineffectual. The only lady in the hall was one who had fallen short of absolute and perfect beauty, merely by the trifling defect of a slight cast in her left eye. But this blemish, minute as it was, so shocked the pure ideal of her soul, rather than her vanity, that she passed her life in solitude, and veiled her countenance even from her own gaze. So the skeleton sat shrouded at one end of the table, and this poor lady at the other.

One other guest remains to be described. He was a young man of smooth brow, fair cheek, and fashionable mien. So far as his exterior developed him, he might much more suitably have found a place at some merry Christmas table, than have been numbered among the blighted, fate-stricken, fancy-tortured set of ill-starred banqueters. Murmurs arose among the guests, as they noted the glance of general scrutiny which the intruder threw over his companions. What had he to do among them? Why did not the skeleton of the dead founder of the feast unbend its rattling joints, arise, and motion the unwelcome stranger from the board?

"Shameful!" said the morbid man, while a new ulcer broke out in his heart. "He comes to mock us!—we shall be the jest of his tavern friends!—he will make a farce of our miseries, and bring it out upon the stage!"

"Oh, never mind him!" said the hypochondriac, smiling sourly. "He shall feast from yonder tureen of viper soup, and if there is a fricassee of scorpions on the table, pray let him have his share of it. For the dessert, he shall taste the apples of Sodom. Then, if he like our Christmas fare, let him return again next year!"

"Trouble him not," murmured the melancholy man, with gentleness. "What matters it whether the consciousness of misery come a few years sooner or later? If this youth deem himself happy now, yet let him sit with us, for the sake of the wretchedness to come."

The poor idiot approached the young man, with that mournful aspect of vacant inquiry which his face continually wore, and which caused people to say that he was always in search of his missing wits. After no little examination, he touched the stranger's hand, but immediately drew back his own, shaking his head and shivering.

"Cold, cold, cold!" muttered the idiot.

The young man shivered too—and smiled.

"Gentlemen—and you, madam,"—said one of the stewards of the festival, "do not conceive so ill, either of our caution or judgment, as to imagine that we have admitted this young stranger—Gervayse Hastings by name—without a full investigation and thoughtful balance of his claims. Trust me, not a guest at the table is better entitled to his seat."

The steward's guarantee was perforce satisfactory. The company, therefore, took their places, and addressed themselves to the serious business of the feast, but were soon disturbed by the hypochondriac, who thrust back his chair, complaining that a dish of stewed toads and vipers was set before him, and that there was green ditch-water in his cup of wine. This mistake being amended, he quietly resumed his seat. The wine, as it flowed freely from the sepulchral urn, seemed to come imbued with all gloomy inspirations; so that its influence was not to cheer, but either to sink the revellers into a deeper melancholy, or elevate their spirits to an enthusiasm of wretchedness. The conversation was various. They told sad stories about people who might have been worthy guests at such a festival as the present. They talked of grisly incidents in human history; of strange crimes, which, if truly considered, were but convulsions of agony; of some lives that had been altogether wretched, and of others, which, wearing a general semblance of happiness, had yet been deformed, sooner or later, by misfortune, as by the intrusion of a grim face at a banquet; of death-bed scenes, and what dark intimations might be gathered from the words of dying men; of suicide, and whether the more eligible mode were by halter, knife, poison, drowning, gradual starvation, or the fumes of charcoal. The majority of the guests, as is the custom with people thoroughly and profoundly sick at heart, were anxious to make their own woes the theme of discussion, and prove themselves most excellent in anguish. The misanthropist went deep into the philosophy of evil, and wandered about in the darkness, with now and then a gleam of discolored light hovering on ghastly shapes and horrid scenery. Many a miserable thought, such as men have stumbled upon from age to age, did he now rake up again, and gloat over it as an inestimable gem, a diamond, a treasure far preferable to those bright, spiritual revelations of a better world, which are like precious stones from heaven's pavement. And then, amid his lore of wretchedness, he hid his face and wept.

It was a festival at which the woful man of Uz might suitably have been a guest, together with all, in each succeeding age, who have tasted deepest of the bitterness of life. And be it said, too, that every son or daughter of woman, however favored with happy fortune, might, at one sad moment or another, have claimed the privilege of a stricken heart, to sit down at this table. But, throughout the feast, it was remarked that the young stranger, Gervayse Hastings, was unsuccessful in his attempts to catch its pervading spirit. At any deep, strong thought that found utterance, and which was torn out, as it were, from the saddest recesses of human consciousness, he looked mystified and bewildered; even more than the poor idiot, who seemed to grasp at such things with his earnest heart, and thus occasionally to comprehend them. The young man's conversation was of a colder and lighter kind, often brilliant, but lacking the powerful characteristics of a nature that had been developed by suffering.

"Sir," said the misanthropist, bluntly, in reply to some observation by Gervayse Hastings, "pray do not address me again. We have no right to talk together. Our minds have nothing in common. By what claim you appear at this banquet, I cannot guess; but methinks, to a man who could say what you have just now said, my companions and myself must seem no more than shadows, flickering on the wall. And precisely such a shadow are you to us!"

The young man smiled and bowed, but drawing himself back in his chair, he buttoned his coat over his breast, as if the banqueting-hall were growing chill. Again the idiot fixed his melancholy stare upon the youth, and murmured—"Cold! cold! cold!"

The banquet drew to its conclusion, and the guests departed. Scarcely had they stepped across the threshold of the hall, when the scene that had there passed seemed like the vision of a sick fancy, or an exhalation from a stagnant heart. Now and then, however, during the year that ensued, these melancholy people caught glimpses of one another, transient, indeed, but enough to prove that they walked the earth with the ordinary allotment of reality. Sometimes, a pair of them came face to face, while stealing through the evening twilight, enveloped in their sable cloaks. Sometimes, they casually met in church-yards. Once, also, it happened, that two of the dismal banqueters mutually started, at recognizing each other in the noon-day sunshine of a crowded street, stalking there like ghosts astray. Doubtless, they wondered why the skeleton did not come abroad at noonday, too!

But, whenever the necessity of their affairs compelled these Christmas guests into the bustling world, they were sure to encounter the young man, who had so unaccountably been admitted to the festival. They saw him among the gay and fortunate; they caught the sunny sparkle of his eye; they heard the light and careless tones of his voice—and muttered to themselves, with such indignation as only the aristocracy of wretchedness could kindle:—"The traitor! The vile impostor! Providence, in its own good time, may give him a right to feast among us!" But the young man's unabashed eye dwelt upon their gloomy figures, as they passed him, seeming to say, perchance with somewhat of a sneer—"First, know my secret!—then, measure your claims with mine!"

The step of Time stole onward, and soon brought merry Christmas round again, with glad and solemn worship in the churches, and sports, games, festivals, and everywhere the bright face of Joy beside the household fire. Again, likewise, the hall, with its curtains of dusky purple, was illuminated by the death-torches, gleaming on the sepulchral decorations of the banquet. The veiled skeleton sat in state, lifting the cypress wreath above its head, as the guerdon of some guest, illustrious in the qualifications which there claimed precedence. As the stewards deemed the world inexhaustible in misery, and were desirous of recognizing it in all its forms, they had not seen fit to re-assemble the company of the former year. New faces now threw their gloom across the table.

There was a man of nice conscience, who bore a bloodstain in his heart—the death of a fellow-creature—which, for his more exquisite torture, had chanced with such a peculiarity of circumstances, that he could not absolutely determine whether his will had entered into the deed, or not. Therefore, his whole life was spent in the agony of an inward trial for murder, with a continual sifting of the details of his terrible calamity, until his mind had no longer any thought, nor his soul any emotion, disconnected with it. There was a mother, too—a mother once, but a desolation now—who, many years before, had gone out on a pleasure-party, and, returning, found her infant smothered in its little bed. And ever since she had been tortured with the fantasy, that her buried baby lay smothering in its coffin. Then there was an aged lady, who had lived from time immemorial with a constant tremor quivering through her frame. It was terrible to discern her dark shadow tremulous upon the wall; her lips, likewise, were tremulous; and the expression of her eyes seemed to indicate that her soul was trembling too. Owing to the bewilderment and confusion which made almost a chaos of her intellect, it was impossible to discover what dire misfortune had thus shaken her nature to its depths; so that the stewards had admitted her to the table, not from any acquaintance with her history, but on the safe testimony of her miserable aspect. Some surprise was expressed at the presence of a bluff, red-faced gentleman, a certain Mr. Smith, who had evidently the fat of many a rich feast within him, and the habitual twinkle of whose eye betrayed a disposition to break forth into uproarious laughter, for little cause or none. It turned out, however, that, with the best possible flow of spirits, our poor friend was afflicted with a physical disease of the heart, which threatened instant death on the slightest cachinnatory indulgence, or even that titillation of the bodily frame, produced by merry thoughts. In this dilemma, he had sought admittance to the banquet, on the ostensible plea of his irksome and miserable state, but, in reality, with the hope of imbibing a life-preserving melancholy.

A married couple had been invited, from a motive of bitter humor; it being well understood, that they rendered each other unutterably miserable whenever they chanced to meet, and therefore must necessarily be fit associates at the festival. In contrast with these, was another couple, still unmarried, who had interchanged their hearts in early life, but had been divided by circumstances as impalpable as morning mist, and kept apart so long, that their spirits now found it impossible to meet. Therefore, yearning for communion, yet shrinking from one another, and choosing none beside, they felt themselves companionless in life, and looked upon eternity as a boundless desert. Next to the skeleton sat a mere son of earth —a haunter of the Exchange—a gatherer of shining dust—a man whose life's record was in his leger, and whose soul's prison-house, the vaults of the bank where he kept his deposits. This person had been greatly perplexed at his invitation, deeming himself one of the most fortunate men in the city; but the stewards persisted in demanding his presence, assuring him that he had no conception how miserable he was.

And now appeared a figure, which we must acknowledge as our acquaintance of the former festival. It was Gervayse

Hastings, whose presence had then caused so much question and criticism, and who now took his place with the composure of one whose claims were satisfactory to himself, and must needs be allowed by others. Yet his easy and unruffled face betrayed no sorrow. The well-skilled beholders gazed a moment into his eyes, and shook their heads, to miss the unuttered sympathy—the countersign, never to be falsified—of those whose hearts are cavern-mouths, through which they descend into a region of illimitable wo, and recognize other wanderers there.

"Who is this youth?" asked the man with a blood-stain on his conscience. "Surely he has never gone down into the depths! I know all the aspects of those who have passed through the dark valley. By what right is he among us?"

"Ah, it is a sinful thing to come hither without a sorrow," murmured the aged lady, in accents that partook of the eternal tremor which pervaded her whole being. "Depart, young man! Your soul has never been shaken; and therefore I tremble so much the more to look at you."

"His soul shaken! No; I'll answer for it," said bluff Mr. Smith, pressing his hand upon his heart, and making himself as melancholy as he could, for fear of a fatal explosion of laughter. "I know the lad well; he has as fair prospects as any young man about town, and has no more right among us, miserable creatures, than the child unborn. He never was miserable, and probably never will be!"

"Our honored guests," interposed the stewards, "pray have patience with us, and believe, at least, that our deep veneration for the sacredness of this solemnity would preclude any wilful violation of it. Receive this young man to your table. It may not be too much to say, that no guest here would exchange his own heart for the one that beats within that youthful bosom!"

"I'd call it a bargain, and gladly too," muttered Mr. Smith, with a perplexing mixture of sadness and mirthful conceit. "A plague upon their nonsense! My own heart is the only really miserable one in the company—it will certainly be the death of me at last!"

Nevertheless, as on the former occasion, the judgment of the stewards being without appeal, the company sat down. The obnoxious guest made no more attempt to obtrude his conversation on those about him, but appeared to listen to the table-talk with peculiar assiduity, as if some inestimable secret, otherwise beyond his reach, might be conveyed in a casual word. And, in truth, to those who could understand and value it, there was rich matter in the upgushings and outpourings of these initiated souls, to whom sorrow had been a talisman, admitting them into spiritual depths which no other spell can open. Sometimes, out of the midst of densest gloom, there flashed a momentary radiance, pure as crystal, bright as the flame of stars, and shedding such a glow upon the mystery of life, that the guests were ready to exclaim, "Surely the riddle is on the point of being solved!" At such illuminated intervals, the saddest mourners felt it to be revealed, that mortal griefs are but shadowy and external; no more than the sable robes, voluminously shrouding a certain divine reality, and thus indicating what might otherwise be altogether invisible to mortal eye.

"Just now," remarked the trembling old woman, "I seemed to see beyond the outside. And then my everlasting tremor passed away!"

"Would that I could dwell always in these momentary gleams of light!" said the man of stricken conscience. "Then the blood-stain in my heart would be washed clean away."

This strain of conversation appeared so unintelligibly absurd to good Mr. Smith, that he burst into precisely the fit of laughter which his physicians had warned him against, as likely to prove instantaneously fatal. In effect, he fell back in his chair, a corpse with a broad grin upon his face; while his ghost, perchance, remained beside it, bewildered at its unpremeditated exit. This catastrophe, of course, broke up the festival.

"How is this? You do not tremble?" observed the tremulous old woman to Gervayse Hastings, who was gazing at the dead man with singular intentness. "Is it not awful to see him so suddenly vanish out of the midst of life—this man of flesh and blood, whose earthly nature was so warm and strong? There is a never-ending tremor in my soul; but it trembles afresh at this! And you are calm!"

"Would that he could teach me somewhat!" said Gervayse Hastings, drawing a long breath. "Men pass before me like shadows on the wall—their actions, passions, feelings, are flickerings of the light—and then they vanish! Neither the corpse, nor yonder skeleton, nor this old woman's everlasting tremor, can give me what I seek."

And then the company departed.

We cannot linger to narrate, in such detail, more circumstances of these singular festivals, which, in accordance with the founder's will, continued to be kept with the regularity of an established institution. In process of time, the stewards adopted the custom of inviting, from far and near, those individuals whose misfortunes were prominent above other men's, and whose mental and moral development might, therefore, be supposed to possess a corresponding interest. The exiled noble of the French Revolution, and the broken soldier of the Empire, were alike represented at the table. Fallen monarchs, wandering about the earth, have found places at that forlorn and miserable feast. The statesman, when his party flung him off, might, if he chose it, be once more a great man for the space of a single banquet. Aaron Burr's name appears on the record, at a period when his ruin—the profoundest and most striking, with more of moral circumstance in it than that of almost any other man—was complete, in his lonely age. Stephen Girard, when his wealth weighed upon him like a mountain, once sought admittance of his own accord. It is not probable, however, that these men had any lessons to teach in the lore of discontent and misery, which might not equally well have been studied in the common walks of life. Illustrious unfortunates attract a wider sympathy, not because their griefs are more intense, but because, being set on lofty pedestals, they the better serve mankind as instances and by-words of calamity.

It concerns our present purpose to say that, at each successive festival, Gervayse Hastings showed his face, gradually changing from the smooth beauty of his youth to the thoughtful comeliness of manhood, and thence to the bald, impressive dignity of age. He was the only individual invariably present. Yet, on every occasion, there were murmurs, both from those who knew his character and position, and from them whose hearts shrank back, as denying his companionship in their mystic fraternity.

"Who is this impassive man?" had been asked a hundred times. "Has he suffered? Has he sinned? There are no traces of either. Then wherefore is he here?"

"You must inquire of the stewards, or of himself," was the constant reply. "We seem to know him well, here in our city, and know nothing of him but what is creditable and fortunate. Yet hither he comes, year after year, to this gloomy banquet, and sits among the guests like a marble statue. Ask yonder skeleton—perhaps that may solve the riddle!"

It was, in truth, a wonder. The life of Gervayse Hastings was not merely a prosperous, but a brilliant one. Everything had gone well with him. He was wealthy, far beyond the expenditure that was required by habits of magnificence, a taste of rare purity and cultivation, a love of travel, a scholar's instinct to collect a splendid library, and, moreover, what seemed a munificent liberality to the distressed. He had sought domestic happiness, and not vainly, if a lovely and tender wife, and children of fair promise, could insure it. He had, besides, ascended above the limit which separates the obscure from the distinguished, and had won a stainless reputation in affairs of the widest public importance. Not that he was a popular character, or had within him the mysterious attributes which are essential to that species of success. To the public, he was a cold abstraction, wholly destitute of those rich hues of personality, that living warmth, and the peculiar faculty of stamping his own heart's impression on a multitude of hearts, by which the people recognize their favorites. And it must be owned that, after his most intimate associates had done their best to know him thoroughly, and love him warmly, they were startled to find how little hold he had upon their affections. They approved—they admired—but still, in those moments when the human spirit most craves reality, they shrank back from Gervayse Hastings, as powerless to give them what they sought. It was the feeling of distrustful regret, with which we should draw back the hand, after extending it, in an illusive twilight, to grasp the hand of a shadow upon the wall.

As the superficial fervency of youth decayed, this peculiar effect of Gervayse Hastings' character grew more perceptible. His children, when he extended his arms, came coldly to his knees, but never climbed them of their own accord. His wife wept secretly, and almost adjudged herself a criminal, because she shivered in the chill of his bosom. He, too, occasionally appeared not unconscious of the chillness of his moral atmosphere, and willing, if it might be so, to warm himself at a kindly fire. But age stole onward, and benumbed him more and more. As the hoar-frost began to gather on him, his wife went to her grave, and was doubtless warmer there;

his children either died, or were scattered to different homes of their own; and old Gervayse Hastings, unscathed by grief—alone, but needing no companionship—continued his steady walk through life, and still, on every Christmas-day, attended at the dismal banquet. His privilege as a guest had become prescriptive now. Had he claimed the head of the table, even the skeleton would have been ejected from its seat.

Finally, at the merry Christmas-tide, when he had numbered four-score years complete, this pale, high-browed, marble-featured old man once more entered the long-frequented hall, with the same impassive aspect that had called forth so much dissatisfied remark at his first attendance. Time, except in matters merely external, had done nothing for him, either of good or evil. As he took his place, he threw a calm, inquiring glance around the table, as if to ascertain whether any guest had yet appeared, after so many unsuccessful banquets, who might impart to him the mystery—the deep, warm secret—the life within the life—which, whether manifested in joy or sorrow, is what gives substance to a world of shadows.

"My friends," said Gervayse Hastings, assuming a position which his long conversance with the festival caused to appear natural, "you are welcome! I drink to you all in this cup of sepulchral wine."

The guests replied courteously, but still in a manner that proved them unable to receive the old man as a member of their sad fraternity. It may be well to give the reader an idea of the present company at the banquet.

One was formerly a clergyman, enthusiastic in his profession, and apparently of the genuine dynasty of those old Puritan divines whose faith in their calling, and stern exercise of it, had placed them among the mighty of the earth. But, yielding to the speculative tendency of the age, he had gone astray from the firm foundation of an ancient faith, and wandered into a cloud region, where everything was misty and deceptive, ever mocking him with a semblance of reality, but still dissolving when he flung himself upon it for support and rest. His instinct and early training demanded something steadfast; but, looking forward, he beheld vapors piled on vapors, and, behind him, an impassable gulf between the man of yesterday and to-day; on the borders of which he paced to and fro, sometimes wringing his hands in agony, and often making his own wo a theme of scornful merriment. This, surely, was a miserable man. Next, there was a theorist —one of a numerous tribe, although he deemed himself unique since the creation—a theorist, who had conceived a plan by which all the wretchedness of earth, moral and physical, might be done away, and the bliss of the millennium at once accomplished. But, the incredulity of mankind debarring him from action, he was smitten with as much grief as if the whole mass of wo which he was denied the opportunity to remedy, were crowded into his own bosom. A plain old man in black attracted much of the company's notice, on the supposition that he was no other than Father Miller, who, it seemed, had given himself up to despair at the tedious delay of the final conflagration. Then there was a man distinguished for native pride and obstinacy, who, a little while before, had possessed immense wealth, and held the control of a vast moneyed interest, which he had wielded in the same spirit as a despotic monarch would wield the power of his empire, carrying on a tremendous moral warfare, the roar and tremor of which was felt at every fireside in the land. At length came a crushing ruin—a total overthrow of fortune, power, and character—the effect of which on his imperious, and, in many respects, noble and lofty nature, might have entitled him to a place, not merely at our festival, but among the peers of Pandemonium.

There was a modern philanthropist, who had become so deeply sensible of the calamities of thousands and millions of his fellow creatures, and of the impracticableness of any general measures for their relief, that he had no heart to do what little good lay immediately within his power, but contented himself with being miserable for sympathy. Near him sat a gentleman in a predicament hitherto unprecedented, but of which the present epoch, probably, affords numerous examples. Ever since he was of capacity to read a newspaper, this person had prided himself on his consistent adherence to one political party, but, in the confusion of these latter days, had got bewildered, and knew not whereabouts his party was. This wretched condition, so morally desolate and disheartening to a man who has long accustomed himself to merge his individuality in the mass of a great body, can only be conceived by such as have experienced it. His next companion was a popular orator who had lost his voice, and—as it was pretty much all that he had to lose—had fallen into a state of hopeless melancholy. The table was likewise graced by two of the gentler sex—one, a half-starved, consumptive seamstress, the representative of thousands just as wretched; the other, a woman of unemployed energy, who found herself in the world with nothing to achieve, nothing to enjoy, and nothing even to suffer. She had, therefore, driven herself to the verge of madness by dark broodings over the wrongs of her sex, and its exclusion from a proper field of action. The roll of guests being thus complete, a side-table had been set for three or four disappointed office-seekers, with hearts as sick as death, whom the stewards had admitted, partly because their calamites really entitled them to entrance here, and partly that they were in especial need of a good dinner. There was likewise a homeless dog, with his tail between his legs, licking up the crumbs and gnawing the fragments of the feast—such a melancholy cur as one sometimes sees about the streets, without a master, and willing to follow the first that will accept his service.

In their own way, these were as wretched a set of people as ever had assembled at the festival. There they sat, with the veiled skeleton of the founder, holding aloft the cypress wreath, at one end of the table; and at the other, wrapt in furs, the withered figure of Gervayse Hastings, stately, calm, and cold, impressing the company with awe, yet so little interesting their sympathy, that he might have vanished into thin air, without their once exclaiming—"Whither is he gone?"

"Sir," said the philanthropist, addressing the old man, "you have been so long a guest at this annual festival, and have thus been conversant with so many varieties of human affliction, that, not improbably, you have thence derived some great and important lessons. How blessed were your lot, could you reveal a secret by which all this mass of wo might be removed!"

"I know of but one misfortune," answered Gervayse Hastings, quietly, "and that is my own."

"Your own!" rejoined the philanthropist. "And, looking back on your serene and prosperous life, how can you claim to be the sole unfortunate of the human race?"

"You will not understand it," replied Gervayse Hastings, feebly, and with a singular inefficiency of pronunciation, and sometimes putting one word for another. "None have understood it—not even those who experience the like. It is a chillness—a want of earnestness—a feeling as if what should be my heart were a thing of vapor—a haunting perception of unreality! Thus, seeming to possess all that other men have— all that men aim at—I have really possessed nothing, neither joys nor griefs. All things—all persons—as was truly said to me at this table long and long ago—have been like shadows flickering on the wall. It was so with my wife and children—

with those who seemed my friends: it is so with yourselves, whom I see now before me. Neither have I myself any real existence, but am a shadow like the rest!"

"And how is it with your views of a future life?" inquired the speculative clergyman.

"Worse than with you," said the old man, in a hollow and feeble tone; "for I cannot conceive it earnestly enough to feel either hope or fear. Mine—mine is the wretchedness! This cold heart—this unreal life! Ah! it grows colder still."

It so chanced, that at this juncture the decayed ligaments of the skeleton gave way, and the dry bones fell together in a heap, thus causing the dusty wreath of cypress to drop upon the table. The attention of the company being thus diverted, for a single instant, from Gervayse Hastings, they perceived, on turning again towards him, that the old man had undergone a change. His shadow had ceased to flicker on the wall.

"Well, Rosina, what is your criticism?" asked Roderick, as he rolled up the manuscript.

"Frankly, your success is by no means complete," replied she. "It is true, I have an idea of the character you endeavor to describe; but it is rather by dint of my own thought than your expression."

"That is unavoidable," observed the sculptor, "because the characteristics are all negative. If Gervayse Hastings could have imbibed one human grief at the gloomy banquet, the task of describing him would have been infinitely easier. Of such persons—and we do meet with these moral monsters now and then—it is difficult to conceive how they came to exist here, or what there is in them capable of existence hereafter. They seem to be on the outside of everything; and nothing wearies the soul more than an attempt to comprehend them within its grasp."

DROWNE'S WOODEN IMAGE

O NE SUNSHINY morning, in the good old times
of the town of Boston, a young carver in wood,
well known by the name of Drowne, stood contemplating a large oaken log, which it was his purpose to
convert into the figure-head of a vessel. And while he discussed within his own mind what sort of shape or similitude
it were well to bestow upon this excellent piece of timber, there came into Drowne's workshop a certain Captain
Hunnewell, owner and commander of the good brig called
the Cynosure, which had just returned from her first voyage
to Fayal.

"Ah! that will do, Drowne, that will do!" cried the jolly
captain, tapping the log with his rattan. "I bespeak this very
piece of oak for the figure-head of the Cynosure. She has
shown herself the sweetest craft that ever floated, and I
mean to decorate her prow with the handsomest image that
the skill of man can cut out of timber. And, Drowne, you are
the fellow to execute it."

"You give me more credit than I deserve, Captain Hunnewell," said the carver, modestly, yet as one conscious of eminence in his art. "But, for the sake of the good brig, I stand

ready to do my best. And which of these designs would you prefer? Here—" pointing to a staring, half length figure, in a white wig and scarlet coat—"here is an excellent model, the likeness of our gracious king. Here is the valiant Admiral Vernon. Or, if you prefer a female figure, what say you to Britannia with the trident?"

"All very fine, Drowne; all very fine," answered the mariner. "But as nothing like the brig ever swam the ocean, so I am determined she shall have such a figure-head as old Neptune never saw in his life. And what is more, as there is a secret in the matter, you must pledge your credit not to betray it."

"Certainly," said Drowne, marvelling, however, what possible mystery there could be in reference to an affair so open, of necessity, to the inspection of all the world, as the figure-head of a vessel. "You may depend, captain, on my being as secret as the nature of the case will permit."

Captain Hunnewell then took Drowne by the button, and communicated his wishes in so low a tone, that it would be unmannerly to repeat what was evidently intended for the carver's private ear. We shall, therefore, take the opportunity to give the reader a few desirable particulars about Drowne himself.

He was the first American who is known to have attempted, —in a very humble line, it is true,—that art in which we can now reckon so many names already distinguished, or rising to distinction. From his earliest boyhood, he had exhibited a knack—for it would be too proud a word to call it genius— a knack, therefore, for the imitation of the human figure, in whatever material came most readily to hand. The snows of a New England winter had often supplied him with a species of marble as dazzling white, at least, as the Parian or the Carrara, and if less durable, yet sufficiently so to correspond with any claims to permanent existence possessed by the boy's frozen statues. Yet they won admiration from maturer judges than his schoolfellows, and were, indeed, remarkably clever, though destitute of the native warmth that might have made the snow melt beneath his hand. As he advanced in life, the young man adopted pine and oak as eligible materials for the display of his skill, which now began to bring him a return of solid silver, as well as the empty praise that had been an apt reward enough for his productions of evanescent snow. He became noted for carving ornamental pump-heads, and wooden urns for gate-posts, and decorations, more grotesque than fanciful, for mantel-pieces. No apothecary would have deemed himself in the way of obtaining custom, without setting up a gilded mortar, if not a head of Galen or Hippocrates, from the skilful hand of Drowne. But the great scope of his business lay in the manufacture of figure-heads for vessels. Whether it were the monarch himself, or some famous British admiral or general, or the governor of the province, or perchance the favourite daughter of the ship-owner, there the image stood above the prow, decked out in gorgeous colours, magnificently gilded, and staring the whole world out of countenance, as if from an innate consciousness of its own superiority. These specimens of native sculpture had crossed the sea in all directions, and been not ignobly noticed among the crowded shipping of the Thames, and wherever else the hardy mariners of New England had pushed their adventures. It must be confessed, that a family likeness pervaded these respectable progeny of Drowne's skill —that the benign countenance of the king resembled those of his subjects, and that Miss Peggy Hobart, the merchant's daughter, bore a remarkable similitude to Britannia, Victory, and other ladies of the allegoric sisterhood; and, finally, that they had all had a kind of wooden aspect, which proved an intimate relationship with the unshaped blocks of timber in the carver's workshop. But, at least, there was no inconsiderable skill of hand, nor a deficiency of any attribute to render them really works of art, except that deep quality, be it of soul or intellect, which bestows life upon the lifeless, and warmth upon the cold, and which, had it been present, would have made Drowne's wooden image instinct with spirit.

The captain of the Cynosure had now finished his instructions.

"And Drowne," said he, impressively, "you must lay aside all other business, and set about this forthwith. And as to the price, only do the job in first rate style, and you shall settle that point yourself."

"Very well, captain," answered the carver, who looked grave and somewhat perplexed, yet had a sort of smile upon his visage. "Depend upon it, I'll do my utmost to satisfy you."

From that morning, the men of taste about Long Wharf and the Town Dock, who were wont to show their love for the arts by frequent visits to Drowne's workshop, and admiration of his wooden images, began to be sensible of a mystery in the carver's conduct. Often he was absent in the daytime. Sometimes, as might be judged by gleams of light from the shop windows, he was at work until a late hour of the evening; although neither knock nor voice, on such occasions, could gain admittance for a visitor, or elicit any word of response. Nothing remarkable, however, was observed in the shop at those hours when it was thrown open. A fine piece of timber, indeed, which Drowne was known to have reserved for some work of especial dignity, was seen to be gradually assuming shape. What shape it was destined ultimately to take, was a problem to his friends, and a point on which the carver preserved a rigid silence. But day after day, though Drowne was seldom noticed in the act of working upon it, this rude form began to be developed, until it became evident to all observers, that a female figure was growing into mimic life. At each new visit they beheld a larger pile of wooden chips, and a nearer approximation to something beautiful. It seemed as if the hamadryad of the oak had sheltered herself from the unimaginative world within the heart of her native tree, and that it was only necessary to remove the strange shapelessness that had incrusted her, and reveal the grace and loveliness of a divinity. Imperfect as the design, the attitude, the costume, and especially the face of the image, still remained, there was already an effect that drew the eye from the wooden cleverness of Drowne's earlier productions, and fixed it upon the tantalizing mystery of this new project.

Copley, the celebrated painter, then a young man, and a resident of Boston, came one day to visit Drowne; for he had recognized so much of moderate ability in the carver, as to induce him, in the dearth of any professional sympathy, to cultivate his acquaintance. On entering the shop, the artist glanced at the inflexible images of king, commander, dame, and allegory, that stood around; on the best of which might have been bestowed the questionable praise, that it looked as if a living man had here been changed to wood, and that not only the physical, but the intellectual and spiritual part, partook of the stolid transformation. But in not a single instance did it seem as if the wood were imbibing the ethereal essence of humanity. What a wide distinction is here, and how far would the slightest portion of the latter merit have outvalued the utmost degree of the former!

"My friend Drowne," said Copley, smiling to himself, but alluding to the mechanical and wooden cleverness that so invariably distinguished the images, "you are really a remarkable person! I have seldom met with a man, in your line of business, that could do so much; for one other touch might make this figure of General Wolfe, for instance, a breathing and intelligent human creature."

"You would have me think that you are praising me highly, Mr. Copley," answered Drowne, turning his back upon Wolfe's image in apparent disgust. "But there has come a light into my mind. I know, what you know as well, that the one touch, which you speak of as deficient, is the only one that would be truly valuable, and that, without it, these works of mine are no better than worthless abortions. There is the same difference between them and the works of an inspired artist, as between a sign post daub and one of your best pictures."

"This is strange!" cried Copley, looking him in the face, which now, as the painter fancied, had a singular depth of intelligence, though, hitherto, it had not given him greatly the advantage over his own family of wooden images. "What has come over you? How is it that, possessing the idea which you have now uttered, you should produce only such works as these?"

The carver smiled, but made no reply. Copley turned again to the images, conceiving that the sense of deficiency which Drowne had just expressed, and which is so rare in a merely mechanical character, must surely imply a genius, the tokens of which had heretofore been overlooked. But no; there was not a trace of it. He was about to withdraw, when his eyes chanced to fall upon a half-developed figure which lay in a corner of the workshop, surrounded by scattered chips of oak. It arrested him at once.

"What is here? Who has done this?" he broke out, after contemplating it in speechless astonishment for an instant. "Here is the divine, the life-giving touch! What inspired hand is beckoning this wood to arise and live? Whose work is this?"

"No man's work," replied Drowne. "The figure lies within that block of oak, and it is my business to find it."

"Drowne," said the true artist, grasping the carver fervently by the hand, "you are a man of genius!"

As Copley departed, happening to glance backward from the threshold, he beheld Drowne bending over the half created shape, and stretching forth his arms as if he would have embraced and drawn it to his heart; while, had such a miracle been possible, his countenance expressed passion enough to communicate warmth and sensibility to the lifeless oak.

"Strange enough!" said the artist to himself. "Who would have looked for a modern Pygmalion in the person of a Yankee mechanic!"

As yet, the image was but vague in its outward presentment; so that, as in the cloud-shapes around the western sun, the observer rather felt, or was led to imagine, than really saw what was intended by it. Day by day, however, the work assumed greater precision, and settled its irregular and misty outline into distincter grace and beauty. The general design was now obvious to the common eye. It was a female figure, in what appeared to be a foreign dress; the gown being laced over the bosom, and opening in front, so as to disclose a skirt or petticoat, the folds and inequalities of which were admirably represented in the oaken substance. She wore a hat of singular gracefulness, and abundantly laden with flowers, such as never grew in the rude soil of New England, but which, with all their fanciful luxuriance, had a natural truth that it seemed impossible for the most fertile imagination to have attained without copying from real prototypes. There were several little appendages to this dress, such as a fan, a pair of ear-rings, a chain about the neck, a watch in the bosom, and a ring upon the finger, all of which would have been deemed beneath the dignity of sculpture. They were put on, however, with as much taste as a lovely woman might have shown in her attire, and could therefore have shocked none but a judgment spoiled by artistic rules.

The face was still imperfect; but, gradually, by a magic touch, intelligence and sensibility brightened through the features, with all the effect of light gleaming forth from

within the solid oak. The face became alive. It was a beautiful, though not precisely regular, and somewhat haughty
aspect, but with a certain piquancy about the eyes and mouth
which, of all expressions, would have seemed the most impossible to throw over a wooden countenance. And now, so
far as carving went, this wonderful production was complete.

"Drowne," said Copley, who had hardly missed a single day
in his visits to the carver's workshop, "if this work were in
marble, it would make you famous at once; nay, I would
almost affirm that it would make an era in the art. It is as
ideal as an antique statue, and yet as real as any lovely
woman whom one meets at a fireside or in the street. But I
trust you do not mean to desecrate this exquisite creature
with paint, like those staring kings and admirals yonder?"

"Not paint her?" exclaimed Captain Hunnewell, who stood
by;—"not paint the figure-head of the Cynosure! And what
sort of a figure should I cut in a foreign port, with such an
unpainted oaken stick as this over my prow? She must, and
she shall, be painted to the life, from the topmost flower in
her hat down to the silver spangles on her slippers."

"Mr. Copley," said Drowne, quietly, "I know nothing of
marble statuary, and nothing of a sculptor's rules of art. But
of this wooden image—this work of my hands—this creature
of my heart—" and here his voice faltered and choked, in a
very singular manner—"of this—of her—I may say that I
know something. A well-spring of inward wisdom gushed
within me, as I wrought upon the oak with my whole
strength, and soul, and faith! Let others do what they may
with marble, and adopt what rules they choose. If I can
produce my desired effect by painted wood, those rules are
not for me, and I have a right to disregard them."

"The very spirit of genius!" muttered Copley to himself.
"How otherwise should this carver feel himself entitled to
transcend all rules, and make me ashamed of quoting them."

He looked earnestly at Drowne, and again saw that expression of human love which, in a spiritual sense, as the artist could not help imagining, was the secret of the life that had been breathed into this block of wood.

The carver, still in the same secrecy that marked all his operations upon this mysterious image, proceeded to paint the habiliments in their proper colours, and the countenance with nature's red and white. When all was finished, he threw open his workshop, and admitted the townspeople to behold what he had done. Most persons, at their first entrance, felt impelled to remove their hats, and pay such reverence as was due to the richly dressed and beautiful young lady, who seemed to stand in a corner of the room, with oaken chips and shavings scattered at her feet. Then came a sensation of fear; as if, not being actually human, yet so like humanity, she must therefore be something preternatural. There was, in truth, an indefinable air and expression that might reasonably induce the query—who and from what sphere this daughter of the oak should be. The strange rich flowers of Eden on her head; the complexion, so much deeper and more brilliant than those of our native beauties; the foreign, as it seemed, and fantastic garb, yet not too fantastic to be worn decorously in the street; the delicately wrought embroidery of the skirt; the broad gold chain about her neck; the curious ring upon her finger; the fan, so exquisitely sculptured in open work, and painted to resemble pearl and ebony;—where could Drowne, in his sober walk of life, have beheld the vision here so matchlessly embodied! And then her face! In the dark eyes, and around the voluptuous mouth, there played a look made up of pride, coquetry, and a gleam of mirthfulness, which impressed Copley with the idea that the image was secretly enjoying the perplexed admiration of himself and all other beholders.

"And will you," said he to the carver, "permit this masterpiece to become the figure-head of a vessel? Give the honest captain yonder figure of Britannia—it will answer his purpose far better,—and send this fairy queen to England, where, for aught I know, it may bring you a thousand pounds."

"I have not wrought it for money," said Drowne.

"What sort of a fellow is this!" thought Copley. "A Yankee, and throw away the chance of making his fortune! He has gone mad; and thence has come this gleam of genius."

There was still further proof of Drowne's lunacy, if credit were due to the rumour that he had been seen kneeling at the feet of the oaken lady, and gazing with a lover's passionate ardour into the face that his own hands had created. The bigots of the day hinted that it would be no matter of surprise if an evil spirit were allowed to enter this beautiful form, and seduce the carver to destruction.

The fame of the image spread far and wide. The inhabitants visited it so universally, that, after a few days of exhibition, there was hardly an old man or a child who had not become minutely familiar with its aspect. Even had the story of Drowne's wooden image ended here, its celebrity might have been prolonged for many years, by the reminiscences of those who looked upon it in their childhood, and saw nothing else so beautiful in after life. But the town was now astounded by an event, the narrative of which has formed itself into one of the most singular legends that are yet to be met with in the traditionary chimney-corners of the New England metropolis, where old men and women sit dreaming of the past, and wag their heads at the dreamers of the present and the future.

One fine morning, just before the departure of the Cynosure on her second voyage to Fayal, the commander of that gallant vessel was seen to issue from his residence in Hanover street. He was stylishly dressed in a blue broadcloth coat, with gold lace at the seams and button-holes, an embroidered scarlet waistcoat, a triangular hat, with a loop and broad binding of gold, and wore a silver-hilted hanger at his side.

But the good captain might have been arrayed in the robes of a prince or the rags of a beggar, without in either case attracting notice, while obscured by such a companion as now leaned on his arm. The people in the street started, rubbed their eyes, and either leaped aside from their path, or stood as if transfixed to wood or marble in astonishment.

"Do you see it?—do you see it?" cried one, with tremulous eagerness. "It is the very same!"

"The same?" answered another, who had arrived in town only the night before. "What do you mean? I see only a sea-captain in his shore-going clothes, and a young lady in a foreign habit, with a bunch of beautiful flowers in her hat. On my word, she is as fair and bright a damsel as my eyes have looked on this many a day!"

"Yes; the same!—the very same!" repeated the other. "Drowne's wooden image has come to life!"

Here was a miracle indeed! Yet, illuminated by the sunshine, or darkened by the alternate shade of the houses, and with its garments fluttering lightly in the morning breeze, there passed the image along the street. It was exactly and minutely the shape, the garb, and the face, which the towns-people had so recently thronged to see and admire. Not a rich flower upon her head, not a single leaf, but had had its prototype in Drowne's wooden workmanship, although now their fragile grace had become flexible, and was shaken by every footstep that the wearer made. The broad gold chain upon the neck was identical with the one represented on the image, and glistened with the motion imparted by the rise and fall of the bosom which it decorated. A real diamond sparkled on her finger. In her right hand she bore a pearl and ebony fan, which she flourished with a fantastic and bewitching coquetry, that was likewise expressed in all her movements, as well as in the style of her beauty and the attire that so well harmonized with it. The face, with its brilliant depth of complexion, had the same piquancy of mirthful mischief that was fixed upon the countenance of the image, but which was here varied and continually shifting, yet always essentially the same, like the sunny gleam upon a bubbling fountain. On the whole, there was something so airy and yet so real in the figure, and withal so perfectly did it represent Drowne's image, that people knew not whether to suppose the magic wood etherealized into a spirit, or warmed and softened into an actual woman.

"One thing is certain," muttered a Puritan of the old stamp. "Drowne has sold himself to the devil; and doubtless this gay Captain Hunnewell is a party to the bargain."

"And I," said a young man who overheard him, "would almost consent to be the third victim, for the liberty of saluting those lovely lips."

"And so would I," said Copley, the painter, "for the privilege of taking her picture."

The image, or the apparition, whichever it might be, still escorted by the bold captain, proceeded from Hanover street through some of the cross-lanes that make this portion of the town so intricate, to Ann street, thence into Dock-square, and so downward to Drowne's shop, which stood just on the water's edge. The crowd still followed, gathering volume as it rolled along. Never had a modern miracle occurred in such broad daylight, nor in the presence of such a multitude of witnesses. The airy image, as if conscious that she was the object of the murmurs and disturbance that swelled behind her, appeared slightly vexed and flustered, yet still in a manner consistent with the light vivacity and sportive mischief that were written in her countenance. She was observed to flutter her fan with such vehement rapidity, that the elaborate delicacy of its workmanship gave way, and it remained broken in her hand.

Arriving at Drowne's door, while the captain threw it open, the marvellous apparition paused an instant on the threshold, assuming the very attitude of the image, and casting over the crowd that glance of sunny coquetry which all remembered on the face of the oaken lady. She and her cavalier then disappeared.

"Ah!" murmured the crowd, drawing a deep breath, as with one vast pair of lungs.

"The world looks darker, now that she has vanished," said some of the young men.

But the aged, whose recollections dated as far back as witch-times, shook their heads, and hinted that our forefathers would have thought it a pious deed to burn the daughter of the oak with fire.

"If she be other than a bubble of the elements," exclaimed Copley, "I must look upon her face again!"

He accordingly entered the shop; and there, in her usual corner, stood the image, gazing at him, as it might seem, with the very same expression of mirthful mischief that had been the farewell look of the apparition when, but a moment before, she turned her face towards the crowd. The carver stood beside his creation, mending the beautiful fan, which by some accident was broken in her hand. But there was no longer any motion in the life-like image, nor any real woman in the workshop, nor even the witchcraft of a sunny shadow, that might have deluded people's eyes as it flitted along the street. Captain Hunnewell, too, had vanished. His hoarse, sea-breezy tones, however, were audible on the other side of a door that opened upon the water.

"Sit down in the stern sheets, my lady," said the gallant captain. "Come, bear a hand, you lubbers, and set us on board in the turning of a minute-glass."

And then was heard the stroke of oars.

"Drowne," said Copely, with a smile of intelligence, "you have been a truly fortunate man. What painter or statuary ever had such a subject! No wonder that she inspired a genius into you, and first created the artist who afterwards created her image."

Drowne looked at him with a visage that bore the traces of tears, but from which the light of imagination and sensibility, so recently illuminating it, had departed. He was again the mechanical carver that he had been known to be all his lifetime.

"I hardly understand what you mean, Mr. Copley," said he, putting his hand to his brow. "This image! Can it have been my work? Well—I have wrought it in a kind of dream; and now that I am broad awake, I must set about finishing yonder figure of Admiral Vernon."

And forthwith he employed himself on the stolid countenance of one of his wooden progeny, and completed it in his own mechanical style, from which he was never known afterwards to deviate. He followed his business industriously for many years, acquired a competence, and, in the latter part of his life, attained to a dignified station in the church, being remembered in records and traditions as Deacon Drowne, the carver. One of his productions, an Indian chief, gilded all over, stood during the better part of a century on the cupola of the Province House, bedazzling the eyes of those who looked upward, like an angel of the sun. Another work of the good deacon's hand—a reduced likeness of his friend Captain Hunnewell, holding a telescope and quadrant—may be seen, to this day, at the corner of Broad and State streets, serving in the useful capacity of sign to the shop of a nautical instrument maker. We know not how to account for the inferiority of this quaint old figure, as compared with the recorded excellence of the Oaken Lady, unless on the supposition, that in every human spirit there is imagination, sensibility, creative power, genius, which, according to circumstances, may either be developed in this world, or shrouded in a mask of dulness until another state of being. To our friend Drowne, there came a brief season of excitement, kindled by love. It rendered him a genius for that one occasion, but, quenched in disappointment, left him again the mechanical carver in wood, without the power even of appreciating the work that his own hands had wrought. Yet who can doubt, that the very highest state to which a human spirit can attain, in its loftiest aspirations, is its truest and most natural state, and that Drowne was more consistent with himself when he wrought the admirable figure of the mysterious lady, than when he perpetrated a whole progeny of blockheads?

There was a rumor in Boston, about this period, that a young Portuguese lady of rank, on some occasion of political or domestic disquietude, had fled from her home in Fayal, and put herself under the protection of Captain Hunnewell, on board of whose vessel, and at whose residence, she was sheltered until a change of affairs. This fair stranger must have been the original of Drowne's Wooden Image.

THE INTELLIGENCE OFFICE

A GRAVE FIGURE, with a pair of mysterious spectacles on his nose and a pen behind his ear, was seated at a desk, in the corner of a metropolitan office. The apartment was fitted up with a counter, and furnished with an oaken cabinet and a chair or two, in simple and business-like style. Around the walls were stuck advertisements of articles lost, or articles wanted, or articles to be disposed of; in one or another of which classes were comprehended nearly all the conveniences, or otherwise, that the imagination of man has contrived. The interior of the room was thrown into shadow, partly by the tall edifices that rose on the opposite side of the street, and partly by the immense show-bills of blue and crimson paper, that were expanded over each of the three windows. Undisturbed by the tramp of feet, the rattle of wheels, the hum of voices, the shout of the city-crier, the scream of the news-boys, and other tokens of the multitudinous life that surged along in front of the office, the figure at the desk pored diligently over a folio volume, of leger-like size and aspect. He looked like the spirit of a record—the soul of his own great volume—made visible in mortal shape.

But scarcely an instant elapsed without the appearance at the door of some individual from the busy population whose vicinity was manifiested by so much buzz, and clatter, and outcry. Now, it was a thriving mechanic, in quest of a tenement that should come within his moderate means of rent; now, a ruddy Irish girl from the banks of Killarney, wandering from kitchen to kitchen of our land, while her heart still hung in the peat-smoke of her native cottage; now, a single gentleman, looking out for economical board; and now—for this establishment offered an epitome of worldly pursuits—it was a faded beauty inquiring for her lost bloom; or Peter Schlemihl for his lost shadow; or an author, of ten years standing, for his vanished reputation; or a moody man for yesterday's sunshine.

At the next lifting of the latch there entered a person with his hat awry upon his head, his clothes perversely ill-suited to his form, his eyes staring in directions opposite to their intelligence, and a certain odd unsuitableness pervading his whole figure. Wherever he might chance to be, whether in palace or cottage, church or market, on land or sea, or even at his own fireside, he must have worn the characteristic expression of a man out of his right place.

"This," inquired he, putting his question in the form of an assertion, "this is the Central Intelligence Office?"

"Even so," answered the figure at the desk, turning another leaf of his volume; he then looked the applicant in the face, and said briefly—"Your business?"

"I want," said the latter, with tremulous earnestness, "a place!"

"A place!—and of what nature?" asked the Intelligencer. "There are many vacant, or soon to be so, some of which will probably suit, since they range from that of a footman up to a seat at the council-board, or in the cabinet, on a throne, or a presidential chair."

The stranger stood pondering before the desk, with an unquiet, dissatisfied air—a dull, vague pain of heart, expressed by a slight contortion of the brow—an earnestness of glance, that asked and expected, yet continually wavered, as if distrusting. In short, he evidently wanted, not in a physical or intellectual sense, but with an urgent moral necessity that is the hardest of all things to satisfy, since it knows not its own object.

"Ah, you mistake me!" said he at length, with a gesture of nervous impatience. "Either of the places you mention, indeed, might answer my purpose—or, more probably, none of them. I want my place!—my own place!—my true place in the world!—my proper sphere!—my thing to do, which nature intended me to perform when she fashioned me thus awry, and which I have vainly sought, all my lifetime! Whether it be a footman's duty, or a king's, is of little consequence, so it be naturally mine. Can you help me here?"

"I will enter your application," answered the Intelligencer, at the same time writing a few lines in his volume. "But to undertake such a business, I tell you frankly, is quite apart from the ground covered by my official duties. Ask for something specific, and it may doubtless be negotiated for you, on your compliance with the conditions. But were I to go further, I should have the whole population of the city upon my shoulders; since far the greater proportion of them are, more or less, in your predicament."

The applicant sank into a fit of despondency, and passed out of the door without again lifting his eyes; and, if he died of the disappointment, he was probably buried in the wrong tomb; inasmuch as the fatality of such people never deserts them, and, whether alive or dead, they are invariably out of place.

Almost immediately, another foot was heard on the threshold. A youth entered hastily, and threw a glance around the office to ascertain whether the Man of Intelligence was alone. He then approached close to the desk, blushed like a maiden, and seemed at a loss how to broach his business.

"You come upon an affair of the heart," said the official personage, looking into him through his mysterious spectacles. "State it in as few words as may be."

"You are right," replied the youth. "I have a heart to dispose of."

"You seek an exchange?" said the Intelligencer. "Foolish youth, why not be contented with your own?"

"Because," exclaimed the young man, losing his embarrassment in a passionate glow,—"because my heart burns me with an intolerable fire; it tortures me all day long with yearnings for I know not what, and feverish throbbings, and the pangs of a vague sorrow; and it awakens me in the night-time with a quake, when there is nothing to be feared! I cannot endure it any longer. It were wiser to throw away such a heart, even if it brings me nothing in return!"

"Oh, very well," said the man of office, making an entry in his volume. "Your affair will be easily transacted. This species of brokerage makes no inconsiderable part of my business; and there is always a large assortment of the article to select from. Here, if I mistake not, comes a pretty fair sample."

Even as he spoke, the door was gently and slowly thrust ajar, affording a glimpse of the slender figure of a young girl, who, as she timidly entered, seemed to bring the light and cheerfulness of the outer atmosphere into the somewhat gloomy apartment. We know not her errand there; nor can we reveal whether the young man gave up his heart into her custody. If so, the arrangement was neither better nor worse than in ninety-nine cases out of a hundred, where the parallel sensibilities of a similar age, importunate affections, and the easy satisfaction of characters not deeply conscious of themselves, supply the place of any profounder sympathy.

Not always, however, was the agency of the passions and affections an office of so little trouble. It happened—rarely, indeed, in proportion to the cases that came under an ordinary rule, but still it did happen—that a heart was occasionally brought hither, of such exquisite material, so delicately attempered, and so curiously wrought, that no other heart could be found to match it. It might almost be considered a misfortune, in a worldly point of view, to be the possessor of such a diamond of the purest water; since in any reasonable probability, it could only be exchanged for an ordinary pebble, or a bit of cunningly manufactured glass, or, at least, for a jewel of native richness, but ill-set, or with some fatal flaw, or an earthy vein running through its central lustre. To choose another figure, it is sad that hearts which have their well-spring in the infinite, and contain inexhaustible sympathies, should ever be doomed to pour themselves into shallow vessels, and thus lavish their rich affections on the ground. Strange, that the finer and deeper nature, whether in man or woman, while possessed of every other delicate instinct, should so often lack that most invaluable one, of preserving itself from contamination with what is of a baser kind! Sometimes, it is true, the spiritual fountain is kept pure by a wisdom within itself, and sparkles into the light of heaven, without a stain from the earthy strata through which it has gushed upward. And sometimes, even here on earth, the pure mingles with the pure, and the inexhaustible is recompensed with the infinite. But these miracles, though he should claim the credit of them, are far beyond the scope of such a superficial agent in human affairs, as the figure in the mysterious spectacles.

Again the door was opened, admitting the bustle of the city with a fresher reverberation into the Intelligence Office. Now entered a man of wo-begone and downcast look; it was such an aspect as if he had lost the very soul out of his body, and had traversed all the world over, searching in the dust of the highways, and along the shady footpaths, and beneath the leaves of the forest, and among the sands of the sea-shore, in hopes to recover it again. He had bent an anxious glance along the pavement of the street, as he came hitherward; he looked, also, in the angle of the door-step, and upon the floor of the room; and, finally, coming up to the Man of Intelligence, he gazed through the inscrutable spectacles which the latter wore, as if the lost treasure might be hidden within his eyes.

"I have lost—" he began; and then he paused.

"Yes," said the Intelligencer, "I see that you have lost—but what?"

"I have lost a precious jewel," replied the unfortunate person, "the like of which is not to be found among any prince's treasures. While I possessed it, the contemplation of it was my sole and sufficient happiness. No price should have purchased it of me; but it has fallen from my bosom, where I wore it, in my careless wanderings about the city."

After causing the stranger to describe the marks of his lost jewel, the Intelligencer opened a drawer of the oaken cabinet, which has been mentioned as forming a part of the furniture of the room. Here were deposited whatever articles had been picked up in the streets, until the right owners should claim them. It was a strange and heterogeneous collection. Not the least remarkable part of it, was a great number of wedding-rings, each one of which had been riveted upon the finger with holy vows, and all the mystic potency that the most solemn rites could attain, but had, nevertheless, proved too slippery for the wearer's vigilance. The gold of some was worn thin, betokening the attrition of years of wedlock; others, glittering from the jeweller's shop, must have been lost within the honey-moon. There were ivory tablets, the leaves scribbled over with sentiments that had been the deepest truths of the writer's earlier years, but which were now quite obliter-

ated from his memory. So scrupulously were articles preserved in this depository, that not even withered flowers were
rejected; white roses, and blush roses, and moss-roses, fit emblems of virgin purity and shamefacedness, which had been
lost or flung away, and trampled into the pollution of the
streets; locks of hair—the golden, and the glossy dark—the
long tresses of woman and the crisp curls of man—signified
that lovers were now and then so heedless of the faith entrusted to them, as to drop its symbol from the treasure-place
of the bosom. Many of these things were imbued with
perfumes; and perhaps a sweet scent had departed from the
lives of their former possessors, ever since they had so wilfully
or negligently lost them. Here were gold pencil-cases, little
ruby hearts with golden arrows through them, bosom-pins,
pieces of coin, and small articles of every description, comprising nearly all that have been lost, since a long time ago.
Most of them, doubtless, had a history and a meaning, if there
were time to search it out and room to tell it. Whoever has
missed anything valuable, whether out of his heart, mind, or
pocket, would do well to make inquiry at the Central Intelligence Office.

And, in the corner of one of the drawers of the oaken cabinet, after considerable research, was found a great pearl,
looking like the soul of celestial purity, congealed and
polished.

"There is my jewel! my very pearl!" cried the stranger,
almost beside himself with rapture. "It is mine! Give it me—
this moment!—or I shall perish!"

"I perceive," said the Man of Intelligence, examining it
more closely, "that this is the Pearl of Great Price."

"The very same," answered the stranger. "Judge, then, of
my misery at losing it out of my bosom! Restore it to me! I
must not live without it an instant longer."

"Pardon me," rejoined the Intelligencer, calmly. "You ask
what is beyond my duty. This pearl, as you well know, is held

upon a peculiar tenure; and having once let it escape from your keeping, you have no greater claim to it—nay, not so great—as any other person. I cannot give it back."

Nor could the entreaties of the miserable man—who saw before his eyes the jewel of his life, without the power to reclaim it—soften the heart of this stern being, impassive to human sympathy, though exercising such an apparent influence over human fortunes. Finally, the loser of the inestimable pearl clutched his hands among his hair, and ran madly forth into the world, which was affrighted at his desperate looks. There passed him on the door-step a fashionable young gentleman, whose business was to inquire for a damask rose-bud, the gift of his lady-love, which he had lost out of his button-hole within an hour after receiving it. So various were the errands of those who visited this Central Office, where all human wishes seemed to be made known, and, so far as destiny would allow, negotiated to their fulfilment.

The next that entered was a man beyond the middle age, bearing the look of one who knew the world and his own course in it. He had just alighted from a handsome private carriage, which had orders to wait in the street while its owner transacted his business. This person came up to the desk with a quick, determined step, and looked the Intelligencer in the face with a resolute eye; though, at the same time, some secret trouble gleamed from it in red and dusky light.

"I have an estate to dispose of," said he, with a brevity that seemed characteristic.

"Describe it," said the Intelligencer.

The applicant proceeded to give the boundaries of his property, its nature, comprising tillage, pasture, woodland, and pleasure-grounds, in ample circuit; together with a mansion-house, in the construction of which it had been his object to realize a castle in the air, hardening its shadowy walls into granite, and rendering its visionary splendor perceptible to the awakened eye. Judging from his description, it was beautiful enough to vanish like a dream, yet substantial enough to endure for centuries. He spoke, too, of the gorgeous furniture, the refinements of upholstery, and all the luxurious artifices that combined to render this a residence where life might flow onward in a stream of golden days, undisturbed by the ruggedness which fate loves to fling into it.

"I am a man of strong will," said he, in conclusion; "and at my first setting out in life, as a poor, unfriended youth, I resolved to make myself the possessor of such a mansion and estate as this, together with the abundant revenue necessary to uphold it. I have succeeded to the extent of my utmost wish. And this is the estate which I have now concluded to dispose of."

"And your terms?" asked the Intelligencer, after taking down the particulars with which the stranger had supplied him.

"Easy—abundantly easy!" answered the successful man, smiling, but with a stern and almost frightful contraction of the brow, as if to quell an inward pang. "I have been engaged in various sorts of business—a distiller, a trader to Africa, an East India merchant, a speculator in the stocks—and, in the course of these affairs, have contracted an incumbrance of a certain nature. The purchaser of the estate shall merely be required to assume this burthen to himself."

"I understand you," said the Man of Intelligence, putting his pen behind his ear. "I fear that no bargain can be negotiated on these conditions. Very probably, the next possessor may acquire the estate with a similar incumbrance, but it will be of his own contracting, and will not lighten your burthen in the least."

"And am I to live on," fiercely exclaimed the stranger, "with the dirt of these accursed acres, and the granite of this infernal mansion, crushing down my soul? How, if I should turn the edifice into an almshouse or a hospital, or tear it down and build a church?"

"You can at least make the experiment," said the Intelligencer; "but the whole matter is one which you must settle for yourself."

The man of deplorable success withdrew, and got into his coach, which rattled off lightly over the wooden pavements, though laden with the weight of much land, a stately house, and ponderous heaps of gold, all compressed into an evil conscience.

There now appeared many applicants for places; among the most note-worthy of whom was a small, smoke-dried figure, who gave himself out to be one of the bad spirits that had waited upon Doctor Faustus in his laboratory. He pretended to show a certificate of character, which, he averred, had been given him by that famous necromancer, and counter-signed by several masters whom he had subsequently served.

"I am afraid, my good friend," observed the Intelligencer, "that your chance of getting a service is but poor. Now-a-days, men act the evil spirit for themselves and their neighbors, and play the part more effectually than ninety-nine out of a hundred of your fraternity."

But, just as the poor fiend was assuming a vaporous consistency, being about to vanish through the floor in sad disappointment and chagrin, the editor of a political newspaper chanced to enter the office, in quest of a scribbler of party paragraphs. The former servant of Doctor Faustus, with some misgivings as to his sufficiency of venom, was allowed to try his hand in this capacity. Next appeared, likewise seeking a service, the mysterious Man in Red, who had aided Buonaparte in his ascent to imperial power. He was examined as to his qualifications by an aspiring politician, but finally rejected, as lacking familiarity with the cunning tactics of the present day.

People continued to succeed each other, with as much briskness as if everybody turned aside, out of the roar and tumult of the city, to record here some want, or superfluity, or desire. Some had goods or possessions, of which they wished to negotiate the sale. A China merchant had lost his health by a long residence in that wasting climate; he very liberally offered his disease, and his wealth along with it, to any physician who would rid him of both together. A soldier offered his wreath of laurels for as good a leg as that which it had cost him, on the battle-field. One poor weary wretch desired nothing but to be accommodated with any creditable method of laying down his life; for misfortune and pecuniary troubles had so subdued his spirits, that he could no longer conceive the possibility of happiness, nor had the heart to try for it. Nevertheless, happening to overhear some conversation in the Intelligence Office, respecting wealth to be rapidly accumulated by a certain mode of speculation, he resolved to live out this one other experiment of better fortune. Many persons desired to exchange their youthful vices for others better suited to the gravity of advancing age; a few, we are glad to say, made earnest efforts to exchange vice for virtue, and, hard as the bargain was, succeeded in effecting it. But it was remarkable, that what all were the least willing to give up, even on the most advantageous terms, were the habits, the oddities, the characteristic traits, the little ridiculous indulgences, somewhere between faults and follies, of which nobody but themselves could understand the fascination.

The great folio, in which the Man of Intelligence recorded all these freaks of idle hearts, and aspirations of deep hearts, and desperate longings of miserable hearts, and evil prayers of perverted hearts, would be curious reading, were it possible to obtain it for publication. Human character in its individual developments—human nature in the mass—may best be studied in its wishes; and this was the record of them all. There was an endless diversity of mode and circumstance, yet withal such a similarity in the real ground-work, that any one page of the volume—whether written in the days before the Flood, or the yesterday that is just gone by, or to be written on the morrow that is close at hand, or a thousand ages hence —might serve as a specimen of the whole. Not but that there were wild sallies of fantasy that could scarcely occur to more than one man's brain, whether reasonable or lunatic. The strangest wishes—yet most incident to men who had gone deep into scientific pursuits, and attained a high intellectual stage, though not the loftiest—were, to contend with Nature, and wrest from her some secret, or some power, which she had seen fit to withhold from mortal grasp. She loves to delude her aspiring students, and mock them with mysteries that seem but just beyond their utmost reach. To concoct new minerals—to produce new forms of vegetable life—to create an insect, if nothing higher in the living scale—is a sort of wish that has often revelled in the breast of a man of science. An astronomer, who lived far more among the distant worlds of space than in this lower sphere, recorded a wish to behold the opposite side of the moon, which, unless the system of the firmament be reversed, she can never turn towards the earth. On the same page of the volume, was written the wish of a little child, to have the stars for playthings.

The most ordinary wish, that was written down with wearisome recurrence, was, of course, for wealth, wealth, wealth, in sums from a few shillings up to unreckonable thousands. But, in reality, this often repeated expression covered as many different desires. Wealth is the golden essence of the outward world, embodying almost everything that exists beyond the limits of the soul; and therefore it is the natural yearning for the life in the midst of which we find ourselves, and of which gold is the condition of enjoyment, that men abridge into this general wish. Here and there, it is true, the volume testified to some heart so perverted as to desire gold for its own sake. Many wished for power; a strange desire, indeed, since it is but another form of slavery. Old people wished for the delights of youth; a fop, for a fashionable coat; an idle reader, for a new novel; a versifier, for a rhyme to some stubborn word; a painter, for Titian's secret of coloring; a prince, for a cottage; a republican, for a kingdom and a palace; a libertine, for his neighbor's wife; a man of palate, for green peas; and a poor man, for a crust of bread. The ambitious desires of public men, elsewhere so craftily concealed, were here expressed openly and boldly, side by side with the unselfish wishes of the philanthropist, for the welfare of the race, so beautiful, so comforting, in contrast with the egotism that continually weighed self against the world. Into the darker secrets of the Book of Wishes, we will not penetrate.

It would be an instructive employment for a student of mankind, perusing this volume carefully, and comparing its records with men's perfected designs, as expressed in their deeds and daily life, to ascertain how far the one accorded with the other. Undoubtedly, in most cases, the correspondence would be found remote. The holy and generous wish, that rises like incense from a pure heart towards heaven, often lavishes its sweet perfume on the blast of evil times. The foul, selfish, murderous wish, that steams forth from a corrupted heart, often passes into the spiritual atmosphere, without being concreted into an earthly deed. Yet this volume is probably truer, as a representation of the human heart, than is the living drama of action, as it evolves around us. There is more of good and more of evil in it; more redeeming points of the bad, and more errors of the virtuous; higher up-soarings, and baser degradation of the soul; in short, a more perplexing amalgamation of vice and virtue, than we witness in the outward world. Decency, and external conscience, often produce a far fairer outside, than is warranted by the stains within. And be it owned, on the other hand, that a man seldom repeats to his nearest friend, any more than he realizes in act, the purest wishes, which, at some blessed time or other, have arisen from the depths of his nature, and witnessed for him in this volume. Yet there is enough, on every leaf, to make the good man shudder for his own wild and idle wishes, as well as for the sinner, whose whole life is the incarnation of a wicked desire.

But again the door is opened; and we hear the tumultuous stir of the world—a deep and awful sound, expressing in another form, some portion of what is written in the volume that lies before the Man of Intelligence. A grandfatherly personage tottered hastily into the office, with such an earnestness in his infirm alacrity that his white hair floated backward, as he hurried up to the desk; while his dim eyes caught a momentary lustre from his vehemence of purpose. This venerable figure explained that he was in search of To-morrow.

"I have spent all my life in pursuit of it," added the sage old gentleman, "being assured that To-morrow has some vast benefit or other in store for me. But I am now getting a little in years, and must make haste; for unless I overtake To-morrow soon, I begin to be afraid it will finally escape me."

"This fugitive To-morrow, my venerable friend," said the Man of Intelligence, "is a stray child of Time, and is flying from his father into the region of the infinite. Continue your pursuit, and you will doubtless come up with him; but as to the earthly gifts which you expect, he has scattered them all among a throng of Yesterdays."

Obliged to content himself with this enigmatical response, the grandsire hastened forth, with a quick clatter of his staff upon the floor; and as he disappeared, a little boy scampered through the door in chase of a butterfly, which had got astray amid the barren sunshine of the city. Had the old gentleman been shrewder, he might have detected To-morrow under the semblance of that gaudy insect. The golden butter-fly glistened through the shadowy apartment, and brushed its wings against the Book of Wishes, and fluttered forth again with the child still in pursuit.

A man now entered, in neglected attire, with the aspect of a thinker, but somewhat too rough-hewn and brawny for a scholar. His face was full of sturdy vigor, with some finer and keener attribute beneath; though harsh at first, it was temp-ered with the glow of a large, warm heart, which had force enough to heat his powerful intellect through and through. He advanced to the Intelligencer, and looked at him with a glance of such stern sincerity, that perhaps few secrets were beyond its scope.

"I seek for Truth," said he.

"It is precisely the most rare pursuit that has ever come under my cognizance," replied the Intelligencer, as he made the new inscription in his volume. "Most men seek to impose some cunning falsehood upon themselves for truth. But I can lend no help to your researches. You must achieve the miracle for yourself. At some fortunate moment, you may find Truth at your side—or, perhaps, she may be mistily dis-cerned, far in advance—or, possibly, behind you."

"Not behind me," said the seeker, "for I have left nothing on my track without a thorough investigation. She flits before me, passing now through a naked solitude, and now mingling with the throng of a popular assembly, and now writing with the pen of a French philosopher, and now standing at the altar of an old cathedral, in the guise of a Catholic priest, performing the high mass. Oh weary search! But I must not falter; and surely my heart-deep quest of Truth shall avail at last."

He paused, and fixed his eyes upon the Intelligencer, with a depth of investigation that seemed to hold commerce with the inner nature of this being, wholly regardless of his external development.

"And what are you?" said he. "It will not satisfy me to point to this fantastic show of an Intelligence Office, and this mockery of business. Tell me what is beneath it, and what your real agency in life, and your influence upon mankind?"

"Yours is a mind," answered the Man of Intelligence, "before which the forms and fantasies that conceal the inner idea from the multitude, vanish at once, and leave the naked reality beneath. Know, then, the secret. My agency in worldly action—my connection with the press, and tumult, and intermingling, and development of human affairs—is merely delusive. The desire of man's heart does for him whatever I seem to do. I am no minister of action, but the Recording Spirit!"

What further secrets were then spoken, remains a mystery; inasmuch as the roar of the city, the bustle of human business, the outcry of the jostling masses, the rush and tumult of man's life, in its noisy and brief career, arose so high that it drowned the words of these two talkers. And whether they stood talking in the Moon, or in Vanity Fair, or in a city of this actual world, is more than I can say.

ROGER MALVIN'S BURIAL

O NE OF THE few incidents of Indian warfare,
naturally susceptible of the moonlight of romance,
was that expedition, undertaken, for the defence of
the frontiers, in the year 1725, which resulted in the well-
remembered 'Lovell's Fight.' Imagination, by casting certain
circumstances judiciously into the shade, may see much to
admire in the heroism of a little band, who gave battle to
twice their number in the heart of the enemy's country. The
open bravery displayed by both parties was in accordance with
civilized ideas of valor, and chivalry itself might not blush to
record the deeds of one or two individuals. The battle, though
so fatal to those who fought, was not unfortunate in its consequences to the country; for it broke the strength of a tribe,
and conduced to the peace which subsisted during several
ensuing years. History and tradition are unusually minute in
their memorials of this affair; and the captain of a scouting
party of frontier-men has acquired as actual a military renown, as many a victorious leader of thousands. Some of the
incidents contained in the following pages will be recognized,
notwithstanding the substitution of fictitious names, by such
as have heard, from old men's lips, the fate of the few com-

batants who were in a condition to retreat, after 'Lovell's Fight.'

The early sunbeams hovered cheerfully upon the tree-tops, beneath which two weary and wounded men had stretched their limbs the night before. Their bed of withered oak-leaves was strewn upon the small level space, at the foot of a rock, situated near the summit of one of the gentle swells, by which the face of the country is there diversified. The mass of granite, rearing its smooth, flat surface, fifteen or twenty feet above their heads, was not unlike a gigantic grave-stone, upon which the veins seemed to form an inscription in forgotten characters. On a tract of several acres around this rock, oaks and other hard-wood trees had supplied the place of the pines, which were the usual growth of the land; and a young and vigorous sapling stood close beside the travellers.

The severe wound of the elder man had probably deprived him of sleep; for, so soon as the first ray of sunshine rested on the top of the highest tree, he reared himself painfully from his recumbent posture, and sat erect. The deep lines of his countenance, and the scattered grey of his hair, marked him as past the middle age; but his muscular frame would, but for the effects of his wound, have been as capable of sustaining fatigue, as in the early vigor of life. Languor and exhaustion now sat upon his haggard features, and the despairing glance which he sent forward through the depths of the forest, proved his own conviction that his pilgrimage was at an end. He next turned his eyes to the companion, who reclined by his side. The youth, for he had scarcely attained the years of manhood, lay, with his head upon his arm, in the embrace of an unquiet sleep, which a thrill of pain from his wounds seemed each moment on the point of breaking. His right hand grasped a musket, and, to judge from the violent action of his features, his slumbers were bringing back a vision of the conflict, of which he was one of the few survivors. A shout,—deep and loud to his dreaming fancy,—found its way in an imperfect murmur to his lips, and, starting even at the slight sound of his own voice, he suddenly awoke. The first act of reviving recollection, was to make anxious inquiries respecting the condition of his wounded fellow traveller. The latter shook his head.

'Reuben, my boy,' said he, 'this rock, beneath which we sit, will serve for an old hunter's grave-stone. There is many and many a long mile of howling wilderness before us yet; nor would it avail me anything, if the smoke of my own chimney were but on the other side of that swell of land. The Indian bullet was deadlier than I thought.'

'You are weary with our three days' travel,' replied the youth, 'and a little longer rest will recruit you. Sit you here, while I search the woods for the herbs and roots, that must be our sustenance; and having eaten, you shall lean on me, and we will turn our faces homeward. I doubt not, that, with my help, you can attain to some one of the frontier garrisons.'

'There is not two days' life in me, Reuben,' said the other, calmly, 'and I will no longer burthen you with my useless body, when you can scarcely support your own. Your wounds are deep, and your strength is failing fast; yet, if you hasten onward alone, you may be preserved. For me there is no hope; and I will await death here.'

'If it must be so, I will remain and watch by you,' said Reuben, resolutely.

'No, my son, no,' rejoined his companion. 'Let the wish of a dying man have weight with you; give me one grasp of your hand, and get you hence. Think you that my last moments will be eased by the thought, that I leave you to die a more lingering death? I have loved you like a father, Reuben, and, at a time like this, I should have something of a father's authority. I charge you to be gone, that I may die in peace.'

'And because you have been a father to me, should I therefore leave you to perish, and to lie unburied in the wilderness?' exclaimed the youth. 'No; if your end be in truth approaching, I will watch by you, and receive your parting words. I will dig a grave here by the rock, in which, if my weakness overcome me, we will rest together; or, if Heaven gives me strength, I will seek my way home.'

'In the cities, and wherever men dwell,' replied the other, 'they bury their dead in the earth; they hide them from the sight of the living; but here, where no step may pass, perhaps for a hundred years, wherefore should I not rest beneath the open sky, covered only by the oak-leaves, when the autumn winds shall strew them? And for a monument, here is this grey rock, on which my dying hand 'shall carve the name of Roger Malvin; and the traveller in days to come will know, that here sleeps a hunter and a warrior. Tarry not, then, for a folly like this, but hasten away, if not for your own sake, for hers who will else be desolate.'

Malvin spoke the last few words in a faultering voice, and their effect upon his companion was strongly visible. They reminded him that there were other, and less questionable duties, than that of sharing the fate of a man whom his death could not benefit. Nor can it be affirmed that no selfish feeling strove to enter Reuben's heart, though the consciousness made him more earnestly resist his companion's entreaties.

'How terrible, to wait the slow approach of death, in this solitude!' exclaimed he. 'A brave man does not shrink in the battle, and, when friends stand round the bed, even women may die composedly; but here—'

'I shall not shrink, even here, Reuben Bourne,' interrupted Malvin. 'I am a man of no weak heart; and, if I were, there is a surer support than that of earthly friends. You are young, and life is dear to you. Your last moments will need comfort far more than mine; and when you have laid me in the earth, and are alone, and night is settling on the forest, you will feel all the bitterness of the death that may now be escaped. But I will urge no selfish motive to your generous nature. Leave me for my sake; that, having said a prayer for your safety, I may have space to settle my account, undisturbed by worldly sorrows.'

'And your daughter! How shall I dare to meet her eye?' exclaimed Reuben. 'She will ask the fate of her father, whose life I vowed to defend with my own. Must I tell her, that he travelled three days' march with me from the field of battle, and that then I left him to perish in the wilderness? Were it not better to lie down and die by your side, than to return safe, and say this to Dorcas?'

'Tell my daughter,' said Roger Malvin, 'that, though yourself sore wounded, and weak, and weary, you led my tottering footsteps many a mile, and left me only at my earnest entreaty, because I would not have your blood upon my soul. Tell her, that through pain and danger you were faithful, and that, if your life-blood could have saved me, it would have flowed to its last drop. And tell her, that you will be something dearer than a father, and that my blessing is with you both, and that my dying eyes can see a long and pleasant path, in which you will journey together.'

As Malvin spoke, he almost raised himself from the ground, and the energy of his concluding words seemed to fill the wild and lonely forest with a vision of happiness. But when he sank exhausted upon his bed of oak-leaves, the light, which had kindled in Reuben's eye, was quenched. He felt as if it were both sin and folly to think of happiness at such a moment. His companion watched his changing countenance, and sought, with generous art, to wile him to his own good.

'Perhaps I deceive myself in regard to the time I have to live,' he resumed. 'It may be, that, with speedy assistance, I might recover of my wound. The foremost fugitives must, ere this, have carried tidings of our fatal battle to the frontiers, and parties will be out to succour those in like condition with ourselves. Should you meet one of these, and guide them hither, who can tell but that I may sit by my own fireside again?'

A mournful smile strayed across the features of the dying man, as he insinuated that unfounded hope; which, however, was not without its effect on Reuben. No merely selfish motive, nor even the desolate condition of Dorcas, could have induced him to desert his companion, at such a moment. But his wishes seized upon the thought, that Malvin's life might be preserved, and his sanguine nature heightened, almost to certainty, the remote possibility of procuring human aid.

'Surely there is reason, weighty reason, to hope that friends are not far distant,' he said, half aloud. 'There fled one coward, unwounded, in the beginning of the fight, and most probably he made good speed. Every true man on the frontier would shoulder his musket, at the news; and though no party may range so far into the woods as this, I shall perhaps encounter them in one day's march. Counsel me faithfully,' he added, turning to Malvin, in distrust of his own motives. 'Were your situation mine, would you desert me while life remained?'

'It is now twenty years,' replied Roger Malvin, sighing, however, as he secretly acknowledged the wide dissimilarity between the two cases,—'it is now twenty years, since I escaped, with one dear friend, from Indian captivity, near Montreal. We journeyed many days through the woods, till at length, overcome with hunger and weariness, my friend lay down, and besought me to leave him; for he knew, that, if I remained, we both must perish. And, with but little hope of obtaining succour, I heaped a pillow of dry leaves beneath his head, and hastened on.'

'And did you return in time to save him?' asked Reuben, hanging on Malvin's words, as if they were to be prophetic of his own success.

'I did,' answered the other. 'I came upon the camp of a hunting party, before sunset of the same day. I guided them to the spot where my comrade was expecting death; and he is now a hale and hearty man, upon his own farm, far within the frontiers, while I lie wounded here, in the depths of the wilderness.'

This example, powerful in effecting Reuben's decision, was aided, unconsciously to himself, by the hidden strength of many another motive. Roger Malvin perceived that the victory was nearly won.

'Now go, my son, and Heaven prosper you!' he said. 'Turn not back with our friends, when you meet them, lest your wounds and weariness overcome you; but send hitherward two or three, that may be spared, to search for me. And believe me, Reuben, my heart will be lighter with every step you take towards home.' Yet there was perhaps a change, both in his countenance and voice, as he spoke thus; for, after all, it was a ghastly fate, to be left expiring in the wilderness.

Reuben Bourne, but half convinced that he was acting rightly, at length raised himself from the ground, and prepared himself for his departure. And first, though contrary to Malvin's wishes, he collected a stock of roots and herbs, which had been their only food during the last two days. This useless supply he placed within reach of the dying man, for whom, also, he swept together a fresh bed of dry oak-leaves. Then, climbing to the summit of the rock, which on one side was rough and broken, he bent the oak-sapling downward, and bound his handkerchief to the topmost branch. This precaution was not unnecessary, to direct any who might come in search of Malvin; for every part of the rock, except its broad, smooth front, was concealed, at a little distance, by the dense undergrowth of the forest. The handkerchief had been the bandage of a wound upon Reuben's arm; and, as he bound it to the tree, he vowed, by the blood that stained it, that he would return, either to save his companion's life, or to lay his body in the grave. He then descended, and stood, with downcast eyes, to receive Roger Malvin's parting words.

The experience of the latter suggested much and minute advice, respecting the youth's journey through the trackless forest. Upon this subject he spoke with calm earnestness, as if he were sending Reuben to the battle or the chase, while he himself remained secure at home; and not as if the human countenance, that was about to leave him, were the last he would ever behold. But his firmness was shaken, before he concluded.

'Carry my blessing to Dorcas, and say that my last prayer shall be for her and you. Bid her have no hard thoughts because you left me here'—Reuben's heart smote him—'for that your life would not have weighed with you, if its sacrifice could have done me good. She will marry you, after she has mourned a little while for her father; and Heaven grant you long and happy days! and may your children's children stand round your death-bed! And, Reuben,' added he, as the weakness of mortality made its way at last, 'return, when your wounds are healed and your weariness refreshed, return to this wild rock, and lay my bones in the grave, and say a prayer over them.'

An almost superstitious regard, arising perhaps from the customs of the Indians, whose war was with the dead, as well as the living, was paid by the frontier inhabitants to the rites of sepulture; and there are many instances of the sacrifice of life, in the attempt to bury those who had fallen by the 'sword of the wilderness.' Reuben, therefore, felt the full importance of the promise, which he most solemnly made, to return, and perform Roger Malvin's obsequies. It was remarkable, that the latter, speaking his whole heart in his parting words, no longer endeavored to persuade the youth, that even the speediest succour might avail to the preservation of his life. Reuben was internally convinced, that he should see Malvin's living face no more. His generous nature would fain have delayed him, at whatever risk, till the dying scene were past; but the desire of existence, and the hope of happiness had strengthened in his heart, and he was unable to resist them.

'It is enough,' said Roger Malvin, having listened to Reuben's promise. 'Go, and God speed you!'

The youth pressed his hand in silence, turned, and was departing. His slow and faultering steps, however, had borne him but a little way, before Malvin's voice recalled him.

'Reuben, Reuben,' said he, faintly; and Reuben returned and knelt down by the dying man.

'Raise me, and let me lean against the rock,' was his last request. 'My face will be turned towards home, and I shall see you a moment longer, as you pass among the trees.'

Reuben, having made the desired alteration in his companion's posture, again began his solitary pilgrimage. He walked more hastily at first, than was consistent with his strength; for a sort of guilty feeling, which sometimes torments men in their most justifiable acts, caused him to seek concealment from Malvin's eyes. But, after he had trodden far upon the rustling forest-leaves, he crept back, impelled by a wild and painful curiosity, and, sheltered by the earthy roots of an uptorn tree, gazed earnestly at the desolate man. The morning sun was unclouded, and the trees and shrubs imbibed the sweet air of the month of May; yet there seemed a gloom on Nature's face, as if she sympathized with mortal pain and sorrow. Roger Malvin's hands were uplifted in a fervent prayer, some of the words of which stole through the stillness of the woods, and entered Reuben's heart, torturing it with an unutterable pang. They were the broken accents of a petition for his own happiness and that of Dorcas; and, as the youth listened, conscience, or something in its similitude, pleaded strongly with him to return, and lie down again by the rock. He felt how hard was the doom of the kind and generous being whom he had deserted in his extremity. Death would come, like the slow approach of a corpse, stealing gradually towards him through the forest, and showing its ghastly and motionless features from behind a nearer, and yet a nearer tree. But such must have been Reuben's own fate, had he tarried another sunset; and who shall impute blame to him, if he shrank from so useless a sacrifice? As he gave a parting look, a breeze waved the little banner upon the sapling-oak, and reminded Reuben of his vow.

Many circumstances contributed to retard the wounded traveller, in his way to the frontiers. On the second day, the clouds, gathering densely over the sky, precluded the possibility of regulating his course by the position of the sun; and he knew not but that every effort of his almost exhausted strength, was removing him farther from the home he sought. His scanty sustenance was supplied by the berries, and other spontaneous products of the forest. Herds of deer, it is true, sometimes bounded past him, and partridges frequently whirred up before his footsteps; but his ammunition had been expended in the fight, and he had no means of slaying them. His wounds, irritated by the constant exertion in which lay the only hope of life, wore away his strength, and at intervals confused his reason. But, even in the wanderings of intellect, Reuben's young heart clung strongly to existence, and it was only through absolute incapacity of motion, that he at last sank down beneath a tree, compelled there to await death. In this situation he was discovered by a party, who, upon the first intelligence of the fight, had been despatched to the relief of the survivors. They conveyed him to the nearest settlement, which chanced to be that of his own residence.

Dorcas, in the simplicity of the olden time, watched by the bed-side of her wounded lover, and administered all those comforts, that are in the sole gift of woman's heart and hand. During several days, Reuben's recollection strayed drowsily among the perils and hardships through which he had passed, and he was incapable of returning definite answers to the inquiries, with which many were eager to harass him. No authentic particulars of the battle had yet been circulated; nor could mothers, wives, and children tell, whether their loved ones were detained by captivity, or by the stronger chain of death. Dorcas nourished her apprehensions in silence, till one afternoon, when Reuben awoke from an unquiet sleep, and seemed to recognize her more perfectly than at any previous time. She saw that his intellect had become composed, and she could no longer restrain her filial anxiety.

'My father, Reuben?' she began; but the change in her lover's countenance made her pause.

The youth shrank, as if with a bitter pain, and the blood gushed vividly into his wan and hollow cheeks. His first impulse was to cover his face; but, apparently with a desperate effort, he half raised himself, and spoke vehemently, defending himself against an imaginary accusation.

'Your father was sore wounded in the battle, Dorcas, and he bade me not burthen myself with him, but only to lead him to the lake-side, that he might quench his thirst and die. But I would not desert the old man in his extremity, and, though bleeding myself, I supported him; I gave him half my strength, and led him away with me. For three days we journeyed on together, and your father was sustained beyond my hopes; but, awaking at sunrise on the fourth day, I found him faint and exhausted,—he was unable to proceed,—his life had ebbed away fast,—and—'

'He died!' exclaimed Dorcas, faintly.

Reuben felt it impossible to acknowledge, that his selfish love of life had hurried him away, before her father's fate was decided. He spoke not; he only bowed his head; and, between shame and exhaustion, sank back and hid his face in the pillow. Dorcas wept, when her fears were thus confirmed; but the shock, as it had been long anticipated, was on that account the less violent.

'You dug a grave for my poor father, in the wilderness, Reuben?' was the question by which her filial piety manifested itself.

'My hands were weak, but I did what I could,' replied the youth in a smothered tone. 'There stands a noble tomb-stone above his head, and I would to Heaven I slept as soundly as he!'

Dorcas, perceiving the wildness of his latter words, inquired no further at the time; but her heart found ease in the thought, that Roger Malvin had not lacked such funeral rites as it was possible to bestow. The tale of Reuben's courage and fidelity lost nothing, when she communicated it to her friends; and the poor youth, tottering from his sick chamber to breathe the sunny air, experienced from every tongue the miserable and humiliating torture of unmerited praise. All acknowledged that he might worthily demand the hand of the fair maiden, to whose father he had been 'faithful unto death'; and, as my tale is not of love, it shall suffice to say, that, in the space of a few months, Reuben became the husband of Dorcas Malvin. During the marriage ceremony, the bride was covered with blushes, but the bridegroom's face was pale.

There was now in the breast of Reuben Bourne an incommunicable thought; something which he was to conceal most heedfully from her whom he most loved and trusted. He regretted, deeply and bitterly, the moral cowardice that had restrained his words, when he was about to disclose the truth to Dorcas; but pride, the fear of losing her affection, the dread of universal scorn, forbade him to rectify this falsehood. He felt, that, for leaving Roger Malvin, he deserved no censure. His presence, the gratuitous sacrifice of his own life, would have added only another, and a needless agony to the last moments of the dying man. But concealment had imparted to a justifiable act, much of the secret effect of guilt; and Reuben, while reason told him that he had done right, experienced, in no small degree, the mental horrors, which punish the perpetrator of undiscovered crime. By a certain association of ideas, he at times almost imagined himself a murderer. For years, also, a thought would occasionally recur, which, though he perceived all its folly and extravagance, he had not power to banish from his mind; it was a haunting and torturing fancy, that his father-in-law was yet sitting at the foot of the rock, on the withered forest-leaves, alive, and awaiting his pledged assistance. These mental deceptions, however, came and went, nor did he ever mistake them for realities; but in the calmest and clearest moods of his mind, he was conscious that he had a deep vow unredeemed, and that an unburied corpse was calling to him, out of the wilderness. Yet, such was the consequence of his prevarication, that he could not obey the call. It was now too late to require the assistance of Roger Malvin's friends, in performing his long-deferred sepulture; and superstitious fears, of which none were more susceptible than the people of the outward settlements, forbade Reuben to go alone. Neither did he know where, in the pathless and illimitable forest, to seek that smooth and lettered rock, at the base of which the body lay; his remembrance of every portion of his travel thence was indistinct, and the latter part had left no impression upon his mind. There was, however, a continual impulse, a voice audible only to himself, commanding him to go forth and redeem his vow; and he had a strange impression, that, were he to make the trial, he would be led straight to Malvin's bones. But, year after year, that summons, unheard but felt, was disobeyed. His one secret thought, became like a chain, binding down his spirit, and, like a serpent, gnawing into his heart; and he was transformed into a sad and downcast, yet irritable man.

In the course of a few years after their marriage, changes began to be visible in the external prosperity of Reuben and Dorcas. The only riches of the former had been his stout heart and strong arm; but the latter, her father's sole heiress, had made her husband master of a farm, under older cultivation, larger, and better stocked than most of the frontier establishments. Reuben Bourne, however, was a neglectful husbandman; and while the lands of the other settlers became annually more fruitful, his deteriorated in the same proportion. The discouragements to agriculture were greatly lessened by the cessation of Indian war, during which men held the plough in one hand, and the musket in the other; and were fortunate if the products of their dangerous labor were not destroyed, either in the field or in the barn, by the savage enemy. But Reuben did not profit by the altered condition of the country; nor can it be denied, that his intervals of industrious attention to his affairs were but scantily rewarded with success. The irritability, by which he had recently become distinguished, was another cause of his declining prosperity, as it occasioned frequent quarrels, in his unavoidable intercourse with the neighboring settlers. The results of these were innumerable law-suits; for the people of New England, in the earliest stages and wildest circumstances of the country, adopted, whenever attainable, the legal mode of deciding their differences. To be brief, the world did not go well with Reuben Bourne, and, though not till many years after his marriage, he was finally a ruined man, with but one remaining expedient against the evil fate that had pursued him. He was to throw sunlight into some deep recess of the forest, and seek subsistence from the virgin bosom of the wilderness.

The only child of Reuben and Dorcas was a son, now arrived at the age of fifteen years, beautiful in youth, and giving promise of a glorious manhood. He was peculiarly qualified for, and already began to excel in, the wild accomplishments of frontier life. His foot was fleet, his aim true, his apprehension quick, his heart glad and high; and all, who anticipated the return of Indian war, spoke of Cyrus Bourne as a future leader in the land. The boy was loved by his father, with a deep and silent strength, as if whatever was good and happy in his own nature had been transferred to his child, carrying his affections with it. Even Dorcas, though loving and beloved, was far less dear to him; for Reuben's secret thoughts and insulated emotions had gradually made him a selfish man; and he could no longer love deeply, except where he saw, or imagined, some reflection or likeness of his own mind. In Cyrus he recognized what he had himself been in other days; and at intervals he seemed to partake of the boy's spirit, and to be revived with a fresh and happy life. Reuben was accompanied by his son in the expedition, for the purpose of selecting a tract of land, and felling and burning the timber, which necessarily preceded the removal of the household gods. Two months of autumn were thus occupied; after which Reuben Bourne and his young hunter returned, to spend their last winter in the settlements.

It was early in the month of May, that the little family snapped asunder whatever tendrils of affection had clung to inanimate objects, and bade farewell to the few, who, in the blight of fortune, called themselves their friends. The sadness of the parting moment had, to each of the pilgrims, its peculiar alleviations. Reuben, a moody man, and misanthropic because unhappy, strode onward, with his usual stern brow and downcast eye, feeling few regrets, and disdaining to acknowledge any. Dorcas, while she wept abundantly over the broken ties by which her simple and affectionate nature had bound itself to everything, felt that the inhabitants of her inmost heart moved on with her, and that all else would be supplied wherever she might go. And the boy dashed one tear-drop from his eye, and thought of the adventurous pleasures of the untrodden forest. Oh! who, in the enthusiasm of a day-dream, has not wished that he were a wanderer in a world of summer wilderness, with one fair and gentle being hanging lightly on his arm? In youth, his free and exulting step would know no barrier but the rolling ocean or the snow-topt mountains; calmer manhood would choose a home, where Nature had strewn a double wealth, in the vale of some transparent stream; and when hoary age, after long, long years of that pure life, stole on and found him there, it would find him the father of a race, the patriarch of a people, the founder of a mighty nation yet to be. When death, like the sweet sleep which we welcome after a day of happiness, came over him, his far descendants would mourn over the venerated dust. Enveloped by tradition in mysterious attributes, the men of future generations would call him godlike; and remote posterity would see him standing, dimly glorious, far up the valley of a hundred centuries!

The tangled and gloomy forest, through which the personages of my tale were wandering, differed widely from the dreamer's Land of Fantasie; yet there was something in their way of life that Nature asserted as her own; and the gnawing cares, which went with them from the world, were all that now obstructed their happiness. One stout and shaggy steed, the bearer of all their wealth, did not shrink from the added weight of Dorcas; although her hardy breeding sustained her, during the latter part of each day's journey, by her husband's side. Reuben and his son, their muskets on their shoulders, and their axes slung behind them, kept an unwearied pace, each watching with a hunter's eye for the game that supplied their food. When hunger bade, they halted and prepared their meal on the bank of some unpolluted forest-brook, which, as they knelt down with thirsty lips to drink, murmured a sweet unwillingness, like a maiden, at love's first kiss. They slept beneath a hut of branches, and awoke at peep of light, refreshed for the toils of another day. Dorcas and the boy went on joyously, and even Reuben's spirit shone at intervals with an outward gladness; but inwardly there was a cold, cold sorrow, which he compared to the snow-drifts, lying deep in the glens and hollows of the rivulets, while the leaves were brightly green above.

Cyrus Bourne was sufficiently skilled in the travel of the woods, to observe, that his father did not adhere to the course they had pursued, in their expedition of the preceding autumn. They were now keeping farther to the north, striking out more directly from the settlements, and into a region, of which savage beasts and savage men were as yet the sole possessors. The boy sometimes hinted his opinions upon the subject, and Reuben listened attentively, and once or twice altered the direction of their march in accordance with his son's counsel. But having so done, he seemed ill at ease. His quick and wandering glances were sent forward, apparently in search of enemies lurking behind the tree-trunks; and seeing nothing there, he would cast his eyes backward, as if in fear of some pursuer. Cyrus, perceiving that his father gradually resumed the old direction, forbore to interfere; nor, though something began to weigh upon his heart, did his adventurous nature permit him to regret the increased length and the mystery of their way.

On the afternoon of the fifth day, they halted and made their simple encampment, nearly an hour before sunset. The face of the country, for the last few miles, had been diversified by swells of land, resembling huge waves of a petrified sea; and in one of the corresponding hollows, a wild and romantic spot, had the family reared their hut, and kindled their fire. There is something chilling, and yet heart-warming, in the thought of these three, united by strong bands of love, and insulated from all that breathe beside. The dark and gloomy pines looked down upon them, and, as the wind swept through their tops, a pitying sound was heard in the forest; or did those old trees groan, in fear that men were come to lay the axe to their roots at last? Reuben and his son, while Dorcas made ready their meal, proposed to wander out in search of game, of which that day's march had afforded no supply. The boy, promising not to quit the vicinity of the encampment, bounded off with a step as light and elastic as that of the deer he hoped to slay; while his father, feeling a transient happiness as he gazed after him, was about to pursue an opposite direction. Dorcas, in the meanwhile, had seated herself near their fire of fallen branches, upon the moss-grown and mouldering trunk of a tree, uprooted years before. Her employment, diversified by an occasional glance at the pot, now beginning to simmer over the blaze, was the perusal of the current year's Massachusetts Almanac, which, with the exception of an old black-letter Bible, comprised all the literary wealth of the family. None pay a greater regard to arbitrary divisions of time, than those who are excluded from society; and Dorcas mentioned, as if the information were of importance, that it was now the twelfth of May. Her husband started.

'The twelfth of May! I should remember it well,' muttered he, while many thoughts occasioned a momentary confusion in his mind. 'Where am I? Whither am I wandering? Where did I leave him?'

Dorcas, too well accustomed to her husband's wayward moods to note any peculiarity of demeanor, now laid aside the Almanac, and addressed him in that mournful tone, which the tender-hearted appropriate to griefs long cold and dead.

'It was near this time of the month, eighteen years ago, that my poor father left this world for a better. He had a kind arm to hold his head, and a kind voice to cheer him, Reuben, in his last moments; and the thought of the faithful care you took of him, has comforted me, many a time since. Oh! death would have been awful to a solitary man, in a wild place like this!'

'Pray Heaven, Dorcas,' said Reuben, in a broken voice, 'pray Heaven, that neither of us three die solitary, and lie unburied, in this howling wilderness!' And he hastened away, leaving her to watch the fire, beneath the gloomy pines.

Reuben Bourne's rapid pace gradually slackened, as the pang, unintentionally inflicted by the words of Dorcas, became less acute. Many strange reflections, however, thronged upon him; and, straying onward, rather like a sleep-walker than a hunter, it was attributable to no care of his own, that his devious course kept him in the vicinity of the encampment. His steps were imperceptibly led almost in a circle, nor did he observe that he was on the verge of a tract of land heavily timbered, but not with pine-trees. The place of the latter was here supplied by oaks, and other of the harder woods; and around their roots clustered a dense and bushy undergrowth, leaving, however, barren spaces between the trees, thick-strewn with withered leaves. Whenever the rustling of the branches, or the creaking of the trunks made a sound, as if the forest were waking from slumber, Reuben instinctively raised the musket that rested on his arm, and cast a quick, sharp glance on every side; but, convinced by a partial observation that no animal was near, he would again give himself up to his thoughts. He was musing on the strange influence, that had led him away from his premeditated course, and so far into the depths of the wilderness. Unable to penetrate to the secret place of his soul, where his motives lay hidden, he believed that a supernatural voice had called him onward, and that a supernatural power had obstructed his retreat. He trusted that it was Heaven's intent to afford him an opportunity of expiating his sin; he hoped that he might find the bones, so long unburied; and that, having laid the earth over them, peace would throw its sunlight into the sepulchre of his heart. From these thoughts he was aroused by a rustling in the forest, at some distance from the spot to which he had wandered. Perceiving the motion of some object behind a thick veil of undergrowth, he fired, with the instinct of a hunter, and the aim of a practised marksman. A low moan, which told his success, and by which even animals can express their dying agony, was unheeded by Reuben Bourne. What were the recollections now breaking upon him?

The thicket, into which Reuben had fired, was near the summit of a swell of land, and was clustered around the base of a rock, which, in the shape and smoothness of one of its surfaces, was not unlike a gigantic grave-stone. As if reflected in a mirror, its likeness was in Reuben's memory. He even recognized the veins which seemed to form an inscription in forgotten characters; everything remained the same, except that a thick covert of bushes shrouded the lower part of the rock, and would have hidden Roger Malvin, had he still been sitting there. Yet, in the next moment, Reuben's eye was caught by another change, that time had effected, since he last stood, where he was now standing again, behind the earthy roots of the uptorn tree. The sapling, to which he had bound the blood-stained symbol of his vow, had increased and strengthened into an oak, far indeed from its maturity, but with no mean spread of shadowy branches. There was one singularity, observable in this tree, which made Reuben tremble. The middle and lower branches were in luxuriant life, and an excess of vegetation had fringed the trunk, almost to the ground; but a blight had apparently stricken the upper part of the oak, and the very topmost bough was withered, sapless, and utterly dead. Reuben remembered how the little banner had fluttered on the topmost bough, when it was green and lovely, eighteen years before. Whose guilt had blasted it?

Dorcas, after the departure of the two hunters, continued her preparations for their evening repast. Her sylvan table was the moss-covered trunk of a large fallen tree, on the broadest part of which she had spread a snow-white cloth, and arranged what were left of the bright pewter vessels, that had been her pride in the settlements. It had a strange aspect—that one little spot of homely comfort, in the desolate heart of Nature. The sunshine yet lingered upon the higher branches of the trees that grew on rising ground; but the shades of evening had deepened into the hollow, where the encampment was made; and the fire-light began to redden as it gleamed up the tall trunks of the pines, or hovered on the dense and obscure mass of foliage, that circled round the spot. The heart of Dorcas was not sad; for she felt that it was better to journey in the wilderness, with two whom she loved, than to be a lonely woman in a crowd that cared not for her. As she busied herself in arranging seats of mouldering wood, covered with leaves, for Reuben and her son, her voice danced through the gloomy forest, in the measure of a song that she had learned in youth. The rude melody, the production of a bard who won no name, was descriptive of a winter evening in a frontier-cottage, when, secured from savage inroad by the high-piled snow-drifts, the family rejoiced by their own fireside. The whole song possessed that nameless charm, peculiar to unborrowed thought; but four continually-recurring lines shone out from the rest, like the blaze of the hearth whose joys they celebrated. Into them, working magic with a few simple words, the poet had instilled the very essence of domestic love and household happiness, and they were poetry and picture joined in one. As Dorcas sang, the walls of her forsaken home seemed to encircle her; she no longer saw the gloomy pines, nor heard the wind, which still, as she began each verse, sent a heavy breath through the branches, and died away in a hollow moan, from the burthen of the song. She was aroused by the report of a gun, in the vicinity of the encampment; and either the sudden sound, or her loneliness by the glowing fire, caused her to tremble violently. The next moment, she laughed in the pride of a mother's heart.

'My beautiful young hunter! my boy has slain a deer!' she exclaimed, recollecting that, in the direction whence the shot proceeded, Cyrus had gone to the chase.

She waited a reasonable time, to hear her son's light step bounding over the rustling leaves, to tell of his success. But he did not immediately appear, and she sent her cheerful voice among the trees, in search of him.

'Cyrus! Cyrus!'

His coming was still delayed, and she determined, as the report had apparently been very near, to seek for him in person. Her assistance, also, might be necessary in bringing home the venison, which she flattered herself he had obtained. She therefore set forward, directing her steps by the long-past sound, and singing as she went, in order that the boy might be aware of her approach, and run to meet her. From behind the trunk of every tree, and from every hiding place in the thick foliage of the undergrowth, she hoped to discover the countenance of her son, laughing with the sportive mischief that is born of affection. The sun was now beneath the horizon, and the light that came down among the trees was sufficiently dim to create many illusions in her expecting fancy. Several times she seemed indistinctly to see his face gazing out from among the leaves; and once she imagined that he stood beckoning to her, at the base of a craggy rock. Keeping her eyes on this object, however, it proved to be no more than the trunk of an oak, fringed to the very ground with little branches, one of which, thrust out farther than the rest, was shaken by the breeze. Making her way round the foot of the rock, she suddenly found herself close to her husband, who had approached in another direction. Leaning upon the butt of his gun, the muzzle of which rested upon the withered leaves, he was apparently absorbed in the contemplation of some object at his feet.

'How is this, Reuben? Have you slain the deer, and fallen asleep over him?' exclaimed Dorcas, laughing cheerfully, on her first slight observation of his posture and appearance.

He stirred not, neither did he turn his eyes towards her; and a cold, shuddering fear, indefinite in its source and object, began to creep into her blood. She now perceived that her husband's face was ghastly pale, and his features were rigid, as if incapable of assuming any other expression than the strong despair which had hardened upon them. He gave not the slightest evidence that he was aware of her approach.

'For the love of Heaven, Reuben, speak to me!' cried Dorcas, and the strange sound of her own voice affrighted her even more than the dead silence.

Her husband started, stared into her face; drew her to the front of the rock, and pointed with his finger.

Oh! there lay the boy, asleep, but dreamless, upon the fallen forest-leaves! his cheek rested upon his arm, his curled locks were thrown back from his brow, his limbs were slightly relaxed. Had a sudden weariness overcome the youthful hunter? Would his mother's voice arouse him? She knew that it was death.

'This broad rock is the grave-stone of your near kindred, Dorcas,' said her husband. 'Your tears will fall at once over your father and your son.'

She heard him not. With one wild shriek, that seemed to force its way from the sufferer's inmost soul, she sank insensible by the side of her dead boy. At that moment, the withered topmost bough of the oak loosened itself, in the stilly air, and fell in soft, light fragments upon the rock, upon the leaves, upon Reuben, upon his wife and child, and upon Roger Malvin's bones. Then Reuben's heart was stricken, and the tears gushed out like water from a rock. The vow that the wounded youth had made, the blighted man had come to redeem. His sin was expiated, the curse was gone from him; and, in the hour, when he had shed blood dearer to him than his own, a prayer, the first for years, went up to Heaven from the lips of Reuben Bourne.

P.'S CORRESPONDENCE

M Y UNFORTUNATE friend P. has lost the thread
of his life, by the interposition of long intervals
of partially disordered reason. The past and present
are jumbled together in his mind, in a manner often productive of curious results; and which will be better understood
after a perusal of the following letter, than from any description that I could give. The poor fellow, without once stirring
from the little white-washed, iron-grated room, to which he
alludes in his first paragraph, is nevertheless a great traveller,
and meets, in his wanderings, a variety of personages who
have long ceased to be visible to any eye save his own. In
my opinion, all this is not so much a delusion, as a partly
wilful and partly involuntary sport of the imagination, to
which his disease has imparted such morbid energy that he
beholds these spectral scenes and characters with no less
distinctness than a play upon the stage, and with somewhat
more of illusive credence. Many of his letters are in my
possession, some based upon the same vagary as the present
one, and others upon hypotheses not a whit short of it in
absurdity. The whole form a series of correspondence, which,
should fate seasonably remove my poor friend from what is
to him a world of moonshine, I promise myself a pious

pleasure in editing for the public eye. P. had always a hankering after literary reputation, and has made more than one unsuccessful effort to achieve it. It would not be a little odd, if, after missing his object while seeking it by the light of reason, he should prove to have stumbled upon it in his misty excursions beyond the limits of sanity.

LONDON, February 29, 1845.

MY DEAR FRIEND:

Old associations cling to the mind with astonishing tenacity. Daily custom grows up about us like a stone-wall, and consolidates itself into almost as material an entity as mankind's strongest architecture. It is sometimes a serious question with me, whether ideas be not really visible and tangible, and endowed with all the other qualities of matter. Sitting as I do, at this moment, in my hired apartment, writing beside the hearth, over which hangs a print of Queen Victoria—listening to the muffled roar of the world's metropolis, and with a window at but five paces distant, through which, whenever I please, I can gaze out on actual London—with all this positive certainty, as to my whereabouts, what kind of notion, do you think, is just now perplexing my brain? Why—would you believe it?—that, all this time, I am still an inhabitant of that wearisome little chamber,—that white-washed little chamber—that little chamber with its one small window, across which, from some inscrutable reason of taste or convenience, my landlord had placed a row of iron bars—that same little chamber, in short, whither your kindness has so often brought you to visit me! Will no length of time, or breadth of space, enfranchise me from that unlovely abode? I travel, but it seems to be like the snail, with my house upon my head. Ah, well! I am verging, I suppose, on that period of life when present scenes and events make but feeble impressions, in comparison with those of yore; so that I must reconcile myself to be more and more the prisoner of Memory, who merely lets me hop about a little, with her chain around my leg.

My letters of introduction have been of the utmost service, enabling me to make the acquaintance of several distinguished characters, who, until now, have seemed as remote from the sphere of my personal intercourse as the wits of Queen Anne's time, or Ben Jonson's compotators at the Mermaid. One of the first of which I availed myself, was the letter to Lord Byron. I found his lordship looking much older than I had anticipated; although—considering his former irregularities of life, and the various wear and tear of his constitution—not older than a man on the verge of sixty reasonably may look. But I had invested his earthly frame, in my imagination, with the poet's spiritual immortality. He wears a brown wig, very luxuriantly curled, and extending down over his forehead. The expression of his eyes is concealed by spectacles. His early tendency to obesity having increased, Lord Byron is now enormously fat; so fat as to give the impression of a person quite overladen with his own flesh, and without sufficient vigor to diffuse his personal life through the great mass of corporeal substance, which weighs upon him so cruelly. You gaze at the mortal heap; and, while it fills your eye with what purports to be Byron, you murmur within yourself—"For Heaven's sake, where is he?" Were I disposed to be caustic, I might consider this mass of earthly matter as the symbol, in a material shape, of those evil habits and carnal vices which unspiritualize man's nature, and clog up his avenues of communication with the better life. But this would be too harsh; and besides, Lord Byron's morals have been improving, while his outward man has swollen to such unconscionable circumference. Would that he were leaner; for, though he did me the honor to present his hand, yet it was so puffed out with alien substance, that I could not feel as if I had touched the hand that wrote Childe Harold.

On my entrance, his lordship apologized for not rising to receive me, on the sufficient plea that the gout, for several years past, had taken up its constant residence in his right foot; which, accordingly, was swathed in many rolls of flannel, and deposited upon a cushion. The other foot was hidden in the drapery of his chair. Do you recollect whether Byron's right or left foot was the deformed one?

The noble poet's reconciliation with Lady Byron is now, as you are aware, of ten years' standing; nor does it exhibit, I am assured, any symptom of breach or fracture. They are said to be, if not a happy, at least a contented, or, at all events, a quiet couple, descending the slope of life with that tolerable degree of mutual support, which will enable them to come easily and comfortably to the bottom. It is pleasant to reflect how entirely the poet has redeemed his youthful errors, in this particular. Her ladyship's influence, it rejoices me to add, has been productive of the happiest results upon Lord Byron in a religious point of view. He now combines the most rigid tenets of Methodism with the ultra-doctrines of the Puseyites: the former being perhaps due to the convictions wrought upon his mind by his noble consort; while the latter are the embroidery and picturesque illumination, demanded by his imaginative character. Much of whatever expenditure his increasing habits of thrift continue to allow him, is bestowed in the reparation or beautifying of places of worship; and this nobleman, whose name was one considered a synonym of the foul fiend, is now all but canonized as a saint, in many pulpits of the metropolis and elsewhere. In politics, Lord Byron is an uncompromising conservative, and loses no opportunity, whether in the House of Lords or in private circles, of denouncing and repudiating the mischievous and anarchical notions of his earlier day. Nor does he fail to visit similar sins, in other people, with the severest vengeance which his somewhat blunted pen is capable of inflicting. Southey and he are on the most intimate terms. You are aware that some little time before the death of Moore, Byron caused that brilliant but reprehensible man to be ejected from his house. Moore took the insult so much to heart, that it is said to have been one great cause of the fit of illness which brought him to the grave. Others pretend that the Lyrist died in a very happy state of mind, singing one of his own sacred melodies, and expressing his belief that it would be heard within the gate of paradise, and gain him instant and honorable admittance. I wish he may have found it so.

I failed not, as you may suppose, in the course of conversation with Lord Byron, to pay the meed of homage due to a mighty poet, by allusions to passages in Childe Harold, and Manfred, and Don Juan, which have made so large a portion of the music of my life. My words, whether apt or otherwise, were at least warm with the enthusiasm of one worthy to discourse of immortal poesy. It was evident, however, that they did not go precisely to the right spot. I could perceive that there was some mistake or other, and was not a little angry with myself, and ashamed of my abortive attempt to throw back, from my own heart to the gifted author's ear, the echo of those strains that have resounded throughout the world. But, by and by, the secret peeped quietly out. Byron—I have the information from his own lips, so that you need not hesitate to repeat it in literary circles—Byron is preparing a new edition of his complete works, carefully corrected, expurgated and amended, in accordance with his present creed of taste, morals, politics and religion. It so happened, that the very passages of highest inspiration, to which I had alluded, were among the condemned and rejected rubbish, which it is his purpose to cast into the gulf of oblivion. To whisper you the truth, it appears to me that his passions having burnt out, the extinction of their vivid and riotous flame has deprived Lord Byron of the illumination by which he not merely wrote, but was enabled to feel and comprehend what he had written. Positively, he no longer understands his own poetry.

This became very apparent on his favoring me so far as to read a few specimens of Don Juan in the moralized version. Whatever is licentious—whatever disrespectful to the sacred mysteries of our faith—whatever morbidly melancholic, or splenetically sportive—whatever assails settled constitutions of government, or systems of society—whatever could wound the sensibility of any mortal, except a pagan, a republican, or a dissenter—has been unrelentingly blotted out, and its place supplied by unexceptionable verses, in his lordship's later style. You may judge how much of the poem remains as hitherto published. The result is not so good as might be wished; in plain terms, it is a very sad affair indeed; for though the torches kindled in Tophet have been extinguished, they leave an abominably ill odor, and are succeeded by no glimpses of hallowed fire. It is to be hoped, nevertheless, that this attempt, on Lord Byron's part, to atone for his youthful errors, will at length induce the Dean of Westminster, or whatever churchman is concerned, to allow Thorwaldsen's statue of the poet its due niche in the grand old Abbey. His bones, you know, when brought from Greece, were denied sepulture among those of his tuneful brethren there.

What a vile slip of the pen was that! How absurd in me to talk about burying the bones of Byron, whom I have just seen alive, and encased in a big, round bulk of flesh! But, to say the truth, a prodigiously fat man always impresses me as a kind of hobgoblin; in the very extravagance of his mortal system, I find something akin to the immateriality of a ghost. And then that ridiculous old story darted into my mind, how that Byron died of fever at Missolonghi, above twenty years ago. More and more I recognize that we dwell in a world of shadows; and, for my part, I hold it hardly worth the trouble to attempt a distinction between shadows in the mind, and shadows out of it. If there be any difference, the former are rather the more substantial.

Only think of my good fortune! The venerable Robert Burns—now, if I mistake not, in his eighty-seventh year—happens to be making a visit to London, as if on purpose to afford me an opportunity of grasping him by the hand. For upwards of twenty years past he has hardly left his quiet cottage in Ayrshire for a single night, and has only been drawn hither now by the irresistible persuasions of all the distinguished men in England. They wish to celebrate the patriarch's birthday by a festival. It will be the greatest literary triumph on record. Pray Heaven the little spark of life within the aged bard's bosom may not be extinguished in the lustre of that hour! I have already had the honor of an introduction to him, at the British Museum, where he was examining a collection of his own unpublished letters, interspersed with songs, which have escaped the notice of all his biographers.

Poh! Nonsense! What am I thinking of! How should Burns have been embalmed in biography, when he is still a hearty old man!

The figure of the bard is tall, and in the highest degree reverend; nor the less so, that it is much bent by the burthen of time. His white hair floats like a snow-drift around his face, in which are seen the furrows of intellect and passion, like the channels of headlong torrents that have foamed themselves away. The old gentleman is in excellent preservation, considering his time of life. He has that cricketty sort of liveliness—I mean the cricket's humor of chirping for any cause or none—which is perhaps the most favorable mood that can befall extreme old age. Our pride forbids us to desire it for ourselves, although we perceive it to be a beneficence of nature in the case of others. I was surprised to find it in Burns. It seems as if his ardent heart and brilliant imagination had both burnt down to the last embers, leaving only a little flickering flame in one corner, which keeps dancing upward and laughing all by itself. He is no longer capable of pathos. At the request of Allan Cunningham, he attempted to sing his own song to Mary in Heaven; but it was evident that the feeling of those verses, so profoundly true, and so simply expressed, was entirely beyond the scope of his present sensibilities; and when a touch of it did partially awaken him, the tears immediately gushed into his eyes, and his voice broke into a tremulous cackle. And yet he but indistinctly knew wherefore he was weeping. Ah! he must not think again of Mary in Heaven, until he shake off the dull impediment of time, and ascend to meet her there.

Burns then began to repeat Tam O'Shanter, but was so tickled with its wit and humor—of which, however, I suspect he had but a traditionary sense—that he soon burst into a fit of chirruping laughter, succeeded by a cough, which brought this not very agreeable exhibition to a close. On the whole, I would rather not have witnessed it. It is a satisfactory idea, however, that the last forty years of the peasant-poet's life have been passed in competence and perfect comfort. Having been cured of his bardic improvidence for many a day past, and grown as attentive to the main chance as a canny Scotsman should be, he is now considered to be quite well off, as to pecuniary circumstances. This, I suppose, is worth having lived so long for.

I took occasion to inquire of some of the countrymen of Burns in regard to the health of Sir Walter Scott. His condition, I am sorry to say, remains the same as for ten years past; it is that of a hopeless paralytic, palsied not more in body than in those nobler attributes of which the body is the instrument. And thus he vegetates from day to day, and from year to year, at that splendid fantasy of Abbotsford, which grew out of his brain, and became a symbol of the great romancer's tastes, feelings, studies, prejudices, and modes of intellect. Whether in verse, prose, or architecture, he could achieve but one thing, although that one in infinite variety. There he reclines, on a couch in his library, and is said to spend whole hours of every day in dictating tales to an amanuensis. To an imaginary amanuensis; for it is not deemed worth any one's trouble now to take down what flows from that once brilliant fancy, every image of which was formerly worth gold, and capable of being coined. Yet, Cunningham, who has lately seen him, assures me that there is now and then a touch of the genius; a striking combination of incident, or a picturesque trait of character, such as no other man alive could have hit off; a glimmer from that ruined mind, as if the sun had suddenly flashed on a half-rusted helmet in the gloom of an ancient hall. But the plots of these romances become inextricably confused; the characters melt into one another; and the tale loses itself like the course of a stream flowing through muddy and marshy ground.

For my part, I can hardly regret that Sir Walter Scott had lost his consciousness of outward things, before his works went out of vogue. It was good that he should forget his fame, rather than that fame should first have forgotten him. Were he still a writer, and as brilliant a one as ever, he could no longer maintain anything like the same position in literature. The world, now-a-days, requires a more earnest purpose, a deeper moral, and a closer and homelier truth, than he was qualified to supply it with. Yet who can be, to the present generation, even what Scott has been to the past? I had expectations from a young man—one Dickens—who published a few magazine articles, very rich in humor, and not without symptoms of genuine pathos; but the poor fellow died, shortly after commencing an odd series of sketches, entitled, I think, the Pickwick Papers. Not impossibly, the world has lost more than it dreams of, by the untimely death of this Mr. Dickens.

Whom do you think I met in Pall Mall, the other day? You would not hit it in ten guesses. Why, no less a man than Napoleon Bonaparte!—or all that is now left of him— that is to say, the skin, bones, and corporeal substance, little cocked hat, green coat, white breeches and small sword, which are still known by his redoubtable name. He was attended only by two policemen, who walked quietly behind the phantasm of the old ex-Emperor, appearing to have no duty in regard to him, except to see that none of the light-fingered gentry should possess themselves of his star of the Legion of Honor. Nobody, save myself, so much as turned to look after him; nor, it grieves me to confess, could even I contrive to muster up any tolerable interest, even by reminiscences of all that the warlike spirit, formerly mani-fested within that now decrepit shape, had wrought upon our globe. There is no surer method of annihilating the magic influence of a great renown, than by exhibiting the possessor of it in the decline, the overthrow, the utter degradation of his powers—buried beneath his own mortality—and lacking even the qualities of sense, that enable the most ordinary men to bear themselves decently in the eye of the world. This is the state to which disease, aggravated by long endur-ance of a tropical climate, and assisted by old age—for he is now above seventy—has reduced Bonaparte. The British government has acted shrewdly, in re-transporting him from St. Helena to England. They should now restore him to Paris, and there let him once again review the relics of his armies. His eye is dull and rheumy; his nether lip hung down upon his chin. While I was observing him, there chanced to be a little extra bustle in the street; and he, the brother of Cæsar and Hannibal—the Great Captain, who had veiled the world in battle smoke, and tracked it round with bloody footsteps—was seized with a nervous trembling, and claimed the protection of the two policemen by a cracked and dolorous cry. The fellows winked at one another, laughed aside, and patting Napoleon on the back, took each an arm and led him away.

Death and fury! Ha, villain, how came you hither? Avaunt! —or I fling my inkstand at your head. Tush, tush; it is all a mistake. Pray, my dear friend, pardon this little outbreak. The fact is, the mention of those two policemen, and their custody of Bonaparte, had called up the idea of that odious wretch—you remember him well—who was pleased to take such gratuitous and impertinent care of my person, before I quitted New England. Forthwith, up rose before my mind's eye that same little white-washed room, with the iron-grated window—strange, that it should have been iron-grated— where, in too easy compliance with the absurd wishes of my relatives, I have wasted several good years of my life. Posi- tively, it seemed to me that I was still sitting there, and that the keeper—not that he ever was my keeper neither, but only a kind of intrusive devil of a body-servant—had just peeped in at the door. The rascal! I owe him an old grudge, and will find a time to pay it yet! Fie, fie! The mere thought of him has exceedingly discomposed me. Even now, that hateful chamber—the iron-grated window, which blasted the blessed sunshine as it fell through the dusty panes, and made it poison to my soul—looks more distinct to my view than does this, my comfortable apartment in the heart of London. The reality—that which I know to be such—hangs like remnants of tattered scenery over the intolerably prominent illusion. Let us think of it no more.

You will be anxious to hear of Shelley. I need not say, what is known to all the world, that this celebrated poet has, for many years past, been reconciled to the Church of England. In his more recent works, he has applied his fine powers to the vindication of the Christian faith, with an especial view to that particular development. Latterly—as you may not have heard—he has taken orders, and been inducted to a small country living, in the gift of the Lord Chancellor. Just now, luckily for me, he has come to the metropolis to superintend the publication of a volume of discourses, treating of the poetico-philosophical proofs of Christianity, on the basis of the Thirty-nine Articles. On my first introduction, I felt no little embarrassment as to the manner of combining what I had to say to the author of Queen Mab, the Revolt of Islam, and Prometheus Unbound, with such acknowledgments as might be acceptable to a Christian minister, and zealous upholder of the Established Church. But Shelley soon placed me at my ease. Standing where he now does, and reviewing all his successive productions from a higher point, he assures me that there is a harmony, an order, a regular procession, which enables him to lay his hand upon any one of the earlier poems, and say, "This is my work!" with precisely the same complacency of conscience, wherewithal he contemplates the volume of discourses above-mentioned. They are like the successive steps of a staircase, the lowest of which, in the depth of chaos, is as essential to the support of the whole, as the highest and final one, resting upon the threshold of the heavens. I felt half inclined to ask him, what would have been his fate, had he perished on the lower steps of his staircase, instead of building his way aloft into the celestial brightness.

How all this may be, I neither pretend to understand nor greatly care, so long as Shelley has really climbed, as it seems he has, from a lower region to a loftier one. Without touching upon their religious merits, I consider the productions of his maturity superior, as poems, to those of his youth. They are warmer with human love, which has served as an interpreter between his mind and the multitude. The author has learned to dip his pen oftener into his heart, and has thereby avoided the faults into which a too exclusive use of fancy and intellect was wont to betray him. Formerly, his page was often little other than a concrete arrangement of crystallizations, or even of icicles, as cold as they were brilliant. Now, you take it to your heart, and are conscious of a heart-warmth responsive to your own. In his private character, Shelley can hardly have grown more gentle, kind and affectionate, than his friends always represented him to be, up to that disastrous night when he was drowned in the Mediterranean. Nonsense, again!—sheer nonsense! What am I babbling about? I was thinking of that old figment of his being lost in the Bay of Spezia, and washed ashore near Via Reggio, and burned to ashes on a funeral pyre, with wine and spices and frankincense; while Byron stood on the beach, and beheld a flame of marvellous beauty rise heavenward from the dead poet's heart; and that his fire-purified relics were finally buried near his child, in Roman earth. If all this happened three-and-twenty years ago, how could I have met the drowned, and burned, and buried man, here in London, only yesterday?

Before quitting the subject, I may mention that Dr. Reginald Heber, heretofore Bishop of Calcutta, but recently translated to a see in England, called on Shelley while I was with him. They appeared to be on terms of very cordial intimacy, and are said to have a joint poem in contemplation. What a strange, incongruous dream is the life of man!

Coleridge has at last finished his poem of Christabel; it will be issued entire, by old John Murray, in the course of the present publishing season. The poet, I hear, is visited

with a troublesome affection of the tongue, which has put a
period, or some lesser stop, to the life-long discourse that has
hitherto been flowing from his lips. He will not survive it
above a month, unless his accumulation of ideas be sluiced
off in some other way. Wordsworth died only a week or two
ago. Heaven rest his soul, and grant that he may not have
completed the Excursion! Methinks I am sick of everything
he wrote, except his Laodamia. It is very sad—this inconstancy of the mind to the poets whom it once worshipped.
Southey is as hale as ever, and writes with his usual diligence.
Old Gifford is still alive, in the extremity of age, and with
most pitiable decay of what little sharp and narrow intellect
the devil had gifted him withal. One hates to allow such
a man the privilege of growing old and infirm. It takes away
our speculative license of kicking him.

Keats? No; I have not seen him, except across a crowded
street, with coaches, drays, horsemen, cabs, omnibuses, foot-
passengers, and divers other sensual obstructions, intervening
betwixt his small and slender figure and my eager glance. I
would fain have met him on the sea-shore—or beneath a
natural arch of forest trees—or the Gothic arch of an old
cathedral—or among Grecian ruins—or at a glimmering fireside on the verge of evening—or at the twilight entrance of
a cave, into the dreamy depths of which he would have led
me by the hand; anywhere, in short, save at Temple Bar,
where his presence was blotted out by the porter-swollen
bulks of these gross Englishmen. I stood and watched him,
fading away, fading away, along the pavement, and could
hardly tell whether he were an actual man, or a thought that
had slipped out of my mind, and clothed itself in human
form and habiliments, merely to beguile me. At one moment
he put his handkerchief to his lips, and withdrew it, I am
almost certain, stained with blood. You never saw anything
so fragile as his person. The truth is, Keats has all his life

felt the effects of that terrible bleeding at the lungs, caused by the article on his Endymion, in the Quarterly Review, and which so nearly brought him to the grave. Ever since, he has glided about the world like a ghost, sighing a melancholy tone in the ear of here and there a friend, but never sending forth his voice to greet the multitude. I can hardly think him a great poet. The burthen of a mighty genius would never have been imposed upon shoulders so physically frail, and a spirit so infirmly sensitive. Great poets should have iron sinews.

Yet Keats, though for so many years he has given nothing to the world, is understood to have devoted himself to the composition of an epic poem. Some passages of it have been communicated to the inner circle of his admirers, and impressed them as the loftiest strains that have been audible on earth since Milton's days. If I can obtain copies of these specimens, I will ask you to present them to James Russell Lowell, who seems to be one of the poet's most fervent and worthiest worshippers. The information took me by surprise. I had supposed that all Keats's poetic incense, without being embodied in human language, floated up to heaven, and mingled with the songs of the immortal choristers, who perhaps were conscious of an unknown voice among them, and thought their melody the sweeter for it. But it is not so; he has positively written a poem on the subject of Paradise Regained, though in another sense than that which presented itself to the mind of Milton. In compliance, it may be imagined, with the dogma of those who pretend that all epic possibilities, in the past history of the world, are exhausted, Keats has thrown his poem forward into an indefinitely remote futurity. He pictures mankind amid the closing circumstances of the time-long warfare between Good and Evil. Our race is on the eve of its final triumph. Man is within the last stride of perfection; Woman, redeemed from the thraldom against which our Sybil uplifts so powerful and so sad a remonstrance, stands equal by his side, or communes for herself with angels; the Earth, sympathizing with her children's happier state, has clothed herself in such luxuriant and loving beauty as no eye ever witnessed since our first parents saw the sunrise over dewy Eden. Nor then, indeed; for this is the fulfilment of what was then but a golden promise. But the picture has its shadows. There remains to mankind another peril; a last encounter with the Evil Principle. Should the battle go against us, we sink back into the slime and misery of ages. If we triumph!—but it demands a poet's eye to contemplate the splendor of such a consummation, and not to be dazzled.

To this great work Keats is said to have brought so deep and tender a spirit of humanity, that the poem has all the sweet and warm interest of a village tale, no less than the grandeur which befits so high a theme. Such, at least, is the perhaps partial representation of his friends; for I have not read or heard even a single line of the performance in question. Keats, I am told, withholds it from the press, under an idea that the age has not enough of spiritual insight to receive it worthily. I do not like this distrust; it makes me distrust the poet. The Universe is waiting to respond to the highest word that the best child of time and immortality can utter. If it refuse to listen, it is because he mumbles and stammers, or discourses things unseasonable and foreign to the purpose.

I visited the House of Lords, the other day, to hear Canning, who, you know, is now a peer, with I forget what title. He disappointed me. Time blunts both point and edge, and does great mischief to men of his order of intellect. Then I stept into the Lower House, and listened to a few words from Cobbett, who looked as earthy as a real clodhopper, or, rather, as if he had lain a dozen years beneath the clods. The men, whom I meet now-a-days, often impress me thus; prob-

ably because my spirits are not very good, and lead me to
think much about graves, with the long grass upon them,
and weather-worn epitaphs, and dry bones of people who
made noise enough in their day, but now can only clatter,
clatter, clatter, when the sexton's spade disturbs them. Were
it only possible to find out who are alive, and who dead, it
would contribute infinitely to my peace of mind. Every day
of my life, somebody comes and stares me in the face, whom
I had quietly blotted out of the tablet of living men, and
trusted never more to be pestered with the sight or sound of
him. For instance, going to Drury Lane Theatre, a few eve-
nings since, up rose before me, in the ghost of Hamlet's
father, the bodily presence of the elder Kean, who did die,
or ought to have died, in some drunken fit or other, so long
ago that his fame is scarcely traditionary now. His powers
are quite gone; he was rather the ghost of himself than the
ghost of the Danish king.

In the stage-box sat several elderly and decrepit people,
and among them a stately ruin of a woman, on a very large
scale, with a profile—for I did not see her front face—that
stamped itself into my brain, as a seal impresses hot wax.
By the tragic gesture with which she took a pinch of snuff,
I was sure it must be Mrs. Siddons. Her brother, John
Kemble, sat behind, a broken-down figure, but still with a
kingly majesty about him. In lieu of all former achievements,
nature enables him to look the part of Lear far better than
in the meridian of his genius. Charles Matthews was likewise there; but a paralytic affection has distorted his once
mobile countenance into a most disagreeable one-sidedness,
from which he could no more wrench it into proper form
than he could re-arrange the face of the great globe itself. It
looks as if, for the joke's sake, the poor man had twisted his
features into an expression at once the most ludicrous and
horrible that he could contrive; and, at that very moment,

as a judgment for making himself so hideous, an avenging
Providence had seen fit to petrify him. Since it is out of his
own power, I would gladly assist him to change countenance;
for his ugly visage haunts me both at noontide and night-
time. Some other players of the past generation were present,
but none that greatly interested me. It behoves actors, more
than all other men of publicity, to vanish from the scene
betimes. Being, at best, but painted shadows flickering on the
wall, and empty sounds that echo another's thought, it is a
sad disenchantment when the colors begin to fade, and the
voices to croak with age.

What is there new, in the literary way, on your side of
the water? Nothing of the kind has come under my inspection, except a volume of poems, published above a year ago,
by Dr. Channing. I did not before know that this eminent
writer is a poet; nor does the volume alluded to exhibit any
of the characteristics of the author's mind, as displayed in his
prose works; although some of the poems have a richness that
is not merely of the surface, but glows still the brighter, the
deeper and more faithfully you look into them. They seem
carelessly wrought, however, like those rings and ornaments
of the very purest gold, but of rude, native manufacture,
which are found among the gold dust from Africa. I doubt
whether the American public will accept them; it looks less
to the assay of metal than to the neat and cunning manufacture. How slowly our literature grows up! Most of our writers
of promise have come to untimely ends. There was that wild
fellow, John Neal, who almost turned my boyish brain with
his romances; he surely has long been dead, else he never
could keep himself so quiet. Bryant has gone to his last sleep,
with the Thanatopsis gleaming over him, like a sculptured
marble sepulchre by moonlight. Halleck, who used to write
queer verses in the newspapers, and published a Don Juanic
poem called Fanny, is defunct as a poet, though averred to

be exemplifying the metempsychosis as a man of business. Somewhat later there was Whittier, a fiery Quaker youth, to whom the muse had perversely assigned a battle-trumpet, and who got himself lynched, ten years agone, in South Carolina. I remember, too, a lad just from college, Longfellow by name, who scattered some delicate verses to the winds, and went to Germany, and perished, I think, of intense application, at the University of Gottingen. Willis— what a pity!—was lost, if I recollect rightly, in 1833, on his voyage to Europe, whither he was going, to give us sketches of the world's sunny face. If these had lived, they might, one or all of them, have grown to be famous men.

And yet there is no telling—it may be as well that they have died. I was myself a young man of promise. Oh, shattered brain!—oh, broken spirit!—where is the fulfilment of that promise? The sad truth is, that when fate would gently disappoint the world, it takes away the hopefullest mortals in their youth;—when it would laugh the world's hopes to scorn, it lets them live. Let me die upon this apophthegm, for I shall never make a truer one!

What a strange substance is the human brain! Or rather— for there is no need of generalizing the remark—what an odd brain is mine! Would you believe it? Daily and nightly there come scraps of poetry humming in my intellectual ear— some as airy as bird-notes, and some as delicately neat as parlor-music, and a few as grand as organ-peals—that seem just such verses as those departed poets would have written, had not an inexorable destiny snatched them from their inkstands. They visit me in spirit, perhaps desiring to engage my services as the amanuensis of their posthumous productions, and thus secure the endless renown that they have forfeited by going hence too early. But I have my own business to attend to; and, besides, a medical gentleman, who interests himself in some little ailments of mine, advises me not to make too free use of pen and ink. There are clerks enough out of employment who would be glad of such a job.

Good bye! Are you alive or dead? And what are you about? Still scribbling for the Democratic? And do those infernal compositors and proof-readers misprint your unfortunate productions, as vilely as ever? It is too bad. Let every man manufacture his own nonsense, say I! Expect me home soon, and —to whisper you a secret—in company with the poet Campbell, who purposes to visit Wyoming, and enjoy the shadow of the laurels that he planted there. Campbell is now an old man. He calls himself well, better than ever in his life, but looks strangely pale, and so shadow-like, that one might almost poke a finger through his densest material. I tell him, by way of joke, that he is as dim and forlorn as Memory, though as unsubstantial as Hope.

Your true friend, P.

P. S. Pray present my most respectful regards to our venerable and revered friend, Mr. Brockden Brown. It gratifies me to learn that a complete edition of his works, in a double-columned octavo volume, is shortly to issue from the press, at Philadelphia. Tell him that no American writer enjoys a more classic reputation on this side of the water. *Is* old Joel Barlow yet alive? Unconscionable man! Why, he must have nearly fulfilled his century! And *does* he meditate an epic on the war between Mexico and Texas, with machinery contrived on the principle of the steam-engine, as being the nearest to celestial agency that our epoch can boast? How can he expect ever to rise again, if, while just sinking into his grave, he persists in burthening himself with such a ponderosity of leaden verses?

EARTH'S HOLOCAUST

O NCE upon a time—but whether in time past or time to come, is a matter of little or no moment—this wide world had become so overburthened with an accumulation of worn-out trumpery, that the inhabitants determined to rid themselves of it by a general bonfire. The site fixed upon, at the representation of the Insurance Companies, and as being as central a spot as any other on the globe, was one of the broadest prairies of the West, where no human habitation would be endangered by the flames, and where a vast assemblage of spectators might commodiously admire the show. Having a taste for sights of this kind, and imagining, likewise, that the illumination of the bonfire might reveal some profundity of moral truth, heretofore hidden in mist or darkness, I made it convenient to journey thither and be present. At my arrival, although the heap of condemned rubbish was as yet comparatively small, the torch had already been applied. Amid that boundless plain, in the dusk of evening, like a far-off star alone in the firmament, there was merely visible one tremulous gleam, whence none could have anticipated so fierce a blaze as was destined to ensue. With every moment, however, there came foot-travellers, women holding up their aprons, men on horseback, wheelbarrows, lumbering baggage-wagons, and other vehicles great and small, and from far and near, laden with articles that were judged fit for nothing but to be burnt.

"What materials have been used to kindle the flames?" inquired I of a bystander; for I was desirous of knowing the whole process of the affair, from beginning to end.

The person whom I addressed was a grave man, fifty years old or thereabout, who had evidently come thither as a looker-on; he struck me immediately as having weighed for himself the true value of life and its circumstances, and therefore as feeling little personal interest in whatever judgment the world might form of them. Before answering my question, he looked me in the face, by the kindling light of the fire.

"Oh, some very dry combustibles," replied he, "and extremely suitable to the purpose—no other, in fact, than yesterday's newspapers, last month's magazines, and last year's withered leaves. Here, now, comes some antiquated trash, that will take fire like a handfull of shavings."

As he spoke, some rough-looking men advanced to the verge of the bonfire, and threw in, as it appeared, all the rubbish of the Herald's Office; the blazonry of coat-armor; the crests and devices of illustrious families; pedigrees that extended back, like lines of light, into the mist of the dark ages; together with stars, garters, and embroidered collars; each of which, as paltry a bauble as it might appear to the uninstructed eye, had once possessed vast significance, and was still, in truth, reckoned among the most precious of moral or material facts, by the worshippers of the gorgeous past. Mingled with this confused heap, which was tossed into the flames by armsfull at once, were innumerable badges of knighthood; comprising those of all the European sovereignties, and Napoleon's decoration of the Legion of Honor, the ribands of which were entangled with those of the ancient order of St. Louis. There, too, were the medals of our own society of Cincinnati, by means of which, as history tells us, an order of hereditary knights came near being constituted out of the king-quellers of the Revolution. And, besides, there were the patents of nobility of German counts and barons, Spanish grandees, and English peers, from the worm-eaten instrument signed by William the Conqueror, down to the bran-new parchment of the latest lord, who has received his honors from the fair hand of Victoria.

At sight of the dense volumes of smoke, mingled with vivid jets of flame, that gushed and eddied forth from this immense pile of earthly distinctions, the multitude of plebeian spectators set up a joyous shout, and clapt their hands with an emphasis that made the welkin echo. That was their moment of triumph, achieved after long ages, over creatures of the same clay and same spiritual infirmities, who had dared to assume the privileges due only to Heaven's better workmanship. But now there rushed towards the blazing heap a gray-haired man, of stately presence, wearing a coat from the breast of which some star, or other badge of rank, seemed to have been forcibly wrenched away. He had not the tokens of intellectual power in his face; but still there was the demeanor—the habitual, and almost native dignity—of one who had been born to the idea of his own social superiority, and had never felt it questioned, till that moment.

"People," cried he, gazing at the ruin of what was dearest in his eyes, with grief and wonder, but, nevertheless, with a degree of stateliness—"people, what have you done! This fire is consuming all that marked your advance from barbarism, or that could have prevented your relapse thither. We—the men of the privileged orders—were those who kept alive, from age to age, the old chivalrous spirit; the gentle and generous thought; the higher, the purer, the more refined and delicate life! With the nobles, too, you cast off the poet, the painter, the sculptor—all the beautiful arts;—for we were their patrons, and created the atmosphere in which they flourish. In abolishing the majestic distinctions of rank, society loses not only its grace, but its steadfastness—"

More he would doubtless have spoken; but here there arose an outcry, sportive, contemptuous, and indignant, that altogether drowned the appeal of the fallen nobleman; insomuch that, casting one look of despair at his own half-burnt pedigree, he shrunk back into the crowd, glad to shelter himself under his new-found insignificance.

"Let him thank his stars that we have not flung him into the same fire!" shouted a rude figure, spurning the embers with his foot. "And, henceforth, let no man dare to show a piece of musty parchment, as his warrant for lording it over his fellows! If he have strength of arm, well and good; it is one species of superiority. If he have wit, wisdom, courage, force of character, let these attributes do for him what they may. But, from this day forward, no mortal must hope for place and consideration, by reckoning up the mouldy bones of his ancestors! That nonsense is done away."

"And in good time," remarked the grave observer by my side—in a low voice however—"if no worse nonsense come in its place. But at all events, this species of nonsense has fairly lived out its life."

There was little space to muse or moralize over the embers of this time-honored rubbish; for, before it was half burnt out, there came another multitude from beyond the sea, bearing the purple robes of royalty, and the crowns, globes, and sceptres of emperors and kings. All these had been condemned as useless baubles; playthings, at best, fit only for the infancy of the world, or rods to govern and chastise it in its nonage; but with which universal manhood, at its full-grown stature, could no longer brook to be insulted. Into such contempt had these regal insignia now fallen, that the gilded crown and tinselled robes of the player-king, from Drury

Lane Theatre, had been thrown in among the rest, doubtless as a mockery of his brother-monarchs, on the great stage of the world. It was a strange sight, to discern the crown-jewels of England, glowing and flashing in the midst of the fire. Some of them had been delivered down from the times of the Saxon princes; others were purchased with vast revenues, or, perchance, ravished from the dead brows of the native potentates of Hindostan; and the whole now blazed with a dazzling lustre, as if a star had fallen in that spot, and been shattered into fragments. The splendor of the ruined monarchy had no reflection, save in those inestimable precious-stones. But, enough on this subject! It were but tedious to describe how the Emperor of Austria's mantle was converted to tinder, and how the posts and pillars of the French throne became a heap of coals, which it was impossible to distinguish from those of any other wood. Let me add, however, that I noticed one of the exiled Poles, stirring up the bonfire with the Czar of Russia's sceptre, which he afterwards flung into the flames.

"The smell of singed garments is quite intolerable here," observed my new acquaintance, as the breeze enveloped us in the smoke of a royal wardrobe. "Let us get to windward, and see what they are doing on the other side of the bonfire."

We accordingly passed round, and were just in time to witness the arrival of a vast procession of Washingtonians— as the votaries of temperance call themselves now-a-days— accompanied by thousands of the Irish disciples of Father Mathew, with that great apostle at their head. They brought a rich contribution to the bonfire; being nothing less than all the hogsheads and barrels of liquor in the world, which they rolled before them across the prairie.

"Now, my children," cried Father Mathew, when they reached the verge of the fire—"one shove more, and the work is done! And now let us stand off, and see Satan deal with his own liquor!"

Accordingly, having placed their wooden vessels within reach of the flames, the procession stood off at a safe distance, and soon beheld them burst into a blaze that reached the clouds, and threatened to set the sky itself on fire. And well it might. For here was the whole world's stock of spirituous liquors, which, instead of kindling a frenzied light in the eyes of individual topers as of yore, soared upward with a bewildering gleam that startled all mankind. It was the aggregate of that fierce fire, which would otherwise have scorched the hearts of millions. Meantime, numberless bottles of precious wine were flung into the blaze; which lapped up the contents as if it loved them, and grew, like other drunkards, the merrier and fiercer for what it quaffed. Never again will the insatiable thirst of the fire-fiend be so pampered! Here were the treasures of famous bon-vivants—liquors that had been tossed on ocean, and mellowed in the sun, and hoarded long in the recesses of the earth—the pale, the gold, the ruddy juice of whatever vineyards were most delicate— the entire vintage of Tokay—all mingling in one stream with the vile fluids of the common pot-house, and contributing to heighten the self-same blaze. And while it rose in a gigantic spire, that seemed to wave against the arch of the firmament, and combine itself with the light of stars, the multitude gave a shout, as if the broad earth were exulting in its deliverance from the curse of ages.

But the joy was not universal. Many deemed that human life would be gloomier than ever, when that brief illumination should sink down. While the reformers were at work, I had overheard muttered expostulations from several respectable gentlemen with red noses, and wearing gouty shoes; and a ragged worthy, whose face looked like a hearth where the fire is burnt out, now expressed his discontent more openly and boldly.

"What is this world good for," said the Last Toper, "now that we can never be jolly any more? What is to comfort the poor man in sorrow and perplexity?—how is he to keep his heart warm against the cold winds of this cheerless earth?—and what do you propose to give him, in exchange for the solace that you take away? How are old friends to sit together by the fireside, without a cheerful glass between them? A plague upon your reformation! It is a sad world, a cold world, a selfish world, a low world, not worth an honest fellow's living in, now that good-fellowship is gone forever!"

This harangue excited great mirth among the bystanders. But, preposterous as was the sentiment, I could not help commiserating the forlorn condition of the Last Toper, whose boon-companions had dwindled away from his side, leaving the poor fellow without a soul to countenance him in sipping his liquor, nor, indeed, any liquor to sip. Not that this was quite the true state of the case; for I had observed him, at a critical moment, filch a bottle of fourth-proof brandy that fell beside the bonfire, and hide it in his pocket.

The spirituous and fermented liquors being thus disposed of, the zeal of the reformers next induced them to replenish the fire with all the boxes of tea and bags of coffee in the world. And now came the planters of Virginia, bringing their crops of tobacco. These, being cast upon the heap of inutility, aggregated it to the size of a mountain, and incensed the atmosphere with such potent fragrance, that methought we should never draw pure breath again. The present sacrifice seemed to startle the lovers of the weed, more than any that they had hitherto witnessed.

"Well;—they've put my pipe out," said an old gentleman, flinging it into the flames in a pet. "What is this world coming to? Everything rich and racy—all the spice of life—is to be condemned as useless. Now that they have kindled the bonfire, if these nonsensical reformers would fling themselves into it, all would be well enough!"

"Be patient," responded a staunch conservative;—"it will come to that in the end. They will first fling us in, and finally themselves."

From the general and systematic measures of reform, I now turned to consider the individual contributions to this memorable bonfire. In many instances, these were of a very amusing character. One poor fellow threw in his empty purse, and another, a bundle of counterfeit or insolvable banknotes. Fashionable ladies threw in their last season's bonnets, together with heaps of ribbon, yellow lace, and much other half-worn milliner's ware; all of which proved even more evanescent in the fire, than it had been in the fashion. A multitude of lovers, of both sexes—discarded maids or bachelors, and couples, mutually weary of one another—tossed in bundles of perfumed letters and enamored sonnets. A hack-politician, being deprived of bread by the loss of office, threw in his teeth, which happened to be false ones. The Rev. Sydney Smith—having voyaged across the Atlantic for that sole purpose—came up to the bonfire, with a bitter grin, and threw in certain repudiated bonds, fortified though they were with the broad seal of a sovereign state. A little boy of five years old, in the premature manliness of the present epoch, threw in his playthings; a college-graduate, his diploma; an apothecary, ruined by the spread of homœopathy, his whole stock of drugs and medicines; a physician, his library; a parson, his old sermons; and a fine gentleman of the old school, his code of manners, which he had formerly written down for the benefit of the next generation. A widow, resolving on a second marriage, slily threw in her dead husband's miniature. A young man, jilted by his mistress, would willingly have flung his own desperate heart into the flames, but could find no means to wrench it out of his bosom. An

American author, whose works were neglected by the public, threw his pen and paper into the bonfire, and betook himself to some less discouraging occupation. It somewhat startled me to overhear a number of ladies, highly respectable in appearance, proposing to fling their gowns and petticoats into the flames, and assume the garb, together with the manners, duties, offices, and responsibilities, of the opposite sex.

What favor was accorded to this scheme, I am unable to say; my attention being suddenly drawn to a poor, deceived, and half-delirious girl, who, exclaiming that she was the most worthless thing alive or dead, attempted to cast herself into the fire, amid all that wrecked and broken trumpery of the world. A good man, however, ran to her rescue.

"Patience, my poor girl!" said he, as he drew her back from the fierce embrace of the destroying angel. "Be patient, and abide Heaven's will. So long as you possess a living soul, all may be restored to its first freshness. These things of matter, and creations of human fantasy, are fit for nothing but to be burnt, when once they have had their day. But your day is Eternity!"

"Yes," said the wretched girl, whose frenzy seemed now to have sunk down into deep despondency;—"yes; and the sunshine is blotted out of it!"

It was now rumored among the spectators, that all the weapons and munitions of war were to be thrown into the bonfire; with the exception of the world's stock of gunpowder, which, as the safest mode of disposing of it, had already been drowned in the sea. This intelligence seemed to awaken great diversity of opinion. The hopeful philanthropist esteemed it a token that the millenium was already come; while persons of another stamp, in whose view mankind was a breed of bull-dogs, prophesied that all the old stoutness, fervor, nobleness, generosity, and magnanimity of the race, would disappear; these qualities, as they affirmed, requiring blood for their nourishment. They comforted themselves, however, in the belief that the proposed abolition of war was impracticable, for any length of time together.

Be that as it might, numberless great guns, whose thunder had long been the voice of battle—the artillery of the Armada, the battering-trains of Marlborough, and the adverse cannon of Napoleon and Wellington—were trundled into the midst of the fire. By the continual addition of dry combustibles, it had now waxed so intense, that neither brass nor iron could withstand it. It was wonderful to behold, how those terrible instruments of slaughter melted away like playthings of wax. Then the armies of the earth wheeled around the mighty furnace, with their military music playing triumphant marches, and flung in their muskets and swords. The standard-bearers, likewise, cast one look upward at their banners, all tattered with shot-holes, and inscribed with the names of victorious fields; and giving them a last flourish on the breeze, they lowered them into the flame, which snatched them upward in its rush towards the clouds. This ceremony being over, the world was left without a single weapon in its hands, except, possibly, a few old King's arms and rusty swords, and other trophies of the Revolution, in some of our state-armories. And now the drums were beaten and the trumpets brayed all together, as a prelude to the proclamation of universal and eternal peace, and the announcement that glory was no longer to be won by blood; but that it would henceforth be the contention of the human race, to work out the greatest mutual good; and that beneficence, in the future annals of the earth, would claim the praise of valor. The blessed tidings were accordingly promulgated, and caused infinite rejoicings among those who had stood aghast at the horror and absurdity of war.

But I saw a grim smile pass over the scarred visage of a stately old commander—by his war-worn figure and rich military dress, he might have been one of Napoleon's famous marshals—who, with the rest of the world's soldiery, had just flung away the sword, that had been familiar to his right hand for half-a-century.

"Aye, aye!" grumbled he. "Let them proclaim what they please; but, in the end, we shall find that all this foolery has only made more work for the armorers and cannon-founderies."

"Why, Sir," exclaimed I, in astonishment, "do you imagine that the human race will ever so far return on the steps of its past madness, as to weld another sword, or cast another cannon?"

"There will be no need," observed, with a sneer, one who neither felt benevolence, nor had faith in it. "When Cain wished to slay his brother, he was at no loss for a weapon."

"We shall see," replied the veteran commander.—"If I am mistaken, so much the better; but, in my opinion—without pretending to philosophize about the matter—the necessity of war lies far deeper than these honest gentlemen suppose. What! Is there a field for all the petty disputes of individuals, and shall there be no great law-court for the settlement of national difficulties? The battle-field is the only court where such suits can be tried!"

"You forget, General," rejoined I, "that, in this advanced stage of civilization, Reason and Philanthropy combined will constitute just such a tribunal as is requisite."

"Ah, I had forgotten that, indeed!" said the old warrior, as he limped away.

The fire was now to be replenished with materials that had hitherto been considered of even greater importance to the well-being of society, than the warlike munitions which we had already seen consumed. A body of reformers had travelled all over the earth, in quest of the machinery by which the different nations were accustomed to inflict the punishment of death. A shudder passed through the multitude, as these ghastly emblems were dragged forward. Even the flames seemed at first to shrink away, displaying the shape and murderous contrivance of each in a full blaze of light, which, of itself, was sufficient to convince mankind of the long and deadly error of human law. Those old implements of cruelty—those horrible monsters of mechanism—those inventions which it seemed to demand something worse than man's natural heart to contrive, and which had lurked in the dusky nooks of ancient prisons, the subject of terror-stricken legends—were now brought forth to view. Headsmen's axes, with the rust of noble and royal blood upon them, and a vast collection of halters that had choked the breath of plebeian victims, were thrown in together. A shout greeted the arrival of the guillotine, which was thrust forward on the same wheels that had borne it from one to another of the blood-stained streets of Paris. But the loudest roar of applause went up, telling the distant sky of the triumph of the earth's redemption, when the gallows made its appearance. An ill-looking fellow, however, rushed forward, and putting himself in the path of the reformers, bellowed hoarsely, and fought with brute fury to stay their progress.

It was little matter of surprise, perhaps, that the executioner should thus do his best to vindicate and uphold the machinery by which he himself had his livelihood, and worthier individuals their death. But it deserved special note, that men of a far different sphere—even of that consecrated class in whose guardianship the world is apt to trust its benevolence—were found to take the hangman's view of the question.

"Stay, my brethren!" cried one of them. "You are misled by a false philanthropy!—you know not what you do. The gallows is a heaven-oriented instrument! Bear it back, then, reverently, and set it up in its old place; else the world will fall to speedy ruin and desolation!"

"Onward, onward!" shouted a leader in the reform. "Into the flames with the accursed instrument of man's bloody policy! How can human law inculcate benevolence and love, while it persists in setting up the gallows as its chief symbol? One heave more, good friends; and the world will be redeemed from its greatest error!"

A thousand hands, that, nevertheless, loathed the touch, now lent their assistance, and thrust the ominous burthen far, far, into the centre of the raging furnace. There its fatal and abhorred image was beheld, first black, then a red coal, then ashes.

"That was well done!" exclaimed I.

"Yes; it was well done," replied—but with less enthusiasm than I expected—the thoughtful observer who was still at my side; "well done, if the world be good enough for the measure. Death, however, is an idea that cannot easily be dispensed with, in any condition between the primal innocence and that other purity and perfection, which, perchance, we are destined to attain, after travelling round the full circle. But, at all events, it is well that the experiment should now be tried."

"Too cold!—too cold!" impatiently exclaimed the young and ardent leader in this triumph. "Let the heart have its voice here, as well as the intellect. And as for ripeness—and as for progress—let mankind always do the highest, kindest, noblest thing, that, at any given period, it has attained to the perception of; and surely that thing cannot be wrong, nor wrongly timed!"

I know not whether it were the excitement of the scene, or whether the good people around the bonfire were really growing more enlightened, every instant; but they now proceeded to measures, in the full length of which I was hardly prepared to keep them company. For instance, some threw their marriage-certificates into the flames, and declared themselves candidates for a higher, holier, and more comprehensive union than that which had subsisted from the birth of time, under the form of the connubial tie. Others hastened to the vaults of banks, and to the coffers of the rich—all of which were open to the first-comer, on this fated occasion—and brought entire bales of paper-money to enliven the blaze, and tons of coin to be melted down by its intensity. Henceforth, they said, universal benevolence, uncoined and exhaustless, was to be the golden currency of the world. At this intelligence, the bankers, and speculators in the stocks, grew pale; and a pick-pocket, who had reaped a rich harvest among the crowd, fell down in a deadly fainting-fit. A few men of business burnt their day-books and legers, the notes and obligations of their creditors, and all other evidences of debts due to themselves; while perhaps a somewhat larger number satisfied their zeal for reform with the sacrifice of any uncomfortable recollection of their own indebtment. There was then a cry, that the period was arrived, when the title-deeds of landed property should be given to the flames, and the whole soil of the earth revert to the public, from whom it had been wrongfully abstracted, and most unequally distributed among individuals. Another party demanded, that all written constitutions, set forms of government, legislative acts, statute-books, and everything else on which human invention had endeavored to stamp its arbitrary laws, should at once be destroyed, leaving the consummated world as free as the man first created.

Whether any ultimate action was taken with regard to these propositions, is beyond my knowledge; for, just then, some matters were in progress that concerned my sympathies more nearly.

"See!—see!—what heaps of books and pamphlets," cried a fellow, who did not seem to be a lover of literature. "Now we shall have a glorious blaze!"

"That's just the thing," said a modern philosopher. "Now we shall get rid of the weight of dead men's thought, which has hitherto pressed so heavily on the living intellect, that it has been incompetent to any effectual self-exertion. Well done, my lads! Into the fire with them! Now you are enlightening the world, indeed!"

"But what is to become of the Trade?" cried a frantic bookseller.

"Oh, by all means, let them accompany their merchandise," coolly observed an author. "It will be a noble funeral-pile!"

The truth was, that the human race had now reached a stage of progress, so far beyond what the wisest and wittiest men of former ages had ever dreamed of, that it would have been a manifest absurdity to allow the earth to be any longer encumbered with their poor achievements in the literary line. Accordingly, a thorough and searching investigation had swept the booksellers' shops, hawkers' stands, public and private libraries, and even the little book-shelf by the country fireside, and had brought the world's entire mass of printed paper, bound or in sheets, to swell the already mountain-bulk of our illustrious bonfire. Thick, heavy folios, containing the labors of lexicographers, commentators, and encyclopediasts, were flung in, and, falling among the embers with a leaden thump, smouldered away to ashes, like rotten wood. The small, richly-gilt, French tomes, of the last age, with the hundred volumes of Voltaire among them, went off in a brilliant shower of sparkles, and little jets of flame; while the current literature of the same nation burnt red and blue, and threw an infernal light over the visages of the spectators, converting them all to the aspect of parti-colored fiends. A collection of German stories emitted a scent of brimstone. The English standard authors made excellent fuel, generally exhibiting the properties of sound oak logs. Milton's works, in particular, sent up a powerful blaze, gradually reddening into a coal, which promised to endure longer than almost any other material of the pile. From Shakspeare there gushed a flame of such marvellous splendor, that men shaded their eyes as against the sun's meridian glory; nor, even when the works of his own elucidators were flung upon him, did he cease to flash forth a dazzling radiance, from beneath the ponderous heap. It is my belief, that he is still blazing as fervidly as ever.

"Could a poet but light a lamp at that glorious flame," remarked I, "he might then consume the midnight oil to some good purpose."

"That is the very thing which modern poets have been too apt to do—or, at least, to attempt," answered a critic. "The chief benefit to be expected from this conflagration of past literature, undoubtedly is, that writers will henceforth be compelled to light their lamps at the sun or stars."

"If they can reach so high," said I. "But that task requires a giant, who may afterwards distribute the light among inferior men. It is not every one that can steal the fire from Heaven, like Prometheus; but when once he had done the deed, a thousand hearths were kindled by it."

It amazed me much to observe, how indefinite was the proportion between the physical mass of any given author, and the property of brilliant and long-continued combustion. For instance, there was not a quarto volume of the last century—nor, indeed, of the present—that could compete, in that particular, with a child's little gilt-covered book, containing Mother Goose's Melodies. The Life and Death of Tom Thumb outlasted the biography of Marlborough. An epic— indeed, a dozen of them—was converted to white ashes, before the single sheet of an old ballad was half-consumed. In more than one case, too, when volumes of applauded verse proved incapable of anything better than a stifling smoke, an unregarded ditty of some nameless bard—perchance, in the corner of a newspaper—soared up among the stars, with a flame as brilliant as their own. Speaking of the properties of flame, methought Shelley's poetry emitted a purer light than almost any other productions of his day; contrasting beautifully with the fitful and lurid gleams, and gushes of black vapor, that flashed and eddied from the volumes of Lord Byron. As for Tom Moore, some of his songs diffused an odor like a burning pastille.

I felt particular interest in watching the combustion of American authors, and scrupulously noted, by my watch, the precise number of moments that changed most of them from shabbily-printed books to indistinguishable ashes. It would be invidious, however, if not perilous, to betray these awful secrets; so that I shall content myself with observing, that it was not invariably the writer most frequent in the public mouth, that made the most splendid appearance in the bonfire. I especially remember, that a great deal of excellent inflammability was exhibited in a thin volume of poems by Ellery Channing; although, to speak the truth, there were certain portions that hissed and spluttered in a very disagreeable fashion. A curious phenomenon occurred, in reference to several writers, native as well as foreign. Their books, though of highly respectable figure, instead of bursting into a blaze, or even smouldering out their substance in smoke, suddenly melted away, in a manner that proved them to be ice.

If it be no lack of modesty to mention my own works, it must here be confessed, that I looked for them with fatherly interest, but in vain. Too probably, they were changed to vapor by the first action of the heat; at best, I can only hope, that, in their quiet way, they contributed a glimmering spark or two to the splendor of the evening.

"Alas, and woe is me!" thus bemoaned himself a heavy-looking gentleman in green spectacles. "The world is utterly ruined, and there is nothing to live for any longer! The business of my life is snatched from me. Not a volume to be had for love or money!"

"This," remarked the sedate observer beside me, "is a book-worm—one of those men who are born to gnaw dead thoughts. His clothes, you see, are covered with the dust of libraries. He has no inward fountain of ideas; and, in good earnest, now that the old stock is abolished, I do not see what is to become of the poor fellow. Have you no word of comfort for him?"

"My dear Sir," said I to the desperate book-worm, "is not Nature better than a book?—is not the human heart deeper than any system of philosophy?—is not life replete with more instruction than past observers have found it possible to write down in maxims? Be of good cheer! The great book of Time is still spread wide open before us; and, if we read it aright, it will be to us a volume of eternal Truth."

"Oh, my books, my books, my precious, printed books!" reiterated the forlorn book-worm. "My only reality was a bound volume; and now they will not leave me even a shadowy pamphlet!"

In fact, the last remnant of the literature of all the ages was now descending upon the blazing heap, in the shape of a cloud of pamphlets from the press of the New World. These, likewise, were consumed in the twinkling of an eye, leaving the earth, for the first time since the days of Cadmus, free from the plague of letters—an enviable field for the authors of the next generation!

"Well!—and does anything remain to be done?" inquired I, somewhat anxiously. "Unless we set fire to the earth itself, and then leap boldly off into infinite space, I know not that we can carry reform to any further point."

"You are vastly mistaken, my good friend," said the observer. "Believe me, the fire will not be allowed to settle down, without the addition of fuel that will startle many persons, who have lent a willing hand thus far."

Nevertheless, there appeared to be a relaxation of effort, for a little time, during which, probably, the leaders of the movement were considering what should be done next. In the interval, a philosopher threw his theory into the flames; a sacrifice, which, by those who knew how to estimate it, was pronounced the most remarkable that had yet been made. The combustion, however, was by no means brilliant. Some indefatigable people, scorning to take a moment's ease, now employed themselves in collecting all the withered leaves and fallen boughs of the forest, and thereby recruited the bonfire to a greater height than ever. But this was mere by-play.

"Here comes the fresh fuel that I spoke of," said my companion.

To my astonishment, the persons who now advanced into the vacant space, around the mountain of fire, bore surplices and other priestly garments, mitres, crosiers, and a confusion of popish and protestant emblems, with which it seemed their purpose to consummate this great Act of Faith. Crosses, from the spires of old cathedrals, were cast upon the heap, with as little remorse as if the reverence of centuries, passing in long array beneath the lofty towers, had not looked up to them as the holiest of symbols. The font, in which infants were consecrated to God; the sacramental vessels, whence Piety had received the hallowed draught; were given to the same destruction. Perhaps it most nearly touched my heart, to see, among these devoted relics, fragments of the humble communion-tables and undecorated pulpits, which I recognized as having been torn from the meeting-houses of New-

England. Those simple edifices might have been permitted to
retain all of sacred embellishment that their Puritan founders
had bestowed, even though the mighty structure of St. Peter's
had sent its spoils to the fire of this terrible sacrifice. Yet I
felt that these were but the externals of religion, and might
most safely be relinquished by spirits that best knew their
deep significance.

"All is well," said I, cheerfully. "The wood-paths shall be
the aisles of our cathedral—the firmament itself shall be its
ceiling! What needs an earthly roof between the Deity and
his worshipper? Our faith can well afford to lose all the
drapery that even the holiest men have thrown around it, and
be only the more sublime in its simplicity."

"True," said my companion. "But will they pause here?"

The doubt, implied in his question, was well-founded. In
the general destruction of books, already described, a holy
volume—that stood apart from the catalogue of human literature, and yet, in one sense, was at its head—had been spared.
But the Titan of innovation—angel or fiend, double in his
nature, and capable of deeds befitting both characters—at
first shaking down only the old and rotten shapes of things,
had now, as it appeared, laid his terrible hand upon the main
pillars, which supported the whole edifice of our moral and
spiritual state. The inhabitants of the earth had grown too
enlightened to define their faith within a form of words, or
to limit the spiritual by any analogy to our material existence.
Truths, which the Heavens trembled at, were now but a
fable of the world's infancy. Therefore, as the final sacrifice
of human error, what else remained, to be thrown upon the
embers of that awful pile, except the Book, which, though a
celestial revelation to past ages, was but a voice from a lower
sphere, as regarded the present race of man? It was done!
Upon the blazing heap of falsehood and worn-out truth—
things that the earth had never needed, or had ceased to

need, or had grown childishly weary of—fell the ponderous church-Bible, the great old volume, that had lain so long on the cushions of the pulpit, and whence the pastor's solemn voice had given holy utterances, on so many a Sabbath-day. There, likewise, fell the family-Bible, which the long-buried patriarch had read to his children—in prosperity or sorrow, by the fireside, and in the summer-shade of trees—and had bequeathed downward, as the heirloom of generations. There fell the bosom-Bible, the little volume that had been the soul's friend of some sorely tried Child of Dust, who thence took courage, whether his trial were for life or death, steadfastly confronting both, in the strong assurance of Immortality.

All these were flung into the fierce and riotous blaze; and then a mighty wind came roaring across the plain, with a desolate howl, as if it were the angry lamentation of the Earth for the loss of Heaven's sunshine; and it shook the gigantic pyramid of flame, and scattered the cinders of half-consumed abominations around upon the spectators.

"This is terrible!" said I, feeling that my cheek grew pale, and seeing a like change in the visages about me.

"Be of good courage yet," answered the man with whom I had so often spoken. He continued to gaze steadily at the spectacle, with a singular calmness, as if it concerned him merely as an observer.—"Be of good courage—nor yet exult too much; for there is far less both of good and evil, in the effect of this bonfire, than the world might be willing to believe."

"How can that be?" exclaimed I, impatiently.—"Has it not consumed everything? Has it not swallowed up, or melted down, every human or divine appendage of our mortal state, that had substance enough to be acted on by fire? Will there be anything left us, tomorrow morning, better or worse than a heap of embers and ashes?"

"Assuredly there will," said my grave friend. "Come hither tomorrow morning—or whenever the combustible portion of the pile shall be quite burnt out—and you will find among the ashes everything really valuable that you have seen cast into the flames. Trust me; the world of tomorrow will again enrich itself with the gold and diamonds, which have been cast off by the world of to-day. Not a truth is destroyed—nor buried so deep among the ashes, but it will be raked up at last."

This was a strange assurance. Yet I felt inclined to credit it; the more especially as I beheld, among the wallowing flames, a copy of the Holy Scriptures, the pages of which, instead of being blackened into tinder, only assumed a more dazzling whiteness, as the finger-marks of human imperfection were purified away. Certain marginal notes and commentaries, it is true, yielded to the intensity of the fiery test, but without detriment to the smallest syllable that had flamed from the pen of inspiration.

"Yes;—there is the proof of what you say," answered I, turning to the observer. "But, if only what is evil can feel the action of the fire, then, surely, the conflagration has been of inestimable utility. Yet, if I understand aright, you intimate a doubt whether the world's expectation of benefit will be realized by it."

"Listen to the talk of these worthies," said he, pointing to a group in front of the blazing pile.—"Possibly, they may teach you something useful, without intending it."

The persons, whom he indicated, consisted of that brutal and most earthy figure, who had stood forth so furiously in defence of the gallows—the hangman, in short—together with the Last Thief and the Last Murderer; all three of whom were clustered about the Last Toper. The latter was liberally passing the brandy-bottle, which he had rescued from the general destruction of wines and spirits. This little

convivial party seemed at the lowest pitch of despondency;
as considering that the purified world must needs be utterly
unlike, the sphere that they had hitherto known, and therefore but a strange and desolate abode for gentlemen of their
kidney.

"The best counsel for all of us, is," remarked the hangman,
"that—as soon as we have finished the last drop of liquor—
I help you, my three friends, to a comfortable end upon the
nearest tree, and then hang myself on the same bough. This
is no world for us, any longer."

"Poh, poh, my good fellows!" said a dark-complexioned personage, who now joined the group—his complexion was indeed fearfully dark; and his eyes glowed with a redder light
than that of the bonfire—"Be not so cast down, my dear
friends; you shall see good days yet. There is one thing that
these wiseacres have forgotten to throw into the fire, and
without which all the rest of the conflagration is just nothing
at all—yes; though they had burnt the earth itself to a cinder!"

"And what may that be?" eagerly demanded the Last
Murderer.

"What, but the human heart itself!" said the dark-visaged
stranger, with a portentous grin. "And, unless they hit upon
some method of purifying that foul cavern, forth from it will
re-issue all the shapes of wrong and misery—the same old
shapes, or worse ones—which they have taken such a vast
deal of trouble to consume to ashes. I have stood by, this
live-long night, and laughed in my sleeve at the whole business. Oh, take my word for it, it will be the old world yet!"

This brief conversation supplied me with a theme for
lengthened thought. How sad a truth—if true it were—that
Man's age-long endeavor for perfection had served only to
render him the mockery of the Evil Principle, from the fatal
circumstance of an error at the very root of the matter! The
Heart—the Heart—there was the little, yet boundless sphere,

wherein existed the original wrong, of which the crime and misery of this outward world were merely types. Purify that inner sphere; and the many shapes of evil that haunt the outward, and which now seem almost our only realities, will turn to shadowy phantoms, and vanish of their own accord. But, if we go no deeper than the Intellect, and strive, with merely that feeble instrument, to discern and rectify what is wrong, our whole accomplishment will be a dream; so unsubstantial, that it matters little whether the bonfire, which I have so faithfully described, were what we choose to call a real event, and a flame that would scorch the finger—or only a phosphoric radiance, and a parable of my own brain!

PASSAGES FROM A RELINQUISHED
WORK

AT HOME

FROM INFANCY, I was under the guardianship
of a village parson, who made me the subject of daily
prayer and the sufferer of innumerable stripes, using
no distinction, as to these marks of paternal love, between
myself and his own three boys. The result, it must be owned,
has been very different in their cases and mine; they being
all respectable men, and well settled in life, the eldest as the
successor to his father's pulpit, the second as a physician, and
the third as a partner in a wholesale shoe store; while I, with
better prospects than either of them, have run the course,
which this volume will describe. Yet there is room for doubt,
whether I should have been any better contented with such
success as theirs, than with my own misfortunes; at least,
till after my experience of the latter had made it too late for
another trial.

My guardian had a name of considerable eminence, and
fitter for the place it occupies in ecclesiastical history, than
for so frivolous a page as mine. In his own vicinity, among
the lighter part of his hearers, he was called Parson Thumpcushion, from the very forcible gestures with which he
illustrated his doctrines. Certainly, if his powers as a preacher
were to be estimated by the damage done to his pulpit

furniture, none of his living brethren, and but few dead ones, would have been worthy even to pronounce a benediction after him. Such pounding and expounding, the moment he began to grow warm, such slapping with his open palm, thumping with his closed fist, and banging with the whole weight of the great Bible, convinced me that he held, in imagination, either the Old Nick or some Unitarian infidel at bay, and belabored his unhappy cushion as proxy for those abominable adversaries. Nothing but this exercise of the body, while delivering his sermons, could have supported the good parson's health under the mental toil, which they cost him in composition.

Though Parson Thumpcushion had an upright heart, and some called it a warm one, he was invariably stern and severe, on principle, I suppose, to me. With late justice, though early enough, even now, to be tinctured with generosity, I acknowledge him to have been a good and a wise man, after his own fashion. If his management failed as to myself, it succeeded with his three sons; nor, I must frankly say, could any mode of education, with which it was possible for him to be acquainted, have made me much better than what I was, or led me to a happier fortune than the present. He could neither change the nature that God gave me, nor adapt his own inflexible mind to my peculiar character. Perhaps it was my chief misfortune that I had neither father nor mother alive; for parents have an instinctive sagacity, in regard to the welfare of their children; and the child feels a confidence both in the wisdom and affection of his parents, which he cannot transfer to any delegate of their duties, however conscientious. An orphan's fate is hard, be he rich or poor. As for Parson Thumpcushion, whenever I see the old gentleman in my dreams, he looks kindly and sorrowfully at me, holding out his hand, as if each had something to forgive. With such kindness, and such forgiveness, but without the sorrow, may our next meeting be!

I was a youth of gay and happy temperament, with an incorrigible levity of spirit, of no vicious propensities, sensible enough, but wayward and fanciful. What a character was this, to be brought in contact with the stern old Pilgrim spirit of my guardian! We were at variance on a thousand points; but our chief and final dispute arose from the pertinacity with which he insisted on my adopting a particular profession; while I, being heir to a moderate competence, had avowed my purpose of keeping aloof from the regular business of life. This would have been a dangerous resolution, any where in the world; it was fatal, in New-England. There is a grossness in the conceptions of my countrymen; they will not be convinced that any good thing may consist with what they call idleness; they can anticipate nothing but evil of a young man who neither studies physic, law, nor gospel, nor opens a store, nor takes to farming, but manifests an incomprehensible disposition to be satisfied with what his father left him. The principle is excellent, in its general influence, but most miserable in its effect on the few that violate it. I had a quick sensitiveness to public opinion, and felt as if it ranked me with the tavern-haunters and town-paupers,—with the drunken poet, who hawked his own fourth of July odes,— and the broken soldier, who had been good for nothing since last war. The consequence of all this, was a piece of light-hearted desperation.

I do not over-estimate my notoriety, when I take it for granted, that many of my readers must have heard of me, in the wild way of life which I adopted. The idea of becoming a wandering story teller had been suggested, a year or two before, by an encounter with several merry vagabonds in a showman's wagon, where they and I had sheltered ourselves during a summer shower. The project was not more extravagant than most which a young man forms. Stranger ones are executed every day; and not to mention my proto-types in the East, and the wandering orators and poets whom my own ears have heard, I had the example of one illustrious itinerant in the other hemisphere; of Goldsmith, who planned and performed his travels through France and Italy, on a less promising scheme than mine. I took credit to myself for various qualifications, mental and personal, suited to the undertaking. Besides, my mind had latterly tormented me for employment, keeping up an irregular activity even in sleep, and making me conscious that I must toil, if it were but in catching butterflies. But my chief motives were dis-content with home, and a bitter grudge against Parson Thumpcushion, who would rather have laid me in my father's tomb, than seen me either a novelist or an actor; two characters which I thus hit upon a method of uniting. After all, it was not half so foolish as if I had written romances, instead of reciting them.

The following pages will contain a picture of my vagrant life, intermixed with specimens, generally brief and slight, of that great mass of fiction to which I gave existence, and which has vanished like cloud-shapes. Besides the occasions when I sought a pecuniary reward, I was accustomed to exercise my narrative faculty, wherever chance had collected a little audience, idle enough to listen. These rehearsals were useful in testing the strong points of my stories; and, indeed, the flow of fancy soon came upon me so abundantly, that its indulgence was its own reward; though the hope of praise, also, became a powerful incitement. Since I shall never feel the warm gush of new thought, as I did then, let me beseech the reader to believe, that my tales were not always so cold as he may find them now. With each specimen will be given a sketch of the circumstances in which the story was told. Thus my air-drawn pictures will be set in frames, perhaps more valuable than the pictures themselves, since they will be embossed with groups of characteristic figures, amid the lake and mountain scenery, the villages and fertile fields, of our native land. But I write the book for the sake of its moral, which many a dreaming youth may profit by, though it is the experience of a wandering story teller.

A Flight in the Fog

I set out on my rambles one morning in June, about sunrise. The day promised to be fair, though, at that early hour, a heavy mist lay along the earth, and settled, in minute globules, on the folds of my clothes, so that I looked precisely as if touched with a hoar-frost. The sky was quite obscured, and the trees and houses invisible, till they grew out of the fog as I came close upon them. There is a hill towards the west, whence the road goes abruptly down, holding a level course through the village, and ascending an eminence on the other side, behind which it disappears. The whole view comprises an extent of half a mile. Here I paused, and, while gazing through the misty veil, it partially rose and swept away, with so sudden an effect, that a gray cloud seemed to have taken the aspect of a small white town. A thin vapor being still diffused through the atmosphere, the wreaths and pillars of fog, whether hung in air or based on earth, appeared not less substantial than the edifices, and gave their own indistinctness to the whole. It was singular, that such an unromantic scene should look so visionary.

Half of the parson's dwelling was a dingy white house, and half of it was a cloud; but Squire Moody's mansion, the grandest in the village, was wholly visible, even the lattice-work of the balcony under the front window; while, in another place, only two red chimneys were seen above the mist, appertaining to my own paternal residence, then tenanted by strangers. I could not remember those with whom I had dwelt there, not even my mother. The brick edifice of the bank was in the clouds; the foundations of what was to be a great block of buildings had vanished, ominously, as it proved; the dry-good store of Mr. Nightingale seemed a doubtful concern; and Dominicus Pike's tobacco-manufactory an affair of smoke, except the splendid image of an Indian chief in front. The white spire of the meeting-house ascended out of the densest heap of vapor, as if that shadowy base were its only support; or, to give a truer interpretation, the steeple was the emblem of religion, enveloped in mystery below, yet pointing to a cloudless atmosphere, and catching the brightness of the east on its gilded vane.

As I beheld these objects, and the dewy street, with grassy intervals and a border of trees between the wheel-track and the side-walks, all so indistinct, and not to be traced without an effort, the whole seemed more like memory than reality. I would have imagined that years had already passed, and I was far away, contemplating that dim picture of my native place, which I should retain in my mind through the mist of time. No tears fell from my eyes among the dew-drops of the morning; nor does it occur to me that I heaved a sigh. In truth, I had never felt such a delicious excitement, nor known what freedom was till that moment, when I gave up my home, and took the whole world in exchange, fluttering the wings of my spirit, as if I would have flown from one star to another through the universe. I waved my hand towards the dusky village, bade it a joyous farewell, and turned away, to follow any path but that which might lead me back. Never was Childe Harold's sentiment adopted in a spirit more unlike his own.

Naturally enough, I thought of Don Quixote. Recollecting how the knight and Sancho had watched for auguries, when they took the road to Toboso, I began, between jest and earnest, to feel a similar anxiety. It was gratified, and by a more poetical phenomenon than the braying of the dappled ass, or the neigh of Rosinante. The sun, then just above the horizon, shone faintly through the fog, and formed a species of rainbow in the west, bestriding my intended road like a gigantic portal. I had never known, before, that a bow could be generated between the sunshine and the morning mist. It had no brilliancy, no perceptible hues; but was a mere unpainted frame-work, as white and ghost-like as the lunar rainbow, which is deemed ominous of evil. But, with a light heart, to which all omens were propitious, I advanced beneath the misty archway of futurity.

I had determined not to enter on my profession within a hundred miles of home, and then to cover myself with a fictitious name. The first precaution was reasonable enough, as otherwise Parson Thumpcushion might have put an untimely catastrophe to my story; but as nobody would be much affected by my disgrace, and all was to be suffered in my own person, I know not why I cared about a name. For a week or two, I travelled almost at random, seeking hardly any guidance, except the whirling of a leaf, at some turn of the road, or the green bough, that beckoned me, or the naked branch, that pointed its withered finger onward. All my care was to be farther from home each night than the preceding morning.

A FELLOW-TRAVELLER

One day at noontide, when the sun had burst suddenly out of a cloud and threatened to dissolve me, I looked round for shelter, whether of tavern, cottage, barn, or shady tree.

The first which offered itself was a wood, not a forest, but a trim plantation of young oaks, growing just thick enough to keep the mass of sunshine out, while they admitted a few straggling beams, and thus produced the most cheerful gloom imaginable. A brook, so small and clear, and apparently so cool, that I wanted to drink it up, ran under the road through a little arch of stone, without once meeting the sun, in its passage from the shade on one side to the shade on the other. As there was a stepping-place over the stone-wall, and a path along the rivulet, I followed it and discovered its source,— a spring gushing out of an old barrel.

In this pleasant spot, I saw a light pack suspended from the branch of a tree, a stick leaning against the trunk, and a person seated on the grassy verge of the spring, with his back towards me. He was a slender figure, dressed in black broadcloth, which was none of the finest, nor very fashionably cut. On hearing my footsteps, he started up, rather nervously, and, turning round, showed the face of a young man about my own age, with his finger in a volume which he had been reading, till my intrusion. His book was, evidently, a pocket-Bible. Though I piqued myself, at that period, on my great penetration into people's characters and pursuits, I could not decide whether this young man in black were an unfledged divine from Andover, a college-student, or preparing for college at some academy. In either case, I would quite as willingly have found a merrier companion; such, for instance, as the comedian with whom Gil Blas shared his dinner, beside a fountain in Spain.

After a nod, which was duly returned, I made a goblet of oak-leaves, filled and emptied it two or three times, and then remarked, to hit the stranger's classical associations, that this beautiful fountain ought to flow from an urn, instead of an old barrel. He did not show that he understood the allusion, and replied, very briefly, with a shyness that was quite out of place, between persons who met in such circumstances. Had he treated my next observation in the same way, we should have parted without another word.

"It is very singular," said I, "though, doubtless, there are good reasons for it, that Nature should provide drink so abundantly, and lavish it every where by the road-side, but so seldom any thing to eat. Why should not we find a loaf of bread on this tree, as well as a barrel of good liquor at the foot of it?"

"There is a loaf of bread on the tree," replied the stranger, without even smiling at a coincidence which made me laugh. "I have something to eat in my bundle, and if you can make a dinner with me, you shall be welcome."

"I accept your offer with pleasure," said I. "A pilgrim, such as I am, must not refuse a providential meal."

The young man had risen to take his bundle from the branch of the tree, but now turned round and regarded me with great earnestness, coloring deeply at the same time. However, he said nothing, and produced part of a loaf of bread, and some cheese, the former being, evidently, home-baked, though some days out of the oven. The fare was good enough, with a real welcome, such as his appeared to be. After spreading these articles on the stump of a tree, he proceeded to ask a blessing on our food; an unexpected cere-mony, and quite an impressive one at our woodland table, with the fountain gushing beside us, and the bright sky glimmering through the boughs; nor did his brief petition affect me less, because his embarrassment made his voice tremble. At the end of the meal, he returned thanks with the same tremulous fervor.

He felt a natural kindness for me, after thus relieving my necessities, and showed it by becoming less reserved. On my part, I professed never to have relished a dinner better, and, in requital of the stranger's hospitality, solicited the pleasure of his company to supper.

"Where? At your home?" asked he.

"Yes," said I, smiling.

"Perhaps our roads are not the same," observed he.

"Oh, I can take any road but one, and yet not miss my way," answered I. "This morning I breakfasted at home; I shall sup at home to-night; and a moment ago, I dined at home. To be sure, there was a certain place which I called home; but I have resolved not to see it again, till I have been quite round the globe, and enter the street on the east, as I left it on the west. In the mean time, I have a home every where or no where, just as you please to take it."

"No where, then; for this transitory world is not our home," said the young man, with solemnity. "We are all pilgrims and wanderers; but it is strange that we two should meet."

I inquired the meaning of this remark, but could obtain no satisfactory reply. But we had eaten salt together, and it was right that we should form acquaintance after that cere-mony, as the Arabs of the desert do; especially as he had learned something about myself, and the courtesy of the country entitled me to as much information in return. I asked whither he was travelling.

"I do not know," said he; "but God knows."

"That is strange!" exclaimed I; "not that God should know it, but that you should not. And how is your road to be pointed out?"

"Perhaps by an inward conviction," he replied, looking sideways at me, to discover whether I smiled; "perhaps by an outward sign."

"Then believe me," said I, "the outward sign is already granted you, and the inward conviction ought to follow. We are told of pious men in old times, who committed themselves to the care of Providence, and saw the manifestation of its will in the slightest circumstances; as in the shooting of a star, the flight of a bird, or the course taken by some brute animal. Sometimes even a stupid ass was their guide. May not I be as good a one?"

"I do not know," said the pilgrim, with perfect simplicity.

We did, however, follow the same road, and were not overtaken, as I partly apprehended, by the keepers of any lunatic asylum in pursuit of a stray patient. Perhaps the stranger felt as much doubt of my sanity as I did of his, though certainly with less justice; since I was fully aware of my own extravagances, while he acted as wildly, and deemed it heavenly wisdom. We were a singular couple, strikingly contrasted, yet curiously assimilated, each of us remarkable enough by himself, and doubly so in the other's company. Without any formal compact, we kept together, day after day, till our union appeared permanent. Even had I seen nothing to love and admire in him, I could never have thought of deserting one who needed me continually; for I never knew a person, not even a woman, so unfit to roam the world in solitude, as he was—so painfully shy, so easily discouraged by slight obstacles, and so often depressed by a weight within himself.

I was now far from my native place, but had not yet stepped before the public. A slight tremor seized me, whenever I thought of relinquishing the immunities of a private character, and giving every man, and for money, too, the right, which no man yet possessed, of treating me with open scorn. But about a week after contracting the above alliance, I made my bow to an audience of nine persons, seven of whom hissed me in a very disagreeable manner, and not without good cause. Indeed, the failure was so signal, that it would have been mere swindling to retain the money which had been paid, on my implied contract to give its value of amusement; so I called in the door-keeper, bade him refund the whole receipts, a mighty sum, and was gratified with a round of applause, by way of offset to the hisses. This event would have looked most horrible in anticipation; a thing to make a man shoot himself, or run a muck, or hide himself in caverns, where he might not see his own burning blush; but the reality was not so very hard to bear. It is a fact, that I was more deeply grieved by an almost parallel misfortune, which happened to my companion on the same evening. In my own behalf, I was angry and excited, not depressed; my blood ran quick, my spirits rose buoyantly; and I had never felt such a confidence of future success, and determination to achieve it, as at that trying moment. I resolved to persevere, if it were only to wring the reluctant praise from my enemies.

Hitherto, I had immensely underrated the difficulties of my idle trade; now I recognized, that it demanded nothing short of my whole powers, cultivated to the utmost, and exerted with the same prodigality as if I were speaking for a great party, or for the nation at large, on the floor of the capitol. No talent or attainment could come amiss; every thing, indeed, was requisite; wide observation, varied knowledge, deep thoughts, and sparkling ones; pathos and levity, and a mixture of both, like sunshine in a rain-drop; lofty imagination, veiling itself in the garb of common life; and the practised art which alone could render these gifts, and more than these, available. Not that I ever hoped to be thus qualified. But my despair was no ignoble one; for, knowing the impossibility of satisfying myself, even should the world be satisfied, I did my best to overcome it, investigated the causes of every defect, and strove, with patient stubbornness, to remove them in the next attempt. It is one of my few sources of pride, that, ridiculous as the object was, I followed it up with the firmness and energy of a man.

I manufactured a great variety of plots and skeletons of tales, and kept them ready for use, leaving the filling up to the inspiration of the moment; though I cannot remember ever to have told a tale, which did not vary considerably from my pre-conceived idea, and acquire a novelty of aspect as often as I repeated it. Oddly enough, my success was generally in proportion to the difference between the conception and accomplishment. I provided two or more commencements and catastrophes to many of the tales, a happy expedient, suggested by the double sets of sleeves and trimmings, which diversified the suits in Sir Piercy Shafton's wardrobe. But my best efforts had a unity, a wholeness, and a separate character, that did not admit of this sort of mechanism.

The Village Theatre

About the first of September, my fellow-traveller and myself arrived at a country town, where a small company of actors, on their return from a summer's campaign in the British Provinces, were giving a series of dramatic exhibitions. A moderately sized hall of the tavern had been converted into a theatre. The performances that evening were The Heir at Law, and No Song No Supper, with the recitation of Alexander's Feast between the play and farce. The house was thin and dull. But the next day, there appeared to be brighter prospects, the play-bills announcing, at every corner, on the town-pump, and, awful sacrilege! on the very door of the meeting-house, an Unprecedented Attraction!! After setting forth the ordinary entertainments of a theatre, the public were informed, in the hugest type that the printing-office could supply, that the manager had been fortunate enough to accomplish an engagement with the celebrated Story Teller. He would make his first appearance that evening, and recite his famous tale of "Mr. Higginbotham's Catastrophe!" which had been received with rapturous applause, by audiences in all the principal cities. This outrageous flourish of trumpets, be it known, was wholly unauthorized by me, who had merely made an engagement for a single evening, without assuming any more celebrity than the little I possessed. As for the tale, it could hardly have been applauded by rapturous audiences, being as yet an unfilled plot; nor, even when I stepped upon the stage, was it decided whether Mr. Higginbotham should live or die.

In two or three places, underneath the flaming bills which announced the Story Teller, was pasted a small slip of paper, giving notice, in tremulous characters, of a religious meeting, to be held at the school-house, where, with Divine permission, Eliakim Abbott would address sinners on the welfare of their immortal souls.

In the evening, after the commencement of the tragedy of Douglas, I took a ramble through the town, to quicken my ideas by active motion. My spirits were good, with a certain glow of mind, which I had already learned to depend upon as the sure prognostic of success. Passing a small and solitary school-house, where a light was burning dimly, and a few people were entering the door, I went in with them, and saw my friend Eliakim at the desk. He had collected about fifteen hearers, mostly females. Just as I entered, he was beginning to pray, in accents so low and interrupted, that he seemed to doubt the reception of his efforts, both with God and man. There was room for distrust, in regard to the latter. At the conclusion of the prayer, several of the little audience went out, leaving him to begin his discourse under such discouraging circumstances, added to his natural and agonizing diffidence. Knowing that my presence on these occasions increased his embarrassment, I had stationed myself in a dusky place near the door, and now stole softly out.

On my return to the tavern, the tragedy was already concluded, and being a feeble one in itself, and indifferently
performed, it left so much the better chance for the Story
Teller. The bar was thronged with customers, the toddy-stick
keeping a continual tattoo, while in the hall there was a
broad, deep, buzzing sound, with an occasional peal of im-
patient thunder, all symptoms of an overflowing house and
an eager audience. I drank a glass of wine and water, and
stood at the side-scene, conversing with a young person of
doubtful sex. If a gentleman, how could he have performed
the singing-girl, the night before, in No Song No Supper?
Or if a lady, why did she enact Young Norval, and now
wear a green coat and white pantaloons in the character of
Little Pickle? In either case, the dress was pretty, and the
wearer bewitching; so that, at the proper moment, I stepped
forward, with a gay heart and a bold one; while the orchestra
played a tune that had resounded at many a country ball,
and the curtain, as it rose, discovered something like a country
bar-room. Such a scene was well enough adapted to such
a tale.

The orchestra of our little theatre consisted of two fiddles
and a clarionet; but if the whole harmony of the Tremont
had been there, it might have swelled in vain, beneath the
tumult of applause that greeted me. The good people of
the town, knowing that the world contained innumerable
persons of celebrity, undreamt of by them, took it for granted
that I was one, and that their roar of welcome was but a
feeble echo of those which had thundered around me, in
lofty theatres. Such an enthusiastic uproar was never heard;
each person seemed a Briareus, clapping a hundred hands,
besides keeping his feet and several cudgels in play, with
stamping and thumping on the floor; while the ladies flourished their white cambric handkerchiefs, intermixed with

yellow, and red bandanna, like the flags of different nations. After such a salutation, the celebrated Story Teller felt almost ashamed to produce so humble an affair as Mr. Higginbotham's Catastrophe.

This story was originally more dramatic, than as there presented, and afforded good scope for mimicry and buffoonry; neither of which, to my shame, did I spare. I never knew the "magic of a name," till I used that of Mr. Higginbotham; often as I repeated it, there were louder bursts of merriment, than those which responded to what, in my opinion, were more legitimate strokes of humor. The success of the piece was incalculably heightened by a stiff queue of horse-hair, which Little Pickle, in the spirit of that mischief-loving character, had fastened to my collar, where, unknown to me, it kept making the queerest gestures of its own, in correspondence with all mine. The audience, supposing that some enormous joke was appended to this long tail behind, were ineffably delighted, and gave way to such a tumult of approbation, that, just as the story closed, the benches broke beneath them, and left one whole row of my admirers on the floor. Even in that predicament, they continued their applause. In after times, when I had grown a bitter moralizer, I took this scene for an example, how much of fame is humbug; how much the meed of what our better nature blushes at; how much an accident; how much bestowed on mistaken principles; and how small and poor the remnant. From pit and boxes there was now a universal call for the Story Teller.

That celebrated personage came not, when they did call to him. As I left the stage, the landlord, being also the postmaster, had given me a letter, with the postmark of my native village, and directed to my assumed name, in the stiff old hand-writing of Parson Thumpcushion. Doubtless, he had heard of the rising renown of the Story Teller, and conjectured at once, that such a nondescript luminary could be no other than his lost ward. His epistle, though I never read it, affected me most painfully. I seemed to see the puritanic figure of my guardian, standing among the fripperies of the theatre, and pointing to the players,—the fantastic and effeminate men, the painted women, the giddy girl in boy's clothes, merrier than modest,—pointing to these with solemn ridicule, and eyeing me with stern rebuke. His image was a type of the austere duty, and they of the vanities of life.

I hastened with the letter to my chamber, and held it unopened in my hand, while the applause of my buffoonry yet sounded through the theatre. Another train of thought came over me. The stern old man appeared again, but now with the gentleness of sorrow, softening his authority with love, as a father might, and even bending his venerable head, as if to say, that my errors had an apology in his own mistaken disicipline. I strode twice across the chamber, then held the letter in the flame of the candle, and beheld it consume, unread. It is fixed in my mind, and was so at the time, that he had addressed me in a style of paternal wisdom, and love, and reconciliation, which I could not have resisted, had I but risked the trial. The thought still haunts me, that then I made my irrevocable choice between good and evil fate.

Meanwhile, as this occurrence had disturbed my mind, and indisposed me to the present exercise of my profession, I left the town, in spite of a laudatory critique in the newspaper, and untempted by the liberal offers of the manager. As we walked onward, following the same road, on two such different errands, Eliakim groaned in spirit, and labored, with tears, to convince me of the guilt and madness of my life.

SKETCHES FROM MEMORY

The Notch Of The White Mountains

IT WAS NOW the middle of September. We had come since sunrise from Bartlett, passing up through the valley of the Saco, which extends between mountainous walls, sometimes with a steep ascent, but often as level as a church-aisle. All that day and two preceding ones, we had been loitering towards the heart of the White Mountains—those old crystal hills, whose mysterious brilliancy had gleamed upon our distant wanderings before we thought of visiting them. Height after height had risen and towered one above another, till the clouds began to hang below the peaks. Down their slopes, were the red path-ways of the Slides, those avalanches of earth, stones and trees, which descend into the hollows, leaving vestiges of their track, hardly to be effaced by the vegetation of ages. We had mountains behind us and mountains on each side, and a group of mightier ones ahead. Still our road went up along the Saco, right towards the centre of that group, as if to climb above the clouds, in its passage to the farther region.

In old times, the settlers used to be astounded by the inroads of the northern Indians, coming down upon them from this mountain rampart, through some defile known only to themselves. It is indeed a wondrous path. A demon, it might be fancied, or one of the Titans, was travelling up the valley, elbowing the heights carelessly aside as he passed, till at length a great mountain took its stand directly across his intended road. He tarries not for such an obstacle, but rending it asunder, a thousand feet from peak to base, discloses its treasures of hidden minerals, its sunless waters, all the secrets of the mountain's inmost heart, with a mighty fracture of rugged precipices on each side. This is the Notch of the White Hills. Shame on me, that I have attempted to describe it by so mean an image—feeling, as I do, that it is one of those symbolic scenes, which lead the mind to the sentiment, though not to the conception, of Omnipotence.

We had now reached a narrow passage, which showed almost the appearance of having been cut by human strength and artifice in the solid rock. There was a wall of granite on each side, high and precipitous, especially on our right, and so smooth that a few evergreens could hardly find foothold enough to grow there. This is the entrance, or, in the direction we were going, the extremity of the romantic defile of the Notch. Before emerging from it, the rattling of wheels approached behind us, and a stage-coach rumbled out of the mountain, with seats on top and trunks behind, and a smart driver, in a drab great-coat, touching the wheel horses with the whip-stock, and reining in the leaders. To my mind, there was a sort of poetry in such an incident, hardly inferior to what would have accompanied the painted array of an Indian war-party, gliding forth from the same wild chasm. All the passengers, except a very fat lady on the back seat, had alighted. One was a mineralogist, a scientific, green-spectacled figure in black, bearing a heavy hammer, with which he did great damage to the precipices, and put the fragments in his pocket. Another was a well-dressed young man, who carried an opera-glass set in gold, and seemed to be making a quotation from some of Byron's rhapsodies on mountain scenery. There was also a trader, returning from Portland to the upper part of Vermont; and a fair young girl, with a very faint bloom, like one of those pale and delicate flowers, which sometimes occur among Alpine cliffs.

They disappeared, and we followed them, passing through a deep pine forest, which, for some miles, allowed us to see nothing but its own dismal shade. Towards night-fall, we reached a level amphitheatre, surrounded by a great rampart of hills, which shut out the sunshine long before it left the external world. It was here that we obtained our first view, except at a distance, of the principal group of mountains. They are majestic, and even awful, when contemplated in a proper mood; yet, by their breadth of base, and the long ridges which support them, give the idea of immense bulk, rather than of towering height. Mount Washington, indeed, looked near to Heaven; he was white with snow a mile downward, and had caught the only cloud that was sailing through the atmosphere, to veil his head. Let us forget the other names of American statesmen, that have been stamped upon these hills, but still call the loftiest —WASHINGTON. Mountains are Earth's undecaying monuments. They must stand while she endures, and never should be consecrated to the mere great men of their own age and country, but to the mighty ones alone, whose glory is universal, and whom all time will render illustrious.

The air, not often sultry in this elevated region, nearly two thousand feet above the sea, was now sharp and cold, like that of a clear November evening in the low-lands. By morning, probably, there would be a frost, if not a snow-fall, on the grass and rye, and an icy surface over the standing water. I was glad to perceive a prospect of comfortable quarters, in a house which we were approaching, and of pleasant company in the guests who were assembled at the door.

Our Evening Party Among The Mountains

We stood in front of a good substantial farm-house, of old date in that wild country. A sign over the door denoted it to be the White Mountain Post-Office, an establishment which distributes letters and newspapers to perhaps a score of persons, comprising the population of two or three townships among the hills. The broad and weighty antlers of a deer, 'a stag of ten,' were fastened at a corner of the house; a fox's bushy tail was nailed beneath them; and a huge black paw lay on the ground, newly severed and still bleeding—the trophy of a bear-hunt. Among several persons collected about the door-steps, the most remarkable was a sturdy mountaineer, of six feet two and corresponding bulk, with a heavy set of features, such as might be moulded on his own blacksmith's anvil, but yet indicative of mother-wit and rough humor. As we appeared, he uplifted a tin trumpet, four or five feet long, and blew a tremendous blast, either in honor of our arrival, or to awaken an echo from the opposite hill.

Ethan Crawford's guests were of such a motley description as to form quite a picturesque group, seldom seen together, except at some place like this, at once the pleasure-house of fashionable tourists, and the homely inn of country travellers. Among the company at the door, were the mineralogist and the owner of the gold opera-glass, whom we had encountered in the Notch; two Georgian gentlemen, who had chilled their southern blood, that morning, on the top of Mount Wash-

ington; a physician and his wife, from Conway; a trader, of
Burlington, and an old 'Squire, of the Green Mountains; and
two young married couples, all the way from Massachusetts,
on the matrimonial jaunt. Besides these strangers, the rugged
county of Coos, in which we were, was represented by half
a dozen wood-cutters, who had slain a bear in the forest
and smitten off his paw.

I had joined the party, and had a moment's leisure to
examine them, before the echo of Ethan's blast returned from
the hill. Not one, but many echoes had caught up the harsh
and tuneless sound, untwisted its complicated threads, and
found a thousand aerial harmonies in one stern trumpet-
tone. It was a distinct, yet distant and dreamlike symphony
of melodious instruments, as if an airy band had been hidden
on the hill-side, and made faint music at the summons. No
subsequent trial produced so clear, delicate, and spiritual a
concert as the first. A field-piece was then discharged from
the top of a neighboring hill, and gave birth to one long
reverberation, which ran round the circle of mountains in an
unbroken chain of sound, and rolled away without a separate
echo. After these experiments, the cold atmosphere drove us
all into the house, with the keenest appetites for supper.

It did one's heart good to see the great fires that were
kindled in the parlor and bar-room, especially the latter,
where the fire-place was built of rough stone, and might have
contained the trunk of an old tree for a back-log. A man keeps
a comfortable hearth when his own forest is at his very door.
In the parlor, when the evening was fairly set in, we held
our hands before our eyes, to shield them from the ruddy
glow, and began a pleasant variety of conversation. The mineralogist and the physician talked about the invigorating
qualities of the mountain air, and its excellent effect on Ethan
Crawford's father, an old man of seventy-five, with the unbroken frame of middle life. The two brides and the doctor's
wife held a whispered discussion, which, by their frequent

titterings and a blush or two, seemed to have reference to the trials or enjoyments of the matrimonial state. The bridegrooms sat together in a corner, rigidly silent, like Quakers whom the spirit moveth not, being still in the odd predicament of bashfulness towards their own young wives. The Green Mountain 'Squire chose me for his companion, and described the difficulties he had met with, half a century ago, in travelling from the Connecticut river through the Notch to Conway, now a single day's journey, though it had cost him eighteen. The Georgians held the album between them, and favored us with the few specimens of its contents, which they considered ridiculous enough to be worth hearing. One extract met with deserved applause. It was a 'Sonnet to the Snow on Mount Washington,' and had been contributed that very afternoon, bearing a signature of great distinction in magazines and annuals. The lines were elegant and full of fancy, but too remote from familiar sentiment, and cold as their subject, resembling those curious specimens of crystallized vapor, which I observed next day on the mountain-top. The poet was understood to be the young gentleman of the gold opera-glass, who heard our laudatory remarks with the composure of a veteran.

Such was our party, and such their ways of amusement. But, on a winter evening, another set of guests assembled at the hearth, where these summer travellers were now sitting. I once had it in contemplation to spend a month hereabouts, in sleighing-time, for the sake of studying the yeomen of New-England, who then elbow each other through the Notch by hundreds, on their way to Portland. There could be no better school for such a purpose than Ethan Crawford's inn. Let the student go thither in December, sit down with the teamsters at their meals, share their evening merriment, and repose with them at night, when every bed has its three occupants, and parlor, bar-room and kitchen are strewn with slumberers around the fire. Then let him rise before daylight, button his great-coat, muffle up his ears, and stride with the departing caravan a mile or two, to see how sturdily they make head against the blast. A treasure of characteristic traits will repay all inconveniences, even should a frozen nose be of the number.

The conversation of our party soon became more animated and sincere, and we recounted some traditions of the Indians, who believed that the father and mother of their race were saved from a deluge by ascending the peak of Mount Washington. The children of that pair have been overwhelmed, and found no such refuge. In the mythology of the savage, these mountains were afterwards considered sacred and inaccessible, full of unearthly wonders, illuminated at lofty heights by the blaze of precious stones, and inhabited by deities, who sometimes shrouded themselves in the snowstorm, and came down on the lower world. There are few legends more poetical than that of the 'Great Carbuncle' of the White Mountains. The belief was communicated to the English settlers, and is hardly yet extinct, that a gem, of such immense size as to be seen shining miles away, hangs from a rock over a clear, deep lake, high up among the hills. They who had once beheld its splendor, were enthralled with an unutterable yearning to possess it. But a spirit guarded that inestimable jewel, and bewildered the adventurer with a dark mist from the enchanted lake. Thus, life was worn away in the vain search for an unearthly treasure, till at length the deluded one went up the mountain, still sanguine as in youth, but returned no more. On this theme, methinks I could frame a tale with a deep moral.

The hearts of the pale-faces would not thrill to these superstitions of the red men, though we spoke of them in the centre of their haunted region. The habits and sentiments of that departed people were too distinct from those of their successors to find much real sympathy. It has often been a matter of regret to me, that I was shut out from the most peculiar field of American fiction, by an inability to see any romance, or poetry, or grandeur, or beauty in the Indian character, at least, till such traits were pointed out by others. I do abhor an Indian story. Yet no writer can be more secure of a permanent place in our literature, than the biographer of the Indian chiefs. His subject, as referring to tribes which have mostly vanished from the earth, gives him a right to be placed on a classic shelf, apart from the merits which will sustain him there.

I made inquiries whether, in his researches about these parts, our mineralogist had found the three 'Silver Hills,' which an Indian sachem sold to an Englishman, nearly two hundred years ago, and the treasure of which the posterity of the purchaser have been looking for ever since. But the man of science had ransacked every hill along the Saco, and knew nothing of these prodigious piles of wealth. By this time, as usual with men on the eve of great adventure, we had pro-longed our session deep into the night, considering how early we were to set out on our six miles' ride to the foot of Mount Washington. There was now a general breaking-up. I scruti-nized the faces of the two bridegrooms, and saw but little probability of their leaving the bosom of earthly bliss, in the first week of the honey-moon, and at the frosty hour of three, to climb above the clouds. Nor, when I felt how sharp the wind was, as it rushed through a broken pane, and eddied between the chinks of my unplastered chamber, did I antici-pate much alacrity on my own part, though we were to seek for the 'Great Carbuncle.'

The Canal-Boat

I was inclined to be poetical about the Grand Canal. In my imagination, De Witt Clinton was an enchanter, who had waved his magic wand from the Hudson to Lake Erie, and united them by a watery highway, crowded with the commerce of two worlds, till then inaccessible to each other. This simple and mighty conception had conferred inestimable value on spots which Nature seemed to have thrown carelessly into the great body of the earth, without foreseeing that they could ever attain importance. I pictured the surprise of the sleepy Dutchmen when the new river first glittered by their doors, bringing them hard cash or foreign commodities, in exchange for their hitherto unmarketable produce. Surely, the water of this canal must be the most fertilizing of all fluids; for it causes towns—with their masses of brick and stone, their churches and theatres, their business and hubbub, their luxury and refinement, their gay dames and polished citizens—to spring up, till, in time, the wondrous stream may flow between two continuous lines of buildings, through one thronged street, from Buffalo to Albany. I embarked about thirty miles below Utica, determining to voyage along the whole extent of the canal, at least twice in the course of the summer.

Behold us, then, fairly afloat, with three horses harnessed to our vessel, like the steeds of Neptune to a huge scallop-shell, in mythological pictures. Bound to a distant port, we had neither chart nor compass, nor cared about the wind, nor felt the heaving of a billow, nor dreaded shipwreck, however fierce the tempest, in our adventurous navigation of an interminable mud-puddle—for a mud-puddle it seemed, and as dark and turbid as if every kennel in the land paid contribution to it. With an imperceptible current, it holds its drowsy way through all the dismal swamps and unimpressive scenery, that could be found between the great lakes and the sea-coast. Yet there is variety enough, both on the surface of the canal and along its banks, to amuse the traveller, if an overpowering tedium did not deaden his perceptions.

Sometimes we met a black and rusty-looking vessel, laden with lumber, salt from Syracuse, or Genesee flour, and shaped at both ends like a square-toed boot; as if it had two sterns, and were fated always to advance backward. On its deck would be a square hut, and a woman seen through the window at her household work, with a little tribe of children, who perhaps had been born in this strange dwelling and knew no other home. Thus, while the husband smoked his pipe at the helm, and the eldest son rode one of the horses, on went the family, travelling hundreds of miles in their own house, and carrying their fireside with them. The most frequent species of craft were the 'line boats,' which had a cabin at each end, and a great bulk of barrels, bales, and boxes in the midst; or light packets, like our own, decked all over, with a row of curtained windows from stem to stern, and a drowsy face at every one. Once, we encountered a boat, of rude construction, painted all in gloomy black, and manned by three Indians, who gazed at us in silence and with a singular fixedness of eye. Perhaps these three alone, among the ancient possessors of the land, had attempted to derive benefit from the white man's mighty projects, and float along the current of his enterprise. Not long after, in the midst of a swamp and beneath a clouded sky, we overtook a vessel that seemed full of mirth and sunshine. It contained a little colony of Swiss, on their way to Michigan, clad in garments of strange fashion and gay colors, scarlet, yellow and bright blue, singing, laughing, and making merry, in odd tones and a babble of outlandish words. One pretty damsel, with a beautiful pair of naked white arms, addressed a mirthful remark to me; she spoke in her native tongue, and I retorted in good English, both of us laughing heartily at each other's unintelligible wit. I cannot describe how pleasantly this incident affected me. These honest Swiss were an itinerant community of jest and fun, journeying through a gloomy land and among a dull race of money-getting drudges, meeting none to understand their mirth and only one to sympathize with it, yet still retaining the happy lightness of their own spirit.

Had I been on my feet at the time, instead of sailing slowly along in a dirty canal-boat, I should often have paused to contemplate the diversified panorama along the banks of the canal. Sometimes the scene was a forest, dark, dense, and impervious, breaking away occasionally and receding from a lonely tract, covered with dismal black stumps, where, on the verge of the canal, might be seen a log-cottage, and a sallow-faced woman at the window. Lean and aguish, she looked like Poverty personified, half clothed, half fed, and dwelling in a desert, while a tide of wealth was sweeping by her door. Two or three miles further would bring us to a lock, where the slight impediment to navigation had created a little mart of trade. Here would be found commodities of all sorts, enumerated in yellow letters on the window-shutters of a small grocery-store, the owner of which had set his soul to the gathering of coppers and small change, buying and selling through the week, and counting his gains on the blessed Sabbath. The next scene might be the dwelling-houses and stores of a thriving village, built of wood or small gray stones, a church-spire rising in the midst, and generally two taverns, bearing over their piazzas the pompous titles of 'hotel,' 'exchange,' 'tontine,' or 'coffee-house.' Passing on, we glide now into the unquiet heart of an inland city—of Utica, for instance—and find ourselves amid piles of brick, crowded docks and quays, rich warehouses and a busy population. We feel the eager and hurrying spirit of the place, like a stream and eddy whirling us along with it. Through the thickest of the tumult goes the canal, flowing between lofty rows of buildings and arched bridges of hewn stone. Onward, also, go we, till the hum and bustle of struggling enterprise die away behind us, and we are threading an avenue of the ancient woods again.

This sounds not amiss in description, but was so tiresome in reality, that we were driven to the most childish expedients for amusement. An English traveller paraded the deck with a rifle in his walking-stick, and waged war on squirrels and woodpeckers, sometimes sending an unsuccessful bullet among flocks of tame ducks and geese, which abound in the dirty water of the canal. I, also, pelted these foolish birds with apples, and smiled at the ridiculous earnestness of their scrambles for the prize, while the apple bobbed about like a thing of life. Several little accidents afforded us good-natured diversion. At the moment of changing horses, the tow-rope caught a Massachusetts farmer by the leg, and threw him down in a very indescribable posture, leaving a purple mark around his sturdy limb. A new passenger fell flat on his back, in attempting to step on deck, as the boat emerged from under a bridge. Another, in his Sunday clothes, as good luck would have it, being told to leap aboard from the bank, forthwith plunged up to his third waistcoat button in the canal, and was fished out in a very pitiable plight, not at all amended by our three rounds of applause. Anon, a Virginia schoolmaster, too intent on a pocket Virgil to heed the helmsman's warning—'Bridge! bridge!'—was saluted by the said bridge on his knowledge-box. I had prostrated myself, like a pagan before his idol, but heard the dull leaden sound of the contact, and fully expected to see the treasures of the poor man's cranium scattered about the deck. However, as there was no harm done, except a large bump on the head, and probably a corresponding dent in the bridge, the rest of us exchanged glances and laughed quietly. Oh, how pitiless are idle people!

The table being now lengthened through the cabin, and

spread for supper, the next twenty minutes were the pleasantest I had spent on the canal—the same space at dinner
excepted. At the close of the meal, it had become dusky
enough for lamplight. The rain pattered unceasingly on the
deck, and sometimes came with a sullen rush against the
windows, driven by the wind, as it stirred through an opening
of the forest. The intolerable dullness of the scene engendered
an evil spirit in me. Perceiving that the Englishman was
taking notes in a memorandum-book, with occasional glances
round the cabin, I presumed that we were all to figure in a
future volume of travels, and amused my ill-humor by falling
into the probable vein of his remarks. He would hold up
an imaginary mirror, wherein our reflected faces would appear
ugly and ridiculous, yet still retain an undeniable likeness to
the originals. Then, with more sweeping malice, he would
make these caricatures the representatives of great classes of
my countrymen.

He glanced at the Virginia schoolmaster, a Yankee by
birth, who, to recreate himself, was examining a freshman
from Schenectady college, in the conjugation of a Greek
verb. Him, the Englishman would portray as the scholar of
America, and compare his erudition to a schoolboy's Latin
theme, made up of scraps, ill-selected and worse put together.
Next, the tourist looked at the Massachusetts farmer, who
was delivering a dogmatic harangue on the iniquity of Sunday
mails. Here was the far-famed yeoman of New-England; his
religion, writes the Englishman, is gloom on the Sabbath,
long prayers every morning and eventide, and illiberality at
all times; his boasted information is merely an abstract and
compound of newspaper paragraphs, Congress debates, caucus
harangues, and the argument and judge's charge in his own
lawsuits. The bookmonger cast his eye at a Detroit merchant,
and began scribbling faster than ever. In this sharp-eyed
man, this lean man, of wrinkled brow, we see daring enter-

prise and close-fisted avarice combined; here is the worshipper of Mammon at noonday; here is the three-times bankrupt, richer after every ruin; here, in one word, (Oh, wicked Englishman to say it!) here is the American! He lifted his eye-glass to inspect a western lady, who at once became aware of the glance, reddened, and retired deeper into the female part of the cabin. Here was the pure, modest, sensitive, and shrinking woman of America; shrinking when no evil is intended; and sensitive like diseased flesh, that thrills if you but point at it; and strangely modest, without confidence in the modesty of other people; and admirably pure, with such a quick apprehension of all impurity.

In this manner, I went all through the cabin, hitting everybody as hard a lash as I could, and laying the whole blame on the infernal Englishman. At length, I caught the eyes of my own image in the looking-glass, where a number of the party were likewise reflected, and among them the Englishman, who, at that moment, was intently observing myself.

The crimson curtain being let down between the ladies and gentlemen, the cabin became a bed-chamber for twenty persons, who were laid on shelves, one above another. For a long time, our various incommodities kept us all awake, except five or six, who were accustomed to sleep nightly amid the uproar of their own snoring, and had little to dread from any other species of disturbance. It is a curious fact, that these snorers had been the most quiet people in the boat, while awake, and became peace-breakers only when others ceased to be so, breathing tumult out of their repose. Would it were possible to affix a wind instrument to the nose, and thus make melody of a snore, so that a sleeping lover might serenade his mistress, or a congregation snore a psalm-tune! Other, though fainter sounds than these, contributed to my restlessness. My head was close to the crimson curtain—the sexual division of the boat—behind which I continually heard whispers and stealthy footsteps; the noise of a comb laid on the table, or a slipper dropt on the floor; the twang, like a broken harp-string, caused by loosening a tight belt; the rustling of a gown in its descent; and the unlacing of a pair of stays. My ear seemed to have the properties of an eye; a visible image pestered my fancy in the darkness; the curtain was withdrawn between me and the western lady, who yet disrobed herself without a blush.

Finally, all was hushed in that quarter. Still, I was more broad awake than through the whole preceding day, and felt a feverish impulse to toss my limbs miles apart, and appease the unquietness of mind by that of matter. Forgetting that my berth was hardly so wide as a coffin, I turned suddenly over, and fell like an avalanche on the floor, to the disturbance of the whole community of sleepers. As there were no bones broken, I blessed the accident, and went on deck. A lantern was burning at each end of the boat, and one of the crew was stationed at the bows, keeping watch, as mariners do on the ocean. Though the rain had ceased, the sky was all one cloud, and the darkness so intense, that there seemed to be no world, except the little space on which our lanterns glimmered. Yet, it was an impressive scene.

We were traversing the 'long level,' a dead flat between Utica and Syracuse, where the canal has not rise or fall enough to require a lock for nearly seventy miles. There can hardly be a more dismal tract of country. The forest which covers it, consisting chiefly of white cedar, black ash, and other trees that live in excessive moisture, is now decayed and death-struck, by the partial draining of the swamp into the great ditch of the canal. Sometimes, indeed, our lights were reflected from pools of stagnant water, which stretched far in among the trunks of the trees, beneath dense masses of dark foliage. But generally, the tall stems and intermingled branches were naked, and brought into strong relief, amid the surrounding gloom, by the whiteness of their decay. Often, we beheld the prostrate form of some old sylvan giant, which had fallen, and crushed down smaller trees under its immense ruin. In spots, where destruction had been riotous, the lanterns showed perhaps a hundred trunks, erect, half overthrown, extended along the ground, resting on their shattered limbs, or tossing them desperately into the darkness, but all of one ashy-white, all naked together, in desolate confusion. Thus growing out of the night as we drew nigh, and vanishing as we glided on, based on obscurity, and overhung and bounded by it, the scene was ghost-like—the very land of unsubstantial things, whither dreams might betake themselves, when they quit the slumberer's brain.

My fancy found another emblem. The wild Nature of America had been driven to this desert-place by the encroachments of civilized man. And even here, where the savage queen was throned on the ruins of her empire, did we penetrate, a vulgar and worldly throng, intruding on her latest solitude. In other lands, Decay sits among fallen palaces; but here, her home is in the forests.

Looking ahead, I discerned a distant light, announcing the approach of another boat, which soon passed us, and proved to be a rusty old scow—just such a craft as the 'Flying Dutchman' would navigate on the canal. Perhaps it was that celebrated personage himself, whom I imperfectly distinguished at the helm, in a glazed hat and rough great-coat, with a pipe in his mouth, leaving the fumes of tobacco a hundred yards behind. Shortly after, our boatman blew a horn, sending a long and melancholy note through the forest-avenue, as a signal for some watcher in the wilderness to be ready with a change of horses. We had proceeded a mile or two with our fresh team, when the tow-rope got entangled in a fallen branch on the edge of the canal, and caused a momentary delay, during which I went to examine the phosphoric light of an old tree, a little within the forest. It was not the first delusive radiance that I had followed.

The tree lay along the ground, and was wholly converted into a mass of diseased splendor, which threw a ghastliness around. Being full of conceits that night, I called it a frigid fire; a funeral light, illumining decay and death; an emblem of fame, that gleams around the dead man without warming him; or of genius, when it owes its brilliancy to moral rottenness; and was thinking that such ghost-like torches were just fit to light up this dead forest, or to blaze coldly in tombs, when, starting from my abstraction, I looked up the canal. I recollected myself, and discovered the lanterns glimmering far away.

'Boat ahoy!' shouted I, making a trumpet of my closed fists.

Though the cry must have rung for miles along that hollow passage of the woods, it produced no effect. These packet-boats make up for their snail-like pace by never loitering day nor night, especially for those who have paid their fare. Indeed, the captain had an interest in getting rid of me, for I was his creditor for a breakfast.

'They are gone! Heaven be praised!' ejaculated I; 'for I cannot possibly overtake them! Here am I, on the "long level," at midnight, with the comfortable prospect of a walk to Syracuse, where my baggage will be left; and now to find a house or shed, wherein to pass the night.' So thinking aloud, I took a flambeau from the old tree, burning, but consuming not, to light my steps withal, and, like a Jack-o'-the-lantern, set out on my midnight tour.

THE OLD APPLE-DEALER

THE LOVER of the moral picturesque may sometimes find what he seeks in a character, which is,
nevertheless, of too negative a description to be
seized upon, and represented to the imaginative vision by
word-painting. As an instance, I remember an old man who
carries on a little trade of gingerbread and apples, at the
depôt of one of our rail-roads. While awaiting the departure
of the cars, my observation, flitting to and fro among the
livelier characteristics of the scene, has often settled insensibly
upon this almost hueless object. Thus, unconsciously to
myself, and unsuspected by him, I have studied the old
apple-dealer, until he has become a naturalized citizen of my
inner world. How little would he imagine—poor, neglected,
friendless, unappreciated, and with little that demands appreciation—that the mental eye of an utter stranger has so often
reverted to his figure! Many a noble form—many a beautiful
face—has flitted before me, and vanished like a shadow.
It is a strange witchcraft, whereby this faded and featureless
old apple-dealer has gained a settlement in my memory!

He is a small man with gray hair and gray stubble beard,
and is invariably clad in a shabby surtout of snuff-color,

closely buttoned, and half-concealing a pair of gray pantaloons; the whole dress, though clean and entire, being
evidently flimsy with much wear. His face, thin, withered,
furrowed, and with features which even age has failed to
render impressive, has a frost-bitten aspect. It is a moral frost,
which no physical warmth or comfortableness could counter-
act. The summer sunshine may fling its white heat upon him,
or the good fire of the depôt-room may make him the focus
of its blaze, on a winter's day; but all in vain; for still the
old man looks as if he were in a frosty atmosphere, with
scarcely warmth enough to keep life in the region about his
heart. It is a patient, long-suffering, quiet, hopeless, shivering
aspect. He is not desperate—that, though its etymology im-
plies no more, would be too positive an expression—but
merely devoid of hope. As all his past life, probably, offers
no spots of brightness to his memory, so he takes his present
poverty and discomfort as entirely a matter of course; he
thinks it the definition of existence, so far as himself is
concerned, to be poor, cold, and uncomfortable. It may be
added, that time has not thrown dignity, as a mantle, over
the old man's figure; there is nothing venerable about him;
you pity him without a scruple.

He sits on a bench in the depôt-room; and before him, on
the floor, are deposited two baskets, of a capacity to contain
his whole stock in trade. Across, from one basket to the other,
extends a board, on which is displayed a plate of cakes and
gingerbread, some russet and red cheeked apples, and a box
containing variegated sticks of candy; together with that
delectable condiment, known by children as Gibraltar rock,
neatly done up in white paper. There is likewise a half-peck
measure of cracked walnuts, and two or three tin half-pints
or gills, filled with the nut kernels, ready for purchasers.
Such are the small commodities with which our old friend
comes daily before the world, ministering to its petty needs

and little freaks of appetite, and seeking thence the solid subsistence—so far as he may subsist—of his life.

A slight observer would speak of the old man's quietude. But, on closer scrutiny, you discover that there is a continual unrest within him, which somewhat resembles the fluttering action of the nerves, in a corpse from which life has recently departed. Though he never exhibits any violent action, and, indeed, might appear to be sitting quite still, yet you perceive, when his minuter peculiarities begin to be detected, that he is always making some little movement or other. He looks anxiously at his plate of cakes, or pyramid of apples, and slightly alters their arrangement, with an evident idea that a great deal depends on their being disposed exactly thus and so. Then, for a moment, he gazes out of the window; then he shivers, quietly, and folds his arms across his breast, as if to draw himself closer within himself, and thus keep a flicker of warmth in his lonesome heart. Now he turns again to his merchandise of cakes, apples, and candy, and discovers that this cake or that apple, or yonder stick of red and white candy, has, somehow, got out of its proper position. And is there not a walnut-kernel too many, or too few, in one of those small tin measures? Again, the whole arrangement appears to be settled to his mind; but, in the course of a minute or two, there will assuredly be something to set right. At times, by an indescribable shadow upon his features—too quiet, however, to be noticed, until you are familiar with his ordinary aspect—the expression of frost-bitten, patient despondency becomes very touching. It seems as if, just at that instant, the suspicion occurred to him, that, in his chill decline of life, earning scanty bread by selling cakes, apples, and candy, he is a very miserable old fellow.

But, if he think so, it is a mistake. He can never suffer the extreme of misery, because the tone of his whole being is too much subdued for him to feel any thing acutely.

Occasionally, one of the passengers, to while away a tedious interval, approaches the old man, inspects the articles upon his board, and even peeps curiously into the two baskets. Another, striding to and fro along the room, throws a look at the apples and gingerbread, at every turn. A third, it may be, of a more sensitive and delicate texture of being, glances shyly thitherward, cautious not to excite expectations of a purchaser, while yet undetermined whether to buy. But there appears to be no need of such a scrupulous regard to our old friend's feelings. True, he is conscious of the remote possibility of selling a cake or an apple, but innumerable disappointments have rendered him so far a philosopher, that, even if the purchased article should be returned, he will consider it altogether in the ordinary train of events. He speaks to none, and makes no sign of offering his wares to the public; not that he is deterred by pride, but by the certain conviction that such demonstrations would not increase his custom. Besides, this activity in business would require an energy that never could have been a characteristic of his almost passive disposition, even in youth. Whenever an actual customer appears, the old man looks up with a patient eye; if the price and the article are approved, he is ready to make change; otherwise, his eyelids droop again, sadly enough, but with no heavier despondency than before. He shivers, perhaps, folds his lean arms around his lean body, and resumes the life-long, frozen patience, in which consists his strength. Once in a while, a schoolboy comes hastily up, places a cent or two upon the board, and takes up a cake or a stick of candy, or a measure of walnuts, or an apple as red cheeked as himself. There are no words as to the price, that being as well known to the buyer as to the seller. The old apple-dealer never speaks an unnecessary word; not that he is sullen and morose; but there is none of the cheeriness and briskness in him, that stirs up people to talk.

Not seldom, he is greeted by some old neighbor, a man well-to-do in the world, who makes a civil, patronizing observation about the weather; and then, by way of performing a charitable deed, begins to chaffer for an apple. Our friend presumes not on any past acquaintance; he makes the briefest possible response to all general remarks, and shrinks quietly into himself again. After every diminution of his stock, he takes care to produce from the basket another cake, another stick of candy, another apple, or another measure of walnuts, to supply the place of the article sold. Two or three attempts —or, perchance, half a dozen—are requisite, before the board can be re-arranged to his satisfaction. If he have received a silver coin, he waits till the purchaser is out of sight, then examines it closely, and tries to bend it with his finger and thumb; finally, he puts it into his waistcoat pocket, with seemingly a gentle sigh. This sigh, so faint as to be hardly perceptible, and not expressive of any definite emotion, is the accompaniment and conclusion of all his actions. It is the symbol of the chillness and torpid melancholy of his old age, which only make themselves felt sensibly, when his repose is slightly disturbed.

Our man of gingerbread and apples is not a specimen of the 'needy man who has seen better days.' Doubtless, there have been better and brighter days in the far-off time of his youth; but none with so much sunshine of prosperity in them, that the chill, the depression, the narrowness of means, in his declining years, can have come upon him by surprise. His life has all been of a piece. His subdued and nerveless boyhood prefigured his abortive prime, which, likewise, contained within itself the prophecy and image of his lean and torpid age. He was perhaps a mechanic, who never came to be a master in his craft, or a petty tradesman, rubbing onward between passably-to-do and poverty. Possibly, he may look back to some brilliant epoch of his career, when there were a hundred or two of dollars to his credit, in the Savings Bank. Such must have been the extent of his better fortune—his little measure of this world's triumphs—all that he has known of success. A meek, downcast, humble, uncomplaining creature, he probably has never felt himself entitled to more than so much of the gifts of Providence. Is it not still something, that he has never held out his hand for charity, nor has yet been driven to that sad home and household of Earth's forlorn and broken-spirited children, the alms-house? He cherishes no quarrel, therefore, with his destiny, nor with the Author of it. All is as it should be.

If, indeed, he have been bereaved of a son—a bold, energetic, vigorous young man, on whom the father's feeble nature leaned, as on a staff of strength—in that case, he may have felt a bitterness that could not otherwise have been generated in his heart. But, methinks, the joy of possessing such a son, and the agony of losing him, would have developed the old man's moral and intellectual nature to a much greater degree than we now find it. Intense grief appears to be as much out of keeping with his life, as fervid happiness.

To confess the truth, it is not the easiest matter in the world, to define and individualize a character like this which we are now handling. The portrait must be so generally negative, that the most delicate pencil is likely to spoil it by introducing some too positive tint. Every touch must be kept down or else you destroy the subdued tone, which is absolutely essential to the whole effect. Perhaps more may be done by contrast, than by direct description. For this purpose, I make use of another cake-and-candy merchant, who likewise infests the rail-road depôt. This latter worthy is a very smart and well-dressed boy, of ten years old or thereabouts, who skips briskly hither and thither, addressing the passengers in a pert voice, yet with somewhat of good breeding in his tone and pronunciation. Now he has caught my eye, and skips across the room with a pretty pertness, which I should like to correct with a box on the ear. "Any cake, sir?—any candy?"

No; none for me, my lad. I did but glance at your brisk figure, in order to catch a reflected light, and throw it upon your old rival yonder.

Again, in order to invest my conception of the old man with a more decided sense of reality, I look at him in the very moment of intensest bustle, on the arrival of the cars. The shriek of the engine, as it rushes into the car-house, is the utterance of the steam-fiend, whom man has subdued by magic spells, and compels to serve as a beast of burden. He has skimmed rivers in his headlong rush, dashed through forests, plunged into the hearts of mountains, and glanced from the city to the desert-place, and again to a far-off city, with a meteoric progress, seen, and out of sight, while his reverberating roar still fills the ear. The travellers swarm forth from the cars. All are full of the momentum which they have caught from their mode of conveyance. It seems as if the whole world, both morally and physically, were detached from its old standfasts, and set in rapid motion. And, in the midst of this terrible activity, there sits the old man of gingerbread, so subdued, so hopeless, so without a stake in life, and yet not positively miserable—there he sits, the forlorn old creature, one chill and sombre day after another, gathering scanty coppers for his cakes, apples and candy—there sits the old apple-dealer, in his threadbare suit of snuff-color and gray, and his grisly stubble-beard. See! he folds his lean arms around his lean figure, with that quiet sigh, and that scarcely perceptible shiver, which are the tokens of his inward state. I have him now. He and the steam-fiend are each other's antipodes; the latter is the type of all that go ahead—and the old man, the representative of that melancholy class who, by some sad witchcraft, are doomed never to share in the world's exulting progress. Thus the contrast between mankind and this desolate brother becomes picturesque, and even sublime.

And now farewell, old friend! Little do you suspect, that a student of human life has made your character the theme of more than one solitary and thoughtful hour. Many would say, that you have hardly individuality enough to be the object of your own self-love. How, then, can a stranger's eye detect any thing in your mind and heart, to study and to wonder at? Yet could I read but a tithe of what is written there, it would be a volume of deeper and more comprehensive import than all that the wisest mortals have given to the world; for the soundless depths of the human soul, and of eternity, have an opening through your breast. God be praised, were it only for your sake, that the present shapes of human existence are not cast in iron, nor hewn in everlasting adamant, but moulded of the vapors that vanish away while the essence flits upward to the infinite. There is a spiritual essence in this gray and lean old shape that shall flit upward too. Yes; doubtless there is a region, where the life-long shiver will pass away from his being, and that quiet sigh, which it has taken him so many years to breathe, will be brought to a close for good and all.

THE ARTIST OF THE BEAUTIFUL

AN ELDERLY man, with his pretty daughter on his arm, was passing along the street, and emerged from the gloom of the cloudy evening into the light that fell across the pavement from the window of a small shop. It was a projecting window; and on the inside were suspended a variety of watches,—pinchbeck, silver, and one or two of gold,—all with their faces turned from the street, as if churlishly disinclined to inform the wayfarers what o'clock it was. Seated within the shop, sidelong to the window, with his pale face bent earnestly over some delicate piece of mechanism, on which was thrown the concentrated lustre of a shade-lamp, appeared a young man.

"What can Owen Warland be about?" muttered old Peter Hovenden,—himself a retired watchmaker, and the former master of this same young man, whose occupation he was now wondering at. "What can the fellow be about? These six months past, I have never come by his shop without seeing him just as steadily at work as now. It would be a flight beyond his usual foolery to seek for the Perpetual Motion. And yet I know enough of my old business to be certain, that what he is now so busy with is no part of the machinery of a watch."

"Perhaps, father," said Annie, without showing much interest in the question, "Owen is inventing a new kind of time-keeper. I am sure he has ingenuity enough."

"Poh, child! he has not the sort of ingenuity to invent anything better than a Dutch toy," answered her father, who had formerly been put to much vexation by Owen Warland's irregular genius. "A plague on such ingenuity! All the effect that ever I knew of it, was to spoil the accuracy of some of the best watches in my shop. He would turn the sun out of its orbit, and derange the whole course of time, if, as I said before, his ingenuity could grasp anything bigger than a child's toy!"

"Hush, father! he hears you," whispered Annie, pressing the old man's arm. "His ears are as delicate as his feelings, and you know how easily disturbed they are. Do let us move on."

So Peter Hovenden and his daughter Annie plodded on, without further conversation, until, in a by-street of the town, they found themselves passing the open door of a blacksmith's shop. Within was seen the forge, now blazing up, and illuminating the high and dusky roof, and now confining its lustre to a narrow precinct of the coal-strewn floor, according as the breath of the bellows was puffed forth, or again inhaled into its vast leathern lungs. In the intervals of brightness, it was easy to distinguish objects in remote corners of the shop, and the horse-shoes that hung upon the wall; in the momentary gloom, the fire seemed to be glimmering amidst the vagueness of unenclosed space. Moving about in this red glare and alternate dusk, was the figure of the blacksmith, well worthy to be viewed in so picturesque an aspect of light and shade, where the bright blaze struggled with the black night, as if each would have snatched his comely strength from the other. Anon, he drew a white-hot bar of iron from the coals, laid it on the anvil, uplifted his arm of might, and was soon enveloped in the myriads of sparks which the strokes of his hammer scattered into the surrounding gloom.

"Now, that is a pleasant sight," said the old watchmaker. "I know what it is to work in gold, but give me the worker in iron, after all is said and done. He spends his labor upon a reality. What say you, daughter Annie?"

"Pray don't speak so loud, father," whispered Annie. "Robert Danforth will hear you."

"And what if he should hear me?" said Peter Hovenden; "I say again, it is a good and a wholesome thing to depend upon main strength and reality, and to earn one's bread with the bare and brawny arm of a blacksmith. A watchmaker gets his brain puzzled by his wheels within a wheel, or loses his health or the nicety of his eyesight, as was my case; and finds himself, at middle age, or a little after, past labor at his own trade, and fit for nothing else, yet too poor to live at his ease. So, I say once again, give me main strength for my money. And then, how it takes the nonsense out of a man! Did you ever hear of a blacksmith being such a fool as Owen Warland, yonder?"

"Well said, uncle Hovenden!" shouted Robert Danforth, from the forge, in a full, deep, merry voice, that made the roof re-echo. "And what says Miss Annie to that doctrine? She, I suppose, will think it a genteeler business to tinker up a lady's watch, than to forge a horse-shoe or make a gridiron!"

Annie drew her father onward, without giving him time for reply.

But we must return to Owen Warland's shop, and spend more meditation upon his history and character than either Peter Hovenden, or probably his daughter Annie, or Owen's old schoolfellow, Robert Danforth, would have thought due to so slight a subject. From the time that his little fingers could grasp a pen-knife, Owen had been remarkable for a delicate ingenuity, which sometimes produced pretty shapes in wood, principally figures of flowers and birds, and sometimes seemed to aim at the hidden mysteries of mechanism. But it was always for purposes of grace, and never with any mockery of the useful. He did not, like the crowd of school-boy artizans, construct little windmills on the angle of a barn, or watermills across the neighboring brook. Those who discovered such peculiarity in the boy, as to think it worth their while to observe him closely, sometimes saw reason to suppose that he was attempting to imitate the beautiful movements of Nature, as exemplified in the flight of birds or the activity of little animals. It seemed, in fact, a new development of the love of the Beautiful, such as might have made him a poet, a painter, or a sculptor, and which was as completely refined from all utilitarian coarseness, as it could have been in either of the fine arts. He looked with singular distaste at the stiff and regular processes of ordinary machinery. Being once carried to see a steam-engine, in the expectation that his intuitive comprehension of mechanical principles would be gratified, he turned pale, and grew sick, as if something monstrous and unnatural had been presented to him. This horror was partly owing to the size and terrible energy of the Iron Laborer; for the character of Owen's mind was microscopic, and tended naturally to the minute, in accordance with his diminutive frame, and the marvellous smallness and delicate power of his fingers. Not that his sense of beauty was thereby diminished into a sense of prettiness. The Beautiful Idea has no relation to size, and may be as perfectly developed in a space too minute for any but microscopic investigation, as within the ample verge that is measured by the arc of the rainbow. But, at all events, this characteristic minuteness in his objects and accomplishments made the world even more incapable, than it might otherwise have been, of appreciating Owen Warland's genius. The boy's relatives saw nothing better to be done—as perhaps there was not—than to bind him apprentice to a watchmaker, hoping that his strange ingenuity might thus be regulated, and put to utilitarian purposes.

Peter Hovenden's opinion of his apprentice has already been expressed. He could make nothing of the lad. Owen's apprehension of the professional mysteries, it is true, was inconceivably quick. But he altogether forgot or despised the grand object of a watchmaker's business, and cared no more for the measurement of time than if it had been merged into eternity. So long, however, as he remained under his old master's care, Owen's lack of sturdiness made it possible, by strict injunctions and sharp oversight, to restrain his creative eccentricity within bounds. But when his apprentice-ship was served out, and he had taken the little shop which Peter Hovenden's failing eyesight compelled him to relinquish, then did people recognize how unfit a person was Owen Warland to lead old blind Father Time along his daily course. One of his most rational projects was, to connect a musical operation with the machinery of his watches, so that all the harsh dissonances of life might be rendered tuneful, and each flitting moment fall into the abyss of the Past in golden drops of harmony. If a family-clock was entrusted to him for repair—one of those tall, ancient clocks that have grown nearly allied to human nature, by measuring out the lifetime of many generations—he would take upon himself to arrange a dance or funeral procession of figures, across its venerable face, representing twelve mirthful or melancholy hours. Several freaks of this kind quite destroyed the young watchmaker's credit with that steady and matter-of-fact class of people who hold the opinion that time is not to be trifled with, whether considered as the medium of advancement and prosperity in this world, or preparation for the next. His custom rapidly diminished—a misfortune, how-ever, that was probably reckoned among his better accidents by Owen Warland, who was becoming more and more absorbed in a secret occupation, which drew all his science and manual dexterity into itself, and likewise gave full employment to the characteristic tendencies of his genius. This pursuit had already consumed many months.

After the old watchmaker and his pretty daughter had gazed at him, out of the obscurity of the street, Owen Warland was seized with a fluttering of the nerves, which made his hand tremble too violently to proceed with such delicate labor as he was now engaged upon.

"It was Annie herself!" murmured he. "I should have known it, by this throbbing of my heart, before I heard her father's voice. Ah, how it throbs! I shall scarcely be able to work again on this exquisite mechanism to-night. Annie—dearest Annie—thou shouldst give firmness to my heart and hand, and not shake them thus; for if I strive to put the very spirit of Beauty into form, and give it motion, it is for thy sake alone. Oh, throbbing heart, be quiet! If my labor be thus thwarted, there will come vague and unsatisfied dreams, which will leave me spiritless to-morrow."

As he was endeavoring to settle himself again to his task, the shop-door opened, and gave admittance to no other than the stalwart figure which Peter Hovenden had paused to admire, as seen amid the light and shadow of the blacksmith's shop. Robert Danforth had brought a little anvil of his own manufacture, and peculiarly constructed, which the young artist had recently bespoken. Owen examined the article, and pronounced it fashioned according to his wish.

"Why, yes," said Robert Danforth, his strong voice filling the shop as with the sound of a bass-viol, "I consider myself equal to anything in the way of my own trade; though I should have made but a poor figure at yours, with such a fist as this,"—added he, laughing, as he laid his vast hand beside the delicate one of Owen. "But what then? I put more main strength into one blow of my sledge-hammer, than all that you have expended since you were a 'prentice. Is not that the truth?"

"Very probably," answered the low and slender voice of Owen. "Strength is an earthly monster. I make no pretensions to it. My force, whatever there may be of it, is altogether spiritual."

"Well; but, Owen, what are you about!" asked his old schoolfellow, still in such a hearty volume of tone that it made the artist shrink; especially as the question related to a subject so sacred as the absorbing dream of his imagination. "Folks do say, that you are trying to discover the Perpetual Motion."

"The Perpetual Motion?—nonsense!" replied Owen Warland, with a movement of digust; for he was full of little petulances. "It can never be discovered! It is a dream that may delude men whose brains are mystified with matter, but not me. Besides, if such a discovery were possible, it would not be worth my while to make it, only to have the secret turned to such purposes as are now effected by steam and water-power. I am not ambitious to be honored with the paternity of a new kind of cotton-machine."

"That would be droll enough!" cried the blacksmith, breaking out into such an uproar of laughter, that Owen himself, and the bell-glasses on his work-board, quivered in unison. "No, no, Owen! No child of yours will have iron joints and sinews. Well, I won't hinder you any more. Good night, Owen, and success; and if you need any assistance, so far as a downright blow of hammer upon anvil will answer the purpose, I'm your man!"

And with another laugh, the man of main strength left the shop.

"How strange it is," whispered Owen Warland to himself, leaning his head upon his hand, "that all my musings, my purposes, my passion for the Beautiful, my consciousness of power to create it—a finer, more ethereal power, of which this earthly giant can have no conception—all, all, look so vain and idle, whenever my path is crossed by Robert Danforth! He would drive me mad, were I to meet him often. His hard, brute force darkens and confuses the spiritual element within me. But I, too, will be strong in my own way. I will not yield to him!"

He took from beneath a glass, a piece of minute machinery, which he set in the condensed light of his lamp, and, looking intently at it through a magnifying glass, proceeded to operate with a delicate instrument of steel. In an instant, however, he fell back in his chair, and clasped his hands, with a look of horror on his face, that made its small features as impressive as those of a giant would have been.

"Heaven! What have I done!" exclaimed he. "The vapor! —the influence of that brute force!—it has bewildered me, and obscured my perception. I have made the very stroke— the fatal stroke—that I have dreaded from the first! It is all over—the toil of months—the object of my life! I am ruined!"

And there he sat, in strange despair, until his lamp flickered in the socket, and left the Artist of the Beautiful in darkness.

Thus it is, that ideas which grow up within the imagination, and appear so lovely to it, and of a value beyond whatever men call valuable, are exposed to be shattered and annihilated by contact with the Practical. It is requisite for the ideal artist to possess a force of character that seems hardly compatible with its delicacy; he must keep his faith in himself, while the incredulous world assails him with its utter disbelief; he must stand up against mankind and be his own sole disciple, both as respects his genius, and the objects to which it is directed.

For a time, Owen Warland succumbed to this severe, but inevitable test. He spent a few sluggish weeks, with his head so continually resting in his hands, that the townspeople had scarcely an opportunity to see his countenance. When, at last, it was again uplifted to the light of day, a cold, dull, nameless change was perceptible upon it. In the opinion of Peter Hovenden, however, and that order of sagacious understandings who think that life should be regulated, like clockwork, with leaden weights, the alteration was entirely for the better. Owen now indeed, applied himself to business with dogged industry. It was marvellous to witness the obtuse gravity with which he would inspect the wheels of a great, old silver watch; thereby delighting the owner, in whose fob it had been worn till he deemed it a portion of his own life, and was accordingly jealous of its treatment. In consequence of the good report thus acquired, Owen Warland was invited by the proper authorities to regulate the clock in the church-steeple. He succeeded so admirably in this matter of public interest, that the merchants gruffly acknowledged his merits on 'Change; the nurse whispered his praises, as she gave the potion in the sick-chamber; the lover blessed him at the hour of appointed interview; and the town in general thanked Owen for the punctuality of dinner-time. In a word, the heavy weight upon his spirits kept everything in order, not merely within his own system, but wheresoever the iron accents of the church-clock were audible. It was a circumstance, though minute, yet characteristic of his present state, that, when employed to engrave names or initials on silver spoons, he now wrote the requisite letters in the plainest possible style; omitting a variety of fanciful flourishes, that had heretofore distinguished his work in this kind.

One day, during the era of this happy transformation, old Peter Hovenden came to visit his former apprentice.

"Well, Owen," said he, "I am glad to hear such good accounts of you from all quarters; and especially from the town-clock yonder, which speaks in your commendation every hour of the twenty-four. Only get rid altogether of your nonsensical trash about the Beautiful—which I, nor nobody else, nor yourself to boot, could never understand—only free yourself of that, and your success in life is as sure as daylight. Why, if you go on in this way, I should even venture to let you doctor this precious old watch of mine; though, except my daughter Annie, I have nothing else so valuable in the world."

"I should hardly dare touch it, sir," replied Owen in a depressed tone; for he was weighed down by his old master's presence.

"In time," said the latter, "in time, you will be capable of it."

The old watchmaker, with the freedom naturally consequent on his former authority, went on inspecting the work which Owen had in hand at the moment, together with other matters that were in progress. The artist, meanwhile, could scarcely lift his head. There was nothing so antipodal to his nature as this man's cold, unimaginative sagacity, by contact with which everything was converted into a dream, except the densest matter of the physical world. Owen groaned in spirit, and prayed fervently to be delivered from him.

"But what is this?" cried Peter Hovenden abruptly, taking up a dusty bell-glass, beneath which appeared a mechanical something, as delicate and minute as the system of a butterfly's anatomy. "What have we here! Owen, Owen! there is witchcraft in these little chains, and wheels, and paddles! See! with one pinch of my finger and thumb, I am going to deliver you from all future peril."

"For Heaven's sake," screamed Owen Warland, springing up with wonderful energy, "as you would not drive me mad—do not touch it! The slightest pressure of your finger would ruin me for ever."

"Aha, young man! And is it so?" said the old watchmaker, looking at him with just enough of penetration to torture Owen's soul with the bitterness of worldly criticism. "Well;

take your own course. But I warn you again, that in this small piece of mechanism lives your evil spirit. Shall I exorcise him?"

"You are my Evil Spirit," answered Owen, much excited— "you, and the hard, coarse world! The leaden thoughts and the despondency that you fling upon me are my clogs. Else, I should long ago have achieved the task that I was created for."

Peter Hovenden shook his head, with the mixture of contempt and indignation which mankind, of whom he was partly a representative, deem themselves entitled to feel towards all simpletons who seek other prizes than the dusty ones along the highway. He then took his leave with an uplifted finger, and a sneer upon his face, that haunted the artist's dreams for many a night afterwards. At the time of his old master's visit, Owen was probably on the point of taking up the relinquished task; but, by this sinister event, he was thrown back into the state whence he had been slowly emerging.

But the innate tendency of his soul had only been accumulating fresh vigor, during its apparent sluggishness. As the summer advanced, he almost totally relinquished his business, and permitted Father Time, so far as the old gentleman was represented by the clocks and watches under his control, to stray at random through human life, making infinite confusion among the train of bewildered hours. He wasted the sunshine, as people said, in wandering through the woods and fields, and along the banks of streams. There, like a child, he found amusement in chasing butterflies, or watching the motions of water-insects. There was something truly mysterious in the intentness with which he contemplated these living playthings, as they sported on the breeze; or examined the structure of an imperial insect whom he had imprisoned. The chase of butterflies was an apt emblem of the ideal pursuit in which he had spent so many golden hours. But, would the Beautiful Idea ever be yielded to his hand, like the butterfly that symbolized it? Sweet, doubtless, were these days, and congenial to the artist's soul. They were full of bright conceptions, which gleamed through his intellectual world, as the butterflies gleamed through the outward atmosphere, and were real to him for the instant, without the toil, and perplexity, and many disappointments, of attempting to make them visible to the sensual eye. Alas, that the artist, whether in poetry or whatever other material, may not content himself with the inward enjoyment of the Beautiful, but must chase the flitting mystery beyond the verge of his ethereal domain, and crush its frail being in seizing it with a material grasp! Owen Warland felt the impulse to give external reality to his ideas, as irresistibly as any of the poets or painters, who have arrayed the world in a dimmer and fainter beauty, imperfectly copied from the richness of their visions.

The night was now his time for the slow process of recreating the one Idea, to which all his intellectual activity referred itself. Always at the approach of dusk, he stole into the town, locked himself within his shop, and wrought with patient delicacy of touch, for many hours. Sometimes he was startled by the rap of the watchman, who, when all the world should be asleep, had caught the gleam of lamp-light through the crevices of Owen Warland's shutters. Daylight, to the morbid sensibility of his mind, seemed to have an intrusiveness that interfered with his pursuits. On cloudy and inclement days, therefore, he sat with his head upon his hands, muffling, as it were, his sensitive brain in a mist of indefinite musings; for it was a relief to escape from the sharp distinctness with which he was compelled to shape out his thoughts, during his nightly toil.

From one of these fits of torpor, he was aroused by the entrance of Annie Hovenden, who came into the shop with the freedom of a customer, and also with something of the familiarity of a childish friend. She had worn a hole through her silver thimble, and wanted Owen to repair it.

"But I don't know whether you will condescend to such a task," said she, laughing, "now that you are so taken up with the notion of putting spirit into machinery."

"Where did you get that idea, Annie?" said Owen, starting in surprise.

"Oh, out of my own head," answered she, "and from something that I heard you say, long ago, when you were but a boy, and I a little child. But, come! will you mend this poor thimble of mine?"

"Anything for your sake, Annie," said Owen Warland— "anything; even were it to work at Robert Danforth's forge."

"And that would be a pretty sight!" retorted Annie, glancing with imperceptible slightness at the artist's small and slender frame. "Well; here is the thimble."

"But that is a strange idea of yours," said Owen, "about the spiritualization of matter!"

And then the thought stole into his mind, that this young girl possessed the gift to comprehend him, better than all the world beside. And what a help and strength would it be to him, in his lonely toil, if he could gain the sympathy of the only being whom he loved! To persons whose pursuits are insulated from the common business of life—who are either in advance of mankind, or apart from it—there often comes a sensation of moral cold, that makes the spirit shiver, as if it had reached the frozen solitudes around the pole. What the prophet, the poet, the reformer, the criminal, or any other man, with human yearnings, but separated from the multitude by a peculiar lot, might feel, poor Owen Warland felt.

"Annie," cried he, growing pale as death at the thought, "how gladly would I tell you the secret of my pursuit! You, methinks, would estimate it rightly. You, I know, would hear it with a reverence that I must not expect from the harsh, material world."

"Would I not? to be sure I would!" replied Annie Hovenden, lightly laughing. "Come; explain to me quickly what is the meaning of this little whirligig, so delicately wrought that it might be a plaything for Queen Mab. See; I will put it in motion."

"Hold," exclaimed Owen, "hold!"

Annie had but given the slightest possible touch, with the point of a needle, to the same minute portion of complicated machinery which has been more than once mentioned, when the artist seized her by the wrist with a force that made her scream aloud. She was affrighted at the convulsion of intense rage and anguish that writhed across his features. The next instant he let his head sink upon his hands.

"Go, Annie," murmured he, "I have deceived myself, and must suffer for it. I yearned for sympathy—and thought—and fancied—and dreamed—that you might give it me. But you lack the talisman, Annie, that should admit you into my secrets. That touch has undone the toil of months, and the thought of a lifetime! It was not your fault, Annie—but you have ruined me!"

Poor Owen Warland! He had indeed erred, yet pardonably; for if any human spirit could have sufficiently reverenced the processes so sacred in his eyes, it must have been a woman's. Even Annie Hovenden, possibly, might not have disappointed him, had she been enlightened by the deep intelligence of love.

The artist spent the ensuing winter in a way that satisfied any persons, who had hitherto retained a hopeful opinion of him, that he was, in truth, irrevocably doomed to inutility as regarded the world, and to an evil destiny on his own part. The decease of a relative had put him in possession of a small inheritance. Thus freed from the necessity of toil, and having lost the steadfast influence of a great purpose—great, at least to him—he abandoned himself to habits from which, it might have been supposed, the mere delicacy of his organization would have availed to secure him. But when the ethereal portion of a man of genius is obscured, the earthly part assumes an influence the more uncontrollable, because the character is now thrown off the balance to which Providence had so nicely adjusted it, and which, in coarser natures, is adjusted by some other method. Owen Warland made proof of whatever show of bliss may be found in riot. He looked at the world through the golden medium of wine, and contemplated the visions that bubble up so gaily around the brim of the glass, and that people the air with shapes of pleasant madness, which so soon grow ghostly and forlorn. Even when this dismal and inevitable change had taken place, the young man might still have continued to quaff the cup of enchantments, though its vapor did but shroud life in gloom, and fill the gloom with spectres that mocked at him. There was a certain irksomeness of spirit, which, being real, and the deepest sensation of which the artist was now conscious, was more intolerable than any fantastic miseries and horrors that the abuse of wine could summon up. In the latter case, he could remember, even out of the midst of his trouble, that all was but a delusion; in the former, the heavy anguish was his actual life.

From this perilous state, he was redeemed by an incident which more than one person witnessed, but of which the shrewdest could not explain nor conjecture the operation on Owen Warland's mind. It was very simple. On a warm afternoon of spring, as the artist sat among his riotous companions, with a glass of wine before him, a splendid butterfly flew in at the open window, and fluttered about his head.

"Ah!" exclaimed Owen, who had drank freely, "Are you alive again, child of the sun, and playmate of the summer breeze, after your dismal winter's nap! Then it is time for me to be at work!"

And leaving his unemptied glass upon the table, he departed, and was never known to sip another drop of wine.

And now, again, he resumed his wanderings in the woods and fields. It might be fancied that the bright butterfly, which had come so spiritlike into the window, as Owen sat with the rude revellers, was indeed a spirit, commissioned to recall him to the pure, ideal life that had so etherealized him among men. It might be fancied, that he went forth to seek this spirit, in its sunny haunts; for still, as in the summer-time gone by, he was seen to steal gently up, wherever a butterfly had alighted, and lose himself in contemplation of it. When it took flight, his eyes followed the winged vision, as if its airy track would show the path to heaven. But what could be the purpose of the unseasonable toil, which was again resumed, as the watchman knew by the lines of lamp-light through the crevices of Owen Warland's shutters? The townspeople had one comprehensive explanation of all these singularities. Owen Warland had gone mad! How universally efficacious—how satisfactory, too, and soothing to the injured sensibility of narrowness and dullness—is this easy method of accounting for whatever lies beyond the world's most ordinary scope! From Saint Paul's days, down to our poor little Artist of the Beautiful, the same talisman has been applied to the elucidation of all mysteries in the words or deeds of men, who spoke or acted too wisely or too well. In Owen Warland's case, the judgment of his townspeople may have been correct. Perhaps he was mad. The lack of sympathy—that contrast between himself and his neighbors, which took away the restraint of example—was enough to make him so. Or, possibly, he had caught just so much of ethereal radiance as served to bewilder him, in an earthly sense, by its intermixture with the common daylight.

One evening, when the artist had returned from a customary ramble, and had just thrown the lustre of his lamp on the delicate piece of work, so often interrupted, but still taken up again, as if his fate were embodied in its mechanism, he was surprised by the entrance of old Peter Hovenden. Owen never met this man without a shrinking of the heart. Of all the world, he was most terrible, by reason of a keen understanding, which saw so distinctly what it did see, and disbelieved so uncompromisingly in what it could not see. On this occasion, the old watchmaker had merely a gracious word or two to say.

"Owen, my lad," said he, "we must see you at my house to-morrow night."

The artist began to mutter some excuse.

"Oh, but it must be so," quoth Peter Hovenden, "for the sake of the days when you were one of the household. What, my boy, don't you know that my daughter Annie is engaged to Robert Danforth? We are making an entertainment, in our humble way, to celebrate the event."

"Ah!" said Owen.

That little monosyllable was all he uttered; its tone seemed cold and unconcerned, to an ear like Peter Hovenden's; and yet there was in it the stifled outcry of the poor artist's heart, which he compressed within him like a man holding down an evil spirit. One slight outbreak, however, imperceptible to the old watchmaker, he allowed himself. Raising the instrument with which he was about to begin his work, he let it fall upon the little system of machinery that had, anew, cost him months of thought and toil. It was shattered by the stroke!

Owen Warland's story would have been no tolerable representation of the troubled life of those who strive to create the Beautiful, if, amid all other thwarting influences, love had not interposed to steal the cunning from his hand. Outwardly, he had been no ardent or enterprising lover; the career of his passion had confined its tumults and vicissitudes so entirely within the artist's imagination, that Annie herself had scarcely more than a woman's intuitive perception of it. But, in Owen's view, it covered the whole field of his life. Forgetful of the time when she had shown herself incapable of any deep response, he had persisted in connecting all his dreams of artistical success with Annie's image; she was the visible shape in which the spiritual power that he worshipped, and on whose altar he hoped to lay a not unworthy offering, was made manifest to him. Of course he had deceived himself; there were no such attributes in Annie Hovenden as his imagination had endowed her with. She, in the aspect which she wore to his inward vision, was as much a creation of his own, as the mysterious piece of mechanism would be were it ever realized. Had he become convinced of his mistake through the medium of successful love; had he won Annie to his bosom, and there beheld her fade from angel into ordinary woman, the disappointment might have driven him back, with concentrated energy, upon his sole remaining object. On the other hand, had he found Annie what he fancied, his lot would have been so rich in beauty, that, out of its mere redundancy, he might have wrought the Beautiful into many a worthier type than he had toiled for. But the guise in which his sorrow came to him, the sense that the angel of his life had been snatched away and given to a rude man of earth and iron, who could neither need nor appreciate her ministrations; this was the very perversity of fate, that makes human existence appear too absurd and contradictory to be the scene of one other hope or one other fear. There was nothing left for Owen Warland but to sit down like a man that had been stunned.

He went through a fit of illness. After his recovery, his small and slender frame assumed an obtuser garniture of flesh than it had ever before worn. His thin cheeks became round; his delicate little hand, so spiritually fashioned to achieve fairy task-work, grew plumper than the hand of a thriving infant. His aspect had a childishness, such as might have induced a stranger to pat him on the head—pausing, however, in the act, to wonder what manner of child was here. It was as if the spirit had gone out of him, leaving the body to flourish in a soft of vegetable existence. Not that Owen Warland was idiotic. He could talk, and not irrationally. Somewhat of a babbler, indeed, did people begin to think him; for he was apt to discourse at wearisome length, of marvels of mechanism that he had read about in books, but which he had learned to consider as absolutely fabulous. Among them he enumerated the Man of Brass, constructed by Albertus Magnus, and the Brazen Head of Friar Bacon; and, coming down to later times, the automata of a little coach and horses, which, it was pretended, had been manufactured for the Dauphin of France; together with an insect that buzzed about the ear like a living fly, and yet was but a contrivance of minute steel springs. There was a story, too, of a duck that waddled, and quacked, and ate; though, had any honest citizen purchased it for dinner, he would have found himself cheated with the mere mechanical apparition of a duck.

"But all these accounts," said Owen Warland, "I am now satisfied, are mere impositions."

Then, in a mysterious way, he would confess that he once thought differently. In his idle and dreamy days, he had considered it possible, in a certain sense, to spiritualize machinery; and to combine with the new species of life and motion, thus produced, a beauty that should attain to the ideal which Nature has proposed to herself, in all her creatures, but has never taken pains to realize. He seemed, however, to retain no very distinct perception either of the process of achieving this object, or of the design itself.

"I have thrown it all aside now," he would say. "It was a dream, such as young men are always mystifying themselves with. Now that I have acquired a little common sense, it makes me laugh to think of it."

Poor, poor, and fallen Owen Warland! These were the symptoms that he had ceased to be an inhabitant of the better sphere that lies unseen around us. He had lost his faith in the invisible, and now prided himself, as such unfortunates invariably do, in the wisdom which rejected much that even his eye could see, and trusted confidently in nothing but what his hand could touch. This is the calamity of men whose spiritual part dies out of them, and leaves the grosser understanding to assimilate them more and more to the things of which alone it can take cognizance. But, in Owen Warland, the spirit was not dead, nor past away; it only slept.

How it awoke again, is not recorded. Perhaps, the torpid slumber was broken by a convulsive pain. Perhaps, as in a former instance, the butterfly came and hovered about his head, and reinspired him—as, indeed, this creature of the sunshine had always a mysterious mission for the artist—reinspired him with the former purpose of his life. Whether it were pain or happiness that thrilled through his veins, his first impulse was to thank Heaven for rendering him again the being of thought, imagination, and keenest sensibility, that he had long ceased to be.

"Now for my task," said he. "Never did I feel such strength for it as now."

Yet, strong as he felt himself, he was incited to toil the more diligently, by an anxiety lest death should surprise him in the midst of his labors. This anxiety, perhaps, is common to all men who set their hearts upon anything so high, in their own view of it, that life becomes of importance only as conditional to its accomplishment. So long as we love life for itself, we seldom dread the losing it. When we desire life for the attainment of an object, we recognize the frailty of its texture. But, side by side with this sense of insecurity, there is a vital faith in our invulnerability to the shaft of death, while engaged in any task that seems assigned by Providence as our proper thing to do, and which the world would have cause to mourn for, should we leave it unaccomplished. Can the philosopher, big with the inspiration of an idea that is to reform mankind, believe that he is to be beckoned from this sensible existence, at the very instant when he is mustering his breath to speak the word of light? Should he perish so, the weary ages may pass away—the world's whole life-sand may fall, drop by drop—before another intellect is prepared to develope the truth that might have been uttered then. But history affords many an example, where the most precious spirit, at any particular epoch manifested in human shape, has gone hence untimely, without space allowed him, so far as mortal judgment could discern, to perform his mission on the earth. The prophet dies; and the man of torpid heart and sluggish brain lives on. The poet leaves his song half sung, or finishes it, beyond the scope of mortal ears, in a celestial choir. The painter—as Allston did—leaves half his conception on the canvass, to sadden us with its imperfect beauty, and goes to picture forth the whole, if it be no irreverence to say so, in the hues of Heaven. But, rather, such incomplete designs of this life will be perfected nowhere. This so frequent abortion of man's dearest projects must be taken as a proof, that the deeds of earth, however etherealized by piety or genius, are without value, except as exercises and manifestations of the spirit. In Heaven, all ordinary thought is higher and more melodious than Milton's song. Then, would he add another verse to any strain that he had left unfinished here?

But to return to Owen Warland. It was his fortune, good or ill, to achieve the purpose of his life. Pass we over a long space of intense thought, yearning effort, minute toil, and wasting anxiety, succeeded by an instant of solitary triumph; let all this be imagined; and then behold the artist, on a winter evening, seeking admittance to Robert Danforth's fireside circle. There he found the Man of Iron, with his massive substance thoroughly warmed and attempered by domestic influences. And there was Annie, too, now trans-formed into a matron, with much of her husband's plain and sturdy nature, but imbued, as Owen Warland still believed, with a finer grace, that might enable her to be the interpreter between Strength and Beauty. It happened, likewise, that old Peter Hovenden was a guest, this evening, at his daughter's fireside; and it was his well-remembered expression of keen, cold criticism, that first encountered the artist's glance.

"My old friend Owen!" cried Robert Danforth, starting up, and compressing the artist's delicate fingers within a hand that was accustomed to gripe bars of iron. "This is kind and neighborly, to come to us at last! I was afraid your Perpetual Motion had bewitched you out of the remembrance of old times."

"We are glad to see you!" said Annie, while a blush red-dened her matronly cheek. "It was not like a friend, to stay from us so long."

"Well, Owen," inquired the old watchmaker, as his first greeting, "how comes on the Beautiful? Have you created it at last?"

The artist did not immediately reply, being startled by the apparition of a young child of strength, that was tumbling about on the carpet; a little personage who had come myster-iously out of the infinite, but with something so sturdy and real in his composition that he seemed moulded out of the densest substance which earth could supply. This hopeful infant crawled towards the new-comer, and setting himself on end—as Robert Danforth expressed the posture—stared at Owen with a look of such sagacious observation, that the mother could not help exchanging a proud glance with her husband. But the artist was disturbed by the child's look, as imagining a resemblance between it and Peter Hovenden's habitual expression. He could have fancied that the old watchmaker was compressed into this baby-shape, and was looking out of those baby-eyes, and repeating—as he now did—the malicious question:

"The Beautiful, Owen! How comes on the Beautiful? Have you succeeded in creating the Beautiful?"

"I have succeeded," replied the artist, with a momentary light of triumph in his eyes, and a smile of sunshine, yet steeped in such depth of thought that it was almost sadness. "Yes, my friends, it is the truth. I have succeeded!"

"Indeed!" cried Annie, a look of maiden mirthfulness peeping out of her face again. "And is it lawful, now, to inquire what the secret is?"

"Surely; it is to disclose it, that I have come," answered Owen Warland. "You shall know, and see, and touch, and possess, the secret! For Annie—if by that name I may still address the friend of my boyish years—Annie, it is for your bridal gift that I have wrought this spiritualized mechanism, this harmony of motion, this Mystery of Beauty! It comes late, indeed; but it is as we go onward in life, when objects begin to lose their freshness of hue, and our souls their delicacy of perception, that the spirit of Beauty is most needed. If—forgive me, Annie—if you know how to value this gift, it can never come too late!"

He produced, as he spoke, what seemed a jewel-box. It was carved richly out of ebony by his own hand, and inlaid with a fanciful tracery of pearl, representing a boy in pursuit of a butterfly, which, elsewhere, had become a winged spirit, and was flying heavenward; while the boy, or youth, had found such efficacy in his strong desire, that he ascended from earth to cloud, and from cloud to celestial atmosphere, to win the Beautiful. This case of ebony the artist opened, and bade Annie place her finger on its edge. She did so, but almost screamed, as a butterfly fluttered forth, and alighting on her finger's tip, sat waving the ample magnificence of its purple and gold-speckled wings, as if in prelude to a flight. It is impossible to express by words the glory, the splendor, the delicate gorgeousness, which were softened into the beauty of this object. Nature's ideal butterfly was here realized in all its perfection; not in the pattern of such faded insects as flit among earthly flowers, but of those which hover across the meads of Paradise, for child-angels and the spirits of departed infants to disport themselves with. The rich down was visible upon its wings; the lustre of its eyes seemed instinct with spirit. The firelight glimmered around this wonder— the candles gleamed upon it—but it glistened apparently by its own radiance, and illuminated the finger and outstretched hand on which it rested, with a white gleam like that of precious stones. In its perfect beauty, the consideration of size was entirely lost. Had its wings overarched the firmament, the mind could not have been more filled or satisfied.

"Beautiful! Beautiful!" exclaimed Annie. "Is it alive? Is it alive?"

"Alive? To be sure it is," answered her husband. "Do you suppose any mortal has skill enough to make a butterfly,—or would put himself to the trouble of making one, when any child may catch a score of them in a summer's afternoon? Alive? Certainly! But this pretty box is undoubtedly of our friend Owen's manufacture; and really it does him credit."

At this moment, the butterfly waved its wings anew, with a motion so absolutely lifelike that Annie was startled, and even awe-stricken; for, in spite of her husband's opinion, she could not satisfy herself whether it was indeed a living creature, or a piece of wondrous mechanism.

"Is it alive?" she repeated, more earnestly than before.

"Judge for yourself," said Owen Warland, who stood gazing in her face with fixed attention.

The butterfly now flung itself upon the air, fluttered round Annie's head, and soared into a distant region of the parlor, still making itself perceptible to sight by the starry gleam in which the motion of its wings enveloped it. The infant on the floor, followed its course with his sagacious little eyes. After flying about the room, it returned, in a spiral curve, and settled again on Annie's finger.

"But is it alive?" exclaimed she again; and the finger, on which the gorgeous mystery had alighted, was so tremulous that the butterfly was forced to balance himself with his wings. "Tell me if it be alive, or whether you created it?"

"Wherefore ask who created it, so it be beautiful?" replied Owen Warland. "Alive? Yes, Annie; it may well be said to possess life, for it absorbed my own being into itself; and in the secret of that butterfly, and in its beauty—which is not merely outward, but deep as its whole system—is represented the intellect, the imagination, the sensibility, the soul, of an Artist of the Beautiful! Yes, I created it. But"—and here his countenance somewhat changed—"this butterfly is not now to me what it was when I beheld it afar off, in the day-dreams of my youth."

"Be it what it may, it is a pretty plaything," said the blacksmith, grinning with childlike delight. "I wonder whether it would condescend to alight on such a great clumsy finger as mine? Hold it hither, Annie!"

By the artist's direction, Annie touched her finger's tip to that of her husband; and, after a momentary delay, the butterfly fluttered from one to the other. It preluded a second flight by a similar, yet not precisely the same waving of wings, as in the first experiment; then, ascending from the blacksmith's stalwart finger, it rose in a gradually enlarging curve to the ceiling, made one wide sweep around the room, and returned with an undulating movement to the point whence it had started.

"Well, that does beat all nature!" cried Robert Danforth, bestowing the heartiest praise that he could find expression for; and, indeed, had he paused there, a man of finer words and nicer perception, could not easily have said more. "That goes beyond me, I confess! But what then? There is more real use in one downright blow of my sledge-hammer, than in the whole five years' labor that our friend Owen has wasted on this butterfly!"

Here the child clapped his hands, and made a great babble of indistinct utterance, apparently demanding that the butterfly should be given him for a plaything.

Owen Warland, meanwhile, glanced sidelong at Annie, to discover whether she sympathized in her husband's estimate of the comparative value of the Beautiful and the Practical. There was, amid all her kindness towards himself, amid all the wonder and admiration with which she contemplated the marvelous work of his hands, and incarnation of his idea, a secret scorn; too secret, perhaps, for her own consciousness, and perceptible only to such intuitive discernment as that of the artist. But Owen, in the latter stages of his pursuit, had risen out of the region in which such a discovery might have been torture. He knew that the world, and Annie as the representative of the world, whatever praise might be bestowed, could never say the fitting word, nor feel the fitting sentiment which should be the perfect recompense of an artist who, symbolizing a lofty moral by a material trifle—converting what was earthly, to spiritual gold—had won the Beautiful into his handiwork. Not at this latest moment, was he to learn that the reward of all high performance must be sought within itself, or sought in vain. There was, however, a view of the matter, which Annie, and her husband, and even Peter Hovenden, might fully have understood, and which would have satisfied them that the toil of years had here been worthily bestowed. Owen Warland might have told them, that this butterfly, this plaything, this bridal-gift of a poor watchmaker to a blacksmith's wife, was, in truth, a gem of art that a monarch would have purchased with honors and abundant wealth, and have treasured it among the jewels of his kingdom, as the most unique and wondrous of them all! But the artist smiled, and kept the secret to himself.

"Father," said Annie, thinking that a word of praise from the old watchmaker might gratify his former apprentice, "do come and admire this pretty butterfly!"

"Let us see," said Peter Hovenden, rising from his chair, with the sneer upon his face that always made people doubt, as he himself did, in everything but a material existence. "Here is my finger for it to alight upon. I shall understand it better when once I have touched it."

But, to the increased astonishment of Annie, when the tip of her father's finger was pressed against that of her husband, on which the butterfly still rested, the insect drooped its wings, and seemed on the point of falling to the floor. Even the bright spots of gold upon its wings and body, unless her eyes deceived her, grew dim, and the glowing purple took a dusky hue, and the starry lustre that gleamed around the blacksmith's hand, became faint, and vanished.

"It is dying! it is dying!" cried Annie, in alarm.

"It has been delicately wrought," said the artist calmly. "As I told you, it has imbibed a spiritual essence—call it magnetism, or what you will. In an atmosphere of doubt and mockery, its exquisite susceptibility suffers torture, as does the soul of him who instilled his own life into it. It has already lost its beauty; in a few moments more, its mechanism would be irreparably injured."

"Take away your hand, father!" entreated Annie, turning pale. "Here is my child; let it rest on his innocent hand. There, perhaps, its life will revive, and its colors grow brighter than ever."

Her father, with an acrid smile, withdrew his finger. The butterfly then appeared to recover the power of voluntary motion; while its hues assumed much of their original lustre, and the gleam of starlight, which was its most ethereal attribute, again formed a halo round about it. At first, when transferred from Robert Danforth's hand to the small finger of the child, this radiance grew so powerful that it positively threw the little fellow's shadow back against the wall. He, meanwhile, extended his plump hand as he had seen his father and mother do, and watched the waving of the insect's wings, with infantine delight. Nevertheless, there was a certain odd expression of sagacity, that made Owen Warland feel as if here were old Peter Hovenden, partially, and but partially, redeemed from his hard scepticism into childish faith.

"How wise the little monkey looks!" whispered Robert Danforth to his wife.

"I never saw such a look on a child's face," answered Annie, admiring her own infant, and with good reason, far more than the artistic butterfly. "The darling knows more of the mystery than we do."

As if the butterfly, like the artist, were conscious of something not entirely congenial in the child's nature, it alternately sparkled and grew dim. At length, it arose from the small hand of the infant with an airy motion, that seemed to bear it upward without an effort; as if the ethereal instincts, with which its master's spirit had endowed it, impelled this fair vision involuntarily to a higher sphere. Had there been no obstruction, it might have soared into the sky, and grown immortal. But its lustre gleamed upon the ceiling; the exquisite texture of its wings brushed against that earthly medium; and a sparkle or two, as of star-dust, floated downward and lay glimmering on the carpet. Then the butterfly came fluttering down, and instead of returning to the infant, was apparently attracted towards the artist's hand.

"Not so, not so!" murmured Owen Warland, as if his handiwork could have understood him. "Thou hast gone forth out of thy master's heart. There is no return for thee!"

With a wavering movement, and emitting a tremulous radiance, the butterfly struggled, as it were, towards the infant, and was about to alight upon his finger. But, while it still hovered in the air, the little Child of Strength, with his grandsire's sharp and shrewd expression in his face, made a snatch at the marvellous insect, and compressed it in his hand. Annie screamed! Old Peter Hovendon burst into a cold and scornful laugh. The blacksmith, by main force, unclosed the infant's hand, and found within the palm a small heap of glittering fragments, whence the Mystery of Beauty had fled for ever. And as for Owen Warland, he looked placidly at what seemed the ruin of his life's labor, and which was yet no ruin. He had caught a far other butterfly than this. When the artist rose high enough to achieve the Beautiful, the symbol by which he made it perceptible to mortal senses became of little value in his eyes, while his spirit possessed itself in the enjoyment of the Reality.

A VIRTUOSO'S COLLECTION

THE OTHER day, having a leisure hour at my disposal, I stept into a new museum, to which my notice was casually drawn by a small and unobtrusive sign: "To be seen here, a Virtuoso's Collection." Such was the simple, yet not altogether unpromising announcement, that turned my steps aside, for a little while, from the sunny sidewalk of our principal thoroughfare. Mounting a sombre staircase, I pushed open a door at its summit, and found myself in the presence of a person, who mentioned the moderate sum that would entitle me to admittance:

"Three shillings, Massachusetts tenor," said he; "no, I mean half a dollar, as you reckon in these days."

While searching my pocket for the coin, I glanced at the door-keeper, the marked character and individuality of whose aspect encouraged me to expect something not quite in the ordinary way. He wore an old-fashioned great-coat, much faded, within which his meagre person was so completely enveloped that the rest of his attire was undistinguishable. But his visage was remarkably wind-flushed, sun-burnt, and weather-worn, and had a most unquiet, nervous, and apprehensive expression. It seemed as if this man had some all-important object in view, some point of deepest interest to be decided, some momentous question to ask, might he but hope for a reply. As it was evident, however, that I could have nothing to do with his private affairs, I passed through an open door-way, which admitted me into the extensive hall of the Museum.

Directly in front of the portal was the bronze statue of a youth with winged feet. He was represented in the act of flitting away from earth, yet wore such a look of earnest invitation that it impressed me like a summons to enter the hall.

"It is the original statue of Opportunity, by the ancient sculptor Lysippus," said a gentleman who now approached me; "I place it at the entrance of my Museum, because it is not at all times that one can gain admittance to such a collection."

The speaker was a middle-aged person, of whom it was not easy to determine whether he had spent his life as a scholar, or as a man of action; in truth, all outward and obvious peculiarities had been worn away by an extensive and promiscuous intercourse with the world. There was no mark about him of profession, individual habits, or scarcely of country; although his dark complexion and high features made me conjecture that he was a native of some southern clime of Europe. At all events, he was evidently the Virtuoso in person.

"With your permission," said he, "as we have no descriptive catalogue, I will accompany you through the Museum, and point out whatever may be most worthy of attention. In the first place, here is a choice collection of stuffed animals."

Nearest the door stood the outward semblance of a wolf, exquisitely prepared, it is true, and showing a very wolfish fierceness in the large glass eyes, which were inserted into its wild and crafty head. Still it was merely the skin of a wolf, with nothing to distinguish it from other individuals of that unlovely breed.

"How does this animal deserve a place in your collection?" inquired I.

"It is the wolf that devoured Little Red Riding-Hood," answered the Virtuoso; "and by his side,—with a milder and more matronly look, as you perceive,—stands the she-wolf that suckled Romulus and Remus."

"Ah, indeed!" exclaimed I. "And what lovely lamb is this, with the snow-white fleece, which seems to be of as delicate a texture as innocence itself?"

"Methinks you have but carelessly read Spenser," replied my guide, "or you would at once recognize the 'milk-white lamb' which Una led. But I set no great value upon the lamb. The next specimen is better worth our notice."

"What!" cried I, "this strange animal, with the black head of an ox upon the body of a white horse? Were it possible to suppose it, I should say that this was Alexander's steed Bucephalus."

"The same," said the Virtuoso. "And can you likewise give a name to the famous charger that stands beside him?"

Next to the renowned Bucephalus stood the mere skeleton of a horse, with the white bones peeping through its ill-conditioned hide. But, if my heart had not warmed towards that pitiful anatomy, I might as well have quitted the Museum at once. Its rarities had not been collected with pain and toil from the four quarters of the earth, and from the depths of the sea, and from the palaces and sepulchres of ages, for those who could mistake this illustrious steed.

"It is Rosinante!" exclaimed I, with enthusiasm.

And so it proved! My admiration for the noble and gallant horse caused me to glance with less interest at the other animals, although many of them might have deserved the notice of Cuvier himself. There was the donkey which Peter Bell cudgelled so soundly; and a brother of the same species, who had suffered a similar infliction from the ancient prophet Balaam. Some doubts were entertained, however, as to the authenticity of the latter beast. My guide pointed out the venerable Argus, that faithful dog of Ulysses, and also another dog, (for so the skin bespoke it,) which, though imperfectly preserved, seemed once to have had three heads. It was Cerberus. I was considerably amused at detecting, in an obscure corner, the fox that became so famous by the loss of his tail. There were several stuffed cats, which, as a dear lover of that comfortable beast, attracted my affectionate regards. One was Dr. Johnson's cat Hodge; and in the same row stood the favorite cats of Mahomet, Gray, and Walter Scott, together with Puss in Boots, and a cat of very noble aspect who had once been a deity of ancient Egypt. Byron's tame bear came next. I must not forget to mention the Erymanthean boar, the skin of St. George's Dragon, and that of the serpent Python; and another skin, with beautifully variegated hues, supposed to have been the garment of the "spirited sly snake," which tempted Eve. Against the wall were suspended the horns of the stag that Shakspeare shot; and on the floor lay the ponderous shell of the tortoise which fell upon the head of Æschylus. In one row, as natural as life, stood the sacred bull Apis, the "cow with the crumpled horn," and a very wild looking young heifer, which I guessed to be the cow that jumped over the moon. She was probably killed by the rapidity of her descent. As I turned away, my eyes fell upon an indescribable monster, which proved to be a griffin.

"I look in vain," observed I, "for the skin of an animal which might well deserve the closest study of a naturalist,— the winged horse Pegasus."

"He is not yet dead," replied the Virtuoso, "but he is so hard ridden by many young gentlemen of the day, that I hope soon to add his skin and skeleton to my collection."

We now passed to the next alcove of the hall, in which was a multitude of stuffed birds. They were very prettily arranged, some upon the branches of trees, others brooding upon nests, and others suspended by wires so artificially that they seemed in the very act of flight. Among them was a white dove, with a withered branch of olive leaves in her mouth.

"Can this be the very dove," inquired I, "that brought the message of peace and hope to the tempest-beaten passengers of the ark?"

"Even so," said my companion.

"And this raven, I suppose," continued I, "is the same that fed Elijah in the wilderness."

"The raven?—no," said the Virtuoso, "it is a bird of modern date. He belonged to one Barnaby Rudge; and many people fancied that the devil himself was disguised under his sable plumage. But poor Grip has drawn his last cork, and has been forced to 'say die' at last. This other raven, hardly less curious, is that in which the soul of King George the First revisited his lady love, the Duchess of Kendall."

My guide next pointed out Minerva's owl, and the vulture that preyed upon the liver of Prometheus. There was likewise the sacred Ibis of Egypt, and one of the Stymphalides, which Hercules shot in his sixth labor. Shelley's sky-lark, Bryant's water-fowl, and a pigeon from the belfry of the Old South Chuch, preserved by N. P. Willis, were placed on the same perch. I could not but shudder on beholding Coleridge's albatross, transfixed with the Ancient Mariner's crossbow shaft. Beside this bird of awful poesy stood a gray goose of very ordinary aspect.

"Stuffed goose is no such rarity," observed I. "Why do you preserve such a specimen in your Museum?"

"It is one of the flock whose cackling saved the Roman Capitol," answered the Virtuoso. "Many geese have cackled and hissed, both before and since; but none, like those, have clamored themselves into immortality."

There seemed to be little else that demanded notice in this department of the Museum, unless we except Robinson Crusoe's parrot, a live phœnix, a footless bird of Paradise, and a splendid peacock, supposed to be the same that once contained the soul of Pythagoras. I therefore passed to the next alcove, the shelves of which were covered with a miscellaneous collection of curiosities, such as are usually found in similar establishments. One of the first things that took my eye was a strange looking cap, woven of some substance that appeared to be neither woollen, cotton, nor linen.

"Is this a magician's cap?" I asked.

"No," replied the Virtuoso, "it is merely Dr. Franklin's cap of asbestos. But here is one which, perhaps, may suit you better. It is the wishing-cap of Fortunatus. Will you try it on?"

"By no means," answered I, putting it aside with my hand. "The day of wild wishes is past with me. I desire nothing that may not come in the ordinary course of Providence."

"Then, probably," returned the Virtuoso, "you will not be tempted to rub this lamp?"

While speaking, he took from the shelf an antique brass lamp, curiously wrought with embossed figures, but so covered with verdigris that the sculpture was almost eaten away.

"It is a thousand years," said he, "since the genius of this lamp constructed Aladdin's palace in a single night. But he still retains his power; and the man who rubs Aladdin's lamp, has but to desire either a palace or a cottage."

"I might desire a cottage," replied I, "but I would have it founded on sure and stable truth, not on dreams and fantasies. I have learned to look for the real and the true."

My guide next showed me Prospero's magic wand, broken into three fragments by the hand of its mighty master. On the same shelf lay the gold ring of ancient Gyges, which enabled the wearer to walk invisible. On the other side of the alcove was a tall looking-glass in a frame of ebony, but veiled with a curtain of purple silk, through the rents of which the gleam of the mirror was perceptible.

"This is Cornelius Agrippa's magic glass," observed the Virtuoso. "Draw aside the curtain, and picture any human form within your mind, and it will be reflected in the mirror."

"It is enough if I can picture it within my mind," answered I. "Why should I wish it to be repeated in the mirror? But, indeed, these works of magic have grown wearisome to me. There are so many greater wonders in the world, to those who keep their eyes open, and their sight undimmed by custom, that all the delusions of the old sorcerers seem flat and stale. Unless you can show me something really curious, I care not to look further into your Museum."

"Ah, well, then," said the Virtuoso, composedly, "perhaps you may deem some of my antiquarian rarities deserving of a glance."

He pointed out the Iron Mask, now corroded with rust; and my heart grew sick at the sight of this dreadful relic, which had shut out a human being from sympathy with his race. There was nothing half so terrible in the axe that beheaded King Charles, nor in the dagger that slew Henry of Navarre, nor in the arrow that pierced the heart of William Rufus,—all of which were shown to me. Many of the articles derived their interest, such as it was, from having been formerly in the possession of royalty. For instance, here was Charlemagne's sheepskin cloak, the flowing wig of Louis Quatorze, the spinning-wheel of Sardanapalus, and King Stephen's famous breeches, which cost him but a crown. The heart of the Bloody Mary, with the word "Calais" worn into its diseased substance, was preserved in a bottle of spirits; and near it lay the golden case in which the queen of Gustavus Adolphus treasured up that hero's heart. Among these relics and heirlooms of kings, I must not forget the long, hairy ears of Midas, and a piece of bread, which had been changed to gold by the touch of that unlucky monarch. And as Grecian Helen was a queen, it may here be mentioned, that I was permitted to take into my hand a lock of her golden hair, and the bowl which a sculptor modelled from the curve of her perfect breast. Here, likewise, was the robe that smothered Agamemnon, Nero's fiddle, the Czar Peter's brandy-bottle, the crown of Semiramis, and Canute's sceptre, which he extended over the sea. That my own land may not deem itself neglected, let me add, that I was favored with a sight of the skull of King Philip, the famous Indian chief, whose head the Puritans smote off and exhibited upon a pole.

"Show me something else," said I to the Virtuoso. "Kings are in such an artificial position, that people in the ordinary walks of life cannot feel an interest in their relics. If you could show me the straw hat of sweet little Nell, I would far rather see it than a king's golden crown."

"There it is," said my guide, pointing carelessly with his staff to the straw hat in question. "But, indeed, you are hard to please. Here are the seven-league boots. Will you try them on?"

"Our modern railroads have superseded their use," answered I; "and as to these cow-hide boots, I could show you quite as curious a pair at the transcendental community in Roxbury."

We next examined a collection of swords and other weapons, belonging to different epochs, but thrown together without much attempt at arrangement. Here was Arthur's sword Excalibar, and that of the Cid Campeador, and the sword of Brutus rusted with Cæsar's blood and his own, and the sword of Joan of Arc, and that of Horatius, and that

with which Virginius slew his daughter, and the one which
Dionysius suspended over the head of Damocles. Here, also,
was Arria's sword, which she plunged into her own breast,
in order to taste of death before her husband. The crooked
blade of Saladin's scimetar next attracted my notice. I know
not by what chance, but so it happened that the sword of
one of our own militia generals was suspended between Don
Quixote's lance and the brown blade of Hudibras. My heart
throbbed high at the sight of the helmet of Miltiades, and
the spear that was broken in the breast of Epaminondas. I
recognized the shield of Achilles, by its resemblance to the
admirable cast in the possession of Professor Felton. Nothing
in this department interested me more than Major Pitcairn's
pistol, the discharge of which, at Lexington, began the war
of the revolution, and was reverberated in thunder around
the land for seven long years. The bow of Ulysses, though
unstrung for ages, was placed against the wall, together with
a sheaf of Robin Hood's arrows, and the rifle of Daniel Boone.

"Enough of weapons," said I, at length; "although I would
gladly have seen the sacred shield which fell from Heaven
in the time of Numa. And surely you should obtain the sword
which Washington unsheathed at Cambridge. But the collection does you much credit. Let us pass on."

In the next alcove we saw the golden thigh of Pythagoras,
which had so divine a meaning; and, by one of the queer
analogies to which the Virtuoso seemed to be addicted, this
ancient emblem lay on the same shelf with Peter Stuyvesant's
wooden leg, that was fabled to be of silver. Here was a
remnant of the Golden Fleece; and a sprig of yellow leaves
that resembled the foliage of a frost-bitten elm, but was
duly authenticated as a portion of the golden branch by
which Æneas gained admittance to the realm of Pluto.
Atalanta's golden apple, and one of the apples of discord,

were wrapt in the napkin of gold which Rampsinitus brought from Hades; and the whole were deposited in the golden vase of Bias, with its inscription: "To THE WISEST."

"And how did you obtain this vase?" said I to the Virtuoso.

"It was given me long ago," replied he, with a scornful expression in his eye, "because I had learned to despise all things."

It had not escaped me that, though the Virtuoso was evidently a man of high cultivation, yet he seemed to lack sympathy with the spiritual, the sublime, and the tender. Apart from the whim that had led him to devote so much time, pains, and expense to the collection of this Museum, he impressed me as one of the hardest and coldest men of the world whom I had ever met.

"To despise all things!" repeated I. "This, at best, is the wisdom of the understanding. It is the creed of a man whose soul,—whose better and diviner part,—has never been awakened, or has died out of him."

"I did not think that you were still so young," said the Virtuoso. "Should you live to my years, you will acknowledge that the vase of Bias was not ill bestowed."

Without farther discussion of the point, he directed my attention to other curiosities. I examined Cinderella's little glass slipper, and compared it with one of Diana's sandals, and with Fanny Elssler's shoe, which bore testimony to the muscular character of her illustrious foot. On the same shelf were Thomas the Rhymer's green velvet shoes, and the brazen shoe of Empedocles, which was thrown out of Mount Ætna. Anacreon's drinking-cup was placed in apt juxtaposition with one of Tom Moore's wine-glasses and Circe's magic bowl. These were symbols of luxury and riot; but near them stood the cup whence Socrates drank his hemlock; and that which Sir Philip Sydney put from his death-parched lips to bestow the draught upon a dying soldier. Next appeared a cluster of tobacco pipes, consisting of Sir Walter Raleigh's, the earliest on record, Dr. Parr's, Charles Lamb's, and the first calumet of peace which was ever smoked between a European and an Indian. Among other musical instruments, I noticed the lyre of Orpheus, and those of Homer and Sappho, Dr. Franklin's famous whistle, the trumpet of Anthony Van Corlear, and the flute which Goldsmith played upon in his rambles through the French provinces. The staff of Peter the Hermit stood in a corner, with that of good old Bishop Jewel, and one of ivory, which had belonged to Papirius, the Roman Senator. The ponderous club of Hercules was close at hand. The Virtuoso showed me the chisel of Phidias, Claude's palette, and the brush of Apelles, observing that he intended to bestow the former either on Greenough, Crawford, or Powers, and the two latter upon Washington Allston. There was a small vase of oracular gas from Delphos, which, I trust, will be submitted to the scientific analysis of Professor Silliman. I was deeply moved on beholding a phial of the tears into which Niobe was dissolved; nor less so, on learning that a shapeless fragment of salt was a relic of that victim of despondency and sinful regrets, Lot's wife. My companion appeared to set great value upon some Egyptian darkness in a blacking jug. Several of the shelves were covered by a collection of coins; among which, however, I remember none but the Splendid Shilling, celebrated by Phillips, and a dollar's worth of the iron money of Lycurgus, weighing about fifty pounds.

Walking carelessly onward, I had nearly fallen over a huge bundle, like a pedlar's pack, done up in sackcloth and very securely strapped and corded.

"It is Christian's burthen of sin," said the Virtuoso.

"Oh, pray let us open it!" cried I. "For many a year I have longed to know its contents."

"Look into your own consciousness and memory," replied the Virtuoso. "You will there find a list of whatever it contains."

As this was an undeniable truth, I threw a melancholy look at the burthen, and passed on. A collection of old garments, hanging on pegs, was worthy of some attention, especially the shirt of Nessus, Cæsar's mantle, Joseph's coat of many colors, the Vicar of Bray's cassock, Goldsmith's peach-bloom suit, a pair of President Jefferson's scarlet breeches, John Randolph's red baize hunting-shirt, the drab small clothes of the Stout Gentleman, and the rags of the "man all tattered and torn." George Fox's hat impressed me with deep reverence, as a relic of perhaps the truest apostle that has appeared on earth for these eighteen hundred years. My eye was next attracted by an old pair of shears, which I should have taken for a memorial of some famous tailor, only that the Virtuoso pledged his veracity that they were the identical scissors of Atropos. He also showed me a broken hour-glass, which had been thrown aside by Father Time, together with the old gentleman's gray forelock, tastefully braided into a brooch. In the hour-glass was the handful of sand, the grains of which had numbered the years of the Cumæan Sibyl. I think it was in this alcove that I saw the inkstand which Luther threw at the Devil, and the ring which Essex, while under sentence of death, sent to Queen Elizabeth. And here was the blood-encrusted pen of steel with which Faust signed away his salvation.

The Virtuoso now opened the door of a closet, and showed me a lamp burning, while three others stood unlighted by its side. One of the three was the lamp of Diogenes, another that of Guy Faux, and the third that which Hero set forth to the midnight breeze in the high tower of Abydos.

"See!" said the Virtuoso, blowing with all his force at the lighted lamp.

The flame quivered and shrank away from his breath, but clung to the wick, and resumed its brilliancy as soon as the blast was exhausted.

"It is an undying lamp from the tomb of Charlemagne," observed my guide. "That flame was kindled a thousand years ago."

"How ridiculous, to kindle an unnatural light in tombs!" exclaimed I. "We should seek to behold the dead in the light of Heaven. But what is the meaning of this chafing-dish of glowing coals?"

"That," answered the Virtuoso, "is the original fire which Prometheus stole from Heaven. Look steadfastly into it, and you will discern another curiosity."

I gazed into that fire,—which, symbolically, was the origin of all that was bright and glorious in the soul of man,—and in the midst of it, behold! a little reptile, sporting with evident enjoyment of the fervid heat. It was a salamander.

"What a sacrilege!" cried I, with inexpressible disgust. "Can you find no better use for this ethereal fire than to cherish a loathsome reptile in it? Yet there are men who abuse the sacred fire of their own souls to as foul and guilty a purpose."

The Virtuoso made no answer, except by a dry laugh, and an assurance that the salamander was the very same which Benvenuto Cellini had seen in his father's household fire. He then proceeded to show me other rarities; for this closet appeared to be the receptacle of what he considered most valuable in his collection.

"There," said he, "is the Great Carbuncle of the White Mountains."

I gazed with no little interest at this mighty gem, which it had been one of the wild projects of my youth to discover. Possibly it might have looked brighter to me in those days

than now; at all events, it had not such brilliancy as to detain
me long from the other articles of the Museum. The Virtuoso
pointed out to me a crystalline stone, which hung by a gold
chain against the wall.

"That is the Philosopher's Stone," said he.

"And have you the Elixir Vitæ, which generally accom-
panies it?" inquired I.

"Even so,—this urn is filled with it," he replied. "A draught
would refresh you. Here is Hebe's cup,—will you quaff a
health from it?"

My heart thrilled within me at the idea of such a reviving
draught; for methought I had great need of it, after travelling
so far on the dusty road of life. But I know not whether it
were a peculiar glance in the Virtuoso's eye, or the circumstance that this most precious liquid was contained in an
antique sepulchral urn, that made me pause. Then came
many a thought, with which, in the calmer and better hours
of life, I had strengthened myself to feel that Death is the
very friend whom, in his due season, even the happiest
mortal should be willing to embrace.

"No, I desire not an earthly immortality," said I. "Were
man to live longer on the earth, the spiritual would die out
of him. The spark of ethereal fire would be choked by the
material, the sensual. There is a celestial something within
us that requires, after a certain time, the atmosphere of
Heaven to preserve it from decay and ruin. I will have none
of this liquid. You do well to keep it in a sepulchral urn; for
it would produce death, while bestowing the shadow of life."

"All this is unintelligible to me," responded my guide, with
indifference. "Life,—earthly life,—is the only good. But you
refuse the draught? Well, it is not likely to be offered twice
within one man's experience. Probably you have griefs which

you seek to forget in death. I can enable you to forget them in life. Will you take a draught of Lethe?"

As he spoke, the Virtuoso took from the shelf a crystal vase containing a sable liquor, which caught no reflected image from the objects around.

"Not for the world!" exclaimed I, shrinking back. "I can spare none of my recollections,—not even those of error or sorrow. They are all alike the food of my spirit. As well never to have lived, as to lose them now."

Without further parley we passed to the next alcove, the shelves of which were burthened with ancient volumes, and with those rolls of papyrus, in which was treasured up the eldest wisdom of the earth. Perhaps the most valuable work in the collection, to a bibliomaniac, was the Book of Hermes. For my part, however, I would have given a higher price for those six of the Sibyl's books which Tarquin refused to purchase, and which the Virtuoso informed me he had himself found in the cave of Trophonius. Doubtless these old volumes contain prophecies of the fate of Rome, both as respects the decline and fall of her temporal empire, and the rise of her spiritual one. Not without value, likewise, was the work of Anaxagoras on Nature, hitherto supposed to be irrecoverably lost; and the missing treatises of Longinus, by which modern criticism might profit; and those books of Livy, for which the classic student has so long sorrowed without hope. Among these precious tomes I observed the original manuscript of the Koran, and also that of the Mormon Bible, in Joe Smith's authentic autograph. Alexander's copy of the Iliad was also there, enclosed in the jewelled casket of Darius, still fragrant of the perfumes which the Persian kept in it.

Opening an iron-clasped volume, bound in black leather, I discovered it to be Cornelius Agrippa's book of magic; and it was rendered still more interesting by the fact that many flowers, ancient and modern, were pressed between its leaves. Here was a rose from Eve's bridal bower, and all those red and white roses which were plucked in the garden of the Temple, by the partizans of York and Lancaster. Here was Halleck's Wild Rose of Alloway. Cowper had contributed a Sensitive Plant, and Wordsworth an Eglantine, and Burns a Mountain Daisy, and Kirke White a Star of Bethlehem, and Longfellow a Sprig of Fennel, with its yellow flowers. James Russell Lowell had given a Pressed Flower, but fragrant still, which had been shadowed in the Rhine. There was also a sprig from Southey's Holly-Tree. One of the most beautiful specimens was a Fringed Gentian, which had been plucked and preserved for immortality by Bryant. From Jones Very,—a poet whose voice is scarcely heard among us, by reason of its depth,—there was a Wind Flower and a Columbine.

As I closed Cornelius Agrippa's magic volume, an old, mildewed letter fell upon the floor; it proved to be an autograph from the Flying Dutchman to his wife. I could linger no longer among books, for the afternoon was waning, and there was yet much to see. The bare mention of a few more curiosities must suffice. The immense skull of Polyphemus was recognizable by the cavernous hollow in the centre of the forehead, where once had blazed the giant's single eye. The tub of Diogenes, Medea's cauldron, and Psyche's vase of beauty, were placed one within another. Pandora's box, without the lid, stood next, containing nothing but the girdle of Venus, which had been carelessly flung into it. A bundle of birch rods, which had been used by Shenstone's school-mistress, were tied up with the Countess of Salisbury's garter. I knew not which to value most, a Roc's egg, as big as an ordinary hogshead, or the shell of the egg which Columbus set upon its end. Perhaps the most delicate article in the whole Museum was Queen Mab's chariot, which, to guard it from the touch of meddlesome fingers, was placed under a glass tumbler.

Several of the shelves were occupied by specimens of entomology. Feeling but little interest in the science, I noticed only Anacreon's Grasshopper and a Humble-Bee, which had been presented to the Virtuoso by Ralph Waldo Emerson.

In the part of the hall which we had now reached, I observed a curtain that descended from the ceiling to the floor in voluminous folds, of a depth, richness, and magnificence which I had never seen equalled. It was not to be doubted that this splendid, though dark and solemn veil, concealed a portion of the Museum even richer in wonders than that through which I had already passed. But, on my attempting to grasp the edge of the curtain and draw it aside, it proved to be an illusive picture.

"You need not blush," remarked the Virtuoso, "for that same curtain deceived Zeuxis. It is the celebrated painting of Parrhasius."

In a range with the curtain, there were a number of other choice pictures, by artists of ancient days. Here was the famous Cluster of Grapes by Zeuxis, so admirably depicted that it seemed as if the ripe juice were bursting forth. As to the picture of the Old Woman, by the same illustrious painter, and which was so ludicrous that he himself died with laughing at it, I cannot say that it particularly moved my risibility. Ancient humor seems to have little power over modern muscles. Here, also, was the Horse, painted by Apelles, which living horses neighed at; his first portrait of Alexander the Great, and his last unfinished picture of Venus Asleep. Each of these works of art, together with others by Parrhasius, Timanthes, Polygnotus, Apollodorus, Pausias, and Pamphilus, required more time and study than I could bestow, for the adequate perception of their merits. I shall therefore leave them undescribed and uncriticised, nor attempt to settle the question of superiority between ancient and modern art.

For the same reason I shall pass lightly over the specimens of antique sculpture, which this indefatigable and fortunate Virtuoso had dug out of the dust of fallen empires. Here was Ætion's cedar statue of Æsculapius, much decayed, and Alcon's iron statue of Hercules, lamentably rusted. Here was the statue of Victory, six feet high, which the Jupiter Olympus of Phidias had held in his hand. Here was a fore-finger of the Colossus of Rhodes, seven feet in length. Here was the Venus Urania of Phidias, and other images of male and female beauty or grandeur, wrought by sculptors who appear never to have debased their souls by the sight of any meaner forms than those of gods, or godlike mortals. But the deep simplicity of these great works was not to be comprehended by a mind excited and disturbed as mine was by the various objects that had recently been presented to it. I therefore turned away, with merely a passing glance, resolving, on some future occasion, to brood over each individual statue and picture, until my inmost spirit should feel their excellence. In this department, again, I noticed the tendency to whimsical combinations and ludicrous analogies, which seemed to influence many of the arrangements of the Museum. The wooden statue, so well known as the Palladium of Troy, was placed in close apposition with the wooden head of General Jackson, which was stolen, a few years since, from the bows of the frigate Constitution.

We had now completed the circuit of the spacious hall, and found ourselves again near the door. Feeling somewhat wearied with the survey of so many novelties and antiquities, I sat down upon Cowper's sofa, while the Virtuoso threw himself carelessly into Rabelais's easy-chair. Casting my eyes upon the opposite wall, I was surprised to perceive the shadow of a man, flickering unsteadily across the wainscot, and looking as if it were stirred by some breath of air that found its way through the door or windows. No substantial figure was visible, from which this shadow might be thrown; nor, had there been such, was there any sunshine that would have caused it to darken upon the wall.

"It is Peter Schlemihl's Shadow," observed the Virtuoso, "and one of the most valuable articles in my collection."

"Methinks a shadow would have made a fitting door-keeper to such a Museum," said I, "although, indeed, yonder figure has something strange and fantastic about him, which suits well enough with many of the impressions which I have received here. Pray, who is he?"

While speaking, I gazed more scrutinizingly than before at the antiquated presence of the person who had admitted me, and who still sat on his bench, with the same restless aspect, and dim, confused, questioning anxiety, that I had noticed on my first entrance. At this moment he looked eagerly towards us, and half-starting from his seat, addressed me.

"I beseech you, kind sir," said he, in a cracked, melancholy tone, "have pity on the most unfortunate man in the world! For heaven's sake answer me a single question! Is this the town of Boston?"

"You have recognized him now," said the Virtuoso. "It is Peter Rugg, the Missing Man. I chanced to meet him, the other day, still in search of Boston, and conducted him hither; and, as he could not succeed in finding his friends, I have taken him into my service as door-keeper. He is somewhat too apt to ramble, but otherwise a man of trust and integrity."

"And—might I venture to ask," continued I, "to whom am I indebted for this afternoon's gratification?"

The Virtuoso, before replying, laid his hand upon an antique dart or javelin, the rusty steel head of which seemed to have been blunted, as if it had encountered the resistance of a tempered shield or breast-plate.

"My name has not been without its distinction in the world, for a longer period than that of any other man alive," answered he. "Yet many doubt of my existence,—perhaps you will do so, to-morrow. This dart, which I hold in my hand, was once grim Death's own weapon. It served him well for the space of four thousand years. But it fell blunted, as you see, when he directed it against my breast."

These words were spoken with the calm and cold courtesy of manner that had characterized this singular personage throughout our interview. I fancied, it is true, that there was a bitterness indefinably mingled with his tone, as of one cut off from natural sympathies, and blasted with a doom that had been inflicted on no other human being, and by the results of which he had ceased to be human. Yet, withal, it seemed one of the most terrible consequences of that doom, that the victim no longer regarded it as a calamity, but had finally accepted it as the greatest good that could have befallen him.

"You are the Wandering Jew!" exclaimed I.

The Virtuoso bowed, without emotion of any kind; for, by centuries of custom, he had almost lost the sense of strangeness in his fate, and was but imperfectly conscious of the astonishment and awe with which it affected such as are capable of death.

"Your doom is indeed a fearful one!" said I, with irrepressible feeling, and a frankness that afterwards startled me; "yet perhaps the ethereal spirit is not entirely extinct, under all this corrupted or frozen mass of earthly life. Perhaps the immortal spark may yet be rekindled by a breath of Heaven. Perhaps you may yet be permitted to die, before it is too late to live eternally. You have my prayers for such a consummation. Farewell."

"Your prayers will be in vain," replied he, with a smile of cold triumph. "My destiny is linked with the realities of earth. You are welcome to your visions and shadows of a future state; but give me what I can see, and touch, and understand, and I ask no more."

"It is indeed too late," thought I. "The soul is dead within him!"

Struggling between pity and horror, I extended my hand, to which the Virtuoso gave his own, still with the habitual courtesy of a man of the world, but without a single heart-throb of human brotherhood. The touch seemed like ice, yet I know not whether morally or physically. As I departed, he bade me observe that the inner door of the hall was constructed with the ivory leaves of the gateway through which Æneas and the Sibyl had been dismissed from Hades.

EDITORIAL APPENDIXES

HISTORICAL COMMENTARY

O N JULY 9, 1842, seven months after the publication of the two-volume Munroe edition of *Twice-
told Tales*, Nathaniel Hawthorne married Sophia
Peabody, and the couple took up residence in the Old Manse
at Concord. "We are as happy as people can be, without
making themselves ridiculous," he wrote to his sister Louisa,
"and might be even happier; but, as a matter of taste, we
chose to stop short at this point." [1] He and Sophia lived
there for over three years, enjoying what they were sure
was an idyllic life. The so-called solitary years of his bachelor-
hood and obscurity lay behind him. He also emerged from
a four-year period when he had written only two adult
sketches: "John Inglefield's Thanksgiving," for the *United
States Magazine and Democratic Review*, March, 1840, and
"A Virtuoso's Collection" for the *Boston Miscellany*, May,
1842. [2] In his introductory sketch for *Mosses from an Old
Manse*, he recalled that upon embarking on this new life
at Concord he intended to create "a novel, that should evolve

[1] July 10, 1842, MS, Essex Institute.
The form "Twice-told" is adopted for reference as Hawthorne's title;
see the Textual Commentary, *Twice-told Tales* (Centenary Edition, 1974),
pp. 546–47.
[2] In that span, Hawthorne was measurer for the Boston customs from
January, 1839, to January, 1841, participated in the Brook Farm community from April to November of 1841, and in 1840–42 was concerned
with publication of the *Grandfather's Chair* series, *Biographical Stories*,
and the second edition of *Twice-told Tales*.

some deep lesson, and should possess physical substance enough to stand alone." Although we may take the statement as playfully ironic, he nonetheless enjoyed what fruits were to be found in his renewed dedication to literature. Between July, 1842, and April, 1845, he published twenty-one new tales and sketches, an accomplishment equalling the most productive of his earlier years. This brief period marks his last sustained creativity in short fiction; thereafter, except for the juvenile collections *A Wonder-Book* and *Tanglewood Tales*, he was to write and publish only five other such pieces. In 1845 he also edited Horatio Bridge's *Journal of an African Cruiser*, the first volume of Wiley and Putnam's Library of American Books, a series for which he was then persuaded to prepare his third major collection, *Mosses from an Old Manse*, in which he included seventeen of his latest tales and sketches. From one vantage point these years testify to Hawthorne's dedication and productivity, but from another they must be seen as a dishearteningly temporary interlude between political appointments. Plagued by ever-increasing financial worries, he sought the security of a government post. When they left Concord in the autumn of 1845, the Hawthornes were obliged by poverty to take shelter with his family at Salem, where in the following spring he became surveyor in the custom house.

In resuming literary pursuits without being ready to write the full-length fiction he perhaps longed to, Hawthorne was confronting again the sad and arduous conditions of magazine publication. He took what measures he could to insure a steady, reasonable income from his writing. That Samuel Goodrich's *The Token* and Park Benjamin's *New-England Magazine* were defunct could scarcely have seemed a misfortune, for he had felt intolerably abused by those editors. Remembering his experiences in the 1830s and reticent about discussing the financial aspect of writing, he manifested in the early 1840s a preference for putting himself in the hands of trustworthy editorial friends—John L. O'Sullivan, James Russell Lowell, Epes Sargent. He was also convinced that New York publication offered him his only real chances for even modest success. In March, 1842, he had travelled to confer with O'Sullivan, editor of the *Democratic Review*, now published in New York, to secure his patronage and to plan book publication through him.[3] It is likely that, in again seeking out O'Sullivan and the *Democratic Review*, where he had published ten pieces in 1837–40 when it was located in Washington, Hawthorne was not only reaffirming friendship with the editor but also—skeptical of the economics of magazine publication—trying to maintain a political visibility upon which a future bureaucratic appointment might depend. From 1843 to 1845, thirteen of his new tales and sketches appeared in the *Democratic Review*, all but "A Book of Autographs" being later collected in the 1846 *Mosses*, along with five pieces solicited by other editors: "The Old Apple-Dealer" from the New York *Sargent's New Monthly Magazine*, January, 1843; "The Hall of Fantasy" and "The Birthmark" from James Russell Lowell's Boston *Pioneer*, February and March, 1843; and, from widely popular magazines of Philadelphia, "Earth's Holocaust" in *Graham's Magazine*, May, 1844, and "Drowne's Wooden Image" in *Godey's Lady's Book*, July, 1844.[4] Three other pieces of the Old Manse years were not collected in *Mosses*: "The Antique Ring" (*Sargent's*, February, 1843), "Little Daffydowndilly" (*Boys' and Girls' Magazine*, August, 1843), and "A Good Man's Miracle" (*Child's Friend*, February, 1844).

Although Hawthorne had no difficulty in placing his work in the best and most popular literary journals of the day,

[3] Hawthorne to Sophia, March 10, 1842, MS, Huntington Library.

[4] For an account of the circulation of these magazines, see Frank Luther Mott, *A History of American Magazine, 1741–1850* (New York, 1930).

there were serious problems. The mortality rate was high for magazines that aspired to depart from popular taste: the *Pioneer*, numbering Edgar Allan Poe, Jones Very, Elizabeth Barrett, and John Greenleaf Whittier among its contributors, lasted only three issues, and *Sargent's* went under after six, having sought to use light periodical literature to the exclusion of essays on religious and political controversies. Through Lowell, Hawthorne was invited by Poe to contribute to the first number of his projected magazine in Philadelphia,[5] but the publication of "The Stylus" was aborted. Such events were not likely to spur Hawthorne or any other serious writer to greater exertions. Even the market for juvenile fiction, which he had previously been enthusiastic about, he was now persuaded had been exhausted. Although he planned in 1843 to write "one or two mythological story books . . . under O'Sullivan's auspices,"[6] nothing materialized, and that September he rejected Samuel Colman's proposal to write a series for *Boys' and Girls' Magazine* on the grounds that "the business has long been overdone."[7]

The low rate of pay by magazines was a discouragement. O'Sullivan had set $3.00 to $5.00 per page at the inception of the *Democratic Review*,[8] and Hawthorne said that he had received "fair compensation" for his early contributions;[9] but at the beginning of 1843, the magazine could pay only $20.00 per article of whatever length, whereas R. W. Griswold, co-editor of *Graham's*, offered $5.00 per page.[10] Haw-

[5] Sophia Hawthorne to her mother, April 20, 1843, quoted in Julian Hawthorne, *Nathaniel Hawthorne and His Wife* (Boston, 1884), I, 273.

[6] Hawthorne to Sophia, March 16, 1843, MS, Huntington Library.

[7] Hawthorne to Colman, September 27, 1843, MS, Berg Collection, New York Public Library.

[8] O'Sullivan to Hawthorne, April 19, 1837, quoted in *Nathaniel Hawthorne and His Wife*, I, 159.

[9] Hawthorne to O'Sullivan, May 19, 1839, MS, Collection of Robert H. Taylor, Princeton, N.J.

[10] F. B. Sanborn, *Hawthorne and His Friends* (Cedar Rapids, 1908), p. 31. Sophia is quoted on Hawthorne's loyalty to the *Democratic Review*:

thorne reported to Lowell when sending him the manuscript of "The Hall of Fantasy" that Sargent offered $5.00 per page, and then remarked with stoic gentility: "If you consider this a fair price, it will satisfy me; if not, you may have the article for whatever your arrangements will allow you to pay."[11] Later, in dispatching "The Birth-mark" to Lowell's partner, Robert Carter, he wrote, "I beg you to assure Mr. Lowell, that I did not intend to make a demand for immediate payment of my last contribution. I merely mentioned a price per page, because he had spoken to me upon the subject; and we get rid of an embarrassment by having such matters definitely fixed."[12]

Hawthorne, despite his patience with Lowell, and acceptance of low rates, found delinquency or failure in payment a continuing unwarranted difficulty. Had he received $5.00 per page for the twenty-one stories published during this period, he would have earned only about $750.00, hardly an amount large enough to sustain himself and his family for three years. As it was, he received much less. Whether Lowell was ever able to pay him at all is uncertain. Sophia wrote to her mother on February 28, 1843, that they looked for $70.00 from Lowell,[13] but on March 16 Hawthorne spoke of the failure of the *Pioneer* with the comment, "Not improbably we shall have to wait months for our money, if we ever get it at all."[14] It was not until early 1846 that Sargent sent $10.00, payment presumably for both the stories he had published. Hawthorne, enjoying the prospects of his custom house post, responded graciously that he had

---

"The last paper he sent to it was a real gift, as it was more than four pages; but he thought its character better suited to the grave *Democrat* than for *Graham's*."

[11] December 17, 1842, MS, St. Lawrence University.
[12] February 1, 1843, MS, Fruitlands Museums.
[13] MS, Berg Collection, New York Public Library.
[14] Hawthorne to Sophia, MS, Huntington Library.

dismissed the debt from his mind, having been "a joint adventurer with you in the Magazine speculation" at "trifling loss." [15] In fact, even in the early months of his marriage, it was only in his journal, open to Sophia's perusal, that he expressed their predicament with composure. In a March 31, 1843, entry, he wrote:

> I have written with pretty commendable diligence, averaging from two to four hours a day; and the result is seen in various Magazines. I might have written more, if it had seemed worth while; but I was content to earn only so much gold as might suffice for our immediate wants, having prospects of official station and emolument, which would do away the necessity of writing for bread. Those prospects have not yet had their fulfilment; and we are well content to wait; because an office would inevitably remove us from our present happy home. . . . Meantime, the Magazine people do not pay their debts; so that we taste some of the inconveniences of poverty, and the mortification—only temporary, however—of owing money, with empty pockets. It is an annoyance; not a trouble.[16]

Hawthorne's financial embarrassment was so extreme, however, that in a letter of March 25 to his friend and benefactor, Horatio Bridge, he had already expressed justifiable impatience and bitterness:

> I did not come to see you [on a recent trip to Salem], because I was very short of cash—having been disappointed in money that I had expected from three or four sources. My difficulties of this sort sometimes make me sigh for the regular monthly payments at the Custom House. The system of slack payments in this country is most abominable, and ought of itself to bring upon us the destruction foretold by Father Miller. It is impossible for any individual to be

[15] The payment came after Hawthorne had written for tear sheets, while preparing copy for *Mosses* (Hawthorne to Epes Sargent, March 3, 1846, MS, St. Lawrence University).

[16] *The American Notebooks,* ed. Claude M. Simpson (Centenary Edition, 1973), p. 367.

just and honest, and true to his engagements, when it is a settled principle of the community to be always behind-hand. I find no difference in any body, in this respect; all do wrong alike. [Deleted name] is just as certain to dis-appoint me in money matters as any pitiful little scoundrel among the booksellers.[17]

It was his best friend, O'Sullivan (almost without question referred to in the letter), whose failures to pay caused Haw-thorne the most anxiety. The demise of other magazines made him more dependent on the *Democratic Review*. In his March 16 letter to Sophia, after speaking of the *Pioneer*, he added, "Nobody pays us. It was very strange—at least in-considerate—in Mr. O'Sullivan not to send some money, my request being so urgent." The *Democratic Review* had by this time published two of Hawthorne's pieces—"The New Adam and Eve" in February, 1843, and "Egotism; or, The Bosom-Serpent" in March. O'Sullivan had in hand "The Procession of Life" for the April issue, and perhaps "The Celestial Rail-road," which would be seen in May. A sixth contribution, "Buds and Bird-Voices," appeared in June, and two stories from the 1832 *Token*—"The Wives of the Dead" (renamed "The Two Widows") and "Roger Malvin's Burial" —were reprinted in the July and August issues respectively.[18] But the earliest documented payment Hawthorne received from O'Sullivan during the Old Manse period did not come until the next December, and was in the amount of $100.00.[19]

[17] MS, Bowdoin College.

[18] It is unlikely that payment was expected or made for these reprints. Hawthorne had earlier allowed stories to be reprinted in *Arcturus* (Haw-thorne to "Gentlemen," December 22, 1841, MS, Duyckinck Collection, New York Public Library). But he did complain about unauthorized use; he wrote to Bridge on April 1, 1844: "the pamphlet and piratical system has so broken up all regular literature, that I am forced to work hard for small gains" (MS, Bowdoin College). He probably had most in mind the numerous reprints of "The Celestial Rail-road."

[19] Sophia Hawthorne Journal, December 1, 1843–January 5, 1844, MS, Berg Collection, New York Public Library.

If that is in fact the only sum Hawthorne received for the six new tales, it represents less than half the standard magazine payment of $5.00 per page. Writing to Bridge again on May 3, he lamented his plight: "It is rather singular that I should need an office, for nobody's scribblings seem to be more acceptable to the public than mine; and yet I shall find it a tough scratch to gain a respectable support by my pen. Perhaps matters may mend; at all events, I am not very eager to ensconce myself in an office, though a good one would certainly be desirable." [20]

Since no office was immediately forthcoming, Hawthorne sought to remedy the situation by writing as much as he could. He and O'Sullivan remained steadfast friends,[21] and Hawthorne, probably realizing that the editor could not command money from the publishers, continued sending pieces to the *Democratic Review*. But he was chagrined and desperate enough that, when an opportunity came, he tried to arrange regular publication in *Graham's*. His letter to Griswold on July 2, 1843, expresses his inability to change his basic writing habits even when faced with economic necessity, and also shows practicality in proposing higher pay for his exclusive services:

> There is a mistake as to my having refused to write for Graham's Magazine; the truth is, I have heretofore had no opportunity to refuse, even had I been so inclined— your own letter being the first intimation that my contributions might be acceptable.
> I am never a very diligent penman in the summer time; and, moreover, I had projected a litle work for children

[20] Horatio Bridge, *Personal Recollections of Nathaniel Hawthorne* (New York, 1893), p. 94.

[21] It was Bridge who effected most toward securing the Salem surveyorship in 1846, Hawthorne concluded, but O'Sullivan waged a tireless campaign in general and especially with Secretary of the Navy George Bancroft. Making inquiries into possible offices, O'Sullivan once jokingly asked Hawthorne what he thought about going to China as a consul (*Nathaniel Hawthorne and His Wife*, I, 284–85).

as this summer's literary labor and amusement, which is still to be begun. I have likewise one engagement to fulfil for a Magazine, before I can undertake any other of the kind. These matters being first disposed of, I shall be very willing to send you an article, and will agree to the terms you propose, rather than take upon myself to settle the marketable value of my productions.

I am advised that the publishers of Magazines consider it desirable to attach writers exclusively to their own establishments, and will pay at a higher rate for such monopoly. If this be the case, I should make no difficulty in forswearing all other periodicals for a specified time— and so much the more readily, on account of the safety of your Magazine in a financial point of view. Should you desire an arrangement of this kind, be pleased, at your leisure, to state the terms of it. I hope to free myself from other engagements by October, at furthest, and shall then be happy to become one of your contributors.[22]

No such arrangement materialized. Griswold left his editorship in October, probably only shortly before Hawthorne sent "Earth's Holocaust" to the magazine. George R. Graham, the remaining editor, perhaps thinking the piece too sombre and unsentimental to be appropriate for his audience, did not print it until the May, 1844, issue. Hawthorne, upset by the delay, thought of demanding the manuscript's return.[23] The story was the only one he ever published in *Graham's*.

Thereafter, having little choice, Hawthorne resumed sending his stories to O'Sullivan, publishing six more *Mosses* tales in the *Democratic Review*: "The Christmas Banquet," January, 1844; "The Intelligence Office," March; "The Artist of the Beautiful," June; "A Select Party," July; "Writings of Aubépine" [including "Rappaccini's Daughter"], December; and "P.'s Correspondence," April, 1845. "A Book of Auto-

22 MS, Berg Collection, New York Public Library.

23 Hawthorne to George Hillard, March 24, 1844, MS, Maine Historical Society.

graphs"—omitted from *Mosses*—appeared in the November, 1844, issue. The one other tale of 1844 that made its way into *Mosses from an Old Manse* was "Drowne's Wooden Image," from *Godey's Lady's Book* for July. Hawthorne's letter to the editor, John Frost, has a businesslike crispness that suggests he was not altogether eager to join the likes of Mrs. Sarah Hale, Mrs. Lydia Sigourney, and Catherine Sedgwick as a regular contributor and to find his fiction appearing among the self-consciously pious, sentimental offerings that characterized this magazine:

> Considering it good policy in a writer to extend and vary his audience as much as possible, I comply with your request for an article. It will make, I suppose, five, or perhaps six, pages of the Lady's Book. It is difficult to regulate the length of an article precisely according to order; as every story has its natural developement, and will be maimed and imperfect, if cut short of it.
>
> By two or three editors, I have been offered twenty-five dollars for articles of such length as might suit myself. As I find it a delicate point to set a price on my own productions, you may have this story at the same valuation, though I do not care to become a regular contributor at that rate. I should have asked the same had it been shorter; and it is less than I could obtain elsewhere for the same amount of matter.
>
> Should either the price or the article fail to satisfy you, have the kindness to send the latter to J. L. O'Sullivan, Esq. (Editor of the Democratic Review) New York City.[24]

Several of Hawthorne's *Democratic Review* sketches manifest an interest in contemporary social problems and clearly represent his attempt to develop a more fully realistic strain in his art. Most readers of Hawthorne, from Poe and Melville to the present, have found the tales of the 1840s generally less satisfactory than those of the 1830s. But no matter how Hawthorne's 1842–45 stories are viewed, their inadequacies are integral to his creative imagination rather than the result

[24] March 11, 1844, MS, Historical Society of Pennsylvania.

of a willingness on his part to indulge in spurious forms that would have perverted the essence of his art. All his work of this period bears the stamp of his imagination. Likewise, although his situation dictated that he try to produce a greater volume of fiction, he followed the habitual rhythms of his creative process and continued to write almost exclusively in the late autumn and winter months. As he once remarked, "An engagement to write a story must in its nature be conditional; because stories grow like vegetables, and are not manufactured, like a pine table." [25]

By the spring of 1844 Hawthorne's creative impetus was clearly, at least for the present, exhausted. For one thing, he had in all probability just completed three of the best tales of this period—"The Artist of the Beautiful," "Rappaccini's Daughter," and "Drowne's Wooden Image"—and the effort must have taken its toll. For another, the birth of his daughter Una on March 3 had sharpened his sense of the futility of writing for the magazines and formalized his resolve to seek a political office. On March 24 he wrote to Hillard, reporting his intention and adding:

> I have business on earth now, and must look about me for the means of doing it. It will never do for me to continue merely a writer of stories for the magazines—the most unprofitable business in the world; and moreover, if there were ever so great a demand for my productions, I could not spend more than a third of my time in this sort of composition. It requires a continual freshness of mind; else a deterioration in the article will quickly be perceptible. If I am to support myself by literature, it must be by what is called drudgery, but which is incomparably less irksome, as a business, than imaginative writing—by translation, concocting of school-books, newspaper-scribbling &c.[26]

[25] Hawthorne to Hillard, July 16, 1841, MS, University of Virginia.
[26] MS, Maine Historical Society. On March 15 he had written to his sister Louisa that a new Democratic administration would assure him a post office or other appointment; otherwise, he intended to join the staff of a paper or magazine (MS, Berg Collection, New York Public Library).

He repeated his intentions on April 1, to Bridge, to whom he wrote, "If we have a Democratic President next year, I shall probably get an office; otherwise, it is to be hoped, God will provide for me and mine in some other way." He added, "the sight of a pen makes me sick." [27] Although his journal entries continued, Hawthorne in the autumn and early winter of 1844–45 could produce only "A Book of Autographs" and "P.'s Correspondence." His journal entry immediately preceding a notation of the germ for "P.'s Correspondence" may well reflect his state of mind: "To represent a man in the midst of all sorts of cares and annoyances—with impossibilities to perform—and almost driven distracted by his inadequacy. Then quietly comes Death, and releases him from all his troubles; and at his last gasp, he smiles, and congratulates himself on escaping so easily." [28]

Horatio Bridge's journal of naval experiences on the west coast of Africa provided the piece of book-manufacture that Hawthorne's imagination now required. Hawthorne had persuaded Bridge to keep a journal, and in a letter to him on April 1, 1844, urged that it be published as a book rather than in a magazine, "and thus make an independent author of you at once." And, he suggested, "My name shall appear as editor, in order to give it what little vogue may be derived from thence—and its own merits will do the rest." [29] Hawthorne spent the first two months of 1845 readying the manuscript,[30] and his efforts to arrange its publication became intertwined with his decision to publish a third collection of short fiction.

Years earlier, in his review of the 1842 *Twice-told Tales*, Evert Duyckinck, who had long been a champion of Haw-

[27] MS, Bowdoin College.
[28] *The American Notebooks*, ed. Simpson, p. 253.
[29] MS, Bowdoin College.
[30] Hawthorne to Duyckinck, March 2, 1845, MS, Duyckinck Collection, New York Public Library.

thorne and was reprinting four of Hawthorne's early tales in *Arcturus*, remarked: "To these [the two volumes of *Twice-told Tales*], the series we are at present publishing in Arcturus, will, we trust, be added and form a third." [31] Hawthorne had a warm affection for Duyckinck, whose "earnest kindness" pleased him and who was representative of "the very friends" for whom his tales and essays were intended. In a letter to Duyckinck on November 26, 1843, he summed up his happiness and trouble: "In short, I have nothing to wish for—except, perhaps, that Providence would make it somewhat more plain to my apprehension how I am to earn my bread, after a year or two." [32] In early 1845, acting as an editor for Wiley and Putnam of New York, Duyckinck conveyed to Hawthorne the firm's offer to publish a book by him. But Hawthorne was no doubt skeptical about the commercial success of another collection of his short fiction. His 1837 *Twice-told Tales* had had to be remaindered, and the 1842 collection had gone through the "humbug of a new edition" in order to be got rid of.[33] He therefore suggested to Duyckinck on March 2 a project that he hoped would bring fame to Bridge and some profit to himself, as editor: "I can offer you nothing of which I claim to be the author; but, for some weeks past, I have been employed in arranging a Journal. . . . Should your judgment of it be favorable, I shall be glad to have it come before the public through your medium." [34]

Duyckinck, however, was insistent in directing Hawthorne's efforts toward a book of his own, and responded with financial inducements and suggestions for a volume of tales:

[31] *Arcturus,* III (April, 1842), 394.

[32] MS, Duyckinck Collection, New York Public Library.

[33] Hawthorne to Hillard, May 29, 1844, MS, Middlebury College. The humbug was advertised in the *Literary World* as late as July 24, 1847. For details on the 1845 issue, see the Historical Commentary, *Twice-told Tales* (Centenary Edition, 1974), pp. 524–26.

[34] MS, Duyckinck Collection, New York Public Library.

Can you let Messrs W & P have some twelve or fifteen of your Tales not published in the two volumes and if possible a few new ones and a Preface—if you choose to write one. The terms Messrs W & P offer are eight cents a copy on the edition, fully equal to one half the profits. The book to be stereotyped and vigorously pushed and for a couple of unpublished Tales to go in the number they would advance you at once One Hundred dollars on a semi-annual settlement. One of the advantages . . . might be, if this first volume is successful and I see no reason to doubt it—the gradual collection and publication of all your Tales in successive volumes. . . .

The following occur to me—Buds and Bird Voices; The Procession of Life; The New Adam & Eve; The Celestial Railroad; Egotism or the Bosom Serpent; Fire Worship; Roger Malvin's Burial; The Two Widows; The Artist of the Beautiful; Writings of M Aubepine; Young Goodman Brown; The History of a Bell in the Knickerbocker, & some late ones in the Democratic.

The copyrights, of course yours & the arrangements made for a definite time.[35]

Thus encouraged, Hawthorne replied on April 7, accepting Duyckinck's proposal after making sure that Bridge's journal would not be forgotten:

Messrs. Wiley & Putnam's proposals, in reference to the volume of tales, seem very liberal, and I shall be glad to take advantage of them, so soon as I find inward and outward quietude enough to write a couple of new stories. Of old tales, I would suggest the following:—"The Virtuoso's Collection," (Boston Miscellany) "The Birth-Mark," (Pioneer) "The New Adam & Eve," "The Artist of the Beautiful," Buds and Bird Voices," "The Procession of Life," "A Select Party," "Aubépine's Writing," "The Celestial Railroad," "Fire-Worship," "Earth's Holocaust" (Graham for, I think, May 1844) "Drowne's Wooden Image" (Godey, May or June 1844). These, with the two new ones, will

[35] March 21, 1845, E. A. Duyckinck Letter Book, MS, Duyckinck Collection, New York Public Library.

probably make up the specified bulk; if not, we will toss in a few make-weights.[36]

Hawthorne added, regarding the possible publication of Bridge's journal, that he would "prefer a per-centage on the sales, rather than to dispose of the book outright. I look for a considerable circulation—more than of my own book proper." He was able to write Bridge on April 17 that the book had been accepted.[37]

The single volume of tales originally planned by both Duyckinck and Hawthorne would have differed significantly from the collection we know as the 1846 *Mosses*. Hawthorne's selections emphasize, not surprisingly, a strong preference for his most recent work. All of the twelve "old" tales he chose had been written within the previous three years, none of them antedating the 1842 *Twice-told Tales*. Once again, in spite of Duyckinck's suggestion, he deliberately rejected "Young Goodman Brown" and "Roger Malvin's Burial" in his initial plans; he also excluded "The Wives of the Dead" and "Egotism; or, The Bosom-Serpent," perhaps wishing to avoid pieces of a darker stripe, whether old or new. Considering their recent reprinting in the *Democratic Review*, his exclusion of "Roger Malvin's Burial" and "The Wives of the Dead" may also have been the result of a wish to avoid "thrice-told tales." The choices reflect likewise a balance between essay-sketches and tales and an attempt to offer as much variety of form, subject, and theme as his recent fiction allowed. His reference to "make-weights" can be taken as a generally reliable indication of his lower regard for the other pieces of this period, especially the recently completed "P.'s Correspondence."

[36] MS, Duyckinck Collection, New York Public Library.
[37] MS, Bowdoin College.

Hawthorne began almost immediately, but to no avail, to try to write the fresh material Duyckinck requested. He never again referred to more than a single story. "I began a story for my book," he wrote to Duyckinck on May 2, "a short time since; but am not in good trim for writing, so that it makes no progress." [38] And on July 1, he explained to the editor his reasons for postponing further efforts:

> My story makes no good progress. There are many matters that thrust themselves between, and hinder my mind from any close approximation to the subject; and for days and weeks together, sometimes, I forget that there is any story to be forthcoming—and am sorry to remember it at last. I am fit for nothing, at present, higher or finer than such another piece of book-manufacture as the Journal. My health is not so good, this summer, as it always has been hitherto. I feel no physical vigor; and my inner man droops in sympathy. . . . Perhaps such sketches would be more easily written after I have pitched my tent elsewhere. That will be in a few months, now. It grieves me to keep you waiting for this story, if it be important that you should have it; but if I were to attempt writing it now, the result would be most pitiable.[39]

He was able at this time, though, to tell Duyckinck what kind of story he wished to write: "It was my purpose to construct a sort of frame-work, in this new story, for the series of stories already published, and to make the scene an idealization of our old parsonage, and of the river close at hand, with glimmerings of my actual life—yet so transmogrified that the reader should not know what was reality and what fancy." "The Old Manse" is in large part a realization of these intentions.

Hawthorne probably did not make another attempt until the following October, after returning with his family to his

[38] MS, Duyckinck Collection, New York Public Library.
[39] MS, Duyckinck Collection, New York Public Library.

mother's home in Salem. Duyckinck, concerned over Hawthorne's silence, wrote to him on October 2: "I hope you will not think me a troublesome fellow if I drop you another line with the vociferous cry MSS! MSS! Mr. Wiley's American series is athirst for the volume of Tales." [40] On October 7, Hawthorne told Bridge that his old chamber was favorable to literary duties and that he had "already begun to sketch out the story for Wiley & Putnam." [41] Writing to Duyckinck on October 10, however, he was less hopeful:

> Here I am . . . in the old dingy and dusky chamber, where I wasted many good years of my youth, shaping day-dreams and night-dreams into idle stories—scarcely half of which ever saw the light; except it were their own blaze upon the hearth. I wish now that I had not burned them; for perhaps there might have been one among them fit—or capable of being made fit—to lead the new collection of tales. However, my youth comes back to me here; and I find myself, sad to say, pretty much the same sort of fellow as of old—and already, though not a week established here, I take out my quire of paper and prepare to cover it with the accustomed nonsense. Doubtless there will be a result of some kind or other, in the course of two or three weeks, so soon as my mind has deposited the sediment of recent anxieties and disturbances.[42]

Hawthorne was disconcerted generally by his persistent lack of money and, more particularly, by the need to bring suit against George Ripley for the remainder of his Brook Farm investment.[43] He had been obliged to borrow $150.00 from Bridge to pay his debts in Concord and had been saved from ignominious flight only by O'Sullivan's payment to him of $100.00 on the first of October.[44] The only literary

[40] MS, Bowdoin College.

[41] MS, Bowdoin College.

[42] MS, Duyckinck Collection, New York Public Library.

[43] Hawthorne to George Hillard, September 6, 1845, MS, University of Rochester.

[44] Hawthorne to Bridge, October 7, 1845, MS, Bowdoin College.

task he was able to complete by the end of 1845 was the editing of B. F. Browne's "Papers of an Old Dartmoor Prisoner," with hopes of its book and serial publication. In his October 10 letter to Duyckinck, he responded to a proposal that he undertake a history of witchcraft. He felt himself not up to the task: "I had often thought of such a work; but I should not like to throw it off hastily, or to write it for the sole and specific purpose of getting $500. . . . such a work, if worthily written, would demand research and study, and as deep thought as any man could bring to it. . . . Perhaps it may be the work of an after time."

Hawthorne persisted in his efforts to write the new piece for his collection, but he had begun to suffer doubts that he would ever be able to finish anything he could admire. He wrote again to Duyckinck on December 24, 1845:

> That wretched tale still refuses to unfold its convolutions— not from any lack of either gentle or compulsory efforts on my part; but I have not now the quiet which has always been my portion aforetime; and therefore nothing prospers with me. I write continually—but am conscious, even at the moment, that I am not writing the true thing; and on re-perusal the next day, it turns out a sad business indeed. Peradventure, I have reached that point in an author's life, when he ceases to effervesce; and whatever I do hereafter must be done with leaden reluctance, and therefore had better be left undone. Do not think me wilfully idle; for it is not so.[45]

In January, 1846, Duyckinck hit upon the idea of expanding to two volumes Hawthorne's new collection of stories. Although the plan appealed to Hawthorne, the reasons for its attractiveness bespeak his lack of enthusiasm for the pieces he was to add. The proposal was for him an occasion to announce to Duyckinck that he would cease writing short fiction:

[45] MS, Duyckinck Collection, New York Public Library.

I like the plan of of [sic] publishing two volumes, and will set about collecting my vagrant progeny forthwith; and as I never mean to write any more stories (the one now in embryo excepted) we will offer this collection to the public as the last that they shall ever be troubled with, at my hands. It is rather a sad idea—not that I am to write no more in this kind, but that I cannot better justify myself for having written at all. As the first essays and tentatives of a young author, they would be well enough—but it seems to me absurd to look upon them as conveying any claim to a settled literary reputation. I thank God, I have grace enough to be utterly dissatisfied with them, considered as the productions of a literary life—or in any point of view whatever; not but what I see the degree of merit they possess. If they were merely spring blossoms, we might look for good fruit hereafter; but I have done nothing but blossom all through the summer. I am ashamed—and there's an end.[46]

Within a month, Hawthorne selected ten more pieces, among them four that antedated the 1837 *Twice-told Tales*: "Roger Malvin's Burial" (1832 *Token*); "Young Goodman Brown" (*New-England Magazine*, April, 1835), and "Mrs. Bullfrog" and "Monsieur du Miroir" (1837 *Token*). Once again, he deliberately omitted "My Kinsman, Major Molineux" (1832 *Token*). On February 22, 1846, still laboring over the new sketch, Hawthorne sent Duyckinck copy for "Part second of the proposed collection" so that it could be readied for the printer, and was confident that "the contents of Part first"—printing of which waited upon the introductory sketch—would soon follow. He had decided upon a title, the choice evidently giving him the same trouble that he would later experience with his romances: "I have bestowed much and solemn consideration upon the title of the book. 'Wall-Flowers from an Old Abbey' occurred to me;—but it is too fine. 'Moss and Lichens from an Old Parsonage';—that

---

[46] January 24, 1846, MS, Duyckinck Collection, New York Public Library.

does not go off trippingly enough. 'Mosses from an Old Manse' suits me rather better; and if my wife agrees with me, so shall the book be christened." In a postscript he added: "We decide on 'Mosses from an Old Manse.' " [47]

In expanding the collection Hawthorne was careful to balance the two volumes in length and variety. In his February 22 letter he noted that the second volume would make "as nearly as I can calculate, just about 175 pages." [48] The number of tales and essay-sketches and the number of original and later selections are likewise evenly distributed in the two volumes. For the second volume Hawthorne combined five of his initial choices with five other recent pieces and "Roger Malvin's Burial," the lengthiest of the earlier tales included. The first volume, when completed, was made up of "The Old Manse," seven of Hawthorne's original selections, one recent sketch, and three tales from the 1830s. He included two pieces which he had once scorned as inferior, "Mrs. Bullfrog" and "Monsieur du Miroir." Years earlier, when choosing pieces for the 1842 *Twice-told Tales*, he had written Sophia: "Sweetest, thou dost please me much by criticizing thy husband's stories, and finding fault with them. I do not very well recollect Monsieur du Miroir; but as to Mrs. Bullfrog, I give her up to thy severest reprehension. The story was written as a mere experiment in that style; it did not come from any depth within me—neither my heart nor mind had any thing to do with it." [49] It is unlikely that either he or Sophia had had a change of mind; rather, Hawthorne decided to use the stories because their humor provides a relief from the sombre tone of most of the other selections. Numerous sequences among the tales and sketches suggest that he tried to dramatize their various differences.

[47] MS, Duyckinck Collection, New York Public Library.
[48] Part I in the 1846 *Mosses* is 207 pages; Part II, 211 pages.
[49] September 16, 1841, MS, Huntington Library.

Though badly needing the advance promised upon delivery of his new sketch, Hawthorne was still unable to compose the introduction for his collection. He was understandably distracted by uncertainty of his political appointment. As the post grew more certain, he commented in a March 3 letter to Sargent, "It is exceedingly convenient for a literary man to be able to ensconce himself in an office, whenever his brain gets weary and his pen blunted." [50] It was not until April 15 that Hawthorne, at last in the custom house and assured of $1,200 a year, finished "The Old Manse" and sent to Duyckinck the rest of the contents of Part I of *Mosses*:

> I send you the initial article, promised so many thousand years ago. The delay has really not been my fault—only my misfortune. Nothing that I tried to write would flow out of my pen, till a very little while ago—when forth came this sketch of its own accord, and much unlike what I had purposed. I like it pretty well, at this present writing; and my wife better than I. It is truth, as you will perceive, with perhaps a gleam or two of ideal light thrown over it—yet hardly the less true for that. I have written it as impersonally as I could, considering the nature of the thing, and do not feel as if there were any indelicacy in it, towards myself or anybody else. [51]

Although Hawthorne did not succeed in writing two fresh tales, "The Old Manse," subtitled "The author makes the reader acquainted with his abode," can be said to provide a loosely rhetorical "frame-work" for the collection. Taken together, at any rate, the introductory sketch and the title of the collection suggest that the writer, the place, and the cumulative vision projected in the tales and sketches shared

[50] MS, St. Lawrence University.

[51] MS, Duyckinck Collection, New York Public Library. On April 18, Hawthorne wrote to Wiley and Putnam that he had drawn upon them for the agreed $100.00 advance payment against royalties (MS, University of Amsterdam).

an organic relationship. The extent to which Hawthorne liked "The Old Manse" can be estimated best by his use of the same quasi-autobiographical mode for "The Custom-House" in *The Scarlet Letter*. Essentially a private person struggling to attract a popular audience, he found in the personal sketch the most congenial possibilities of presenting himself as a public personage who would mediate between his fiction and his readers.

Referring to Part II, Hawthorne wrote Bridge on March 1, 1846, that "My tales, I suppose, are by this time in press." [52] Although he requested to see the proof-sheets for "The Old Manse," being "anxious about the accuracy of the press, in relation to this article," [53] the book was printed without Hawthorne's reading proof. Duyckinck apparently raised a last-minute objection to the title, for Hawthorne wrote him on April 30 defending it: " 'Manse' seemed objectionable to me, at first, for the same reason as to you; but it was our familiar epithet for the old house; and, besides, the word is not exclusively Scotch, but antique English as well. But I suppose everybody will take it to be a Scotticism." [54] Upon seeing a specimen copy, on June 10 he commented to Duyckinck that the book "seemed rather stale to me; but my wife was pleased to like it." [55] It is worth noting that, among the fifty copies he ordered for his own distribution, he remembered his political supporters Senators Atherton and Fairfield.

The collection was published as volumes XVII and XVIII of Wiley and Putnam's Library of American Books and a set was deposited for copyright on June 5, 1846. The first

[52] MS, Bowdoin College.

[53] Hawthorne to Duyckinck, April 15, 1846, MS, Duyckinck Collection, New York Public Library. For a discussion of the text and of copies of *Mosses* annotated by Hawthorne, see the Textual Commentary and Bibliographical Information, pp. 541–48, 561.

[54] MS, Duyckinck Collection, New York Public Library. Several reviewers found regrettable the title's quaint and pedantic quality.

[55] MS, Duyckinck Collection, New York Public Library.

printing was issued in two volumes with paper covers at
$1.00 for the set and in a clothbound two-volumes-in-one
format at $1.25. An English issue of American sheets, bear-
ing the London imprint of Wiley and Putnam, was published in July, 1846.[56] Two more American printings bearing
the 1846 date appeared before the break-up of the firm of
Wiley and Putnam in the spring of 1848, at which time Putnam retained the plates. Hawthorne wrote to Bridge, on
October 26, 1846, that "My 'Mosses' seems to have met with
good acceptance."[57] No publisher's records exist, however, to
indicate the size of the printings or the success of the work
as a publishing venture. Putnam reprinted the plates in 1850,
1851, and 1852, for a total of six printings—now exploiting
Hawthorne's fame on the title page: "By Nathaniel Hawthorne. Author of 'The Scarlet Letter.'" On February 10,
1853, apologizing that the amount was not larger, he
sent Hawthorne a check for $144.09 for *Mosses* sales in
1851 and 1852, indicating that within that period between
750 and 1,150 copies had sold.[58]

After the appearance of *The Scarlet Letter*, Hawthorne's
editor, James T. Fields, urged publication of his tales
through Ticknor, Reed, and Fields. *Twice-told Tales*, un-

[56] The Bibliographical Information notes further details, including a
pirated English edition. In 1853, Hawthorne was to write to Ticknor in
London of another proposal: "Before I reached England, a man named
Wm. S. Orr, of Amen Corner, Paternoster Row, had directed a letter
hither expressing his intention to publish an illustrated edition of the
'Mosses,' and offering me £50. . . . In a subsequent letter to my clerk,
he requests that the preceding letter should not be delivered to me—
thereby indicating that he wishes to back out of his proposal. Of course, he
is entirely at liberty to do so; but if he is really going to publish a handsome edition of the 'Mosses,' I should be glad to correct the proof-sheets;
for there are several errors in the American edition. Will you be kind
enough to call, and look into the matter? Do not say anything about the
£50. It is a matter for him to settle with his own liberality and conscience,
and cannot be bargained for on my part" (August 6, 1853, MS, Berg
Collection, New York Public Library). The proposal never came to
fruition.
[57] MS, Bowdoin College.
[58] See the Bibliographical Information, pp. 568–69.

changed except for a preface added by Hawthorne, was published in the spring of 1851, and a new collection, *The Snow-
Image*, that autumn. Fields wrote to Hawthorne on January
14, 1851, concerning *Mosses*: "How much longer will Putnam's contract hold? I hope we shall have that Book when
the five years are out as we intend to push yr. books a-la-
Steam Engine, and do better for you than any other house." [59]
And on March 26, Fields reaffirmed his intention: "While
in N.Y. I shall try to buy of Putnam 'The Mosses.' I think
it will be a nice thing to have all your works issued by one
house. I do not imagine Putnam will be inclined to sell
the plates of the Mosses but I shall make an effort to buy
them." [60] But it was not until 1854 that Putnam sold the
plates. In the meantime, Hawthorne had already completed
his major phase as a writer of full-length fiction, having
published his three mature American romances.

In July, 1853, Hawthorne sailed to England, enjoying a
political appointment from Franklin Pierce as reward for a
campaign biography of the successful presidential candidate
in 1852. To Fields, who knew that Hawthorne's consular
duties at Liverpool would keep him from extensive writing,
the time must have seemed propitious for another attempt
to secure *Mosses* for his firm and thus to hold the author's
name before the public. In March, 1854, he was at last
able to purchase Putnam's plates and he immediately made
plans to publish. He sent Hawthorne a copy of the 1846
Mosses to review for printer's copy, and Hawthorne returned
it on April 13 "after a careful revision," having found the
reading "a very disagreeable task." Hawthorne commented,
"Upon my honor, I am not quite sure that I entirely comprehend my own meaning in some of these blasted allegories"—
but with an ambivalence characteristic of his attitudes toward

[59] MS, Berg Collection, New York Public Library.
[60] MS, Berg Collection, New York Public Library.

his earlier work, he added, "Yet certainly there is more in it than the public generally gave me credit for, at the time it was written."[61]

In his letter Hawthorne made one suggestion about adding to the collection: "The story of 'Rappaccini's Daughter' was published in the Democratic Review about the year 1844; and it was prefaced by some remarks on the celebrate[d] French author (a certain M. de l'Aubepine) from whose works it was translated. I left out this preface, when the story was republished; but I wish you would turn to it in the Democratic, and see whether it is worth while to insert it in the new edition. I leave it altogether to your judgement." It is possible that Hawthorne deleted the passage in 1846 because, since it had paid tribute briefly to O'Sullivan and the *Democratic Review*, he may have felt that even such innocent remarks would run the risk of endangering a political appointment. In 1854, however, writing from the consulate, he must have felt secure from such criticism and now decided to restore the preface and to acknowledge in print his affection and esteem for his old friend just as he had done for Bridge in the preface to *The Snow-Image* and would later do for Pierce in *Our Old Home* (1863). Fields's senior partner W. D. Ticknor now inquired about the existence of still other uncollected pieces that Hawthorne might be willing to publish, so that the firm in expanding the collection could give it a claim to novelty. Hawthorne's reply, on June 7, betrays only a limited interest in the scheme:

> You put me to my trumps by asking for additional matter for the "Mosses"; for I considered myself exhausted on that score, long ago. Nevertheless, there is "Feathertop"—which is about as good as any of them. Let that go in. It has just occurred to me, moreover, that in the New England

[61] MS, Huntington Library.

Magazine, when published by Park Benjamin, many of the stories appeared which are now collected in the "Twice-told Tales"; and the publication of them was commenced with about ten or more pages of introductory matter, which, I think, will do very well to publish as an article in the "Mosses". It should be separated from all extraneous stuff (which, if I recollect rightly, may be done easy enough,) and may be called "passages from a relinquished work"— or something of that kind. I believe the title was "The Itinerant Storyteller." There are other detached passages of mine, scattered through Park Benjamin's volumes of that magazine; and Fields would readily recognize them. Let him do as he pleases about inserting any or all of them;—only being careful to put in nothing that he does not feel absolutely certain about. The beginning, and the conclusion, of the "Itinerant Storyteller" are there at an interval of some months, and are written quite up to the usual level of my scribblings.[62]

With "Feathertop" Hawthorne had finally savored a triumph over the exigencies of periodical publication. Approached by J. S. Dwight on behalf of *Sartain's Union Magazine* for an article, Hawthorne, the successful romance writer, answered on November 23, 1851, that he had a story which he would sell for $100.00.[63] On December 4 he wrote to John Sartain, rejecting an apparent proposal that he contribute regularly:

> The story in question, according to the best estimation I can form, would make somewhere above twenty of such pages as Ticknor's editions of my books. It is quite long enough for a magazine story; but I should not at all wonder if you should not consider it worth, to you, the price named in my note to Mr Dwight. Most certainly, I myself would not pay it, were I in the chair editorial.
>
> As regards regular contributions, I could not enter into any engagement. These magazine stories make a great draft

[62] MS, Berg Collection, New York Public Library.

[63] MS, Beinecke Library, Yale University. The Historical Commentary of *The Snow-Image, and Uncollected Tales* (Centenary Edition, 1974) relates events of the publication of Hawthorne's other short fiction written after the Old Manse period.

upon an author's time and thoughts—much greater, in proportion both to the bulk of matter and the compensation—than a long romance. I happened to have a little time, just before leaving Lenox, which I could not fill up better than by writing this story; otherwise I should not now have had it on hand. The value of the article may perhaps be enhanced, from the circumstance that there is nothing more of the same kind in the market.[64]

Sartain was, as Hawthorne anticipated, either unwilling or unable to pay the price. After learning from Dwight that *Graham's* finances were shaky,[65] Hawthorne offered the tale on December 15 to R. W. Griswold, now editor of the *International Magazine*, who had invited him to publish a series of monthly tales:

As regards the proposition for twelve short tales, I shall not be able to accept it; because experience has taught me that the thought and trouble, expended on that kind of production, is vastly greater, in proportion, than what is required for a long story. . . .

I have by me a story which I wrote just before leaving Lenox, and which I thought of sending to Dr. Bailey of the National Era, who has offered me $100. for an article. But, being somewhat grotesque in its character, and therefore not quite adapted to the grave and sedate character of that Journal, I hesitate about so doing, and will send it to the International, should you wish it at the price above-mentioned. The story would make between twenty and thirty of such pages as Ticknor's editions of my books—hardly long enough, I think, to be broken into two articles for your magazine; but you might please yourself on that point. I cannot afford it for less than $100, and would not write another for the same price.[66]

Hawthorne received other offers to write magazine fiction, Griswold printed the tale in two parts in February and March, 1852, and apparently paid Hawthorne promptly. Although

[64] MS, University of Virginia.

[65] Hawthorne to Dwight, December 10, 1851, MS, St. Lawrence University.

[66] MS, Huntington Library.

including one from Putnam the following year, he adamantly refused them.

In his June 7, 1854, letter, Hawthorne remarked that Fields, or the critic E. P. Whipple, could "patch up" a sketch to be put in the middle of the new collection, "where it will not attract so much notice." Together with "Feathertop," the 1854 *Mosses* contained two additions which were central parts of the long-since abandoned collection "The Story Teller." "The Story Teller. No. I" and "The Story Teller. No. II" (*New-England Magazine*, November–December, 1834), excepting "Mr. Higginbotham's Catastrophe"— already included in *Twice-told Tales*—were entered as "Passages from a Relinquished Work." After two introductory paragraphs of framework were deleted, "Sketches from Memory. No. I" and "The Canal-Boat" section of "Sketches from Memory. No. II" (*New-England Magazine*, November–December, 1835) were included as "Sketches from Memory." [67] The remainder of "Sketches from Memory. No. II" was not included, perhaps out of respect for Hawthorne's wish that as little old material as possible be used, but more likely because the new edition of *Mosses* was already fuller than the 1851 *Twice-told Tales*. Given the Hawthorne reference in the letter to "an interval of some months," it is possible that he also had in mind "Fragments from the Journal of a Solitary Man," a sketch which may originally have been intended as the conclusion to "The Story Teller," but which Benjamin failed to publish in the *New-England Magazine* and took with him to the *American Monthly*, where it appeared in July, 1837.

Although no other additions were made to the collection, Ticknor and Fields promoted sales by describing it as a new edition "Carefully Revised by the Author." This second edi-

[67] Hawthorne, had he seen "The Canal-Boat" before it was added to the collection, probably would have deleted a voyeuristic passage; see pp. 435–36.

tion was published in two volumes on August 15, 1854, numbering 1,000 sets at a price of $1.50, with Hawthorne's royalty at 10 percent, or 15 cents per set. Some 10,000 copies were issued during Hawthorne's lifetime. *Mosses*, which in his initial conception contained, with one exception, pieces associated with the 1842–45 years, came finally to include tales and sketches composed over the twenty-year period of Hawthorne's career as a writer for magazines.

The 1846 edition provided the occasion for two of the most memorable statements in nineteenth-century American literary criticism: Poe's "Tale Writing—Nathaniel Hawthorne" and Melville's "Hawthorne and His Mosses." [68] Most reviews received the volumes cordially, and although several expressed major reservations, none of them—not even Poe's celebrated attack on Hawthorne's allegorical bent—failed to recognize and reaffirm Hawthorne's basic genius. As the title of his essay suggests, Poe addressed himself not to *Mosses from an Old Manse* specifically but to a revaluation of Hawthorne's whole career and achievement as a writer of short fiction. But those reviewers who explicitly compared *Mosses* with *Twice-told Tales* preferred the newer collection without exception. Charles W. Webber of the *American Whig Review* commented that "in the 'Mosses of an Old Manse,' it seems to us that his life has deepened since that which gave us 'The Twice-told Tales'. . . . " Samuel W. S. Dutton observed in the *New Englander* that "the more he writes the better he writes" and that the *Mosses* volumes were "decidedly superior" to the *Twice-told*. And Melville pronounced extravagantly

[68] *Godey's Lady's Book*, XXXV (November, 1847), 252–56 and *Literary World*, VII (August 17 and 24, 1850), 125–27 and 145–47. In addition to Poe's and Melville's reviews, this discussion draws upon the following notices and essays: *Graham's Magazine*, XXIX (August, 1846), 107–8; *Athenæum* (August 8, 1846), 807–8; *American Whig Review*, IV (September, 1846), 296–316; *New Englander*, V (January, 1847), 56–69; *Blackwood's Magazine*, LXII (November, 1847), 587–92; *Graham's Magazine*, XLV (November, 1854), 492.

that "whatever Nathaniel Hawthorne may hereafter write, 'The Mosses from an Old Manse' will be ultimately accounted his master-piece." Melville's essay is full of rhetorical strategies, one of which—his pretence that he had also read *Twice-told Tales* and *The Scarlet Letter* closely—seems to make his praise still more remarkable. A year later, however, he had changed his judgment. He wrote to Duyckinck that *Twice-told Tales* "far exceed the 'Mosses'—they are, I fancy, an earlier vintage from his vine. Some of those sketches are wonderfully subtle." [69]

Other critics, however, writing omnibus reviews of Hawthorne's works, continued to give *Mosses* the higher place. Amory Dwight Mayo, for example, felt that *Mosses* was to *Twice-told Tales* "what paintings in oils are to sketches in water colors." [70] There is, he claimed, "greater maturity of development" in the later collection and "a more decided treatment, more vivid and definite portrayal of character." E. P. Whipple, whom Hawthorne came to think the most perceptive of his critics, concluded in 1860 that the later group of stories is "intellectually and artistically an advance from the 'Twice-Told Tales.' " [71]

Various of the reviewers understandably found themselves, as they had with *Twice-told Tales,* hard pressed to give a name to Hawthorne's short fiction. *Graham's* described the work as "an exquisite collection of essays, allegories, and stories, replete with fancy, humor and sentiment." Dutton saw it comprised of "various Tales, Essays, Allegories, and

[69] *The Letters of Herman Melville,* ed. Merrell R. Davis and William H. Gilman (New Haven, 1960), p. 121.

[70] "The Works of Nathaniel Hawthorne," *Universalist Quarterly,* VIII (July, 1851), 272–93.

[71] "Nathaniel Hawthorne," *Atlantic Monthly,* V (May, 1860), 614–22. Hawthorne wrote to Fields that he had seen "a really keen and profound article by Whipple, in which he goes over all my works, and recognizes that element of unpopularity which (as nobody knows better than myself) pervades them all. I agree with almost all he says" (April 26, 1860, MS, Huntington Library).

Pieces—we know of no term more specific which will answer our purpose." Melville, essentially unconcerned with generic distinctions, relied on metaphorical terms, referring to individual pieces as "apples" and "Mosses" as well as "chapters," "stories," and "sketches." *Blackwood's* judged "the happier specimens of Mr. Hawthorne's writing . . . those papers which we cannot better describe than as so many American *Spectators* of the year 1846—so much do they call to mind the style of essay in the days of Steele and Addison." Poe, on the other hand, while attempting a formal definition of "that class of composition" called "the brief prose tale," saw Hawthorne's work, along with Addison's and Irving's, exemplifying a species he designated as "the natural," a kind of composition stemming solely from "understanding" and thus having only a "lower degree" of true originality than poetry.

Not knowing otherwise how to describe Hawthorne's idiom, the reviewers conventionally compared him with other writers. *Graham's* said he "is even a finer and deeper humorist . . . than Addison or Goldsmith, or Irving." Chorley's *Athenæum* review saw resemblances to Tieck, Töpffer, and Bunyan. *Blackwood's* was the first of numerous attempts to define the marked differences between Hawthorne's work and Poe's: "whereas Mr. Poe is indebted to whatever good effect he produces to a close detail and agglomeration of facts, Mr. Hawthorne appears to have little skill and little taste for dealing with matter of fact or substantial incident, but relies for his favourable impression on the charm of style, and the play of thought and fancy." Webber hailed Hawthorne's "Ethical Conservatism" and said that he "is to the Present and the Future what Charles Lamb was to the Past." In his ability to walk "that difficult line and narrow between the Natural and Supernatural" Hawthorne is fully the equal of Scott, Fouqué, and Coleridge. Hawthorne's style reminded Dutton of Addison's, Lamb's, and Scott's. In another vein

Melville, disparaging foreign models—"we want no American Goldsmiths; nay, we want no American Miltons"—insisted on Shakespeare as the only worthy comparison: "Not a very great deal more, and Nathaniel were verily William."

Although Poe mentions only briefly one tale in *Mosses*—"Young Goodman Brown," in order to condemn it for its "mysticism"—all the other reviewers single out various pieces for special comment. The enthusiasm for tales and essay-sketches is equally strong. The first review in *Graham's* shows a preference for the sketches: "The Old Manse," "Buds and Bird-Voices," "The Hall of Fantasy," "The Celestial Railroad," "The Procession of Life," "P.'s Correspondence," and "Earth's Holocaust" are "among the most striking in the collection; and . . . among the best productions of American literature." In 1854, *Graham's*, repeating its praise of "The Old Manse" and "Earth's Holocaust," finds especially memorable "The Birth-mark," "Young Goodman Brown," "Rappaccini's Daughter," "Egotism," "The Artist of the Beautiful," "The Christmas Banquet," "Drowne's Wooden Image," and "Roger Malvin's Burial," and calls "P.'s Correspondence" "one of the most ingenious and striking of all Hawthorne's works." Chorley is most impressed with "Rappaccini's Daughter," "The Birth-mark," and "Young Goodman Brown" among the tales and sees "The Celestial Rail-road" and "Earth's Holocaust" as "in the grandest style of allegory." *Blackwood's* calls "Roger Malvin's Burial" the best of the narratives but generally prefers the *Spectator*-like papers—"The Intelligence Office," "The Old Apple-Dealer," and "The New Adam and Eve." It too mentions "The Celestial Rail-road" favorably and concludes with an extract illustrating the successful humor of "Mrs. Bullfrog." "The Birth-mark" and "The Artist of the Beautiful," however, are seen as having "some palpable improbability which mars the effect of the whole" and is the "most serious defect in his stories." The reviewer found impossibly unrealistic Aylmer's attitude towards his wife as well as Owen Warland's passion for the beautiful. "Unfortunately, in Mr. Hawthorne's stories, it is the human being himself who is not probable, nor possible." Webber praises "The Old Manse," "The New Adam and Eve," and "Earth's Holocaust" as illustrations of "the universality of Hawthorne's mind, and his honestly philosophical readiness to recognize all truths, of whatever character." He reserves a special place for "Young Goodman Brown" as the finest "Tale of the Supernatural" in American literature, for "A Virtuoso's Collection" as exemplary of Hawthorne's "Humanizing the Unreal," and for "Rappaccini's Daughter" as evidence that Hawthorne is the "true Poet" and the "highest Philosopher." Dutton cites passages from "Buds and Bird-Voices" and "Snow-flakes" to illustrate Hawthorne's descriptions of natural scenery and his "quick and accurate and comprehensive eye of the true painter." "The New Adam and Eve," "The Intelligence Office," "P.'s Correspondence," "The Hall of Fantasy," "The Procession of Life," "The Artist of the Beautiful," and especially "The Celestial Rail-road" are evidence that Hawthorne is a good-natured but effective satirist of the "faults and foibles and errors of individuals and cliques, of schools, and communities, and ages." On the other hand, Dutton finds "Young Goodman Brown" incomprehensible because the moral lesson it was obviously designed to teach "is not apprehended by nine out of ten of intelligent readers." Melville, admiring all the "chapters," celebrates their variety: "The Old Apple-Dealer" for "depth of tenderness" and "boundless sympathy with all forms of being," "Monsieur du Miroir" for "mystical depth," "The Intelligence Office" for "symbolizing of the secret working in men's souls," and "The Christmas Banquet" and "Egotism" for Hawthorne's "blackness, ten times black."

Various long-standing critical issues surfaced in the reviews. Whereas the *Blackwood's* reviewer thought that Hawthorne was one of those "American writers [who] frequently remind

us of models of composition somewhat antiquated with ourselves," Webber, Dutton, and Melville considered *Mosses* as
gratifying proof that the call for a genuinely national literature had been fully and gracefully answered. Webber found
that Hawthorne's "manly self-reliance" and "quiet, unobtrusive dignity" repudiated the insinuation that "the vice of
our national temperament is exaggeration—exaggeration in
everything." Dutton, disparaging the faults common in other
American writers, congratulated Hawthorne for his natural,
quiet style, in which there is "nothing strained, and no painfully manifest aim and effort to be brilliant and effective."
Melville, decrying the imitative tendencies of Irving, described
Hawthorne as one of "those writers who breathe that un-
shackled, democratic spirit of Christianity in all things, which
now takes the practical lead in this world, though at the same
time led by ourselves—us Americans." The questions of
Hawthorne's lack of popularity and of the allegorical nature
of much of his fiction, however, were the most substantive
problems addressed, and Poe and Melville were the critics
who attended to them most forcefully and defined sharply the
two antithetical responses that were to persist in critical assess-
ments of Hawthorne.

Poe's essay is not so much a review of *Mosses* as it is, at
least ostensibly, an attempt to account for Hawthorne's being
"*the* example, *par excellence,* in this country, of the privately-
admired and publicly-unappreciated man of genius." Poe
assumes throughout that "it is, in fact, the excitable, undisci-
plined and child-like popular mind which most keenly feels
the original." Melville, on the other hand, wants to correct
the popular view of Hawthorne as a "sequestered, harmless
man, from whom any deep and weighty thing would hardly
be anticipated." His central assumption, moreover, is that
"it is the least part of genius that attracts admiration," and
thus he is drawn toward those very aspects of Hawthorne's

imagination that repel Poe. For Poe, influenced by Hawthorne's remarks in "The Old Manse," the author's "books
afford strong internal evidence of having been written to
himself and his particular friends alone," his friends being
Longfellow, Lowell, and others of Poe's literary adversaries
associated with the Concord and *North American Review*
group. Such elite readers always judge an author not by
what he actually does but "by what he evinces a capability
of doing." Melville, however, finds Hawthorne, like Shakespeare, beyond the grasp of the common reader because of
his depth of intellect. Asserting that "Failure is the true test
of greatness," Melville affirms the romantic view Poe tries
to negate: "the immediate products of a great mind are not
so great as that undeveloped and sometimes undevelopable
yet dimly-discernible greatness, to which those immediate
products are but the infallible indices."

The reason Poe gives for Hawthorne's lack of popularity
is that, instead of being commendably original, Hawthorne
has only a "uniform . . . peculiarity," a monotone that "tasks
and startles the intellect." Hawthorne's failure to attract a
wide audience can no longer be a cause of amazement because
he is monotonously allegorical—monotonous, that is, "at that
point which, having the least concern with Nature, is the
farthest removed from the popular intellect, from the popular
sentiment and the popular taste." Just as allegory repels the
masses, "who, seeking in this literature amusement, are positively offended by instruction," so also does it violate Poe's
cardinal tenet—the unity of the *"single effect"*— the end of
which is "pleasure." Hawthorne's "metaphysical originality,"
then, makes him guilty of what Poe later termed the "heresy
of *The Didactic*," for it assumes that literature aims at the
expression of "Truth" as well as "Beauty." Melville, on the
other hand, wrestling at the time with the relationship
between fact and spiritual significance in *Moby-Dick*, found

Hawthorne most worthy precisely because his "deeply thinking mind" confronted demanding and magnificent ideas and
seemed captivated by the "terrific thought" of "Original Sin."
Thus, for Melville, Hawthorne takes his place beside "Shakspeare and other masters of the great Art of Telling the
Truth."

Poe's reversal of the favorable opinions he had expressed
in his 1842 review of *Twice-told Tales* is rooted in various
circumstances. Since that time Poe himself had been the
target of negative reviews. In *Graham's* (February, 1845)
James Russell Lowell had attacked Poe's criticism because
"he seems sometimes to mistake his phial of prussic-acid for
his inkstand." And in the *North American Review* (October,
1846) C. C. Felton had dismissed Poe's tales as belonging
to "the forcible-feeble and the shallow-profound school." Such
events probably fed Poe's animus regarding Hawthorne. And
Hawthorne himself may unwittingly have fanned the flames
when, sending Poe a presentation copy of *Mosses* on June 17,
1846, he wrote:

> I have read your occasional notices of my productions with
> great interest—not so much because your judgment was, on
> the whole, favorable, as because it seemed to be given in
> earnest. I care for nothing but the truth; and shall always
> much more readily accept a harsh truth, in regard to my
> writings, than a sugared falsehood.
>
> I confess, however, that I admire you rather as a writer
> of Tales, than as a critic upon them. I might often—and do
> often—dissent from your opinions, in the latter capacity,
> but could never fail to recognize your force and originality
> in the former.[72]

Both Hawthorne and his wife were most pleased by Melville's
essay, and Sophia, still unaware that Melville was the author,
wrote Duyckinck—who, as editor of the *Literary World,* had
helped Melville revise the statement—to say that the reviewer

[72] MS, Collection of Henry Bradley Martin.

was "the first person who has ever in *print* apprehended Mr. Hawthorne." [73]

Nevertheless Hawthorne's own remarks to Fields in 1854 about not comprehending "some of these blasted allegories" suggest that ultimately Poe's judgment had had a more lasting influence on him. Indeed, Melville himself had come close to agreeing with Poe's assessment. In his 1851 letter to Duyckinck, he had said that he regarded Hawthorne "as evincing a quality of genius, immensely loftier, & more profound, too, than any other American has shown hitherto in printed form." But he had also complained that "Still there is something lacking—a good deal lacking—to the plump sphericity of the man. What is that?—He doesn't patronise the butcher—he needs roast-beef, done rare."

Mosses from an Old Manse, including tales and sketches written more than twenty years apart, spans more fully than *Twice-told Tales* and *The Snow-Image* Hawthorne's entire career as a writer. The two editions, comprising a collection written in years that were punctuated by three political appointments, are an epitome of Hawthorne's continuing efforts to reconcile the claims of the life of the imagination with those attaching to an active involvement in the real world. *Mosses* is at once a measure of his failure and of his greatness. Years later, addressing himself to the question of his popularity, Hawthorne wrote to Fields:

> My own opinion is, that I am not really a popular writer, and that what popularity I have gained is chiefly accidental, and owing to other causes than my own kind or degree of merit. Possibly I may (or may not) deserve something better than popularity; but looking at all my productions . . . with a cold and critical eye, I can see that they do not make their appeal to the popular mind. It is odd enough, moreover, that

[73] September 29, 1850, MS, Duyckinck Collection, New York Public Library.

my own individual taste is for quite another class of works than those which I myself am able to write. If I were to meet with such books as mine, by another writer, I don't believe I should be able to get through them. Have you ever read the novels of Anthony Trollope? They precisely suit my taste; solid and substantial, written on the strength of beef and through the inspiration of ale, and just as real as if some giant had hewn a great lump out of the earth and put it under a glass case, with all its inhabitants going about their daily business, and not suspecting that they were made a show of.[74]

Clearly, Hawthorne deserved something better than popularity, just as American literature needed something different from Trollope's novels. Melville, the man who initially came to an appreciation of Hawthorne through his *Mosses*, knew this and said so magnificently when, having finished *Moby-Dick*, he wrote: "In Token of my admiration for his genius, This book is inscribed to NATHANIEL HAWTHORNE."

J. D. C.

[74] February 11, 1860, MS, Huntington Library.

TEXTUAL COMMENTARY

THE EDITORIAL PROBLEMS in *Mosses from an Old Manse* differ according to the categories of textual transmission into which the various tales and sketches fall. Except for the introductory "The Old Manse," all of the pieces in the original two volumes of 1846 had been printed in periodicals or in *The Token,* and Hawthorne had looked them over and marked clippings with different degrees of care to correct and revise the text in preparation for the printer. Certain of the pieces were reprinted in other journals after their initial appearance, but no new authority entered the text and the original publication was used as printer's copy, with the exception of "Roger Malvin's Burial," which derives from the *United States Magazine and Democratic Review* reprint of the *Token* appearance.

The possibility exists, although the case is far from certain, that Hawthorne read proof on the stories that were first printed in *The Token*—"Mrs. Bullfrog," "Monsieur du Miroir," and "Roger Malvin's Burial." In a letter accompanying the manuscript of "The Birth-mark" on February 1, 1843, Hawthorne wrote to the *Pioneer* editor, Robert Carter, "It would be a great satisfaction to me to look over the proofs of this article, which might be sent me by mail; but if you are pressed for time, it is not essential. I abhor errors of the press—and but seldom escape them." [1] Hawthorne may have corrected this story, therefore, since the changes that appear to be authorial in the 1846 *Mosses* are relatively minor. Whether he asked for or received proof for "The Hall of Fantasy," published in the preceding issue of *Pioneer*, is not known; his letter concerning "The Birth-mark" could be taken to suggest that he had not. The majority of the tales, then, had been printed in various periodicals—although chiefly in the *Democratic Review*—from manuscript, probably without authorial proofreading, and no doubt with variable degrees of editing. It is also relatively certain that Hawthorne would not have recovered the manuscripts.

Under these circumstances when he came to annotate the clippings that were to serve as printer's copy for the 1846 *Mosses*, he would have been conscious of errors that needed correction in the periodicals, some of which had been carelessly printed. Probably the opportunity for revision in the sense of any recasting was secondary in his mind to correction, except in such stories as "Monsieur du Miroir," where he made a massive cut and a minor one, or "The Hall of Fantasy" which he also cut heavily. These cuts are interesting. Some suspicion of Sophia Hawthorne's influence attaches to the first cut in "Monsieur du Miroir" following "visage" at 161.30, since the only purpose of the deletion is to remove a reference to Hawthorne's being flushed with drink. The second—after "counterfeit" at 162.21—might have been made to reduce the length, but since it contains a brief reference to drinking-places and an extensive one to churchgoing which might lead a reader to believe that Hawthorne did not take formal religion very seriously, one cannot discount Sophia's advice here as well. If the case were more certain, an editor might be emboldened to restore these passages on the grounds of external censorship even though Hawthorne had certainly agreed to their removal. The various excisions in "The Hall

[1] MS, Fruitlands Museums, Harvard, Mass.

of Fantasy" appear to be motivated more definitely by Hawthorne's own views, like the short cut made in "P.'s Correspondence." They concern themselves exclusively with the removal of a series of names of American authors, various of them his friends, with an account of their actions in the Hall. Although intended to be cordial, the original text could be narrowly construed as critical, since one's presence in the Hall is not necessarily a flattering mark. It seems clear that Hawthorne removed these passages because of the ambiguity of tone, and what might seem to be an air of personal criticism, despite the fact that he liked to honor his friends and fellow authors in print.

The only other recasting in the 1846 volumes comprises the addition of a few extra details that occurred to his fancy while he looked over "A Virtuoso's Collection." [2] The rest in some small degree exhibit casual stylistic revision that Hawthorne could scarcely have distinguished very closely in his own mind from correction. Hawthorne had nothing new to say in this edition of his sketches except to provide a suitable introductory essay to link the tales as best he could to a common background, and he was content to let them stand as they had initially appeared save for a few refinements of style and what he would consider to be the correction of real error. Since we lack most of the manuscripts, the line between correction and revision in 1846 is often an uncertain one. Obviously, Hawthorne was in no position to recollect his exact words in the lost manuscript when he had only a periodical clipping before him. In "The Celestial Rail-road," for example, the *Democratic Review* had printed a remarkably faithful reproduction of his manuscript wording.[3] Only

[2] See the Explanatory Note in *The American Notebooks*, ed. Claude M. Simpson (Centenary Edition), p. 575, on new exhibits for the Virtuoso noted by Hawthorne in his journals.

[3] The restyling of accidentals in the printing shop is, of course, no indication of failure to follow copy since such house styling was a normal procedure.

five substantive variants slipped through—an omission of "he", alterations of "and a" to "as a" and of "bound for" to "bound to", a misreading of Hawthorne's hand "lurid" as "livid", and the sophistication of "year" to "years' "—none of them an obvious error.[4] In preparing the copy for 1846, Hawthorne did not recognize three of the changes, but he restored "lurid" and, rather remarkably, the "and a" of manuscript. This record of the *Democratic Review* care is paralleled by similar careful treatment of "Buds and Bird-Voices," printed the next month in June, 1843. There is a slip of MS, "-window" as plural, an error by contamination in following "flourish" with "only", a sophistication of "strike" to "strikes", and of "farther" twice changed to "further" (none recovered by Hawthorne in 1846).[5] Otherwise, the reproduction of "Buds and Bird-Voices" is faithful to the substantives and relatively conservative in its restyling of accidentals.

The record of *Graham's*, which printed "Earth's Holocaust," was decidedly less admirable, and Hawthorne's care in 1846 was not equal to the task. Thirteen substantive differences from the manuscript appear in *Graham's*, and six accidentals affecting the forms of words.[6] In only one case, "would" to "could" at 396.30, a substantive difference was restored in 1846, and only two of the accidental variants, whether or not by chance, were brought into conformity with manuscript usage—"toward" to "towards" at 383.16 and "afterward" to "afterwards" at 385.18. Other examples of "towards" at 390.19 and of "afterwards" at 396.22 were not restored, and when one considers the 1846 corruption "upwards" for MS and *Graham's* "upward" at 386.7, the likelihood is that Hawthorne was not responsible for even the restorations at 383.16 and 385.18. In fact, as argued in the

[4] Historical Collation 195.8, 200.6, 200.28, 201.30, and 206.10.

[5] Historical Collation 151.6, 151.14, 152.8, 154.27, and 157.7.

[6] Historical Collation listing, 381.18 through 404.3. See also the Textual Note 381–404 on "Earth's Holocaust."

Textual Note, it is possible that Hawthorne attempted no correction or revision whatever in this clipping either because he had a false confidence that the *Graham's* text had been well printed or because he had lost interest in the piece. If the latter is the reason, "Earth's Holocaust" would join the early "Roger Malvin's Burial" and "Mrs. Bullfrog," which were not reviewed for the 1846 *Mosses*.

In general, Hawthorne was less interested in the early works he had inserted to fill the collection than in his later pieces. "Young Goodman Brown" may have two small revisions (unless these were compositorial), at 85.15 and 87.15, but that is all. The three available manuscripts for earlier printed pieces offer little evidence to assess Hawthorne's typical annotation of copy for the 1846 edition. A further difficulty appears in that the indifferent variants (constituting the majority of the differences) from copy in 1846 that are compositorial are not always easy to distinguish from possible Hawthorne corrections and revisions, particularly because Hawthorne did not read the proof for these volumes.[7]

We have only one real control to evaluate the general fidelity of 1846 *Mosses* to its copy—the introductory "The Old Manse" set from manuscript but not proofread. This piece comes off very badly indeed, there being no less than thirty-seven compositorial substantive variants in its thirty-

[7] On April 15, 1846, Hawthorne posted the manuscript of "The Old Manse" to Duyckinck and remarked, "I shall feel anxious about the accuracy of the press, in relation to this article, and therefore beg you to send me the proof-sheets of it." On April 30, he complained, "The proof-sheet has not yet made its appearance" (MSS, Duyckinck Collection, New York Public Library). The rest is conjecture. That Hawthorne did not specify proofs for pieces from the magazines but only for the manuscript essay would seem to indicate that he trusted the proofreaders to take care of the pieces already once printed. The lack of further mention of proofs for "The Old Manse," and the large number of errors in the 1846 printing, suggest that proofs were never sent Hawthorne; his corrections of a few of the more obvious misprints in three presentation copies of *Mosses* (see the Bibliographical Information, p. 561) supply further evidence. In 1854 Hawthorne was able to return over a third of the original readings; see below, p. 548.

one pages of text as printed in 1846. One notes the difficulty between singulars and plurals that had afflicted "Earth's Holocaust" in "fragment" for MS "fragments" (8.20), a tinkering with usage as in "An humbler" for Hawthorne's "A humbler" (9.3), the false correction of 10.8 "have" to "has", 14.4 "nor" to "or", 30.5 "afflicts" to "afflict", and a shifting of 20.10 "writer's" to the plural genitive. There is betrayed an insistence not only on number and concord but on parallel structure as at 33.2 "nor have ever" changed to "nor have I ever", and on agreements of verbs as at 33.9, where "hastened" is changed to "hasten" and the meaning quite altered. Some variants are simple misreadings of Hawthorne's script, as "country" for "county" (9.26), "any" for "airy" (14.11), "substance" for "subsistence" (10.29), "lonely" for "lovely" (21.34), "where" for "whence" (25.20), "severe" for "serene" (30.14), and "cleared" for "cleaned" (33.20). Some differences are difficult to account for on simple grounds of misreading but may represent free substitution when the MS did not seem entirely legible: "beautified" for "beautiful" (7.21), "floating" for "flung" (28.26). But "improvement" of the text may, instead, be behind such variants as "speculations" for "ejaculations" (17.12) or "magic" for "tranquil" (29.19). One cannot expect the same fidelity in setting from manuscript as in setting from printed copy; nevertheless, the record of the 1846 compositor(s) of "The Old Manse" is a disturbing one, for almost every variant makes sufficient sense and indeed might have caused trouble for an editor if the external circumstances had not, fortunately, forbidden the possibility of authority in these 1846 variants. Hawthorne does not seem to have read the proof for this piece, nor for the rest of the collection. It is demonstrable, however, that the proofreading at the printing shop or editorial office left much to be desired, and it does not give one confidence in the care taken with the rest of the volume where fewer errors might have been anticipated owing to the nature of the copy.

At any rate, the lack of fidelity to copy in setting from manuscript exemplified in "The Old Manse" appears to be repeated in "Earth's Holocaust," where some assumptions can be made about the extent of the error since the manuscript is also present as a control. The degree of error in the 1846 setting of "Earth's Holocaust" is relatively independent of any possible marking of the clipping by Hawthorne. It may reflect the work of some inferior compositor: certainly, not all texts have been similarly corrupted in 1846 although others exhibit the same trail of errors. For example, there is no evidence that Hawthorne touched the copy for "Mrs. Bullfrog"; yet in its eight-and-a-half pages in 1846 the compositor "corrects" the colloquial grammar in dialogue of 134.9 "broke" to "broken", drops the article "a" from the phrase "like a calves foot jelly" (133.9), and removes the inversion in "did she" (134.22). In the twenty-three pages of "Roger Malvin's Burial" the compositor, again setting from printed copy, sophisticated the verbs by returning to the indicative when Hawthorne had written in the subjunctive (355.16) "die . . . lie" changed to "dies . . . lies", perhaps misunderstood the sense in substituting "former" for "foremost" (341.35), and altered the tense of 346.15 "shrank" to "shrink", removed the relative pronoun "that" (357.26), adjusted usage in changing 344.19 "her have" to "her to have", misunderstood the syntax in omitting "or" (346.6), blatantly interfered with the vocabulary by substituting "shadows" for "shades" (357.22) and carelessly changed "backward" (353.30) to "backwards". The error "bow" for "bough" at 360.10 may be a misunderstanding or some form of memorial lapse. Given the length of the story this total of nine variants does not compare with the proportion in "Earth's Holocaust," also set from printed copy but much more corrupted.

Owing to the impossibility of distinguishing the work of the compositors who set the 1846 volumes, a marked disproportion between different sketches in the number of variants from magazine copy need not have a mechanical origin, always,[8] for Hawthorne himself gave quite unequal attention to different pieces.

Certainly a firm line can be drawn between the complete lack of alteration in the early "Mrs. Bullfrog," "Roger Malvin's Burial," or "Earth's Holocaust," and the cuts in "The Hall of Fantasy," the additions in "A Virtuoso's Collection," or in the copy of "The Procession of Life." [9] But when the question is stylistic—one of distinguishing between Hawthorne's correction and minor revision of the periodical clippings, and the compositorial departures from copy that the controls indicate may be expected from at least one workman—quantity of variation is not necessarily evidence, as may be observed in "Earth's Holocaust." Moreover, attention given a story in 1854 is not necessarily a sign of any particular interest in 1846. A touched-up clause in "Drowne's Wooden Image," for example, at 311.16–17, does not necessarily indicate continuing interest in the story, for only three small verbal variants (311.19, 313.11, and 315.18) accompany it. Although a few manifest errors of *Godey's Lady's Book* are corrected in this story in 1846, like 307.33 "Carrara" for "Carrera", 309.15 "Town" for "Tower" and 309.30 "act" for "fact", what may be revisions are freely mixed with 1846 errors. It is clear that the frequent difficulty with singulars and plurals observed in "The Old Manse" is seen again here in the 1846 "image" for magazine "images" (310.15), and other mistakes occur like "perplexing" for "perplexed" (314.32) and the loss of "his" from "of his friend" (319.24).

8 The clustering of variants toward the end of "Earth's Holocaust" may reflect a change of compositors, although the earlier part is higher in error than it should be.

9 See the Textual Note 207–22 on "The Procession of Life."

A number of substitutions not clearly compositorial suggest that in the 1846 copy, the author has been at work here and there, but invariably to distinguish his touch from compositorial substitutions is not an easy task. Given the occasional omission of necessary words elsewhere in 1846, as indeed at 319.24 in this tale, is the omission of Godey's "very" at 306.18 authorial or compositorial? Is 1846 "do" for "would" at 307.1 a contamination from the preceding phrase "do my best", or an authorial touching-up? In this case the repeated "do" is so awkward as to lead one to guess that it is an error; but a question remains whether the compositor objected at 309.4 to "workmanship" and substituted the more literal "image" (on the analogy of "image" at 310.15 but especially at 308.19). The reference to "morning" at 309.14 goes back to the opening line at 306.1 and hence might not seem clear to a compositor who had forgotten it; but was it he or Hawthorne who substituted "moment"? Since the controls, and the other texts, exhibit a shifting back and forth between "a" and "the", one might readily guess that 1846 "a sculptor's rules" (313.22) is not likely to be authorial when Godey's reads "the". Yet the harder reading "transfixed . . . in" (316.6) seems more likely to be Hawthorne's than the conventional "transformed . . . with" of the magazine, and so does "now astounded" (315.22) for Godey's "now to be astonished". Demonstration is scarcely possible whether 1846 "muttered" (313.32) or Godey's "murmured" is one or the other although conjecture may assign it to Hawthorne. On the other hand, the omission of "all" (314.33) serves no useful purpose and appears a line below the clearcut error in 1846 of "perplexing" for "perplexed" (314.32); this is simpler to assign to the compositor than the omission of "very" before "fellow" (306.18). The omission of "being" from "but, quenched" (320.3–4) certainly improves the syntactical logic by referring "quenched in disappointment" to

Drowne and not, as originally, to "a brief season". One hopes Hawthorne would have recognized the anomaly of his original construction. Yet although the substitution of "Who" for "What" at 316.10 sharpens the reference, and is a natural change, at least one of the compositors was a stickler for literal grammar and might have been the agent as easily as Hawthorne. Of the twenty-two substantive variants in this tale, then, aside from three obvious corrections, seven are almost certainly compositorial, eight are probably authorial, and four remain in reasonable doubt. For them—at a minimum—it is an open question whether the 1846 text of this story can be thought to have enough general authority for an editor to follow the revised version in such doubtful cases (as has in fact been done) instead of the original.

It is unfortunate that Hawthorne's copy-reading for the preparation of the Ticknor and Fields edition of *Mosses* produced no more return to the original readings in "Drowne's Wooden Image" as a guide, than that of "his" at 319.24, "What" at 316.10, and "images" at 310.15. Copy for the 1854 edition was the Wiley and Putnam edition of 1846, marked up by Hawthorne in England. On April 13, 1854, he wrote Fields from Liverpool, "I return the copy sent me, after a careful revision." He asked Fields to find "Rappaccini's Daughter" in its *Democratic Review* appearance, and to decide if the preface there should be returned to the story. On June 7, Hawthorne wrote to Ticknor, who had asked for additional matter, that he could suggest only one story, "Feathertop," but told him to search through *New-England Magazine* for uncollected parts of the old "Story Teller" project, and for other travel sketches.[10] These

[10] Hawthorne to Fields, MS, Huntington Library; to Ticknor, MS, Berg Collection, New York Public Library. Hawthorne had confidence in Fields's taste and sometimes delegated proofreading to him although not with any general authority to revise. To Ticknor, Hawthorne wrote, "If I

additions appear, in the 1854 *Mosses*, as "Passages from a Relinquished Work," the association suggested by Hawthorne in his letter to Ticknor, and, as originally titled, "Sketches from Memory." As for the question of proofs having been sent him in England, other letters from Hawthorne to Ticknor exist, of April 30, May 5, May 12, June 16, June 23, June 27, July 7, July 20, and August 3.[11] No mention of proofs occurs in this correspondence, which Ticknor seems to have preserved carefully. Since stereotyping was dated August 15, insufficient time remained after the June 7 letter asking for the copy search, for the typesetting, the minimum of a month for the round trip from Boston to Liverpool, and the reading itself.

It is clear from the internal evidence as well as his statement to Fields in the April 13 letter, that Hawthorne thought he had performed the duty of preparing printer's copy quite conscientiously. No copy-changes appear in "Mrs. Bullfrog" or in "Fire-Worship," nor can any be assigned to "Feathertop," "Passages from a Relinquished Work," "Sketches from Memory," or the preface to "Rappaccini's Daughter." Elsewhere, corrections were erratic. In the prefatory "The Old Manse," which he was correcting for the first time in 1854 after having observed errors in the 1846 printing and marked several in presentation copies, he made at the most ten revisions of joint MS-1846 readings; but he did manage to correct fifteen of the 1846 errors even though he passed over twenty-one further errors without notice, some of these serious ones such as "substance" for "subsistence" at 10.29, "rummage them" for "rummage among them" at 19.30, "blessed" for "blissful" at 27.30, "severe" for "serene" at 30.14, and

---

had the Magazine at hand, I could patch up an article in five minutes; and Fields can do it just as well, and without any trouble at all. If he should already have sailed, Whipple will doubtless do it."

11 MSS, Berg Collection, New York Public Library.

"cleared" for "cleaned" at 33.20. Corrections in 1854 of 1846 errors could occur only if Hawthorne by chance recalled his original phrase or found that the 1846 reading grated on his ear for style or sense. Although they are in the minority in "The Old Manse," he did weed out a number of 1846 errors;[12] and of course when 1854 confirms the periodical source in other sketches by returning to it from the 1846 variant one has a particularly valuable test for authority, whether the 1854 decision was advertent or inadvertent. Thus in "Young Goodman Brown," which had scarcely been touched in 1846, the 1854 text restores four substantive readings (75.22, 77.6, 85.15, and 87.15), makes the revision at 86.10 of "figure" for "apparition"; an almost certain sophistication of "or" for "nor" at 82.3 and another probable one in changing the singular possessive "widow's" at 87.12 to the plural possessive. In "Buds and Bird-Voices," if "or" for 1846 "nor" at 149.3 is a grammatical "correction" by the printer, Hawthorne made only one change in 1854, substituting "always" for "only" following "flourish" at 151.14 to avoid a repetition, although this change was possibly compositorial as well. If it were not for the correction in "Monsieur du Miroir" of 1846 "Lado" to "Ladurlad" at 164.9, the 1854 sophistications "last" for "least" at 161.23 and "mysterious" for "mysteries" at 171.13 might well throw more doubt on the authority of "delusive" for 1846 "illusive" at 170.19 (see the Textual Note). In "The Celestial Rail-road" the confusion between conductor and engineer is straightened out at 190.9 and 190.27, though not at 189.30; the MS readings "by making" (186.8), "a truthful" (194.25), and "into" (197.2) are restored for 1846 "to make", "truthful", and "in"; but the questionable 1846 variant from MS "in the

[12] See the Historical Collation: 5.27, 7.21, 8.20, 9.3, 14.11, 17.12, 17.17, 18.11, 20.10, 21.34, 25.20, 27.20, 29.19, 33.9, and 33.15.

dispute" (188.9) to "in a dispute" and the omission of "that" (190.21) are repeated, along with other 1846 variants from MS that may or may not be authorial, with particular reference to the suspicious "in a dispute". The 1854 "fatten them" for idiomatic MS "fat them" (197.4) is probably compositorial. In "The Procession of Life" the record is a sorry one when 1854 follows seven 1846 errors,[13] corrects only two (211.5 and 221.14) and offers only three revisions, at 219.12, 221.11, and 222.13.

"Rappaccini's Daughter" was given more of what can properly be called stylistic revision in 1854 than any other piece. Here "Lombard" was corrected to "Paduan", "the" to "this", "with" to "withal", "in" to "was", "should . . . have" to "ought . . . to have", "under" to "if taught by", "the heart" to "the depths of the heart", "Giovanni" to "he" and "his" to "Giovanni's", "borders" to "borders of Time", and "hand" to "hands".[14] At 109.2 the relative pronoun "that" was inserted, probably by authority; and a misleading punctuation adjusted at 125.16 from a probable compositorial misreading in the first setting of Hawthorne's script exclamation as a question mark. Twice the 1846 reading was returned to the magazine form: the added "very" of 1846 was deleted from "shuddered nervously" at 127.2–3, and the error "perfume" was returned to "perfumed" at 97.31. It is probable that the 1854 indicative "comes" for Hawthorne's conditional "come" at 115.10 is an error, and one can be suspicious of the usual printer's alteration of characteristic "nor" at 103.24 to "or". Not all of the sketches exhibit this special interest evinced in "Rappaccini's Daughter," for the differentiation seems to show that his marking of copy in 1854 was guided, much like that in 1846,

13 See the Historical Collation: 207.3, 210.11, 213.31, 215.29, 216.11, 219.3–4, and 219.21.

14 At 94.2, 96.5, 100.16, 102.6, 105.7, 111.19, 112.10, 114.29, 114.31, 126.8, and 126.33.

by his continuing rapport with the story rather than a more general desire to insure correctness throughout.[15]

The exceptional care given "Rappaccini's Daughter," "The Christmas Banquet," and "The Procession of Life" in 1846 is in marked contrast to the treatment of other stories, and it provides a relatively good example of the general authority of the 1854 variants that Hawthorne marked in the 1846 copy. That the 1854 edition was set with greater fidelity than was the 1846 edition can be confirmed by the few controls that are available for material added in 1854 and not overseen by Hawthorne. For example, no substantive variants appear in the preface to "Rappaccini's Daughter." In "Feathertop" three typos occur—"Rgiby" for "Rigby" (226.26), "mild" for "mile" (224.16), and "-flabs" for "-flaps" (225.14), this last a faithful reproduction of the 1846 copy. In "Passages from a Relinquished Work," "and a wise" (406.17) becomes "and wise"; "dry-good" (410.6) is modernized to "dry goods", as had also been the case in "The New Adam and Eve" at 251.4; "clarinet" replaced "clarionet" (419.22), and "cue" supplanted "queue" (420.12). In "Sketches from Memory," "a corner" at 425.12 becomes "the corner" and 437.27 "hat" becomes "cap" in what is perhaps an editorial change. The record of the substantives in following copy is excellent. However, some errors do appear that might not have been present had Hawthorne read the proofs.

[15] In Hawthorne's April 13 letter to Fields, avouching (not altogether accurately) that he had given the copy "a careful revision;" he continued: "When I wrote those dreamy sketches, I little thought that I should ever prepare an edition for the press amidst the bustling life of a Liverpool consul. Upon my honor, I am not quite sure that I entirely comprehend my own meaning in some of these blasted allegories; but I remember that I always had a meaning—or, at least, thought I had. I am a good deal changed since those times; and to tell you the truth, my past self is not very much to my taste, as I see myself in this book. Yet certainly there is more in it than the public generally gave me credit for, at the time it was written. But I don't think myself worthy of very much more credit than I got. It has been a very disagreeable task to read the book."

From this survey of typical transmission of copy from manuscript to journal, from journal to the 1846 edition, and from 1846 to 1854, several general assumptions can be formulated that have a bearing on the editorial treatment of the texts. The magazines are of mixed quality in their fidelity, as shown by the four examples where a manuscript is available to serve as a control, or when Hawthorne in 1846 set himself to correct the clippings—as for "Rappaccini's Daughter" or "The Procession of Life"—for the press. The general inference is that ordinarily he did not read proof for magazine publication. Whether or not the relatively extensive alterations in the 1846 "Rappaccini's Daughter" or "The Procession of Life" mean that he had not read proof for these tales in the *Democratic Review* but had done so for at least some of the others first printed in this journal to which less attention was given in 1846 is not to be determined. The evidence of the further revision made in "Rappaccini's Daughter" in 1854 suggests, on the contrary, that no conjectures should be made from the evidence of 1846 alterations and instead that his current interest in a story was the chief determinant in whether he went over it with any particular care. The marking of magazine clippings for 1846 was erratic; perhaps something of value to a critic can be drawn from the evidence about his treatment of special stories in the collection as reflecting his own views about the literary quality of the work. Early tales he was inclined to slide over, whereas a few of the later and apparently favorite pieces engaged his closer attention. In general the alterations he made for 1846 were corrections and minor stylistic revisions, but the special nature of the material in "Monsieur du Miroir" and "The Hall of Fantasy" led to extensive cuts; only in "A Virtuoso's Collection" was new material added. In no case was any piece recast and rewritten. It is just possible to speculate that to some limited extent, also, the amount of care he expended in 1846 was governed by his confidence in the carefulness of the magazine's printing of his manuscripts; if so, his confidence was misplaced in "Earth's Holocaust" published in *Graham's*.

For the 1846 edition Hawthorne marked the printer's copy but did not see the proofs. For 1854 the position was the same since (in England) he read over a copy of the 1846 edition and gave it what he stated to be a careful reading but one that on the evidence was as erratic as his correction of copy for 1846 and governed by substantially the same principles.

In each case, the earliest known example has been chosen as Centenary copy-text, the manuscript when available but otherwise the periodical publications. These last are closer by one step than 1846 to the accidentals of the lost manuscripts; and in respect to these have a textual authority which though far from absolute is yet superior to the reprints in the two book collections.[16] Into the accidental texture of these copy-texts are inserted the substantive variants from 1846 and then 1854 that appear to represent Hawthorne's own intentional and authoritative markings of the 1846 printer's copy and later, in 1854, of the 1846 volume insofar as these markings can be identified. Certain principles govern this selection. When controls are present as in the manuscript of "The Old Manse," the extremely careless nature of the 1846 typesetting is clearly revealed. That this compositorial corruption of copy was not confined to such a work set from manuscript but could be equally present from time to time in work set from printed copy can be demonstrated in "Earth's Holocaust," where a manuscript is also present as evidence.

[16] In relatively few cases is it possible to distinguish what may be occasional Hawthorne alterations of the accidentals in 1846 and 1854 from the respective house stylings which overlay the texture, each of which would have occurred after he had approved of the printer's copy.

It would seem, therefore, that the 1846 edition is not corrupt throughout but has its degrees of corruption probably concentrated in the work of one compositor, whose areas of typesetting, however, cannot be strictly delimited by any bibliographical evidence.

Since Hawthorne did not see proof for 1846, he had no opportunity to repair the damage, except as was presented to him in 1854 when his memory of the pieces was far dimmer and he confessed himself often out of sympathy with what he had earlier written. The 1854 copy-alterations are scarcely so extensive or valuable as they would have been if performed in 1846, and on the evidence it is clear that they by no means remove all the textual corruption that penetrated the 1846 edition along with Hawthorne's own authoritative markings of the printer's copy. No infallible tests exist to distinguish authority from corruption in these mixed 1846 readings when they are not in turn altered in 1854. Certain common classes of error can be isolated and rejected with relative consistency, such as the switches between singulars and plurals and the reverse, as well as the confusion of "a" and "the". An omitted word is often suspicious. The more indifferent the variant in 1846 that does not agree with Hawthorne's known stylistic characteristics, the more likely it is to be compositorial and to be rejected. Clusters of suspicious variants within a group of pages or within a story make the tests for relatively neutral variation in the same area the more severe. In general, although it is demonstrable that for most stories Hawthorne did indeed correct and revise the printer's copy, the evidence suggests that it would be dangerous in the extreme to rely for decision on the general authority of 1846 as a revised edition. Instead, each variant must be viewed on its merits but with the editorial requirement that it should have some positive evidence in its favor other than its appearance in 1846 if it is to be accepted as authoritative. Such positive evidence rests on the critical assessment of the variant as conforming to Hawthorne's known preferences, and in some part on the evaluation of the amount of correction and revision that the text suggests he gave to any individual story. As with "Rappaccini's Daughter," when the text indicates that it was set by one of the better 1846 compositors and that a number of clearly authoritative revisions are present, a considerable majority may be accepted. In contrast, the known views that Hawthorne had about such inferior work as "Mrs. Bullfrog," and the negative evidence of the variants themselves, suggest that no 1846 difference is acceptable in such a story, despite the relatively clean typesetting. In a sketch like "The Procession of Life," which we know he marked with care, the very large number of variants in 1846 calls for special scrutiny; and when it can be shown that some differ in their kind from the authoritative variants in, say, "Rappaccini's Daughter," and that most of these show the kinds of corruption theoretically to be associated with the work of an inferior compositor, the presence of authorial revisions in the copy does not prevent the rejection of a considerable number of readings according to their association with the categories of error found elsewhere.

The case is altered for the majority of the variants in the 1854 edition. The evidence from control texts that the 1854 typesetting was much more faithful to copy than that of 1846—especially in the bad patches in 1846—promotes the general reliability of its variation, as does the internal evidence of the variants themselves, with especial relation to the occasional ones that restore the earlier readings from the corruption of 1846. That 1854 is not impeccable goes without saying, and an occasional sophistication can be detected, as remarked.[17] But on the whole the 1854 substantive differ-

---

[17] See also "lightest" for "slightest" (55.4), "with which" for "of which" (60.31), "sharply" for "sharp" (133.18), "last" for "least" (161.23), "mys-

ences from 1846 appear to be authorially based, and thus they have ordinarily been accepted on their merits as well as on the background evidence that gives 1854 a general authority. However, the agreement of 1854 with an 1846 variant is no confirmation whatever of the authority of the 1846 change and has had no effect on the editor's evaluation of the 1846 reading. Hawthorne's copy-reading in 1854 was by no means so informed that he could be expected to detect more than a few plausible corruptions of the original periodical, transmitted through 1846, when the materials lay in the distant past and were not available for consultation. It is surprising, indeed, that consciously or not he recognized and changed back to their original form as many 1846 variants as he did.

Since the copy-text for most of the tales exists only in printed form and has already been styled by a printing house to remove mechanical lapses in the lost manuscripts, not very many changes need making in the accidentals. The punctuation is acceptable with but few exceptions, and insofar as Hawthorne's characteristic spellings were reproduced in the periodicals they have been retained, although no effort has been made to secure uniformity between the various tales in respect to recognized variant spellings: each copy-text is treated as independent and has not been altered unless it is internally variant and a choice to normalization is thus possible on evidence contained within the individual copy-text. Some small amount of capitalization to restore Hawthorne's personifications has been indulged in, however, as a form of independent emendation. Whenever possible, documentary authority is avouched; but it must be

---

terious" for "mysteries" (171.13), and "to sell" for "of selling" (442.11). On the evidence of Hawthorne's preference for "nor" as late as *The Marble Faun*, the 1854 changes to "or" at 82.3, 103.24, and 461.29, must be removed from authority.

understood that in all such cases the documents need not have authority in the readings and the choice of personification is, in actuality, an independent editorial one when it appears in an unauthoritative document—meaning one that Hawthorne is not supposed to have corrected substantively—just as much as if no document witnessed the emended reading.

The result is an eclectic text that within the limitations of the documentary evidence attempts to purify the basic copy-texts, as well as the two revised editions, of error and to include the authoritative readings which Hawthorne inserted as revisions in the 1846 and the 1854 printer's copy insofar as bibliographical logic guiding critical assessment can succeed in establishing authority among some hundreds of variants.

The English editions have no separate authority and hence are not represented in the collations, nor do any American editions after 1854 contain further authorial revision.

In this collection, copy-texts have general authority for accidentals, and substantive emendations are judged by the authority of their sources; editorial corrections reject printer's errors presumably missed by Hawthorne in his reviews, and return his characteristic spellings when misreading or house-styling is considered the agent of variance. Normalizations of spelling, capitalization, and word-division are made in the individual texts by use of the prevailing form. Hawthorne's undifferentiated use of "further" and "farther" is kept, and his spelling is modernized only when the obsolete would confuse the sense. A full statement of editorial principles is included in the first four volumes of the Centenary Edition.

F. B.

BIBLIOGRAPHICAL INFORMATION

T HE FOLLOWING INFORMATION is in two sections, the first dealing with the editions of *Mosses from an Old Manse*, and the second with the histories of individual tales and sketches in the collections.

I

Publication of the first edition of *Mosses from an Old Manse*, according to the Library of Congress copyright deposit copy, was on June 5, 1846. Volume I contains all the pieces from "The Old Manse" through "The Procession of Life," and volume II "The New Adam and Eve" through "A Virtuoso's Collection." (In 1854, "Feathertop" was added to the first volume and "Passages from a Relinquished Work" and "Sketches from Memory" were placed following "Earth's Holocaust" within the second.) The *Wiley and Putnam's Literary Newsletter* (October, 1846), p. 79, lists *Mosses* at $1.25 in the two-volumes-in-one, clothbound issue, or $1.00 in paper (50¢ per volume, the price printed on the wrapper).

First Printing, American Issue

MOSSES | FROM | AN OLD MANSE. | BY NA-
THANIEL HAWTHORNE. | IN TWO PARTS. |
PART I. [PART II.] | NEW YORK: | WILEY AND
PUTNAM. | [short rule] | 1846.

I: [1]²⁺¹ 2–9¹² 10⁶ [11]², also signed at \$5r; sig. [1]
is a folio and a singleton tipped in to sig. 21r; 107 leaves;
pp. [i–vi] [1] 2–207 [208]; p. i has the series half-title
(p. ii blank); p. iii is the title page; p. iv: '[rule]
ENTERED according to Act of Congress, in the year
1846, by | WILEY & PUTNAM, | In the Clerk's
Office of the District Court for the Southern District
of New York. | [rule] | [brace to the left: wavy rule] |
R. CRAIGHEAD's Power Press, | 112 Fulton Street. |
[brace to the right: wavy rule] | T. B. SMITH, Stereo-
typer, | 216 William Street.'; the contents are listed on
p. v (p. vi blank); pp. 1–207 have the text, with p. 208
blank.

II: [1]²⁺¹ 2–9¹² 10⁶ [11–12]²; also signed at \$5r; sig.
[1] is a folio and a singleton tipped in to sig. 21r; 109
leaves; pp. [i–vi] [1] 2–211 [212]; series half-title is
on p. i (p. ii blank); p. iii is the title page; p. iv has the
copyright notice and imprint, as vol. I; the contents are
listed on p. v (p. vi blank); pp. 1–211 have the text (p.
212 blank).

Although the paper wrappers belong to the binding and
are not integral to the printed sheets, bibliographers have
traditionally distinguished "issues" of the book by noting
wrapper variants and the appearance or omission of printers
and stereotypers on the copyright pages of the text.[1]

[1] Prominent among bibliographers dealing with the question are Wallace
Hugh Cathcart, in *Bibliography of the Works of Nathaniel Hawthorne*

The wrappers, as the text, were printed from stereotype plates. No variants have been seen in the inside front and rear covers, but the outside front cover exists in two states and the outside rear cover in five states, requiring new stereotype plates for each variant state.

Outside front cover, state 1: first line of text has "and hoping well, . . . "; second line has "them-"; vertical measurement from "PART I." to "NEW YORK AND LONDON." is 3/4 inch.

Outside front cover, state 2: first line of text has "and hoping well . . . "; second line has "them"; vertical measurement from "PART I." to "NEW YORK AND LONDON." is 5/8 inch.

Five states of the outside rear wrapper can be distinguished as follows:

state 1: volumes I–X of Wiley and Putnam's Library of American Books listed; five titles "In Preparation."

state 2: volumes I–XVI listed; five titles "In Immediate Preparation."

state 3: volumes I–XVIII listed; no titles in preparation (*BAL* 7598, state A).

state 4: volumes I–XX listed (*BAL* 7598, state B).

state 5: volumes I–XXII listed (*BAL* 7598, state C).

It was the custom of Wiley and Putnam's Library of

(Cleveland, 1905), p. 29, and in *First Editions of the Works of Nathaniel Hawthorne . . . Exhibited at the Grolier Club* (New York, 1905), p. 25; Richard Curle, *Collecting American First Editions* (Indianapolis, 1930), pp. 154–55; Carroll A. Wilson, *Thirteen Author Collections of the Nineteenth Century* (New York, 1950), p. 138; Jacob Blanck, *A Bibliography of American Literature* (New Haven and London, 1963), IV, item 7598; and Merle Johnson, *Merle Johnson's American First Editions* (Waltham, Mass., 1965), 4th ed., p. 222. Taken together, their accounts contain enough contradictions, varied interpretations of the evidence, and shifting definitions of terms to warrant a close examination of the relationship between wrapper states and printings of the text.

American Books to update wrapper advertisements with each new publication. Updating of the rear plate of the *Mosses* wrappers to state 3, the first to include volumes XVII and XVIII, *Mosses* itself, apparently did not occur until after a few wrappers with *Mosses* on the front cover had been printed. The more common state of the front wrapper is state 1 (only three copies of state 2 have been seen); the most common state of the rear wrapper is state 3 (only one copy each of states 1 and 2 have been seen). Pairing of outside front and rear wrapper plates was done at the discretion of the printer, who filled bindery orders as needed; no priority should be assigned to a particular combination.[2] The distinction between states of the wrappers as binding variants only and variants in the printed sheets of the text must be maintained.

Printing distinctions in the text of the two volumes for copies with the title-page date 1846 are based on four kinds of evidence: copyright notice and imprint; collational formula; presence or absence of integral advertisements in volume II, sig. 10; and type-batter in each volume. Each printing and issue will be treated separately, with the evidence for every distinction presented fully.[3]

[2] A copy with state 2 front wrappers, at Princeton University, for example, is paired with state 4 rear wrappers in both volumes, bound to a second printing of the text, while a copy in the Berg Collection, New York Public Library, pairs a state 2 front with a state 5 rear wrapper in volume II, bound to a first printing of the text.

[3] Thirty-four copies of volume I and thirty-two of volume II, identifiable on all points as first printing, American issue, have been examined. These are at the Berg Collection, New York Public Library (seven copies of volume I and eight of volume II), Yale University (four of volume I and three of volume II), the Library of Congress (two of volume I and one of volume II), Concord, Mass., Public Library (two of volume I and one of volume II), five of both volumes each at the Houghton Library, Harvard University, and Ohio State University, two of both volumes each at Rare Books Division, New York Public Library, Washington University, St. Louis, Mo., and the University of Virginia, and one of both volumes each at the Ohio Historical Society, Columbus, the Essex Institute, Salem, and the University of Pennsylvania.

Hawthorne wrote to E. A. Duyckinck on April 30, 1846, to order ten complimentary copies of the first printing for distribution among friends.[4] While these copies did not pass through Hawthorne's hands, other presentation copies, signed by him, exist in various collections. Three of the latter, all of the first printing, American issue, inscribed to George S. Hillard (in the Berg Collection, New York Public Library), Ralph Waldo Emerson, and Sarah B. Shaw (in the Houghton Library, Harvard University), have pencilled hand-cancels in Hawthorne's autograph, all in the text of "The Old Manse," the essay he had not seen in proof.

The Emerson and Shaw copies have two similar hand-cancels: I, 19.6, "n" in "lonely" cancelled and "v/" written in the margin; and I, 26.12, the second "magic" in the line cancelled and "tranquil" written in the margin. The Hillard copy has these cancels and adds a third: I, 24.17, a caret between "now." and "It", and a paragraph symbol written in the margin. The first two cancels return the readings to manuscript, and the return was made by Hawthorne in marking printer's copy for the 1854 Ticknor and Fields edition. The paragraph indention, however, appears neither in manuscript nor in the 1854 edition. Hawthorne either forgot about it or changed his mind back to the manuscript paragraphing when correcting copy in 1854.[5]

First Printing, English Issue

MOSSES | FROM | AN OLD MANSE. | BY NATHANIEL HAWTHORNE. | IN TWO PARTS.

[4] MS, Duyckinck Collection, New York Public Library.

[5] Another copy in the Berg Collection, New York Public Library, inscribed to Robert Manning, has no hand-cancels. A survey of all major library holdings has failed to turn up further examples. Other copies having Hawthorne's corrections, clear demonstrations of his concern for the accuracy of his texts, may well exist.

| PART I. [PART II.] | LONDON: | WILEY &
PUTNAM, 6, WATERLOO PLACE. | [short rule] |
1846. | [ENTERED AT STATIONERS' HALL.]
Title page is a cancel (verso blank), inserted between
the series half-title and the contents leaves; collation,
pagination, and contents are otherwise as first printing,
American issue.

Note: Two advertisements for the English issue, in
the *Literary Gazette* of July 11 and *Publisher's Circular*
of July 15, indicate that approximately five weeks
elapsed between publication of the American issue and
shipment of sheets to London, printing of the cancel
title leaf, and binding in two volumes, cloth only (no
copies of the English issue have been seen in paper
wrappers out of twenty-four copies examined in various
libraries).

Because the American and English issues were bound in
their respective countries, the sheets show two methods of
opening. The American sheets were opened conventionally
by cutting across the outside edges, but the English sheets
were opened signature-by-signature, by slicing from within
the outer folds. Thus English-issue copies show which leaves
had been conjugal at the outside before opening. This page-
edge evidence is sufficient to narrow the imposition formula
for the first printing of sigs. 2–9 of both volumes to a sheet
of twelves, work-and-turn (either Savage #23 or #24).[6] This
formula would require a sheet size of at least 21 3/4 by 20
inches, each leaf being 7 1/4 by 5 inches. Page-edge evidence
is insufficient to show the imposition of I, sigs. [1], 10, and
[11], and II, sigs. [1], 10, [11–12], totalling twenty-four

[6] William Savage, *A Dictionary of the Art of Printing* (London, 1841),
p. 340.

leaves. How these were divided into twelve-leaf sheets can only be conjectured.

An anomaly in the weight of the paper in I, sig. 10 only, in four of twenty-eight copies calibrated, may show part of the sequence of imposition.[7] Thickness of the paper in all other signatures was calibrated at .004–.005 inches, but sig. 10 in these four copies measured .006–.007 inches, a difference easily verifiable by the texture and relative stiffness of the paper. Paper-weight variation is not insignificant because it requires press adjustment. That this variant shows up in hardbound copies of the American issue only may mean that, during the run of the last sheet imposed (sig. 10 of volume I), the pressman exhausted the paper stock and, rather than hold up printing, adjusted the press for a heavier stock to finish the run. Thus I, sig. 10, a six-leaf gathering, comprised half of the last sheet to be imposed; the other six leaves of the gathering consisted of II, sig. 10, I, sig. [11] and II, sigs. [11 and 12], sig. [1] of both volumes, or—a fourth and remote possibility—duplicate plates of I, sig. 10. At any rate, the paper variant points to the possibility that the earliest sheets imposed went to England and later sheets became the American issue.

Second Printing

Title is as first printing, American issue, in both volumes; copyright notice and imprint, as first printing in volume I; in II the page is blank. Collation and pagination of volume I are also at first printing; volume II collates [1]$^{2+1}$ 2–9^{12} 10^{12}; II, 212: 'NEW AND VAL-

[7] All four copies are hardbound American issues of the first printing, at Ohio State University. Copies checked in other collections did not have the anomaly.

UABLE | BOOKS, | PUBLISHED BY | WILEY AND PUTNAM. | NEW YORK: | [short rule] | 1846.' II, sig. 10 has two leaves of ads following p. 212; copies have been seen with the final leaf or final two leaves excised before binding.

Machine collation of eight copies dated 1846, both volumes, at Ohio State University, revealed 41 examples of type-batter within the printings of volume I, and 31 examples within volume II. For purposes of distinguishing printings, only one example from each gathering showing new batter in that printing is listed here:

I, [1], [iii].5	PARTS $_\wedge$
I, 2, 17.7	ser $_\wedge$
I, 3, 28.1	fire
I, 5, 81.2	heart
I, 6, 104.1	been
I, 7, 121.29–30	biscuits . . . merely
I, 8, 155.1	scrape
I, 9, 180.33	blasted
II, 2, 3.33	it
II, 3, 36.29	heard
II, 4, 50.33	it
II, 5, 72.33	than
II, 6, 100.32	had
II, 7, 141.0	141
II, 8, 161.5	energetic,

Type-batter alone distinguishes the first and second printings of volume I. That the two were made close together is evidenced by three copies observed of the one-volume, hard-cover binding that mix a first printing of one volume with a second printing of the other.[8]

[8] These are at Yale University, Georgetown University, and the Library of Congress. Otherwise, nine copies of both volumes identified as second

Third Printing

The title page is as first printing in both volumes. Copyright notice in volume I is as first printing; imprint has the stereotyper, Smith, only. Volume II has no copyright notice; a reset imprint has '[brace to the left, wavy rule] | WILLIAM OSBORN, PRINTER, | TRIBUNE BUILDINGS. | [brace to the right, wavy rule] | T. B. SMITH, STEREOTYPER | 216 WILLIAM STREET.' Collation of Vol. I is $[1]^{2+1}$ 2–9^{12} 10^{8}; Vol. II collates as second printing, except that II, sig. 10 has no ads, p. 212 being blank.

Words showing type-batter introduced in the third printing:

I, [1], 5.13	LIFE∧
I, 2, 10.33	apophthegm∧
I, 4, 61.30	it
I, 5, 81.2	heart
I, 6, 101.5	self∧
I, 7, 125.13	Bull∧
I, 8, 163.2	proverbial
I, 9, 172.4	had
I, 10, 201.31	alms-house
II, 3, 39.5	proba∧
II, 4, 57.1–8	[batter through center of page]
II, 5, 88.29	tumult
II, 8, 145.0	145
II, 9, 169.33	school

Note: *BAL* 7598 cautions that copies with mixed sheets may exist. Only one such copy has been seen, in the Berg Collection, New York Public Library, of vol-

---

printing have been seen, two each at the Houghton Library, Harvard University, Princeton University, and Boston Public Library, and one each at the Library of Congress, Peabody Institute, Baltimore, and Case-Western Reserve University.

ume I, mixing the prelims of a first or second printing with the text of a third printing.[9]

Third Printing, John Wiley Issue

The firm of Wiley and Putnam dissolved in the spring of 1848.[10] Their agreement called for Putnam to retain all literary titles, except for Ruskin's works, and for Wiley to keep the scientific material.[11] But *Mosses* was split so that both publishers retained a share of the title. The plates went to Putnam, but the unbound sheets of the third printing were kept by Wiley, who cancelled the title-copyright leaf, rearranged the prelims, and bound them in one volume in his Library of Choice Reading series.

MOSSES | FROM | AN OLD MANSE. | BY | NA-THANIEL HAWTHORNE. | [short rule] | PARTS I. & II. | [short rule] | NEW YORK: | JOHN WILEY, 161 BROADWAY, | AND 13 PATERNOSTER ROW, LONDON. | [short rule] | 1849. Signed: $[1]^4$ $2–10^{12}$, $2–10^{12}$; gathered: $[1]^{1+1+1+1}$ $2–9^{12}$ 10^8 $[11–19]^{12}$ (sig. [1] is four tipped-in leaves; one or both of the final two leaves of sig. [19] may be excised before binding); [i–viii] [1] 2–207 [208], [1] 2–211 [212–

---

[9] Ten copies of the third printing have been examined, two at the Berg Collection, New York Public Library, and one each at Yale University, Columbia University, Ohio State University, the University of Virginia, the J. Pierpont Morgan Library, the Newberry Library, Houghton Library, Harvard University, and the Massachusetts Historical Society, Boston.

[10] Ads in *Literary World* demonstrate the breakup. Putnam, calling himself "Publisher and Importer of Foreign Books," placed his "List No. I" in III (March 4, 1848), 98. John Wiley's first ad as "Importer, Publisher, and Bookseller" appeared in III (April 1, 1848), 180, and he advertised himself as "of the late firm of Wiley and Putnam" in III (April 8, 1848), 200.

[11] Henry Walcott Boynton, "Wiley and Putnam," *The First One Hundred and Fifty Years* (New York, 1957), p. 34.

216]; pp. i–ii blank, p. iii is the title page; p. iv is blank, p. v lists the contents of Part I; p. vi is blank; the contents of Part II are on p. vii, with p. viii blank; the text is as the 1846 Wiley and Putnam issue.[12]

Fourth Printing

MOSSES | FROM | AN OLD MANSE. | BY NA-THANIEL HAWTHORNE. | AUTHOR OF "THE SCARLET LETTER," ETC., EEC. | New Edition [in Gothic type]. | NEW YORK: | GEORGE P. PUT-NAM, 155 BROADWAY. | [short rule] | 1850.

Part I: [1]$^{2+1}$ 2–9^{12} 10^6 [11]^2; pp. [i–vi] [1] 2–207 [208]; pp. i–ii are blank; the title is on p. iii (p. iv blank); p. v has the contents of Part I; p. vi is blank; the text is as the first printing.

Part II: [1]^2 2–9^{12} 10^6 [11]^4; pp. [i–iv] [1] 2–211 [212]; p. i: 'MOSSES FROM AN OLD MANSE. | [short rule] | PART II. '; (p. ii blank); the contents are listed on p. iii (p. iv blank); the text is as the first printing, with p. 212 blank.

Note: The two parts were bound together in one volume. This printing can be dated approximately by Hawthorne's letter to Bridge, August 7, 1850: "Your surmise as to Putnam's failure was wholly groundless. He has paid up the balance due me, and appears to be in the full tide of success. He has just got out a new edition of my Mosses." [13]

[12] Two copies have been seen, in the Berg Collection and the Newberry Library.

[13] MS, Bowdoin College. Two copies of the fourth printing have been een, at Ohio State University.

Fifth Printing

Title is as fourth printing, except '1851.'; Part I: $[1]^{2+1}$ $2-9^{12}$ 10^{12-4}, with the final four leaves excised before binding; pagination and contents are as the fourth printing. Part II: $[1]^2$ $2-9^{12}$ 10^{12-2}, with the final two leaves excised before binding (pagination and contents as fourth printing).[14]

Sixth Printing

Title is as fourth printing, except '1852.'; Part I: $[1]^{2+1}$ $2-9^{12}$ 10^8 (pagination and contents as fourth printing); Part II: $[1]^2$ $2-9^{12}$ 10^{10} (pagination and contents as fourth printing).

Note: Machine collation of a first printing, American issue, against a sixth printing shows no plate changes in either volume except for type-batter increasing with each printing.[15]

No publisher's records of the early years of the Wiley and Putnam firms are extant. The number of copies of the 1846 printings are therefore impossible to determine. Some evidence exists, however, to indicate the number of copies of the three printings of 1850–52. On February 10, 1853, Putnam wrote to Hawthorne, "Annexed is an account of the sales of the *Mosses* up to the first of January, and for the balance due you ($144.09) a check is enclosed." Since, according to Hawthorne's letter to Bridge of August 7, 1850,

[14] Two copies examined, at the New York Public Library and Harvard College Library.

[15] Two copies of the sixth printing were examined at Ohio State University. A third copy, collating as a sixth printing but having a title page dated 1851 is at the University of Michigan.

Putnam had settled the account up to that date, the check for $144.09 was payment only for the three printings after 1849. George Haven Putnam, commenting on his father's letter of 1853, erroneously claims that *Mosses* was first published in 1851, then adds, "two years after the publication my father was able to report a total sale not exceeding 750 copies." [16] George Haven Putnam's calculation is based on a copyright of fifteen percent on the retail price of $1.25 per volume.

The copyright, however, was probably ten percent. In his letter of March 21, 1845, E. A. Duyckinck reported to Hawthorne Wiley and Putnam's offer of "eight cents a copy on the edition, fully equal to one half the profits." [17] But on August 26, 1845, Duyckinck wrote to John Greenleaf Whittier that the proposed Library of American Books would "allow ten per cent on the retail price." [18] At a copyright of ten percent, therefore, the payment would represent some 1,150 copies.

Mosses from an Old Manse was in print throughout the eight years that Wiley and Putnam, and then George P. Putnam, owned the plates. These include four years before the publication of *The Scarlet Letter* in 1850 marked Hawthorne's rise to fame. The fact of six printings in six years, along with steady sales, makes *Mosses* Hawthorne's first commercially successful book.

At least three printings of the pirated English edition appeared prior to the Ticknor and Fields edition of 1854. The first printing is *Mosses from an Old Manse* (London: George Routledge & Co., 1851), in one volume, using the 1846 Wiley and Putnam edition as printer's copy, but omitting "The Virtuoso's Collection." It was advertised in

[16] George Haven Putnam, *George Palmer Putnam: A Memoir* (New York, 1912), pp. 195, 215.

[17] Duyckinck Letter Book, MS, Duyckinck Collection, New York Public Library.

[18] Ibid.

the *Athenæum,* September 13. Two later printings are dated 1852 and 1853.

In March of 1854 Putnam put up for auction plates, copyrights, engravings, bound volumes, and unbound sheets of various works, including *Journal of an African Cruiser* and *Mosses from an Old Manse.* Some eleven works were sold at this Bangs Brothers trade sale; the plates of *Mosses,* subject to copyright, were bought by Ticknor and Fields of Boston for $290.00, a figure that included plates of *African Cruiser* and J. R. Lowell's *A Fable for Critics.*[19]

The second edition, the first Ticknor and Fields edition of *Mosses,* was published on October 28, 1854, according to *Cost Books* entry B78b: the two-volume set retailed for $1.50, and Hawthorne's payment was ten percent on 900 copies of the 1,000 printed. "Feathertop" was added to volume I, and "Passages from a Relinquished Work" and "Sketches from Memory," to volume II, at Hawthorne's suggestion.[20]

MOSSES FROM AN OLD MANSE. | BY | NATHANIEL HAWTHORNE. | IN TWO VOLUMES. | VOL. I [VOL. II.] | NEW EDITION, | CAREFULLY REVISED BY THE AUTHOR. | BOSTON: | TICKNOR AND FIELDS. | M DCCC LIV.

I: signed: $[1]^8$ $2-18^8$; gathered: $[1]^8$ 2^4 $[3-24]^{8/4}$; 144 leaves; pp. [1–2] 3 [4] 5–286 [287–288]; p. 1 has the title; copyright and stereotype notices are on p. 2; p. 3 lists the contents for vol. I (p. 4 blank); the text is on pp. 5–286, with pp. 287–288 blank.

[19] *Norton's Literary Gazette,* I (April 1, 1854), 159; and *The Cost Books of Ticknor and Fields,* ed. Warren S. Tryon and William Charvat (New York, 1949), p. 292, entry B78b.

[20] Hawthorne to Ticknor, June 7, 1854, MS, Berg Collection, New York Public Library.

II: signed: $[1]^8$ $2-18^8$ 19^6; gathered: $[1]^8$ 2^4 $[3-24]^{8/4}$; $[25]^6$; 150 leaves; pp. $[1-2]$ 3 $[4]$ 5–297 $[298–300]$; the title is on p. 1; p. 2 is as vol. I; contents of vol. II are on p. 3; p. 4 is blank; pp. 5–297 have the text (pp. 298–300 blank).

The *Cost Books* entry shows the sheet size to be 22 by 37 inches. Page-edge evidence is lacking, but one side of a sheet would impose a total of 24 pages (48 pages per sheet), given the page size of 7 by 4 1/2 inches. The sheets are gathered in an alternating 8- and 4-leaf pattern, making imposition in half-sheet of 24's with two signatures. Savage #33, "Sheet of Twelves with Two Signatures, Sixteen and Eight Pages," provides the layout if the two formes are combined to make a half-sheet of 24's, work-and-tumble.

The *Cost Books* and unpublished Cost Books show the plates of the Ticknor and Fields edition of *Mosses* to have been imposed twenty-five times, five during Hawthorne's lifetime, for a total of 10,043 copies of the two volumes. Machine collation of an 1854 first printing against a copy bearing a copyright date of 1880 reveals plate repairs entering in the thirteenth printing of May 26, 1871, when *Mosses* was included in the Library Edition, but no substantive alterations.

II

Recorded here are the individual pieces of the *Mosses from an Old Manse* in their descent from copy-text manuscript or first printed appearance to the stereotyped 1854 Ticknor and Fields collection. Hawthorne's Journal sources are remarked, as "*Notebooks* 235.15, 364.31–34" for "Fire-Worship"; the numbers are page / line citations to text and associated Explanatory Notes in *The American Notebooks*, ed. Claude M. Simpson (Centenary Edition, [Columbus, Ohio, 1973]). Further references to the tales may be found in the index of *The American Notebooks*.

The numerous unauthoritative reprintings of the tales are not listed, since they have no bearing on the Centenary text.

The *Mosses from an Old Manse* collections are referred to as *MOM* 1846 and 1854.

The Old Manse

Notebooks 237.17–28, 250.19–24, 252.26–29, 318.12–319.5, 320.23–25, 320.29–321.29, 322.20–26, 324.18–325.5, 325.17–26, 326.5–9, 326.15–327.26, 328.26–330.22, 338.5–339.29, 341.34–342.26, 348.7–349.5, 350.2–9, 350.17–20, 350.25–29, 354.24–30, 359.22–360.24, 393.4–24.

Manuscript (Manuscript Division, New York Public Library), copy-text: Eight folios, folded size 9 7/8 by 7 3/4 inches, in black ink on white wove unwatermarked paper, rectos and versos. First recto carries title, and each first recto of following folios is numbered by Hawthorne, as "(2ᵈ sheet)". There is now pencil pagination at top outer corners.

Printer's marks, by manuscript pagination (1846 *Mosses* page-line in parentheses): 1 (1), in ink: "Phair" at top left; 2 (3.3), ink bracket before "In"; 5 (5.3), in ink: "Kitchener" at top left; 9 (9.8), in ink: "Rosette" at indent; 13 (13.8), before "gusts" a pencil bracket, erased words preceding and under it; 17 (16.19), in ink "Phair" at indent; 17 (17.11), in pencil: "office" above a bracket before "same"; 23 (22.24), ink bracket before "seen," and name at left margin cancelled by pencil; 25 (25.1), pencil bracket before "austerity," and pencil "25/2" at left margin; 29 (29.1), pencil "28" above "egotist"; 30 (29.13), pencil step bracket between "quality" and "that."

First printed appearance: *MOM* 1846 I, 1–31. *MOM* 1854 I, 5–42.

The Birth-mark

Notebooks 20.13–15, 158.3, 165.23–25, 26–28, 184.26, 235.24.

Pioneer, I (March, 1843), 113–19. By Nathaniel Hawthorne. *MOM* 1846 I, 32–51; 1854 I, 43–66.

A Select Party

Notebooks 242.15.

United States Magazine and Democratic Review, XV (July, 1844), 33–40. By Nathaniel Hawthorne. *MOM* 1846 I, 52–68; 1854 I, 67–86.

Young Goodman Brown

New-England Magazine, VIII (April, 1835), 249–60. By the author of "The Gray Champion." *MOM* 1846 I, 69–84; 1854 I, 87–105.

Rappaccini's Daughter

Notebooks 184.4, 222.13–15, 237.17–28.

United States Magazine and Democratic Review, XV (December, 1844), 545–60, as "Writings of Aubépine" with the

interior title "Rappaccini's Daughter." By Nathaniel Hawthorne. *MOM* 1846 I, 85–118; 1854 I, 106–49.

Mrs. Bullfrog

Notebooks 11.24–27.

The Token and Atlantic Souvenir. Boston: Charles Bowen,
1837, pp. 66–75. By the author of "Wives of the Dead."
MOM 1846 I, 119–27; 1854 I, 150–60.

Fire-Worship

Notebooks 235.15, 364.31–34.

United States Magazine and Democratic Review, XIII
(December, 1843), 627–30. By Nathaniel Hawthorne. *MOM*
1846 I, 128–36; 1854 I, 161–71.

Buds and Bird-Voices

Notebooks 341.14–34, 374.18–21, 375.11–15, 380.9ff.,
382.7–9.

Manuscript (C. E. Frazer Clark, Jr., collection), copy-
text: Five disjunct leaves, 10 by 8 inches, of white wove
paper written in black ink on rectos and versos through the
fourth and concluding on recto of the fifth. The leaves are
tipped onto mounting paper and bound in a green leather
volume. Creases show folding of the manuscript for mailing.
Rectos and versos are numbered 1 through 9 by Hawthorne,
and his markings "(2ᵈ sheet)" and "(3ᵈ sheet)" indicate
original folio state.

Printer's marks: page 3 (Centenary 145.23) pencil signature "Gilman" in space at end of paragraph; page 8 (Centenary 145.23), ink bracket before "trees" and interlined

inked box with "Sig. 77 609", one page off pagination of the *Democratic Review*, where "trees" begins page 608, and signature 77 starts on 609.

First printed appearance: *United States Magazine and Democratic Review*, XIII (June, 1843), 604–8. By Nathaniel Hawthorne. *MOM* 1846 I, 137–46; 1854 I, 172–83.

Monsieur du Miroir

Notebooks 15.10–11.

The Token and Atlantic Souvenir. Boston: Charles Bowen, 1837, pp. 49–64. By the author of "Sights from a Steeple." *MOM* 1846 I, 147–58; 1854 I, 184–98.

The Hall of Fantasy

Pioneer, I (February, 1843), 49–55. By Nathaniel Hawthorne. *MOM* 1846 I, 159–72; 1854 I, 199–215.

The Celestial Rail-road

Notebooks 70.19, 238.21–24.

Manuscript (anonymous collector), copy-text: Five folios, folded dimensions 10 by 8 inches, and a half folio of the same size. All have been trimmed. The third folio is on wove white paper faded to gray; the others are on wove pale blue. The first five folios are inscribed in black ink on both rectos and versos; the sixth (half-folio) only on recto. Two horizontal creases are evidence of folding for mailing. Rectos are numbered by Hawthorne at top right corners, and the folios after the first are marked on first recto "(2^d sheet)" and so on. The manuscript is now bound; the folios are separated by portraits following the second and the fourth, and other non-manuscript material follows the sixth.

Printer's marks (*Democratic Review*, May, 1843, page-line in parentheses): 1 (515), upper left corner, "sig. 45" and, in ink, "Gilman"; 5 (516.49b), "Whipple" at indent; 9 (518.39b), "Gilman" in space at end of paragraph; 13 (520.45a), in pencil, "Whipple" at indent; 18 (522.10b), in pencil, "Stevens" at indent.

First printed appearance, *United States Magazine and Democratic Review*, XII (May, 1843), 515–23. By Nathaniel Hawthorne. MOM 1846 I, 173–92; 1854 I, 216–39.

The Procession of Life

Notebooks 15.12–13, 14–18; 22.19–23.5.

United States Magazine and Democratic Review, XII (April, 1843), 360–66. By Nathaniel Hawthorne. MOM 1846 I, 193–207; 1854 I, 240–58.

Feathertop

Notebooks 185.8–11, 286.14–27.

Manuscript (Morgan Library), partial copy-text: Eleven leaves, 7 3/4 by 9 5/8 inches, blue wove paper with an octagonal blind-stamp, detail undecipherable, in upper left corner. The manuscript is written in black ink on both sides of the leaves, which are now framed in tapes, with no record of disjunction of folios. Hawthorne's paging begins with ordinals at top center, "(2ᵈ)" through "(13th)" and then in cardinal numbers through "(20)".

Printer's marks (*International Magazine*, February–March, 1852, page-lines in parentheses): 1 (182), upper left corner, in pencil: "Corner", and at lower left margin in ink, "183" and brackets dividing "scarecrow" (183.1a) and before "himself" (183.2a); 5, in pencil: "Jewel" in space following "scarecrow" (184.28a); 7, in ink, "185" and bracket before "nothing" (185.1a); 10, above text, in ink: "Jewel" cancelled by pencil, and undecipherable mark at left margin before "With" (333.1a); 13, in pencil: "Corner" at indent (334.34a); 17, in pencil: "Carter" at indent (335.66b); 19, in ink: "Jewell" in space following "itself" (336.57b), with line drawn down to "321" before "A figure" (327.1a).

First printed appearance, copy-text for final three paragraphs beginning at Centenary 245.34 "While thus muttering . . .": *International Monthly Magazine of Literature, Science, and Art*, V (February 1, 1852), 182–86, and V (March 1, 1852), 333–37. By Nathaniel Hawthorne. *MOM* 1854 I, 259–86.

The New Adam and Eve

Notebooks 21.18–24.
United States Magazine and Democratic Review, XII (February, 1843), 146–55. By Nathaniel Hawthorne. *MOM* 1846 II, 1–21; 1854 II, 5–29.

Egotism; or, The Bosom-Serpent

Notebooks 22.1–3, 228.6–7.
United States Magazine and Democratic Review, XII (March, 1843), 255–61. By Nathaniel Hawthorne. *MOM* 1846 II, 22–37; 1854 II, 30–48.

The Christmas Banquet

Notebooks 20.21–21.8, 167.3–5, 235.12, 237.17–28.
United States Magazine and Democratic Review, XIV

(January, 1844), 78–87. By Nathaniel Hawthorne. *MOM* 1846 II, 38–58; 1854 II, 49–74.

Drowne's Wooden Image

Godey's Magazine and Lady's Book, XXIX (July, 1844), 13–17. By Nathaniel Hawthorne. *MOM* 1846 II, 59–73; 1854 II, 75–91.

The Intelligence Office

Notebooks 23.6–10.
United States Magazine and Democratic Review, XIV (March, 1844), 269–75. By Nathaniel Hawthorne. *MOM* 1846 II, 74–89; 1854 II, 92–110.

Roger Malvin's Burial

The Token. Boston: Gray and Bowen, 1832, pp. 161–88. No attribution. Reprinted in *United States Magazine and Democratic Review*, XIII (August, 1843), 186–96. *MOM* 1846 II, 90–112; 1854 II, 111–38.

P.'s Correspondence

Notebooks 22.16–17, 253.21–254.2.
United States Magazine and Democratic Review, XVI (April, 1845), 337–45. By Nathaniel Hawthorne. *MOM* 1846 II, 113–32; 1854 II, 139–62.

Earth's Holocaust

Notebooks 23.27–29, 185.29–30, 237.10–16.

Manuscript (Lilly Library, Indiana University) copy-text: Five folios, folded size 9 3/4 by 7 3/4 inches, and one disjunct leaf of same size; white wove, unwatermarked paper, written in black ink faded to brown, on both sides of folios and on the recto only of the disjunct leaf, a total of 21 pages. Hawthorne numbered the folios, as, "(2ᵈ sheet)". Two marks of printers for *Graham's* appear: a short double divider in pencil on page 15 above line 6, and below it a name in pencil, possibly "McKeeley."

First printed appearance: *Graham's Lady's and Gentleman's Magazine*, XXV (May, 1844), 193–200. By Nathaniel Hawthorne. MOM 1846 II, 133–55; 1854 II, 163–90.

Note: Autograph-pages written by Hawthorne in 1864 at the request of John P. Kennedy, for photo-reproduction in a volume of such autograph writings, were adapted from "Earth's Holocaust" 141.13–142.21. The abridgements and alterations of the copied passage do not represent any intention of changing the sketch itself. The three disjunct leaves of manuscript are in the University of Texas Library Rare Books Collection.

Passages from a Relinquished Work

New-England Magazine, VII (November, 1834), 352–58: "At Home," "A Flight in the Fog," and "A Fellow Traveller," under the heading "The Story Teller. No. I."; ibid., VII (December, 1834), 449–59: "The Village Theater," "Mr. Higginbotham's Catastrophe," and conclusion after the Higginbotham narrative, under the heading "The Story Teller.

No. II." No attribution. ("Mr. Higginbotham's Catastrophe" was extracted by Hawthorne for the 1837 *Twice-told Tales*, and so does not appear in *Mosses.*) MOM 1854 II, 191–210.

Sketches from Memory

New-England Magazine, IX (November, 1835), 321–26: "The Notch" and "Our Evening Party among the Mountains," under the title "Sketches from Memory. By a Pedestrian. No. I."; ibid., IX (December, 1835) 398–409: "The Canal-Boat" (with other sketches as "Sketches from Memory. By a Pedestrian. No. II."). MOM 1854 II, 211–30.

The Old Apple-Dealer

Notebooks 59.22, 222.22.
Sargent's New Monthly Magazine of Literature, Fashion, and the Fine Arts, I (January, 1843), 21–24. By Nathaniel Hawthorne. MOM 1846 II, 156–63; 1854 II 231–39.

The Artist of the Beautiful

Notebooks 158.3, 165.26–28, 185.26, 242.12.
United States Magazine and Democratic Review, XIV (June, 1844), 605–17. By Nathaniel Hawthorne. MOM 1846 II, 164–91; 1854 II, 240–73.

A Virtuoso's Collection

Notebooks 23.21–23, 30.11, 51.24, 184.18, 227.23, 235.12, 241.12, 242.24, 243.22–24, 252.23–25.

Boston Miscellany of Literature and Fashion, I (May, 1842), 193–200. By Nathaniel Hawthorne. MOM 1846 II, 192–211; 1854 II, 274–97.

J. M.

TEXTUAL NOTES

4.11 old] The regular form that Hawthorne wrote throughout this sketch is "old Manse". Since he apparently did not see proof, the ten 1846 settings of "Old Manse" are unauthoritative, especially since the MS copy "old" is followed five times. The 1854 text capitalizes these five to print, uniformly, "Old Manse". One might take it that "old Manse" could in fact have been the name of the house in the manuscript, but two pieces of evidence suggest the contrary. In various passages, the house is called simply "the Manse"; and the collection title would not have read "an" if the house had "The Old Manse" as its formal reference. In Hawthorne's letter of February 22, 1846, to Evert Duyckinck (MS, Duyckinck Collection, New York Public Library), he wrote of his search for a title, " 'Wall-Flowers from an Old Abbey' occurred to me. . . . 'Moss and Lichens from an Old Parsonage'. . . . 'Mosses from an Old Manse' suits me rather better. . . . " Here the uses of *old* are clearly no part of a name, and the capitalization is that necessary in the title of a book. In addition, in Hawthorne's letter to Duyckinck on April 30 (MS, Duyckinck Collection, New York Public Library) defending the chosen title, he explained, " 'Manse' was our familiar epithet for the old house."

We cannot know whether, as seems possible, the compositor of the 1854 edition changed his 1846 copy to "Old" in the five remaining variant occurrences of "old", or whether Hawthorne made these uniform in preparing copy. We do know that Hawthorne altered a few mistakes in marked presentation copies of the 1846 *Mosses*, but did not change any of the five appearances of "old" nor the ten of "Old". Moreover, the uniformity of "Old" in 1854 demonstrates that he did not trouble to reduce in its copy any of the 1846 capitalizations. Under the circumstances of the relatively careful survey given this sketch in 1854, when he returned many readings to manuscript, it seems difficult to believe that if Hawthorne had recognized a violation of his intention in "Old" he would not have altered the capitalization. One may suggest that whereas Hawthorne thought of the Manse frequently as "the old Manse"—a standard phrase although not the actual name of the house—the phrase with its capital "Old" may simply have made no impression on him. By the time of his finishing the sketch on April 15, the book's title was already in his mind, and it is to the book that he alludes at 34.1 when he speaks of giving up his literary life for a political appointment, "from the Old Manse into a Custom-House!" The history of the texts in this as in the other volumes demonstrates that when Hawthorne did not recognize an unauthoritative variant in the 1846 *Mosses* and passed it on in 1854 unaltered, no argument can be made that he thereby "approved" it. Since in this sketch "Old Manse" conflicts with the book's title, the Centenary Edition re-introduces the original "old Manse" in its occurrences in manuscript as the only authoritative form.

13.18 closest] Whether 1854 "closest" for MS "closer" is a printer's sophistication or Hawthorne's own second thought is hard to decide. Since on the evidence of "afforded" (5.14) and "the Paphian" (5.16–17) from 1846 "offered" and "Paphian", Hawthorne in correcting the copy for 1854 did occasionally devote care to exact meaning and small points of syntax (despite the large number of indifferent 1846 corruptions that he passed), an argument can be made for the authority of the 1854 variant. The 1846 comparative "closer" is not an error but it was subject to a misunderstanding in that its reference back to "the fruit of trees that he did not plant" implied that any apple had a *close* resemblance to those in Eden but the apples he is writing about are closer in their resemblance than those from trees one had oneself planted with toil. Only two forms are being compared, and the comparative is technically correct. Yet an ambiguity does linger, and it may be that Hawthorne tried to resolve the problem by changing the comparative to the superlative, which in effect alters the meaning to: "If any apple has a resemblance to those of Eden, then trees that one has not oneself planted bear apples that come the closest of all earthly apples to Eden because they seem to partake of free bounty." This then agrees with the following remark, "I relish best the free gifts of Providence."

15.10 borne] This is only the other spelling for "born" and by no means signifies *carried*.

52.17 wrapt] The form "wrapt" in the *Pioneer* clearly follows its copy, no matter what the meaning. That is, if the sense is *rapt* in 1854, then "wrapt" is simply an old-fashioned spelling unlikely to occur to a compositor reading "rapt" in his copy. If the sense is *wrapped*, then the old-fashioned form with final -*t* can be paralleled in this collection, as in "stept" (86.15), "skipt" (89.11), "undreamt" (419.26), and even "past" (466.20) for *passed*. In either case, then, the reading is not likely to be compositorial. Whether "rapt" in 1854 is an authorial change or a modernization such as the 1854 compositors occasionally indulged in can scarcely be determined. We know that Hawthorne may have read proof for the *Pioneer* printing, and he had the chance to alter the reading in preparing the 1846 copy. It may be that only in 1854 did he see the possible ambiguity caused by his older spelling. It may also be that the form in 1854 is simply a printer's modernization, like "grizzly" for "grisly" at 445.29. The safer course is to retain Hawthorne's original spelling but to note that the 1854 "rapt" almost certainly offers the intended meaning.

55.29 that earth] The change in 1846 from *Pioneer* "that" to "the", repeated in 1854, is so indifferent on the surface as to be of suspect authority, especially since "the earth" echoes "the best" and may have been contaminated by it. However, a precise and important meaning is wrapped up in the phrase. At 42.22 and 47.2 "the earth" clearly means the planet, whereas at 42.25 and 49.8 "earth" means the dirt, the material from which life springs and to which it returns. This latter meaning receives its most important statement at 55.12–13 in Aylmer's "Matter and Spirit—Earth and Heaven". The problem at 55.29, then, focuses on whether *matter* is intended, as in the *Pioneer*, or the planet as in the 1846 reading. In the latter, Georgiana would, almost inevitably, be calling herself the best that the world had produced. This was the common view of her lovers but it has little pertinence here. The key comes in the preceding part of her speech, "that, with so high and pure a feeling". This phrase is linked with earlier statements about Aylmer's spiritual aspirations, especially, "He handled physical details, as if there were nothing beyond them; yet spiritualized them all, and redeemed himself from materialism by his strong and eager aspiration towards the infinite. In his grasp, the veriest clod of earth assumed a soul" (49.4–8). Thus with a "high and pure . . . feeling", by the removal of the Crimson Hand Aylmer unwittingly unbinds the knot of Matter and Spirit and so works out Hawthorne's statement that "[Nature] permits us, indeed, to mar, but seldom to mend" (42.32–33). Georgiana's dying words sum up this moral. Aylmer has not rejected the best that the world could offer but instead the highest product of matter: "Nature assimilates all her precious influences from earth and air, and from the spiritual world, to create and foster Man, her masterpiece" (42.24–26). The Hand was not a blemish but a token of the union of spirit and matter. Thus "that earth" must be correct, for "the earth" would destroy Hawthorne's careful distinction and would obscure his irony at this crucial point in the story. It is the fact that Georgiana is a human being that makes her the best that earth has produced among all other forms of life.

60.31 of which] The 1854 change to "with which" may have been the printer's error through contamination by "With a generosity" but perhaps even Hawthorne's own responsibility if he had been momentarily confused, especially since the further change of "the" to "an" in 1854 could be doubtfully authorial. Grammar does not permit the substitution of "with" for "of": *he alone sets us the example of a generosity with which we will glance merely at his nobler attributes.*

74.1 Goodman Brown] Whether or not so marked by Hawthorne, the 1846 capitalization of "Goodman" (as well as that of "Deacon", 78.23 *et seq.* and "Goody", 78.24 *et seq.*) is required and the magazine's "goodman", "deacon", and "goody" are wrong when attached to names, even though it is probable that they so stood in Hawthorne's manuscript. "Goodman Brown" like "Deacon Gookin" conforms to the old custom of prefixing one's occupation as a title to one's name, like *Farmer John* or *Lawyer Jones*. However, the lower-case title, as at 76.32 and 77.24, is acceptable in all texts without the name.

94.32 the fountain] The 1846 alteration of magazine "the fountain" to "a fountain" appears to be another in the series of interchanges between these articles characteristic of the 1846 typesetting. It would be absurd to take it that Giovanni is generalizing here about fountains in general as spirits, but only about this particular fountain.

109.2 that] The addition of the relative "that" in 1854 is taken as authorial. In other places in the present edition the addition in 1846 is also assigned as an authoritative revision and its omission from copy as an error. Hawthorne's manuscripts have many examples of the relative "that" interlined as a revision: see for example, the apparatus to the *Blithedale Romance* 111.33 and 149.13; the *House of the Seven Gables* 179.23; *Our Old Home* 32.32, 89.8, 96.24, 191.8, 257.1–4, 257.15–16, 264.12, 330.32; and the *Marble Faun* 139.33, 307.20. In "Feathertop", "that" is added by interlineation at MS 17.10 (241.20 of this text).

134.9 broke] As an indication of the unauthoritative nature of the 1846 variants in this story, one may compare the normalization in 1846 of colloquial "broke" in dialogue of the *Token*, with which one may compare "Wives of the Dead," in *Snow-Image*: "I judged you wouldn't mind being broke of your rest".

134.22 did she] The very awkwardness of the *Token* phrase, and the likelihood that Hawthorne read proof for his early *Token* stories, suggest that "did she" was authorial. It is not impossible to conceive that this could be the only change that Hawthorne made in the *Token* copy for 1846; but the fact that this is a make-weight tale of which Sophia had earlier dis-

approved joins with Hawthorne's more or less casual treatment
of all his early work in *Mosses* to suggest that he skimmed it, if
he read it at all, and made no alterations. The compositor was
quite capable of attempting to straighten out the syntax.

138.8 clouded] In view of "clouded sky" in "Buds and Bird-
Voices" (151.1), one is forced to take it that it was not Hawthorne who here revised his idiom but instead that it was the
compositor who sophisticated to the more conventional phrase.

141.11 dusky] The change from the *Review's* "dusty" to 1846
"dusky" seems required. The hearth would become dusty with
use, of course, but this was a fault that would be repaired not
only in the morning (142.1) but by a good housewife and her
servant whenever needed. The word "dusty" would be appropriate only if the reference were to "one long, lonesome night after
another". But the nights are remarked at 143.14–17, and the
"jets of flame" there from the raked-over coals have no relation
to "only now and then betraying his wild nature, by thrusting
his red tongue out of the chimney-top." This can refer only to
the heaping-on of wood to make a strong blaze, and thus the
praise of the fire on "dusty hearth" or "dusky hearth" is supposed
to cover both day and night, and any reference to the condition
of the hearth relating only to one or to the other period is impossible. Under this requirement the only sensible reading is
"dusky", for to insinuate that except for the morning sweeping
the hearth was customarily dusty would be a serious housekeeping
criticism. The hearth would be swept, ordinarily, whenever fresh
wood was put on the fire and thus attention directed to it. On the
other hand, "dusky" is a suitable word, for the hearth extended
to the back of the fireplace, and the recess forming the fireplace
would be removed from the light and thus "dusky" compared to
the lighting in the rest of the room. Since light is fire's nature,
it is being praised for consenting to dwell in a place that ought to
be repugnant because it is dark.

141.34 element has] The variant "elements have" in 1846 is a
clear case of misunderstanding and sophistication. The "element"
is the fire, one of the four primary elements, which has been
gnawing the tree trunks for hours and thus leaving only remnants.

The compositor mistook the sense and thought that it should have been the elements of wind and rain, outdoors, that had gnawed the remnants.

143.18 latter] The 1846 "later" is a normalization of a form that Hawthorne preferred: see 150.1, "latter autumn".

151.14 flourish] The sense of MS is clear and economical. It would seem that by contamination from "only" in 151.14 the *Democratic Review* compositor added "only" after "flourish" and the error was not corrected in 1846. However, either the editor or compositor of 1854 (or possibly Hawthorne) noticed the feeble repetition of "only" and substituted "always", which does not alter the original sense but is not required. The agent of the 1854 alteration is not to be determined; but even if it were Hawthorne himself, the change would have been made under a misapprehension. Thus an editor has no choice but gladly to let MS stand as Hawthorne intended when he wrote the essay.

153.34–154.1 departed . . . have] Reference to the typesetting in the *Democratic Review* makes it reasonably clear that this omission in 1846 is a mechanical eyeskip and not a revision in the copy by Hawthorne. The "betaken" occurs in the line immediately below the "have" of "have departed". The sentence, since it still made sense, was evidently not remarked by Hawthorne.

167.21 ray] The singular here agrees with the following singulars "lamp-light" and "fireside". The 1846 plural "rays" may exhibit the same sort of misunderstanding or casual sophistication found more obviously at 170.4 where correct *Token* "companion" becomes the 1846 error "companions".

169.33 nature] The capitalization of this word in 1854 must be a printer's error. Hawthorne personifies *Nature* when he is referring to *Mother Nature*—the external world—but not when he is writing about human nature, as here, or at 151.17 in "Buds and Bird-Voices," for instance.

170.18 is himself] Some doubt must inhere in the authority of the 1846 alteration "himself is" from the *Token* "is himself",

the more particularly because Hawthorne was fond of such in-
versions, as "did she" changed probably without authority by
1846 to "she did" at 134.22. Only a slight chance of a significant
difference in meaning exists here, for it would be too subtle to
remark on the possibility that in the *Token* form the narrator
might also be thought of as a "wanderer from the spiritual
world"; the reference is quite clearly back to the invisible beings
posited in 170.8–14.

170.19 illusive] The 1854 alteration "delusive" of *Token* and
1846 "illusive" (surely authorial) is somewhat suspect as the
only 1854 change in the 1846 text that is not an error in this
story except for the correction at 164.9. The change to "delusive"
agrees with its use at 167.33 and removes any ambiguity about
the meaning of "illusive" as *illusory*. Nevertheless, the original
use of "illusive" is so firmly Hawthorne's as to cast doubt on the
1854 substitute as a printer's sophistication. For example, see "The
Custom-House" in *The Scarlet Letter*, p. 35.19–24, "Moonlight
. . . is a medium the most suitable for a romance-writer to get
acquainted with his illusive guests"; and *The Blithedale Romance*,
p. 154.10–12, " . . . that illusive torment (like the ache of a
limb long ago cut off) by which a past mode of life prolongs
itself into the succeeding one."

174.6 reposited] The unfamiliar *Pioneer* "reposited" was an
open invitation to the 1846 compositor to emend. But *to reposit*
is *to store*, even *to deposit*, and hence it is very difficult to conceive of the *Pioneer* compositor either inventing the word as a
substitute or creating it as a misprint. Sophistication in 1846
seems to be the only answer.

195.7 itself] The manuscript attests to the authority of this
somewhat difficult reading, for it would be natural, as in 1846,
to put the formation of the almost articulate words back to the
murmurs, shrieks, and whispers. However, for the blast itself to
form the words is perhaps even more accurate. The possibility
must be recognized that Hawthorne himself may have smoothed
out a difficulty in the 1846 copy, but the sense so strongly
attracts the plural that the 1846 compositor is the better agent

to whom to assign the change, as in the clearcut case of 141.34 discussed above.

207–22 The Procession of Life] In a letter of April 15, 1846, to Evert Duyckinck (MS, Duyckinck Collection, New York Public Library), Hawthorne wrote that he was enclosing all copy for the first volume of *Mosses* except for "The Procession of Life," which, he wrote, "is so inaccurately printed that I must write out a new copy. It shall be sent you in two or three days after you receive this—before the printers can possibly want it." Then, after completion of the letter, over its subscription he wrote, "P.S. I have sent the Procession of Life, so that you now have all." If the present editor's judgment is correct, eight 1846 substantive errors appear at 207.3, 210.11, 211.5, 216.11, 219.3–4, 219.21, 221.14, and 222.13, in addition to the 1846 removal of what seems to be the necessary personification capitalization of "Disease" at 208.25 and 210.13, the modernization of the *Democratic Review* "alarum" to "alarm" at 213.31, and the reprinting of uncharacteristic "toward" at 221.11. These are all mistakes in 1846 about which there can be little question, for they fall into the familiar category of errors found elsewhere in this collection. On the other hand, in fifteen substantive readings 1846 alters the *Democratic* copy to create new words or forms (207.7, 207.13, 208.26, 208.30, 209.31, 210.19, 211.23, 211.26, 212.10, 212.24, 213.21, 213.23, 219.4, 219.16, and 220.21). Not all of these are certain authorial revisions or corrections, but given the care that Hawthorne manifestly devoted to the piece they may be accepted even with some reservations about 208.30 and 211.26. No clearcut error in the *Democratic* seems to have been overlooked and transferred to 1846 except a required comma missing after "unutterably" at 212.4, and possibly the omission of "to" at 220.21, both of these changed in 1854. The question is, whether the fifteen probable authorial changes would have necessitated recopying. The answer is, of course, that if these were all to which Hawthorne objected they could readily have been altered by marking the clipping: the 1846 edition does not so materially alter what could be regarded as incorrect *Democratic* accidentals as to lead these in any real sense to motivate Hawthorne's drastic proposal. The matter is of considerable importance, since if

Hawthorne did in fact submit a fair copy to Wiley and Putnam, a case could be made for it as the proper copy-text for the present edition despite the fact that the fair copy would have been one of a printed version which would therefore pass on to the copy a number of features not characteristic of the original manuscript. What evidence we have suggests the contrary. It is highly suspicious that after writing the letter and promising to copy out the manuscript, the printer's copy is enclosed with the same letter. Unless Hawthorne delayed mailing the letter there would not have been much time for a transcript of this length to have been made. Secondly, not only do no clear signs exist of an intervening transcript between the *Democratic* and the 1846 appearance, but there is some slight positive evidence against such a transcript. It is difficult to believe, for instance, that Hawthorne at 221.11 would faithfully copy out from the *Democratic* the form "toward", or that—heavy parenthetical punctuator that he was—he would not in a copy have added the necessary comma after "unutterably" (212.4), missing in the *Democratic* and in 1846. In short, the very strong probability is that the printer's copy for "The Procession of Life" was an annotated clipping like the rest and that the copy-text should remain the *Democratic* first publication. The numerous errors that afflict the 1846 *Mosses* in this sketch may safely be laid to the compositor who elsewhere mixed up singulars and plurals, switched "a" and "the", and sometimes omitted words. Since Hawthorne never saw the proof, these post-copy errors remained and were mostly repeated in 1854.

207.3 of a] Despite the repetition of the phrase as "the Chief-Marshal" in all texts at 221.20, the *Democratic* reading "of a Chief-Marshal" is probably right, and the 1846 change to "of the" is likely another of the frequent unauthoritative switches between "a" and "the" that make up a category of variants in 1846 not to be assigned to the author without firmer evidence than is present here.

207.7 train] Ordinarily one would assume that 1846 "train" for magazine "trail" was a typo. But, in fact, here the people are moving in spaced organization; they "train" themselves to enhance the dignity and importance of the procession. On the principle of the difficult reading, therefore, and with the knowledge that Hawthorne deplored the *Democratic* errors in this sketch and concerned himself to correct them, "train" has been adopted as an 1846 correction of what is presumed to be the *Democratic's* easy sophistication of the original in the lost manuscript.

210.19 human pride . . . human rank] The 1846 addition of "human" before "rank" seems to be authorial for the purpose of distinguishing this order of worldly rank from the "order of rank" of Disease (210.15). One may speculate, however, on the possibility that in fact "human" was intended to be transferred from before "pride" to "rank" but in error the first was not deleted. The case is not so certain, however, as to permit emendation, tempting as is the hypothesis.

211.26 brethren] The omission of *Democratic* "these" in 1846 before "brethren" is not impossible as a compositorial cleaning-up of confused modification, but it is by no means impossible for Hawthorne, looking for errors in the copy. To have "these" modify "brethren" presents no difficulty, but an anomaly develops when it must also apply equally to "sisterhood" parallel with "brethren". The simplest solution was to omit it so that "brethren and sisterhood" became more generalized than in the *Democratic* text.

216.11 chambers] It is possible, of course, that under the spell of the other singulars in this series Hawthorne altered the *Democratic* "chambers" to "chamber". But the original reading could not have been an error, and the singular as a revision is suspect. That is, the singular "alms-house" properly takes its place in the series and the plural "chambers" merely modifies it. Thus the singular series permits "chambers" and the sense almost requires it.

219.16 more] Whether the change to "more" in 1846 from *Democratic* "much" is authorial or not is impossible to decide. It is certain that Hawthorne's characteristic "much" is authentic in the *Democratic;* hence if 1846 is a legitimate variant it was intended as a revision of the sense. Both versions are acceptable, however, the *Democratic* making the better literal sense and the

1846 the better metaphorical. Although the change might have been irresistible to an "improving" compositor such as one encounters here and there in 1846, the added contrast is not impossible for an author to contrive, even though one would hardly suppose it had suggested itself and been discarded in the lost manuscript inscription.

241.29 ceiling] It is moot whether in Hawthorne's time the old variant spelling "cieling" which Hawthorne consistently used would not be considered a real misspelling, by ordinary cultivated standards. At least the compositors of his works, although often respecting his other old-fashioned spellings, invariably altered this one. See also the occurrence at 400.10 in the manuscript of "Earth's Holocaust."

270.24 were it] The 1854 variant "should it be" is very likely authorial; however, the point is that it revises an error "where it" in the 1846 copy, and one cannot be sure that Hawthorne ungarbled the error back to "were it" before deciding on the form of his substitution in the 1854 proof. The normal conjecture is that "should it be" would not have revised "were it" if it had stood in 1846. Thus there seem to be sufficient grounds to retain the original authoritative reading of the *Democratic* and to reject the also authoritative revision of 1854 since the later reading did not immediately revise the *Democratic* form but instead the 1846 intermediate error.

294.22 had] The change from the *Democratic* "had" to "has" in 1846 is unusual because it represents the only shift from the past perfect to the perfect in a passage otherwise cast exclusively in the preterite and past perfect. The change may have been triggered by what is taken to be the authorial alteration of "smothered" to "smothering"; but whether Hawthorne also altered "had" to "has" is doubtful because of the abrupt shift in the tense that is, in fact, not required by the change "smothering". In 1846 occur several examples where a precisionist compositor tinkered with the grammar, not always with happy results (see, for example, Textual Notes for 346.15, 355.16, 373.7). In the present case it is possible that the compositor was influenced not alone by "smothering" but also by the preceding phrases "but a desolation now" and "ever since" and so created the error albeit with good intentions. The "now", for instance, does not refer to time contemporaneous to the reading of the story but instead with the past time of the preterite narrative, the date of the banquet.

295.27 leger] This acceptable old spelling found in 1854, and altering the conventional "ledger" of the magazine and 1846, is definitely authorial, on the evidence of the manuscript of "Earth's Holocaust" (394.15). It is difficult to avoid the conclusion that the spelling was marked by Hawthorne in the 1846 copy for 1854 and is a sign of his occasional scrupulousness, even though in this same story he let pass the obvious error "hunter" at 295.26.

297.8 more] At first sight the addition of this word in 1846 may seem odd, for the guest had made no recorded attempt to address anyone in the company. Probably the preceding phrase "as on the former occasion" governs the intention, and Hawthorne meant that although at the first banquet the young man talked until rebuffed (292.13–29), at this second banquet he made no further attempt to speak.

297.19 mystery] 1846 "mysteries" for the *Democratic* "mystery" appears to be another of the unauthoritative shifts between singular and plural observable in the typesetting, like the demonstrable error in this story of "lesson" for magazine "lessons" (see Textual Note, 299.7) and probably "eye" for "eyes" at 294.27. One may compare the singular use of "mystery" in a similar manner in "who might impart to him the mystery—the deep, warm secret— the life within the life—which . . . is what gives substance to a world of shadows" (301.18–21).

299.7 lessons] The fact that 1846 is in error in reading "lesson" for *Democratic* "lessons" is demonstrated by the plural verb "have been studied" which has "lessons" as its subject.

300.4 domestic happiness] The 1854 omission of "domestic", which seems to be a required adjective, is odd since it appears to narrow Hastings's actual seeking of happiness exclusively to his marriage and thus to exclude his wealth and public position as having been sought as means to happiness as well. It is not convincing to argue that the omission has its purpose by giving marriage as an illustration only, without limiting the search to just one area. The contrary is in fact true. However, this 1854 variant cannot be viewed without reference to the one a few words earlier in which "munificent liberality" is altered to "magnificent liberality". This is also an odd change, partly because "magnificent" had appeared in the form "magnificence" only three lines above in 1846 (299.34) and Hawthorne was not accustomed to write such feeble repetitions, particularly as a revision. In most circumstances common revision would seem more likely than common compositorial error; but this circumstance appears to be a special one. It is significant that both changes affect words that are at the end of a line in 1846, "munificent" being divided "mu-/nificent" and "domestic" appearing at the line ending immediately below. This suggests some mechanical reason for the 1854 variants, probably compositorial reconstruction of copy defective because of inking or a torn-off piece. Aiding this mechanical explanation is the fact that the division of "munificent" could suggest to the compositor that "nificent" starting the next line at the left would be reconstructed as "magnificent". In the line below "domestic" we find that the division of the final word is "chil-/dren". Here the context would create no difficulty in supplying any missing letters, whereas the illegibility of "domestic" might defy guesswork and lead to the omission of the word since sufficient sense was made without it. The case seems so plausible, and the 1854 variants so inexplicable as authorial revisions, that the present textual editor has felt some confidence in retaining the 1846 readings. Since some defect like frisket bite or bad inking would probably have been noticed by Hawthorne in reading over the 1846 copy, and since no observed example of the 1846 edition has a defect here, it is probably necessary to hypothesize some damage to the page subsequently, such as a tear, or an ink blot, that caused the ends of at least two lines in the 1846 page used to set 1854 to be illegible.

304.29 chillness] The probable correctness of the original *Democratic* reading as against the 1846 version "chilliness" is indicated by "chillness" at 443.19 in "The Old Apple-Dealer."

314.32 perplexed] The 1846 variant "perplexing" followed by 1854 for magazine "perplexed" seems to be a memorial error triggered by the preceding participle "enjoying". At best one could argue that if he changed the reading Hawthorne intended the admiration not simply to be "perplexed"—of the mixed nature of reverence and fear he had described at 314.10–16—but the feeling itself as being perplexing to those who admired; that is, that Copley and the beholders had a sense of a more heightened consciousness of their divided attitude than would be furnished simply by "perplexed". But this interpretation puts an intolerable strain on "perplexing", which still needs an object. The normal object would be Copley, observing the admiration of the other beholders; but he is himself associated with the "perplexing admiration" and it would be ridiculous to take it that the admiration of the others was perplexing to him. Despite the several seemingly authoritative substantive changes made in 1846, then, it would seem that the present variant is an error and that Hawthorne did not recognize it in 1854.

346.15 shrank] The variant "shrink" in 1846, followed by 1854, seems to depend upon "shall impute blame" but it brings the action into the reader's present in a manner that does not suit the context. Since no single one of the 1846 variants is demonstrably Hawthorne's in this story, and several (such as 341.35 and 346.6) are manifest errors, the odds against this present doubtful reading are too long.

355.16 die . . . lie] The uncertainty whether any 1846 reading in this story is authorial extends to the present variant, in which 1846 changed its copy to "dies . . . lies". The present editor takes this change to be a mistaken compositorial tinkering with the grammar. It is easy to see how "neither of us" could be interpreted as requiring the singular; what the compositor failed to recognize was the subjunctive.

357.22 shades] Although most of the unauthoritative 1846 readings are related forms to the original words, an occasional real substitution like "shadows" here, can take place. All other variants in this tale can be rejected with a clear conscience; it is unlikely that Hawthorne made this simple and relatively indifferent alteration of his poetic language.

370.20 reminiscences of] The dropping of the magazine phrase in 1846 would appear to be an eyeskip. One can imagine Hawthorne removing the phrase, perhaps, but the remaining modification "by all that" creates a problem of usage that requires a different preposition.

373.7 was] The 1846 change of "was" to "are" is puzzling because the strictures must apply to the past and make nonsense if focussed on the present. It would seem that the compositor was a literalist and felt that the perfect "has thereby avoided" required the normal present instead of the *Democratic* preterite. However, the change produces false grammar in that the singular "was" properly referred to the singular "use" whereas the 1846 "are" has been mistaken as referring to the dependent "of fancy and intellect". The same sort of change in 1846 may be observed in "shrink" for "shrank" at 346.15. See also the Textual Note to 294.22.

381–404 Earth's Holocaust] The central problem of this sketch is the authority of the 1846 variants, and, indeed, the question whether Hawthorne annotated the *Graham's* clipping in any respect, or had enough (misplaced) confidence in it to pass it without the careful scrutiny afforded at least a few of the other pieces. The concrete evidence does not favor the correctness of the 1846 text. In a quite unexampled manner, nine substantive variants originating in *Graham's* were repeated without change in 1846, as well as seven or eight accidentals forms affecting usage. In no case was a *Graham's* variant from MS corrected, although when in 1854 Hawthorne prepared printer's copy he altered four substantives back to the MS readings (381.13, 383.10, 400.2, 401.16) and perhaps two of the accidentals (390.19, 396.22) while at the same time making only one seemingly authoritative revision (392.28). The emphasis only on correction (such as it was) in 1854 instead of on revision confirms what the evidence of 1846 itself suggests, either that Hawthorne was convinced that the text stood as he wanted it, or that he was so little interested in the piece that he was indifferent to the niceties of its style. If Hawthorne—against the tendency in other of the later sketches—failed to see and to correct nine substantive copy-errors in 1846, although in 1854 identifying four introduced in 1846, the question must be raised whether any of the alterations originating in 1846 are his. A curious cluster of variants occurs on pages 151–52 of 1846, in which eight alterations are concentrated (Centenary 399.23–401.25). Normally this could be interpreted as a sign of close authorial attention, and indeed only one—"lamentations" for "lamentation" (401.16)—seems incorrect, and this is changed back to the original in 1854. Yet this mistake, and an earlier one in which 1854 restores "embellishments" to the MS reading "embellishment" (400.2), casts some doubt on the whole group, particularly on the other switches between singular and plural at 400.11, 401.3, and 401.4 not touched in 1854. In the light of the two 1854 corrections, it would be difficult, indeed, to justify any of the 1846 changes of this kind as authorial, particularly because such doubtful variants are by no means confined to this one sketch. If these six differences are not Hawthorne's, then it is likely that nothing else in 1846 can be positively identified as his, especially given the 1854 correction of variants at 381.13 and 383.10. The editorial theory for this sketch, therefore, is to admit no alterations of the manuscript copy-text save only the *Graham's* corrections of MS errors at 385.15, 387.9, 397.4, and 400.27, and the single 1854 revision at 392.28. Although the restoration of four 1846 errors to their MS purity made by 1854 indicates that Hawthorne read the copy with some care, its repetition of a number of the 1846 errors can scarcely be thought to confirm their authority. Hawthorne cannot be held accountable for the 1854 errors of "ribbons" for "ribands" (382.34) and "farther" for "further" (399.2) but he failed to notice the fifteen readings in which 1846 had repeated *Graham's* corruptions. It follows that no weight can be given to the validity of the new 1846 readings simply because 1854 agrees with seventeen of them, especially since in this group "comes" at 384.22 is clearly a sophistication, "upwards" at 386.7 an uncharacteristic Hawthorne usage, and "mountain fire" at 399.21 a simple misprint. In addition, 1854 perpetuates the nonsensical question marks initiated by *Graham's* for exclamations at 395.9 and 403.28, and the wrong spelling of MS "Sydney" at 388.20.

384.22 come] Hawthorne's subjunctives were fair game for compositors as in the 1846 variant "comes". A similar and even clearer misinterpretation is the change of 355.16 "die . . . lie" to "dies . . . lies".

388.12 ribbon] MS "ribbon" agrees with the singular "lace"; the 1846 "ribbons" is another example of the unauthoritative changes from singular to plural characteristic of that edition.

390.24 all together] The *OED* does not encourage the belief that the early confusion of "all together" and "altogether" continued much beyond the King James Bible. It does not appear that Hawthorne was being deliberately archaic here but instead was writing what probably must in his own day be classed as a misspelling. That it was not necessarily casual may be indicated by the event that in quoting this passage in an autograph leaf of 1864 (MS, University of Texas) he again wrote "altogether" as in the manuscript.

399.24 this great] The more specific "this" from MS seems required to distinguish the "Act of Faith" proposed in burning the religious symbols from the traditional ceremony associated with the phrase, a conventional use that seems to have misled the 1846 compositor.

442.11 of selling] 1854 "to sell" replaces the magazine's natural idiom "of selling", repeated in 1846, with an unnatural phrase, perhaps by contamination from preceding "to excite" and "to buy" and even "to be no need" or "to our old friend's feelings". Hawthorne was not likely to be the agent of this change.

444.7–8 nor has] That 1846 is here repairing a *Sargent's* error "nor as" seems reasonably clear, for to have "as yet been driven" refer back to the "has never" involves a tangle from which Hawthorne needed to be extricated if it had been original. Whether he was himself the agent is slightly doubtful, although on the basis of the addition of "old" at 446.5 (which repeats "old friend" at 440.33) he made at least one change in the text and thus can be shown to have looked through it.

445.13 serve as] Again, whether or not authorial, this 1846 change from "serve him as" removes a serious difficulty in reference. The "steam-fiend" is the subject of "He has skimmed" but the reference is rather ambiguous until the end of the sentence is reached, for "He had skimmed" could seem to refer, more expectedly, to "man". The original "to serve him" brings in "him" as man in close juxtaposition to "He" as steam-fiend and promotes the confusion further. The omission of this "him", then, helps to clarify the problem in reference and thus could well be authorial.

445.29 grisly] An old variant spelling existed in this word although the latest reported by the OED is in Sir Walter Scott in 1810. Nevertheless, it would be wrong to regard "grisly" as a misspelling, and 1854 "grizzly" is almost certainly no more than a typical compositorial modernization.

458.18 process] The 1846 variant "progress", repeated in 1854, seems to be a compositorial error, as indicated by the unidiomatic retention of the preposition "of" appropriate for "process" but not for "progress", which would require "in".

470.23 overarched] The word "overreached" in 1846 is probably a curious sophistication or misreading. The authority of the *Democratic* "overarched" seems to be attested by "overarching shade" at 24.3.

EDITORIAL EMENDATIONS IN
THE COPY-TEXT

Except for silent typographical modernizations remarked on in "The Centenary Texts: Editorial Procedures," prefixed to volume I (as "A Preface to the Text") and appended to volumes II–IV of this edition, every editorial change from copy-text is listed here. Also noticed are certain editorial decisions against emendation, marked *stet.* The titles of individual pieces are followed by symbols (identified below) for copy-text and for texts in which emended forms could have appeared. For each entry, the accepted reading, at the left of the bracket, is followed by the first appearance of the emendation, and then by any rejected reading and its source. An asterisk indicates that the crux is discussed in a Textual Note. In recording punctuation variants, a wavy dash ⁓ represents a word before the bracket, and a caret ∧ indicates the absence of a punctuation mark. Hawthorne's characteristic spellings are restored (as his "z" misread as "s" by compositors), but copy-texts cover a period of years during which Hawthorne's spelling habits varied, especially for doublet forms (as 'stopt / stopped') and for hyphenation of compounds; no attempt has been made to impose uniformity on such spellings between one periodical or annual and another.

BM   *Boston Miscellany of Literature and Fashion*
DR   *United States Magazine and Democratic Review*

G   *Graham's Lady's and Gentleman's Magazine*
GL   *Godey's Magazine and Lady's Book*
IM   *International Monthly Magazine*
NE   *New-England Magazine*
P   *Pioneer*
SM   *Sargent's New Monthly Magazine*
T   *The Token*
46   *Mosses from an Old Manse*, Wiley and Putnam, 1846
54   *Mosses from an Old Manse*, Ticknor and Fields, 1854

THE OLD MANSE (MS,46,54)

Note:	(H) is annotated 46; see Textual Commentary, p. 541.
3.13	highway] 46; high-way MS
*4.11	old] *stet* MS
5.14	afforded] 54; offered MS-46
5.20	Puritan] 54; puritan MS-46
6.3	little,] 54; ∼₍ MS-46
6.14	bank. He] 54; ∼; he MS-46
8.3	heaven] 54; Heaven MS-46
11.24	We] 54; —we MS-46
11.29	had that been] 46; had that had been MS
11.31	successors—] 54; ∼; MS-46
12.33	currants] 46; currents MS
*13.18	closest] 54; closer MS-46
14.27	Art] 54; art MS-46
*15.10	borne] *stet* MS
15.25	Nature] 54; nature MS-46
15.25	then] 54; omit MS-46
15.32	outbuildings] CENTENARY; ∼₍∼ MS-46; ∼-∼ 54
15.35	Time] 54; time MS-46
16.1–2	rain-drops; the] 54;∼—∼. The MS-46
16.11	penetrate; but] 54; ∼. But MS-46

16.19	universe,] 54; ~; MS-46
17.16	Bible] 54; bible MS-46
18.26	Papistry] 54; papistry MS-46
20.4	par.] 46; ~∧ MS
21.9	Lightly] 46; Lighty MS
21.12–13	Mussulman. He] 54; ~; he MS-46
21.24	so] 54; *omit* MS-46
21.26	wood-paths] CENTENARY; woodpaths MS-46
22.13	foliage,] 54; ~; MS-46
22.16	has] 54; had MS-46
22.25	Oriental] 54; oriental MS-46
23.10	-vines] 46; -Vines MS
24.1	Nor] 54; ¶Nor MS-46
24.26–27	partakes] 46; ~, MS
26.17	¶Did] 54; *no* ¶ MS-46
26.17	Ah,] 54; ~; MS-46
27.7	them,] 46; ~; MS
27.20	¶It] (H); *no* ¶ MS-54
27.22	this!] 54; ~. MS-46
28.31	sofa,] 54; ~; MS-46
29.6–7	rest—rest] 54; ~. Rest MS-46
29.7	trouble.] 54; ~! MS-46
29.13	accomplishment] 46; accomplish-| MS
29.26	sleep] 54; Sleep MS-46
30.11	writing, to] 54; writing it, to MS-46
31.15	universe; but] 54; ~. But MS-46
32.23	which] 46; which|which MS
33.16	chestnut] 46; chestnuts MS
34.4	hoped] 54; had hoped MS-46
34.20	even] 54; *omit* MS-46

THE BIRTH-MARK (P,46,54)

37.4	a union] 54; an union P-46
39.20,55.18	recognized] 46; recognised P
39.25	glance,] 46; ~: P

40.17, *et seq.*	Aminadab] 46; Aminidab *P*
42.21	medicinal] 46; medical *P*
48.22	their] 46; its *P*
49.24	recognize] 46; recognise *P*
*52.17	wrapt] *stet P*-46
54.14	eyelid] 46; ~-~ *P*
55.25	perfect!"] 46; ~!∧ *P*
*55.29	that earth] *stet P*

A Select Party (DR,46,54)

*60.31–32	of which . . . the example] *stet DR*-46
60.34	a humble] 54; an humble *DR*-46
62.8	easy-chair] Centenary; ~∧~ *DR*-54
63.28	jointed-doll] 46; painted doll *DR*
64.15	came] 54; had come *DR*-46
64.16	life,] 46; ~∧ *DR*
64.21	dim] 46; dire *DR*
64.32	amused] 46; caused *DR*
66.32	Dwight, and Freneau] 54; Dwight, Freeneau *DR*; Dwight, Freneau 46
69.2	this] 54; *omit DR*-46
70.15	by] 46; hy *DR*
71.21	chair] 46; chain *DR*
71.29	Master Genius] 54; ~-~ *DR*-46
73.10–11	away, . . . drowned] 46; away, and drowned *DR*
73.13	convoy] 46; convey *DR*

Young Goodman Brown (NE,46,54)

*74.1 et seq.	Goodman Brown] 46; goodman Brown *NE*
75.20 et seq.	traveller] 46; traveler *NE*
76.14	King] 46; king *NE*
77.4	kept—'] 54 (~—"); ~'— *NE*; ~"— 46

77.6	Well said] 46; Good NE
77.13	King] 54; king NE-46
78.23 *et seq.*	Deacon Gookin] 46; deacon Gookin NE
78.24 *et seq.*	Goody] 46; goody NE
79.13	But— . . . it?—] 54; ~, . . . ~? NE-46
79.17	bane—'] 54; ~'— NE; ~"— 46
81.12	travellers] 46; travelers NE
84.25	aflame] 54; a flame NE-46
85.28	mournful] 46; solemn NE
86.10	figure] 54; apparition NE-46
86.24	Gookin] 46; ~, NE
86.32	race] 46; grave NE
87.22	yours] 46; your's NE
87.24	which] 46; ~, NE
89.25	Bible] 54; bible NE-46

Rappaccini's Daughter (DR,46,54)

92.26	Père . . . Mère] 54; père . . .—mère DR
93.26,94.8,94.14	Signor] CENTENARY; signor DR-54
94.2	Paduan] 54; Lombard DR-46
94.10	No;] 54; ~: DR-46
94.13	that he] 46; *omit* that DR
94.15	Signora] CENTENARY; signora DR-54
*94.32	the fountain] *stet* DR
95.1	perishable] 46; *omit* DR
96.5	this] 54; the DR-46
96.8	Giovanni] 46; Givoanni DR
97.19	garden path] 54; ~-~ DR-46
98.29,107.16	Nature] 54; nature DR-46
98.30	daughter,] 46; ~ˌ DR
99.4,99.12,119.16	Professor] CENTENARY; professor DR-54
99.12	Doctor] CENTENARY; Dr. DR-54
100.16	withal] 54; with DR-46
100.16	Signor] 54; signor DR-46
101.4	cried] 46; cries DR
102.6	was] 54; in DR-46
103.13	window,] 46; ~ˌ DR

103.29   Now,] 54; ~ₐ DR-46
103.32–33   feet; . . . shivered;] 54; ~!— . . . ~!
                 DR-46
103.33   dead—] 54; ~!— DR-46
104.28   this] 46; the DR
105.7   ought Giovanni to have] 54; should Giovanni
                 have DR-46
105.25–26   yet hope and dread] 46; *hope* and *dread* DR
106.9   Professor's] CENTENARY; professor's DR-54
107.3   human, interest] 54; ~ₐ~, DR-46
107.11   other] 46; o[*undotted* i]her DR
107.16   Nature's] 54; nature's DR-46
107.31   shall] 46; should DR
108.2   lad] 46; bud DR
*109.2   that] 54; omit DR-46
109.29   will] 46; wil (*batter*) DR
110.2   Oriental] 54; oriental DR-46
110.33   not by the desire,] 46; not the desireₐ DR
111.19   if taught by] 54; under DR-46
112.10   depths of the] 54; *omit* DR-46
112.30–31   daylight] 54; day-light DR-46
114.29   he] 54; Giovanni DR-46
114.31   Giovanni's] 54; his DR-46
115.12   hand] 46; head DR
123.17   Approach] 46; "~ DR
123.25–26   reassured] 54; re-assured DR; re-|assured 46
123.30   my] 46; any DR
124.12   thunder-] 46; wonder- DR
125.6   Rappaccini] 46; Rappacini DR
125.16   science!] 54; ~? DR-46
126.8   of Time] 54; *omit* DR-46
126.33   hands] 54; hand DR-46

MRS. BULLFROG (*T*,46,54)

*134.9   broke] *stet T*
*134.22   did she] *stet T*

| 134.32 | unreasonable] 46; ~, T |
| 137.17 | 'The] 46;∧~ T |

FIRE-WORSHIP (DR,46,54)

*138.8	clouded] *stet* DR
*141.11	dusky] 46; dusty DR
*141.34	element has] *stet* DR
*143.18	latter] *stet* DR
144.2	fiend] 46; fires DR
144.17	urn] 46; urns DR
145.4	Alas!] 46; ~, DR
146.22	seemed] 46; seems DR
147.6	cold] 46; *omit* DR

BUDS AND BIRD-VOICES (MS,DR,46,54)

149.18	corpselike] DR (~-~); corpslike MS
*151.14	flourish] *stet* MS
151.17	though they] 46; but MS-DR
152.13	hour] 46; *omit* MS-DR
153.5	moss-covered] DR; ~∧~ MS
*153.34–154.1	departed . . . have] *stet* MS
154.5	tree-tops] DR; ~∧~ MS

MONSIEUR DU MIROIR (T,46,54)

161.30	visage. All] 46; *see* Historical Collation T
162.21–22	counterfeit. ¶In my age] 46; *see* Historical Collation T
163.4	hardware] 46; hard ware T

164.9	Ladurlad] 54; Lauderlad *T*; Lado 46
165.9	moonlight] 46; ~-~ *T*
165.27	had been] 46; been *T*
166.18	bed-chamber] 46; ~ₐ~ *T*
166.31	hereafter,] 46; ~ₐ *T*
*167.21	ray] *stet T*
*169.33	nature] *stet T*-46
*170.18	is himself] *stet T*
*170.19	illusive] *stet T*-46

THE HALL OF FANTASY (P,46,54)

172.19	recognizes] 46; recognises *P*
173.7–8	lives—if not . . . dream. At] 46; lives. At *P*
*174.6	reposited] *stet P*
175.18–19	them. ¶A] 46; them. In the most vivacious of these, I recognised Holmes. ¶A *P*
175.26–27	heart. ¶"Thank] 46; *see* Historical Collation *P*
176.3	had not heretofore] 46; has not hitherto *P*
180.12	recognized] 46; recognise *P*
180.14–15	they. ¶It] 46; *see* Historical Collation *P*
180.27	nonsense,—] 46; ~,ₐ *P*
180.27–28	throng. ¶Yet] 46; *see* Historical Collation *P*
180.29	fellowship] 46; brotherhood *P*
181.3,183.13	recognize] 46; recognise *P*
185.15	who had been sent] 46; whom Dr. Collyer had sent *P*
185.15–16	in magnetic] 46; in the magnetic *P*
185.23	prophecy] 46; prophesy *P*

THE CELESTIAL RAIL-ROAD (MS,DR,46,54)

188.15–16	Station House] 54; ~-~ MS-46
189.28	Greatheart?"] DR; ~?", MS

189.30	engineer] CENTENARY; conductor MS-54
190.9,27	engineer] 54; conductor MS-46
192.3	we] DR; we we MS
*195.7	itself] stet MS-DR
196.20	more, certainly,—] 46; more∧—certainly, MS-DR
197.2	there;] 46; ~, MS-DR
200.8	Yet,] 54; ~∧ MS-46
201.3	transaction] 46; bargain MS-DR
202.7	Mr. Foot-it-to-Heaven] 46; Mr. Go-the-old-way MS-DR
202.25	Fair] 54; fair MS-46
203.9	long since] 46; omit MS-DR
205.24	steam ferry-boat] DR; ~-~∧~ MS

THE PROCESSION OF LIFE (DR,46,54)

*207–22	The Procession of Life] see Textual Note
*207.3	of a] stet DR
*207.7	train] 46; trail DR
207.13	taken] 46; continued DR
208.26	other] 46; other common DR
208.30	with gold] 46; with much gold DR
209.1	toes,] 46; ~∧ DR
209.31	heart's] 46; hearts' DR
*210.19	human rank] 46; rank DR
211.22	far-descended] 46; ~∧~ DR
211.23	match] 46; watch DR
*211.26	brethren] 46; these brethren DR
212.4	unutterably,] 54; ~∧ DR-46
212.10	funereal] 46; funeral DR
212.24	dwelling-house] 46; dwelling-place DR
213.21	them] 46; the DR
213.23	arts, or] 46; arts, literature, or DR
*216.11	chambers] stet DR
219.4	those] 46; those suitable DR
219.12	to] 54; omit DR-46

*219.16	more] 46; much DR
220.21	State] 46; state DR
220.21	to] 46; in DR
221.11	towards] 54; toward DR-46
221.25–26	pale horse] 46; Pale Horse DR
222.13	echoes] 54; passes DR; pass 46

FEATHERTOP (MS,IM,54)

224.4	New England] IM; ~-~ MS
225.1	corporosity] CENTENARY; corporcity MS-54
232.2	world,] 54; ~ₐ MS-IM
234.26	glistened] IM; glistenened MS
239.23	a-light] CENTENARY; alight IM-54
240.17	looking-glass] IM; ~ₐ~ MS
241.9	guest,)] CENTENARY; ~), MS; ~,ₐ IM-54
*241.29	ceiling] IM; cieling MS
243.21	coruscating] IM; corruscating MS
243.23	pipe-bowl] IM; ~ₐ~ MS
246.2	continued.] 54; ~, IM (MS lacking)

THE NEW ADAM AND EVE (DR,46,54)

248.31	an inner] 46; the inner DR
249.16–17	situation] 46; category DR
252.7	upward] CENTENARY; upwards DR-54
252.10–11	deep reverberating] 54; deep and reverberating DR-46
253.2	towards] 54; to DR-46
258.24	come] 54; came DR-46
260.5	Nature] 54; nature DR-46
264.7	opportunities are] 46; opportunities of wisdom are DR
264.14	columns] 46; volumes DR

264.16	as if it] 54; as it *DR-46*
266.14	We] 46; Ye *DR*
266.25	wherewith Nature] 54; wherewith kind Nature *DR-46*

Egotism; or, The Bosom-Serpent (DR,46,54)

268	Bosom-Serpent] CENTENARY; ~ʌ~ *DR-54*
268.14	aright] 46; right *DR*
*270.24	were it] *stet DR*
271.31–32	whatsoever] 46; whatever *DR*
273.6	that] 46; *omit DR*
273.21	it be] 54; *omit DR-46*
274.9	gloried] 46; glorified *DR*
274.13	and a] 46; *omit* a *DR*
274.23	out] 46; *omit DR*
275.17	has stung] 46; stung *DR*
276.19	depreciated] 54; deprecated *DR-46*
277.16	man;] 54; ~: *DR-46*
281.8–9	whether, and when, to] 46; whether to *DR*
282.6	had] 46; has *DR*
283.31	but] 46; *omit DR*

The Christmas Banquet (DR,46,54)

288.13	and, in] 54; *omit* in *DR-46*
290.4	of the feast] 46; *omit DR*
292.2	lore] 46; love *DR*
292.33	Cold] 54; cold *DR-46*
293.15	noonday] 54; ~-~ *DR-46*
294.3	cypress wreath] 54; ~-~ *DR-46*
294.6	recognizing] 46; re-organizing *DR*
*294.22	had] *stet DR*
294.23	baby] 46; babe *DR*

294.23	smothering] 46; smothered *DR*
*295.27	leger] 54; ledger *DR*-46
*297.8	more] 46; *omit DR*
*297.19	mystery] *stet DR*
297.20	exclaim,] 54; ~; *DR*-46
*299.7	lessons] *stet DR*
300.1	travel] 46; travels *DR*
*300.4	domestic] *stet DR*-46
301.23	caused] 46; causes *DR*
302.9	merriment.] 46; ~∧ *DR*
303.23	enjoy] 46; envy *DR*
*304.29	chillness] *stet DR*

DROWNE'S WOODEN IMAGE (GL, 46, 54)

306.18	the fellow] 46; the very fellow *GL*
307.2	Here—"] CENTENARY; ~"— *GL*-54
307.3	and scarlet] 46; and a scarlet *GL*
307.33	Carrara] 46; Carrera *GL*
308.2	were,] 46; ~∧ *GL*
309.4	image] 46; workmanship *GL*
309.15	Town] 46; Tower *GL*
309.18	daytime] 54; ~∧~ *GL*; ~-~ 46
309.30	act] 46; fact *GL*
311.16–17	deficiency which . . . so rare] 54; deficiency, so rare *GL*-46
311.19	heretofore] 54; *omit GL*-46
313.11	and] 54; *omit GL*-46
313.24	heart—"] CENTENARY; ~"— *GL*-46; ~,"— 54
313.28	faith!] CENTENARY; ~? *GL*; ~. 46–54
313.32	muttered] 46; murmured *GL*
*314.32	perplexed] *stet GL*
315.18	Even had] 54; Had *GL*-46
315.22	now astounded] 46; now to be astonished *GL*
316.6	transfixed . . . in] 46; transformed . . . with *GL*

317.15	Copley,] 46; ∼∧ GL
319.26	streets] 46; Streets GL
320.3–4	but, quenched] 46; but, being quenched GL

The Intelligence Office (DR,46,54)

321.19	leger-like] 54; ledger-like DR-46
324.1	Man of Intelligence] CENTENARY; man of intelligence DR-54
325.14	sad] 46; said DR
326.24	owners] 46; owner DR
326.24	claim] 46; reclaim DR
326.31	wedlock;] 54; ∼: DR-46
327.16	time] 54; while DR-46
328.25	eye;] 46; ∼: DR
329.26,31	burthen] CENTENARY; burden DR-54
330.20	and their] 54; and for their DR-46
331.21	a few] 46; others DR

Roger Malvin's Burial (T,DR,46,54)

337.12	unfortunate] DR; unforunate T
337.19 *et seq.*	recognized] DR; recognised T
338.5	oak-leaves] DR; ∼∧∼ T
340.30	here—'] 54 (∼ —"); ∼'— T; ∼"— DR-46
340.31	Bourne,'] DR (∼,"); ∼;' T
340.32	Malvin.] 54; ∼, T; ∼; DR; ∼: 46
341.35	recover of] DR; recover T
342.15	distant,] 54; ∼; T-46
343.4	other.] 54; ∼, T-46
343.25	himself] 54; *omit* T-46
343.32	downward] 46; downwards T-DR
*346.15	shrank] *stet* T-DR

· 615 ·

347.19	recognize] *DR*; recognise *T*
348.4	and—'] 54 (~—"); ~'— *T*; ~"— *DR*-46
348.21	further at the] 54; farther at that *T*-46
348.30	death';] CENTENARY; ~;' *T*; ~:" *DR*-46
348.31	a few months] 54; two years *T*-46
351.34	asunder] *DR*; assunder *T*
352.32	Fantasie] 46; Fantasiē *T*-*DR*
353.3	latter] 54; larger *T*-46
354.8	these] 54; *omit T*-46
*355.16	die . . . lie] *stet T*-*DR*
357.1	symbol] *DR*; cymbol *T*
*357.22	shades] *stet T*-*DR*
358.27–28	report had] 54; report of the gun had *T*-46

P.'s Correspondence (DR,46,54)

362.25	from] 46; for *DR*
363.2	Memory] 54; memory *DR*-46
363.9	compotators] 46; competitors *DR*
364.3	lordship apologized] 54; lordship had apologised *DR*-46
364.21	Methodism] 54; methodism *DR*-46
364.25	his] 46; his own *DR*
366.5	had] 46; has *DR*
366.32	hobgoblin;] 46; ~: *DR*
367.24	when] 46; while *DR*
367.27	reverend] 46; reverent *DR*
368.19–20	I suspect] 54; I did suspect *DR*-46
369.33–34	past? I had] 54; *see* Historical Collation *DR*-46
*370.20	reminiscences of] *stet DR*
371.17	up rose] 46; uprose *DR*
371.28	the iron-] 54; that iron- *DR*-46
372.14	manner] 54; mode *DR*-46
372.19	reviewing] 46; viewing *DR*
*373.7	was wont] *stet* was *DR*
374.15	our] 46; your *DR*

374.30	my mind] 54; my own mind DR-46
375.8	never] 54; not DR-46
376.21	that] 46; *omit* DR
377.11	Drury Lane] 54; ⁓⸱⁓ DR-46
378.2	Providence] 54; providence DR-46

EARTH'S HOLOCAUST (MS,G,46,54)

*381–404	Earth's Holocaust] *see* Textual Note
*384.22	come] *stet* MS-G
385.15	of coals] G; of of coals MS
387.9	not worth] G; not an worth MS
387.13	commiserating] G; commisserating MS
*388.12	ribbon] *stet* MS
*390.24	all together] altogether MS-G
392.28	consecrated] 54; *omit* MS-46
397.4	unregarded] G; ungreguarded MS
398.8–9	book-worm] G; ⁓ₐ⁓ MS
*399.24	this] *stet* MS-G
400.10	ceiling] G; cieling MS
400.27	Heavens] CENTENARY; Heaven's MS; heavens G-54

PASSAGES FROM A RELINQUISHED WORK (NE,54)

405	Passages from a Relinquished | Work | At Home] 54; The Story Teller. | No. I. | At Home. NE
409.28	but] 54; But NE
411.21	travelled] 54; traveled NE
411.27	Traveller] 54; Traveler NE
414.7	Oh] CENTENARY; O NE-54
414.25	travelling] 54; traveling NE

417.13	The Village Theatre] 54; The Story Teller. | No. II. | The Village Theatre. *NE*
417.14	-traveller] 54; -traveler *NE*
419.6	deep,] 54; ∼∧ *NE*
420.3–5	as Mr. Higginbotham's Catastrophe. ¶This] 54; as | Mr. Higginbotham's Catastrophe. ["Mr. Higginbotham's Catastrophe" follows, as printed in *Twice-told Tales*.] ¶This *NE*
420.5–6	there presented, and] 54 (*editorial emendation*); here presented to the reader, and *NE*

Sketches from Memory (*NE*,54)

422	Sketches from Memory. | The Notch of the White Mountains] 54; Sketches from Memory. | By a Pedestrian. | No. I. | [Introduction follows; *see* Historical Collation.] | The Notch. *NE*
423.3 *et seq.*	travelling] 54; traveling *NE*
425.26 *et seq.*	travellers] 54; travelers *NE*
427.3	Quakers] 54; quakers *NE*
427.13	Snow] 54; snow *NE*
428.17	than that] 54; that that *NE*
429.14	looking] 54; lookgin *NE*
429.29	The Canal-Boat] 54 (∼∼∧∼); *see* Historical Collation *NE*
430.1	Lake] 54; lake *NE*
430.5	Nature] 54; nature *NE*
431.2	Genesee] 54; Genessee *NE*
433.24	Bridge] 54; bridge *NE*
434.20	Schenectady] 54; Schnectady *NE*
435.8	and shrinking] 54; and skrinking *NE*
435.28	ceased] Centenary; cease *NE*-54
438.7	fire; . . . death;] Centenary; ∼: . . . ∼: *NE*; ∼, . . . ∼, 54
438.23	"long level,"] Centenary; '∼∼,' *NE*-54

The Old Apple-Dealer (SM,46,54)

439	Apple-Dealer] 46; ~∧~ SM
*442.11	of selling] *stet* SM
*444.7–8	nor has] 46; nor as SM
444.11	Author] 46; author SM
445.3	cake,] 46; ~∧ SM
*445.13	serve as] 46; serve him as SM
*445.29	grisly] *stet* SM
446.5	old] 46; *omit* SM

The Artist of the Beautiful (DR,46,54)

447.14	watchmaker] 54; watch-maker DR-46
448.4	Poh] 54; Pooh DR-46
450.12	Nature] 54; nature DR-46
451.17	eyesight] 54; ~-~ DR-46
452.14	it,] 54; it∧ DR; *omit* 46
453.9	Well;] Centenary; ~∧ DR; ~, 46–54
453.17	can never] 54; never can DR-46
453.28	won't] 54; wont DR-46
455.1	scarcely] 46; carcely DR
455.12	treatment.] 46; ~∧ DR
456.25	paddles] 46; pulleys DR
*458.18	process] *stet* DR
458.20	itself.] 46; ~∧ DR
459.19	spiritualization] 46; spiritualisation DR
460.3	Annie] 46; Anne DR
465.7	fairy] 46; fancy DR
466.25	reinspired] 46; reïnspired DR
467.32	a proof] 46; proof DR
469.1	seemed] 46; seem DR
469.7	husband.] 46; ~∧ DR

*470.23   overarched] *stet* DR
472.24   secret . . . secret] 46; sweet . . . sweet DR
475.22   was yet] 54; yet was DR-46

A Virtuoso's Collection (BM,46,54)

476.8   staircase] 54; ⌣⌣ BM-46
476.17   great-coat] Centenary; ⌣ₐ⌣ BM-46;
                 greatcoat 54
479.22   snake,"] 46; ⌣,' BM
480.20–22   This . . . Kendall."] 46; *omit* BM
483.8–10   hair and . . . breast. Here] 46; hair. Here BM
483.32   of the] 46; cf the BM
484.18   Boone] 54; Boon BM-46
486.8   Van Corlear] 46; van Corlear BM
486.12   Papirius] 46; Papyrius BM
486.24   Egyptian] 46; Egyptain BM
487.25–27   And . . . salvation.] 46; *omit* BM
488.22–25   laugh, . . . fire. He then] 46; laugh. He then
                 BM
488.28   Great Carbuncle] 54; great carbuncle BM-46
489.3   out] 54; *omit* BM-46
490.3   spoke,] 54; ⌣ₐ BM-46
490.28–31   Alexander's . . . it.] 46; *omit* BM
491.25   Psyche's] 54; Psyché's BM-46
492.34   undescribed] 46; undiscribed BM
493.25   frigate] 54; *omit* BM-46
494.4   Schlemihl's] 46; Schlemil's BM

WORD-DIVISION

1. *End-of-the-Line Hyphenation in the Century Edition*

Possible compounds hyphenated at the end of a line in the Centenary text are listed here if they are hyphenated within the line in the copy-text. Exclusion from this list means that a possible compound appears as one unhyphenated word in the copy-text. Also excluded are hyphenated compounds in which both elements are capitalized.

3.4	black-ash	24.21	will-|of-the-whisps
4.33	long-hidden	29.27	age-long
5.26	willow-tree	30.26	self-involved
6.5	willow-branches	31.27	mountain-
6.16	battle-smoke		atmosphere
6.31	mountain-torrent	42.16	cloud-region
6.34	water-power	46.33	re-appeared
9.4	stone-wall	69.1	wind-stirred
9.6, 32.14	moss-grown	72.29	thunder-storm
11.16	wind-rocked	73.4	meteor-lighted
13.2	bread-fruit	73.10	three-cornered
13.26	market-gardener	76.13	dinner-table
18.26	sledge-hammer	80.1	fellow-traveller
23.2	pond-lily	84.14	meeting-house
24.13	banquetting-hall	84.34	to-and-|fro
24.15	red-gleaming	87.21	blood-spot

90.1	grand-children	225.14	button-holes
93.24	ill-furnished	227.1	chimney-corner
98.20,	matter-|of-fact	230.9	over-peopled
451.31		232.14	night-fog
112.30	day-light	243.33	well-ordered
113.5	gem-like	251.7	watch-word
124.22	heart-broken	261.1	wished-for
130.12	looking-glass	261.23	bank-notes
139.7	half-a-dozen	269.21	snake-possessed
144.28	half-asleep	275.30	copper-head
145.1	air-tight	281.26	serpent-tribe
149.32	snow-drifts	289.32	fancy-tortured
157.18	up-springing	294.10	blood-stain
162.22	ball-room	301.11	long-frequented
163.11	temperance-man	307.15	figure-head
167.22	lamp-light	308.9	pump-heads
168.32	ill-treatment	308.18	ship-owner
175.29	laurel-gatherers	314.34	master-piece
176.30	every-day	316.10	sea-captain
178.11	gum-elastic	318.8	witch-times
183.10	new-born	321.12	show-bills
191.30,	rail-road	326.26	wedding-rings
202.8		328.33	mansion-house
196.1	church-music	334.22	To-morrow
198.22	Clog-|the-spirit	337.4	well-remembered
198.23	Wind-of-|doctrine	343.29	oak-leaves
199.10,	Smooth-|it-away	355.30	thick-strewn
201.15,203.2		370.15	light-fingered
202.28	soap-bubble	374.17	foot-passengers
203.23	Flimsy-|faith	381.21	foot-travellers
204.2	creeping-plants	383.6	worm-eaten
206.8	smoke-wreath	383.18	gray-haired
209.20	house-painters	385.11	precious-stones
211.8	drawing-rooms	388.17	hack-politician
211.11	silk-gowned	391.7	cannon-foundries
213.2	alms-house	392.10	terror-stricken
219.19	broad-brim	398.3	heavy-looking
222.6	stuff-jacket	398.8	book-worm
223.17	corn-patch	409.33	lattice-work

413.21	home-baked	441.27	frost-bitten
426.12	trumpet-tone	450.6	school-boy
432.22	dwelling-houses	455.5	clock-work
433.12	good-natured	455.14	church-steeple
437.30	forest-avenue	477.1	all-important

2. End-of-the-Line Hyphenation in the Copy-Texts

The following possible compounds are hyphenated at the ends of lines in the copy-text. The Centenary form, as listed below, represents Hawthorne's predominant usage within the copy-texts or, lacking such examples, in contemporaneous Hawthorne manuscripts.

3.5	twelvemonth	47.14	lifetime
3.12	roadside	53.20	overspread
3.17	passer-by	55.3,143.5	rose-color
9.29	battle-field	56.11	self-same
12.3	windfall	57.17	sunshine
12.26	weed-grown	59.8	footstep
15.26	willow-tree	60.10	earth-incrusted
15.30	splash-|splash-splashing	60.13	easy-chair
		60.29	superhuman
20.23	looking-glass	64.8	dream-lady
20.25,	above-mentioned	67.8	arm-in-|arm
189.16		72.6	ice-creams
24.21	hobgoblins	72.7	whip-syllabubs
25.1	mint-mark	73.3	long-past
25.10	tomorrow	88.32	grave-yard
25.22	overshadowed	91.6	pen-and-|ink
31.22	shining-one	98.29	thought-worn
33.28	angel-gifts	100.30	black-letter
42.26	masterpiece	102.32	orange-colored
43.17	under-worker	105.14	fever-pitch
46.30	furnace-room	112.6	queen-like

125.8	flower-odors	225.26	maple-leaves
128.7	thunder-stricken	229.2	witchcraft
130.2	dry-goods	230.2	good-for-|nothing
135.28	thin-visaged	230.3	patchwork
138.13	ice-encrusted	230.25	cottage-kitchen
141.2	tea-kettle	234.19	scarecrow
141.18,146.19	fireside	247.15	sea-shore
141.29	window-panes	251.4	dry-good
142.5	arm-chair	252.25	foretaste
142.23	crisscross	254.29	plague-spot
143.23	chimney-place	256.10	harp-strings
144.3	thunder-storm	257.23	dwelling-place
145.27	forefathers	258.20	dinner-party
148.21	stone-wall	260.28	news-boy
149.29	to-morrow	265.33	worn-out
152.1	by-gone	273.31	snake-like
152.3	flower-shrubs	275.25	close-fisted
154.5	tree-tops	275.34	bosom-serpents
155.22	four-|and-twenty	280.1	bosom-fiend
161.21	twin-children	281.25	half-opened
162.6	fever-heat	287.9	eye-caverns
162.19	copper-washed	287.9	skeleton-jaws
162.25	dress-circle	287.18	skeleton-arm
175.18	to-and-|fro	289.32	fate-stricken
176.5,276.12	fellow-men	294.7	re-assemble
194.32	half-extinct	301.9	Christmas-tide
195.2	cavern-mouth	306.14	figure-head
195.25	pale-cheeked	308.10	gate-posts
203.4	silver-mine	311.26	life-giving
204.2	half-overgrown	315.35	silver-hilted
206.18	heart-quake	316.11	shore-going
210.11	nation-sweeping	325.33	wo-begone
211.9	nose-gay	327.3	moss-roses
211.24	backwoodsman	328.14	button-hole
214.21	frost-work	334.18	To-morrow
215.3	bond-servants	345.29	forest-leaves
223.19,227.8	blackbirds	356.25	grave-stone
224.29	pudding-stick	362.19	whereabouts

371.28	iron-grated	443.15	waistcoat
379.26	parlor-music	443.33	passably-to-|do
379.26	organ-peals	444.8	household
380.5	proof-readers	444.30	cake-and-|candy
381.4	worn-out	445.12	steam-fiend
384.10	new-found	446.21	life-long
387.14	boon-companions	447.6	pinchbeck
388.13	half-worn	449.27	gridiron
394.15	day-books	449.33	schoolfellow
396.28	long-continued	450.32	rainbow
407.23	tavern-haunters	451.31	watchmaker's
412.21	pocket-Bible	453.23	cotton-machine
412.30	oak-leaves	456.2	daylight
418.13	school-house	456.22	bell-glass
424.3,427.21	opera-glass	462.30	townspeople
426.25	fire-place	463.13,473.14	watchmaker
427.2	bridegrooms	469.11	baby-eyes
432.1	money-getting	476.7	sidewalk
434.23	ill-selected	480.27	water-fowl
435.1	close-fisted	493.7	fore-finger
435.27	peace-breakers	494.34	breast-plate
439.5	word-painting		

3. Special Cases

The following possible compounds are hyphenated at the end of the line in both copy-text and Centenary Edition. Words appear here in the adopted Centenary form, which is obscured by line-end hyphenation.

18.9	ill-starched	157.1	mile-wide
59.7	re-echoed	157.8	overflowed
91.4	countrymen	209.32	pale-cheeked
110.18	offspring	212.34	sailor-boy
139.32	rail-car	219.13	handicraftsmen

220.27	weak-framed	322.16	ill-suited
223.21	scarecrow	326.23	white-washed
224.17,226.15		368.24	peasant-poet's
263.13	thanksgiving	369.18	half-rusted
275.22	gentleman's	378.4	night-time
285.27	likewise	438.16	packet-boats
310.23	outvalued	471.26	day-dreams
316.21	townspeople	488.9	chafing-dish

HISTORICAL COLLATION

Substantive variants from copy-text are listed chronologically in descent of the texts of individual pieces through the stereotype 1854 collection to the Centenary Edition. Also listed are copy-text errors not forming accepted words.

Rejected first-edition substantive variants head all lists but those of four pieces where rejections of manuscript copy-text precede those of the first printed appearance.

Following the title of each piece are the symbols (identified below) for copy-text and successive appearances. For each entry, the Centenary reading to the left of the bracket is followed by the rejected variant with its origin and other editions using it. Unlisted editions may be taken to agree with Centenary.

BM   *Boston Miscellany of Literature and Fashion*
DR   *United States Magazine and Democratic Review*
G   *Graham's Lady's and Gentleman's Magazine*
GL   *Godey's Magazine and Lady's Book*
IM   *International Monthly Magazine*
NE *New-England Magazine*
P   *Pioneer*
SM   *Sargent's New Monthly Magazine*
T   *The Token*

46 *Mosses from an Old Manse*, Wiley and Putnam, 1846
54 *Mosses from an Old Manse*, Ticknor and Fields, 1854

The Old Manse (MS,46,54)

Note:	(H) is annotated *Mosses*; see Textual Commentary, p. 541.
5.14	afforded] offered MS-46
11.29	had that been] had that had been MS
12.33	currants] currents MS
13.18	closest] closer MS-46
21.24	so] *omit* MS-46
22.16	has] had MS-46
24.1	Nor] ¶Nor MS-46
26.17	¶Did] *no* ¶ MS-46
27.20	¶It] (H); *no* ¶MS-54
29.13	accomplishment] accomplish- MS
30.11	writing, to] writing it, to MS-46
32.23	which] which which MS
33.16	chestnut] chestnuts MS
34.4	hoped] had hoped MS-46
34.20	even] *omit* MS-46
5.27	eaves] eves 46
7.21	beautiful] beautified 46
8.20	fragments] fragment 46
9.3	A humbler] An humbler 46
9.26	county] country 46–54
10.8	have] has 46–54
10.29	subsistence] substance 46–54
11.8	an exquisite] *omit* an 46–54
11.14	amid] and 46–54
12.34	this] his 46–54
13.12	the summer] *omit* the 46–54
14.4	nor] or 46–54
14.11	airy] any 46

15.10	borne] born 46–54
17.6	Saints'] Saint's 46–54
17.12	ejaculations] speculations 46
17.17	towards] toward 46
18.11	at] to 46
19.30	among] *omit* 46–54
20.10	writer's] writers' 46
21.30	straight-laced] strait-laced 46
21.34	lovely] lonely 46
25.11	a house] the house 46–54
25.12	overhung] overhang 46–54
25.20	whence] where 46
27.16	these] those 46–54
27.20	alive, at] alive, and at 46
27.30	blissful] blessed 46–54
28.26	flung] floating 46–54
29.19	tranquil] magic 46
30.5	afflicts] afflict 46–54
30.14	serene] severe 46–54
30.30	this free] the free 46–54
33.2	nor have ever] nor have I ever 46–54
33.9	hastened] hasten 46
33.15	strewing the green] strewing green 46
33.20	cleaned] cleared 46–54
5.16–17	the Paphian] Paphian 54

THE BIRTH-MARK (P,46,54)

37.4	a union] an union P-46
40.17 et seq.	Aminadab] Aminidab P
42.21	medicinal] medical P
48.22	their] its P
38.2	Aylmer] Aylmar 46
44.25	such rapture] such a rapture 46–54
54.3	round] around 46–54

55.29	that earth] the earth 46–54
52.17	wrapt] rapt 54
55.4	slightest] lightest 54

A Select Party (DR,46,54)

60.34	a humble] an humble DR-46
63.28	jointed-doll] painted doll DR
64.15	came] had come DR-46
64.21	dim] dire DR
64.32	amused] caused DR
66.32	Dwight, and Freneau] Dwight, Freeneau DR; see also 46
69.2	this] omit DR-46
70.15	by] hy DR
71.21	chair] chain DR
73.10–11	away, . . . drowned] away, and drowned DR
73.13	convoy] convey DR
58.5	fantastically] fanatically 46
66.32	Dwight, and Freneau] Dwight, Freneau 46
60.31	of which] with which 54
60.32	the example] an example 54
67.7	John] Joel 54

Young Goodman Brown (NE,46,5 4)

77.6	Well said] Good NE
84.25	aflame] a flame NE-46
85.28	mournful] solemn NE
86.10	figure] apparition NE-46
86.32	race] grave NE
75.22	overhead] overheard 46
77.6	interpreting] interrupting 46
79.20	receipt] recipe 46–54

85.15	revered] reverend 46
87.15	fathers'] father's 46
82.3	nor] or 54
87.12	widow's] widows' 54

RAPPACCINI'S DAUGHTER (DR,46,54)

94.2	Paduan] Lombard DR-46
94.13	that he] omit that DR
95.1	perishable] omit DR
96.5	this] the DR-46
96.8	Giovanni] Givoanni DR
100.16	withal] with DR-46
101.4	cried] cries DR
102.6	was] in DR-46
104.28	this] the DR
105.7	ought Giovanni to have] should Giovanni have DR-46
105.25	yet] omit DR
107.11	other] o[undotted i]her DR
107.31	shall] should DR
108.2	lad] bud DR
109.2	that] omit DR-46
109.29	will] wil DR
110.33	not by the] not the DR
111.19	if taught by] under DR-46
112.10	depths of the] omit DR-46
114.29	he] Giovanni DR-46
114.31	Giovanni's] his DR-46
115.12	hand] head DR
123.30	my] any DR
124.12	thunder-] wonder- DR
125.6	Rappaccini] Rappacini DR
126.8	of Time] omit DR-46
126.33	hands] hand DR-46
91.1–93.8	Introductory passage omitted 46
94.32	the fountain] a fountain 46

97.31	perfumed] perfume 46
127.2–3	shuddered nervously] shuddered very nervously 46
103.24	nor] or 54
115.10	come] comes 54

Mrs. Bullfrog (T,46,54)

133.9	a calves foot] calves-foot 46; *see also* 54
134.9	broke] broken 46–54
134.22	did she] she did 46–54
129.18	reconciling] recognizing 54
133.9	a calves foot] calf's-foot 54
133.18	sharp] sharply 54

Fire-Worship (DR,46,54)

141.11	dusky] dusty DR
144.2	fiend] fires DR
144.17	urn] urns DR
146.22	seemed] seems DR
147.6	cold] *omit* DR
138.8	clouded] cloudy 46–54
141.34	element has] elements have 46–54
143.18	latter] later 46–54
145.24	to] with 46–54

Buds and Bird-Voices (MS,DR,46,54)

151.17	though they] but MS-DR
152.13	hour] *omit* MS-DR
151.6	-window] -windows DR-54

151.14	flourish] flourish only DR-46; *see also* 54
152.8	strike] strikes *DR*-54
154.27, 157.7	farther] further *DR*-54
149.3	nor] or 46
153.34–154.1	departed . . . have] *omit* 46–54
151.14	flourish] flourish always 54

Monsieur du Miroir (*T*,46,54)

161.30

visage. All] visage. If we chance to meet, when I am pale with midnight study, or haply flushed with a mere sip of silver-top champagne, the poor fellow is sure to exhibit an aspect of worn-out or over excited energy, graduated precisely to my own. All   *T*

162.21–22

counterfeit. ¶In my age] counterfeit. ¶Intimate as, in some respects, we may be said to be, the reader will hardly conceive my ignorance in regard to many important points of M. du Miroir's mode of life. I never yet could discover, nor even guess, what is his business or pastime, in the long space which sometimes elapses without an interview between us. He seldom goes into society, except when introduced by me. Yet, occasionally, I have caught a dim glimpse of M. du Miroir's well-known countenance, gazing at me from the casement of some aristocratic mansion where I am not a guest; although, quite as often, I grieve to say, he has been imprudent enough to show himself within the dusty panes of the lowest pot-houses, or even more disreputable haunts. In such cases, meeting each other's eyes, we both look down abashed. It must not be concealed, however, that, while holding my course amid the week-day bustle which flows past a church, I have discerned my friend through the lofty windows, doubtless enjoy-

ing a private audience of Religion, who sits
six days in her deserted fane, and sees all
the world the seventh. With what sect he
worships on the Sabbath, indispensable as
the point is to a proper judgment of his moral
character, I absolutely never knew. When
the bells fling out their holy music, I generally see him, in his best black suit, of the
same pattern as my own, and wearing a mild
solemnity of aspect, that edifies me almost as
much as the sound orthodoxy of my reverend
pastor. But we meet no more, till the services
are ended. Whether he goes to church with
the Episcopalians, to chapel with the Method-
ists, or to the synagogue with the Jews—
whether perverted to Roman Catholic idolatry, or to Universalist or Unitarian infidelity—is a matter which, being no controver-
sialist, M. du Miroir keeps to himself. Of
course, however exemplary in his worldly
character, he cannot expect my full confidence, while there remains the slightest ambiguity on this head. ¶In my age   *T*

164.9	Ladurlad] Lauderlad *T; see also* 46
165.27	had been] been *T*
164.9	Ladurlad] Lado 46
167.21	ray] rays 46–54
170.4	companion] companions 46–54
170.18	is himself] himself is 46–54
161.23	least] last 54
170.19	illusive] delusive 54
171.13	mysteries] mysterious 54

THE HALL OF FANTASY (*P*,46,54)

173.7–8	lives—if not . . . dream. At] lives. At *P*
175.18–19	them. ¶A] them. In the most vivacious of these, I recognised Holmes. ¶A *P*

175.26–27   heart. ¶"Thank] heart. Bryant had come hither from his editor's room, his face no longer wrinkled by political strife, but with such a look as if his soul were full of the Thanatopsis, or of those beautiful stanzas on the Future Life. Percival, whom to see is like catching a glimpse of some shy bird of the woods, had shrunk into the deepest shadow that he could find. Dana was also there; though, for a long time back, the public has been none the richer for his visits to the Hall of Fantasy; but, in his younger days, he descended to its gloomiest caverns, and brought thence a treasure of dark, distempered stories. Halleck, methought, had strayed into this purple atmosphere rather by way of amusement, than because the strong impulse of his nature compelled him hither; and Willis, though he had an indefeasible right of entrance, looked so much like a man of the world, that he seemed hardly to belong here. Sprague had stept across from the Globe Bank, with his pen behind his ear. Pierpont had come hither in the hope, I suppose, of allaying the angry glow of controversy; a fire unmeet for such an altar as a poet's kindly heart. ¶In the midst of these famous people, I beheld the figure of a friend, whom I fully believed to be thousands of leagues away. His glance was thrown upward to the lofty dome, as who should say, Excelsior. ¶"It is Longfellow!" I exclaimed. "When did he return from Germany?" ¶"His least essential part—that is to say, his physical man—is probably there at this moment, under a water-spout," replied my companion. "But wherever his body may be, his soul will find its way into the Hall of Fantasy. See; there is Washington Irving too, whom all the world supposes to be enacting the grave character

of Ambassador to Spain." ¶And, indeed, there
stood the renowned Geoffry Crayon, in the
radiance of a window, which looked like the
pictured symbol of his own delightful fancy.
Mr. Cooper had chosen to show himself in a
more sombre light, and was apparently medi-
tating a speech in some libel case, rather than
a scene of such tales as have made him a
foremost man in this enchanted hall. But,
woe is me! I tread upon slippery ground,
among these poets and men of imagination,
whom perhaps it is equally hazardous to
notice, or to leave undistinguished in the
throng. Would that I could emblazon all
their names in star-dust! Let it suffice to
mention indiscriminately such as my eye
chanced to fall upon. There was Washington
Allston, who possesses the freedom of the hall
by the threefold claim of painter, novelist,
and poet; and John Neal, whose rampant
muse belches wild-fire, with huge volumes of
smoke; and Lowell, the poet of the generation that now enters upon the stage. The
young author of Dolon was here, involved
in a deep mist of metaphysical fantasies. Epes
Sargent and Mr. Tuckerman had come hither
to engage contributors for their respective
magazines. Hillard was an honorary member of the poetic band, as editor of Spenser,
though he might well have preferred a claim
on his own account. Mr. Poe had gained
ready admittance for the sake of his imagination, but was threatened with ejectment,
as belonging to the obnoxious class of critics.
¶There were a number of ladies among the
tuneful and imaginative crowd. I know not
whether their tickets of admission were
signed with the authentic autograph of
Apollo; but, at all events, they had an un-

doubted right of entrance by courtesy. Miss
Sedgwick was an honored guest, although
the atmosphere of the Hall of Fantasy is not
precisely the light in which she appears to
most advantage. Finally, I saw Mr. Rufus
Griswold, with pencil and memorandum-
book, busily noting down the names of all
the poets and poetesses there, and likewise
of some, whom nobody but himself had suspected of ever visiting the hall. ¶"Thank   P

176.3   had not heretofore] has not hitherto P
180.14–15   they. It] they. There was a dear friend of mine
among them, who has striven with all his
might to wash away the blood-stain from the
statute-book; and whether he finally succeed
or fail, no philanthropist need blush to stand
on the same footing with O'Sullivan. ¶In the
midst of these lights of the age, it gladdened
me to greet my old friends of Brook Farm,
with whom, though a recreant now, I had
borne the heat of many a summer's day,
while we labored together towards the perfect life. They seem so far advanced, however, in the realization of their idea, that
their sun-|burnt faces and toil-hardened
frames may soon be denied admittance into
the Hall of Fantasy. Mr. Emerson was likewise there, leaning against one of the pillars,
and surrounded by an admiring crowd of
writers and readers of the Dial, and all manner of Transcendentalists and disciples of
the Newness, most of whom betrayed the
power of his intellect by its modifying influence upon their own. He had come into
the hall, in search, I suppose, either of a fact
or a real man; both of which he was as
likely to find there as elsewhere. No more
earnest seeker after truth than he, and few
more successful finders of it; although, some-

times, the truth assumes a mystic unreality
and shadowyness in his grasp. In the same
part of the hall, Jones Very stood alone,
within a circle which no other of mortal
race could enter, nor himself escape from.
¶Here, also was Mr. Alcott, with two or three
friends, whom his spirit had assimilated to
itself and drawn to his New England home,
though an ocean rolled between. There was
no man in the enchanted hall, whose mere
presence, the language of whose look and
manner, wrought such an impression as that
of this great mystic innovator. So calm and
gentle was he, so holy in aspect, so quiet in.
the utterance of what his soul brooded upon,
that one might readily conceive his Orphic
Sayings to well upward from a fountain in
his breast, which communicated with the
infinite abyss of Thought. ¶"Here is a prophet," cried my friend, with enthusiasm—"a
dreamer, a bodiless idea amid our actual
existence. Another age may recognise him
as a man; or perhaps his misty apparition
will vanish into the sunshine. It matters
little; for his influence will have impregnated
the atmosphere, and be imbibed by generations that know not the original apostle of
the ideas, which they shall shape into earthly
business. Such a spirit cannot pass through
human life, yet leave mankind entirely as he
found them!" ¶"At all events, he may count
you as a disciple," said I, smiling; "and doubtless there is the spirit of a system in him, but
not the body of it. I love to contrast him
with that acute and powerful Intellect, who
stands not far off." ¶"Ah, you mean Mr.
Brownson!" replied my companion. "Pray
Heaven he do not stamp his foot or raise
his voice; for if he should, the whole fabric

	of the Hall of Fantasy will dissolve like a smoke-wreath! I wonder how he came here?" It *P*
180.27–28	throng. ¶Yet] throng, among whom I must not forget to mention Mrs. Abigail Folsom, though by no means as a type of the whole. ¶Yet *P*
180.29	fellowship] brotherhood *P*
185.15	who had been sent] whom Dr. Collyer had sent *P*
185.15–16	in magnetic] in the magnetic *P*
174.6	reposited] deposited 46–54

The Celestial Rail-road (MS,DR,46,54)

189.30	engineer] conductor MS-54
190.9,27	engineer] conductor MS-46
192.3	we] we we MS
201.3	transaction] bargain MS-*DR*
202.7	Mr. Foot-it-to-Heaven] Mr. Go-the-old-way MS-*DR*
203.9	long since] *omit* MS-*DR*
195.8	—he would] —would *DR*-54
200.6	and a] as a *DR*
200.28	years] years' *DR*-54
201.30	bound for] bound to *DR*-54
206.10	lurid] livid *DR*
186.8	by making] to make 46
188.9	in the dispute] in a dispute 46–54
190.21	that] *omit* 46–54
194.25	a truthful] *omit* a 46
195.7	itself] themselves 46–54
195.28–29	called to him] called him 46–54
197.2	into] in 46
197.4	fat] fatten 54

The Procession of Life (DR,46,54)

207.7	train] trail DR
207.13	taken] continued DR
208.26	other] other common DR
208.30	with gold] with much gold DR
209.31	heart's] hearts' DR
210.19	human rank] *omit* human DR
211.23	match] watch DR
211.26	brethren] these brethren DR
212.10	funereal] funeral DR
212.24	dwelling-house] dwelling-place DR
213.21	them] the DR
213.23	arts, or] arts, literature, or DR
219.4	those] those suitable DR
219.12	to] *omit* DR-46
219.16	more] much DR
220.21	to] in DR
221.11	towards] toward DR-46
222.13	echoes] passes DR; *see also* 46
207.3	of a] of the 46–54
210.11	pestilences] pestilence 46–54
211.5	we] *omit* 46
213.31	alarum] alarm 46–54
215.29	Do] Does 46–54
216.11	chambers] chamber 46–54
219.3–4	the prospect] a prospect 46–54
219.21	has] had 46–54
221.14	praise] phrase 46
222.13	echoes] pass 46
221.26	Revelations] Revelation 54

Feathertop (MS,IM,54)

225.1	corporosity] corporcity MS-54
234.26	glistened] glistenened MS

241.29	ceiling] cieling MS
243.21	coruscating] corruscating MS
224.15	there's] there is *IM-54*
225.14	-flaps] flabs *IM-54*
226.5	rusty] dusty *IM-54*
226.9	knobby] nobby *IM-54*
228.7	pretty] my pretty *IM-54*
228.21	palms] hands *IM-54*
233.2–3	deepest of] deepest part of *IM-54*
234.9	which] *omit IM-54*
235.11	its] his *IM-54*
237.7	wrists] wrist *IM-54*
238.8	deportment] department *IM-54*
239.11	still] *omit IM-54*
239.26	do] did *IM-54*
239.27	a-blaze] a blaze *IM*; ablaze 54
242.26	that] *omit IM-54*
244.15	farther] further *IM-54*
245.2	snuffling] sniffling *IM-54*
224.16	mile] mild 54
237.5	gentleman] gentlemen 54
242.22	of person] of a person 54

The New Adam and Eve (DR,46,54)

248.31	an inner] the inner *DR*
249.16–17	situation] category *DR*
252.7	upward] upwards *DR-54*
252.10–11	deep reverberating] deep and reverberating *DR-46*
253.2	towards] to *DR-46*
258.24	come] came *DR-46*
264.7	opportunities are] opportunities of wisdom are *DR*
264.14	columns] volumes *DR*
264.16	as if it] as it *DR-46*
266.14	We] Ye *DR*

266.25	wherewith Nature] wherewith kind Nature DR-46
247.9	loosen] lessen 46–54
251.26	Poh] Pooh 46
259.10	answers] answered 46–54
263.11	upward] upwards 46–54
263.19	observes] observed 46–54
263.26	unconjectured] unconjectural 46
251.4	dry-good] dry goods 54

Egotism; or, The Bosom-Serpent (DR,46,54)

268.14	aright] right DR
270.24	were it] where it 46; see also 54
271.31–32	whatsoever] whatever DR
273.6	that] omit DR
273.21	it be] omit DR-46
274.9	gloried] glorified DR
274.13	and a] omit a DR
274.23	out] omit DR
275.17	has stung] stung DR
276.19	depreciated] deprecated DR-46
281.8–9	whether, and when, to] whether to DR
282.6	had] has DR
283.31	but] omit DR
269.19	of discussion] of a discussion 54
270.24	were it] should it be 54

The Christmas Banquet (DR,46,54)

288.13	and in] omit in DR-46
290.4	of the feast] omit DR
292.2	lore] love DR
294.6	recognizing] re-organizing DR

294.23	baby] babe *DR*
294.23	smothering] smothered *DR*
297.8	more] *omit DR*
300.1	travel] travels *DR*
301.23	caused] causes *DR*
303.23	enjoy] envy *DR*
288.17	faithlessness] faithfulness 46
294.22	had] has 46–54
294.27	eyes] eye 46–54
295.26	haunter] hunter 46–54
297.19	mystery] mysteries 46–54
299.7	lessons] lesson 46–54
304.29	chillness] chilliness 46
304.33	joys] joy 46–54
300.3	munificent] magnificent 54
300.4	domestic] *omit* 54

Drowne's Wooden Image (GL,46,54)

306.18	the fellow] the very fellow *GL*
307.3	and scarlet] and a scarlet *GL*
307.33	Carrara] Carrera *GL*
309.4	image] workmanship *GL*
309.15	Town] Tower *GL*
309.30	act] fact *GL*
311.16–17	deficiency which . . . so rare] deficiency, so rare *GL*-46
311.19	heretofore] *omit GL*-46
313.11	and] *omit GL*-46
313.32	muttered] murmured *GL*
315.18	Even had] Had *GL*-46
315.22	now astounded] now to be astonished *GL*
316.6	transfixed . . . in] transformed . . . with *GL*
320.3–4	but, quenched] but, being quenched *GL*
307.1	would] do 46–54
309.14	morning] moment 46–54
310.15	images] image 46

313.22	a] the 46–54
314.32	perplexed] perplexing 46–54
314.33	all] *omit* 46–54
316.10	What] Who 46
319.24	of his friend] of friend 46

The Intelligence Office (DR,46,54)

325.14	sad] said *DR*
326.24	owners] owner *DR*
326.24	claim] reclaim *DR*
327.16	time] while *DR*-46
330.20	and their] and for their *DR*-46
331.21	a few] others *DR*
322.13	years] years' 46–54
322.33	on a throne] or a throne 46–54
325.24	has] had 46–54

Roger Malvin's Burial (T,DR,46,54)

337.12	unfortunate] unforunate *T*
341.35	recover of] recover *T*
343.25	himself] *omit* *T*-46
343.32	downward] downwards *T-DR*
348.21	further at the] farther at that *T*-46
348.31	a few months] two years *T*-46
351.34	asunder] assunder *T*
353.3	latter] larger *T*-46
354.8	these] *omit* *T*-46
357.1	symbol] cymbol *T*
358.27–28	report had] report of the gun had *T*-46
339.1	to his] in his *DR*-54
343.15	our] your *DR*-54
347.3	In] ¶In *DR*-54

351.34	affection] affections DR-54
354.25	Massachusetts] Massachusetts' DR-46
341.35	foremost] former 46
344.19	her have] her to have 46-54
346.6	or] *omit* 46
346.15	shrank] shrink 46–54
353.30	backward] backwards 46–54
355.16	die . . . lie] dies . . . lies 46–54
357.22	shades] shadows 46–54
357.26	felt that it] felt it 46
360.10	bough] bow 46
337.6	judiciously] judicially 54

P.'s Correspondence (DR,46,54)

362.25	from] for DR
363.9	compotators] competitors DR
364.3	lordship apologized] lordship had apologized DR-46
364.25	his] his own DR
366.5	had] has DR
367.24	when] while DR
367.27	reverend] reverent DR
368.19–20	I suspect] I did suspect DR-46
369.33–34	past? I had] past? Bulwer nauseates me; he is the very pimple of the age's humbug. There is no hope of the public, so long as he retains an admirer, a reader, or a publisher. I had DR-46
371.28	the iron-] that iron- DR-46
372.14	manner] mode DR-46
372.19	reviewing] viewing DR
374.15	our] your DR
374.30	my mind] my own mind DR-46
375.8	never] not DR-46
376.21	that] *omit* DR
361.6	a perusal] the perusal 46–54

362.7	February 29] February 25 46
365.1	severest] sincerest 46–54
367.16	spark] spirit 46–54
370.16	his] the 46–54
370.20	reminiscences of] *omit* 46–54
373.7	was wont] are wont 46–54
378.11	voices] voice 46–54

EARTH'S HOLOCAUST (MS,G,46,54)

385.15	of coals] of of coals MS
387.9	not worth] not an worth MS
390.24	all together] altogether MS-G
392.28	consecrated] *omit* MS-46
397.4	unregarded] ungreguarded MS
400.27	Heavens] Heaven's MS
381.18	of evening] of the evening G-54
382.31	armsfull] armfuls G-54
383.18	towards] toward G
383.20	some star] some stars G; *see also* 46–54
383.27	in his] to his G-54
385.18	afterwards] afterward G
385.24	round] around G-54
386.29	had] *omit* G-54
388.20	Sydney] Sidney G-54
390.11	those] these G-54
390.19	towards] toward G-46
390.33	scarred] seared G-54
391.7–8	cannon-founderies] cannon-founders G; cannon founders 46–54
392.11	legends] legend G-54
393.28	attained to] *omit* to G-54
395.25	encyclopediasts] encyclopedists G-54
396.22	afterwards] afterward G-46
396.30	could] would G
404.3	inner] inward G-54
381.1	in time] in the time 46–54

381.13	of moral] or moral 46
383.7	instrument] instruments 46–54
383.10	the] these 46
383.16	and same] and the same 46–54
383.20	some star] a star 46–54
384.22	come] comes 46–54
385.5	times] time 46–54
386.7	upward] upwards 46–54
388.12	ribbon] ribbons 46–54
399.21	mountain of fire] mountain fire 46–54
399.24	this] the 46–54
399.30	had] *omit* 46–54
400.2	embellishment] embellishments 46
400.11	worshipper] worshippers 46–54
401.3	cushions] cushion 46–54
401.4	utterances] utterance 46–54
401.16	lamentation] lamentations 46
402.23	will] would 46–54
382.34	ribands] ribbons 54
399.2	further] farther 54

Passages from a Relinquished Work (*NE*, 54)

405	Passages . . . At Home] The Story Teller. | No. I. | At Home. *NE*
414.7	Oh] O *NE*-54
417.13	The Village Theatre] The Story-Teller. | No. II. | The Village Theatre. *NE*
420.3–5	as Mr. Higginbotham's Catastrophe. ¶This] as | Mr. Higginbotham's Catastrope. [*followed by the story*] ¶This *NE*
420.5–6	there presented, and] (*editorial bridge*); here presented to the reader, and *NE*
406.17	and a wise] *omit* a 54
410.6	dry-good] dry goods 54
416.4	a muck] amuck 54
419.22	clarionet] clarinet 54

419.26   undreamt] undreamed 54
420.12   queue] cue 54

Sketches from Memory (*NE*,54)

422   Sketches from Memory . . . White Mountains]
             Sketches from Memory. | By a Pedestrian. |
             No. I. | We are so fortunate as to have in
             our possession the portfolio of a friend, who
             traveled on foot in search of the picturesque
             over New-England and New-York. It con-
             tains many loose scraps and random sketches,
             which appear to have been thrown off at
             different intervals, as the scenes once ob-
             served were recalled to the mind of the writer
             by recent events or associations. He kept no
             journal nor set down any notes during his
             tour; but his recollection seems to have been
             faithful, and his powers of description as
             fresh and effective as if they had been tasked
             on the very spot which he describes. Some of
             his quiet delineations deserve rather to be
             called pictures than sketches, so lively are the
             colors shed over them. The first which we
             select, is a reminiscence of a day and night
             spent among the White Mountains, and will
             revive agreeable thoughts in the minds of
             those tourists who have but just returned
             from a visit to their sublime scenery. | The
             Notch. *NE*
428.17   than that] that that *NE*
429.14   looking] lookgin *NE*
429.29   The Canal-Boat] Sketches from Memory. | By
             a Pedestrian. | No. II. | We present to our
             readers a few more of the loose sketches from
             our friend's portfolio, which, we think, will,
             more clearly than those of the last month,
             shew the truth of our remark, that, like the

careless drawings of a master-hand, they shadow forth a power and beauty, that might be visibly embodied into life-like forms on the canvass. 'The Afternoon Scene' and 'The Night Scene' will, we trust, suggest subjects to our landscape painters. The former, which has the mellow richness of a Claude, might be exquisitely done by Doughty; and young Brown, whose promise is as great as the hopes of his friends, could employ his glowing pencil upon no subject better adapted to call forth all his genius, than the latter. | The Canal-Boat. *NE*

434.20	Schenectady] Schnectady *NE*
435.8	and shrinking] and skrinking *NE*
435.28	ceased] cease *NE*-54
425.12	a corner] the corner 54
432.15	further] farther 54
437.27	hat] cap 54

The Old Apple-Dealer (*SM*,46,54)

444.7–8	nor has] nor as *SM*
445.13	serve as] serve him as *SM*
446.5	old] *omit SM*
442.30	the price] price 46–54
442.11	of selling] to sell 54
442.29	a stick] *omit* a 54
445.29	grisly] grizzly 54

The Artist of the Beautiful (*DR*,46,54)

448.4	Poh] Pooh *DR*-46
453.17	can never] never can *DR*-46
455.1	scarcely] carcely *DR*

456.25	paddles] pulleys *DR*
460.3	Annie] Anne *DR*
465.7	fairy] fancy *DR*
467.32	a proof] proof *DR*
469.1	seemed] seem *DR*
472.24	secret . . . secret] sweet . . . sweet *DR*
475.22	was yet] yet was *DR*-46
449.1	soon] seen 46
452.14	known it, by] known by 46
456.1	never] ever 46–54
457.12	ones] one 46–54
458.18	process] progress 46–54
462.27	has] had 46–54
469.10–11	was looking] looking 46–54
470.23	overarched] overreached 46–54
473.17	the sneer] a sneer 46–54
475.4	of] if 46
461.29	nor] or 54
466.20	past] passed 54

A Virtuoso's Collection (*BM*,46,54)

480.20–22	This . . . Kendall."] *omit BM*
483.8–10	hair and . . . breast. Here] hair. Here *BM*
483.32	of the] cf the *BM*
484.18	Boone] Boon *BM*-46
486.8	Van Corlear] van Corlear *BM*
486.12	Papirius] Papyrius *BM*
486.24	Egyptian] Egyptain *BM*
487.25–27	And . . . salvation.] *omit BM*
488.22–25	laugh, . . . fire. He then] laugh. He then *BM*
489.3	out] *omit BM*-46
490.28–31	Alexander's . . . it.] *omit BM*
492.34	undescribed] undischbed *BM*
493.25	frigate] *omit BM*-46
494.4	Schlemihl's] Schlemil's *BM*
478.24	its] his 46–54

479.22   wall] walls 46–54
479.23   the stag] a stag 46–54
483.32   Campeador] Campeodor 46
484.13   department] apartment 46–54
492.5   and a] and an 46
482.18   further] farther 54
485.22   farther] further 54
487.31   Faux] Fawkes 54

ALTERATIONS IN THE MANUSCRIPTS

A Centenary key is given to the left of the bracket, and a description of the alteration follows; "above" indicates inter-lineation, and "over," inscription in the same space. The presence of a caret is always noticed. Not listed are inter-lineations repeating originals for clarity, mendings for clarity, or alterations over undecipherable originals.

THE OLD MANSE

4.1	remote] over wiped-out 'dim'
4.1	privacy.] above cancelled 'retirement'
4.29	rustling] over wiped-out 'great la'
5.1	gold,] interlined with a caret
5.10	physical] above cancelled 'material'
5.17	our] above cancelled 'the'
5.20	These] over wiped-out 'it' and period inserted after preceding 'around'
5.22	sternly] above cancelled 'fiercely'
5.33	books] precedes wiped-out comma
6.3	little] 'li' over wiped-out 'ol'
6.3	old] 'ld' over wiped-out 'd'
6.29	From] over wiped-out 'Owing'
6.29	indolence] interlined with a caret
7.6	of] interlined with a caret
7.9	on the] over wiped-out 'of the'

7.21	circumstances] over wiped-out 'influences'
7.25	lovely] above cancelled 'beautiful'
7.28	Each] over wiped-out 'The shadow'
7.28	tree] over wiped-out 'of'
7.29	grass] over wiped-out 'glass'
8.3	adequate] 'ad' over wiped-out 'aq'
8.6	human] over wiped-out 'soul'
8.9	city—] dash cancels comma
8.27	western bank,] over wiped-out 'other side' and precedes cancelled 'of the river' and inadvertently undeleted comma
8.28	grown] over wiped-out 'sprung'
8.29	fertilized] over wiped-out 'moistened'
9.2	memorial.] precedes cancelled sentence 'A humbler . . . parsonage.' which was then written below in new paragraph
9.6	grave—] dash over wiped-out comma
9.7	stone] over wiped-out 'gran'
9.12	of] over wiped-out 'f'
9.17–18	the inhabitants below.] 'the' over 'its' and 'below.' interlined with a caret which deletes period after 'inhabitants'
9.24	what] interlined with a caret
9.25	been] above cancelled 'continued'
10.15	brother man] above cancelled 'fellow-creature'
10.23	interest] over wiped-out 'and'
10.24	breadth—] dash over wiped-out comma
11.6	rudeness] 'r' altered from 'i'
11.6	in the] 'in' interlined with a caret
11.8	shapes] above deleted 'makes'
11.19	broad] over wiped-out 'day'
12.3	early] 'arly' over wiped-out 'rly'
12.4	branches] 'hes' over wiped-out 'es'
12.26	offer] over wiped-out 'eve'
12.33	were] 'w' over wiped-out 'ch'
13.7	tormented me with] over wiped-out 'were being tormented with'
13.7	neither] 'n' over wiped-out 'th'
13.16	-life,] over wiped-out ', who'

14.6	observed] 'o' over wiped-out 's'
14.14	too,] over wiped-out 'also,'
14.18	upon] over wiped-out 'on'
14.28	the] over wiped-out 'my'
14.30	Providence] precedes wiped-out comma
15.22	out of doors] 'of' follows wiped-out hyphen
15.28	water] over wiped-out 'rain'
15.30	and] follows wiped-out comma
17.4	on] over wiped-out 'one'
17.6	title] above cancelled 'name'
17.16	I] over wiped-out 'he'
17.17	such] over wiped-out 'which'
17.29	entry;—] dash added after following word inscribed
17.31	improbably] 'a' over wiped-out 'I'
17.33	the garret] over wiped-out 'a garret'
18.6	ironing—] 'ironing' over wiped-out 'swee'; dash cancels comma
18.7	labor—] dash cancels comma
18.13	receptacle] 'ptacle' over wiped-out 'pcle'
18.24	profound] above cancelled 'deep'
18.26	Catholic] 'Ca' over wiped-out 'cl'
18.26	papistry] initial 'p' over wiped-out 'P'
19.13	beneath] over wiped-out 'in the'
19.23	So long as] interlined with a caret above cancelled 'While'
19.28	These] altered from 'They'
19.29	elder] 'I' over wiped-out 'd'
20.3	the specific gravity of] interlined with a caret
20.14	the better world on] over wiped-out 'Heaven on a Gothic stai'
20.15	flying] 'ying' over wiped-out 'ee'
20.21	epochs] over wiped-out 'time fr'
20.26	austere] over wiped-out 'gi'
20.28	nothing] 'n' over wiped-out 'half'
20.33	which] over wiped-out 'and whi'
21.2	age—] dash deletes comma
22.20	original] over wiped-out 'reflection'
22.24	then] interlined with a caret

22.32	In] over wiped-out 'At'
23.1–2	and illuminate] above 'the dark'
23.4	which] over wiped-out ', as'
23.7	due] over wiped-out 'suc'
23.7	stole] over wiped-out 'stept'
23.10	Grape-vines] 'Grape-' interlined with a caret before 'Vines inadvertently left capitalized
23.13	in] over wiped-out comma
23.17	branches] above cancelled 'boughs'
23.23	We] 'W' over wiped-out 'I'
23.26	anger or alarm.] above cancelled 'alarm or remonstrance'
23.26	Ducks—that] dash deletes comma; 'that' over wiped-out 'th'
23.27	since the] over wiped-out 'the live-long'
23.27	eve—] dash deletes comma
24.15–16	fire, red-gleaming] 'fire, red-' over wiped-out 'red gleam'
24.26–27	partakes] precedes wiped-out comma
24.27	may] 'm' over wiped-out 'b'
25.8	on] over wiped-out 'and'
26.2	had] interlined with a caret
26.5	cities] 'c' over wiped-out 'h'
27.7	flowers—] dash deletes comma
27.8	year—] dash deletes comma
27.30	promise] over wiped-out 'blissf'
28.10–11	the branches were] interlined with a caret
28.25	him] interlined with a caret above cancelled 'them'
28.31	on] over wiped-out 'at'
29.4	give] over wiped-out 'the'
29.11	from earliest youth,] interlined with a caret
30.1	dewy] 'ewy' over wiped-out 'ie'
30.6	hitherto] above cancelled 'that has been'
30.6	attempted] over wiped-out possible 'tried'
30.16–17	encountered] over wiped-out 'met with'
31.2	midnight of the] interlined with a caret
31.3	burning] 'bu' over wiped-out 'be'
31.5	hitherto] 'h' over wiped-out 'b'

31.8	which] over wiped-out 'who fla'
31.29	giddiness] above cancelled 'kindness'
32.2	character] interlined with a caret
32.3	draw] 'd' over wiped-out 'm'
32.3–4	become imbued] 'become im' over wiped-out 'be imbued'
32.7	immovable] 'vable' over wiped-out 'veab'
32.12	Mine] 'ine' altered from 'y'
32.13	honored] over wiped-out 'rea'
32.16	woods,—] dash added after following word inscribed
32.19	sacredly individual to] 'ly' added to 'sacred'; 'individual to' over wiped-out 'to be revealed'
32.21–22	from my pen] over wiped-out 'hitherward'
32.23	which swell around] interlined with a caret above cancelled 'haunt'; 'which' on previous line inadvertently undeleted
32.26	my own!] over wiped-out 'all my ow'
33.10	breezy] interlined with a caret
33.11	the depths of a] over wiped-out 'a breezy hill-side'
33.13	Carpenters] over wiped-out 'Wor'
33.15	strewing] follows cancelled 'and'
33.20	cleaned] over wiped-out 'brushed'
33.23	venerable] 'able' over wiped-out 'ble a'
33.30	as uncertain] 'as' over wiped-out 'kno'
34.20	most] over wiped-out 'so'
34.21	profess] original following 'ed' erased
34.25	will receive them the] over wiped-out 'as the last offering, the last'
34.32	sunshine] first 'n' over wiped-out 's'
34.34	and that,] interlined with a caret
34.34	seen] above cancelled 'shown him'
34.34	whatever] 'wh' over wiped-out possible 'ab'
35.1	old Manse] above cancelled 'house'
35.1	he] over wiped-out possible 'bee'
35.3	an antique] 'an' interlined with a caret, 'anti' over wiped-out 'on a'

Buds and Bird-Voices

148.18	season] over wiped-out 'frost'
149.3	to labor] 'to' interlined with a caret
149.8	winter] 'win' over wiped-out 'Win'
149.17	white] interlined with a caret
150.15	an instant] 'an' mended from 'a' and 'instant' above cancelled 'moment'
152.19	melancholy] 'me' over wiped-out 'old'
152.28	primal] above cancelled 'first'
153.13	its faint] originally 'a faint'; 'a' mended to 'its' and 'faint' wiped out and reinscribed
153.23	it] over wiped-out 'al'
153.33	race.] original following 'They seem mostly to have departed now, or else to have' cancelled
154.7–8	their loud clamor] interlined with a caret
154.17	stationary] 's' over wiped-out 'al'
154.21	confidently] 'con' over wiped-out 'eff'
154.29	songsters] over wiped-out 'minstrels'
154.30	man's] over wiped-out undeciphered word ending in 'le'
154.32	orchard-trees] hyphen replaces comma and 'trees' interlined with a caret
156.3	there came] over wiped-out possible 'thereafter'
156.18–19	A bee . . . flowers.] interlined with a caret
156.29	overflowing] initial 'o' over wiped-out 'f'
157.5	usual] initial 'u' over wiped-out 'f'

The Celestial Rail-road

190.9	comes] over wiped-out 'cond'
191.5	tail] 'i' over wiped-out 'l'
191.5	thunder-bolt] '-bolt' over wiped-out 'bolt'

192.11	unanimity] above crossed-out 'unamity'
193.12	disastrously] 'astrously' over wiped-out 'tasrously'
193.17	ditch] 'tch' over wiped-out 'ch'
193.28	its] over erased 'the'
194.32	Directors] 'D' over wiped-out 'd'
195.8	have] interlined with a caret
195.12	and] over wiped-out 'with'
195.28	fellow] interlined with a caret
197.19	As I] over wiped-out 'It bein'
197.20	is] interlined with a caret
198.24	doctrine] 'd' over wiped-out 'D'
199.18	Fair] 'F' over wiped-out 'f'
199.28	her most] over wiped-out 'to be her'
199.31	which] 'wh' over wiped-out 'and'
200.11	questionable] preceding 'very' crossed out
201.15	ogling] over possible 'vie'
201.21	Stick-] 'ck' over wiped-out 'k'
201.31	right] above crossed-out 'truth'
202.30	were] 'w' over wiped-out 't'
203.14	constructed] 'c' over wiped-out 'of'
203.32	train] 'tr' over wiped-out 'of'
205.10	had] over wiped-out 'were'
205.18	secure of as] over wiped-out 'as secure of'
205.22	you] over wiped-out 'th'
206.2	Oh] 'O' over wiped-out 'I'
206.11	Fiend] 'F' over wiped-out 'f'
206.19	Dream] 'D' over wiped-out 'd'

FEATHERTOP

223.9	mother] a final 's' wiped out
224.7	humor] interlined with a caret
224.10	hobgoblin] 'g' over wiped-out 'b'
224.15	Besides,] 's' over wiped-out comma
224.32	left] 'l' over wiped-out 'f'
225.2	and this] over wiped-out 'This was'; preceding semicolon cancels period

225.22	on] interlined with a caret between 'it' and comma
225.26	which] interlined with a caret
225.30	Louis] 'is' over wiped-out 's'
226.5	in which] 'in w' over wiped-out 'which'
226.22	shape,] interlined with a caret
226.23	countenance] above cancelled 'face'
226.23	appeared] 'ap' over wiped-out 'shr'
227.16	dabble] above cancelled 'have dabbled'
227.18	no] interlined with a caret
227.32	singular] 'sin-' interlined above cancelled 're-' and 'gular' interlined above cancelled 'markable'
228.15	extending] interlined with a caret
228.16	There] 'Th' over wiped-out 'wh'
228.27	in like manner] 'in like m' over wiped-out 'likewise'
228.27	assumed a] over wiped-out 'appeared to'
229.4	I] over wiped-out 'can'
229.5	better] 'er' over wiped-out 're'
229.10	again] initial 'a' over wiped-out 'g'
229.13	her] 'h' over wiped-out 'th'
229.21	analyze] above cancelled 'examine'
229.24	outstretched] 'ched' over wiped-out 'hed'
230.12	nature, (like] parenthesis cancels comma; comma added after 'nature'
230.22	head] interlined with a caret
230.25	unhappy] 'un' over wiped-out 'pu'
231.10	vollies] 'voll' over wiped-out 'whiff'
232.1	merely] above cancelled 'only'
232.4	nothing!] a second exclamation point wiped out
232.14	babble] 'l' over wiped-out 'b'
232.17	made] above cancelled 'seen'
232.19	said] above cancelled 'answered'
232.23	loudly] over wiped-out 'heartily'
233.2	So now] over wiped-out 'Such were'
233.6–7	ten years before] interlined with a caret
233.10	the coin] interlined with a caret
233.10	"With] ' "Wi' over wiped-out 'That'
233.10	Mother] 'th' over wiped-out 'f'

233.13	the adventurer] cancelled 'new' following 'the'
233.14	dame] over wiped-out 'woman'
233.15	introduce himself] 'introduce him-' over wiped-out 'make him' and 'self' over wiped-out 'self'
233.18	who stood at] over wiped-out 'in the neighboring'
233.26	wrinkled] over wiped-out 'withe'
234.2	Put] over wiped-out 'But'
234.20	perfectly] interlined with a caret
234.22	its lips] 'elf' wiped out after 'its' and 'lips' interlined with a caret
235.12	soon] over wiped-out 'soon h'
235.22	a fresh] 'a' over wiped-out 'fr'
236.3	else] over wiped-out 'tha'
236.14	Feathertop] 'F' over wiped-out 'f'
236.15	of feathers] interlined with a caret
236.32	a pair of splendid] over wiped-out 'splendid scarlet breeches'
237.1	disorder] 'dis-' above cancelled 'cover' and 'order' interlined with a caret
237.13	as often] 'as' over wiped-out 'of'
238.11	Canada] over wiped-out 'Quebec'
238.20	delicacy of] interlined with a caret
238.26	a compliment] 'a com' over wiped-out 'compl'
239.5	requital] 'r' over wiped-out 'f'
239.28	indeed,] the comma over wiped-out exclamation point
239.29	Polly] 'P' over wiped-out 'p'
240.6	here] above cancelled 'now'
240.15	preparation] 'p' over wiped-out 'pr'
240.19	than the former] interlined with a caret
240.21	every gesture] 'every' interlined above cancelled 'all her' and final 's' of 'gestures' wiped out
240.23	pretty] 'p' over wiped-out 'p'
240.25	himself;] semicolon over wiped-out period
240.25–26	when she] over wiped-out 'because she'
240.27	might] over wiped-out 'could'
240.29	parlor-door] 'door' interlined with a caret and hyphen added after 'parlor'
241.20	that] interlined with a caret

241.22	convinced] following comma and 'he became convinced' cancelled
241.27	along] 'alo' over wiped-out 'fr'
242.1	hand] over 'arm'
242.5	constraint] 'cons' over wiped-out 'fear'
242.7	an earlier] above cancelled 'some'
242.14	after] interlined with a caret
242.25	perceive] following 'that' cancelled
242.26	and] over wiped-out 'any'
242.31	him] interlined with a caret
242.34	having] 'h' over wiped-out 'at'
243.17	no matter what he did] over wiped-out 'no matter how he looked'
243.19	an] over 'in'
243.24	silly] over wiped-out 'poor'
243.27	throwing himself] 'ing him' over wiped-out 'himself'
244.12	a picture] 'a' over 'an' and 'picture' above cancelled 'image'
244.19	an Illusion] 'an' over wiped-out 'a', and 'I' over wiped-out 'p'
244.22	just] interlined with a caret
244.31	in] over wiped-out 'on'
245.16	myself] 'If' over wiped-out 'f'
245.18	Snatching] 'And' cancelled before 'snatching' and 's' altered to 'S'
245.20	straw] 'st' over wiped-out 'ta'
245.24	was] above cancelled 'seemed'
245.33	know] above cancelled 'see'

EARTH'S HOLOCAUST

381.4	trumpery] 'trum' over wiped-out 'trash'
381.21	moment] 'ent' over wiped-out 'et'
381.22	women] following 'with their aprons' was cancelled
382.8	a grave] 'a' over wiped-out 'agr'

382.16	suitable] 'sui' over 'o'
382.18	now] 'n' over wiped-out 'c'
382.19	like a] 'a' interlined with a caret
383.13	a joyous] 'a' over wiped-out 'the'
383.33–34	refined and] 'and' interlined with a caret
383.34	cast] over wiped-out 'gave'
384.8	own] over wiped-out 'half-'
384.12	shouted] over wiped-out 'cried a'
384.13	henceforth] over wiped-out 'fr'
384.13	dare] over wiped-out 'dares'
385.2	as] over wiped-out 'of'
385.9	fallen in that spot, and] 'there,' cancelled after 'fallen' and 'in that spot,' interlined with a caret
385.10–11	ruined monarchy] over wiped-out 'fallen mon'
385.24	accordingly] 'cco' over wiped-out 'co'
386.7	as of yore] interlined with a caret
386.15	bon-vivants—] 'bon-' over wiped-out 'bonv'; dash cancels comma
386.20	pot-house] '-house' over wiped-out 'house'
386.24	as] over wiped-out 'and'
386.29	muttered expostulations] 'mut' over wiped-out 'many'; 'ex' over wiped-out 'p'
387.1	Last] over wiped-out 'last'
387.17	true] over wiped-out 'st'
387.18	by the loss] over wiped-out 'by course'
389.5	fling] over wiped-out 'throw'
389.18	So long as] over wiped-out 'These things'
389.32	prophesied] over wiped-out 'exclaim'
390.3	time] 'me' over wiped-out 'ne'
390.4	as] interlined with a caret
390.4	numberless great] 'great' over wiped-out 'grat'
390.8	the fire] 'the' interlined with a caret
390.11	slaughter] 's' over wiped-out 'S'
390.27	henceforth] 'henc' over wiped-out 'thence'
391.15	wished] 'd' over wiped-out 's'
391.25	Reason] 'Rea' over wiped-out 'rea'
392.4	contrivance] 'riv' over wiped-out 'iv'
392.19	made] altered from 'was'

392.21	reformers] 'rm' altered from 'm'
392.25	uphold] over wiped-out 'uphold th'
392.30	benevolence—] dash over wiped-out comma
393.4	instrument] 'in' over wiped-out 'so'
393.17	the] over wiped-out 'it'
393.21	attain] above cancelled 'reach'
394.3	higher] 'i' altered from 'o'
394.8	enliven] over wiped-out 'elive'
394.27	arbitrary] initial 'ar' over wiped-out 'ab'
396.18	"The] over wiped-out 'The'
397.27	instead] 'a' over wiped-out 'd'
398.11	inward] 'ward' over wiped-out 'wad'
399.4	"Believe me] over wiped-out ' "Take my wo'
401.10	Child of Dust] 'C' over wiped-out 'c'; 'D' over wiped-out 'd'
401.13	Immortality] 'Imm' altered from 'im'
401.23	spoken. He continued] period over wiped-out comma; 'He continued' over wiped-out 'and who contin'
401.30	everything]'every' over 'anyth'
402.12	the pages of] interlined with a caret
403.3	known] preceded by wiped-out 'un'
403.7	that—] dash deletes comma
403.7	liquor—] dash deletes comma
403.11	fellows] over wiped-out 'frie'
403.14	than] 'n' over wiped-out 't'
404.3	many] 'ny' over wiped-out 'y'
404.11–12	phosphoric] 'horic' over wiped-out 'oric'